SHADOW

SHADOW

The Scavenger Trilogy
Book One

K. J. PARKER

An *Orbit* Book

First published in Great Britain by Orbit 2001

ISBN 0-7394-4266-X

Typeset in Horley by M Rules

Printed in the USA

Orbit
A Division of
Little, Brown and Company (UK)
Brettenham House
Lancaster Place
London WC2E 7EN

Chapter One

He opened his eyes and looked down. He had no idea where he was.

A long way below, he could see a man's body lying in churned-up mud beside a river. It lay sideways, as if in bed, one cheek submerged in a shallow pool, still enough to form a mirror. That struck him as a pleasantly absurd symmetry; one side of the man's face buried in mud, the other side duplicated by the reflection. There were red splashes in the pool that could be blood or, just as easily, something far less melodramatic. At first he assumed it was a peaceful scene, until it occurred to him to wonder why anybody would choose to sleep in such a position.

Then he heard voices. That was what put him on notice that something was wrong; because one voice belonged to the sleeper, the other quite definitely seemed to be coming from the reflection.

'I've had it with you,' the sleeper's voice said. 'I can't take any more of this; it's all completely out of control and I just don't want to know you any more. And look at me when I'm talking to you.'

(Instinctively he knew that the unconscious body was his own.)

'You've said all this before,' the reflection replied. 'You don't mean it. I'm not listening.'

'The hell with you,' the sleeper replied furiously. 'You know, that's probably what I hate about you the most, the way you just look away every time I say something you don't want to hear. Just for once, why can't you listen to me?'

'Because you never say anything worth listening to,' the reflection said. 'Oh come on, I've heard it all before. You aren't going to leave me, you wouldn't last five minutes without me to take care of you. On your own, you're nothing.'

'My God,' the sleeper said, after a pause. 'I'm listening to you, and I can't believe we ever had anything in common. Get out of here, go away. I don't want to see you ever again.'

'Really.'

'Yes, really. Can't you understand *anything*? From now on, as far as I'm concerned, you're dead.'

'Charming.'

'More than that, even. You never existed. I've never heard of you. I don't know your name, or where you come from, or what you've been or done – especially that, for God's sake.'

The reflection laughed insultingly. 'Oh, right,' it said. 'And of course, all that was just me. You were never involved. You never did *anything*.'

'No,' replied the sleeper, 'I never did. It was all you. And now you're gone, completely out of my mind, like pulling a bad tooth. You were never here. You never existed.'

'If that's what you want,' said the reflection, sounding offensively reasonable. 'But I don't think you want anything of the sort. You need me. You'll be back. Same as the last time.'

'No—'

'Same as the last time,' the reflection repeated, 'same as always. But I'll leave you to figure that out for yourself. You'll know where to find me.'

'Like hell,' shouted the sleeper. 'I'd sooner die first.'

'We'll see,' the reflection said; then the body stirred and lifted its head, and the movement shattered the reflection, scattering it in waves out to the edges of the pool.

He opened his eyes and looked up. He felt dizzy and his head was splitting. Just now he'd had the most unpleasant feeling, as if he'd been floating in the air and looking down at himself; but that wasn't how it was at all. Instead, he could see the black silhouette of a crow. It circled a couple of times, then turned into the slight breeze to slow itself down, opened its wings like a sail and glided down, pitching on the chest of a dead man who was lying next to him, a yard or so away. Having landed, the crow lifted its head and stared at him, as if to suggest that he had no right to be there. He remembered about crows; they'll sit in a tree watching you for hours at a time, and they won't stir till you leave. But they can't count; you want to nail a crow with a stone or a sling-shot, take someone with you as you walk to the hide; when you're ready, send your friend out and the crow will watch him till he's out of sight, then he'll lift himself into the air on his big, stiff wings, sail in and pitch, right where you want him to be. Very smart birds, crows, with an instinctive knowledge of how far a man can throw a stone, but useless at figuring.

He meant to wave his arms and shout, because you always chase off crows, on principle. All he could manage, it turned out, was a vague flap of his hand and a croak in the back of his throat. It was enough to do the job, however, and the crow opened its wings and lifted, proclaiming as it went the subtle treachery of humans who lie still pretending to be dead, just to fool hard-working scavengers.

Just scaring off a bird was enough to make him feel dizzy and sick all over again. He lay back and stared at the sky, waiting for his memory to come back and explain to him how he came to be lying out in the open next to a dead body. Once he knew that, he'd know what to do; meanwhile, it'd do no harm to close his eyes again, just for a moment—

'I had to make him go away,' somebody said. He recognised it as his own voice, the sleeper's voice from the dream, or hallucination, or vision, or whatever the hell it had been. 'He was always trouble, nothing but trouble and sorrow. We'll be much better off without him, you wait and see.'

Will we? he wanted to ask.

'Just put him completely out of your mind,' the voice replied. 'Trust me, I know him. Whatever happens, we've got to be better off without him.'

So he opened his eyes again, sat up and looked round. He found that he was in the bottom of a combe, with a rain-swollen river running down the middle. The water had slopped out on to the grass on either side, and where he was lying was churned up into a filthy mess of mud and brown standing pools. In it lay dead bodies, some on their backs, some face down and almost submerged. He was filthy himself, with a black tidemark a hand's span above both knees, and he was missing one boot, presumably sucked off when he'd stumbled into a boggy patch.

It's all right, he told himself, it'll all come back in a moment. He forced himself to stand up, in spite of violent protests from his head and knees. That gave him a better view, a broader perspective, but still none of it made any sense.

He looked down at the dead man lying next to where he'd been, trying to read him through the mud. A soldier, because he was wearing armour (boiled leather cuirass and pauldrons, cheap and cheerful and fairly efficient so long as you fight in the dry; over that a rough woollen cloak so sodden with blood and dirty water that it could've been any colour; trousers the same, the toes of the boots just sticking up out of the mud); cause of death was either the big puncture wound in the pit of the stomach or the deep slash that started under the right ear and carried on an inch or so into the leather of the cuirass, just above the collarbone. His face was just an open mouth and two open eyes, with drying mud slopped incongruously on the eyeballs, but whether it was a friend or an enemy he couldn't say.

He counted. Two dozen bodies, more or less (he could easily have missed one in the mud), and half of them were dressed like the first one he'd looked at; the other half were scruffier, tattier but kitted out in better armour – good steel scale, fine protection but expensive and a bitch to keep clean – and clothes that had once been good-quality civilian stuff. They didn't mean anything to him either, and that bothered him a lot, so he went to the trouble of pulling each of them out of the swamp, wiping the muck off their faces so he could see their eyes, but it didn't get him anywhere. Quite the opposite, in fact, since he went in over his knees more than once in the slough, and the thought of being stuck there, unable to move and with nobody living to pull him out, wasn't a cheerful one. Fortunately, by going flat on his face and clawing hard at the grass with his hands until the mud let go of his knees, he managed to get away with it. Apparently that was something he had a knack for.

By now he was painfully tired and painfully thirsty. Even so, he didn't fancy the river, at least not until after he'd lugged out the two bodies, lodged in a big patch of briars, whose blood was fouling the water. Then he drank, and that made him feel much better, though not inclined to stir much from where he was lying, belly down, back in the mud again. But it occurred to him that if the bodies he'd just cleared out of the stream were still bleeding, it followed that the fighting must've been quite recent – and that there had been two sides to the fighting, and he didn't know which one he belonged to. It could easily be the case that the friends of one side or the other were out looking for them, that they could show up here at any moment. Of course, they might be his friends too, and overjoyed to see that he'd made it. Or they might not.

He lay in the dirty water, unable to make up his mind. It could be that he was on the home side, that this was his native valley and when his memory came back he'd simply walk home over the hills, have a bath and go to bed. Or he might be the last survivor of a raiding party, trapped a hundred miles behind enemy lines, in which case his only chance of ever getting out alive would be to find his own people quickly, before they gave him up for dead and withdrew. Or they might all be dead, and every living soul he'd be likely to meet would be his enemy, ready to kill him on sight. He thought about that, and realised that he hadn't a clue what he looked like. If he knew that, surely it'd give him some idea of which side he'd been on.

He found a pool large enough to show him his reflection, but the face he saw in it could have been anybody, some stranger. He saw a man with his hair plastered down over his face with mud, a tidemark down one side of his face, traces of clotted blood gathered in the socket of the left eye; two days' growth of beard, a long, straight nose, someone who was either younger than he looked or older than he felt; a mess. No armour, nothing that looked like military uniform or the clothes the other side were wearing (he was thinking of them as the other side, but only because the first body he'd come across was one of the uniformed soldiers) and no empty scabbard or sheath to suggest he'd been carrying a weapon. One civilian left alive, two dozen dead soldiers. Of course, any moment now he'd remember it all and everything would make sense – assuming he lived that long.

Big assumption. Give him five, ten minutes and he'd have his life back again, he'd know what to do. How long would it take for a troop of cavalry to get from the skyline to the river-bank? Two minutes, maybe three. In many ways he wasn't as smart as a crow, but he could figure. It was time to go.

Halfway up the western side of the combe was a small clump of tall, thin trees with a little scrubby patch of ferns and briars tangled round the edge, enough to hide a man in if he didn't mind getting scratched all to hell. It was as good a place as any to lie up and wait for himself to come back. (*But if I'm hidden, how will I know where to look for me? Because it's the only scrap of cover in this whole valley, fool. Obvious place to look.*) As an afterthought, he dragged a left boot off the nearest dead man and crammed his foot into it – a size too big, much better than a size too small; as a second afterthought, he pulled off the man's cloak and sword-belt, squelched ten paces up the slope, thought about going back to look for a rations bag or a water bottle, decided against it. After all, he'd only be laid up there for half an hour, an hour at most, just as long as it took him to remember himself.

He put up two crows as he bustled a way through the briars; *they must hate me,* he thought, *I've been doing nothing but get in their way ever since I woke up.* They circled a couple of times, swearing at him, then headed off due south, flying awkwardly and with obvious effort, like a man wading through mud.

Something was happening down below by the river. He crawled to the edge of the briar tangle, where he could see.

A dozen horsemen, soldiers, were riding at a smart gallop over the opposite crest. As they felt the soft ground under their horses' hooves, they slowed down – dangerously easy for a horse to slip and break a leg on a slope in the mud – and walked the rest of the way. Before they reached the river, the man in front held up his hand, a signal to halt; then he dismounted, gave his reins to the man behind him, and walked carefully (not wanting to go arse over tip in front of the men) to the edge of the muddy slough. Didn't have to see his face to sense the hesitation before he stepped into it – horror at what he was looking at, shock at the death of friends, or he really didn't want to get his shiny black riding boots covered in mud and filth.

The horseman – he was a soldier, no question about it; but infuriatingly, his clothes and armour didn't match with either side, he was wearing a knee-length mailshirt (terrifyingly expensive, and after an hour or so your neck and shoulders start hurting like you wouldn't believe) and a tall conical helmet bulled up to a mirror shine, and a small round shield, bowcase and quiver were slung over his back – the soldier squelched through the mud like a fine lady crossing a farmyard, knelt beside the nearest body and peered at it, lifting the head; gently let it back, moved on to the next, and the next. He was examining the bodies from both sides with the same care and respect (if they were enemy bodies, would you lift the head gently then lower it softly again after you'd looked, or would you just use the toe of your boot?). And he was definitely looking for something or someone, rather than examining them for cause of death or any other evidence of how the fight had gone. *Conclusion: they're looking for me. Maybe; or they're looking for someone else who was supposed to be here, but who escaped or got taken away.* That was a thought; he'd been assuming that these two dozen dead men had fought to the death, each killing the other in a graceful act of symmetry so as to leave him the perfect puzzle when he came round. Bad assumption, made for the sake of keeping the problem confined. Bad assumption; all assumptions bad, though some worse than others, like assuming the battle had been for or about him, or that it hadn't. This was no time to trust or take chances; better to keep well clear, like the crows, and wait till all the humans had gone and it was safe.

Whatever else the horseman may have been, he was efficient and quick in making his inspection, and when he was through he dragged himself back on his horse (he was tired, too, probably anxious to get home, change into some dry footwear, have something to eat) and gave the signal to move on. They didn't go back the way they'd come, he noticed; instead they followed the combe parallel to the river until they were out of sight over the horizon.

Getting out of the briar tangle was significantly harder than getting in . . . The brambles ran their fingers down his face and tugged at his clothes like children wanting attention, as if they were sorry to see him go. *Affection,* he remembered, *I guess I've known what that feels like. But it was easier to get out of my life than a patch of briars.*

Nothing had changed; still the river, the mud and the bodies. He had a feeling it would get dark in the next hour or so. He still couldn't remember anything, not his name or his nationality, or why he was here or what had happened. For the first time, he made himself contemplate the possibility that he could be like this for days, or weeks – and what would happen to his life while he was away from it? For all he knew it was about to catch fire or boil over, or starve to death; or maybe he'd walk out of this and back into it and nobody would realise he'd even been away. No doubt about it, he was frightened, and the worst part of that was not knowing what he ought to be frightened of. Taking a deep breath, he made a resolution: to be afraid of *everything,* on principle, until he was sure it was safe. It worked for the crows, after all; and so far they were the only role models for survival that he had.

Ah yes, survival; not just a matter of keeping out of the way of swords and spears, you also had to eat and drink. He had an idea that a lot of people found it hard enough to manage even with their memories intact; it was difficult, not something that came by light of nature. It would probably be a good idea to get away from here and go somewhere else, somewhere he could find food and shelter, a change of clothes, the things he'd need in order to be still alive when his life decided to come back (idiotic, suddenly to remember that he was the crown prince or an incredibly wealthy merchant seconds before dying of starvation or exposure). The thought made him smile – *so what am I supposed to do, settle down and get a job? Hell, I don't even know if there's anything I can do.* Walking into some village – assuming there were villages nearby for walking into – and telling people the truth; that didn't appeal to him for some reason, too dangerous. Maybe the first village he came to would turn out to be the one where he'd been captured after a life of highway robbery, where the soldiers had collected him to take him back to the city to stand trial. Maybe he'd been there before, hours or days earlier, to burn or pillage or maybe just to collect taxes—

It was starting to rain. He looked up at the sky, which was grey and low. Heavy rain about to set in for a long time, not a comforting thought. He could be sensible and crawl back under the briars till it passed over (but he didn't want to do that) or he could start walking and hope he found a wood or a barn, something like that. As for a direction to walk in, he had no idea, other than a certain reluctance to go either where the horseman had come from or gone to. That still left him with a choice between east and west, far more choice than he actually wanted. He chose west because that was where the rain was coming from, and it was marginally less uncomfortable having it at his back than in his face.

He felt a certain degree of anxiety as he walked over the skyline to look down into the next valley, but when it appeared there was nothing much to see; no familiar landmarks to jog his memory, no column of bloodthirsty soldiers advancing on him with swords drawn. Instead there was a gentle slope falling away to a heather-covered plain, across which was a road. He didn't know why exactly, but he knew that a road was a good thing, potentially. A road could take him in the right direction, towards people who might help him. There were other things it could do, of course, but he preferred not to think about them.

The boot he'd taken from the dead man became uncomfortable pretty quickly; being too big, it rubbed his heel and instep, and it was full of muddy water. It occurred to him that he might want to go back, find a boot that fitted a little better, and while he was at it he could scrounge around for other things he might need – a better cloak, something to eat, money, all the advantages the dead could offer to a man

making a start in life. He decided against it, though the decision was irrational. He couldn't keep going back there; if he
went back, maybe the next time he wouldn't be able to leave.
At any rate, he had to do *something*, and walking away down
the road was probably as good a choice as any.

*No more choices, please. Take all the choices away, and I'll be
a happy man.* He shook his head, and was glad he hadn't said
that aloud, just in case someone was listening. When he
reached the road he didn't stop. East was slightly uphill, west
was slightly downhill, so he went west. See? Another choice
successfully made, in a rational manner with due regard to
prudent self-interest, and no need even to break stride for it.

After that he walked for a long time, until it was too dark to
go any further. He hadn't noticed any houses, forests, rivers,
other roads, there was nowhere to reach, so when he felt it
wasn't safe to walk any further (last thing he needed was a
twisted ankle) he stopped, lay down with the spare cloak rolled
up as a pillow and tried to go to sleep. Perversely, he couldn't.
Instead he lay with his eyes open, feeling the rain tapping his
face, with nothing to see however hard he looked. When he
started to feel cramp coming on he shifted over on to his side
but the sensation of rain falling in his ear wasn't pleasant. He
stood up, wondered about walking a little further, chose not to,
lay down again. All the while his mind was looking hard and
there was nothing to see there either.

That night lasted a long time. He tried to make use of the
time by taking stock, making a rational analysis of his position
and the options available to him, laying plans, figuring out.
That didn't work. Instead he kept coming back to a sound in
the back of his mind. At first it was just a suggestion, a shape
made out of noise, but the more he tried to ignore it the clearer
it became, until he recognised it as a tune (music would be
overstating it). Where it had come from he didn't know.
Possibly it was a genuine memory, or possibly it was something he'd just made up (in which case, he hoped very much

that when his memory came back, he wouldn't turn out to be a professional musician)—

> *Old crow sitting in a tall thin tree,*
> *Old crow sitting in a tall thin tree,*
> *Old crow sitting in a tall thin tree,*
> *And along comes the Dodger and he says, 'That's me.'*

Once it was stuck in his mind, like a stringy scrap of meat lodged between two teeth, there was no escaping it; quite probably he lay there humming it under his breath for an hour, not listening to it, not thinking, just following the shape of the sounds round and round in a dance. It did occur to him that if it was a memory, it was a stupid one to have chosen, like dashing back into a burning house to save one odd sock. Unfortunately there weren't any more where that came from, so he tried to pass the time by making up another verse, an experiment that had the dubious merit of disproving once and for all the professional songwriter theory.

Perhaps it was because he was listening so closely to the song that he didn't hear the cart until it was almost too late; or perhaps he'd finally fallen asleep after all, and simply dreamed he was humming the same tune over and over again. In any event, the cart was suddenly there – the sound of creaking axles, iron tyres crushing the heather stalks, the breath of the horses – and if he hadn't jumped out of the way it would have rolled right over him.

The cart noises stopped, and he heard a man's voice swearing in the dark, the first words he could remember having heard. He picked himself up and tried to see, but all he could make out was a vague shape.

'Stupid bloody fool,' the man was yelling into the rain. 'Could've startled the horses, could've bloody well killed me.' The man sounded like he was drunk, which might explain why he was driving a cart at night without even a lantern.

'Got a good mind to give you a smack round the head for that, stupid bloody clown.'

Any thoughts of trying to hitch a ride evaporated. *Wonderful*, he thought. *Even drunks driving carts want to attack me. If this sort of thing happens to me all the time, no wonder I'm having trouble getting my memory back. Who'd want to remember a lot of stuff like this?*

He heard the sound of boots crushing heather, and a noise that had something to do with metal that his instincts didn't like at all. 'Teach you a damn lesson,' the voice said. 'Teach you to go jumping out at people in the middle of the night.'

'For God's sake, you idiot, leave it alone.' That was a woman's voice, coming from where he reckoned the cart was. 'Get back in and sleep it off, before you do yourself an injury.'

'You shut up,' the man's voice replied. 'Gotta teach him a lesson, roads aren't safe otherwise.' That was useful; it gave him a fix on where the drunk was. Now all he had to do was walk quietly away in the opposite direction, and everything would be fine.

Instead he contrived to put his foot in a pothole and go down hard on his face. A stone found his cheekbone, jarring him painfully enough to make him cry out. What the drunk made of the sound he never found out; best guess was that he took it for a challenge or a battle-cry, because the next sound was that of a sword blade cutting empty air as the drunk drew and slashed at where he thought his enemy ought to be. All wrong, of course, but a drunk waving a sharp object about in the dark can be just as dangerous as a well-trained swords-man – worse, in some cases, since his moves are irrational, therefore impossible to read and predict. Staying still was probably the best policy, except that the drunk was very close now, so close that he could easily blunder into him. More choices, more decisions . . . Just for once, couldn't something contrive to happen on its own, without him having any say in the matter?

He decided to run; after all, nothing to be gained here . . . He got up as quietly as he could; but the drunk appeared to have taken root, he couldn't hear his footsteps or breathing any more. That was bad.

'Got you, you bastard!' A loud swish and a disturbance in the air told him that the drunk was fencing at shadows again, this time uncomfortably close. He backed away, as quietly as he could (and that was very quietly indeed, apparently), and was just starting to think he'd made it when something hit him in the back. It turned out to be the back wheel of the cart.

'Is that you?' the woman's voice called out nervously.

That didn't help. The drunk must have assumed that he was trying to get in the cart, to steal it or kill the woman or whatever. He roared angrily and charged, and the chunk of wood on bone announced that he'd run into something, probably the boom. Anyhow, it was a fix of sorts, enough information to let him decide which direction was away. It was just bad luck that the woman chose that moment to start fooling around with a tinderbox.

There would still have been time to run, he decided later; he'd got that wrong, that was all there was to it. In the event, as soon as he heard flint and steel noises he froze, torn between running and some dumb notion of getting underneath the cart and hiding there. While he was still trying to make his mind up, the drunk came blundering in his direction, still swiping with his sword. He felt the slipstream, a cold breeze on his face—

—And the rest was pure instinct. He could have sworn he'd forgotten all about the sword he'd taken from the dead man in the river combe, but in the time it took him to figure out what he was doing his hand had found the hilt and started to draw. The first he knew about it was the sound of steel in flesh (no other sound like that in the world, a hissing, sucking, solid, meaty noise) and the shock of impact travelling up his arm to his shoulder.

His first thought was that the drunk had cut him. It was only the heavy thump of a body hitting first the side of the cart then the ground that started him wondering if in fact it had been the other way round. Then he realised there was something in his right hand, and remembered about the dead soldier's sword, which he hadn't even looked at all day. *What the hell did I do that for?* he asked himself, just as the woman's fourth attempt at lighting the tinderbox succeeded, and the small orange glow caught the corner of his eye.

Light to see by, growing quickly as she applied the tinder to the wick of a lamp. As the lamp opened up the darkness like a folded blanket, he saw first his hand around the hilt of a sword, and beyond that something like a sack or a pile of bed-clothes, slumped at the base of the cart's front wheel.

'Who the hell are you?' said the woman's voice, somewhere above his head.

He'd have answered if he could. Instead he knelt down and turned the body over. Interestingly, the cut started just under the right ear and carried on down to the collarbone. Of course, that may have been pure random chance.

'He's dead,' he announced, superfluously.

'Fuck,' the woman said. 'Oh, that's bloody marvellous, that is.'

This time he looked round, surprised at her tone of voice, which suggested a lame horse or a broken wheel. She was holding the lamp up in front of her, so all he could see was a vague reflection of light off her face and one white hand. He wondered whether it would be safe to put his sword away, then realised he'd just done it.

'Bloody marvellous,' the woman repeated. 'Now what am I going to do?'

All he could think of to say was, 'I'm sorry,' because he was. That didn't seem to impress the woman very much.

'You're sorry,' she said. 'Thank you, but that's a fat lot of good. What the hell did you have to go and do that for?'

He looked at her. 'He was trying to kill me,' he said.

'Was he?' She didn't seem surprised, or particularly interested. 'He always was a bloody fool, and a liability. I should never have let him get his hands on the stuff. God knows, he was dumb enough sober. Oh *hell*,' she added. 'Just my typical rotten luck.'

Maybe if he'd still had his memory, he'd have known how to cope with the situation. Just then the lamp guttered – the rain, presumably, or the wind – and went out. He caught his breath. He'd never have a better chance to make a run for it, and surely it had to be the most, the only sensible thing to do. Instead he waited patiently while she scraped and swore at the tinderbox.

'Let me try,' he heard himself suggest.

'Get lost.' There was the orange glow again, followed by ivory lamplight. 'There used to be a glass bell for this lamp, but the bloody fool dropped it. Never knew anybody quite so clumsy. Here, let's have a look at you.' She swung the lamp towards him; this time he caught the instinct in plenty of time and suppressed it, letting his hand fall off the sword hilt and back to his side. 'My God,' she said, 'what the hell have you been up to? You look like you just went for a swim in the slurry pit.'

'Thank you,' he replied. 'Actually, that's not far off . . .'

'Whatever.' She moved the lamp a little closer to his face. He made an effort to keep still. 'Who did you say you are?'

'I was asleep,' he replied. 'Your cart nearly ran me over. Then he came after me with a sword. When he got too close, I must have just lashed out. I'm sorry.'

'You keep saying that.' He could just make out her eyes, by the reflection of the lamp in them. 'And that's not what I asked. Who are you?'

This time he couldn't resist saying it, because it had been a long day and he was past caring. 'You know,' he said, 'that's a very good question.'

Chapter Two

'What kind of an answer is that?' she said.

He recognised the tone of voice: disapproval, impatience, stop-being-silly-this-is-serious. 'Straight answer, I'm afraid,' he replied, yawning. 'I haven't a clue who I am. I got bashed over the head' – no need for awkward details just now – 'and I can't remember anything. I've been wandering about all day, and—'

'Oh,' the woman said. 'I see. Still doesn't give you any right to go killing people in the middle of nowhere.'

He couldn't help frowning at that; why was the location so important? 'I'm sorry,' he said, for a third time. 'It was him or me. Whoever I am, I'd rather not get killed by some drunk for not lying still and getting run over. Who was he?' he went on. 'Your husband?'

The woman laughed. 'Do me a favour,' she said. 'No, he was my god.'

'Your what?'

'My god. And a bloody hard time I had finding him, too. Waste of effort that turned out to be.'

Let's assume there's a rational explanation. 'What are you talking about?' he asked, as gently as he could manage.

'What? Oh, I see what you mean. He wasn't a *real* god,' the woman explained. 'Actually, I don't believe in gods; well, it'd be rather hard to do that in my line of work.'

'Really? What's that?'

'I'm a priestess.'

He sighed. Maybe if he could remember anything he'd know that the world was usually like this, though in all conscience he found that hard to imagine. 'You're a priestess,' he repeated.

'Not a real one, you fool. Just like he wasn't a real god. Come on, use your head. Or did you get all your brains knocked out along with your memories?'

'Oh, I see,' he said. 'You're—' He couldn't think of a polite way of saying it: swindlers, conmen, coney-catchers. 'Impersonators,' he said.

'I like that,' she replied. 'Divine impersonators. That's us, or at least it was, till you showed up. He was the god and I was his priestess. We drive round the towns and villages taking the rubes for money. It's a living.' She sighed. 'Or it was. Now what the hell am I going to do?'

He laughed, although he had an idea it wasn't tactful. 'You and me both,' he replied, and as he said the words he thought of something. 'Where are you going next?' he asked.

'What?' She sounded preoccupied. 'Oh, there's a small town half a day to the west, we were headed there. No point going now, of course, except I suppose I could sell the cart, that'd probably be enough to get me to Josequin. Except I just left there, getting out of Josequin was the whole bloody *point* . . .'

'What's the town called?'

'Cric.'

'Cric,' he repeated. 'No.'

'What do you mean, no? Oh, I get you, you wanted to see if it sounded familiar. It doesn't, I take it.'

'No, unfortunately.' He slumped down on to his heels and rubbed his face with his hands. 'Not to worry,' he said, 'I'll get there eventually. I must do, or I'm really in trouble.'

'If you like—' That was a different tone of voice; a little sympathy, and there was something she wanted, too. 'If you like,' she said, 'I'll take you there in the cart. After all, no skin off my nose.'

He looked up. 'Thank you,' he said. 'That'd be kind.'

'No trouble. We'll stay here till it's light. I suppose we'd better bury him, too.' This time there was something else in her voice, the way she said *him*; a deliberate transfer, from valuable asset lost to nuisance to be dealt with. Nothing if not pragmatic, this woman. 'I'm going to get under the cart.'

'Why?'

'Because it's dry under there, you fool. You may be so drenched it doesn't matter, but I was nice and snug under the cover before – well, all this. And a fine priestess I'll sound like with a streaming cold.'

Ah, he thought, *so that's what she wanted.* 'Mind if I get under there too?' he asked.

'You'd be an idiot not to,' she replied. 'It's raining.'

They lay side by side in the dark, the underside of the cart a hand's span from their faces. 'My name's Copis,' she said.

'Copis,' he repeated. 'No, that's not familiar. Not unfamiliar, either. Not anything, really.'

She laughed. 'Thank you very much,' she said. 'Actually, I'd be surprised if it was. It's not a Bohec name, you see. I'm from Torcea, right on the other side of the bay.'

'None of that means anything to me,' he replied.

'Really? You don't even know where you are? That's . . .' She paused for a moment, presumably marshalling her thoughts. 'All right,' she said, 'it's like this. Actually, I'm having problems with this, because geography really isn't my strong point, but we're just south of the Mahec River – does that mean anything to you?'

'No.'

'Oh. Right, then. There's the Mahec, which starts in the eastern mountains and runs west to the sea, I think I've got that the right way round. South of the Mahec there's this big hilly plain – can you have a hilly plain? Well, you know what I mean. Moorland and hills and valleys, mostly too high for growing anything, so the towns and villages are down in the valleys. In the middle of that is Josequin, which is the only city worth a damn north of the Bohec. Still nothing?'

'No,' he replied, 'but it's very interesting. What's the Bohec?'

'That's another river,' she replied, 'more or less parallel with the Mahec, much bigger and more important, because ships can sail right up as far as Mael – Mael Bohec, that's its full name – and there's three other big cities: Boc Bohec on the west coast, Weal Bohec about a day inland and Sansory two days upriver from Mael. Got that?'

'I think so.'

'Well done. Anyhow, it's another two days due south from the Bohec to the south coast – that's the bay – and it's a day's sail from one of the south coast ports straight across the bay to Torcea, where I come from, but of course you can only do that in summer; the rest of the year you have to go the long way round, to the east. Due west's just open sea, of course, and nobody's got the faintest idea what's on the other side of it. And that's all, really. At least, they're the only places I've ever been to, and they're enough to be going on with.'

He was feeling drowsy, but this was all good, solid information, as good as tools or weapons. 'Thank you,' he said. 'And where are we, right now?'

She laughed. 'Oh, we're nowhere much,' she said. 'We're at least three days from Josequin; actually, Weal or Mael would be closer, but there's two lots of mountains in the way.'

'Have you got anything to eat?'

'Yes,' she answered. 'In the cart. Lift the lid off the box, you'll find a jar. Josequin biscuits.' She laughed. 'And if they don't refresh your memory, you really aren't from around here.'

Josequin biscuits turned out to be round, flat and thin, slightly bigger than the palm of his hand; oatmeal sweetened with honey, and there were bits of nuts and raisins in them as well. He didn't remember them, and they'd have been a little too sweet for his taste if he hadn't been so hungry. He ate two.

'It's one of the odd things about this racket,' Copis said. 'Either you're starving on the road between jobs, or you're eating wonderful stuff like that – only delicacies are fit for the god, you see. Salmon, smoked lamb, partridges, peacock – plenty of that kind of thing, but if you want a stack of griddle cakes and a hunk of cooking cheese, forget it. Same with drink. If you'd told me five years ago there'd come a day when I'd swap a jug of wine for an equal measure of milk, I'd have laughed in your face. Truth is, though, I never did like wine much. How about you? You don't know, I suppose.'

'No.'

'Oh well.' He could sense that she was about to ask. 'You know,' she went on, 'I've been thinking. I've lost my partner, you're at a loose end till you get your memory back. Seems a bit silly for both of us to wander around the place with no means of earning a living.'

'You want me to do what he did. Pretend to be a god.'

She giggled. 'Not *a* god. *The* god. Oh damn, I suppose I've got to explain that, too. Have I?'

'It'd help.'

'All right, then. Lately – let's say the last ten years, give or take a year – a lot of people, especially up here, have started believing in this new god – well, he's not new exactly, he's in all the old stories, but he was supposed to have gone away, and he's due to come back just before the end of the world. Really he's kind of a mixed blessing, because he sorts out the good from the bad, however you define that kind of thing, and if you've been good you get to survive and inherit the earth, while if you're bad the enemy's going to get you. For the enemy,' she went on, 'read the pirates, or that's the way people are taking it, and you can't blame them, all things considered. Of course it's all just a load of old rubbish. But you know what they say: opportunities and mushrooms.'

'Opportunities and mushrooms what?'

'Grow up out of horseshit,' she explained. 'So what do you think? I mean,' she added, 'it's not as if you're spoilt for choice, is it?'

He laughed. 'I was thinking earlier,' he said, 'about how all of a sudden every damn thing was a choice; all the options you could ever wish for, and no reason for favouring one over the other. I don't know,' he went on. 'What if we show up in some place and it turns out I've been there before and they recognise me?'

'Come on,' she said. 'Wouldn't that be a good thing?'

'That depends,' he replied, 'on what I'd been doing the last time I was there. Suppose I really am one of these pirates, for instance.'

'Then you wouldn't need to have any worries on that score,' Copis replied. 'Nobody knows what they look like. Guess why. Their standard operating procedure is no survivors. Makes it all much simpler really, doesn't it?'

'All right, then,' he said, stifling a yawn with the back of his hand. 'But the moment my memory comes back, chances are I'll be off and away like a hare. So long as that's understood . . .'

'That's fine,' she replied. 'So, welcome to the team. I suppose I'd better tell you what the job entails.'

'Later,' he muttered, as his eyelids started to get heavy. 'I've had a long day.'

She was saying something when he fell asleep, and the dream opened for him, almost impatiently, like a child who's been promised a walk. Remembering was easy here; he remembered

the short man and the dead man in the barn and the woman –
but when he looked round, everything was different.

This time he was standing beside a fountain in the middle
of a courtyard. He was much younger here, and his reflection
in the edge of the pool showed him a round, slightly chubby
face topped by a tangle of reddish curls and with the first
scruffy traces of a beard. He turned his head, because there
was someone standing behind him.

'Ready?'

He watched himself nod, as the other man (perhaps a year
or two older, dressed in the same plain white shirt and rather
elegant grey trousers) opened a wooden box and handed him a
knife. He picked it up and looked at it thoughtfully, examining
it as if the details mattered to him. It was a good-looking knife,
as knives go; the blade was about seven inches long, double-
edged and gently tapering to a point, the hilt was ivory, carved
with a spiral pattern. It looked expensive and either new or
very carefully looked after. He wondered why it was important.

'Remember,' the other man said, 'he'll start off going for
your face, trying to scare you. Keep your guard up, don't let
him in close, you'll be fine. What you'll need to be doing is
using your feet – don't let him make you play his game, up and
down in a straight line. Use your back foot, try and get round
him all the time, don't be afraid to use left-hand blocks –
you're quicker than him; he's bigger and stronger but that
really shouldn't come into it. Let him wear himself out, and
then he'll get sloppy and drop his guard. He's only got to do it
once, after all, and you're home and dry. Got that?'

For a moment, he hadn't been paying attention; he'd been
looking at the statue that formed the centrepiece of the fountain. Not beautiful, by any stretch of the imagination, but
striking: a crow, very realistically rendered, holding a gold
ring in its beak.

(*Ah, now I know where I am, I'm back inside my memory. So
that's all right.*)

He nodded. 'It's all right,' he said, 'I ought to be able to handle this. To be honest, I'm more concerned about what's going to happen afterwards.'

That seemed to annoy the other man. 'Don't think about that,' he said. 'Really, you mustn't. Anything like that could distract you, put you in two minds at the crucial moment. As far as you're concerned, all you're here to do is stick that knife in his ribs. We'll handle the rest, don't you worry.'

It was beautifully cool in the courtyard, near the water. When the other man wasn't looking, he reached out and cupped a little in his hand; when he sipped, he made a soft slurping noise and immediately felt embarrassed.

'All right,' the other man said, peering round a column and through the courtyard gate, 'he's coming. You know what to do. Good luck.'

(I know what to do, do I? This'll be interesting.)

He grinned in reply, slid the knife into his sash behind his back and moved away from the fountain towards the gateway, where he couldn't be seen by anyone coming in from the main yard. The other man sat down on a bench in the shadows on the west side of the yard, pulled out a book, opened it at random and started to read. Not long afterwards, he saw a shadow coming in through the gateway and recognised it as his cue. Timing was important here; he counted under his breath, one, two, then started to walk briskly towards the gate. After five steps he collided heavily with the man whose shadow he'd just seen. Without stopping to catch his breath, he said his line, 'Watch out, you bloody fool. Why can't you look where you're going?'

The man he'd just walked into had caught him, holding him by the elbows so he wouldn't fall over. 'I do apologise,' he said. 'My fault. Terribly sorry.'

A big man, this newcomer, over six feet tall, broad-shouldered, with long, straight black hair, a thick beard with maybe five or six grey hairs in it, and noticeably gentle brown eyes. He was smiling. No good at all.

'That's not good enough,' he improvised. 'Crashing into me like that, you could have done me an injury.' He sounded nervous, and he had an unpleasant feeling that the big man had picked up on it. Nevertheless; 'Someone ought to teach you a lesson,' he went on, trying to make that nervousness sound like anger and not making a very good job of it.

'I said I'm sorry,' the man replied, letting go of his arms. 'I'm in a bit of hurry, that's all, and I wasn't thinking. You aren't hurt, are you?' he added.

'No. That's not the point.' This was all wrong; this dreadful man, this enemy of the empire, should be as easy to provoke as a wasps' nest. Instead it was like trying to pick a fight with a pillow. 'You barge around like you own the place – well, you don't. Not yet, anyhow.'

That got his attention; but instead of getting angry he just seemed curious. Damnation, he's figured it out, I've given the game away. He knows he's being set up.

'What a strange thing to say,' the man replied. 'And I'm very sorry I've upset you. It was just an accident, that's all.'

'I don't think so.' Out of the corner of his eye he could see the other man, his friend, looking embarrassed, shooting him a trust-you-to-cock-it-up look from behind the pages of his book. Now that did make him angry. 'I think you did it on purpose—'

'How could I have? I didn't even know you were there.'

'You did it on purpose,' he ground on, 'because you enjoy pushing people like us around, you like shoving us about because it makes you feel big. Well, we'll see how big you are.' And, on that really quite unsatisfactory line, he pulled the knife out, took a step back and crouched in the best coaching-manual fashion.

The big man looked at him and sighed. 'I see,' he said. He didn't move. 'Your idea?' he asked.

'I don't know what you mean.' It was exquisitely embarrassing standing there in the second defensive guard (weight on the back foot, head and arms well forward, left elbow up, right hand low), talking back to an enemy who was upright, unarmed, with hands folded across his chest. 'Come on,' he said, aware that his voice was getting higher and higher the more flustered he became. 'Scared, are you?'

'Yes,' the man replied (he didn't look it). 'People waving knives at me generally have that effect.' Damn it, he was starting to walk backwards, he was getting away. This *wasn't meant to happen* – it was time to do something. If he just walked away, and then told people about what'd just happened, how he'd been set up . . . Feeling wretchedly stupid, he stepped forward sharply with his left leg, threw a feint to the head and converted it into a thrust to the groin. The man blocked him easily with his left hand and punched him on the nose with his right.

He hadn't been expecting that; it was bad form, common, to punch in a knife fight. And it *hurt* . . He staggered back three or four steps, managed not to drop the knife; if the man had followed up, he'd have had no chance. But he didn't; he was turning his back, leaving. With a shout of dismay he jumped forward again, misjudging the distance because the punch had left him groggy, but he managed to grab the man's shoulder and pull him round. The man's right hand came up fast to take the knife away from him; as he pulled it away, like a child protecting a toy from an angry parent, the side of the man's hand brushed against it and drew blood.

He was appalled at the sight of it, for some reason; he felt so stupid . . . But the man was still trying to get the knife; he hopped back two-footed and steadied himself. 'For God's sake,' his friend was shouting behind him. He made a conscious effort, pretended he was back in the fencing school, about to perform an exercise. Come on, he was *good* at this . . . He struck out, narrowly missing the ball of the man's right shoulder (but at least it was a legitimate fighting shot, not like that horrible confused grabbing and pulling away), and brought his arm back and down for a stomach thrust. The big man (his eyes were cold now) blocked that with his left forearm to the wrist, reached behind his back and drew his own knife (at last; I thought we'd never get there . . .). He was so relieved that he didn't realise he was out of position and horribly open until it was almost too late.

But, as his friend had said earlier, he was quick. Another jump back, and he landed well, on the balls of his feet, good balance. The man was serious now, either angry or resigned; his back was bent too, his hands forward and low. The knife in his hand was one of those long, thin, square-section stilettos, the kind engineers and artillerymen carry, with a scale of inches engraved on the blade – no cutting edges, but extremely efficient for stabbing with. For the first time it occurred to him that he might easily get killed . . . He shivered, felt his stomach churn. He was an expert fencer, sure, but this was the first time in his life he'd ever tried to kill anybody, or face someone who was trying to kill him. He didn't like it at all.

The hell with it, he thought, and tried his best shot. It was a complex manoeuvre, made up of three parts – feint at the eyes, drop low for another feint to the hands, snap back up for a killing shot to the head – but it was a guaranteed match-winner if it worked and he'd practised it over and over again. The man stepped back on the first feint, read it (as he was meant to do), moved his left arm to block the blow shot, read that too—

—And what he should have done, if he'd learned his knife-fighting in the Purple Ring instead of an alley behind some dockside tavern, was sidestep for a counterattack, right into the path of the oncoming blade. Instead, quite improperly, he switched his weight on to his right foot and struck out hard with his left. The boot landed squarely in the younger man's crotch. He dropped his knife and doubled over, hearing his own shriek of pain as he found himself suddenly and unexpectedly staring at the grass between his feet. *Fuck, I'm going to die,* he thought, just as the older man's left fist crashed into the side of his head and dumped him on the ground.

For a long time, nothing happened. He was lying on his left arm, not really aware of very much beside the splitting pain in his head and groin. He heard his friend screaming, 'You *idiot!*' but he was past caring now about what other people thought of him; in fact, nothing really registered apart from his extreme discomfort. Then he saw the man's boots coming towards him – that's it, he'll finish me off now, oh well – and tried to move, but he was wasting his time.

The other man lifted his right foot and kicked him hard in the stomach.

'All right,' he heard the man say, 'you can get up now. And you—' Presumably to his friend, though it hardly mattered. 'You stay out of it. Don't I know you from somewhere?'

'I don't think so,' his friend stuttered – spineless bastard! Get him for that . . . 'I was just sitting here . . .'

'Yes, all right.' The man sounded annoyed, that was all. 'And I do know you, come to think of it. You're Galien – I beg your pardon, *Prince* Galien. Your idea, was it?'

'No, really,' Galien replied, terrified. 'Like I said, I was just . . .'

'Bugger off.'

'But I . . .'

'I said bugger off.' Apparently Galien did as he was told because he heard nothing more from him; instead he felt the man's hand on his collar, hauling him up. His legs weren't working very well, and he ended up hanging off the man's hand, like a little kid. 'And you, Tazencius,' the man was saying, 'you really ought to know better. You really thought you could pull off something like this? You two?'

'Let go of me,' he gasped.

'All right,' the man said, and let go. Of course, he ended up back on the ground again. He had the feeling he'd turned his ankle over. 'Now then, when you're ready.' He felt himself being hauled up again, like a fish on a line, and found himself looking straight into the man's face. 'You clown,' the man said.

'You—' It was all he could manage to keep himself from bursting into tears. 'You're going to tell my father, aren't you?'

Oh, the scorn in the man's eyes . . . 'No,' he said. 'That'd only make things worse, he'd have to punish you and then *everybody* would hate me, instead of just nearly everybody. Dear God, what is it with you people? Can't you just leave me alone?'

'I'm sorry.' He said it without thinking, because it was what he felt. Suddenly the man smiled.

'You're sorry,' he repeated. 'Well, that's all right, then.' He let go. 'Apologise nicely, or it's straight up to bed and no pudding. You lot, you're amazing.' But he didn't seem angry any more; the contempt was still there, but it probably always had been. And it was tolerant contempt, the sort he sometimes caught sight of in the eyes of the older servants, the ones who'd been at court a long time. 'Now go away,' the man went on, 'before somebody comes along and sees us. And listen, Tazencius; next time you and your devious cousin want to play at politics, don't try picking a fight with a soldier, or you might get hurt; and you're a prince, and I've sworn to protect all the members of the royal family with my life, including, God help us all, you. I'd hate to get drawn into a fight with a grown-up just to stop you getting your silly throat cut. Got that?'

He nodded and started to back away.

'Hold on,' the man said, 'you've forgotten something.'

'Have I?'

The man stooped down, picked something up. 'Your knife,' he said. 'Can't leave things like this lying about; somebody might cut himself on it. Worth a lot of money, too,' he added. 'A year's pay, when I was your age.' He handed it over solemnly. 'Watch out,' he warned, 'it's sharp.'

'Thank you,' he said automatically.

'You're welcome.'

'Actually—' Why was he saying this? Just making conversation. 'Actually it isn't my knife, it's Galien's.'

'Mind you give it back, then,' the man replied. 'His idea, was it?'

He nodded. 'Yes.'

'Thought so. Takes after his father.' The man looked at him seriously. 'Really,' he said, 'you want to stay away from him. You think he's on your side, but he isn't.' Then he looked sad, and added, 'Nobody is, that's the bloody awful thing about it.'

For some reason, he was shocked. 'Nobody?'

'Nobody.' The man's eyes were large and soft. 'Except possibly me, but you shouldn't count on it.'

He took a deep breath. 'Tell me something, General,' he said quietly. 'Whose side *are* you on? Really?'

'Really?' The man smiled. He was the sort of man who preferred to smile if he could. 'You know, I wish I knew, sometimes.'

'But, General . . .'

But, General . . .

'What did you say?' asked the woman, Copis, in the dark beside him.

He woke up. 'Huh?'

'Did you just say something?'

'I don't think so.'

'I thought I heard you say something.'

He rubbed his eyes. 'Maybe you did,' he said. It was just starting to get light. In spite of everything he'd hoped that somehow he'd wake up and all his memories would be back. They weren't. On the other hand, he could remember what had happened the previous day, from the moment when he woke up in the mud. That was something, after all. 'We'd better get going,' he said, realising as he tried to move that he'd cricked his neck horribly in his sleep. Also, his head hurt.

'All right,' Copis replied. It occurred to him, as they both scrambled out from under the cart, that he hadn't seen her yet, except as a vague presence behind a lantern. He waited until her head and shoulders appeared on the other side of the cart. Of course, she was looking at him too.

'You need to get a wash,' she said. 'Badly.'

He hadn't been expecting beauty, of course, so he wasn't disappointed. On the other hand, she looked younger than she sounded – somewhere between thirty and forty, probably nearer thirty but ground down a bit by a hard and wearing life. She had a sharp face, with a pointed nose and chin, high cheekbones and very dark eyes, and reddish hair tied back out of the way, as if she couldn't be doing with it. She was wearing a man's riding coat, very faded and rather tatty at the neck.

'If you've quite finished staring,' she said, and climbed up on to the box. 'You can sit in the back for now. No offence, but you smell of mud.'

Come to think of it, he hadn't seen himself either – he wasn't inclined to count the reflection he'd seen in the clouded water of the flood pools back by the river. 'All right,' he said, 'find a river or a stream or something and I'll wash it off. There wouldn't be any dry clothes in the back there, would there?' he added.

'Yes,' she replied over her shoulder as she moved the horses on. They were both sluggish and restive after standing all night in the traces. 'Of course he was taller than you, and bigger across the shoulders. You'll look like you're wearing your big brother's hand-me-downs.'

Maybe they are, at that; anything's possible. 'Doesn't matter,' he replied. 'I'm still soaked to the skin here.'

She was looking straight ahead. 'Under the cover,' she said. 'You'll find a blanket roll, they're inside that. And there's his god robes, of course; won't matter so much with them, they're all loose and flowing, fit anybody.'

The dead man's clothes were much too big, just as she'd said they'd be, but the waxed hide of the cover had kept most of the rain out. The simple act of putting on dry clothes turned out to be a moment of sublime luxury – *would I have enjoyed that so much if I knew who I was? Probably not* – and afterwards he sat with his legs dangling over the edge of the tailboard, quite happy simply not to be wet.

'That'll have to do,' Copis called out, some time after. 'Right, you have a wash while I have a pee. Don't be too long about it.'

It was a beautiful place, wherever it was. Below the road, on the right-hand side, the ground fell away quite steeply into a small combe, so carefully folded into the moor that it'd be easy to miss if you weren't paying attention. A stream ran down the middle of the combe, draining into what was either a large pond or a very small lake, according to mood and preference, before breaking over a natural dam of boulders and falling fifteen feet or so into a churning white mess hemmed in by a tangled border of briars, ferns, docks and cow parsley. Below that the stream ran fast and thin over a rocky bed and soaked away into a bog. Two thin thorn trees flanked the splash, and he saw a pair of crows sitting in the stiff branches of the nearest tree, facing perversely into the wind.

A glance at the brown, peat-soaked water of the top pool left him with the conclusion that bathing in it wouldn't leave him any cleaner than he was already, so he picked his way round the edge and scrambled down the rocks to the splash. Off to the left of it was a little basin of calm water, overhung by a broad, flat stone, as handy as a table. Pushing his way through the ferns he took off his clothes and piled them up on the flat stone, then walked into the splash. It was cold enough to make him wince, and the spray hit him in the face, blinding him for a moment. He walked in until the water was up to his

neck, ducked his head under the surface and worked his fingers through his hair, feeling the caked mud and blood loosen.
One of the crows got up, flew a circuit round the pool, and
pitched in the other tree.

Too cold to stay in longer than absolutely necessary . . . He
hopped out on to the stone table, dragged his clothes back on
over his wet skin, then lay down on his stomach and looked at
his face in the still water of the basin.

So that's me, he thought. *Oh well.*

He didn't know what he'd been expecting, but it wasn't the
sad, rectangular face that he saw, with its long, straight nose
and pointed chin, and the eyes were downright miserable,
completely out of keeping with the exhilarating feeling of the
cold water on his skin and the blood tingling in his cheeks.
He'd been expecting someone younger, someone as young as
he felt, but even though his hair was slicked back and wet he
could see streaks of grey at the temples and sides, fringing his
small, flat ears. He could see the smooth, slightly dark blem-
ish of an old scar, running down from the corner of his left eye
to the middle of his cheekbone, and another on the same side,
the length of a thumbnail, where the web of his mouth had
been split.

Disappointed . . . He felt as if he'd been promised a house
and given a falling-down old barn, with a bare plank door
stiff on its hinges and ivy picking the mortar out from between
the stones. Not a cheerful face, by any means; waterproof,
and that was about all you could say for it.

'Hurry up.' He heard Copis' voice, away at the top of the
combe. 'What are you doing down there, for pity's sake?'

'Just a moment,' he called back. One last look at the face –
it was frowning, and the frown settled easily into grooves it
had worn for itself. He picked up a pebble and flipped it
through the middle of the face's forehead.

Chapter Three

'A war,' he repeated. 'What's that about?'

Copis looked at him severely down her nose. 'You mean you don't – you really have lost your memory, haven't you? Oh well. It's like this,' she went on. 'Long story, so pay attention. The emperor – you do know about the emperor, don't you?'

'No.'

All morning the road had looked pretty much the same, a grey and brown ribbon across a green and brown surface, not even straight. In the distance on either side were the vague shapes of hills, but they were hazy, indistinct. Low cloud, Copis said, usual for this time of year. In autumn and winter it was low cloud, in spring it was mist and in summer it was heat-haze. Put another way, you never got to see the hills, not that they were all that interesting anyway.

'Oh, bloody hell,' she sighed. 'All right. How's the best way to explain this? We live in the empire, all right? This is the northern end, the bit that doesn't really matter very much; the emperor and the capital and all that stuff, they're on the other side of the bay, where I come from. Clear so far?'

'More or less.'

'Excellent. Now then, about six days north of the Mahec – you remember what I told you about the Mahec?'

'It's a river. Somewhere.'

'That's right, and it's the frontier, or at least where the frontier used to be. I don't suppose many people know where it really is these days, and probably they aren't telling. Things aren't going well for the empire right now, if you see what I mean.'

'I see.'

'Anyway,' Copis went on, 'about five years ago the emperor sent a new general to take over on the frontier; and it's the usual story, after getting thumped a few times he came back and drove the enemy away over the mountains, and so on and so forth; and then he announces that he's taking over everything north of the Bohec – heard it all before, of course; in fact, I wonder why they still bother, they should know by now it usually ends in tears. I can't remember the exact figure, but it's something like seventy emperors in the last hundred and fifty years, and maybe a dozen of them died in their beds. Silly, really.'

'Yes,' he replied, for want of anything better to say. A flock of geese flew overhead, very high, as if they wanted nothing to do with what was beneath them.

'And you mean to tell me you'd forgotten all that?' There was a new colour in her voice now, slight suspicion. 'You must be really bad if you don't even remember about the empire.'

He decided to take the risk. 'There's something else, isn't there?' he said.

'No.'

'Yes, there is. Please,' he went on. 'I don't care what it is, even if it's bad. I'd rather find out now than later.'

'Really,' she said, 'it's nothing.'

He reminded himself that he didn't have the luxury of getting angry. Only people who know who they are can do that.

'Please,' he repeated. 'It doesn't matter to me how bad it is, all I want to do is find out who I am. That's all that matters. If there's something else—'

'Oh, all right, then.' She didn't sound at all happy. 'I was just thinking, if you don't know about the empire, maybe it's not because you've forgotten – you couldn't just *forget*, no matter what. Maybe it's because you didn't know to begin with.'

'Because I'm a foreigner, you mean?'

The cart ran over a stone, jolting them both. Copis swore, then composed herself, a swift and impressive transition.

'You don't sound like one,' she said thoughtfully. 'On the other hand, how the hell would I know what one of them would sound like? Actually, all this time we've been talking I've been trying to place your accent, and I can't. And I'm very good at accents, so that ought to mean something.'

He closed his eyes. 'Please explain,' he said.

'All right. What I'm getting at is – this is difficult. Do you know who the pirates are?'

'Pirates,' he repeated. 'I know what the word means.'

She sighed. 'Obviously you don't, then. That's really hard to believe, but I believe you; just don't expect anybody else to, that's all. We call them the pirates, though it's not the right word to describe them; it's what we thought they were when they first showed up, fifty or sixty years ago. Actually, we don't really know anything about them, that's the most scary part of it. They come out of apparently nowhere, we think from the west. Usually they sail right up to one of the cities on the coast, but sometimes they land way up north and sneak down through the mountains; or when they attack on the other side of the bay they'll come up through the forests; amazing, how they manage it.' She hesitated for a moment, fiddled with the reins. 'Anyway, the first thing we know about it is a sudden attack, another city looted and burned down, and they're gone again. Nobody knows where they're from, or who they are – oh, there's plenty of stories, but nobody really *knows* – and they must have trashed, oh, fifteen, twenty major cities over the last fifty years. Now and again they run into the soldiers; we've never once beaten them in a battle, of course, they always wipe the floor with us, but from time to time they find a few bodies, sometimes they say they've caught one alive. But nobody seems to know anything, except possibly imperial intelligence if they've really ever caught one; we don't even know what colour their hair is, or what their faces look like, anything like that. The best guess is that it's all being kept a deadly secret, because if we really knew about them it'd cause such a panic there'd be riots and God knows what else.'

'And you think I may be one of them.'

She thought for a moment before replying. 'To be honest with you, no,' she said. 'But of course, I don't know what to think. All my life pirates have been great big hairy, ugly monsters, so naturally I wouldn't expect one of them to sound like a human being. I don't know,' she added. 'How the hell would I know if you're one of them when I don't know the first thing about them?'

He considered this. 'You wouldn't,' he said. 'I guess that puts you and me in the same position. All either of us knows about me is what we can both see. You're still at an advantage, of course.'

She grinned. 'That's the way I like it,' she said.

As the sun rose, the low cloud (or mist, possibly even heat-haze; it wasn't actually freezing) lifted a little, and he thought he could see darker green patches on the sides of the distant hills that might be forests, or at least wooded combes and valleys. He could see a very long way from where they were, but what was the point in having such excellent visibility when there was nothing to look at except couch grass and the occasional stone?

'Are you sure there's a town in this direction?' he asked.

'Of course I'm sure. Otherwise we wouldn't be going this way.'

He shrugged. 'Sorry,' he said. 'I was just wondering. It's all so empty.'

'Used not to be, before the war.'

'Which war?'

'Whichever. But yes, there's definitely a town called Cric. Which is just as well, since you've eaten three of our biscuits and there's nothing else after they're gone. Unless, of course, you'd care to hop off the cart and go catch a rabbit or something?'

'I haven't seen any rabbits.'

'Neither have I. Maybe they don't want to be seen. I wouldn't want people looking at me if I was a rabbit. Especially hungry people.'

'I haven't seen anything,' he went on, 'except a few birds, crows and the like. You'd think there'd be something alive out here besides us.'

'Don't ask me,' she replied. 'I was brought up in a city, I don't really know about animals and things. As far as I'm concerned there's cities, and everything else is just the gaps in between. This,' she added, 'is a big gap.'

There didn't seem much point in discussing the matter further, so he went back to thinking about the face he'd seen in the pool. Me, he thought; that's all I am. How did I come to look so thoroughly miserable? Of course, I suppose I've got a right to be miserable now – except that I'm not, so maybe this is a good thing, a fresh start or something. Maybe I've walked away from a life that I never really liked, which is why I'm in no hurry to remember it . . .

He looked behind. He'd caught sight of something, a flash of metal in the pale sunlight.

'What's so interesting?' Copis asked.

'I don't know. Stop the cart.'

'All right. But if all you've seen is a thrush or something, I'm going to be very annoyed.'

It was hard to tell, because of the low cloud; he screwed up his eyes and concentrated, making distinctions between tones of colour. 'Something behind us,' he said. 'There it is again, look. Something's flashing in the sun.'

'Oh.' Copis seemed to think that was serious enough; she stood up on the box and shaded her eyes with her hand. 'Where?'

'Directly behind us. Probably someone on the road.'

'Damn.' She sat beside him. 'Point,' she said. He pointed. 'Yes, you're right, I saw it too.'

'You sound worried,' he said.

'Think about it,' she replied. 'Just the two of us, nowhere to hide. And metal flashing in the sun suggests armour to me.'

'Well,' he said, 'what do you think we should do?'

'Easy,' she replied. 'You get out of my cart and start running. With any luck, by the time they're close enough to see you, you'll be far enough away that they won't assume I'm anything to do with you. Which I'm not,' she added, with a little more feeling than was polite.

'All right,' he said, and started to climb off the cart.

'No,' she said wearily. 'Come back. After all, you're wearing different clothes, you aren't all muddy any more. And if they ask, I'll just tell them the truth.'

He hesitated. 'It's all right,' he said. 'You don't owe me anything.'

'Of course I don't,' she replied. 'But on the other hand, if you're some rich prince or long-lost hero, there ought to be money in it if I'm the one who saved you from bleeding and starving to death. That's me,' she added gloomily, 'a born optimist.'

She moved the cart on; a steady walk, no point in forcing the pace. As they watched, the flash turned into three riders, and when they were close enough, he saw that they were nothing like any of the soldiers he'd seen so far; they wore round, broad-brimmed steel helmets and no armour, and each one had a bow and quiver on his back and a curved sword at his side. They were riding fast, as if they were in a hurry to catch up with something.

'I think I made the wrong decision,' said Copis. 'I've seen an awful lot of soldiers over the years, but never any like them.'

'Oh.' He frowned. 'I can still run for it if you like.'

'No point,' she said. 'Let's hope they're nothing to do with you. I hate hoping,' she added. 'It's like rubbing dock leaves on a nettle sting. They tell you it helps, but does it hell as like.'

The riders came up to them very quickly. One passed them and blocked the way, while the others closed in on either side.

'You in the cart,' said the man in front.

'Me?' he called out, rather pointlessly, since the rider was staring at him.

'Stay where you are. Don't move.'

Copis looked at him. 'You can understand what they're saying?'

'Yes.'

'I can't.'

The two riders in flank held their position while the third man slid off his horse and walked up to the cart. 'You,' he said, 'take your hat off. I want to see your face.'

'All right,' he replied.

The man looked at him and nodded. 'Right,' he said.

'You know who I am, then?'

'Oh yes,' the rider replied. 'I know exactly who you are.'

'Then would you mind—?'

The rider reached up and grabbed his arm, pulling him on to his feet. With his other hand, he was drawing his sword. 'Shut up,' he said, and pulled again. Then Copis kicked him in the face.

It wasn't a very hard kick, or particularly well aimed, but it was enough to make the rider lose interest for a moment. 'Go

on, run,' she hissed, and it struck him that it would be rude
not to do what she told him to, though he wished she hadn't
got involved. But there it was; he jumped down off the cart
and made a quick mental estimate of how far away the rider's
horse was and how long it'd take him to get to it. Too long.
Meanwhile the rider was ignoring Copis and drawing his
sword, so he jumped on to the boom, grabbed him by the
throat and pushed him down. The rider landed awkwardly on
his back, giving him enough time to jump off the boom and
kick him hard on the chin; then he stooped down and
grabbed the sword. It seemed to fit his hands, almost as if it
was a part of him that he'd had amputated years ago and
which had suddenly grown back. That was just as well,
because as the left-side rider rode up and slashed at him he
was able to parry the cut squarely and in good time, opening
the rider up for a thrust under the armpit. The moves came
easily, faster than he could think. Probably, he reflected as the
man slipped out of the saddle and hit the ground, I've done
this before.

The other rider was wrong-sided, of course; he'd either
have to turn and go round the back of the cart, or go all the
way round the front of the horses. That helped. He watched
as the rider hesitated, then came forward, presumably anxious
to get to him before he could mount up on either of the spare
horses. He waited till the other man was level with him, then
hopped back on to the boom and made a dive under his horse's
legs.

The rider wasn't expecting that. He swished airily with his
sword but was far too late to connect with anything, then
craned his neck to see if he could find out what his opponent
was up to. He didn't have to wait long to find out; a moment
later his horse squealed with pain and started bucking furiously, throwing him. When he hit the ground his eyes closed
reflexively for a second; when he opened them again, he saw
his enemy scrambling out of the way of the horse – he'd

slashed its belly open – and heading for him. He made it to his feet just in time to get in the way of a slanting cut that sliced into him at the junction of neck and shoulder and went on to bite into his spine.

The third rider was on his feet, looking around desperately for some kind of weapon. He made the wrong choice; the left-side rider's body was too far away and his enemy came back over the boom at him and cut him down before he had a chance.

'My God,' Copis said. Presumably she didn't intend it as a pun. Her face was as white as milk and she was shaking. He crossed back over the boom one last time, to grab hold of the maimed horse's head and cut its throat.

'It was them or us,' he said, and noticed with interest that his voice was level, calm. 'As soon as you kicked the first one the only way out for us was to kill them all. You don't offer force to soldiers and get away with it.'

She took a couple of deep breaths, probably fighting back the urge to throw up. 'Actually,' she said, 'you're right. How did you know that?'

'I just do,' he replied. 'My guess is this isn't the first time I've had to deal with a situation like this.' He looked down at his hands and arms, which were splattered with blood; it reminded him of how they'd looked earlier that day, when he'd been flecked with spray from the waterfall. 'Actually, it was all fairly easy,' he added. 'I knew what to do, didn't have to stop and think – probably that was the difference between them and me. I'm sorry,' he added.

'Are you? Why?'

'Well . . .' He waved a hand at the dead bodies. 'Not a pretty sight,' he said.

She shuddered. 'Seen worse,' she said. 'Tell me, what would you have done if I hadn't kicked that man?'

'I don't know,' he replied. 'I was more interested in the fact that he seemed to know who I was.'

'He was going to kill you, right there on the spot.'

'Small price to pay for knowledge.'

She muttered something under her breath, 'Oh, for God's sake,' or words to that effect. He was kneeling beside the man he'd spoken to. 'You really didn't understand what he was saying?'

'No, and I speak seven languages.'

'Good God. How many languages are there?'

'Lots,' she replied. 'What are you looking for?'

He looked up at her. 'Money,' he said. 'Also anything of value that we can sell, so long as it's not the sort of thing that'll get us into trouble.'

'Another instinct?'

'Yes,' he replied. 'Apparently I'm one of nature's scavengers.'

As it turned out, none of the dead men had anything of any real value on them, apart from their clothes and weapons, which they obviously daren't take. But each of them had half a loaf and a two-fist-sized slab of hard white cheese in his saddlebag, and one of them also had a thick slice of rather elderly bacon and three apples.

'Worth more to us than money,' he said.

'Matter of opinion,' she replied.

There was a boggy patch a couple of hundred yards away. He carried the bodies over there, one at a time, and slid them into a still, black pool, which was just about deep enough to cover them. The dead horse was too much trouble to hide or bury, but he stripped the harness and tack off the other two and dumped them, before chasing the horses off. 'Not worth the risk,' he explained, when Copis protested. 'For all I know, there's ways of telling a cavalry horse: regulation shoes, that sort of thing. All right, let's get out of here.' He was painfully aware of the bloodstains on his clothes, but he couldn't quite face the thought of crawling back into his own, still completely sodden garments (and besides, he didn't want to be

wearing the clothes he'd woken up in the next time they met
somebody . . .).

They drove on in silence for the next hour. Then Copis
said, 'Well, at least somebody must know who you are. Pity
they weren't more friendly.'

'I was thinking that,' he replied. His arms and back were
starting to stiffen up after their bout of brief but violent exercise. 'At last I meet somebody who can tell me the one thing I
want to know above everything else, and a few moments later
I've killed them.' He frowned. 'You know,' he went on, 'it'd
probably be best if I left you soon. If there's a welcome like
that waiting for us in this town of yours, we might not get out
of it so easily.'

She shook her head. 'Don't be a bastard,' she replied. 'You
think I'm going to let you run out on me after putting me
through all that? In your dreams.'

That struck him as a strange attitude, but he was still trying
to figure out why she'd forced the issue earlier by kicking the
rider. He could think of at least three explanations, but none
of them felt right. 'If that's the way you feel about it,' he said.
'But at the very least, as soon as we come in sight of the place,
you go on ahead. I'll follow up on foot and meet up with you
there.'

'Not a chance,' she replied firmly. 'You're the god in the
cart, remember? It's got to be done properly, or else we'll *really*
be in trouble.'

Well, that fitted in with explanation number two, but he
still wasn't convinced. 'All right, then,' he said. 'I still figure
it's a bloody stupid risk to take.'

'So's being born,' she replied, as if that was any kind of an
argument.

Later, she told him about the god act.

'Your name's Poldarn,' she said. 'At least, that's the name
we've been using, and there's no reason why we shouldn't stick
with it.'

'Poldarn,' he repeated, 'No, doesn't mean anything to me.'

She laughed. 'I'd be absolutely amazed if it did,' she replied. 'You see, the god these people believe in hasn't got a name, it's forbidden or some such crap, at least until the second coming. So we had to make one up. At least, I didn't make it up exactly, it's a real name.'

'A real god's name?'

'There aren't any real gods, silly. No, it's something I remembered from when I was a kid, actually. The alley we lived in, there was a builder's yard, and they had stacks and stacks of roof tiles, all piled up as high as a haystack, and my brother and I used to play in there sometimes. Strictly against the rules, of course – I can see why, thinking back, because those stacks weren't meant for clambering about all over, and if one of 'em had collapsed we'd have been squashed like bugs. Anyway,' she went on, 'we used to play hide and seek, and I have this crystal-clear picture of myself hiding among these stacks, tucked away in a little child-sized hole only I knew about, and lying there for what seemed like hours at a time while my brother looked for me, and all that time I was reading the maker's name stamped on the tiles, over and over again: Poldarn House Torcea, Poldarn House Torcea, in exactly the same place on thousands upon thousands of tiles. Of course, I hadn't got a clue about how they made the things, I thought it was a little man with a chisel or something, and it beat me how on earth he was able to get it so exactly precise every single time . . . Anyhow,' she said, frowning, 'that's why I had this name Poldarn floating around in my head, and that's what we called the god. So now you're Poldarn.'

'Right,' he replied. 'Named in honour of a brick. Why not, after all?'

'You don't like it.'

'I think it's a wonderful name,' he said irritably. 'Or at least, it has a hell of a lot going for it as against nothing at all.'

'Fine,' she replied. 'That's settled, then. Now, the way we do the show is like this . . .'

The first thing they saw was the remains of a charcoal burners' camp, stranded in the middle of a broad, flat plain covered with tree stumps.

'I think they used to use up something like four square miles of forest a year,' Copis said. 'At least, that's what I heard once. It's one of the reasons why it's so bleak and boring in these parts. There's old iron mines scattered about all through here, from the Mahec down to Sansory – nearly all worked out, of course – and they used charcoal to smelt the ore, or whatever the technical terms are. A hundred and fifty years ago, all this lot was forest.'

'You don't say.'

'Oh, it's worse the other side of the Bohec. They cleared that about, what, seventy years ago, and it's incredible in some places. Where they cut the trees and left the top branches, it's all grown over with briars and weeds and stuff, all tangled up like a thorn hedge a mile thick. From time to time there's big fires, in the dry season. Nothing else could ever clear it.'

He thought about that as he stared at the fire pits and slagheaps, submerged under thick mats of nettles and docks, and the countless lopped trunks, like the dead bodies after a battle. 'What did they need all that iron for?' he asked.

'There was an imperial armoury at Weal Bohec,' Copis replied. 'It supplied all the soldiers in the province. The foundry there turned out something like a thousand tons of iron a year. Don't ask me how I know all this,' she added. 'Useless information just gets stuck in my head, like flies in a spider's web.'

'Lucky you.'

She laughed. 'Yes, well,' she said. 'Probably it was one of the customers told me, when I worked in the cat-house in

Josequin. My God, didn't some of them love the sound of their own voices . . . ? Worst part of the job, really, and that's saying something.'

She hadn't mentioned that before, not that it mattered. It was an interesting thought that this desert of couch grass and bog had once been a great forest. Interesting that even the landscape could lose its memory so completely, could go from being so full to so empty. For some reason, he almost found it comforting.

'Anyway,' he said, 'the town's just ahead, is it?'

'Should be,' she replied. 'Pretty soon we'll start seeing the smoke.'

'Smoke?'

'There's still a foundry there,' Copis explained. 'Only reason for having a town out in the middle of all this. I think they make a living from scavenging bits of stuff from the old worked-out mines, bits the original miners missed or couldn't be bothered to go after. They burn peat now, since they can't use charcoal.'

That was an interesting thought, too; having used up everything that grew in it, they were using up the ground itself. It hadn't occurred to him that iron was so destructive.

The further they went, the drearier the landscape became. Here and there he saw big briar tangles, which he took to be overgrown loppings, such as Copis had described earlier, and a fair sprinkling of derelict buildings – sheds and stores, built low out of rough-cut stone blocks, with broken-backed slate roofs drowning in creepers and nettles. A very predatory kind of place, he decided, where the people ate up the ground and the ground swallowed up the buildings, killers and carrion-feeders, making up a cycle.

'I hope the town's a bit more cheerful than this,' he said. 'It'd depress me, living somewhere like this.'

'For all you know,' she replied, 'this is home.'

'Now there's a charming thought.'

He kept looking for smoke, but there wasn't any, just the usual low cloud (or mist, or possibly heat-haze) that blurred the distinction between ground and sky. Copis, who'd been assuring him that any moment now they'd encounter the first outlying farms and workshops, stopped talking entirely; she was staring at the skyline like a bird, scanning from a great height. There were more buildings now, but still all derelict, the skeletons of houses and barns. There were dry-stone walls, so overgrown with grass and weeds that they looked like banks; a few boundary stones, sticking up like the remaining teeth in an old man's mouth; details like a stone watering-trough split by the frost, a deer hunter's high seat fallen on its side and sinking among the nettles, a millstream clogged with weeds, a dovecote bald of thatch and leaning at an angle on its post.

'Actually,' Copis said, in an unusually subdued tone of voice, 'you get this sort of thing all over the place. It's where a whole village gets called up for military service; they're marched off to the wars somewhere and they don't come back. Either the government resettles the families somewhere else – that's what they're supposed to do, at any rate – or the people who were left behind just go away, to a town or wher-ever. All these little wars they keep having use up a lot of manpower.'

They stumbled on the town quite unexpectedly, just as it was starting to get dark; what was left of the ruined walls had grown over so quickly that at first they mistook them for more briar clumps, and it was only when they began noticing angles of brick and stone peeping out from under the weeds, like the edge of the bone in a bad fracture, that they realised what they were looking at. It had happened within, say, the last ten years. Long enough for several seasons of rain to have washed most of the soot off the ruined walls, for the scattered timbers to have been bleached grey or green under a thin slime of lichen, for the crows to have pecked the skulls and bones as clean as a good child's plate. Here and there the remains of a door still hung off its hinges, a few rafters framed the sky over a gutted house, a few paving stones peeped out from under the grass; a few moments of the old normality, incongruous among the new growth. They were looking at the final stages of the change from scab to scar; another year or so and there would be nothing here but a healed-over ruin, its sharp edges all rounded off by rain, wind and growth, its bones covered with new green flesh. The turf and ground and stones would lose their memory and begin all over again.

'Oh,' Copis said.

She didn't say anything else for a long time. Instead the cart rumbled sedately down what used to be the main street, now a pattern in the grass, and if from time to time something brittle crunched under the heavy wheels, it could just as easily have been something innocuous, like a potsherd.

'All right,' Copis said, 'we'll just have to press on to Josequin, assuming it's still there, of course. We'll have to work some of the poxy little villages south of the city. They're a miserable lot, but better than nothing.'

He'd been looking around, taking note, like an observer from a neutral country. 'Who do you think did this?' he asked. 'The pirates?'

She shrugged. 'That's the likeliest bet,' she replied. 'But it could have been somebody's army, making an example. Or one of the free companies, of course. I'm not sure it matters terribly much any more.'

She stopped the cart in front of the biggest remaining structure, which still had about a third of its roof intact. 'We might as well stay here tonight,' she said, yawning. 'Accommodation's probably not up to much, but at least it won't cost us anything. Got to look on the bright side,' she added.

'What do you think this place used to be?' he asked as he unyoked the horses.

'No idea,' she replied. 'Either the temple or the foundry, nothing else would have rooms this size. You can go and explore if you want to. I'm going to get some sleep. I find the end of the world makes me feel tired like a dog. Oh, and you can forget about anything to eat. That bread and cheese we picked up from your cavalry friends is going to have to see us to Josequin, unless you fancy spit-roasted horse and a long walk.'

While there was still a smudge of light to see by, he picked his way through the building, stepping gingerly over fallen roof beams and rafters, taking care to avoid the places where the floorboards had started to rot. The temple, he guessed, rather than the foundry, since the rooms were all empty, and foundry gear would be too heavy to carry away as plunder, unless that had been what they'd come for in the first place. Besides, he thought, where else would the god Poldarn spend the night but in a temple?

As he was feeling his way back in the dark he stubbed his toe on something and looked down to see what it was. It turned out to be a fat yellowish blob, about the size of a child's head, cold to the touch, smooth and metallic, and heavier than it looked when he tried to lift it. The part of the building he was in had been gutted by fire, leaving nothing but a few rafters. *I think I know what this is,* he thought. *Could come in handy, at that.* He thought for a moment, then went outside through a gap in the wall and followed the side of the building round to where they'd left the cart. There was a nice space in the back, under a couple of mouldy old blankets, just the right size, and not the sort of place where anybody would think to look in the usual run of things. As a final test, he found Copis' small knife and scratched the surface of the lump; it caught the moonlight and flashed, like a distant helmet. That was the good stuff, all right.

Not that he didn't trust her, of course, but there was no immediate need to tell her right now, and it'd make a pleasant surprise for her once they reached somewhere comfortable and safe where he could dispose of it. The contents of somebody's strongbox, he guessed, melted down and fused by the heat, losing the memory of its original shape but not its intrinsic virtues – nice upbeat comparison, he told himself. Things could be getting better.

Chapter Four

*B*urn the village, he says. In this rain? Who's he kidding?
(I'm asleep, he reminded himself. This is a very
realistic dream, so I must remember; I'm asleep, it's
isn't really . . .)

*You, quit complaining. Make yourself useful, go and see if
you can find some lamp oil or something. Lamp oil and straw.
Well, don't just stand there.*

(He remembered the argument, between the body in the
water and its reflection. He knew that the body in the water
wouldn't let him keep this dream – *put it back, it's dirty, you
don't know where it's come from.* That was a great pity.)

*It's all very well him saying lamp oil, but there isn't any.
Tallow, yes. Candles. No oil lamps. And the straw's all wringing
wet, look. You'll never get that to burn in a thousand years.*

(He could try and keep hold of it, he supposed, but he
didn't know how, and anyway, the body in the water would
find it wherever he hid it and take it away from him. If only he
could keep just a bit of it, a corner, something that would jog
his memory—)

Cooking oil; that'll do. Light the thatch from inside, it'll burn better. Yes, all right, you're tired. So am I. But the sooner we start, the sooner we finish.

(Just a little bit of himself, as a souvenir; something to remember himself by. Was that really so much to ask? Did the body in the water always have to know best?)

You three – God almighty, why's it always you three? All right, let's see what you've got. Oh, bloody hell, didn't you hear what he said about no prisoners?

He could see the short man, the one who'd been shouting, but the others – he was one of them – had their backs to him, he couldn't see their faces. Two of them, the other two, were dragging a woman along with them. They'd got hold of her by the wrists, her arms stretched wide like guy-ropes, and as they hauled they lifted her off the ground so that her trailing feet left a line in the wet grass.

She isn't a prisoner, Scaptey, she's spoils of war. Perfectly legitimate. You heard the foreigner, he expressly said plunder's allowed.

The short man was giving them all a don't-try-my-patience look, as if they were children explaining why they should be allowed to keep a stray dog that had followed them home from the market. An interesting face, that man had, and clearly legible. His eyes said that he was too tired to be angry and almost too tired to care, but they couldn't keep the woman. He wished he could see their faces too. Apart from the one who was him, though, he hadn't a clue who they were.

He decided to move closer, leaving the problem behind, like a horse tethered to a rail. At least there were people he knew in the dream.

Oh, the hell with it— 'Oh, the hell with it,' Scaptey, the short man, said. 'Do what you like, so long as you're done and ready to go by the time the rest of them get back. And make sure this place gets torched, right? The boss is in a bad enough mood as it is, and it'll be me that gets a boot up the arse if there's anything still standing.'

(Of course, he realised, I'm Scaptey. Not the man he was yelling at. I just didn't recognise myself, that's all. He looked again.)

Wearily, Scaptey trudged across the courtyard and sat down on a barrel. For the last two hours he'd had to think of everything – their position, the enemy's position, possible traps and ambushes, the scary moment when it looked like they'd break through the far left of the line, the danger of pursuing too far and breaking order, the weather, the time of day – there'd be no point winning the battle if they took too long about it and missed their pickup, that'd be worse than losing . . . Then, when the enemy broke and ran and a man might be justified in thinking he'd done enough for one day, even more to think about and bear in mind: a village to plunder and burn, survivors to root out and deal with, followed by the aggravation of rounding up the rest of the party (just when they were starting to enjoy themselves), getting the plunder loaded on to the carts, sweeping up the stragglers, men who were too drunk or exhausted to move (and it didn't help having the boss's only son along for the ride; he couldn't very well bawl him out along with the rest of the bunch, but he couldn't let him run wild either, in case he got himself hurt or lost). Then he'd have just enough time to make a final check, every last damn thing, to make sure it'd all been done properly, before moving out and facing that long, gruelling march through the hills at double pace to get to the beach in time for the pick-up. All that to come . . . Right now he was still feeling groggy and sick after being bashed over the head with a big axe during the actual fighting. That reminded him. He unbuckled his helmet and examined it. Sure enough, there was a dent in the bowl just above the right temple, big enough to hide a walnut in. Some hit that'd been. If the fool had known to aim with the horn of the axe instead of the forte of the blade (like he was always telling his lads to do) he'd be dead now, or lying in the wet grass waiting to drown in air. As it was, he'd have to put up with this badly dented helmet until he could get it to an armourer and have the pit raised out, which could be days or even weeks. Needless to say, the inside of the dent was just nicely placed to press against the nerve and give him those splitting headaches that lasted all day . . .

Bastard locals, he thought; no bounty for killing the likes of them, and if they kill you, you're dead. Oh yes, plunder – but what could they possibly have here that was worth stealing? It was exactly the sort of junk people filled their houses with at home, the sort of thing you'd probably give to the tinker just to free up the space. Getting your head bashed in over somebody's grandmother's copper saucepan and a few clothes pegs; it was never worth it, even to prove a point.

And it was still raining; what joy. The collar of his cloak was completely sodden, trickling water down his back and chest to places he couldn't reach without stripping off all his armour. There wasn't really much point in getting under cover now, he was soaked through already, but it occurred to him that in one of the houses there might just be something to eat or drink, and he hadn't had time to do either for at least a day. It'd only take a moment or so; nobody would miss him for that long, and he was, after all, the conquering hero—

What's the plan?

(He knew that voice, from somewhere. Couldn't quite place it right now, didn't care. Didn't want to go back where that voice was coming from. He decided to pretend he hadn't heard.)

—And he was back again, in the village; he recognised it immediately (its name was on the tip of his tongue) but now it was much later, and the place was much brighter, since the vague, dirty sunlight strained through too many clouds had been replaced by keen orange firelight from dozens of burning houses. *So this is who I am*, he thought, as he watched himself, the tired and stressed-out short man, watching his people loading heavy-looking barrels and jars on to a cranky-looking farm cart.

'Load of junk,' one of the men was muttering. 'Back home they'd pay you to take it on.'

Perfectly true, Scaptey thought. 'You,' he snapped, 'do your work and keep your face shut. I've had just about enough of you for one day. Next man who talks gets to walk home, understood?'

They were good lads really, of course, or at least no worse than several others, and it was probably just bad luck and coincidence that his boys got all the shitty jobs . . . like this one, and the one before, and the one before that. As he was thinking, he was counting heads (an instinctive thing, something he did automatically every five minutes or so; probably mothers of large families do the same) and suddenly he realised he was three short. A scowl crossed his face. No prizes for guessing which three.

(Out of the corner of his mind's eye, he saw a crow pitching in a tall, thin tree. In its beak, improbably enough, was a gold ring. That was wrong; it's jackdaws who thieve useless shiny objects, crows have more sense. He thought about it for a while but it didn't make sense, so he went back to being Scaptey.)

He nudged the tall man, Raffen, in the back. 'Keep your eye on them till I get back,' he said. 'We're on a schedule, remember?' Then he walked fast – didn't his legs ever ache, but no time to bother with that now – towards the barn where he'd seen them last.

'I thought I told you—' he shouted into the darkness; then the light caught up with him, and he saw the three men he'd been looking for. One of them was lying face down in a tangled mess of old, dusty straw, and the other two were on their knees beside him.

'Fuck it,' he said, 'now what?' They didn't reply, but he didn't need them to. He'd seen enough dead bodies, after all.

'She killed him,' the bald one said—

(The bald one. Damn it, I know his name, I just can't quite . . .)

'Who? Oh, you mean your playmate you found earlier?'

'She had a knife,' the other one said, not looking up at him. 'She waited till afterwards, then she stuck him and ran. Must've had it hidden somewhere, God only knows where.'

He didn't say, *I told you so*. Well, it was done; nothing he could do except find out who'd died, clear up as best he could. He knelt down and turned the body over.

It had to be Tursten, of course; it had to be the boss's only son, on his first ever trip away from home. Look after him, Scap, the boss had told him, make sure he doesn't come to any harm, I know I can trust you. All through the battle he'd been so careful – one eye on his opponent's sword arm, the other on young master Tursten – and now he'd turned his back for five minutes and somehow, with incredible ingenuity, the young bastard had managed to find a way to get himself killed. Fantastic, Scaptey thought gloomily.

The bald man shook his head. 'She was too bloody quick,' he replied. 'I was putting my boots on, he was taking a leak. He—' He looked down at the dead man, then quickly away. 'It was his turn, you see; we take it in turns to kill the prisoners, well, it's a bloody rotten job, it's only fair. So he was meant to be doing that, while we—'

'She got away,' Scaptey said. 'Bugger.' He sighed, just a trifle melodramatically. It was, of course, the General Order Number One: a clean sweep every time, get them all or don't bother coming back. But in practice, in reality, it wouldn't be the first time. There were always a few accidents, like this, or some soft-hearted fool who wasn't up to killing a woman or a kid. Nobody had to know; where was the harm? 'All right,' he said, 'I'll deal with you two later, you can rely on that. Meanwhile, this didn't happen. She never existed. He died when a beam fell on his head, but we'll say he died fighting, for morale, same as usual. Now put a torch to this lot and go and do some work for a change. And don't think you've got away with anything, because you haven't.'

They looked up at him now; a dumb sort of pleading look,

because they didn't want to leave their friend. He had no patience with that – once they're dead they're dead; reorganise priorities, be concerned only with the living. 'Get out of here or you'll feel my boot up your arse,' he said. 'I'll clean up here.'

They left, because they had no choice in the matter. He watched them out, then went outside and pulled a bundle of thatch out of the low eaves, walked across to the next building and lit it. The barn caught fire easily enough; it drank the fire like a thirsty man just waking up from a bad dream, and he didn't have to wait long before the roof caved in, throwing a huge cloud of gorgeous orange sparks into the sky, to light his dead comrade's way to heaven. *So that's all right,* he thought. *A beam's bound to have fallen on him in all that lot, so I'll be telling the truth.* He looked back once more – too soft by half, always was – then made for the carts as quickly as he could.

(*Strange,* he thought, watching Scaptey walk away. *Earlier I could've sworn I was the dead man, the one who just got killed by the woman. Must, must try and remember all this when I wake up—*)

What's the plan?

(Damn it. Her again.)

'I said,' Copis repeated, 'what's the plan? Do we just breeze in like we owned the place (which of course we do, since you're a god and I'm your prophet), or do we sneak in and try and find out if they're likely to want to lynch you first?'

Poldarn (he liked the name; it suited him) stretched his cramped legs and yawned. 'Sorry,' he said. 'I think I may have dozed off for a moment there.'

'Oh, for crying out loud.' She glared at him, but since he didn't immediately freeze and turn to stone she went on, 'If you ask me, we should just go in and see what happens. These are extremely superstitious people, rubes. They probably won't even dare look at your face, for fear of being struck dumb or something.'

It had taken them five days to reach the nearest village – five days on the same straight, unchanging, incredibly boring road, with precious little to eat; it occurred to him that Copis might be letting the prospect of actually doing something, followed by a good meal, blind her to the potential dangers. 'I'm not so sure,' he said. 'So far, you excepted, everybody I've met since I can remember has wanted to kill me. Maybe we should play this by ear.'

She shook her head. 'You're letting a few unfortunate experiences cloud your judgement,' she said. 'Besides, if they catch us skulking around spying on them, we'll never be able to make them believe we're the second coming. Gods don't sneak around the place to see if it's safe, they march straight in and take what they want. I've explained this to you before, but I guess you weren't listening.'

The village lay below them, a mile away down a gentle slope that formed one side of a wide, shallow valley. All they could see was the pattern of the fields, without walls or hedges, and a few paler specks in the distance, the thatched roofs of buildings. The air was chilly and slightly damp – low cloud, probably – and there was a strong smell of rain. From this distance, of course, it was impossible to distinguish anything as small as a living creature.

'If our luck's anything to go by,' Poldarn grumbled, 'when we get there we'll find they're all dead.'

'Don't joke about it,' Copis replied. 'If they're all dead, so are we, unless they've left something we can eat. Look, we can stay up here arguing all day, or we can do as I say. Your choice.'

'I hate choices,' Poldarn said. 'All right, you know best. I wish we'd had a chance for a quick wash before we did this, though. I don't think gods are supposed to smell quite as strongly as we do.'

'Like I told you, they're rubes. They won't notice.'

There speaks a born city-dweller, he thought. Still, it was clear she'd made up her mind, and besides, he couldn't very well spend the rest of his life in the wilderness for fear of meeting an enemy. That'd be like dying of thirst because you didn't trust the water.

The differences between the village and the town they'd been to earlier were quite obvious. The village had only one street, if you could dignify the ribbon of mud between the doorsteps with the name, and the houses (small weather-boarded square boxes under greying thatch, all old – no signs that anybody had built a new house here in the last hundred years) were strung out along it in a straight line, like specks of dust on a worm. That presented a problem – no town square, no obvious place to stop and set up the stall. 'Keep your eyes peeled for a smithy,' Copis said. 'Chances are that's what passes for a public building.' There wasn't one, however, or at least nothing that looked like one from the outside; likewise no mill, chapel or common granary. There was, however, a tower—

('That's not a tower,' Poldarn whispered. 'Towers go up. That goes sideways.'

'It's a short tower. Rubes, remember?')

—A square, squat windowless building two story's high, with one massive door and a flat, crenellated roof, right at the far end of the village. It was considerably bigger than any other building in the place, and the walls were made of stone.

'Four dormitories built round a courtyard,' Copis explained, keeping her voice down so as not to be heard by the small crowd of old men, women and children that had been following them all the way down the street, warily keeping their distance, like crows. 'Quite common in places that got torched a hundred years or so ago and then rebuilt. When the enemy show up they drive the stock into the middle and snuggle down till the bad people have gone away. Probably built over a grain-pit. Good idea so long as there's only a few of the enemy; otherwise it's just making their job easier.'

The door was open wide enough to drive the cart through

into the courtyard without stopping. The interior was a bare, square cattle pen with a churned mud floor ('Been used recently,' Copis observed. 'Which suggests they've had trouble here lately') and a few post-and-rail fences to divide the space up into compartments – one pen for the cows, another for the goats, another for the pigs, and so on; no problem telling which pen had been which, just look at the floor, or sniff. Copis drove the cart into the goat pen, which was the biggest, jumped down and tied up to a rail. She didn't say anything or look at the crowd, who carried on staring at them both in silence.

So far, all according to plan. Nothing could be done until the kids had run out to the fields and called the men back, during which time, Copis had stressed in her briefing, it was vital that he sit absolutely still up on the box, avoiding all eye contact and not making a sound. He'd thought that would probably be pretty difficult to pull off when she'd first told him about it; in the event, it was the next thing to impossible. Though the old men and women all kept as still as gateposts, some of the children were waving or making faces; he could see them out of the corner of his eye, though he was careful to keep staring at the line between the top of the roof and the sky. Timing, of course, was everything; the critical moment had to come as near as possible to noon. The god outfit was excruciatingly heavy and uncomfortable and he wished that he'd had an opportunity to get used to wearing it on the way here, but it had been raining on and off all the way and, as Copis had pointed out, gods don't drive into town looking like drowned rats. That was another dangerous variable. It didn't look as if it was going to rain in the next hour or so, but after that it'd be touch and go; they could risk rushing the act and losing the thread, or they could play it out at the proper pace and risk a cloudburst, which would scupper their credibility in a few moments, or they could time it exactly right and use the rain as part of the act (really impressive if they pulled it off, disastrous if they didn't). It didn't help his nerves to reflect that the penalty for screwing up was anything between getting pelted with donkey shit and a selection of nasty, painful ways to die; whereas in towns, Copis had told him, charlatans are treated with a certain degree of good humour, out in the sticks they don't take kindly to being made fools of.

Eventually the men showed up and pushed their way through to the front of the crowd. Poldarn was annoyed that he couldn't look directly at these people, since he wanted to study the shapes of their faces, the variations of hair and eye colour, the range of height and build. From what he'd been able to see out of the corner of his eye, they seemed to have more in common with the dead soldiers he'd found next to him when he first woke up than with their enemies or either detachment of cavalry, but there wasn't a great deal in it either way. Mostly the men were wearing plain, light brown shirts, coats and trousers, basic homespun dyed grey and faded by the sun and rain; the women, blouses and long, heavy skirts of the same material, plain, yellow-white scarves and shawls over their heads and wrapped round their necks to cover their hair. Mostly their faces were poor, thin and ugly, though he guessed that that told him more about his background than the reality of their situation. That information, however, was far more useful to him than an insight into the daily lives of a bunch of – what was that word? Rubes? He had a strong feeling that he wasn't one of them.

Now that the men were here, still nothing happened . . . They watched in silence while Copis carried on with her chores (spinning them out, he guessed, though she wasn't obvious about it) and still the only sounds were the shuffling of feet in the mud, the occasional cough or sneeze, and a little muted chatter among the children, occasionally cut off by a hissed 'Sssh!'

No reason, of course, why it shouldn't go on like this indef- initely. Copis had explained the basic premise – gods are so far above the concerns of mortals that they don't even notice them unless a human intermediary points them out; the god is only partly there, in any event, like the summit of a mountain poking up above a blanket of low cloud. It went without saying that there was nothing the mortals had that the god could possibly want. His human companion, on the other hand, needed food and shelter just like anybody else, and if these weren't provided for her unsolicited, she'd demand them as of right. Saying thank you was out of the question (you don't thank the ground for letting you tread on it) and as for curing warts or telling fortunes . . .

'You came up the road, then,' a man said.

Copis didn't answer. She hadn't heard him. Probably she was too busy listening to other, better voices inside her head. There was a very good reason why she shouldn't answer, but offhand Poldarn couldn't remember what it was.

Some time later, long enough for Copis to curry-comb the horses' manes, the same man said, 'Reckon you've been on the road a few days. Not many folks travelling about, this time of year.'

'No,' Copis replied, and went on with what she was doing.

At that point the sun came out from behind a cloud, and Poldarn (who was suffering agonies from cramp) raised both hands in front of him, palms outwards, to let her know that he was going for the Special Effect. She didn't give any indication that she'd seen his signal, but that was how they'd planned it, so he had to assume she was ready and hope for the best.

The Special Effect was the heart and soul of the act. Wired to the rim of the silly brass-and-glass-paste diadem he wore round his head was one particular lump of glass that was rather special. Copis had explained that it acted as a sort of funnel for daylight – it was something to do with its shape, she'd explained – and if you held it up to the sun just so it concentrated the light into a tiny point that grew hot enough to start a little fire. They were common enough on Torcea, where people had known about them for hundreds of years and used them instead of tinderboxes (at least they used to; it had been a fad, and they were now distinctly old-fashioned) and called them burning-glasses. The trick, which he'd had plenty of time to practise on the long trudge across the moor, was to catch a beam of light in this glass without making it obvious that he was up to something and concentrate it on the small twist of sulphur-impregnated twine that stuck up out of the thick paper packet that Copis had painstakingly inserted into one of the apples he'd found in the dead horseman's saddlebag.

She'd told him what to do next – as soon as the wick starts to smoulder, pick up the apple and hold it where they can all see, count to three and throw it as high as you can in the air; and she'd given him a fairly vague idea of what to expect. But since her supply of Special Effects was severely limited and she had no way of getting any more after they were all used up, it was out of the question to waste one on mere practice. He'd assumed she'd been exaggerating.

On its own the mysterious appearance of a wisp of smoke curling up out of a perfectly ordinary-looking apple was enough to get the crowd's attention; when the wick started to crackle and throw off sparks, like overheated iron hammered on the anvil, they stared and made some muffled horrified-fascination noises. They reared back when he suddenly rose up and threw the burning apple into the air. When it vanished in a red and green fireball, accompanied by a devastating roll of thunder—

'At that point,' Copis had told him, 'it can go one of two ways. Either they'll go flat on their faces and worship you as a god, or we both get thrown down a well as sorcerors. I guess the uncertainty is part of the fun.'

Fortunately, she'd continued, there's always some woman near the front who looks at you and says, 'What the hell was that . . . ?'

'Always?' he'd asked.

'Always so far,' she'd replied.

'Ah. Exactly how many times have you done this, by the way?'

'Four.'

Fifth time lucky . . . 'What the hell was that?' gasped a woman near the front, as the rest of the crowd shuffled backwards with varying degrees of urgency.

'What, that?' Copis' face was a study in boredom. 'I suppose he must have seen an evil spirit. There seem to be more of them about than usual this year.'

The woman stared at her. 'And what did he just do, then?'

'Killed it, of course,' Copis said, brushing caked mud off her spare boots.

'What with?'

Copis looked up, frowning disapprovingly. 'For pity's sake,' she said. 'Haven't you people ever seen a thunderbolt before?'

Apparently they hadn't; not one like that, at any rate. They'd stopped trying to back away and were straining to get a good view. 'So who's he, then?' asked a voice at the back.

'You mean you—?' Copis looked shocked; horrified, even. 'Give me strength,' she muttered. 'I'd heard people were ignorant out here, but I'd have thought even the likes of you would recognise Poldarn when you saw him.'

Short, anxious pause. 'Who?' asked a younger woman near the front.

Copis rubbed her forehead, as if in some pain. 'What do you mean, who? Poldarn the god, of course. How many Poldarns do you think there are? Now would you all mind either going away or keeping quiet? I'm very tired, and I've got a lot to do tomorrow.'

Poldarn, as still as a statue up on the cart, couldn't see their faces or make out exactly what they were saying; neither was necessary. The tone of their frantic, muted buzzing told him all he needed to know. It was difficult not to grin – Copis had warned him specifically about that – but he managed it.

It was a long time before anybody spoke. Eventually an old man on the far right-hand edge of the crowd piped up. 'That's his name, is it? Poldarn?'

Copis (who was doing the other boot now) nodded without looking up.

'I never knew he had a name.'

'Well, he does,' Copis said.

'So what's he doing here, then?'

At this, the rest of the crowd started shushing the old man in furious disapproval (good sign, excellent sign). Slightly intimidated but afraid of losing face, the old man repeated the question.

Copis sighed. 'Not that it's any of your business,' she said, still looking at the heel of the boot, 'but he's on his way to Josequin.' She smiled bleakly, as if at a private joke. 'Let's say he has business there,' she added.

That shut them all up; no need to ask what the 'business' might be. A young woman somewhere in the middle of the crowd started to cry, and the lonely sound in the middle of so much horrified silence made Poldarn feel distinctly uncomfortable. It was all very well for Copis to talk about not feeling sorry for the marks, who were only rubes and peasants, not to mention a damn sight better off than they were, but this was real fear and heartbreak, and conjuring it up for the sake of scrounging some food and a place to sleep struck him as no way to behave. Too late to worry about that now, though.

Some men, presumably whatever passed for community leaders in those parts, were whispering together heatedly somewhere at the back. The debate ended abruptly, and one of them shuffled through the crowd to address Copis, asking her in a subdued, almost pleading voice if there was anything they could do to please the god.

'Yes,' she replied. 'Be quiet.'

That wasn't what they'd been expecting to hear, but they did it anyway, while Copis carried on with her chores (now she was darning a hole in a sock). Crowds, however, aren't very good at keeping still and quiet for long periods of time, and after a while someone asked the question again.

Copis frowned. 'All right,' she said, in the manner of someone inventing jobs for a small child who insists on helping Mummy. 'The god doesn't need anything, of course, but I'm mortal, and I have to eat and drink. Bread, bacon, cheese, beans, dried fruit, that sort of thing. Beer rather than wine; wine gives me heartburn.'

Business was quite brisk after that, and the back of the cart quickly filled up with provisions. At first the donors tried to tell Copis their names, but she shooed them away, making the point that the god knew exactly who had given what, because he knew everything, and furthermore he wasn't the slightest bit inclined to fool about with the workings of destiny just because one human had given another a slab of slightly mouldy cheese, so really it didn't matter anyway. The effect of this negative attitude was that the next wave of offerings were substantially better quality, the idea presumably being that even a god would be persuaded to bend a rule or two in consideration of the finest plaster-sealed soft ewe's milk cheese with chives.

When there wasn't any room left in the cart, and neither the god nor his priestess had displayed any interest or caused any more explosions, the crowd subsided a little, though nobody showed any signs of being ready to go home. Copis hadn't anticipated that. Even she couldn't spin out her chores for ever, so she announced that it was time for her to meditate, and if they knew what was good for them they'd leave her well alone while she was at it. She then sat down cross-legged on the ground, laid the backs of her hands on her knees, closed her eyes and slowed her breathing right down – very impressive to watch, Poldarn had to admit, though he could only just see her at the very edge of his vision. For his part he was suffering the agonies of the damned, at first from cramp and strain, later from an overwhelming urge to close his eyes and go to sleep – which was, of course, the one thing he mustn't do, under any circumstance. All in all, he figured, defrauding honest villagers of their meagre resources struck him as desperately hard, gruelling work, far more so than digging peat or pushing the big saw in a sawmill, and he wasn't sure he was up to it. One thing was certain; he'd have earned his pay by the time they got out of there.

They've got to shove off soon, he told himself as the excruciating vigil carried on into the night, *they've all got to go to work in the morning; they can't afford to lose a night's sleep.* This turned out to be a serious underestimation of rural piety; furthermore, the heartless creatures sent to their houses for lanterns and torches, which put paid to his hopes of being able to nod off unnoticed in the dark.

Some time later – about two hundred and fifty years, by Poldarn's estimation – Copis came out of her trance, got up slowly and lifted a small wooden box down from the cart. He recognised it, and wondered what on earth she was up to, since there was nothing in there but half a loaf of extremely elderly bread that she'd insisted on keeping, even when they were both hungry. She opened the box, took out the loaf and scraped off some of the thick coating of blue mould on to a little dish with the edge of her small knife. Then she shut the box and looked round.

In spite of being told not to, the villagers had brought out a sad assortment of their sick and infirm, ranging from a young man with a missing arm to an old, old woman swaddled up in blankets who looked like she didn't stand much chance of lasting out the night. Copis stood up and walked backwards and forwards, occasionally leaning forward to take a closer look, feel for a temperature, or roll back an eyelid. She didn't say a word, but after she'd inspected all the various exhibits she pointed to four of them and clapped her hands suddenly for attention. She explained that she'd examined the casualties through the god's eyes, and seen that these four could be saved without upsetting the complex patterns of destiny. In the dish were the scrapings of the god's own food; mixed with garlic juice and swallowed four times a day for ten days, it would cure them and, provided they were properly grateful, they ought to carry on to live long and useful lives. Should anybody else presume to eat the god's food, she warned, she wasn't prepared to be responsible for the consequences, which might well include blindness, madness or death.

There was a loud murmur of wonder from the crowd, as the relatives of the chosen four stepped up to receive their share of the blue dust. When the little ceremony was over, Copis announced that she now had to go into a very deep trance indeed, in order to tell the god what she'd done and ask him to make the necessary arrangements; it was essential, she added, that she wasn't disturbed, else she, the four sick people and anybody else in a day's radius might suffer some unpleasant consequences. She'd rather they went away completely, but if they insisted on coming back shortly after first light, she would probably be through with her trance by then. Then she knelt down, crossed her legs and closed her eyes.

A few moments later they had the place to themselves.

'It's all right,' she hissed softly, 'they've gone. Not far, though; I think they're all sitting outside in the street. You can relax for a bit, but don't make any noise.'

'Actually,' Poldarn whispered back, 'I think I'm stuck. You've got no idea—'

'Ssh.' She got up slowly and walked round the courtyard, still in character. 'I can't see anybody,' she whispered, kneeling down again, 'but that doesn't mean anything. There could easily be kids or something up on the roofs.'

'Would it be all right if I went to sleep?'

She thought for a moment. 'I suppose so,' she said. 'But you'd better stay where you are. You snore when you sleep lying down.'

'I don't. Do I?'

He closed his eyes; and the next thing he knew it was just starting to get light, and Copis was surreptitiously prodding his foot with a stick. 'Let's get out of here,' she said, 'before they come back.'

'You bet,' Poldarn replied. 'For one thing, if I don't take a leak in the next few minutes, I'll either burst or explode.'

'Told you not to drink anything before we started, but you wouldn't listen.'

She had the horses into the shafts and harnessed up in no time at all. The cart was considerably heavier than it had been when they arrived, and there was a nasty moment when it looked like it was going to get stuck in the mud. Luckily it pulled free when Copis applied the switch to the horses' backs, and they were moving.

'Not long now,' she whispered. 'Of course, we've got to stay in character for a while after we leave, just in case anybody follows.'

'Oh hell,' Poldarn muttered, as his mind filled with a nightmare vision of a whole villageload of disciples following the cart all the way to Josequin. Mercifully that didn't happen, though the crowd hung back watching at a safe distance until the cart was over the skyline and out of sight.

'Now?' Poldarn asked anxiously.

'All right.'

He jumped down from the cart, landed painfully, and hobbled round behind the back wheel. 'You know,' he said, some time later, 'I can't imagine anything quite so wonderful as a really good piss after a night of torture. It's almost like a spiritual thing, you know?'

'Shut up and get back on the cart,' Copis replied. 'And keep the chatter down until we're at least an hour further on. You just can't be too careful in this line of work.'

By the time she'd sounded the all-clear he was on the verge of falling asleep again, and only a precisely accurate kick on his left anklebone brought him round at the last moment. He opened his eyes and groaned.

'It's all right,' she said, 'we're clear.'

'You woke me up to tell me that?'

She frowned. 'You weren't the only one who didn't get any sleep.'

'I suppose so,' he replied. 'What the hell are we going to do with all this food?'

'Sell it,' she said. 'Aside from the stuff we need, of course. We'll get a good price for it in Josequin, especially the bacon.'

'I've been meaning to ask you,' he said. 'That stuff you gave the sick people. It wasn't poisonous, was it?'

She laughed. 'Good God, no. Why would I want to poison a bunch of people I don't even know?'

'That's all right then, so long as you're sure. I mean, bits of mould scraped off an old loaf—'

'Actually,' she interrupted, 'it's the best cure for fevers and the like I've ever come across.'

'That was what was wrong with them, was it?'

She nodded. 'Always one or two in every crowd,' she said. 'Wonderful publicity. In a few days' time those four'll be up and about again, utterly convinced the god snatched them out of the jaws of death; they'll tell their friends, word'll spread round the villages, and the next time we work in these parts they'll welcome us with cries of joy and we won't have to bother with all that messing about at the start. Not to mention,' she added with a sigh, 'wasting a firework.'

'A what?'

'The thing that goes bang.'

'Ah, right.' He rubbed his left shoulder, which was still

painful. 'I was meaning to ask you about that. What are those things?'

She smiled. 'Used to be as common as anything in the southern provinces of the empire, back when the empire still had some southern provinces. Apparently it's a mixture of charcoal and sulphur and some kind of white powder you make by distilling urine—'

'You're kidding.'

'That's what I was told,' Copis said. 'Mix it all up, set light to it, and—well, you saw for yourself. Now, of course, nobody from the south ever comes across the desert, and people have forgotten about the things. It was seeing a box of them in Josequin market that gave me the idea for the act, actually. Of course, the man who sold them to me hadn't got the faintest idea what they're for.'

'What happens when we run out?'

'Well, we could try and figure out the recipe for ourselves, if you don't mind peeing into a bottle for a week or so. Or we could think of a different act.'

He didn't reply. She'd reminded him of a rather unsettling train of thought that'd been rattling about in his head for a day or so: how long was he going to do this for, travelling round swindling people for a living? He'd tried to reassure himself that it couldn't be for very long, since any day now he'd get his memory back and it'd all be over . . . And when he repeated this bedtime story to himself in the early hours of the morning, he had to face the fact that his memory might never come back, and that his entire life could be fitted easily into a small cart and carried aimlessly from village to village, still leaving room for several hundredweight of improperly obtained provisions.

'Can I go to sleep now?' he asked.

'I suppose so,' Copis replied. 'If you insist. It's just that it gets very boring, driving this cart for hours at a time with nobody to talk to.'

He smiled. 'Tough,' he said, and closed his eyes, only to find that he couldn't get to sleep after all. He opened them again, and saw a man sitting beside the road about a hundred yards away, apparently doing something to a small wagon.

'We ought to stop and help, really,' Copis said. 'Tradition of the road, and all that.'

'All right,' Poldarn replied. 'Do you know anything about mending broken carts?'

'No.'

When they got close enough to be able to see what he was doing, however, it became apparent that he had the problem well in hand. The offside shaft was broken, so he'd taken out the horse and raised the yoke on a little cairn of stones so as to take the weight off the broken part, and now he was wrapping something round it to hold it together.

'That won't work, surely,' Poldarn said.

'Ah.' Copis nodded toward a bucket of water standing next to the front nearside wheel. 'You see that?' she said. 'What he's done is, he's got some strips of rawhide from somewhere, soaked them for a few hours in the water, and now he's wrapping them round the break. As the rawhide dries out, it shrinks a whole lot and tightens itself round the snapped timbers. When I was a girl, my dad used to mend broken hammer handles and things that way. Works like a charm.'

Poldarn was impressed. 'You know all sorts of things, don't you?'

'Oh yes,' she said. 'No shortage of information. None of it any use, but all good stuff.'

Even though the man didn't seem to need any help, they stopped and asked anyway. The man assured them that he was fine, he'd be on his way by morning; meanwhile, he had something to eat and a nice wagon to sleep under in case it rained. Then he looked hard at Poldarn.

'I know you,' he said.

Poldarn felt as if he'd just been punched in the stomach. 'Do you?'

'Never forget a face,' the man said. 'It was at an inn some-where – either Josequin or Mael, can't remember which. We spent the evening playing dominoes. I won twelve quarters.'

Poldarn took a deep breath. 'All right,' he said. 'Tell me everything you know about me.'

'That's easy,' the man replied, with a slightly bewildered grin. 'You're a rotten dominoes player. That's about it.'

'What do you mean, that's it?'

'That's it.'

Before he realised what he was doing, Poldarn had vaulted off the cart, grabbed the man's throat with both hands and slammed him back hard against the wheel of his wagon. 'What else do you know about me?' he said, tight-lipped. 'Come on, this is important.'

'Really,' the man said, gasping for breath, 'that's all. We were staying at the same inn, I asked if you wanted to play, you said yes. Look, if it's the money that's bothering you—'

Poldarn shook his head. 'I couldn't give a damn about it,' he said. 'Try and remember. Anything at all.'

'All *right*. Just stop throttling me, will you?'

Poldarn relaxed, a little. 'Well?'

'I don't know. What sort of thing do you want me to tell you about?'

'Anything,' Poldarn yelled. 'Any bloody thing at all. I've lost my memory; I got bashed on the head, and now I haven't got a clue who I am or where I live or anything. So if we've met before . . .'

The man shook his head. 'God's honest truth,' he croaked, 'all I can remember is playing the game. I think you were dressed pretty much like you are now.'

Poldarn nodded. 'These were the clothes I was wearing when I came round,' he said, 'after I got bashed. What else?'

'Really, that's all. Well, apart from the fact that you had

twelve quarters on you. I guess that says something about you. Now let go, for God's sake, before you choke me.'

Reluctantly, Poldarn relaxed his grip. The man stepped away from him to one side and rubbed his throat. 'All right,' Poldarn said. 'At least try and remember where it was. Who knows, maybe they'd remember me there.'

'I told you, I—' The man took another step away. 'Hold on, though,' he said. 'It was the Patience Rewarded, in Josequin. That's right, I remember now; it was fair week, and we'd both turned up late so they shoved us in the annexe, along with the stable boys and the like. I complained about having to pay full price just to sleep in the tack room. You told me to be grateful for that, since it gets so busy in town when the fair's on. And that was when I suggested the game.' He screwed up his forehead, as if he was trying to lift an anvil with his eyebrows. 'We played four games, I won all four, and then you didn't want to play any more. So I curled up on my blanket and went to sleep, and when I woke up the next morning you'd gone. And that's it, I swear to God. Nothing else.'

Poldarn stared at him. 'That's it?'

'I just said so, didn't I?'

'All right, all right. Come on then, who do you think I am? What do I do for a living, where do I come from, what sort of accent do I have? Anything at all is better than nothing.'

The man thought for a moment. 'Can't place the accent at all,' he said. 'But around Josequin you hear all kinds of accents; it's not something you worry about. If I had to guess, I'd say you were a southerner, probably from across the bay, like your – hell, I was about to say your wife here, but presumably she isn't.'

'Just someone I met on the road,' Poldarn said. Copis, who was getting more and more impatient, looked daggers at him for saying that, but didn't interrupt. 'So what line of work am I in? Come on, you should be able to make a good guess at that.'

He shrugged. 'Probably something involving travel, because you seemed to be an old hand at staying at inns, like I am, and I'm a courier by trade, though I don't think you are.' He closed his eyes. 'I'm trying to see if I can remember whether you had a horse or whether you were walking,' he said. 'No joy, though. If I've really got a hazard a guess, I'd say you're either something to do with the military or a government type of some sort. But that's reaching, it really is; more to do with your manner than anything else, if you get my meaning.'

Poldarn thought about that, then laughed bitterly. 'You mean I push people around when I want something? Maybe; but I think the circumstances—'

'Oh, sure. In your shoes, maybe I'd react the same way, I really couldn't tell you. It's the next best thing to impossible to imagine something like that.'

Poldarn breathed out slowly. 'The Patience Rewarded, you said.'

'That's right. It's near the Westgate, just before you get to the—'

'I know where it is,' Copis interrupted. 'Talking of which, we've got to get going if we want to be there before dark.' She was starting to get very twitchy, and Poldarn could see why, but the damage was done now. 'Thank you,' he mumbled. 'And I'm sorry—'

The man shook his head. 'That's all right,' he said. 'I guess you're entitled, at that. Best of luck finding out. Try the Patience; could be that you stay there all the time, and they know all about you. They're a good enough crowd there, at any rate.'

Leaving him and going on their way was almost painful, as if he'd lost his child at the fair and was going home without him. At least Copis had the sense not to give him a hard time about the security breach, more tact than he'd given her credit for.

'So how far away is Josequin?' he asked, trying not to sound desperate.

'From here? Oh, we should be there before dark.' She plied the switch to get the horses moving a little faster. He was grateful to her for that.

'Josequin Fair?' he asked, more to distract himself than because he wanted to know. 'Sounds big and important.'

'It is,' she replied, and she managed to keep talking about it for a long time, telling him far more about it than anybody could ever want to know. She was still explaining a couple of hours later, when they saw the smoke.

At first he thought it was just low cloud (or mist, though not heat-haze this time), but it was the wrong shape and colour; it moved differently in the wind. After a while they could smell it. Neither of them said a word. There wasn't really anything to say.

They came over the crest of a small hill, more or less the only bit of high ground they'd encountered all day. From the top they had a fine view down over a dead level plain. Josequin lay in the middle of it.

From where the city should have been there rose the smoke of countless fires; long past the stage where the flames swell up into the sky and the smoke is thick and black, more likely it was the smoke from the really hot embers, still glowing two or even three days later.

'You said I had business there,' Poldarn murmured.

'Yes,' Copis replied. 'I did say that.' She was gazing at the mess, her eyes very round. 'It was just something to say, that was all. I didn't mean anything by it.'

'No,' he said. 'I don't suppose you did.'

Chapter Five

The bonecarver's stall had some new lines: bone and stagshorn spoons as well as the usual horn offerings, bone-handled penknives, tiny bottles with no obvious uses whatsoever, a few shoe buckles, a beautiful chess set, exactly the sort of thing every visitor to Weal Bohec was expected to take home with him as a souvenir. The offcomer nudged his way good-humouredly to the front and asked to see a pair of calipers.

'Lovely work, though I say so myself,' yawned the stallholder. 'Solid brass hinge and legs and look, there's a calibrated scale engraved just here.'

'My word,' said the offcomer, impressed. 'Calibrated in what?'

The stallholder looked puzzled. 'How d'you mean?' he said.

'What's it calibrated in? We use different weights and measures where I come from, you see. As do most of the places I go. What's the scale on this?'

The stallholder shrugged his round shoulders. 'Nothing in particular,' he said. 'I just put in some marks, to be helpful.

They're all exactly the same distance apart,' he added reas-
suringly.

The offcomer nodded. 'I'm sure they are,' he said. 'But
what distance would that be? Local standard? Guild standard?
Or just something you made up out of your head?'

'Look,' the stallholder said, 'do you want to buy them or
not? Because I've got customers waiting.'

The offcomer looked round, then turned back. 'I'll think
about it,' he said. 'Thank you so much.'

The stallholder grunted, put the calipers back in their
proper place on the velvet roll, and turned his attention else-
where. When he next looked in that direction, the offcomer
was gone. He didn't notice.

Four stalls down, the shoemaker was doing good business
with a range of cheap wooden patens. It wasn't a local timber,
the offcomer noticed; most likely they'd come as ballast on one
of the big grain freighters from the other side of the bay. Stuff
like that always went down well in Weal Bohec, where people
were so careful with their money that they'd rather buy a
rough, splintery piece of wood with a leather strap round it
that didn't fit for one and a half bits than pay two and a half
for a pair of tailored leather shoes. As a result, quality goods
were always cheap here because of the lack of demand. The
offcomer particularly liked the look of a pair of tooled pigskin
riding boots, Guild manufacture, with double-stitched seams
and silver hobnails. Five silvers across the bay, three and a
half here. He wondered why the Guild tolerated this place.

'I'll think about it,' he said automatically, as the shoemaker
urged him to try them on.

'Won't take you a minute,' the shoemaker urged him. 'Go
on, best quality. Imported. They may not be here when you
come back.'

The offcomer smiled. 'I'll risk it, thanks,' he said. 'I'll only
be gone a moment.'

'A lot can happen in a moment.'

'Very true.' He smiled and raised his hand, in the universal gesture of polite refusal. The shoemaker's face fell.

'You want me to put them under the counter for you?' he said. 'So I won't go selling them to someone else by mistake?'

The offcomer shook his head. 'That'd be restraint of trade,' he replied. 'They cut your ears off for that where I come from.'

That was a lie, of course. The offcomer had been born in a little village, miles away from the nearest Guild town. But it was enough to shut up the shoemaker, who went back to selling patens. Just in time.

Across the way from the row of stalls were the main steps leading up to the exchange, the most grandiose and impressive building in Weal Bohec. A few people were coming down the steps already, traders and traders' scouts, hurrying ahead with the hot news from the morning session. The offcomer took a step back and watched them. There were a few boys, glad to be out in the fresh air after a morning crouched on the peg stools of the exchange; a couple of middle-aged characters wearing house livery with the unmistakable air of generic henchmen; a few elderly runners who'd been doing the same work for forty years. There was always plenty of bustle around the exchange, promoting the idea, almost unique to Weal Bohec, that business is something that can only be done in a state of mild hysteria.

After the first hurtling outriders came the Serious Men. The idea was that the more Serious you were, the longer it took you to leave the hall, since all the real transactions were carried out in the corridors and courtyards after the meeting itself had ended. The slow walk of a Serious trader making his way from the chapter house to the front gate was one of the great sights of Weal Bohec, a magnificent exhibition of the art of walking as slowly as humanly possible without actually stopping. Conventionally, a Serious Man wouldn't dream of covering the distance in less time than it takes to chop down a fifteen-year-old ash tree with a small hand-axe. Truly Serious men, such as the legendary Gransenier Astel Voche, or Huon Tage, six times president of the chapter, had been known to leave the chapterhouse at noon and not get outside until dusk without ever coming to an actual full stop.

The offcomer knew all of this, of course, so he leaned up against a pillar of the Portico of Probity and Diligence, made sure that he had a clear view of the gateway, took an apple from his sleeve and started to crunch. He ate slowly, savouring the rare and expensive flavour of a genuine Bohec Sweet Pippin, a variety carefully nurtured and interfered with over centuries to make it taste more like a peach than an apple; in other cities, when they wanted peaches they ate peaches, but that was never the Weal Bohec way. From time to time he had to dab the rather overabundant juice off his chin with his sleeve.

He was just worrying the last few fibres of edible flesh off the core when the first Serious Men sauntered out from between the worn, anthropomorphic pillars of the gateway (traditionally, they were supposed to represent Prosperity and prudence, but since their faces had been worn away centuries ago by itinerant shoe repairers sharpening their knives on them it wasn't possible to be certain any more). The offcomer spared them a glance, but as he'd expected his man wasn't one of them. He took a last nibble at the remains of his apple, folded it in a handkerchief (the Bohec city statutes prescribed savage fines for a man of quality who wilfully littered the streets, though of course these rules didn't apply to the lower orders, who couldn't be expected to obey them) and tucked it in his pocket. It was pleasant in the shade after a morning in the sun, and the justly famous aftertaste of the apple was well worth savouring.

In the event, he was looking the other way when his man finally came out, an uncharacteristic piece of carelessness that he could only attribute to the extreme comfort of his

surroundings. It was the flash of the silver lining of the man's
gown as he pushed back his sleeve that caught the offcomer's
eye – a brief, subliminal moment of information that he
absorbed unconsciously, the way a circling hawk notices the
first, tiniest movement of his prey on the ground below. He
pushed himself away from the pillar with his elbows and
sauntered across the street on an interception course, deli-
cately plotted so that he'd carelessly blunder into his man
just before he turned the corner.

The man was deep in some complicated discussion with
another, almost equally Serious trader; they were walking arm
in arm like an old married couple (it was a tradition that
tended to disconcert offcomers until they found out it was
quite normal and simply indicated trust), and both men's
bodyguards were holding back a respectful three paces or so.
Bodyguards were only for show in Weal Bohec, of course;
one wore them in the same way that one wore a jewelled and
enamelled sword or a lovely but useless wafer-thin gold
breastplate. Cheapskates' bodyguards were often just their
clerks dressed up in fancy padded gambesons, but Serious
Men hired serious thugs simply as an exercise in the art of
wasting money gracefully.

The offcomer knew exactly what he was doing. The
moment of collision gave him just enough time to grab his
man's sleeve with his right hand, as if stopping himself from
going off balance and falling over, while the fingers of his left
hand drew back the hem of his robe and the thumb located
the hilt of his sword, twisted round in the sash so as to be
unobtrusively hidden under his armpit without showing
through the line of his coat. While he was graciously apolo-
gising to his man for his clumsiness, he was letting go of the
mark's lapel with his right hand, while his left thumb had
found the guard of the sword and was easing it half an inch
out of the tight mouth of the scabbard. At the precise
moment that his man opened his mouth to say that it was an

accident, perfectly all right, his left fingers tightened round the scabbard throat and gave the little sideways twist that brought the hilt to exactly the right angle for the best draw, and his right hand swooped, a perfect, totally economical gesture. He drew his knuckles down the hilt like a man stroking his lover's cheek until his little finger encountered the guard. Then he flipped his hand over, wrapped his fingers round the hilt, and drew.

Moments make up everything, the way potsherds and bits of broken glass make up a mosaic, but the draw is the supreme moment, the one piece of the mosaic that incorporates the whole pattern, the ultimate fraction. In religion, the perfect draw doesn't even happen. There is no interval between the sword's quiet slumber in the scabbard and the start of the cutting process. In practice, of course, there has to be a moment, and a moment is a thing susceptible of quantification, capable of being measured with a pair of calipers. There has to be a moment between peace and violence, between one version of history and another, a piece of time in which the thing could go either way. The knack is to make it as small as possible.

The offcomer knew exactly what he was doing, and so his man was still talking at the moment when the top inch of the upswinging blade sliced through his throat, cutting his last word neatly in half.

Job done.

There remained the rather more demanding issue of getting away with it, so, as soon as he was certain he'd made the kill, he put the dead man out of his mind entirely and quickly assessed the remaining obstacles; this process took about as long as it takes for a raindrop to fall from your hair to your nose, or for a cat to hear a footstep.

While the blade was still following through, he moved his back foot through ninety degrees in the direction of the other Serious Man, so that he was lined up for the second-position downwards cut ('dividing the earth from the heavens', as the religious rather charmingly call it). The cut followed on from the initial slice so quickly and fluently that it looked to be part of the same movement, but of course it was an entirely separate moment, the clearing away of an inconvenient body. The third and fourth movements cut down the bodyguards before they'd noticed anything was the matter – three perfect diagonal slices, severing the neck to the bone. All four men were still standing when the offcomer, having flicked the blood off his sword blade, looped it back and slid it elegantly into the scabbard.

'Thank you so much,' he said in a calm, clear voice, then he nodded politely, took two steps back, and slipped back between the columns of the portico just as the dead bodies toppled over and slid to the ground. It was two or three heart-beats before anybody noticed, and by then the offcomer was on the other side of the street, having quietly snuck through the portico arcade and emerged in the gap between two stalls. By the time the first woman screamed he was examining the base of a small brass jar for casting flaws.

'Yes, well,' the stallholder replied, when he pointed them out, 'they all have those. But you can't see them, and what the eye doesn't see the heart doesn't grieve over. Tell you what,' he added, suspecting that his moment was passing too quickly, 'you can have them both for seven.'

The offcomer frowned. 'Six and a half.'

'All right.' The stallholder nodded, like a guilty man accept-ing the court's verdict. 'You want them wrapped? Wrapping's a quarter extra.'

The offcomer shook his head. He'd noticed a spot of blood, about the size of a small fly, on the back of his left hand, and he eased it off against his right wrist as he replied. 'No thanks,' he said. 'I'll have them as they are. Oh, and while I'm at it, what'll you take for the inkwell? That's north country work, isn't it?'

When the fuss had died down, he walked back to the inn, bolted the door of his room behind him and lay down on the bed. He didn't get the shakes any more. That was an indulgence he'd gradually learned to do without by absorbing the trauma and filing it away in the back of his mind to be dealt with on a rainy day. Instead he calmly accepted the passing of the moment, the transition between one sequence of events and another, the comforting fact that he'd got away with it again. Already the fear had been contained and subdued and lived only in his memory, along with all those close shaves and embarrassing childhood misdemeanours that made him cringe when he thought about them. The ability to accept, to digest, to be nourished by one's own fear was one of the great joys of religion, or so he liked to believe. It was, after all, rather more spiritually respectable than admitting he was just addicted to the draw, like some dangerous freak in a street gang.

Being classically trained and thorough, he hung around Weal Bohec for the rest of the day, keeping his ears and eyes open, gathering potentially useful background information and local colour. After a thoroughly enjoyable dinner at the Blaze of Glory, a place he'd always wanted to try but had never had time for during any of his previous visits, he went to bed early and slept well before making an early start the next morning. The innkeeper told him that he hoped he'd enjoyed his stay in Weal Bohec and would come again. He replied that it was more than likely.

His journey home was long and tiresome. For some reason, the rain had chosen to come nearly a month early, and the first big storm caught him out on the road in the back of an uncovered carrier's cart halfway between Weal Bohec and Bealvoy. In the time it takes for a good cook to peel an onion his coat and hat were so completely saturated that he could feel the water trickling down his skin. The bed of the cart was flooded a finger-joint deep, and the smell of drenched cloth

was overpowering. Fairly soon he stopped trying to cower
under the brim of his hat – it was thoroughly waterlogged
anyway, with the result that he was getting wetter wearing it
than he would've been bare-headed. Instead he sat upright,
blinked rain out of his eyes and tried to pretend he was in a
nice, deep bath that he hadn't had to pay for.

As usual, the first storm of the season only lasted a very
short time, but its after-effects stayed with him for the rest of
the afternoon. Since he had nowhere to rest his feet except the
floor of the cart, he was still sitting with water seeping
through the seams of his boots long after the actual rain had
stopped. As for anything not made of metal in his pockets or
his luggage, he resigned himself to the fact that it was ruined
for ever. When the sun finally came out and started to dry him
off, he was sure he could hear the creak of cracking boot and
belt leather, and feel the hug of his clothes shrinking around
him. A thin dribble of coloured water running across the back
of his hand confirmed his suspicion that the stallholder who'd
sold him the gown had indeed been lying when he claimed the
dyes were waterfast.

Sudden heavy rain plays havoc with dry roads and baked
earth. Lakes and rivers that hadn't been there when he left
Weal Bohec blocked the cart's way, forcing tedious detours
that themselves ended in obstruction. As a result they didn't
make Bealvoy until just after dark (rumbling and splashing
down a rutted sunken track that had suddenly decided to be a
riverbed instead with only the light of a single swaying coach-
lamp to see by was rather more adventurous than he'd have
liked) and of course all the inns were full up with wet,
stranded travellers. Instead of a room to himself with a nice
warm fire and a jug of hot wine and cinnamon, he had to
make do with a corner of an overcrowded common room that
stank of wet bodies, too far away from the fire to get dry.
Even so he managed to get some sleep, out of which he was
awoken just before dawn by the carter, who wanted to get on

the road early before the rest of the previous day's delayed traffic added to the misery. That left him with a headache that stayed with him all day, made worse every time the cart bumped over a pothole or slithered in a boggy patch. Early sunshine, oppressively hot and stiflingly humid, dried his clothes out, just in time for the noon cloudburst, which left him soggier than he'd been the day before. By the time the cart finally rolled into Deymeson he was in that last, most desperate stage of wetness where you just don't care or notice any more.

What he wanted to do more than anything else was to crawl off to his quarters in the back cloister, bank up a big, unseasonal, totally non-regulation fire, and sweat out his incipient cold fever before it had a chance to get a grip. Instead he did his duty and dragged himself up six flights of deep, wide marble steps to the Father Tutor's lodgings. Because the rains hadn't reached Deymeson yet, the Father Tutor had the shutters and doors open so he wouldn't suffocate in the heat of the night.

'Where did you get to?' the Father Tutor demanded. 'You do realise it's after compline; you should've been back here in time for morning chapter.'

'It rained.'

The Father Tutor looked at him. 'I'd gathered that,' he said. 'You'd better get out of those wet clothes, before you catch a chill. Anyway,' he went on, 'I know how things went in Weal Bohec. It's a shame I had to hear about it from a travelling chair-mender rather than one of my own brothers, but at least I know.'

It occurred to him to explain how he'd decided to stay over an extra night, and how he'd been ambushed by the weather, whereas this chair-mender had obviously started earlier and escaped the rains altogether. He decided not to; he was too wet to be able to put over such a complex narrative coherently. Instead he nodded.

'It's also a pity,' the tutor went on, 'that you couldn't get the job done without killing that other trader. I shouldn't have to remind you that the whole purpose of the exercise was to send a nice clear message to the directors and the Guild; by killing someone who had nothing to do with it, you've muddied the waters. That chair-mender told me it was a simple robbery.'

'I'm sorry.' The brother tried not to notice the clammy texture of his gown across his knees. 'I didn't really have much choice in the matter. I had to go through him to get to the bodyguards; there simply wasn't time to step round him.'

The tutor shook his head. 'You're missing the point,' he said. 'If this other trader spoiled the moment by being in the wrong place, you should have waited for another moment when it was all clear.' He sighed. 'I don't want to have to dispose of another director, but if it's all gone wrong I'll probably have to, and you'll have done all this for nothing. And we'll be a week behind.'

He bowed his head, ashamed. 'I'm sorry,' he repeated. 'I should have thought three times and cut once. It won't happen again.'

'It's all right.' The tutor's lips twitched in a brief smile. 'These things happen, and you aren't the first to make a mistake like that. Certainly you won't be the last.' The smile broadened. 'I did something very similar when I wasn't much older than you are, but the world didn't actually come to an end.' He closed his large hands around the carved arms of his chair and pulled himself to his feet with a show of great effort (complete nonsense, of course, the brother knew; Father Tutor was as supple and strong as a man half his age, but he liked playing at being older). 'Which reminds me,' he went on. 'Have you heard the news from Josequin?'

The brother thought for a moment, as a drop of water trickled out of his wet hair and slid down his forehead. 'You mean about the council elections?' he asked. 'Well, yes. I feel they display a rather disturbing trend, if you ask me.'

'Ah. You haven't.' The Father Tutor poured himself a very small glass of wine. 'And it's funny that you should mention disturbing trends.' He took a little sip, more like a nibble. 'Josequin was destroyed four days ago.'

The brother felt as if he'd just fallen off his horse. 'Destroyed,' he repeated.

'Burned to the ground,' the Father Tutor said. 'Apparently no survivors – if that's true, it's quite remarkable, nobody at all left alive out of a population of nearly a hundred thousand. But our scouts in that area are generally very reliable, and they made a point of stressing the considerable numbers of dead bodies they saw in the ruins. And it's not unprecedented, of course, especially for a land-locked city, affording no easy means of escape by water.'

'My mother's family came from Josequin,' the brother said.

'Really.' The Father Tutor frowned, but decided not to upbraid him for the breach of protocol. Members of the order were supposedly forbidden to refer to their mundane families on pain of extreme penance, but in this case he was prepared to overlook the lapse. 'Now, you may be asking yourself how the fall of Josequin could possibly be relevant to the matter in hand.'

The brother looked up. 'I'm sorry, Father,' he said. 'You were saying.'

'Quite all right. What bearing, you may ask, do these events at Josequin have on the Weal situation?' He nibbled a little more of his wine, and sat down again. 'The connection is, I confess, tangential at best; possibly no more than a coincidence, or a combination of popular hysteria and poor reporting. However, I believe it's worth following the matter up, if only to eliminate an extraneous factor.'

The brother straightened up a little, aware of his lapse from grace. 'Please explain,' he said.

'A day before the attack on Josequin – at least, we think so; the exact order of events is necessarily vague, as you'll appreciate in a moment – a man and a woman appeared in the small village called Sierce, a day's ride from Josequin, and announced that they were, respectively, the god Poldarn and his priestess. After performing either a miracle or a conjuring trick, depending on interpretation, and purporting to cure a number of villagers suffering from respiratory disorders, they declared that they had business in Josequin, and left.' He frowned very slightly. 'You'll understand why I feel this matter ought to be looked into, however trivial it may appear. For what it's worth, at this stage I'm inclined to the view that it's a coincidence and the two people involved are merely charlatans making a living from the gullibility of country people. That said, I'm committing the cardinal sin of forming an opinion on the basis of insufficient information. Your job, accordingly, will be to purge me of my sin by going to this village and compiling a full report, if possible finding and interviewing these people and ideally bringing them here for detailed questioning.'

It wasn't just the discomfort of his wet clothes that made the brother squirm at that moment. Squeamish he definitely wasn't – you couldn't teach novices the eight approved cuts if you didn't have an unusually strong stomach – but the religious concept of detailed questioning always troubled him. It was typical of the polished efficiency and dislike of waste that detailed interrogations doubled as anatomy lecturers, with a class of novices standing respectfully at the back of the room taking notes in their tablets, their lecturer pointing out, naming and describing the function of each organ and component as it was laid open by the interrogator's scalpel. That said, the practice was a thoroughly effective way of both obtaining and conveying important information, and it wasn't the place of a brother to criticise.

'Sierce,' he repeated. 'Near Josequin.' He hesitated. 'I suppose it'd be best if I set off immediately,' he said, doing his best not to sound very sad indeed. 'While the scent's still fresh, as it were.'

The Father Tutor smiled; his expression was warm, almost human (though he wouldn't have taken that as a compliment). 'I think you've missed enough offices as it is without skipping nocturns and prime as well. I suggest you restore your composure with a nice hot bath in front of the fire – and yes, theoretically it's still a month too early, but you can say twenty lines of penance while you're scrubbing your back – and that'll put you in a properly relaxed and contemplative frame of mind for divine service. If you set off immediately after prime tomorrow, I imagine there'll still be something of a trail for you to follow.'

It was, of course, a criticism; every act of compassion in religion was a tacit accusation of weakness, every allowance made for frailty a concession to inadequacy. Nevertheless, the brother thought as he squelched through the south cloister on his way to his quarters, it's prideful sin to imagine oneself better than one actually is, and twenty lines was a small price to pay for a warm bath and an extracurricular scuttle of coals on the fire. The pint of distinctly non-canonical mulled wine with cloves would be an entirely separate transgression, worth at least another twenty lines, but that wasn't a problem. Over the years he'd learned the knack of reciting very quickly indeed.

One bath and fifty lines' worth of wine later he wrapped himself up in his warmest, heaviest blanket and walked across the cloister to the library. Just after midnight was the best time for quiet, comfortable research – there wasn't much point in going to bed with only a couple of hours to go before nocturns, and there wasn't much point in his going investigating if he didn't know what he was supposed to be looking for. As it turned out he had the place almost to himself. One or two of the library monks were fussing about in the stacks, putting back the last of yesterday's books, making a start on tomorrow's requisitions, and there were two or three of the older brothers scattered about among the lecterns, fast asleep (with bursarial autumn still a month away, the library was warmer than their quarters, for one thing). He took down a copy of the Concordance and a couple of other likely sources of information, pulled a stool up close to the fireplace, and looked up Poldarn in the index.

Poldarn, he read; *also Poldan, Polodan; cf. the Tulicite Boliden (s.v.). A deity much revered at one time in the provinces of Satn, Morevish and Thurm* (make that the former provinces of Satn, Morevish and Thurm; it was two hundred years since the southern empire had been lost, though of course the Concordance, even in its latest edition, wouldn't admit that) *but little known outside them; the cult spreading to Tulice in the reign of Allectus IV and thence, fleetingly, to the home provinces. A minor god of discord, prophecy, fire, war and death, mostly favoured by artisans, craftsmen and the uneducated middle classes of small towns. Possibly as a result of the conflation of the Morevish Poldarn with the Tulicite Boliden (primarily a god of labour and the forge, thence fire in general, hence the confusion with the apocalyptic qualities of the better-established Morevish deity), also revered by those engaged in trades or crafts based on the employment of fire and heat, including smiths, founders, charcoal-burners, glaziers, potters, brick and tile manufacturers, bakers and others likely to employ fire in a forge, foundry or oven. In the brief imperial cult, most popular among the forementioned trades and among freelances and mercenary soldiers, whose practice it was to invoke the aid and forgiveness of the god when committing a captured town or city to the flames. Enjoyed a brief vogue at court and among persons of quality in the reign of Trebonian II, substantially as a god of death and transition; thence in philosophical theories propounded by the southernmost Thurmian schools, a patron of change and reincarnation – the conceit being the agency of fire to purge, purify and reshape matter, as in the melting down of metals and the refinement of gold; subsequent peripheral mentions in the writings of the alchemical movement in the south, in which the* god was represented by the symbol of the crow (a carrion bird being deemed an appropriate image for the transition of dead matter into living matter by an impure agency), holding in its beak a golden ring (the gold referring to immutability, the ring to the cycle of death and rebirth) – in this context, cf. the paradoxical conceit whereby Poldarn loses his memory at the start of his journey (crude allegory for scrap metal losing its original shape when melted down in the furnace) and regains it only after encompassing the destruction of the world, presumably – though nowhere explicitly stated – in favour of the better world to come (i.e., after the molten metal has been recast in a new shape in the mould; on which, see Venercius, 36, II, n.). Thereafter in general decline, his cult decaying into superstition and folklore; latterly represented by a tradition of a god riding through rural areas in a wagon escorted by a female acolyte, his circular journey signifying the cycle of transhumance in pastoral societies, the solar cycle, et cetera. (Note also the variant tradition in which Poldarn departs across the sea after planting, travels to a mysterious unknown island and returns in time for harvest; some conflation suspected here with the historical figure of Kjartan Bollidan, leader of the Unferth Penal Colony expedition during the reign of Eucleptus III; Kjartan's supporters maintained that he would one day return across the sea to overthrow the empire and free the oppressed; this did not, of course, happen, but the cult of personality lingered for over a century in some remote country districts.) Some literary references in the poetry of the Mannerist school under Iaco III and Caratacus, mainly referring to the alchemical character noted above and deteriorating into fixed epithet and cliché (e.g., 'Poldarn's journey' fig., for a circle, 'Poldarn's winged servant' for a carrion bird, 'Poldarn's sleep' for forgetfulness, 'riding beside Poldarn' or 'driving Poldarn's cart' as euphemisms for terminal illness or other such prospect of certain death, etc., in Staso, passim); now obsolete in preferred usage except as an archaism or referential. See also: Thurmites; Mannerists; Tulice; labour, patrons of; solar deities.

Well then, the brother thought, and now we know. He'd had an idea the name was familiar from somewhere; presumably he'd come across it at some stage when he'd been reading for finals, and it had lain hidden in the hayloft of his memory ever since, useless and unobtrusive, its purpose forgotten like some rusty old tool you find hanging in a dark corner of the barn. Curious, perhaps, to pick such an out-of-the-way god to impersonate; certainly not one the rubes in the villages would be likely to have heard of. He grinned; he could narrow his search down to renegade scholars, rogue Mannerist poets and southerners. In the countryside between the Mahec and Bohec rivers, anybody belonging to any of those categories would stick out like a turd in a cake shop.

Even so, it all seemed reasonably straightforward; nevertheless, he amused himself by chasing up a few references until the bell went for nocturns. He shuffled into chapel with the rest of them, took his place at the back of the middle section of stalls designated for the junior ordained, and spent the first quarter of an hour gazing meditatively at the distinctly uncanonical sculpted frieze that spiralled round the column nearest to him. The column was one of the best-kept secrets in the order; it stood in a blind spot in the field of view from the lecterns and pulpits, which presumably was how it had escaped the notice of the Father Abbot who'd commissioned the chapel decorations three centuries ago, and it was an unspoken convention of the order that when one was promoted to a level of dignity and grace where one couldn't possibly sanction such things, one conveniently forgot all about it, along with all the other guilty secrets and pleasures of the junior orders. Great art it definitely wasn't; come to that, it wasn't even biologically accurate, having presumably been put up there by a chapel monk who'd only ever read about such things; but it was fun, a little scrap of permitted rebellion in the stronghold of the Rule.

A lifetime of practice enabled him to snap out of his reverie

in plenty of time to join in the hymns and responses, and as
his mouth shaped the words (far too familiar by now to mean
anything) he turned his mind to the divine Poldarn and the
practicalities of his mission.

Going openly, as a religious, in garb and observing the Rule,
he might expect a certain degree of co-operation from the
pious and the fanatical that he wouldn't get as a casual trav-
eller. On the other hand the order wasn't unduly popular
outside its own lands at the best of times. These days, with
bizarre cults springing up all over the place and crazy people
burning down granaries in the name of the coming apocalypse, he might find garb made him unhelpfully conspicuous,
not to mention a target for every overstressed hysteric with a
grudge and a hayfork. (For some reason, the order had never
got around to developing an approved course of combat for
sword against hayfork, and as a result experienced brothers
tended to treat the weapon with a healthy degree of respect. A
fine weapon it was, too, with the potential for some quite
sophisticated parries and disarms. One day, perhaps . . .)

In that case (they were singing the 'Father, In Thy Mercy')
he'd need a persona, something from the order's catalogue of
appropriate identities for spies and infiltrators. He gave the
matter some thought, but nothing obvious sprang to mind.
Most of the personas in the catalogue were designed for the
gathering of political, military and commercial intelligence in
mind; the idea that one day there might be a need for an
undercover scholar would seem not to have occurred to the
early fathers, in spite of their quite awesome ability to predict
virtually any possible contingency. In a way it pleased him
to have come up with an angle that wasn't covered by the
Rule; when he got back, assuming he was still alive and had
managed to achieve his objective, he'd be able to write it up as
a paper, possibly even submit it for adjudication towards the
junior fellowship he was surely in line for.

They knelt for prayer, and he dutifully herded all such

thoughts out of his head as he opened his mind for the voice of the Divine. And, as always, the Divine chose not to speak to him on that particular day; and then they stood and sang the 'Perfect Grace', allowing him to continue with his train of thought.

Apart from a religious, what sort of person goes around the countryside asking questions about gods, prophecies, strange happenings, miracles and magic? Offhand, he couldn't think of anybody. Nor were they the kind of topic that'd be likely to crop up in ordinary taproom conversation, except in passing, without the level of detail necessary for his observations. Very well, then; he'd have to approach the problem from another angle. There was, for example, always force; a man at the head of a column of cavalry can ask any question he likes and expect a detailed and civil answer. But that would be clumsy, as well as constituting an embarrassing show of strength at a time when the order preferred to stay quiet. Father Tutor wouldn't like it at all, and might well suspect that he was doing it to be annoying, as a protest against being sent on what was palpably a penance assignment. Not force, then; what did that leave? Wandering lunatic? Surprisingly effective in some cases, though pretty gruelling, and the outskirts of Josequin were a long way away; sheer hell to have to stay in such a disagreeable character all that time, on foot, sleeping in ditches . . .

All right then, what about the other extreme? What about a wealthy eccentric, an amateur scholar compiling material for a book about – let's see, how about 'some observations concerning popular superstitions in the northern provinces', something like that? Oh, he'd suffered enough of the works of such fatuous dilettanti in his youth – still the primary sources for several topics, even though the lecturers complained bitterly about their inaccuracy and lack of scientific method. There weren't nearly so many of them nowadays – not many people could afford the time or the money, even if they had the interest – but the stereotype would still be recognised (translated into village speech, it'd come out as 'bloody nuisance with too much money and time on his hands, coming round here asking bloody stupid questions' – an accurate enough assessment, at that). At least it'd have the advantages of allowing him to sleep in a bed at an inn instead of curled up under a bush; he'd be able to ride and carry a couple of changes of clothing, eat whatever passed for a good meal.

So engrossed was he in planning the details of his new persona that he didn't notice that the service was over, even though he'd correctly chanted the responses and sung the hymns (automatic, like the draw; and there were some who said that only the man who no longer thinks about praying can actually pray, since in reflexive action there is no thought, and without thought there can be no doubt – 'the hand believes that the sword is in the sash; the heart believes that the divine is there,' as someone or other so memorably put it). He came to just as the choir monks were starting to file out of the chapel, quickly reminded himself of who he was and what he was due to do next, and hurried back to his quarters to start getting ready.

Chapter Six

'No point trying the act in Sansory,' Copis had said earlier that day. 'Wouldn't work. If a god were to show up in Sansory they'd kidnap him and hold him to ransom.'

The first thing they saw after they'd driven under the amazingly high arch of the city gate was a fight. They had no option but to stay and watch, since the crowd of enthusiastic spectators had jammed the street solid and it was perfectly clear that nobody was going anywhere until there was a result. The participants were two old men: one was tall, bald and stooping, and the shaggy fringe of white hair around the back of his head was streaked with blood from two deep scalp wounds on his crown; the other was just under average height, with grey spikes plastered across his forehead and a palpably smashed jaw. They were fighting with quarterstaffs, which clattered together with a sound like a fast-running capstan as they struck and parried faster than Poldarn could follow. It didn't take him long to see why both men's wounds were to the head; it was clearly the primary target in quarterstaff play, with a few shots being reserved for the solar plexus, groin, kneecaps and elbows. The stamina and ferocity of the fighters was quite awe-inspiring, as was their apparent ability to take punishment. The bald man, for example, misjudged a ward and was jabbed in the teeth (he hadn't had many to start with), followed by two lightning-fast cracks to either temple, a savage downward blow in the middle of his forehead, and an upward cut directly under his chin that knocked his head back so sharply that Poldarn was sure his neck must have been broken. But, after staggering back three or four paces, still managing to dodge a shot or two while he was at it, he found a wall to back into and straighten himself up again, and launched himself at his enemy with a feinted jab to the throat, instantly converted into another feint to the groin, and carried home as a slanting smash to the cheekbone that sprayed the first three rows of the crowd with a fine mist of blood. Then it was the other man's turn to stagger for a moment; three or four exchanges later, however, they were back to being evenly matched, both of them moving as fast and as fluently as ever.

Poldarn leaned over to whisper. 'Does this sort of thing . . . ?'

'All the time,' she replied, her eyes fixed on the fight. 'It's part of their rich and unique cultural heritage. Whee!' she added, as the shorter man stepped into his enemy's attack, deliberately taking a sickening blow to his left temple so as to close and slam his staff into the other man's groin. 'You must admit, they put on a good show here.'

Even the bald man couldn't keep standing up after a shot like that one. He doubled up, his head bobbing forward, straight into a chin-lifter even more blood-curdling than the one he'd planted on the other man a few moments before. It was followed up by four crushing side blows, two to each ear, and rounded off by a left-to-right lowhand cross that broke his nose and set it back at a truly bizarre angle, leaving him crumpled up on the ground like a child who's just fallen out of a tree. After that he didn't move at all. The shorter man, having kicked him in the ribs a few times in the interests of total security, spat on his face and hobbled awkwardly away, using his staff as a crutch.

'One thing we must do while we're here,' Copis said, 'is try the smoked lamb. It's *the* local speciality. Apparently, it's something to do with the kind of wood they use.'

Now that there was nothing left to see, the crowd dissolved, like earth becoming mud under heavy rain. Copis edged the cart carefully through the mass of bodies.

'You were staring,' she explained. 'One thing you must never do in a place like this is stare. You'll see a lot worse than that while you're here, I promise you.'

'Sorry,' Poldarn said. 'It just seemed so pointless, that's all. I mean, at their age wouldn't it be simpler to wait a few years and see which one of them outlives the other?'

Copis laughed. 'I suspect you're a country boy,' she replied. 'Nobody in the city waits for anything if they can help it. Which is strange,' she added, 'since living in a city means you're bound to spend a large slice of your life standing around in queues or waiting for the traffic to clear; you'd have thought patience would've become a survival trait by now. Right,' she said, stopping the cart without warning, to the extreme disgust of the traffic behind her, 'let's try here.'

'What are we going to do?' Poldarn asked, as she jumped down and made the reins fast to a tethering-post. The carter who'd been following them squeezed his cart past between their wheels and the opposite pavement, his face bright red with rage as he yelled abuse at them. Copis didn't seem to notice.

'See if we can sell all this stuff, of course,' she replied. 'Pull down a couple of jars while I talk to the stallholder. Well, come on. We're blocking the road.'

The stallholder turned out to be a small man, almost spherical, with a smooth, shiny bald head and a pointed nose, like a carrot. He was sorry, but he didn't buy small quantities, no matter how cheap they might be. His regular order with the plantation agents was finely calculated to give him exactly the amount of stock in hand that he could be sure of getting rid of before it went green and started to sprout; anything extra he bought would be money thrown away. Copis pointed out that at the prices they were asking he could almost give it away, thereby attracting new customers to his stall and increasing his sales without hurting his margins. That suggestion made the stallholder very sad, because, as he pointed out, every bushel of cut-price flour he sold meant another bushel of full-price flour, which he'd already paid for, that he wouldn't be able to get shot of; in effect, he'd be waging a price war against himself. Besides, he explained, he had a Guild charter and a quota; if he bought or sold more or less than what was written down on his licence and the Guild found out about it, that'd be twenty years of hard work out of the window. Not worth it for a dubious chance of making a few extra quarters. Sorry.

'He meant it,' Copis said, frowning, as she climbed back into the cart and pulled out, nearly causing a nasty accident. 'I hadn't realised the Guild had got this far. Bloody nuisance. Never mind,' she added, 'at least we won't go short of things to eat for a while.'

'What's the Guild?' Poldarn asked.

'Long story,' Copis replied, ducking to avoid a low-hanging sign. 'Tell you later. Well, that solves the problem of which inn to stay at. The cheapest.'

Poldarn nodded. 'We'll have to ask someone,' he said.

'No need,' Copis replied, pulling a face. 'It's the one thing everybody knows about Sansory.'

It was a pleasant relief to discover that he could read; the sign over the wide archway was black with soot and mould but he could still make out the words Charity and Diligence in big red letters against a faded gold-leaf background. 'Used to be a religious order,' Copis explained as they passed under the arch. 'All the inns and brothels in these parts were religious houses once, only really changed when the monks started charging for board and lodging. I guess that's the coach-house over there.'

Poldarn saw a huge shed in front of them, nearly twice the size of the ruined temple they'd slept in at Cric. Next to it was an even bigger shed; next to that, a massive square stone building, with fluted white columns and a flight of twelve broad, shallow marble steps leading up to a pair of bronze doors, still awe-inspiring despite a thick layer of verdigris. The steps themselves were nearly invisible for the huge number of people sitting on them, bunched up together like calves in a pen. They ranged from scruffy to bundles of rags, and mostly they sat still and quiet, staring at the ground or straight in front of them. In the doorway itself stood two very large men with folded arms and grim expressions on their faces. When one of the scruffy people got up and tried to push past them through the doorway, they grabbed him by his arms, lifted him off his feet and threw him down the steps like a bale of straw. He landed badly, his fall partly broken by a couple of the silent sitters who hadn't got out of the way in time. There was a little bit of shrill cursing, which didn't seem to bother the men in the doorway at all, and then things settled down again.

'Typical Sansory,' Copis said as they waited for someone to come and open the coach-house door. 'They couldn't pay their tab, so they're slung out and the house keeps their tools and stuff. Without their tools, they can't earn any money to pay off their tab and redeem their tools. So they sit and wait for something to happen. Like I told you, this is pretty much a place where you stop because you can't go any further.'

The doors opened eventually, and two very silent, very efficient grooms unyoked the horses and led them away, while two others manhandled the cart into a stall in a long line that stretched the length of the shed. Another man, who'd kept perfectly still while the others were working, then handed them a little bone counter with a number on it – Copis explained that so many carts and wagons passed through the Charity every day that the stablemaster couldn't be expected to remember them all, hence the little ticket with the stall number on it. There was a hole drilled at the top, through which Copis passed a piece of hemp cord she'd picked up off the floor (it was covered in the stuff). She tied the ends together, hung it round her neck and tucked it away out of sight. 'Lose the ticket, lose the cart,' she said. 'It's that kind of place. Now you can see why I'd have preferred something a bit less basic.'

'What about our things?' Poldarn asked, thinking of the big lump of gold hidden by the tailgate. 'The fireworks and all the rest of our stuff. Do you think they'll be safe there?'

Copis grinned. 'Guaranteed,' she replied. 'Tradition of the house: no fighting, no stealing, except by order of the management. I don't know if you noticed the two porters on the main door; it's a fair bet there's at least a dozen more like them inside, and as many again in the staff barracks waiting for their shift. Free company men, probably; it's one of the usual careers for when you've had enough of the road.'

Getting up the steps past the silent sitters looked like it would be next to impossible; but Copis exhibited a thoroughly efficient technique that basically consisted of treading hard on the hands and ankles of anybody who didn't shift out of the way, and Poldarn followed nervously in her wake. The owners of the squashed fingers and joints swore at them, but didn't bother to look up; instead, they mumbled their curses into the air, like sleepy monks saying their responses.

The porters at the main door looked at them closely but let them pass (the man behind them wasn't so lucky, and ended up on his back on the stairs) and they found themselves in an enormous hallway. The ceiling was so high that Poldarn had to lean his head back as far as it would go in order to see the paintings, still startlingly beautiful despite the effects of decades of smoke and grime on their colours and gold leaf. The mosaics on the walls were even finer, though only a few patches were still discernible. He found that he couldn't afford to stand gawping for long, however. There were too many people in the hallway, moving too fast. For her part, Copis barged her way through to a trestle table set up in the far left corner; she came back some time later with two more bone tickets, one of which she handed to him.

'These aren't quite so precious,' she said. 'We have to show them to get food or a place to sleep in the dormitory. Still, if you lose yours you'll end up outside with the rest of the poor sad people, because that's the last of our money. We'd better give some thought to how we're going to get some more.'

Again he thought about the lump of gold, and probably would have mentioned it if she'd stayed put long enough to let him. Instead she started pushing and slithering her way to the door. 'To be honest with you,' she explained, when they were back in the fresh air again, 'I don't like it much in there. A bit too crowded, and I'm not desperately keen on the smell. Let's go and find the junk market, see if we can get something for your predecessor's boots.'

The fifth boot stall they tried in the junk market was buying, and they came away with three and a half quarters, a quarter more than Copis had been expecting. 'Which means he figures he can get five,' she pointed out, as they turned sideways to squeeze through a narrow gap between two barrows. 'Wonder why rubbish like that's going so dear. Panic, probably; because of what happened to Josequin. People get scared, prices go up. Fact of life.'

There was something about the goods for sale in the junk market that Poldarn found familiar, though he couldn't quite work out what it was. It was only when they had to stand and wait beside a clothing stall while a wide cart went by and he saw a big brown stain around a hole in a tunic that he realised where all the stuff came from.

'That's right,' Copis confirmed, when he asked her. 'It's one of the biggest businesses in town. Someone told me once that three-quarters of all the stuff stripped off bodies on battle-fields ends up in Sansory market sooner or later. It's because so many of the free companies have their headquarters here, and all the others have at least a recruiting office or a dormitory. They're all in the upper town, of course; they wouldn't be seen dead down here in the Sump.'

'Pity,' Poldarn said. 'If only I'd known, we could have made some money here.'

'What do you mean?'

He remembered; he hadn't told her about the two dozen dead men he'd woken up with. Hadn't got round to it, and it was too late now. 'Oh, I was just thinking about those horse-men we ran into,' he said.

'True. But at the time we weren't planning on coming here. And used military equipment isn't the safest thing in the world to carry around with you, especially if you've come by it the hard way, like we did.'

'Fair enough,' he said. 'Well,' he added, stopping and look-ing about him, 'at least nobody's burned it down yet. Makes a pleasant change as far as I'm concerned.'

The stalls were colourful, if nothing else, and (as Copis was at pains to point out) you'd be unlikely to see anything like them anywhere else in the empire. There was a whole stall full of helmets, for instance, well over half of them crushed, cut or punctured in some way; the ones on the back shelves had been straightened, beaten out and patched, while the rest were presumably as the gleaners had found them. There were several stalls selling nothing but loose links for mailshirts, and behind them two or more old women were slowly dismantling shirts that were too badly damaged to be worth repairing. One old woman would cut the rivets with a big pair of shears, while another opened out the rings with two pairs of pinchers and dropped them in a copper basin by her feet. You could have had your choice of half-pairs of marching boots; three stalls sold only left boots, whereas four sold only right. There were belt stalls, buckle stalls, tunic, cloak and trouser stalls, button stalls, stalls selling plates, pots, pans and cauldrons, stalls with neat trays of horn buttons, bone and steel needles, sharpening stones and belt loops for carrying them in; stalls selling knapsacks, water bottles, blankets and tents. There were racks of tools for blacksmiths, armourers, farriers, carpenters and a host of other trades; also spades, shovels, picks and even a few wheelbarrows; folding chairs, tables and beds. It was hard to think of anything that wasn't there, in some shape or form, right down to fur-lined slippers, books and musical instruments, though their comparative rarity suggested that they'd come from the bodies of senior officers rather than ordinary footsloggers.

'Seen enough yet?' Copis asked, trying to detach him from a display of thick woollen socks. 'This lot gives me the creeps, if you must know.'

Poldarn shrugged. 'I was just looking around,' he said. 'After all, if I see something I remember, like a uniform I may have worn once, or some distinctive-looking kit from the bodies of people I used to fight against, it might set the ball rolling and help me remember the rest.'

She clicked her tongue. 'You're not still on about that, are you?' she said wearily. 'Look, if I were you I'd let it go. After all,' she added, lowering her voice, 'there's a chance that if it does all come flooding back, it'll be stuff you really don't want to know. Or me, for that matter. Leave it alone, is my advice.'

Before Poldarn had a chance to state his views on the matter, Copis looked up at the sky and announced that they'd better be getting back if they didn't want to miss dinner. As if to reinforce her point, she added that it'd be quicker if they took a short cut through the scrap market. 'This way,' she said firmly and walked away quickly, so that he had to run a few steps in order to keep up.

The scrap market filled up a long, quite narrow alley between the back of the Faith and Hope (formerly the prebendary temple) and the outer wall of the garden of one of the big commercial houses. There were stalls on both sides, leaving only just enough room for two files of pedestrians, or one cart; it seemed a profoundly illogical place in which to buy and sell large quantities of bulk metal, but Poldarn was quickly learning that logic had very little to do with the design or growth of cities. Here, Copis explained as they shoved and weaved their way through, was where all the busted and mangled metalwork left lying about on battlefields ended up, the stuff that was only fit for cutting up or the melt.

The explanation wasn't really necessary; the stock in trade crowded round him as he passed – piles of crushed and mangled breastplates, with rust clotting on the sharp edges of rips and punctures, crates and barrels of sword blades broken at the forte or sheared at the tang, spearheads snapped off at the top of the socket, arrowheads with their points curled in like seashells, plackets and beavers and gorgets twisted into bizarre shapes, coats of scales and coats of plates with the memory of the killing wound frozen in the distortion of the metal, where other metal had passed through and been drawn out. Each ruined artefact was as eloquent as a witness in a trial, recording its own failure – a bardische cracked along a flaw, exposing the white, gritty grain; a helmet torn apart along a welded seam; an overtempered spearhead bent double; links of a mail-shirt whose rivets had pulled through the eyes under the force of an axe cut. It was like some kind of eternal damnation of metal, where each piece was condemned to stay for ever in the image of that last moment of inadequacy, the point at which it had betrayed its owner or simply given up trying to hold the shape its maker had given it. In every tear, puncture, fracture and distortion was a memory of its own death – was that how the souls of evil men are punished, Poldarn thought idly, by being frozen for all time in the moment of agonised transition?

He hoped not, since he had no idea what he'd done and therefore couldn't repent and seek salvation, and he didn't want to end up on a stall in some crowded market of scrapped souls.

'What the hell do people want with all this junk?' he asked.

Copis grinned. 'It may look like junk to you, but it's prettier than a field of buttercups to some people. Just think of that town we passed through, where they'd cut down all the trees for charcoal. It costs a small fortune to make good iron, and as much again to turn it into steel, and here's all the raw material you could ever want, all ready to be heated up and bashed into any shape you like, none of that tedious mucking about with smelting and rolling and hammering into blooms. It's all good stuff, this,' she went on, gesturing vaguely at the heaps and piles. 'They don't make armour and weapons out of any old rubbish. Where else could you get best oil-hardening steel at twenty quarters a hundredweight?' She realised that Poldarn was looking at her oddly. 'I had a regular who was in the scrap trade,' she explained. 'Really loved his work, I guess, he'd go on for hours about what he called the poetry of it all – you know, taking something that was all busted up and finished with and turning it into something new and useful. I've got to admit, the idea of that appealed to me in a funny sort of a way. I mean, if you've got to have wars, it's nice that someone can get something useful out of it at the end.'

Poldarn nodded gravely. 'It's just a shame they can't do the same sort of thing with all the dead bodies,' he said.

'Don't you believe it.' Copis shook her head. 'There's bonemeal, and compost; and they say the ash from funeral pyres makes wonderful lye, for soap and perfumes and stuff. I've never heard of anybody making a business out of it, but then, it's not the sort of thing you'd admit to, not if you didn't want to turn off all your potential customers. I mean, one block of soap looks pretty much like another; who knows or cares where it came from?'

'You're joking, aren't you?'

'Yes,' Copis admitted. 'Probably. It was the look on your face. I had no idea you were so squeamish.'

'Am I?'

'Apparently. My guess is that in your previous life you were some kind of clerk, spent your life perched on a stool copying out letters and yelling the place down if you nicked your finger when you sharpened your pen.'

He looked seriously at her. 'Do you think that's a possibility?'

'Anything is possible, but that would be pretty low down the list.'

The evening meal at the Charity and Diligence consisted of boiled leeks and red cabbage in a thin grey gravy, with a slab of coarse barley bread the size of a roof slate and a wedge of hard white cheese. 'Nourishing,' Copis remarked with her mouth full, 'wholesome, and tastes disgusting. Welcome to the city.'

The dining-room, which had served the same function when the building was still a religious house, was almost as big as the hall. There were four long lines of tables and benches on either side, enough room for three hundred people who didn't mind their neighbours' elbows in their gravy. It was full, and extremely noisy. From time to time a server passed up and down the aisles with a big earthenware jug; it was just as well that they'd managed to get places at the top end of a table, near the kitchens and the buttery, since the jugs never seemed to make it further than a third of the way down the line before running dry. Catching the server's attention was a simple matter of sticking out an arm or a knee. The paintings on the ceiling weren't quite as fine as those in the hallway, but the frescoes on the walls must have been exquisite at one time, before the damp got behind them and levered them out in handfuls. 'Scenes from scripture,' Copis told him with a yawn, when he asked. 'Not that I'm any expert; half of these don't mean anything to me. But there's Actis stealing the sun from the giants – bloody silly story, that – and that one's Cadanet sieving the stars, assuming that big round thing's meant to be a sieve, and the one next to it is Sthen and Theron drinking the sea.' She hesitated for a moment, then looked at him. 'You haven't got a clue what I'm talking about, have you?' she said.

He looked away. 'I know what you're thinking,' he said. 'We must have different gods where I come from.'

'Well . . .' She shrugged. 'I don't want to know. Eat your dinner before it gets cold.'

That seemed a sensible suggestion, and while he was doing it he tried not to look at the walls or the roof. It stood to reason, though; a man might forget his name and family, but something as basic as scripture (or mythology, or fairy-tales, whatever you liked to call it) ought to have stuck somewhere, along with language and how to tie knots and which hand to wipe your bum with. Even if they'd been knocked back into the scrap, seeing pictures that told the stories ought surely to bring them huddling back into the light. But she was right: none of it meant anything to him, except . . .

He froze, halfway through chewing his last slab of cheese. He'd recognised one of them, he was sure of it. He'd recognised it, but it was so familiar that he hadn't noticed it; his mind had pushed past it in search of something more interesting. He looked round, had to look three times before he found it—

'That one,' he said, pointing. 'Over there, just under the window.'

Copis frowned at him. 'I'd really rather we didn't go into this,' she said.

'Yes,' he replied irritably, 'but I think I know what it is. That big man with the white beard, isn't he just about to open that box? And when he does, I think something escapes.'

'That's right,' Copis said, sounding excited. 'The four seasons. The old man is Cadanet, of course, and—'

'Cadanet,' he replied. 'Yes, I knew that. And his wife – that'll be the thin woman with the funny hat—'

'Veil of stars, actually, but—'

'Her name,' he went on, closing his eyes, 'is Holden. She gave him the box.'

'You've got it.' Copis nodded frantically. 'Go on, what else can you remember? Where did she get the box from?'

He clenched his fists, as if trying to squeeze the information out between his fingers. 'No,' he said, 'I don't know that. But it was some kind of trick.'

'That's it,' Copis said. 'Olfar gave her the box while Cadanet was sleeping.'

'And before he opened it, it was always summer?'

'Exactly.' Copis breathed a sigh of relief. 'You've no idea how relieved I am to hear you say that.'

He thought for a moment before answering. 'All right,' he said, 'but it doesn't prove anything. Just because I remember one story . . .'

'It's a start,' Copis interrupted. 'And it's a pretty basic story, the fall from grace. I think the first time I heard it was when I was four. Maybe even earlier than that, because everything before I was six is really just a jumble. What I mean is, it'd be one of the first ones you learned, so it stands to reason it'll be one of the first you remember. Assuming it works like that,' she added.

'Assuming.'

'Well, I don't know, do I? And why have you got to be so downbeat about everything? It gets on my nerves sometimes.'

He grinned. 'Who's being downbeat? I've actually remembered a name. You have no idea . . .' He paused; another picture had caught his eye. Irritatingly, it was too high up and far away for him to be able to see it clearly, but he could definitely make out a man and a woman in a cart, with a burning town in the background. He pointed at it.

'What?' Copis said.

'There,' he replied. 'Top left corner. It's in shadow from where we're sitting, but—'

'My God, yes, fancy that.' Copis leaned back to get a better view, jogging the elbow of the woman sitting next to her; she swore, and went back to her food. 'You know,' she said, 'that's odd. I could've sworn the cart was my idea.'

'What do you mean by that?'

'When I was a little girl, the end-of-the-world god rode around the place on a black horse with a white spot on its forehead. But there weren't any black horses with white spots in my price range when I was figuring out the act, so I went for a cart instead. Yes, that's definitely off.'

'Stay there,' he said, getting up. 'I'm going to have a closer look.'

From the other end of the room, staring directly up at it, he could see rather more detail. The man, for instance, had a short black beard and a golden crown of some kind (nothing at all like the tiara-thing they used in the act), and while he was brandishing what was presumably meant to be a thunderbolt in his left hand, he was holding an oddly shaped curved sword in his right. The burning town was just a random pattern of black silhouetted squares and rectangles, but the carthorses were both skewbalds, just like the two the grooms had led away to the stables. The part that really caught his attention, however, was the other panel of the painting, which he hadn't been able to see at all from where he'd been sitting. The man in it was definitely the same one as in the first panel; no sign of the woman or, indeed, the cart, but here were two other men standing with him, one on either side, and he was walking down the gangplank of a ship towards a landscape of green grass and decidedly unnaturalistic sheep.

He was about to turn away when someone bumped into him. Instead of swearing at him, the man apologised, which Poldarn took to indicate that he was an offcomer too. 'No problem,' he mumbled, expecting the man to go away. But he didn't.

'Looking at the painting?' the man asked.

'What? Oh, yes. Rather good, isn't it?'

The man grinned. 'I think it's awful,' he replied. 'But it's an interesting subject. Actually, I've just come twelve days' ride to see it.'

Poldarn turned his head and looked at him. He was enormous, the size and shape of a bear who'd got himself apprenticed to a blacksmith; he had a short black beard, just like the man in the picture, a small stub nose and very big round brown eyes. He was smiling.

'Professional curiosity,' the man explained. 'It's the only known pictorial representation of this particular myth this side of Morevish. Pity it had to be in a shithole like this, really.'

Poldarn nodded, not quite sure what to make of him. 'Maybe if you come back later,' he said, 'after dinner's over, you could get a better look at it—'

'Oh, I will,' the man replied. 'And I'll hire some ladders, possibly even a scaffolding team; also a whole bunch of clerks to draw it for me – I never was any good at drawing, even when I was a kid. I haven't come all this way just to gawp at it from down here and then go home.' He smiled. 'You don't recognise me, do you?' he added.

'No.'

The man laughed. 'Oh well,' he said. 'Makes a pleasant change, really. My name's Cleapho.'

That was obviously meant to mean something without further explanation. Poldarn's face must have betrayed his thoughts, because the man laughed again. 'It's all right,' he said, 'don't worry about it. Like I said, it's actually rather nice not to be recognised for once. So,' he went on, and Poldarn could feel the man observing him. 'You just like the look of it, do you?'

Poldarn nodded. 'What's the story behind it, do you know?'

'Yes. Do you?'

Strange edge to his voice when he asked that. 'Not a clue,' Poldarn replied. 'But I'd like it if you'd tell me.'

Cleapho nodded, having apparently satisfied himself about some point or other. 'It's a southern legend,' he said. 'Morevish, Tulice, Thurm, places like that. Not very widely known these days – I mean, that picture's something like three hundred years old, possibly older. The man in the cart is a god, and he's bringing the end of the world. The female's just some priestess; in some versions of the story she's got a name, Machaira, but that's probably a later gloss. The first scene is where he burns down a major city; and that's an interesting thing, because there's a version of the story where the city that gets burned at this stage in the story is supposed to be somewhere in the north, between two great rivers, which could just about be taken to mean Josequin – well, you can see the topicality, can't you? Unfortunately, that version's pretty late and a very poor source in any case – Mannerist epic poetry, thoroughly unreliable, they used to make up any old stuff and chuck it in just to get the rhymes – so it probably doesn't represent a genuine tradition or anything, just some rich dilettante's imagination. It'll be easier, of course, when I can get up there and read the writing.'

'Writing?' Poldarn squinted. 'I can't see any.'

'You wouldn't, not from down there. It's a religious thing, doesn't matter whether you or I can read the writing, it's not us it's addressed to. Lots of bloody stupid things like that in religion; they sound clever the first time you hear them, and then they're just annoying. You know,' he went on, stroking his beard, 'three hundred years is probably on the conservative side. It's difficult, of course, trying to put a date on religious painting, because styles don't change the way they do with commercial stuff. Another religious thing,' he added with a deep, rather exaggerated sigh; Poldarn got the impression that Cleapho was sharing a private joke with himself. 'Anyway,' he went on, 'as I was saying, it could be considerably older than that, though of course I'm no expert. Interesting, though.'

'I suppose so,' Poldarn said.

'But not to you, evidently. And there's no harm in that, either.' The man was chuckling again. Whatever the private joke was, it was clearly very funny. 'It's annoying that some bloody fool saw fit to smash a damned great window right through the interesting bit,' he said. 'Of course nobody mentioned that to me before I left Torcea, or I wouldn't have been quite so eager to come all this way. After all, the beginning of the story's pretty well cut and dried; it's the ending that's the problem. But instead of an ending, all we've got is a window. You know, that's probably highly symbolic, though what of I haven't a clue.'

'You were telling me the story,' Poldarn reminded him.

'What? Oh yes, so I was. Where had I got to?'

'The god had just burned down a city.'

'Right, yes. Now, this is where the story gets a bit complicated, because it all depends on which version you're following. In the Tulicite version, for instance, that's the point where he meets the maker of false images – though there's a translation issue there, because the Tulicite word *trahidur* can also mean a worshipper of false gods, a confidence trickster or one of those people who clips little bits of silver off the coins, basically you can take your pick. Maker of false images sounds better, though. Well, that's the Tulicite version. In the Morevish version – well, there's two Morevish versions, but in the preferred texts the meeting with the maker of false images – only in this version he's the man who makes little bronze statues of demons and brings them to life – well, the meeting with him comes after he fights and overcomes the Saviour of the People, who's the only man on earth who could stop him and save the world – he doesn't, though, it's a very gloomy myth – except that there's a tradition in some of the later Mannerists that may well be derived from a Morevish source that we don't have any more, in which he murders all the priests of the true faith before he overcomes the Saviour, which you'd normally just dismiss out of hand as some

Mannerist trying to be clever, if it wasn't for the fact that in the Thurm tradition, which as far as we can tell is much, much older at this point, the Saviour bit comes before the maker of false images, in fact before the old woman in the hut *and* the false images *and* the drink from the lonely fountain but *after* the visit to the museum of lost souls, which is downright perverse, if you ask me.'

'I see,' Poldarn said. 'If you'll . . .'

'And there, of course,' Cleapho went on, 'is where it really starts to get screwed up; because suddenly out of nowhere about three hundred and twenty-five years ago along comes this purely domestic tradition, right out of the blue with no warning, where the god in the cart isn't actually Poldarn but Poldarn's *son*, would you believe, and the battle with the Saviour comes right after the museum—'

'Excuse me,' Poldarn interrupted, 'but what was that name you just mentioned?'

'Poldarn. Him,' Cleapho explained, pointing at the picture. 'The one we've been talking about all this time.'

'Poldarn?'

'That's right.'

Poldarn took a deep breath. 'That's the god's name, is it?'

Cleapho frowned, looking puzzled. 'Well, of course. Didn't you know that? Sorry, I'd assumed you knew, otherwise why would you be interested in the painting? Yes, that's the name. Southern, originally.'

'And hundreds of years old?'

'More than hundreds of years down in Morevish and Thurm. More like thousands. They're very conservative down there, hardly ever change their gods. Not like us.' At that point he appeared to notice something and swore under his breath. 'Look,' he said, 'you'll think I'm very rude but I've just realised I've left my escort and about a dozen porters standing about in the courtyard – I came straight here, you see, from the jetty – so I really ought to go and sort them out, before

they assume I've been murdered and tear the place apart looking for me. If you're interested in all this, catch me a bit later
on and I'll tell you some more. Bye for now.'

Before Poldarn could say anything, Cleapho had marched
briskly down the aisle and slipped out through the door; it was
rather shocking that anything that size could be moved so fast
without a crane and rollers, at the very least. Poldarn took one
last look at the picture and headed back to his place at table, to
find that Copis had come up the aisle and was only a few feet
away.

'You do know who that was you were talking to, don't you?'
she hissed.

Poldarn, who'd been about to say something else, frowned.
'He said his name was Cleapho,' he replied.

'That's right, Cleapho,' Copis said, actually sounding
bewildered for once. 'Cleapho, the emperor's personal chaplain. Even I recognised him, and it's years since I was last in
Torcea.'

'Torcea,' Poldarn repeated.

'That's right. You know, where the emperor lives. I must
have heard him preach in temple – oh, dozens of times. And
it's not a voice you forget.'

Poldarn hadn't noticed anything specially distinctive about
it, but that wasn't the subject he wanted to talk about. 'You
said you got the name off a roof tile,' he said.

'What?'

'You know, the name. Poldarn. You said it was the name of
a brickworks.'

Copis looked even more confused. 'It is.'

'No it's not,' Poldarn told her. 'It's the name of this god I'm
supposed to be, and that man Cleapho—'

'Outside,' Copis interrupted. 'Before somebody hears us.'

So they went outside, and found a corner of the yard that
wasn't overlooked or near anything else. 'He told me,' Poldarn
said angrily, 'that this Poldarn is a real god, from somewhere

away down south, and there's all sorts of stories about him, including one where he drives round in a cart with a priestess burning down cities. You must've known that; it can't be a coincidence. So why did you tell me you'd picked the name at random?'

'I did,' Copis said. 'It must just be a coincidence, that's all. Look, forget about all that now, it isn't important. Do you realise you've just spent ten minutes talking to one of the most powerful men in the whole empire?'

'What?' Poldarn said, disconcerted. 'I thought you said he was some sort of priest.'

'That's right, some kind of priest. And the emperor's some kind of government official. What the hell's he doing here? And what were you talking to him about for all that time?'

Poldarn was so bewildered that it took him a moment to remember. 'The picture,' he said. 'He told me he'd come all the way from somewhere – Torcea, I think – just to look at that picture. Then he started telling me the story, only he kept sidetracking himself.'

Copis shook her head. 'Cleapho's probably the cleverest man in the empire,' she said. 'If he was talking to you all that time, it wasn't just passing the time of day. What did you tell him? About us, I mean?'

'Nothing. He didn't ask.'

'No, you're missing something. He wouldn't make it sound like he was asking. The likes of him don't talk to the likes of you for a quarter of an hour unless it's a national emergency.'

Poldarn shook his head. 'He said the painting was three hundred years old. If it's an emergency, it can't be a very urgent one.'

'No.' Copis put on her decisive face. 'Something's going on. I don't know or care what it is, but I don't want to get mixed up in it. Let's go to Mael Bohec while we still can.'

'We've only just got here.'

'So? Anything special you were planning on doing while we're here?'

Once again he thought of the lump of fused gold in the back of the cart, and what better time to tell her about it than now? Somehow, though, it didn't feel right; whether it was the thought of how she'd react when she found out he'd been keeping the good luck from her, or perhaps a little scrap of suspicion, a trace element from the stranger he used to be that had survived the melt, or something else that was buried too deep to be found. 'I just don't see what the problem is, that's all,' he said. 'If this Cleapho's so very important, why the hell should he have the slightest interest in us?'

She looked at him. 'Define us,' she said. 'Oh, I know exactly who I am. You, on the other hand . . .'

He hadn't thought of that. Something the big, bearded man had said, *You don't recognise me, do you?* It had seemed to fit the context perfectly well at the time. Remembered in isolation, it could be made to mean all sorts of things. 'You think he knows who I am? From before . . .'

Copis looked away. 'I didn't say that.'

'You think he knows me,' Poldarn said, raising his voice a little. 'What's more, you think I'm the reason he's here.'

She tried to walk away but he grabbed her arm. He was gripping hard enough to hurt, but she didn't say anything about it. 'You think a man like that'd come all this way just to look at a mouldy old painting?'

Poldarn let go a little. 'It's a religious painting. He's a priest. For all I know it could be really, incredibly important.'

'Did he make it sound like it was, when he was talking to you?'

'How should I know? I don't know how priests talk. I don't know how anyone talks.' He closed his eyes, breathed out, tried to clear his mind. 'Think about it. You're suggesting he's come here on purpose to find me. How the hell would he

know to find me here? Even we didn't know we were coming
here till a few days ago. How long would it have taken him to
get here from Torcea? Or are you saying he just packed a bag
and set off on the off chance that he might bump into me
somewhere in the northern provinces?'

Copis pulled a face. 'Yes, all right,' she said irritably, 'point
taken. It's not just unlikely, it's impossible.' She lifted her head
and looked him in the eyes. 'I still think we should clear out of
here,' she said. 'When someone like that suddenly turns up, no
civic reception or marching bands or little girls coming forward to present bouquets of flowers, it means something's
up. Which means trouble. Which means sensible people like
me leave town. Which is why—'

She was staring at something over his shoulder. He turned
his head to see what it was, and saw two soldiers walking
quickly across the yard towards them. Once again, they didn't
look anything like any of the other soldiers he'd seen; they
were magnificent creatures in burnished steel breastplates and
gorgets with plumed open-face helmets carried in the crooks
of their arms. Their clothes were clean and pressed, and their
boots weren't even muddy. No prizes for guessing who they'd
arrived with.

For a very brief moment Poldarn felt himself making a
tactical assessment, but this wasn't some open plain in the
middle of nowhere, without witnesses or bystanders, and
besides, his sword was back in the cart. He dismissed the
option from his mind. That left running away or staying put
and finding out what was going on. Another choice. What
fun.

'Next time I say we should leave town,' Copis hissed, but he
shook his head. The soldiers were headed straight for them; no
chance now that they'd turn out to be on their way somewhere else, nothing to do with them. It was at times like this,
he reflected, that he really wished he knew what his real name
was.

The soldiers stopped about a yard in front of them and, amazingly, saluted. Not having a clue about how to salute back, he kept still and waited for them to say something. Which they did.

'Lord Cleapho's compliments,' was what they said, 'and would you both care to join him for dinner?'

Chapter Seven

'Thanks,' Copis said, 'but we've just eaten.'

The soldier smiled. 'You can't call the slop they dish up in there food,' he said. 'And besides,' he added, nodding at Poldarn, 'he barely touched his, he was too busy looking at the pictures. This way.'

Poldarn stepped between Copis and the soldier. 'Just a moment,' he said. 'While I was in there eating my dinner, you were watching me?'

'Not me,' the soldier said, 'but you were being watched. What do you take us for, peasants?'

Copis was tugging at his sleeve like a little girl, trying to warn him about something. He took no notice. 'Then you know who I am?' he said.

'Of course we do,' the soldier replied, looking at him. 'Now can we please get out of sight, before everybody in Sansory figures out what's going on?'

Copis was pulling hard now; he was tempted just to push her away, but instead he turned round and asked, 'What?'

'I'm going back inside,' she said. 'You don't need me there.' She was looking at the soldier. 'Really you don't.'

The soldier shrugged. 'You can do what the hell you like,' he said to her, then turned back to Poldarn. 'Now come on, before you get me into trouble.'

It didn't look like he had any choice in the matter, which suited him fine. He'd had enough of choices to last him. 'All right,' he said. 'After you.'

The soldier led the way; his colleague waited for a moment, then fell in behind Poldarn, making him walk fast to avoid having his heels trodden on. Whoever he was, they weren't in awe of him to any serious extent.

'All right,' he said to the first soldier, 'who do you think I am?'

The soldier laughed without turning round. 'I could tell you exactly who I think you are,' he said, 'but I'm not supposed to insult His Grace's guests. Low doorway, mind your head.'

The door led through into a little hidden courtyard, beyond which was another small archway leading to a narrow spiral staircase, with an uncomfortably steep pitch and rate of turn; by the time they reached the top, Poldarn was tired and more than a little dizzy. The soldier knocked three times on a very solid-looking oak door, and they went through into a cramped, circular room, presumably the top of some tower. In the middle of the room was a plain round table, with two straight-backed chairs; Cleapho was sitting in one of them, and there were three or four brass tubes with the ends of rolled-up papers sticking out of them. Two more soldiers stood behind Cleapho's chair, in front of another stout door. No sign of any food, drink, cups, plates or cutlery.

'You're a bloody fool,' Cleapho said, frowning. 'What the hell was all that about?'

Poldarn opened his mouth to speak, but realised that he didn't know where to begin. Before he had a chance to order his thoughts, Cleapho went on: 'I know it's all part of the mystique, this deliberately walking around in plain sight

because you're so cool and daring, but next time please leave
me out of it. Dear God; when I saw you standing there looming over me, I nearly had a heart attack.' He shook his head,
then went on, 'I'm assuming you've got plenty of your people
here, because this' – he indicated the four soldiers – 'is all I've
brought, and after your stunt in the hall I'm starting to feel
nervous. Damn it,' he added, 'I'm not used to this sort of
thing, all this cloak-and-dagger stuff. If this is the way you
conduct business, I'm not sure I want to get involved with
you.'

I could try and explain, Poldarn thought. *And I could end up
at the bottom of those stairs with a broken neck. Still, this man
knows who I am. It'd be nice to find that out, even if I don't live
very long to savour the knowledge.* 'Please,' he said, as appeas-
ingly as he could, 'I want you to listen to this as patiently as
you can. I promise I'm not fooling about. You see—'

'Oh, forget it,' Cleapho interrupted. 'If you get some kind
of morbid pleasure out of taking silly risks, that's up to you.
Let's get down to brass tacks; to be precise, this business up
the road. The point is, I appreciate why you did it, but it was
too early. Tazencius and his people aren't ready. He hasn't
even started recruiting openly yet – dammit, he hasn't had
anything to recruit *for*, that's my point, there's been no
build-up, just this; suddenly, wham. And if this is your idea
of an *opening* gambit, please put your ear up against the
stable pump and wash your brain out, because the supply of
large cities in these parts is somewhat limited; we can't go
torching one a week until Tazencius has got his act together,
we'll run out of the bloody things. Unless we can get
Cronan—'

He stopped short, held up his hand for silence. Something
was going on down below.

'Shit,' Cleapho said. 'Oh, that's wonderful. You two, hold
them on the stairs.' The two soldiers who'd brought him there
disappeared immediately through the door they'd just come

through. 'We'll go out this way, on to the roof. That's assuming,' he added with a scowl, 'that they aren't up there already, which they probably are. God, what a mess.'

He stood up, as the other two soldiers pushed open the door behind them and led the way into a dark passage. 'Well, come on,' he said. 'I had an idea you'd be more trouble than you're worth. Next time, maybe Tazencius'll listen to me, instead of teaming up with a bunch of pirates.'

Poldarn could hear unsettling noises from the stairwell: shouting, banging, sharp, crisp metallic noises. It occurred to him that Cleapho had just sent two men to their deaths and they'd obeyed him without a moment's hesitation, obedience being for them an instinctive action, like the drawing of a sword. He decided to follow Cleapho.

The passage led out into the open air. To his right was a battlement, below which he could just see the main courtyard; on his left was the sloping side of the roof, presumably of the refectory (though he wasn't at all sure; going up the spiral staircase had messed up his sense of direction). It was just starting to get dark, and the yard was flooded with yellow light from the chambers beneath. 'Well, that's all right, then,' Cleapho was saying as the soldiers in front of them kicked open another door that apparently led into the refectory roof-space, ducked under the low lintel and climbed in. 'It's just as well one of us took the trouble to figure out the geography of this place. And I thought you were the one who was supposed to be so careful about details.'

Then it started to go badly. One of the soldiers who'd just gone through backed out again, struggling to draw his sword but without enough room to do so. It was a moment or so before Poldarn noticed the blood on his face. Cleapho swore, pushed past the soldier and started to run. Before Poldarn could follow him, someone else came through the doorway – another soldier, or at least a man in a mailshirt with a sword; he swung at the wounded guard, who ducked out of the way as another man emerged and lunged at him with a halberd, stabbing him just under the lower lip of his breastplate. The guard made a quiet, wordless noise, and then the man with the halberd pushed hard, shoving him backwards over the battlement like someone pitching hay. Then he turned to face Poldarn, while his colleague set off after Cleapho.

Poldarn stared at the halberd blade, then quickly at the man behind it, then back at the weapon. He seemed to hear a voice in the back of his mind: *watch the blade, not the man, it's the blade that'll kill you if you don't.* He didn't recognise the voice but he could appreciate the value of what it was telling him. His enemy (assuming he was an enemy, not a rescuer) seemed more concerned with keeping him where he was than attacking him, but Poldarn reckoned he'd had enough of holding still and waiting to see what happened. It didn't look like there were any more of them coming up from the roofspace – no sound of footsteps or signs of movement – which implied that if he could get past this man he might have a means of escape. That was good; life had just become a lot simpler.

The trick would be to get a firm grip on the halberd shaft without being stabbed or sliced in the process. He started forwards; then, just before he was due to stick himself on the point of the halberd, he slid his rear foot down, ducked his head out of the way and let himself fall backwards on to his outstretched right hand, grabbing for the halberd shaft with his left. Disconcertingly, the soldier tried to pull the blade out of the way, as if determined not to let him hurt himself, but Poldarn was quicker anyway, got his grip and jerked the halberd out of the man's hands just as he hit the ground. The other man jumped out of the way, unable to decide for a moment whether or not to draw his sword; someone else, it appeared, who had problems with choices. He'd just made up his mind to draw when Poldarn scrambled to his knees, swung his shoulders round and threw the halberd, hitting him on the little strip of bare flesh above the collar of the mailshirt.

The bone of his neck deflected the blade a little and it flew out over the courtyard, but the man wasn't a factor any more; Poldarn was clear to get away through the door. Simplify; always simplify.

He had to duck to get through the doorway into the roof-space, and the passageway he found himself in was pitch dark. His fingers recognised the feel of rough-sawn timber on either side of him. He kept his head well down, guessing that there wasn't enough room to stand upright. It occurred to him that he should have taken the dead soldier's sword, in case he had more fighting to do, but he wasn't inclined to go back for it; fairly soon the enemy at the foot of the spiral staircase would get past the two men Cleapho had sent to die (what great cause were they dying for, he wondered; did they know what it was? Did they approve?). It would be nice to get as far down this passage as he could before they came in after him. It was likely that the passage led somewhere, or else how had the two enemy soldiers appeared from it? As to where it led, he hadn't a clue, but that held true of all passages, roads, avenues, paths and doorways as far as he was concerned. At least it appeared to be straight, without turnings to left or right to mar his brief illusion of simplicity.

The boards under his feet creaked, and he felt cobwebs in his face (they made him shudder; apparently he was one of those people who don't much care for spiders. He made a mental note, coloured in one more tiny part of the bare outline, and moved on). Every few steps he stopped briefly to listen – for footsteps in front or behind, noises from below that might tell him which part of the inn he was above – but he heard nothing helpful. He carried on, making the most of his unhindered progress. One step following another. Easy.

He nearly fell through the trapdoor at the end of the corridor; all that saved him was the intuitive feeling of being about to rest his weight on nothing, which made him hesitate and prod for a feel of the floor with his toe. Having found out that there was a hole, he knelt down and explored its extent with his fingertips; it was about a shoulder's width square, which suggested a trapdoor or a hatch. Shuffling along on his backside, he let his legs dangle over the side until his heels located what he took to be the rungs of a ladder.

It was a long climb down, and still it was too dark for him to be able to make out anything, not even vague shapes or different tones of shadow, so his sight was as useless to him as his memory. He only realised he'd reached the bottom when his heel jarred on a solid surface, and some cautious exploration with his toe confirmed that he was at the foot of the ladder, standing on something thicker and more solid than boards. Now, of course, he had to choose a direction to go in. The feeling was familiar, and he was getting heartily sick of it.

He took a deep breath, turned left and started to walk, holding his hands in front of his face in case there were any low beams or other unpleasantnesses. Twelve paces or so brought him to a wall – rough brickwork, quite a distinctive texture. He felt his way along it, bearing left again, and was rewarded by a different texture, planed wood, a doorframe and a door. Next he found cold metal, a ring about a hand's span wide. Pulling it achieved nothing, but turning it resulted in a flood of yellow light.

That complicated matters. He dodged out of the way of it, but not before he'd caught sight of someone running towards him, a man carrying a weapon. He flattened his back against the wall and, as the man came through the doorway, kicked the back of his knee, sending him stumbling to the ground. He tried to get up, but Poldarn was in a perfect position to bring a knee sharply up under the man's chin; his head shot back too quickly, too far; he landed on his shoulder, and the sound of his head hitting the ground was loud and heavy.

As good a way of announcing myself as any, if there's any more of them nearby. Well, he couldn't stay in the dark for ever. He stepped through the doorway into the cruel and unwelcome light and saw that he was in a small, empty room, which might once have been a scullery or store. He was facing yet another open door, through which he could see a big fire in a stone hearth, and machinery suspended in front of it from brackets mounted in the wall. He could feel the fire's heat from where he was standing, and hear the clattering of ratchets and clockwork from the machine; there were strange-looking tongs and ladles and cutting tools in racks on the walls or hanging from the lower beams, and at the edge of his vision was an enormous copper vessel, a crucible or cauldron. It was only when he noticed the small pile of cabbages on the table in the middle of the room that he realised it must be a kitchen, and the ferocious machine was a spit.

Somehow the thought that he was standing outside a kitchen made him feel both relieved and foolish, though he knew perfectly well that both emotions were unjustified. He listened again, heard nothing helpful, and tried in vain to remember what the buildings had looked like from the outside, in particular, whether there was direct access from the refectory to the kitchens. Common sense suggested that there should be, but common sense didn't seem to have had much to do with the design of this place. Then he remembered that when he'd sat down to dinner he'd noticed a fireplace as big as this one in the wall at the near end of the hall. Intuitively, he decided that the dining-hall fireplace and this one shared the same chimney, being divided by the wall directly in front of him, in which case the doorway to his left would lead to open air and flagstones; the food would go out of this door on a long stretcher, down the wall five yards, and into the back door of the hall to the serving-table, where the servers would collect and distribute it. He gasped with relief, like a man putting his head up above water after being under for a little bit too long. For once, he actually knew which way to go.

At that point, the door opened. Through it came another soldier of the type he'd decided were the enemy; he was wearing the same kind of mailshirt and holding the same kind of halberd. The pattern repeated; clarity, then complication. It was like some kind of board game.

'Bloody hell,' the soldier said. 'I thought it was you.'

Poldarn hadn't been expecting that; he'd been anticipating something straightforward and easy to deal with, such as a halberd blade shoved in his face. 'You know me?' he asked.

'What? It's me, you idiot, Sergeant Lovick. You been getting bashed on the head a lot lately or something? Quick,' he went on, before Poldarn had a chance to reply, 'straight out the door behind me, takes you across the yard to the stables, you can get a horse and clear out. I never saw you. Right?'

'But just a . . .'

'I said quick. Before you get us both killed.'

'What you said just now,' Poldarn protested. 'About getting bashed on the head. That's what happened, I can't remember anything. Can you—?'

Sergeant Lovick (whoever the hell he was) scowled horribly at him. 'Pack it in, will you? Haven't got time for your stupid jokes right now. Look, if anybody comes then so help me, I'll have to kill you. Go on, clear off, now.'

Poldarn could feel anger about to explode inside his head; there wasn't much he could do about it, even though he knew how much it could complicate matters. 'No,' he shouted. 'Not till you tell me.'

'I said, I haven't got time . . .' The man was getting angry too. 'Bloody hell, chief, can't you take anything seriously?'

Chief? Why couldn't he have used my name instead? Thoughtless, inconsiderate bastard. 'I'm not joking, you idiot. Look, can't you at least tell me my name? Do that, I promise I'll go. Word of honour.'

Before Sergeant Lovick could say anything the door behind him opened; another soldier came in, saw Poldarn; his face instantly filled with anger. 'It's all right,' Lovick said loudly, not looking round, 'I've got him, he's mine. You get back and tell them . . .'

'Hell as like,' the newcomer said. 'Kill the bugger now, have done with it.'

Lovick shook his head. 'Our orders were . . .' he began.

'Screw the orders,' the other man said, taking two steps forward, his halberd at guard. 'Not worth the risk. You try and take this bastard alive, he'll do us both before we can get him across the yard. Oh come on, man, don't be so bloody pathetic.'

Lovick's face didn't change, but suddenly he was two strides closer and the move he was making with his halberd was either a killing thrust to the face or a feint to mask an equally lethal cut to the right temple. More choices.

Poldarn decided to cheat by circumventing both possibilities. He took a standing jump backwards, which gave him a yard of clear space, then threw himself to the right, drawing the sergeant into a clubbing stroke with the butt of the halberd. The sergeant dutifully obliged, and in the fraction of a second before the steel butt-shoe crunched into the bone of his skull, he grabbed the wooden shaft and pulled hard left, drawing the beard of the cutting edge deep into the web of Lovick's right hand. As anticipated, the shock and pain were enough to make him lose his grip, and as soon as Poldarn had control of the weapon he reversed the pull into a brisk upward thrust. He misjudged it a little because Lovick flinched, and instead of driving the point into his throat he caught him square in the left eye; just as good, if not better. Before the dead man could fall backwards he pushed again, throwing the body the way a builder's labourer throws a shovelful of dirt. The other soldier had to step to his right to avoid it, and in doing so walked into a thrust to the groin, which he avoided just in time. It didn't do him much good, since it was only a feint; the killing blow hit him in the ear, and the shock of steel bursting through layers of bone and membrane jarred down the halberd shaft into Poldarn's arm, wrenching a muscle and making him grunt with pain.

From complicated back to simple in a few easy moves. He let the dead man's own weight draw him off the halberd spike, then laid the weapon across the table and rubbed his forearm where he'd hurt it. *Just my luck*, he thought; it didn't take much imagination to see how, if there was going to be more of this sort of thing, a pulled muscle or a sprain or a cramp, anything that detracted from the perfection of these instinctive plays he somehow knew how to make, could easily be enough to kill him. The anger that had been building up before the fight, when Lovick wouldn't answer him, tell him the one word he needed to know (and he could have said it so easily, it wouldn't have cost him anything; damn it, quite likely it would've saved his life) – all that anger was still there but directed now against these two selfish, malicious men who'd kept knowledge from him and damaged his right arm when he needed it most. It only made it worse that one of them had apparently been a friend.

The door was still open. He stopped and listened before he looked through it. There didn't seem to be anybody about. He picked up the halberd, then put it back; even though he was having to work out so much from first principles, he was fairly sure that wandering around the courtyard of a busy inn with a bloodstained halberd in his hands wasn't a good idea. Besides, he'd managed without quite well so far, and whenever he'd needed a weapon there had always been someone on hand to give him one.

It was quite dark outside by this time, although there were lanterns on sconces all round the yard. He stood for a moment outside the door – yet another choice: go to the dormitory or the refectory and try to find Copis, or do what Lovick had advised, head for the stables, or compromise and make for the coach-house, to retrieve the cart or, at the very least, the big lump of fused gold that was bound to come in useful sooner or later . . .

He decided on the compromise, mostly because the coach-house door was directly opposite, only a few seconds away. Of course, there was a fair chance of finding more soldiers there, waiting for him, but that was true of the whole inn, and quite possibly the whole world. Simplify: to the coach-house.

The coach-house was empty; no grooms and no soldiers. And no cart. That made him angry, but it wasn't unexpected, by any means; in fact, he'd resolved on a contingency plan before he even pushed open the door. This consisted of taking the back way out of the coach-house, which (if he was remembering straight) would take him into a little narrow alley that led to the hay store, which had its own direct access to the stables. Once he'd got a horse and was out into the main courtyard, the likeliest problem would be if the soldiers, the enemy, had thought to close the main gate – in which case he'd have to forget about the horse and shin over the wall somewhere. He tried to recall a suitable point for climbing over while he was saddling up the sturdy grey gelding he'd chosen, and he'd just brought to mind an ideally suitable wicket gate in the back wall of the tower courtyard as he rode through the open main gate, thereby rendering all his diligence and foresight redundant. *Always the way,* he thought resentfully. *Just when you've managed to get all eventualities covered, along comes a stroke of good luck, and it's all been for nothing.*

The streets were disconcertingly quiet, which made him wonder whether there was some kind of curfew in Sansory. The basic premise he'd founded his careful strategy on was that once he was outside the Charity and Diligence he'd be able to melt away into a crowd within seconds and become invisible; as it was, the sound of his stolen horse's hooves on the cobbles struck him as being probably the loudest noise ever made since the creation of the world.

Another choice: abandon the horse and make his way slowly but rather more unobtrusively to the nearest gate, or rely on speed and to hell with the racket. He didn't need to be told that he had no way of making an intelligent decision without knowing one vital fact, namely whether the city gates were shut at night, and if so, when.

Common sense, he thought. Why bother having gates at all if you don't close them at night? Furthermore, it'd be shameful to make the same mistake twice and fail to look at the problems that lay beyond the accomplishment of his immediate objective, getting out of town. On foot, on the north road or west along the riverbank, he'd be exposed and vulnerable; with a horse, at least he stood a chance of outrunning anybody who might be after him. If he could find somewhere quiet to sit still and wait till morning, he wouldn't have to give up the horse, but unless the enemy were stupid or in a hurry, wouldn't they think to watch the gates? Irrelevant, of course, if the gates were shut already. Complications were springing up all around him, snagging him like bindweed growing up through ivy. As for all the implications of what had happened to him that day, he really didn't want to think about them.

On his left he noticed something that looked highly promising: an empty coach-house, its doors open just wide enough to allow him to ride through without scraping his knees. He decided to accept it as an omen or portent advising him to lie low and wait for morning, which suited him fine. He was, he realised, exhausted.

He unsaddled the horse and tied it to a ring conveniently set in the wall, then closed the door and used a couple of lengths of wood he found on the floor to wedge it shut. It wasn't completely dark inside; a little moonlight seeped in through the gaps in the roof where slates were missing, and he was able to move about by judging the textures of shadows. His chores finished, he sat up against the far wall, his legs stretched out in front of him, and closed his eyes.

Probably he was far more tired than he thought, because the next thing he saw was a waterwheel towering above him, triangles of blue sky blurred in the gaps of the turning frame. Behind it was a high brown wall built of large, carefully shaped blocks of sandstone, at whose foot the mill-leat lapped and splashed through a dense filter of brambles, weeds and rushes. Beside the wheel grew a tall, thin pear tree, in whose leafless branches, not surprisingly, perched two crows. One of them had a stick in its beak – just a plain, ordinary twig. The other gripped a gold ring, but it was having trouble with it, and after a few failed attempts to get it under control it let the thing fall into the thick grass at the foot of the tree.

Ah, he thought, *symbolism. But I like this dream more than the last one, and the one before. More homely. Cosier.*

Judging by the position of the sun it was mid-afternoon, while the yellow quality of the light, the bare branches and the slight but palpable nip in the air suggested late autumn. General Cronan sat up and looked for a distant line of hills obscured by mist (or low cloud, or heat-haze); instead he saw trees all around him, covering dramatic scarps and slopes on either side of the river from which the mill-leat had been carefully drawn off. At the junction of river and leat there was an extremely impressive dam and lock – he hadn't a clue how it worked, but it involved two leadscrews with painted iron turn-wheels and a bunch of heavy-toothed cogs obscured by a generous smearing of thick black grease. A raft of sodden brown and red leaves floated on the still water of the dam pool, supporting his earlier observations about the time of year.

He walked over to the pool and looked at his reflection. (Him again, he thought, as the crows resentfully spread their wings and flapped out of the pear tree, and then he remembered that last time he was the young, stupid nobleman called Tazencius who'd tried to kill the man whose face he could see in the water.) He found the cut, which started an inch or so above the hairline and ran sideways to just over his left ear; not so bad after all, in spite of the alarming quantity of blood.

Apparently he'd been wrong about that particular helmet; it had done a pretty good job after all.

A single drop of blood trickled down over his eyebrow and fell into the water, dissolving into a small, veined brown cloud. Absently he wiped away the rest of it from his forehead with the base of his thumb, and dismissed the injury to a very low place in his priorities ladder. Instead, he turned his mind to the more important issues: the battle, the fate of the empire, the future of civilisation as he knew it, all of which were going on in that wood over there, without him to keep an eye on them. That was bad.

But just for once he didn't want to go back and get on with the job. It came to something when a desperate hand-to-hand fight with a larger, stronger, younger enemy, from which he'd barely escaped with his life, was nothing more than an annoying distraction from his work, an aggravating and inconvenient waste of time . . . Surely they could spare him for just a quarter of an hour, until he'd had a chance to have a rest and a drink of water, and maybe even stop bleeding.

He smiled; not likely. He turned to face the wood, trying to remember the way he'd come (he hadn't been paying too much attention, on account of being chased by the enemy; a poor excuse, not much better then *the dog ate my homework*, but the best he could do at the moment), and noticed a flattened patch in the random hedge of briars, where he'd burst through on his way out. Going back in that way in cold blood wasn't an inviting prospect, but he knew his own sense of direction too well to trust it. If he didn't retrace his steps exactly, he'd end up hopelessly lost. Standing in front of a divine tribunal and explaining to the immortal gods that he hadn't been there to save the empire because he'd taken a wrong turning in a wood was an even less appealing thought than the brambles.

He retrieved his sword, only to find that the blade was hopelessly notched about four inches down from the point, useless; he left it where it was, found the body of his enemy and nervously rolled it over with his foot. Beyond question the man was dead; he was practically in two pieces, so that if by some horrible miracle he did get up again, he'd fall apart like a badly built lean-to. Nevertheless he was the enemy, and if he could cause trouble, he would – for example, by having dropped or thrown his sword where it couldn't be found when it was needed.

After a frustrating search, Cronan eventually found it a good five yards away in the middle of a tall and awkward bed of nettles. He managed to dislodge it with the toe of his boot, wasting valuable time as he did so, and bent down to pick it up. It was the first time he'd handled one of these semi-mythical objects, the dreaded raider backsabres. He'd been expecting it to be wrist-breakingly heavy, but it wasn't; if anything, it felt lighter and livelier in the hand than his own government-pattern sword, the kind he'd drilled with every day for twenty years. That surprised him, and he took a moment to look at it critically and objectively, as a piece of equipment rather than as an icon of the looming apocalypse.

It was as long as his arm, from the point of his shoulder to the tip of his outstretched middle finger, though nearly a third of that length was the two-handed grip, protected by the spectacular inward-curving horns on the blade side that swept out above and below the hand to form the pommel and hand-guard. The blade itself curved sharply forward and down, making the sword look as if it was the wrong way up, until it flicked back up again a finger's length from the point to form a swan's beak. Underneath the edge flared out, widening as it followed the inward curve, ending in a thin, flat cutting section nearly a palm's breath across, at which point it followed the upwards sweep of the topside, giving the blade the appearance of a dolphin leaping. Just below the spine of the blade was a broad, shallow fuller that followed the profile of the curve, lightening it without sacrificing strength and throwing the centre of percussion forward into the pit of the hook. As a practitioner of the trade of cutting human tissue, Cronan could see that it was, quite simply, the most perfect instrument for shearing through flesh and bone ever made, incapable of development or improvement, since any change to the design must inevitably detract from its perfection. It was, accordingly, a deeply disturbing object, being proof that the people who made it weren't just very tall, very strong and very ferocious, all attributes that could be dealt with quite easily using existing procedures and techniques; they were also intelligent, perceptive and thorough. Now that was something to worry about.

In the short term, however, he now had something to fight with, if he had to, not to mention an unexpected but valuable ally in his forthcoming battle with the brambles; and the rest had done him good, as well. All he had to do now was find out where the war had got to, and he'd be right back on schedule.

Back inside the wood it was dark, wet and complicated. For a while he made good progress in spite of everything, stepping high over tangles of briar, crashing sideways through brushwood and the dead branches of fallen trees, ducking under swiping shoots of bramble like a man in a swordfight. The further he went, however, the less familiar it looked, until he was forced to acknowledge that, in spite of his good intentions, he'd managed to come the wrong way after all, and every brave, energetic step he took was taking him further away from where he wanted to be. He stopped and relaxed, noticing for the first time how heavy and cramped his legs had become, and looked around for some point of reference.

But Cronan was from Thurm province, where trees came in by road with their branches already neatly trimmed away; he'd never learned to tell them apart. So he tried to remember details of how he'd got to the clearing with the watermill. He recalled that at one point the ground was boggy and soft under the leaf-mould; here it was firm and damp rather than sodden wet. Boggy ground suggested the presence of a stream, or at least a valley or fold between two ridges; here, the ground was level, although rising in a gentle slope away from him. Pretty well everything, in fact, was different, as if he'd wandered out of one story and into another without noticing the transition. He hadn't a clue where he was, or which way was north, or how far off the right track he'd come, and all this time, presumably, the war and history were going on without him, disasters (which would be his fault for ever) could be happening only a hundred yards or so away to his left, or his right, and he wasn't there to take charge or responsibility. He felt as if a god had picked him up and put him away in a box, and for the first time in a long time, General Cronan felt afraid.

That wouldn't do, not for a moment. Walking through woods, he told himself, was easy. People did it all the time, woodcutters and poachers and all manner of people with far less brains and common sense than he had. Chances were that he hadn't come more than a few hundred paces from the clearing; maybe the sensible thing would be to swallow his pride, retrace his steps and start again. At least that way there'd be some kind of logical progression behind his actions, instead of this aimless blundering about.

So he tried that, and fairly soon he stopped and admitted to himself that he was now in another completely new and unknown place, a dense thicket of holly on the side of a dry, rocky slope. The holly saplings stood so close together that he couldn't squeeze between them. 'We'll see about that,' he told himself and set about clearing a path with the backsabre. Thanks to the weapon's exceptional cutting and edge-holding abilities, he cleared a path nearly six yards long before he became too exhausted to stand.

Of course, he still had the option of retracing his steps . . . This time, he did make it back to the clearing, though for some reason he couldn't begin to imagine he was on the other

side of it, facing the front gate of the millhouse. That bothered him, as did the discovery that the man he'd killed wasn't
there any more.

He searched until he found a patch of blood on the grass
and his own discarded sword. There were bootprints in the
soft mud beside the millstream that didn't fit his own boots.
He sat down at the foot of the pear tree and thought about the
implications of that, with special regard to the implications for
his latest idea, of staying where he was and waiting for someone to come and fetch him. On the tramp back from the holly
glade, that had seemed an extremely sensible idea; on the
other hand, if the men who'd been here since he left the place
had carefully retrieved the dead man's body, it suggested that
they were the enemy, and if they'd come here once, they could
just as easily come back. It was one of those awkward problems; the more you think about it, the harder it gets. He hated
those.

When he considered the matter rationally, he knew that he
had no choice but to go back into that loathsome wood and
find his people, the war and his life as quickly as possible.
Irrationally, though, he couldn't quite bring himself to stand
up, partly because he was worn out, partly because it was
quiet and peaceful here, wherever it was, and being here took
no effort at all. Of course, he couldn't stay put indefinitely.
Sooner or later he'd need something to eat, and of course he
had responsibilities, vitally urgent ones that couldn't spare
him for a moment. If only, he thought, he could have some
kind of warranty or affidavit confirming that if he went back
in the wood he'd get hopelessly lost all over again and end up
coming back here over and over again; then he'd have no
choice but to stay and wait and see what happened. Even the
prospect of a half-platoon of the enemy bursting out of the
undergrowth didn't bother him as much as it probably should
have done. After all, if there were parties of them roaming
about the edges of the battle, he'd be just as likely to run into

them in the wood as out here, and if he stayed where he was there was some chance that he'd hear them coming long before they saw him, and he'd have time to hide or withdraw.

Maybe the battle was over by now. Maybe, depending on the outcome of the battle, the war was over, too; in which case, supposing the enemy had prevailed, the empire and civilisation and the world as he knew it would also be over, and staying here, learning how to snare rabbits, repairing and working the mill, would be a supremely wise choice. Perhaps he'd been brought here by the direct intervention of the divine Poldarn, who'd thereafter been at great pains to keep him here by rearranging the forest to prevent him from leaving. Poldarn, as everybody knew back home, worked in mysterious ways, to the point where the people of Thurm had stopped trying to figure them out and let the god get on with it. If the god had brought him here for a reason, stripped him of his responsibilities and the burdens of his previous life, it would be blasphemy to move from the shade of this tree. Maybe – it hadn't occurred to him before – the crow sitting in the branches above his head, watching him with patent disapproval, was Poldarn himself, directing the flow of events from a high place like a general on a battlefield. And maybe these thoughts (and the dizziness and nausea) had something to do with the bash on the head the dead man had given him – the dead man who wasn't here any more; even dead people can leave this misbegotten clearing, so why not me?

He fell asleep (*and in that sleep, he wondered, is he dreaming of a man hiding in a coach-house in the back alleys of Sansory?*) and when he woke up there were a couple of dozen men standing watching him, and another one kneeling beside him with a worried look on his face. For a moment he couldn't remember who they were or who he was.

'Cronan? Are you all right? What the hell's been happening to you?'

Then he remembered, and the return of his memory was like the family coming home from the fair, lighting a fire in the hearth and pulling out chairs and tables for dinner. 'I think so,' he replied. 'Who won?'

The man – his name was Feron Amathy and he was an ally, not a subordinate – grinned at him. 'We did, of course. Beat the crap out of them. Caught up with Allectus a mile or so beyond the ford; he's waiting for you back at the camp, or at any rate his head is. Cheer up, you miserable bastard, you've just saved the empire. Again.'

'Have I?' Cronan replied. 'That's nice.' Then he was sick, all down the front of Feron Amathy's mailshirt—

He woke up. It was pitch dark, and he had no idea where he was. Unaccountably, he had the feeling that recently he'd been walking in a forest, but that was obviously nonsense, because he was lying on stone and he could smell horseshit. Then he remembered. He was in a coach-house . . .

Chapter Eight

The horse had done him a favour. It was already starting to get light, and when he opened the door a little and peered through the crack he could see people moving about in the streets, carts and wagons and barrows complicating the flow of traffic. Wherever he was going to go today, he'd have to go slowly. There were too many people in the way to make sudden headlong flight a viable option.

He saddled up and led the horse out into the alley. The rising sun obligingly told him which way was east, the direction he'd decided to follow, but unfortunately the alley ran north–south, and he couldn't remember offhand which way he'd come the night before. He didn't really want to find himself back in the vicinity of the Charity and Diligence if he could help it. Most of the traffic in the alley was heading south, and at this time of day it seemed likely that they'd be going towards the centre of town; from there, he reckoned, he ought to be able to find the main east road. Of course, if the enemy were even slightly interested in him and if they knew what he looked like (he had no idea, of course, whether they did or not), they would almost certainly be watching all the gates, and probably the market district as well. On the other hand, if Cleapho and his people were his friends and if they'd secured reinforcements, they'd still be watching the gates for him too.

Obviously I don't want to be caught. Maybe I don't want to be rescued either. The more tiny scraps of his past he accumulated, the less he liked the smell and taste of it. He thought about that as he threaded his way through the streets, following the general tendency of the traffic. He thought about the gods he'd seen painted on the refectory walls; perhaps one of them had taken pity on him and snatched him out of the hands of his enemies, painting over his past and knocking a window through his future. Maybe he ought to take the hint.

Leaving town, he decided, probably wasn't worth the risk, at least for now. That simplified things. The alley joined a main thoroughfare, and he followed that for a long time, until he caught sight of a large open-air ring off to his left. It was crowded with men and horses, and money was changing hands. That gave him an idea.

It was, of course, a stolen horse, but in any market in a city this size, it stood to reason that there'd be plenty of people who specialised exclusively in stolen horses. He wandered round the ring for a while observing faces and eavesdropping on negotiations, until he was satisfied he'd found one.

'I want to sell my horse,' he told him.

The man looked at him, then at the horse, and rubbed his chin. 'Not sure,' he said. 'What are you asking?'

Poldarn smiled. 'Make me an offer,' he said.

The man frowned. 'Just a moment,' he replied, then, without looking round, he bellowed, 'Acka!' at the top of his voice. A few seconds later, he did it again.

Acka turned out to be the name of a woman, his wife or just possibly his mother. She trudged back from the rail, where she'd been talking to another woman, and scowled at him. 'What d'you want?' she asked.

'Man wants to sell his horse.'

Acka shrugged, as if to say that with people like that, what can you expect? She gave the horse a very quick glance and said, 'How much?'

'Won't say. Says I should make him an offer.'

Acka rubbed a sore-looking patch on her ear with the palm of her hand. 'I don't know,' she said. 'We're overspent as it is.' She walked round the horse a couple of times, looking very sad. 'If it was a skewbald,' she said, 'that'd be different. That man from the cavalry was back yesterday, wanting skewbalds. I'm not sure,' she concluded. 'It depends how much he wants for it.'

'Make me an offer,' Poldarn repeated.

The woman pulled up one of the horse's front hooves and glanced at it. 'Wants shoeing, too,' she said. 'It's all money. Tell him we can't go above thirty.'

From what he'd gathered during his scouting tour of the market, thirty wasn't bad. 'Thirty-five,' he said. 'And I keep the saddle and tack.'

The man looked at Acka; Acka shook her head. 'Thirty-five all in,' she said, 'and we're not doing ourselves any favours. Girth's nearly rubbed through, look, and the snaffle's not worth having.'

Poldarn nodded. 'All right,' he said, holding out his hand for the money. 'You're a tight-fisted bunch in these parts, though.'

Acka fumbled in her apron pocket and produced seven silver coins. 'Ought to count himself lucky, instead of complaining,' she said, taking a firm grip of the reins. 'We'll be lucky if we see our money back on this one inside of a month.'

Poldarn took the money, nodded politely and walked away, taking care not to look round. He wasn't sure how much money thirty-five quarters was, but it was thirty-five quarters more than he'd had the night before, and he'd got rid of a piece of potentially incriminating evidence against himself, all without killing anybody, or even drawing blood. Already he was finding his new life rather more congenial than his old one.

The next thing to do was get out of sight, or at least off the streets, where there might be a risk of running into his enemies or his friends. Where there's a livestock market there's always at least one inn; in Sansory, it was called the Integrity and Honour, and of course it was full of farmers and horse traders and other similar people with loud voices and a good deal of personality. He bought a small jug of beer and some bread and cheese for two quarters, found an empty corner of the settle, just big enough for a crow to perch on, and sat down.

The men next to him were talking about some war or other. One of them, a small, thin man with very bony wrists, was saying that General Cronan had beaten Allectus, he'd beaten General Taino, and if anybody could beat the raiders, it was him. The old man to his right didn't agree; Cronan wasn't bad for a southerner, but nobody could beat the raiders; Allectus might have done it if he hadn't gone to the bad, he'd had imagination, not like the rest of them. Cronan, in the old man's opinion, didn't have imagination, and the raiders would chop him up and feed him to their children.

A round-faced man with a short beard and a new-looking blue wool shirt figured that Cronan might be able to beat the raiders if he ever got the chance, but that was hardly likely; with two major victories to his name, with the confidence and loyalty of the army and the love of the people, he was clearly too much of a security risk to be let loose in the provinces. Even if he didn't want to seize the throne and become emperor, nobody would ever believe that he didn't; in fact, as far as the man in the blue shirt was concerned, Cronan's days were numbered, and he'd been living on borrowed time ever since he won against General Taino.

The thin-wristed man and a number of the others in the group agreed with that, and even the old man nodded a couple of times. It was a tragedy, the blue-shirted man went on, but it was inevitable given the state the empire was in. Meanwhile, if anybody was going to take on the raiders and stand a chance of beating them, it would almost certainly be Feron Amathy.

A moment later, it became apparent that the blue-shirted man had said something controversial, if not downright offensive. The old man scowled and shook his head; someone else just out of Poldarn's line of sight made a rude noise and called Feron Amathy a bastard and a couple of other things Poldarn didn't catch. Nobody seemed inclined to disagree, or if they did they weren't about to risk saying so in a public place. The blue-shirted man held up his hands; all right, he said, he could understand how they felt, he felt pretty much the same way; and no, of course he didn't hold with some of the things the Amathy house had done over the years, nobody in their right mind could. The fact remained: Feron Amathy was at best a freelance, at worst a bandit chieftain and mass murderer, but he was also a first-class soldier, and since the empire had a habit of locking up its own first-class soldiers or making sure they met with accidents, who else was there? Besides, he went on, having quietened down his audience, to fight the raiders you didn't want a decent, honourable type who followed the rules of war, you wanted an evil bastard; and nobody fitted those specifications better than Feron Amathy. Of course, he added after a short pause, whether a victorious Amathy house would prove any easier to live with than the raiders was another matter entirely, the only ray of hope in the gloom being that if he did win, he'd be that much more likely to turn his thoughts towards the rich, fat cities across the bay, and with any luck he'd bugger off over there and leave the northern provinces in peace.

The old man pointed out that Feron Amathy was an evil, murdering something or other that Poldarn didn't quite catch, and furthermore he had it on good authority that a fair few of the burnings and mass slaughters blamed on the raiders were the work of the Amathy house, who thought nothing of butchering women and children to make sure there weren't any witnesses. A young man with big ears said he wasn't sure he believed that, but Feron Amathy was definitely a nasty piece of work, and entrusting the safety of the province to him would be like setting a wolf to guard the chicken shed. The man in the blue shirt said he wouldn't put anything past the Amathy house, and that all the free companies were pretty well as bad as each other, though the Amathy house was probably the worst of the lot, but take away the imperial army and the free companies and who did that leave to fight off the raiders? Well?

There was a short, resentful silence. Then the old man said that it was Feron Amathy who did for Allectus by changing sides halfway through the battle, though nobody could tell him he hadn't fixed it with Cronan well in advance; it was a tragedy for the empire, what had happened to Allectus – nobody had ever really proved that he'd decided to try and seize the throne, and even if he had he'd surely have made a better fist of the job than the halfwit they had doing it now. Allectus, he maintained, wouldn't have been afraid of the raiders, or the free companies, or anybody.

A big man in a soot-blackened leather apron coughed nervously and suggested that the reason why nobody could stop the raiders was that they were a judgement visited on the empire by the gods. That remark had the effect of killing the conversation stone dead for quite some time as the rest of the company tried to make up its mind whether they should ignore him or refute his line of argument. Before they could reach a decision, the nervous man added that it was all very well them laughing and saying it was all a parcel of kids' stories, but what about the god in the cart who turned up at that village and predicted the fall of Josequin, exactly the way it turned out to have happened?

The man in the blue shirt replied that it was a coincidence, nothing more. The nervous man didn't agree; not only had the god foretold the destruction of the city, he'd also healed the sick and raised the dead, and they didn't have to take his word for it, they could go and ask Bigal the drover, whose nephew had gone through that village a fortnight later and heard all about it from the villagers themselves.

Apparently Bigal the drover's credibility was good with some of the company, because they looked thoughtful and didn't say anything. The blue-shirted man, however, shook his head and chuckled; as it happened, he said, a neighbour of his had been talking to a carter who'd seen this so-called god not once but twice; once at the village outside Josequin, and once about six weeks earlier, in a town whose name he couldn't remember off-hand on the other side of the Mahec; and the curious thing was, the god in the village outside Josequin hadn't looked anything like the god he'd seen up north; so it stood to reason that one of them was a fake, and as far as the blue-shirted man was concerned, it was the one who was supposed to have predicted the fall of the city. Furthermore, he added, the fake god hadn't healed all the sick and raised the dead; according to his neighbour's friend the carter, it was just a couple of dead people and a dozen or so of the sick, and their friends and families had paid the priestess pretty well for the privilege.

The nervous man looked shocked and sad, and didn't say anything; the rest of the company kept quiet too, weighing their natural scepticism against the undoubted authority of Bigal the drover. After a while the bony-wristed man stood up and said that he had a living to earn even if the rest of them didn't, and if Perico could spare an hour from speculating about the gods and the end of the world, maybe he'd get on and shoe his black mare, like he'd promised to do that morning. The nervous man nodded guiltily and left with him; the man in the blue shirt finished his drink and went away; and it wasn't long before Poldarn had the settle to himself.

Without the conversation to distract him, he found himself thinking about Copis, though it wasn't a train of thought he was happy with. Sure, he couldn't blame her in the least for clearing out as soon as she smelled trouble – she'd been absolutely right, and she'd done her level best to warn him, too, and of course she didn't know about the lump of fused gold in the back of the cart because he hadn't trusted her enough to mention it, so that was his fault, too. Nevertheless, he was sorry she'd gone, particularly in such a hurry; if they had to part company, he'd have liked a few moments just to thank her, since she'd practically saved his life that night when he met her, and in spite of all the trouble he'd caused her she'd never let him down or even really complained. More to the point, she was the only friend he had, but he couldn't help but reflect that she'd certainly be a good deal safer away from him, given his habit of attracting trouble like a fresh honeycomb drawing wasps. On the positive side, at least he wasn't going to have to pretend to be the god in the cart again. That was an experience he was in no hurry to repeat.

The inn wasn't nearly as crowded as it had been when he came in, and the taproom was empty enough now to make a man sitting on his own after everyone else had gone back to work look conspicuous. It was time he was going as well.

This time he carried on past the livestock market and headed for the centre of town. There were a lot of people in the streets now, far more than he'd seen before, and they all seemed to have a definite destination in mind. He allowed himself to be swept along with them, and eventually found himself in what he recognised as the main square of the city.

It was so crowded that after a while he couldn't go any further, so he scrambled up on the back of a big stone lion, like a man standing on a stepping stone in the middle of a river, and tried to make out what was going on.

The central third of the square was divided up with posts

and railings into a series of stalls, rather like the livestock market had been, but these stalls were full of men and women, all crammed in together, and a walkway had been roped off right the way round the edge. There he saw some other people, not nearly so tightly packed, and they were looking over the people in the pens – mostly just glancing, but occasionally stopping for a closer look, and now and again shouting and beckoning to attract attention. Poldarn watched as one of the penned-up people, after talking to a man on the outside for a while, scrambled over the rail and followed the man he'd been talking to down the walkway and out of sight. At once two or three men from the crowd tried to climb into the pen, whereupon a couple of harassed-looking men with long sticks appeared out of the crowd and pushed all but one of them back.

This was so curious that he had to ask someone. He didn't have long to wait; a young man of about nineteen jumped up on the lion's back beside him, rubbing his shin and pulling a face. He asked the young man what was going on.

The young man didn't understand the question.

'I'm new in town, you see,' Poldarn said. 'Actually, I'm from Thurm.' (He dredged the name up from the cellars of his mind just in time.) 'Whatever this is, we don't have anything like it back home.'

'Really?' The young man clearly found that hard to believe. 'Then how do you people find work if you don't have hiring fairs?'

Ah, he thought, *right*. 'Oh, we've got them all right,' he replied confidently. 'We just don't do it like this, that's all.'

'Oh,' the young man said, and went back to examining his shin. Meanwhile, two more men had been chosen from the pens, and a dozen or so others had tried to take their places and been herded back by the men with sticks. Poldarn got the impression that in Sansory there were more people needing work to do than there was work to go round; he remembered what Copis had told him, about this being a place you ended up in. Depressing thought.

All the same, he was going to have to start earning a living soon, and if this was how you went about finding work in Sansory it'd probably be a good idea to get in line. First, though, he did a little more reconnaissance, and fairly soon worked out that each stall represented a trade. That complicated the issue, since he didn't have one. 'Excuse me,' he said.

The young man looked at him.

'Sorry to bother you again,' he said, 'but what do you do if you don't have a trade? Where do you go to find someone to take you on?'

The young man grinned. 'No trade? At your age? In that case, you might as well forget it.'

Poldarn frowned. 'Maybe,' he said. 'But assuming I'm mad enough to try, what's the drill?'

'Suit yourself,' the young man replied equably. 'Look, you see that big pen there, right at the back? You go there. I'll tell you, though; if you get in the line now, and if you're really lucky, you might just get in the pen by the time the fair closes.'

'I see. And when's that?'

'Day after tomorrow.'

'Fine.' Poldarn frowned. 'All right,' he said, 'which trade's in most demand these days?'

The young man thought for a moment. 'That's a tough one,' he said. 'Clerks, probably. Not just copy clerks, mind; I'm talking about counting-house clerks, the sort who can do figuring and accounts and stuff.'

That didn't sound promising. Nevertheless, Poldarn asked which pen the clerks were in. The young man pointed; it was only slightly less crowded than the others.

'Of course,' the young man went on, 'what they're really crying out for these days is drill instructors – you know, for the companies. Only they've got their own fair, end of the month. And it's not here, it's in Mael.'

'Not much help to me, then,' Poldarn replied. 'Is there anything in that line around here?'

The young man shook his head. 'Not unless you could do
bodyguarding,' he added. 'Mind you, there's a line of work
where there's always more jobs than bloody fools wanting to
do them. There's a reason for that, though.'

Poldarn had the feeling he was being set up as a straight
man. But that didn't matter. 'Oh? What's that?'

'They keep getting killed, of course,' the young man replied
with a grin. 'You'd have to be mad or bloody desperate to go in
for that game.'

Poldarn nodded. 'I expect you're right,' he said. 'So where
do I go to get taken on?'

It wasn't hard to find, in spite of the young man's rather
elliptical directions: a small booth, rather than a stall, on the
far western edge of the market. There were a couple of sad-
looking types sitting outside, and three large men lounging in
the doorway. Poldarn asked if he could get through. They
didn't move. He asked again. One of the large men told him
all the jobs were taken, and suggested that he should go away.
Poldarn wasn't inclined to believe him, since over his shoulder
he could see a line of men inside the booth waiting to be
inspected. When he pointed this out to the men in the doorway, one of them tried to push him out of the way.

A few moments later, a man in a long plush robe came out
of the booth. He looked at the three men lying on the ground,
and then at Poldarn.

'You're hired,' he said.

'Thank you,' Poldarn replied, rubbing his elbow where he'd
made it worse by jarring it on someone's teeth. 'When do I
start?'

'Right away, if you like,' the man said. 'What did they do to
you?'

Poldarn shrugged. 'They didn't want me to apply for the
job.'

'Oh.' The man frowned. 'Serves them right, then. What's your name?'

'Poldarn.'

The man raised an eyebrow. 'That's interesting,' he said. 'Southerner?'

Poldarn nodded. 'From Thurm province,' he said, hoping he wasn't making a big mistake.

'That figures,' the man replied. 'My father always used to say they're all a bunch of vicious psychotics in Thurm. My name's Falx, by the way; Falx Roisin.'

'Pleased to meet you,' Poldarn said. 'May I ask what line of work you're in?'

Falx grinned. 'You really aren't from these parts, are you?' he said. 'I'm a carter.' He smiled. 'Just like any other carter, really, except that last time I looked I had over a hundred carts. Plus six hundred horses, a dozen warehouses, more clerks than anybody could possibly have a use for, and what they do all day I'll probably never understand. Most people in Sansory know me, for one reason or another.'

'I see,' Poldarn said. 'But you need a bodyguard.'

Falx nodded. 'Well, sort of,' he said. 'More like a sergeant-at-arms, if you know what that is. Look, I don't like standing about in the middle of all this chaos, even if you do. My house is just across the way. Come and have a drink.'

If Falx Roisin seemed rather more affable than Poldarn would have expected for a man who owned so many carts and horses, that probably wasn't a bad thing. Falx led the way: down an alley into a small square, down another alley, over a bridge across something that looked like a stream and smelt like a drain, through an archway into a courtyard filled with carts, so tightly packed together that Poldarn had to edge sideways to get through. Beyond that was a big, flat-roofed brick building, which Poldarn assumed was one of the warehouses Falx had referred to. Once inside, though, he realised it wasn't.

The most bewildering thing about it was the colour. Every

square inch of wall, ceiling and floor was either painted or covered with mosaic, depicting a wide range of subjects from deceptively realistic vases of flowers and bowls of fruit to cavalry battles and storms at sea to scenes from religion to elegant pornography. The quality of the work was as diverse as the subject matter, and since all the colours were fresh and none of the mosaics were scuffed or chipped it was a reasonable assumption that they were fairly new and that Falx Roisin had commissioned them.

'I like your pictures,' Poldarn said, lying.

It was the right thing to say. 'Thank you,' Falx replied. 'My son – that's the eldest boy – he's the painter; my daughter and my niece do the mosaics. Later on I'll show you the long gallery; what used to be the drying-loft when this place was a flax warehouse. Nearly all my family are artistic, in one way or another.'

Poldarn nodded. If there were a lot of art-lovers in Sansory, that would explain the need for bodyguards. Falx pulled out one of the two chairs (painted all over, except for the parts covered with ivory and lapis lazuli inlay) that were the only furniture in the room, and waved Poldarn into the other.

'I think I ought to warn you,' he said, as a door opened behind him, apparently in the middle of the sail of a large, rather impractical ship, and a woman came in carrying a jug of wine and two cups on a little brass tray with legs. 'Because you're not from around here, you can't be expected to know what you're getting into. I believe in being straight with people.'

Poldarn nodded again. If Falx required absolute honesty from all his workers, sooner or later he was going to have to point out that the laughing dryad on the wall just above Falx's head had one leg that was drastically longer than the other, but he hoped it wouldn't come to that. He tried not to stare, but it wasn't easy.

'The fact is,' Falx went on, 'your predecessors didn't live

very long. I've had five men doing your job in the last eighteen months; one left after a week, in the middle of the night, and the others—' He sighed. 'Sent 'em home to their families for burial, it seemed like the least I could do. And of course it doesn't cost me anything.'

It was very good wine; light and sweet without being cloying. 'What does the job involve, exactly?' Poldarn asked.

'Well, part of it's genuine bodyguarding,' Falx replied, 'and that aspect of it's relatively safe. I don't pick fights if I can help it, and people don't tend to pick fights with me as a rule; certainly not twice. It's the other part where it starts getting dangerous. You see,' he went on, pouring himself a refill, 'I send a lot of letters, for other people: important messages, letters of credit, business negotiations, the sort of thing you don't want to entrust to just anybody who happens to be going in the right direction. It's very good business once you've got a reputation for making sure the letter gets there, and since I've got carts and couriers going all over the place all the time I can make good money with no additional costs. The trouble is,' he went on, fidgeting with the stem of his cup, 'I have some customers in that line who are very good customers, very good indeed, which means that if they want a letter carried, I can't really refuse to handle it, even if I've got an idea it's likely to be trouble.'

Poldarn frowned. 'You can tell in advance?'

'From where it's going and who's sending it, yes.' Falx nodded. 'Complicated stuff you don't need to bother yourself with. Anyway, when I'm lumbered with one of those letters, I don't really have any choice, I've got to send someone along with it to make sure it gets through. Nine times out of ten, it does. The tenth time – well, forty letters, four dead guards. How are you at mental arithmetic?'

Poldarn thought for a moment. 'Forty letters in eighteen months,' he said. 'That's nearly one a week. How far do these letters have to go?'

'Depends,' Falx replied with a shrug. 'Some of them a day either way; some of them it's a ten-day round trip. Just the job for someone who likes to get out and about a bit.'

'I can see that,' Poldarn said. 'And these other four men. What sort of things happened to them?'

'Let me see.' Falx steepled his fingers around his nose. 'Gusson was loss of blood – got stabbed in the stomach on the road, beat them off all right, didn't actually notice he'd been carved up till he reached the next town and tried to get down off the cart. Bello – I liked him, good sense of humour – he got shot with a crossbow at long range; one moment he was there, the driver told me, the next minute gone, just like that. Hell of a thing to happen. The man after him, name's on the tip of my tongue, he got opened up with a halberd in an inn halfway between Weal and Boc. They tried to make out it was a bar fight, but whatsisname was the quiet type, didn't go in for all that. Stupid part of it was, he was on his way back, they must have been watching the inn and hadn't realised he'd already delivered the letter. And Sullis, he had his head bust with a quarterstaff, not half an hour from the Eastgate; he'd probably have made it if it hadn't been chucking it down with rain, so that people were hurrying past and not likely to notice someone lying in a ditch at the side of the road. Generally, it's just two or three of them, never more than five; discharged soldiers, free company stragglers, well, you know the sort, I'm sure.'

Up in the far corner of the room, Poldarn happened to notice, there was a picture of a large dark bird. At first he thought it was a crow, but when he moved his head a little to one side, he realised it was meant to be a peacock.

'Anyway,' Falx said, 'that's the work. I was paying Sullis forty quarters a month, with board and expenses. You can have forty-five if you're interested.'

Without much of a frame of reference to go by, Poldarn wasn't quite sure how much forty-five quarters was. He thought of the price of a plate of bread and cheese, a horse, a crushed and straightened breastplate. On that basis, it sounded like good money. 'Fifty,' he said. 'And you'll save money in the long run, because I haven't got any family to be shipped back to.'

Falx looked at him for a moment, then laughed. 'You've got a sense of humour too,' he said. 'I like that. All right, fifty; after all, it's a rotten job, you'll earn it. I don't suppose you've got any references,' he added. 'No, I guessed not. Wouldn't expect you had, or you wouldn't be interested in the job. Still, I've been hiring men for twenty-five years on the basis of snap judgement; only been wrong twice and they were both clerks. You'll do.'

That appeared to be that; Falx finished his drink and stood up. 'Equipment,' he said, 'weapons, kit in general. Got any?'

Poldarn shook his head. 'I tend to use other people's, so I don't have any of my own.'

Clearly, Falx wasn't quite sure what to make of that. 'Doesn't matter,' he said. 'I'll take you along to the stores, they can sort you out there, and I'll get the duty foreman to show you your quarters, all that sort of thing. Anyway,' he added, 'welcome to the Falx house, and here's hoping this is the start of a long and happy association.'

Sense of humour? Poldarn wondered. On balance, probably not. They left the gorgeously painted hallway by a different door, crossed a small, enclosed yard and entered another building, essentially a half-size replica of the first. This one wasn't painted, however.

'Right,' Falx said, as an elderly man in a leather apron came out from a back room to meet them. 'This is Eolla, my foreman; marvellous chap, been with the house since my father's time. Eolla, this is Poldarn, he's the new – he's taking over Sullis' job. Give him what he needs, make him feel at home, you know the drill better than I do. All right?'

Eolla nodded gravely. 'Poldarn, did you say?' he asked.

'That's right.'

'Ah.' Eolla dipped his head and formally noticed Poldarn for the first time. 'Southerner?'

'Yes,' Poldarn replied, wishing he'd thought of another name. 'From Thurm.'

'You don't say. Right, you leave him with me, that'll be fine.' He clamped a proprietorial hand on Poldarn's shoulder. He had a grip like a leg vice. 'Anything else?'

Falx shook his head. If Poldarn didn't know better, he'd have imagined his new master was intimidated by the old man. 'I'll be getting on, then,' he said. 'There shouldn't be anything for you for a day or so, so you just settle in.'

Eolla looked at him and dipped his head again, as if to say *dismissed*. Falx withdrew briskly, shutting the door behind him. 'You're right,' Eolla said, as soon as the latch dropped, 'he's scared stiff of me. Good reason. Made his life hell when he was a boy.' He turned round – not just his head, his whole body – and looked Poldarn over from head to foot in a single long glance, the way Acka had looked over the stolen horse. 'And if you're from Thurm I'm the king of the pixies,' he went on. 'Not that I could give a damn where you're from. Doesn't matter where you're *from*, it's where you're at that counts.' He held the stare a moment or so longer. Poldarn stared back. Eolla laughed. 'You're all right,' he said, and held out a hand, which Poldarn took. 'Like he said, I'm Eolla. Actually, I'm not; my name's Eola Catariscas, but Falx Garaut – that's the old man – he could never be bothered to say it right, and Falx Roisin, don't suppose it's ever occurred to him to check, no reason why it should. So I got used to being Eolla. Doesn't bother me, been called a lot worse. Where are you really from?'

Poldarn grinned ruefully. 'I don't know,' he said.

Eolla raised an eyebrow. 'Well,' he said, 'that's a new one. Why don't you know?'

'I had an accident,' Poldarn replied, 'about five years ago.

Don't ask me what happened; all I know is that I woke up in a ditch with a lump on my head the size of an apple. The first town I came to I asked them the name of the place and they told me it was called Josequin. So I guess you could say I'm from there.'

'Is that a fact?' Eolla shrugged his broad, thin shoulders. 'All right, then,' he said. 'And what've you been doing with yourself since?'

Poldarn laughed. 'Nothing very exciting,' he said. 'As soon as I figured I wasn't going to get my memory back in a hurry I started looking round for work, something to do, a place to live, all that. No skills, of course, but it wasn't long before I realised I had what you could call an aptitude for fighting; whether it's training or just a knack I was born with I have no idea. There was a living to be made at it in Josequin.'

Eolla nodded; he seemed to do that a lot. 'Guild town,' he said. 'Stands to reason. Never went there, never will now, of course. Can't say I'm bothered. You were lucky, then, being out of town at the time.'

'I'd left Josequin a few weeks earlier,' Poldarn replied. 'For my health.'

That seemed to constitute a satisfactory answer. 'Anyway,' Eolla said, 'you follow me, we'll go out the back and get you fitted out. Let's see, now. Two changes of clothes, three pairs of boots, two hats, one hood, two belts, loaded staff, plain staff, big and small satchel, plate, cup, big and small knife, lamp, oil, wick, tinderbox, three blankets, leather bottle, heavy coat and gambeson since you'll be on the road, and you can choose a weapon from the rack.' He grinned. 'Takes most people a lifetime to gather that much stuff, and here it's all given to you, compliments of the house, a whole life. Second-hand, of course,' he added. 'Falx house is generous, but we're not made of money. This way.'

One wall of the back room was lined with tall wooden bins; they walked down the line and Eolla rummaged about in each one in turn until he found something he reckoned would suit or fit. 'Practice,' he explained. 'Fifty years in the stores, I can tell a man's size the moment I lay eyes on him. Sorry,' he added, 'we're low on hats right now, this'll be too big, so you'll need to stuff some straw in the crown.'

Eolla didn't offer any account of where it had all come from, and Poldarn didn't ask. One of the shirts had a brown stain between the shoulder blades, but it had been neatly and carefully darned; a critical and final moment in one man's life, patched up with wool and issued to someone else. It was all good, serviceable stuff, none of it frayed or worn out. It occurred to Poldarn as he watched the old man skimming through the contents of the bins that he seemed to know each piece individually, then he realised that quite probably he'd issued most of them before, to some other new associate of the Falx house, two or twenty years ago. People come and go, but the things go on for ever, going out of the bins and being put back there.

'Properly speaking,' Eolla was saying, 'helmet's not included since you're not regular guard squad, but if you don't tell anybody, I won't. Try this.' He reached under a bench (without looking; he seemed to know by touch where everything was, like a blind man) and produced a narrow-brimmed brown felt hat. It was too heavy to be what it looked like, and when Poldarn turned it over he saw it was lined with neatly butted steel plates.

'Far as I know, never been tested,' Eolla said, 'so I can't promise it works. But it's most likely better than nothing.'

Poldarn put it on; a surprisingly good fit, maybe slightly too big. 'Thank you,' he said.

'Pleasure,' the old man replied. 'That was made for Falx Garaut's brother Tocco – nervous little man, he was, always fretting about getting beaten up or stabbed. So the old man got him a first-class gambeson – more a coat of plates, really, nothing but the best – and a collar lined with steel splints, and that hat. Did him no good in the long run, mind, but it was a kind thought.'

Eolla didn't seem inclined to enlarge on the fate of Falx Tocco, and Poldarn wasn't inclined to ask; but the hat seemed a good idea, regardless of its origins. He added it to the pile of his newly acquired possessions, which had grown to a substantial size.

'Right,' Eolla said, 'that's everything except weapons, they're in the locker here. Oh, unless – can you read?'

Poldarn nodded.

'Always a good idea, very useful.' Eolla stooped down and pulled out a big wooden trunk. 'Falx Roisin, he's very keen on reading, likes to encourage it in the house.' He raised the lid and let it drop; the trunk was full of books. There were bound books, in wood and leather covers, and rolled books, in handsome brass tubes. 'All religious, of course,' Eolla added with a slight sigh. 'But you're allowed two, since you'll be on the road. Falx Roisin figures it helps pass the time, keeps a man out of mischief.'

'Right.' Poldarn looked at the contents of the box. None of them had titles. 'What do you suggest?' he said.

Eolla shrugged. 'Haven't a clue,' he said. 'Not bothered, myself. If I were you, I'd go for the biggest, since you're getting them for nothing.'

That seemed entirely logical to Poldarn, so he picked out two bound books, both of them a full hand's span thick. 'Wrap your coat round one,' Eolla pointed out, 'makes a decent enough pillow. Worth thinking of these things if you're on the road all the time.' He pulled open a door that Poldarn hadn't noticed before and disappeared through it. Poldarn followed and waited for him to light the lamp with his tinderbox.

'Weapons locker,' Eolla said, superfluously. One wall was covered with racks for polearms – halberds, guisarms, bardiches, pollaxes, glaives; in the near corner there was a big barrel, with the hilts of long straight-bladed swords sticking up like roses in a vase; on another wall there was a rack of axes and two-handed swords, heads and points downwards. In the far corner was another trunk, similar in size and shape to the bookbox.

'What's in there?' Poldarn asked.

Eolla chuckled. 'Good question,' he replied. 'Nothing to do with you's the short answer. Still, you can take a look if you want.'

'I was just asking,' Poldarn said. 'If they're not on offer—'

'Ah go on, take a look,' the old man interrupted. 'Not something you're likely to see every day.'

So Poldarn lifted the lid and looked inside. He saw two dozen swords, all more or less the same. For a moment he wondered where he'd seen the like before; then he remembered. The wall painting at the Charity and Diligence. His namesake, the god in the cart, had been waving around something fairly similar.

'Pick one up if you like,' the old man said. 'Go on.'

Poldarn didn't want to seem rude, so he did as he was told. It was as long as his arm, from the point of his shoulder to the tip of his outstretched middle finger, though nearly a third of that length was the two-handed grip, protected by the spectacular inward-curving horns on the blade side that swept out above and below the hand to form the pommel and handguard. The blade itself curved sharply forward and down (*I may have seen one of these before, he thought*), making the sword look as if it was the wrong way up, until it flicked back up again a finger's length from the point to form a swan's beak. Underneath the edge flared out, widening as it followed the inward curve, ending in a thin, flat cutting section nearly a palm's breath across, at which point it followed the upwards sweep of the topside, giving the blade the appearance of a dolphin leaping. Just below the spine of the blade was a broad, shallow fuller that followed the profile of the curve, lightening it without sacrificing strength and throwing the centre of percussion forward into the pit of the hook. Neat, Poldarn thought.

'Like it?' Eolla said.

'Yes,' Poldarn replied.

'Tough.' The old man laughed. 'Not for issue, those. You know what they are?'

'Swords,' Poldarn said. 'Or do they have a special name?'

'Probably,' Eolla said. 'But nobody knows what it is, or nobody that's telling. They're raider backsabres. Been there ten years, to my certain knowledge. God alone knows how the old man came by them. Anyhow, they don't leave this room, and I know exactly how many's in there, in case you were wondering.'

Poldarn shrugged and put the sword back where he'd got it from. 'Don't worry,' he said. 'I'll be happy with what I'm given, thank you very much.'

'That's the ticket,' Eolla said, closing the lid. 'Well, in that case, let's see what we've got.' He reached down into the sword barrel. 'Try this,' he said. 'Now this is a nice piece. Religious, look, just right for indoors and cramped spaces – like the box of a cart, for instance.'

Poldarn took the sword. It was short, less than two feet long, curved and single-edged, with a grip just about big enough for two hands. He drew it an inch or two from the scabbard. The blade was polished like a mirror, or the surface of a pool on a still day, except for a wavy, cloudy line running parallel to the cutting edge about a finger's width in.

'Religious?' he asked. 'What does that mean?'

Eolla looked at him. 'Must've been a smart old bang on the head you took,' he said. 'Religious, like the temple fencers. Don't worry about it,' he added, as Poldarn carried on looking bewildered. 'It means it's a nice piece of kit, too good to be in the barrel, by rights, but I like to have a few bits and pieces for a good cause. Will that do you?'

Without thinking Poldarn had undone his belt and wrapped a double loop round the mouth of the scabbard. 'I think so,' he said, tightening the buckle, and his hand dropped to the hilt and he drew—

'Very sweet,' Eolla said, frowning slightly. 'Where'd you learn to do that? Oh, of course, you wouldn't know.'

Poldarn had sheathed the sword without realising. 'You do, though,' he said.

The old man shrugged. 'I've seen men who can draw that fast before. Temple fencers. If you can do that – well, figure it for yourself. Of course, you could've learned it somewhere else. Maybe you picked it up from a book, or worked it out for yourself, I don't know.'

Poldarn took a step closer. It seemed to him that the old man didn't like that much. 'But you don't think so,' Poldarn said.

'No,' Eolla replied, stepping sideways towards the door. 'If you want my opinion, you learned that in the temple.'

'What temple?' Poldarn asked.

Chapter Nine

'Good afternoon,' the brother called out, leaning forward a little in his saddle and wiping rain out of his eyes. 'I wonder, can you tell me if I'm on the right road for Cric?'

The two rubes looked up at him as if a trapdoor had just opened in the sky and he'd stepped out of it, silhouetted against a dazzling mandala of pure white light. 'You what?' the older man said.

'Cric,' the brother repeated, slowly and loudly. 'There's a village by that name somewhere around here, isn't there?'

What the hell the two rubes thought they were doing, scrabbling about on their knees in the peat-mud in the driving rain, he couldn't begin to imagine. At least, they were building a dry-stone wall; but in weather like this, with the rain lashing down on them? On the other hand, they gave every impression of not having noticed the rain, or the wind.

The older man nodded, tipping water off the brim of his tatty leather hat. 'Keep on the road an hour, maybe two, that'll fetch you to Cric.'

'Thank you,' the brother said. 'I should make it there by nightfall, then.'

'Maybe.'

'Is there an inn there, somewhere I can put up for the night?' the brother persevered.

'No.'

'I see. Thank you, you've been incredibly helpful.' He turned his face back into the rain and nudged his horse on with a slight pressure of his heels. He could feel the rubes staring at his shoulder blades all the way to the skyline.

The lousy weather cut visibility down to spitting distance and he was sure he didn't see a single living thing on the road, so how everybody in Cric knew he was coming he had no idea. But they did; they were standing out under their porches or watching out for him from haylofts, dozens of them – women and children mostly, with a few old men and invalids peering over their shoulders. That was disconcerting for someone who'd spent a lifetime learning how to be too boring to be worth noticing. He looked round for some logical place to stop, an inn or forge or other community centre, but there wasn't one, just a miserable-looking tower at the far end of town, which was bound to be cold and damp and foul-smelling. What he wanted was a nice extravagant fire, some hot soup and warm spiced wine, if possible a bath hot enough to scald the feathers off poultry. No chance.

Plenty of houses, nothing at all to choose between them. He scowled under his hat; there were times when he hated the very concept of choice. Doctrine wasn't terribly keen on it either, he remembered – *choice and doubt come between the hand and the hilt, they constitute fatal obstacles to the perfection of the draw; God neither doubts nor chooses, God's thoughts and actions are simultaneous and identical.* Lauctans, Fifth Homily of the Edge, XIV, 2. Stuff choice, then; he pulled up, jumped off the horse, tied it to the nearest porch post and banged on the nearest door.

Bearing in mind that he'd seen six women of various ages and a seven-year-old boy gawping at him from the loft hatch, it was pretty stupid of them to pretend not to be at home. He banged again, waited a little longer, then lifted the latch and walked in.

. That stare, again; *I really must do something about this second head,* he thought as seven pairs of eyes stuck into his face like bradawls, *it's turning out to be a liability.* Years ago he'd been to a place where they still had the quaint old custom of sticking the heads of criminals up on pikes in the market square. That was it; he knew he'd seen that expression somewhere before.

'Excuse me for barging in like that,' he said cheerfully, dislodging a small torrent of water on to the dried-clay-and-cowshit floor as he took off his hat, 'but I don't think you heard me knock, and it's raining. You wouldn't happen to know of somewhere I could hire a bed for the night?'

The magic of the word *hire* unfroze them like the secret incantation waking up the sleeping giants in the old kids' story. 'Not round here,' the oldest woman said. 'But you could stop here, I s'pose. We got room.'

'Splendid,' the brother replied. 'Would three quarters a night be enough, do you think? It's probably only for tonight, but I may have to stop over tomorrow if I don't finish my work in time to get to the next inn by nightfall.'

There was a younger woman sitting next to the old matriarch whose face showed that she didn't believe there was such a sum as three quarters in the whole world, unless you melted down the wheel tyres of the wagon of the moon and ran the bloom under a coining-press. 'That'll do fine,' the old woman said. 'And this is my daughter Melja.'

If Melja's part of the deal, he thought, *I'll try my luck next door. Not giving offence is one thing, but there's limits.* 'Pleased to meet you,' he said, with a slight bow. 'My name is Monach.'

(Monach was, of course, just the word for 'monk' in southern pidgin Torcean, but it was easy to remember, and nobody had figured it out in all the years he'd been using it.)

He clinked four quarters in the palm of his hand, then put them down on the table. 'Any chance of something to eat?' he asked. 'And I suppose a bath would be out of the question.'

He supposed dead right, but after a shocked silence the matriarch prodded Melja in the ribs and she vanished into the back room and came back almost immediately with the end of a loaf and a block of greyish cheese that looked startlingly like the medium-grit waterstone he used for sharpening halberds. Nothing to drink with it, but of course he hadn't asked for it; the moral being, with rubes, specify exactly.

As it turned out, the cheese was too crumbly to have made a good waterstone, though the bread would probably have done the job at a pinch. 'Is that all you want, then?' the old woman asked when he couldn't face any more. He nodded. She shrugged. 'That'll be just two quarters, then,' she said.

He paid up, dipping his head to her in sincere respect as he did so. He'd been to a lot of places, been rooked and shaved by some of the best short-changers and cheese-scrapers in the business. This old woman, though, was something else.

They were all still there, of course. Seven pairs of needle-sharp eyes, pressing on him like a headache, and they showed absolutely no sign of moving so long as he was there. So he stood up, wincing slightly at the touch of very wet, cold cloth against his skin. 'Do you think you could tell me who's in charge here?' he said.

'You what?'

Something under the table was sniffing his leg, pressing a cold, wet nose against his ankle. He really didn't want to know what it was. 'You know,' he said, 'like a town council, parish board, levy and muster committee, burial club – anything like that,' he added, trying not to sound as wretched as he felt. 'I've got some questions to ask, and I need to know who to see.'

The old woman appeared to have lost the power of speech. 'Nothing like that here,' My Daughter Melja said eventually. 'No call for it in these parts. Bloody fuss,' she added, dismissing all hierarchies everywhere with a rather magnificent hint of pride. 'What kind of questions?' she added, her eyebrows crowding together.

'Nothing terrible,' he replied, smiling weakly. 'I'm not the government or anything. Truth is,' he ground on, feeling like a man pouring wine into the sand, 'I'm a scholar.'

'A what?' the old woman interrupted.

'A scholar. I like to learn things about – well, things. Religion,' he added quickly, before any of them could ask *What things?* 'Not that I'm a priest or anything. I'm just interested.'

There was a long silence; then the old woman shook her head, as if wondering sadly how it had come to this, and said that maybe he should go over to the old man's place, because he knew all manner of interesting stuff. The edge she put on the word *interesting* would probably have cut silk in its own weight.

'Thank you,' the brother said. 'Which old man would that be?'

The old woman pursed her lips; then she reached out sideways and grabbed the eight-year-old boy. 'Ebit'll show you the way,' she said. 'And then he'll come straight back, or I'll clip his ear so it'll make his head spin.' The boy muttered something and took a short, nervous step forward. 'Straight back, mind,' the old woman added.

Ebit led him down and across the street. They were all still there, under their porches and up in their lofts. Absolutely nothing whatsoever better to do, he guessed. Ebit stopped outside a plank door that was grey with age where it wasn't green with mould, and lifted the latch. 'In there,' he said, as if he was feeding a condemned man to the timber wolves at Torcea Fair.

'Thank you,' the brother answered, ducking his head as he walked in.

It was almost completely dark inside, apart from a faint orange glow from the last embers of a fire. He found a table by walking into it, and leaned his hands on the rough-sawn top. No sign of an old man, or sound of breathing apart from his own. Rustic humour? Or had the old boy died and nobody had noticed yet? In support of the latter theory was the extremely strong smell; though nauseating, however, it wasn't quite the odour of decaying flesh. Or at least, not exclusively.

'Over here,' said a voice in the shadows. 'By the fire.'

'Ah,' the brother said. 'Sorry, I didn't see you there. My name's—'

'Monach.' It was a very dry, thin voice, tenuous as the glow of the dying coals, but it wasn't a rube voice. The brother was very good at accents, but this was one he couldn't begin to place.

'That's right,' he said. 'How did you know my name?'

The voice laughed. 'Lefit Melja's eldest girl was listening under the window when you told her mother,' it said. 'She guessed they'd send you over here when they'd taken some money from you. So you're the priest, are you?'

Shrewd, too; as if it had experience in interrogation. 'Well,' Monach replied, 'sort of. Actually, I'm not a priest – not ordained or anything. I'm more of an amateur scholar, a bit of a dilettante really.'

Slight pause. 'It's all right,' the voice said, 'I know what the words mean, I'm just thinking about it.' Thin laugh; essence of laughter, strained and purged so many times that all the flavour had been lost. 'I've passed your test, but you haven't passed mine, or at least not yet. It takes me so long to think things through these days.'

Monach shifted uneasily. 'What's to think through?' he said. 'I haven't even told you what I'm here for yet.'

'Don't need to,' the voice replied gently. 'I ask myself, what's a priest – I'm sorry, what's a *scholar* doing in Cric, assuming he's not hopelessly lost on the road? It's got to be something to do with the god in the cart. And if it's something to do with that, then yes, I suppose you could be a gentleman scholar, or you could be a priest; and there's all sorts of different kinds of religious, so if you're a priest, what sort are you?' A soft, dry chuckle. 'Twenty years ago I'd have had the answers before you were through the door; not now, though. So suppose you help me along and tell me the answer. It'll save you an hour or so, if you're in a hurry.'

Definitely not a rube. 'By all means,' Monach replied. 'My name is Sens Monach; you may just have heard of my father, Sens Reuden, if you were ever in the military. I'm his younger son. Anyway, I've been making a study of manifestations of the divine for twenty years, gathering material for a book, and so when I heard about this god in the cart business—'

Loud coughing fit; then: 'Yes indeed, I've heard about General Sens. I never heard he had two sons, never heard he didn't. It's perfectly possible, I suppose; if Sens had a younger son, he could well have turned out idle and bookish – often the way with a self-made man. I'll say this for you: if you're a liar you're a conscientious one.' Slight pause, and a muffled scraping noise, possibly the foot of a chair on a stone floor. 'So you want to hear about the god in the cart.'

Monach perched on the edge of the table; it wobbled a bit. 'Yes please,' he said.

'All right. You'll have to excuse the dark, by the way,' the voice added. 'It rests my eyes and I can't afford to waste charcoal. If you've brought your own lamp, though, you can feel free to light it.'

'Left it in my saddlebag,' Monach replied truthfully. 'It doesn't matter. I can remember well enough without having to take notes.'

'Good.' Pause, and more scraping. 'I expect you're curious

about me, too,' the voice said (still the same weary, strained tone, slow delivery of words). 'And yes, I'm wandering off the subject, but you'll have to bear with me, sometimes I like to talk while I'm thinking. I don't suppose they told you my name.'

'No.'

'That's good, too. Let's see. My household name is Jolect, and my family name's nothing to interest you; but you may want to have a name to call me by. You're Monach and I'm Jolect.' Another of those laughs. 'For the sake of argument, at any rate.'

'If you say so,' Monach replied.

'Now then. Who I am, I'm a retired soldier. I was born here, and when I was through with my work, I came back here, and here I've been ever since. But I've seen a thing or two, Brother Monach – oh, I'm sorry, there I was still thinking you're a priest. I've seen a thing or two around the empire, let me tell you, and I know a little more about some things than my neighbours. Is that about in line with what you'd imagined?'

Monach laughed in spite of himself. 'Almost,' he said. 'I had you down for a religious yourself, possibly a renegade from the order. I suppose the room being in darkness put that thought into my head, but you've explained about that, so I must've been mistaken. After all, not everybody who sits in the dark is hiding from something.'

'I must also apologise,' Jolect went on, 'about the smell. When I was a soldier I was more than usually fussy about my kit – I used to annoy the drill sergeant no end because he couldn't ever find fault with it. These days, though, it's a terrible effort to stand up, let alone do all the cleaning and tidying and throwing away.' A sigh. 'An old woman used to come in and see to the place, but she died. Hardly surprising, she was older than me. I don't like it much, this mess,' the voice said, 'but it's not as if I have a choice.'

'I can imagine it must be hard to bear,' Monach replied. 'I like things neat and tidy myself, though I hope I don't take it to extremes. Of course, it's easy to be fastidious when you've always had people to tidy up after you. About the god in the cart—'

'Oh yes. Let me see, now, what's the best way to explain? I suppose it depends on whether you believe in the gods. Do you?'

'Yes,' Monach answered promptly. 'Well, up to a point, at any rate.'

'I see. And do you believe in a god called Poldarn?'

'Yes. At least, I see no reason not to believe in him, though I don't actually know very much about him. But that should-n't make any odds. After all, I don't know very much about the forests of northern Beltach, but I believe that they exist.'

'That's an interesting approach,' the voice said. 'Very well; if you believe in Poldarn, then he was here a month or so ago.'

'And if I don't?'

'Then some very bad people pretending to be Poldarn were here a month ago. Or another god passed through here in a cart, and for reasons best known to himself he pretended to be Poldarn.' The voice laughed. 'Let me put it another way. If there are such things as gods, there was one in the cart. I'm sceptical about virtually everything, but that's a fact.'

Monach smiled in the dark. 'And if there's no such thing as gods?'

'Ah. In that case, some very bad people who could raise the dead, heal the sick, predict the future and call lightning down out of the sky passed through here not long ago in a cart, but they weren't gods. Exactly the same as a god, but different.'

Monach nodded. 'And you saw all this?' he said.

'Oh yes. I can still see, you know, and I can hear, and people in these parts answer my questions truthfully. I saw the thunderbolt, I saw the healing and the raising from the dead, and I heard the prophecy. I was at the back of the crowd, mind you, having to peer over Pein Annit's shoulder, but I saw it.'

'And you believed?'

'I believe that I saw what I saw. Of course, the woman who was with him wasn't really a priestess. She was a Torcean, about your age, quite pretty in a blanched sort of a way. She didn't believe; I suspect she thought she was a confidence trickster.'

'Really,' Monach said, in a rather strained voice. 'How could you tell?'

'She was afraid,' Jolect said. 'It wasn't particularly warm, but she was sweating – the ends of her fringe were stuck together in little spikes, and there were dark patches in the cloth of her gown under the arms and in the small of her back. She was trying quite hard to take no notice of us – a very good performance, well thought out – but she couldn't help flicking very quick glances at us out of the corner of her eye; I don't suppose she even knew she was doing it, but she was. Also there were inconsistencies in what she told us, things she simply couldn't have said if she actually believed. Oh, and the people she gave medicine to didn't get better; she made a false diagnosis, though it's hard to blame her for that. She thought they had pneumonia, and what they really had was deer-tick fever. The symptoms are almost exactly the same in the early stages.'

Monach took a deep breath. 'So she was a fraud, then.'

'Beyond doubt. I didn't say anything, of course; she'd done me no harm, and nobody would've believed me, in any case. And it didn't matter. If the god is genuine, what difference does it make if the priest isn't what he claims to be? Or even if he doesn't believe.'

'Quite,' the brother muttered. 'All right, you've explained why the priestess was a fraud. Why was the god genuine?'

Another laugh. 'I thought I'd told you that. Because he

raised the dead, healed the sick, made thunder and forecast the future.' A pause. 'The thunder could have been a fraud, of course, because it is possible to manufacture thunder artificially. But it could just as easily have been the real thing.'

Monach thought about that for a moment. 'The same could be true of the healing,' he said. 'Perhaps the god wasn't a god, just a good doctor.'

'What an intelligent young man you are,' the voice said. 'But not in this case, since he didn't give them a medicine or examine them, or do any of the things doctors do.'

'Ah,' Monach interrupted. 'Then how can you be sure it was the god who healed them, if he didn't do anything?'

Another scrape, as if someone was shifting his weight in a chair with one shrunken leg. 'Because when he arrived in town there were four men and two women dying of marsh fever – which, as I'm sure you know, is always fatal if it lasts beyond the second week; and during the night he was here all four of them sweated out the fever and woke up the next morning, and now they're fully recovered. And Lassic Nurico's daughter died just after they arrived, and Pons Quevi a couple of hours later; they were quite dead, I saw their bodies myself and found no pulse or signs of life, and they were taken over to the Fennas' barn and laid out for burial. And in the morning they were alive again, and they're still alive now. What more proof do you need?'

Monach rubbed his chin. 'There are other possible explanations,' he said.

'Of course.' The voice clicked its tongue. 'But Seuro Eliman's boy climbed up into the rafters of the tower courtyard roof and watched the god most of the night, and he told me the god sniffed six times and sneezed twice; and if you've heard or read the stories about Poldarn you'll know that when he cures disease he sniffs, and when he raises the dead he sneezes. And I heard that when I was a boy, so it's not something made up after the fact. As for the prophecy, the priestess said he had business in Josequin, and Josequin was burned to the ground.'

'Coincidence?' Monach suggested.

A laugh, which turned into a dry, painful-sounding cough. 'Veusel says in the second book of his commentaries that five or more consecutive coincidences may be construed as proof of a doubted or disputed proposition. You can't argue with Veusel, he's been part of the syllabus for two hundred years.'

Monach, who'd suffered painfully from Veusel's commentaries in his youth, remembered just in time that he wasn't a monk any more. 'Who's Veusel?' he asked.

Silence. The sound of fingernails tapping on the arm of a chair, as Monach remembered that although he wasn't a monk, he was an enthusiastic amateur scholar. *Damn*, he thought.

'So, yes,' the voice resumed, 'you could say it was all coincidence, and you could say it was a man and a woman in the cart, not the god. Of course, I find it easier to believe because I saw him and you didn't. But I can't show you what I saw, I can only tell you various facts and leave you to draw your own conclusions. What else would you like to know?'

Monach was getting cramp from sitting on the table for so long. 'What did they look like?' he asked.

'The woman,' the voice said, 'was about medium height for a Torcean, with a narrow face, pointed nose and chin, high cheekbones, dark brown hair; I wasn't close enough to see the colour of her eyes, but they were dark too. She was wearing a dark blue dress, probably from Torcea; I don't know anything about women's fashions so I can't give you any technical details – it's a sad gap in my knowledge. I believe that you can tell how old a dress is and where it came from if you know about such things, and of course that could be useful in a case like this.'

'Thank you,' Monach replied. 'And what about the man? I mean the god.'

'He looked like Poldarn,' the voice replied. 'Just like he does in all the statues and paintings and ivory carvings and engravings on the backs of mirrors. Which reminds me, going back to the question of proof. Jira Fider, the miller's wife, had a gold ring that belonged to her great-grandmother. She took it off to wash some shirts – the hot water makes her fingers swell, and it was a tight fit at the best of times – and put it down on the step while she was working; a black bird dropped out of the plum tree, picked the ring up in its beak and flew away. She assumed it was a jackdaw, but for some reason they've never been common in these parts. That was the morning of the day they came. Coincidence, of course.'

Monach rubbed his eyes. 'When you say he looked like Poldarn—'

'The cart,' the voice continued, 'was just a cart, and if you can find anybody who can describe it in any detail I'll give you six quarters. All carts that are just carts look the same, you see. Fortunately I don't believe that there's such a thing as just a cart, so I took a careful look. It was a short two-horse back-sprung haulier's cart, painted grey a long time ago and neglected since, with one grab-handle missing from the box and a patch welded on to the front offside tyre. I think that's all the facts I can remember. If you like we can talk a bit more about metaphysics, or I can tell you some stories about my life as a soldier; you could go back and check the references, to give you an idea of the quality of my memory and powers of observation. I'd rather not, though, since you might use them to work out who I could be; somebody important who was at the same battles as I was. Purely by coincidence, you understand.'

'That's all right, really,' Monach said. 'Besides, if I believed you were something other than an ordinary retired soldier, I think I know who I'd reckon you are. And if you were him—'

'Which I'm not.'

'Oh, I believe you. But if that person was still alive and living in obscurity in a village somewhere, I can see why he'd rather nobody knew who he really was.'

'So can I,' Jolect replied. 'Actually, I knew him once. Quite well. He might have amounted to something, you know, if it hadn't been for General Cronan and a good deal of bad luck.'

Monach smiled. 'I think so too,' he said. 'Thank you for your help.'

'My pleasure. You can give me a small amount of money if it makes you feel any better. Money isn't actually worth anything here, but one or two of the grander farmers' wives collect it, to show how sophisticated they are, and usually they'll trade food and firewood for it. Your hostess, for instance.'

'She's one of the grander farmers' wives?'

'Nearest thing Cric has to royalty,' the voice replied. 'I've heard it said she's got a pair of shoes she's never even worn once.'

Once it got around the village that he'd spent an hour talking to the old man, Monach found it much easier to get people to talk to him, and he spent the evening trudging from house to house, asking the same questions and getting roughly the same answers. He found Pons Quevi, who confirmed that he'd been dead but couldn't remember anything about it that was worth listening to, and Seuro Eliman's boy, who'd watched Poldarn from the roof, and various others who'd been sick or thought they'd been sick, or who remembered thinking they saw strange blue glowing lights hovering over the god's head, or snakes that slithered under the cart while the priestess was meditating. It was good corroborative evidence, but since he hadn't really doubted the accuracy of what the old man had told him, he felt he needn't really have bothered. When it was dark he went back to the Lefit house and was shown a pile of old rugs he was to be allowed to sleep on, in the corner near the economical fire. He lay for a while, listening, trying to match the various snores to the members of the household, wondering if the old man really was General Allectus (who'd died, no question about that; but so had Pons Quevi, and he'd talked to him for half an hour), until his eyes closed, and—

—And opened again, and he saw a crow sitting on his chest, its round black eyes filled with disgust and contempt. In its beak was the gold ring he wore round his neck on a chain *(since when did I wear a gold ring round my neck on a chain? Since this dream started, presumably)* and it jerked its neck, trying to pull it free. He felt the chain tweak the back of his neck and tried to lift his hand to shoo the bird away; it took an unexpected amount of effort. The crow let go of the ring and pulled itself into the air with its broad heavy wings, squawking bitterly.

He was out in the open somewhere, lying on his back in deep, sticky mud. Next to him there was a dead body; lots of dead bodies, soldiers. He sat up, pushing away the surge of panic, and looked round to see where he was.

He found that he was looking at the bottom of a combe, with a rain-swollen river running down the middle. The water had slopped out on to the grass on either side, and where he was lying was churned up into a filthy mess of mud and brown standing pools. In the mud lay the dead bodies, some on their backs, some face down and almost submerged. He was filthy himself, with a tidemark of black mud a hand's span above both knees, and he was missing one boot, presumably sucked off when he'd stumbled into a boggy patch.

I can't remember anything, he realised. *What a horrible feeling, thank God this is only a dream.* He forced himself to stand up, in spite of violent protests from his head and knees. That gave him a better view, a broader perspective, but still none of it made any sense.

He looked down at the dead man lying next to where he'd been, trying to read him through the mud. A soldier, because he was wearing armour (boiled leather cuirass and pauldrons, cheap and cheerful and fairly efficient so long as you fight in the dry; over that a rough wool cloak so sodden with blood and dirty water that it could've been any colour; trousers the same, the toes of the boots just sticking up out of the mud); cause of death was either the big puncture wound in the pit of the stomach or the deep slash that started under the right ear and carried on an inch or so into the leather of the cuirass, just above the collarbone. His face was just an open mouth and two open eyes, with drying mud slopped incongruously on the eyeballs, but whether it was a friend or an enemy he couldn't say.

Yes, it's only a dream; but if I've lost my memory and forgotten who I am, maybe I won't be able to get back out of it when it's supposed to be over. How will I know how to find my body again when it wakes up? I could be stranded here for ever.

He was about to yell, 'Hello, is anybody there,' as loud as he could when he stopped and realised there had been a battle here; what if someone did hear him and turned out to be the enemy? Hopeless, he stood staring at the mud and the bodies, horribly aware that he hadn't the faintest idea what he should do. Then the crow, which had been circling patiently, glided down towards him on the slight breeze, turned into it to brake and pitched on the face of one of the soldiers, and (because it was a dream) melted away into the wound as the soldier sat up and wiped his own brains out of his eyes.

'Hello,' the soldier said.

'You're dead,' Monach replied.

The soldier nodded. 'Though a tactful person would've found a more roundabout way of telling me. Still, you've just had a very nasty bump on the head, bad enough to make you start seeing things, so I suppose I can make allowances. Yes, I'm dead, but so was Pons Quevi. Allow me to introduce myself. My name's Poldarn.'

'Oh,' Monach said.

'Just "Oh". Not "Pleased to meet you, I've come a long way". And I suppose a little respect, or just a tiny bit of worship – no, apparently not.' He grinned lopsidedly, the stretching of the muscles of his face further widening the deep cut that ran from eyesocket to chin. 'It's all right, I can make allowances for mortal frailty. You were looking for me. What can I do for you?'

Monach took a step backwards. 'With – respect,' he mumbled, 'I wasn't actually looking for *you* – not the real you, I mean. I was sent to find out about someone going round in a cart saying they're you. That's all.'

'But the someone in the cart is me,' Poldarn replied. 'Will I do? Or are you going to insist that I produce the cart and show you the patch on the tyre? I can do that if you like, but it'd be a lot of extra work, and I'm rather pushed for time as it is. I can be in two places at the same time but my mortal counterparts can't. So we can skip the cart then, can we?'

'What? Oh, yes, of course.'

'Thank you. So, let's get down to cases. What do you want to know?'

Monach took another step backwards, and felt something solid under his heel. He didn't want to think about what it might be. 'I'm sorry,' he said, 'I can't have explained terribly well. It's not you I need to find out about; we know all about you, back at the order.'

Poldarn looked intrigued. 'All about me?'

Monach nodded. 'Yes. I looked you up before I left.'

'So you know all about me too?'

'Yes. Well, not *all*, obviously. But everything I needed to know—'

Poldarn smiled. 'Oh, I agree, we can skip all the irrelevant detail. Go on, then. I can't wait to hear all the things I need to know about myself.'

Monach took a deep breath, and resisted the urge to back away further. 'I'm sorry,' he repeated. 'I really am expressing myself very badly indeed. My mission – I was sent to find out about two people in a cart, who passed through a village called Cric—'

'Cric.' Poldarn dipped his head. 'Thanks, I'll make a note of it. Is that far from here?'

'I don't know. I don't know where this is.'

'Neither do I,' Poldarn replied. 'Please bear in mind,' he added, pulling blood-matted hair out of the hole in his temple, 'you aren't the only one who's had a nasty bump on the head. Still, now at least I've got somewhere to head for. Any idea where I go from there?'

'Josequin,' Monach answered without thinking.

'Ah, got you. So Josequin's next, after Cric. I have an idea what I've got to do, you see, it's just the order I'm supposed to do it in that's a little vague.'

Monach felt as if he'd just done something seriously wrong, though he wasn't sure what it could be. 'Josequin was burned down,' he said, 'a week or so ago. Everybody was killed, there were no survivors. The god in the cart predicted it; that's why I was sent to find out—' He hesitated. The god was looking at him.

'News to me,' Poldarn said. 'If a city the size of Josequin was burned down, I'm pretty sure I'd have heard about it. But anyway, thank you. It's just as well someone's seen fit to tell me what I'm supposed to be doing, and where.'

Then Monach realised what he'd done wrong. Josequin hadn't been destroyed yet; the god in the cart hadn't yet been to Cric. 'Just a moment,' he said.

'Let's get this straight,' Poldan went on, bending down and picking a sword up out of the mud. It was a backsabre, like the one Cronan found in the wood, or the ones hidden in the trunk in the Falx house. 'From here I go to Cric. In Cric I predict the fall of Josequin; then I go to Josequin. What happens after that?'

'No,' Monach said (and he remembered who he was, and

that he had family in Josequin). 'It doesn't have to happen like that. If you don't go to Cric, maybe Josequin won't get burned down.'

Poldarn nodded. 'And we couldn't have that, could we? Thank you, you've been incredibly helpful. Someone like me needs someone like you to keep things on track. If ever I need another priest, I'll definitely bear you in mind.' He wiped the mud off the sabre and hung it from his belt by the pommel-hook. 'Where do I go after Josequin?' he asked. 'Let's see, Sansory would be the logical choice, it's nearer than Mael. Or better still, Deymeson, for a wide variety of excellent reasons. I assume you know, since you did all that background reading.'

The weight of what he'd done made Monach stagger, and his hand dropped instinctively to his sword hilt. 'You mustn't go to Josequin,' he said. 'Thousands of people live there.'

Poldarn was smiling. 'Not for much longer. You do know who I am, don't you? Or didn't the books mention it?'

Grip the mouth of the scabbard with the left hand and turn it ninety degrees to the left. Place the side of the left thumb against the hilt and press it gently forward to free the sword in the scabbard. Lay the back of the right hand on the grip. 'I can't let you go to Josequin,' Monach said. 'My family lives there.'

'You don't know who I am,' Poldarn said sadly. 'What a pity, I was hoping you could tell me. But everybody I meet who knows me seems to die. Mostly I kill them. You've no idea how frustrating that is; and I'm only doing my job. It's not as if I have any choice in the matter.' He took a step forward; the middle finger of his right hand touched the pommel-hook of the backsabre. 'I go where people ask for me,' he said. 'It's not as if I'm not invited. Now get out of my way.'

'No.'

Another step forward. One more after that would bring him inside Monach's circle, the distance around him that he

could reach with his sword from the draw. He'd been trained
for twenty years to draw and strike as soon as the enemy came
into his circle, to the point where the action became automatic, involuntary. It wasn't as if he'd have any choice in the
matter.

'You were the one who came looking for me,' Poldarn
pointed out gently. 'You asked for me.'

Poldarn lifted his foot, crossed the circumference of the
invisible circle. Flip the right hand over and take a firm hold
on the grip. Draw; right hand and right foot together, step
into the enemy's circle as you cut. A brother of the order
who's been trained in the draw need fear nothing on earth,
there's nothing, not even a god, he can't kill.

Poldarn stepped backwards and dropped the backsabre, as
Monach flicked the blood off the blade; the dead god was still
standing when the ricasso clicked back into the mouth of the
scabbard. Then he slumped and fell, splashing Monach's face
with mud. The crow spread its wings and flew slowly away, as
somewhere behind him Father Tutor shook his head and
sighed. 'You've got to stop doing things like that,' he said.
'You're becoming a liability to the order. I told you to *find*
him, not—'

Monach opened his eyes; and the dream spread its wings and
flapped away back into the darkness, carrying the memory of
what he'd seen gripped in its beak. The old woman was standing over him, prodding him with her toe.

'Breakfast,' she said. 'Fried oatmeal and cheese. Two quarters.'

Monach nodded. He hated fried oatmeal. He was in Cric,
so Josequin must have fallen in spite of him. He recalled that
thought and wondered what the hell it meant.

Chapter Ten

Poldarn woke up out of a bad dream. There were crows in it, and a god who'd talked to him, and a lot of frightening stuff he was glad to see the back of. He opened his eyes and saw something familiar: the back wheel of a cart, turning steadily.

'You're awake, then,' muttered the carter. 'That's good. You know, for a top-of-the-line security guard, you spend a lot of time sleeping. Maybe the gods send you warnings in dreams.'

Poldarn sighed. It was a pity that the carter had taken against him so early, given that they were going to be spending the next four days together. The resentment was understandable, he supposed; he was being paid three times as much as the carter, and the carter was doing all the work (he'd offered to do a share of the driving, but the carter had just scowled suspiciously at him and not replied).

'I'm sorry,' he said mildly. 'It's very boring, sitting here with nothing to do. Sleeping helps pass the time.'

The carter flicked away a wasp with his left hand. 'You snore,' he said. 'And you talk in your sleep. Never knew anybody like it for rabbiting on. Crazy stuff, a lot of it.'

'Really?' Poldarn sat up a little. 'What sort of thing?'

'Don't ask me. I got better things to do than listen.'

Tactical error, Poldarn realised; by expressing an interest, he'd made the carter unwilling to tell him. Still, it wasn't too late to change tack.

'I don't believe you,' he said. 'I've never noticed that I talk in my sleep.'

'Well of course you haven't,' the carter said. 'Think about it.'

Poldarn shook his head. 'Somebody would have mentioned it by now,' he maintained. 'Especially if I really said lots of crazy stuff.'

'Oh, it was crazy all right,' the carter replied. 'Bloody weird, sometimes. All about wars and battles and dead bodies lying around the place; that's when you aren't talking to the gods. What you need is a double dose of rhubarb, clean you out a bit.'

'I thought you said you weren't listening.'

'I wasn't. But you talk so loud I couldn't help hearing bits of it. No choice of mine, I promise you.'

'Give me an example,' Poldarn said. 'Otherwise I'll know you're just bullshitting me.'

The carter laughed. 'You asked for it,' he said. 'What about just now, when you were jabbering away; first it was somebody called Ciartan, next it was General Cronan, then it was the bloody emperor, if you please – I got an idea that's probably treason, dreaming nutty dreams about the emperor – and then, like that wasn't bad enough, you started talking to the gods. "No, I won't do it," you were saying – yelling, more like it, I didn't know where to look. Kept on saying the same thing over and over again, "I won't do it, I won't do it." I'd have woken you up, only they say if you wake someone up when they're having nutty dreams, sometimes they stick like it. I'm telling you, it was better fun than the pantomime.'

Poldarn nodded. 'Glad you enjoyed it,' he said. 'I really wish I could remember some of it. After all, why should you have all the fun?'

The carter shook his head. 'And before that,' he said, 'when you were being Feron Amathy – though why you'd want to be a vicious little creep like that, God only knows. There you were, giving orders – "Burn the houses," you were shouting, "burn the houses, don't let any of them escape." Turned me up just listening to you.'

'Who's Fern Amathy?'

The carter scowled again. 'That's not funny,' he said. 'There's some things you shouldn't make jokes about. People can get offended.'

Poldarn sighed. It was just starting to get dark, and a big flock of rooks were streaming by high overhead, making for a stand of thin larches. 'I wasn't trying to be funny,' he said. 'Seriously, I'm not from around here. Not even from this side of the bay. And I don't recognise the name.'

'You're kidding.'

'No.'

'Oh.' The carter looked at him sideways, as if checking to see if he had an extra finger on either hand now that he knew he was an offcomer. 'Should've known, I suppose, by your voice.'

'My voice?'

'Yeah, your voice. You talk funny. Well, maybe not funny where you come from, but you know what I mean. You don't talk *right*.'

Poldarn shrugged. He'd made a resolution, he reminded himself; not interested any more. 'Be that as it may,' he said. 'Who's Fern Amathy?'

'Not Fern,' the carter said. 'Feron. Feron Amathy. Runs the biggest free company this side of the bay. Real bastard.'

Free company; ah yes, a euphemism for a band of mercenaries. He'd already gathered that they weren't popular. 'In what way?' he asked.

'Any way you care to name, really. Like, there's a lot of people who reckon it's not the raiders who go around burning down towns and cities, it's the Amathy house, and they kill all the people to make sure there's no witnesses to give the game away. Not all the towns and cities,' the carter added, after a moment's reflection. 'It's when they're between jobs with nothing to do, they go around doing that sort of stuff and blaming it on the raiders. Real bastards, like I said.'

'I agree with you,' Poldarn said, 'if it's really them.'

'Stands to reason,' the carter replied, though he didn't enlarge on it. 'And then there's how he treated General Allectus. There's a lot of people had time for General Allectus, he wasn't half as bad as he's been made out. And even if he was no better than the others, there wasn't any call for Feron Amathy to go changing sides like he did, right in the middle of the battle. That's unprofessional, that is. I mean, before that, if you hired a free company, all right, it's usually a bad move regardless of how things go in the war, but at least you could be pretty sure they wouldn't stab you in the back. Now, though, they're all doing it, and the upshot is, instead of being over nice and quick and clean, these bloody little wars keep dragging on and on, with one lot changing sides, then another lot going over to the other side, backwards and forwards like two mules ploughing. Chaos.'

'I can imagine that it would be,' Poldarn replied. 'And it sounds like you're right about this Feron Amathy. God knows what he was doing in my dream, though.'

The sun was setting fast, and they were just coming under a thick patch of fog (or mist, or low cloud); the effect of the sunset through the mist was fine and slightly disturbing, like drops of blood falling in still, muddy water. Poldarn started to feel anxious, though he couldn't think why.

It must have shown in his face, because the carter noticed it. 'What are you getting all twitchy about?' he asked suspiciously. 'Is it trouble?'

'I don't know,' Poldarn replied.

'You bloody well ought to, you're the one with the finely honed instincts you're getting paid all that money for. Should we stop here, or go back, or what?'

'I said, I don't know,' Poldarn said. 'I can't see anything that looks wrong. Mind you, I can't really see anything at all. Maybe that's all it is.'

'You mean you're afraid of the dark.' The carter made a clicking noise with his teeth, one of his many annoying habits. 'That's not good enough, is it?' he said reproachfully. 'You're supposed to be able to smell trouble before it happens, that's what you're here for. Well, is it trouble or isn't it?'

'I just told you, I don't know,' Poldarn said impatiently.

The carter stood up and pulled on the reins. 'That's it,' he said, 'I'm stopping right here. You can go on ahead and see what the matter is.'

Poldarn couldn't help grinning. 'What, and leave you here all alone and unprotected? That's not what I'm paid for.'

'Yes, but you're the one carrying the bloody letter.'

'Yes, but they don't know that.'

'Who doesn't know that?'

'Search me.' Poldarn jumped down from the cart and pulled his hat out from under the cover. 'I could do with stretching my legs, I suppose. You want my advice? If I were you, I'd get down off there, climb under the cart and keep still and quiet. That way, they'll think you've gone off too.'

'Who, for God's sake?'

Poldarn shrugged. 'Suit yourself,' he said. 'Don't say I didn't warn you.'

Muttering hurtful things under his breath, the carter hopped down and vanished under the bed of the cart. 'Don't hang around,' he hissed in a very loud whisper. 'See what's out there and come straight back, you hear me?'

'Shh,' Poldarn replied, and walked into the mist.

It was the very last of the sunset, the last glow of heat left in the cooling embers of the day, just enough orange and red light to see a few yards by until the glow rolled back on the wall of cloud. It wasn't fear, Poldarn decided, more a sense of unease, as if he was missing something important, relevant and useful. He tripped over a stone and scampered a few steps before regaining his balance.

'Hello?' a man's voice called out from somewhere in the cloud.

'Hello yourself,' Poldarn called back. 'Where are you?'

'Over here,' the voice said, uselessly. 'Can you help me? I think I've broken my leg.'

It was an interesting, attractive voice, high-pitched, full of character, the accent probably denoting high birth and refinement, though that was just a guess. 'How did you manage that?' Poldarn called back, straining to get a fix on where the voice was coming from.

'Bloody pheasant got up right under my feet, startled my horse, the miserable thing threw me. I think I landed badly or something.' Deliberate cheerfulness laid over repressed panic: either genuine or a good actor. Poldarn reassured himself that his sword was in his belt, and headed off the road towards where he reckoned the voice was coming from. When he figured he was close, he turned a right angle, walked fifteen paces, turned another right angle and hoped he hadn't missed his mark. The idea, of course, was to come up behind whoever it was, in case it was an ambush, but if he'd got it wrong he could find himself in even worse trouble than if he hadn't bothered at all.

But he was vindicated, eventually; in front of him he could make out the shape of a man, sitting with his back to him, his legs spread out in a thoroughly uncomfortable-looking position that couldn't have been voluntary. A few steps closer and he could just see a horse grazing a few yards further on. So far, so good. He waited, wondering where all these instincts had come from, looking and listening for anything that might suggest that he and the man with the broken leg weren't the only people there. When he was as near satisfied as he could reasonably expect, he closed in a step or two, keeping the trunk of a tall, thin tree between himself and the man (so he'd be able to see the man's face while remaining hidden himself), and cleared his throat.

The other man started, did something unfortunate to his leg, and yelped with pain. 'Bloody hell,' he said, twisting his head round, 'where did you come from?'

'I was talking to you just now,' Poldarn said.

'Yes, but you were – oh, I see. Cautious beggar, aren't you? Come over here, where I can see you.'

Poldarn took another look round the tree. The man was older than he'd thought, middle to late forties by the grey hair over his ears; strikingly good-looking all the same, in a boyish kind of way, with sharp, distinct features and large brown eyes. He was also liberally splattered with mud. He looked harmless enough, and Poldarn was fairly sure he was alone, so he came out from behind the tree and moved forward.

'Oh bloody hell,' the stranger said, staring at him, his face changing completely. 'For pity's sake, what are *you* doing here? Are you out of your mind, or what?'

On balance, Poldarn decided, he'd have preferred it if the man had jumped up and pulled a knife. He was surprised by his own reaction. What he really wanted to do was turn around and walk away, and he couldn't quite understand why, but the urge was so strong he found it hard to resist.

'You know me,' he said.

'I thought I did,' the stranger replied. 'I mean, I'm used to you pulling some bloody stupid stunts but this is going too far, even by your standards. Have you got the faintest idea what they'll do to me if we're seen together? If you've got a death-wish, that's absolutely fine. Just leave me out of it. I'm sick and tired of rescuing you every time you get it into your head to do something crazy.'

'No, really,' Poldarn said (and he felt like there was an enormous weight on his chest, so heavy he could hardly breathe). 'You don't understand.'

The stranger was looking round. 'This is the last time, got it?' he said angrily. 'Absolutely the last time. For God's sake, anybody with half a brain would've taken the hint by now. I don't know,' he went on, shaking his head eloquently, 'somebody up there must hate me. It all goes round and round, like a windmill. First I'm in the shit up to my elbows, under guard, on my way to Torcea for a long chat with my dear cousin. Then suddenly it all gets better; a little money changes hands, I give them the slip and I'm on my way home; then the bloody pheasant, and I'm lying there in a heap with a bust leg. And if that wasn't enough, *you* have to show up.' A thought seemed to occur to him. 'Big coincidence, that,' he added, 'though I suppose even you couldn't have arranged the pheasant. No, I'm probably just being paranoid, though where you're concerned, normal criteria don't seem to apply, for some reason. What she sees in you, I have no idea.' He rubbed his chin, thinking something over, and appeared to reach a decision. 'Look, I can get you past the soldiers, so long as you keep your face shut; that's assuming none of them know you by sight, but we may just get lucky. You're alone?'

'No,' Poldarn said. Simply keeping still was an almost unbearable effort; he'd just realised exactly how frightened he was. Up till then he'd been too preoccupied to notice. But the fear was there, no doubt about it, just starting to well up and flow (it's the same way with a deep cut: there's a second or so after the impact when the flesh is numb and nothing seems to be happening; then the bleeding starts, and suddenly you get a much clearer idea of where your priorities lie).

Let's get out of this alive first, Poldarn decided. *The other stuff can wait.* 'Listen,' he said, 'I'm only a delivery man, we're taking a load of stuff to the city.' (Of course, he could just leave the man lying and walk away, as his instincts urged him to. That would be the simplest thing, and the safest, if there was danger. A sensible man would do that, without hesitation. But that begged the question of who was supposed to be being rescued, and there appeared to be some doubt on that score.) 'Can you please tell me what this is all about?'

'Oh, give it a rest, can't you?' The stranger stared at him as if he was mad. 'I've had it with you,' he said. 'God only knows what possessed me to get mixed up with a lunatic like you in the first place. If it was just me, I'd have the soldiers kill you now, tell them you're a footpad or something, simply to be shot of you.' He sighed. 'Still, can't really do that, she'd never forgive me. All right; now keep quiet and I'll get us out of this, somehow. Who's the man with you?'

Poldarn shrugged. 'He's a carter, from the Falx house. His name's Gotto. That's all I know about him.'

'The Falx house.' The stranger closed his eyes. 'Oh, it just gets better and better. Can't you simply cut his throat and dump him somewhere? No, forget it, that'd be too risky, Falx Roisin would be bound to figure out what's going on.'

Poldarn doubted that, from what he'd seen of his employer, but then what did he know about anything?

'You're sure he doesn't know who you are?' the stranger went on. 'Hey, did I just say something funny?'

Poldarn shook his head. 'Sorry,' he said. 'If you'd just listen—'

'Oh no. I listened to you the last time, and now look at me. Did you say you've got a cart?'

'Yes.'

The stranger frowned. 'Not so bad, after all. You know, maybe there's actually a way out of this. If we could only slide past the soldiers without them seeing me – you know, that could work out rather well. You're still a dangerous lunatic who ought to be put down, but we might just get away with it. You're *sure* the carter doesn't know?' He lifted his head sharply. 'Shut up,' he whispered, 'someone's coming.

Sorry,' he continued, his voice changing effortlessly back to the charming drawl he'd used earlier, 'that's not a very friendly way to say hello to your saviour. Please forgive me; I'm not used to misfortune, it makes me edgy.'

Poldarn glanced round, and saw that the carter was peering at them from behind a tree. He hadn't heard him approaching, so either bewilderment was turning him deaf or the stranger had exceptional hearing.

'Who's this?' the carter asked. He wasn't quite close enough to see the stranger's face; he was holding off, just out of range, like a canny rook circling a feed trough.

'Fell off my horse,' the stranger said, 'and broke my stupid leg. I was wondering, do you think you could possibly give me a lift as far as Mael? If you're headed that way, that is.'

The carter came out from behind his tree, radiating curiosity like a watchman's brazier. 'I don't know about that,' he said. 'We're not supposed—'

'Of course,' the stranger said, 'I can make it worth your while.'

The carter stopped dead in his tracks. 'I don't know,' he repeated. 'Got my job to think about.'

'It'd be no fun at all riding all that way with a broken leg,' Poldarn said, mostly just to break the silence before it choked him. 'I suppose you'd better hitch a ride with us.'

The man's face was a study in relief. 'That's very kind of you,' he said.

Poldarn shrugged. 'We're headed that way anyway,' he said, walking round the back of him so the man couldn't turn and look at his face without hurting himself badly. He wondered if he was doing the right thing, but he simply didn't have enough facts to go on. Soldiers, the stranger had said, and a lot of stuff about danger and risk. For his part, Poldarn decided, he mostly wished he was somewhere else. Here was the past come to visit, like one's least favourite relatives calling unannounced at the worst possible time. He envied the stranger the fluency with which he'd changed faces, and wondered if it was something that could be acquired with practice, like skill at arms, or whether you had to be born with it, like being able to divine water with a twig or read minds. He wished he could do something like that; walk over the top of complexity, like a fly skittering across a pool.

He reached down and pulled the stranger up by the hand on to his good leg and caught him before he could topple over. He put his shoulder under the man's arm. 'Nice and steady,' he said. 'It's not far to the cart. Here, Gotto, give me a hand.'

The mist cleared as soon as they got down off the high ground, but it was dark and the road was rutted and soft, and the carter's temper wasn't improving. 'The hell with this,' he said, after a jolt nearly broke the axle and made the stranger yelp with pain. 'I say we stop here for the night. It's at least two more hours to Vauc Dosime, and I've had enough.'

There didn't seem to be much point in arguing, although, as Poldarn pointed out (just to be difficult), they didn't have any food with them, and nothing to build a fire with. The carter didn't bother to reply, so presumably he didn't think much of either argument. Poldarn could also have pointed out that there was only one blanket, namely the one the carter was sitting on, but he felt that that could lead to unpleasantness and bad feeling, so he let the matter slide. There was always the cart cover (though it still had about half a gallon of water collected in its folds after the late afternoon rain) and his coat; on the other hand, he felt obliged to offer that to the stranger.

'No, it's all right, really,' the stranger replied. 'I've caused you enough trouble as it is.'

Poldarn shook his head. 'Take the damn coat,' he said.

The stranger grinned and accepted. 'If you're sure,' he replied.

'I offered, didn't I?' He fished in his satchel for the small flask of strong spirits that Eolla had advised him never to travel without and offered it to the stranger. As he did so he caught sight of the carter looking sideways at them both. He felt painfully exposed; the silence was unnatural, not appropriate for a rescue, a good deed. Some small talk was called for.

'Have you got friends in Mael who'll look after you?' he asked.

'No; but it's all right, my—' The stranger paused, searching for the right word. 'The people I'm with have an office there, lodgings for couriers and travellers, that sort of thing. I'll be all right.'

'Sounds like a fairly big concern,' Poldarn said. 'Mercantile? Banking?'

'That sort of thing,' the man replied calmly. 'How about you?'

'We're in the dried fish and sausage business,' Poldarn said. 'Just our luck that we get held up on the way there, of course. If we were on the way home, we'd be fully loaded with dried tuna and blood sausage, not to mention a couple of jars of Mael beer.'

'Just my luck,' the stranger said, 'I missed a treat. But there you go, you don't always make your own luck.'

'I suppose not,' Poldarn said. 'Well, get some sleep if you can. We're going to have to try to make up time tomorrow, so it won't be very comfortable.'

Judging by the sound of his breathing, the stranger had no trouble at all getting to sleep; remarkable, if there was any truth in what he'd said about the danger they were both in. Poldarn, on the other hand, was wide awake. He pulled his collar up around his chin and drew his sleeves down as far as they'd go, but it didn't help much. It was a cold night, even if it wasn't raining, and there seemed to be rather more of it than was actually necessary.

About three hours before dawn, by Poldarn's reckoning, he was startled out of a train of thought concerning his unusually broad knowledge of languages and dialects and the implications that went with it by what he thought might have been the sound of someone coughing quite some way away in the direction they'd come from. He listened carefully for a while, but there was nothing else to hear, and it could just as easily have been a fox as a human. Nevertheless he sat up enough so that he could get to his sword if he had to. Perversely, he was now starting to feel drowsy; although he couldn't see the back of his own hand, he knew that if he closed his eyes, even for a moment, he'd be fast asleep in no time. He lifted and shook his head; that helped, though only for a short while.

He'd come to the conclusion that it was all his imagination, egged on by Falx Roisin's colourful account of what had happened to his predecessors, combined with the stranger's dark mutterings about soldiers (whom they were supposed to be slipping past without being seen, with the implication that their lives depended on it), when he heard what was without doubt the sound of two pieces of metal grating together, as it might be the rim of a shield against a tasset or a sword chape against a greave. He caught his breath and dug his elbow into the carter's back.

'Wake up,' he hissed.

'Piss off,' the carter mumbled.

He dug rather harder this time, and the carter sat up with a shudder. 'What the bloody—?'

'Quiet.' There must have been something in his voice that impressed the carter, who did as he was told for the first time since they'd started working together. 'There's someone coming.'

'So what?' the carter muttered. 'It's a road. You get people on roads, it's life.'

'Shh.' This time, it was a creak; a stiff boot, perhaps, or shifting weight on a belt. The carter heard it too; Poldarn could feel the cart move slightly as he jumped in his seat and started rummaging on the floor for the sack he kept his sword in. That gave him an idea. As quietly as he could, so the carter wouldn't know he'd gone, he slipped over the side of the cart and dropped to the ground, reaching out with his toes to ease himself down. On the sides of his feet (the quietest way; how come he knew that?) he walked round to where he figured the tailgate must be, feeling his way with the back of his outstretched left hand, then stopped and worked out a mental diagram, marking the strategic points and relevant distances. He'd almost completed this task when he remembered the stranger's horse, which for some reason the carter had tethered separately from their own, behind the cart. He added it to the schematic in his mind, just in case it proved important later.

There were two of them, at least; he heard a muffled cough somewhere in front of him, and a rustle of cloth away to his right. Aggravating; why weren't they keeping to the road? The only reason he could think of was that they knew where the cart was and wanted to sneak up and surround it, which implied that they probably weren't going to turn out to be friendly. Was the whole world like this, he wondered; and if so, how the hell was it still inhabited at all?

Someone walked past him, only a foot or so away, breaking into his circle. He kept his hand away from his sword hilt with an effort, confining himself to placing his toe behind the back of the other man's knee and pushing. He heard the man go down, took an educated guess as to where his neck would be, and trod lightly there with the side of his foot. Judging by feel, he'd guessed about right.

'Shh,' he whispered. Then he waited to find out what would happen.

'Gian,' someone called out. 'Are you all right?'

Gian, wisely, didn't answer. His friend repeated the enquiry, and some other faint noises suggested to Poldarn that one – or more – of the invisible strangers was heading in his direction. That was what he'd wanted to happen, but it occurred to him that he hadn't really thought it through; the idea of leaving the cart in the first place was to avoid being in a place where any-body could find him, to be a free agent in the darkness. Now he'd effectively told them where he was and invited them to come to him. He had the advantage of a hostage, of course, but they didn't know that.

'Stay where you are,' he called out, 'or I'll break his neck.'

(Fine. If they do as they're told, all we have to do is stay perfectly still till dawn. Piece of cake.)

'Who's there?' another voice shouted back.

'You first,' Poldarn replied. 'Who are you, how many, and what are you doing sneaking about in the dark?'

Gian squirmed slightly under his foot; a little additional pressure soon fixed that.

'I'm Captain Olens of the domestic cavalry,' the voice said confidently, 'second regiment, fifth detachment, seventeenth squadron, forty-third platoon. Who the hell are you?'

Poldarn grinned. 'Nobody important,' he replied, 'except that I'm standing on your friend's neck, and if anybody does anything I don't like, I'll kill him. Understood?'

'Understood,' Captain Olens said nervously.

'Splendid.' Poldarn turned his head towards where he fig-ured the cart should be. 'Gotto,' he yelled, hoping the carter was still there, alive and awake. 'Gotto, are you there?'

'Yes,' the carter replied. 'What the hell's going on?'

Poldarn paused to listen, then replied, 'No idea. Get the lantern lit and we'll find out.'

Now came the awkward part. He stooped down, taking care not to compromise his balance and give Gian an oppor-tunity to escape or attack, slid his sword quietly from the scabbard with his right hand and felt for Gian's hair with his left. He connected and wound a loop of it round his fingers, to serve as a handle. 'Shh,' he repeated, as quietly as he could, shifted his foot off Gian's neck and pulled on the hair at the same time as he straightened up. Gian came up with him, and as soon as they were both upright he let him feel the edge of the sword against his neck. Then he pushed him forward. Disaster would be bumping into someone. Success would be getting to the tailgate of the cart without letting go of Gian or killing him. Rather to his surprise, he achieved success without any serious complications.

The key, he figured, was the stranger's horse, which they'd picked up on the way. He located it by colliding with it softly, and drew himself and his prisoner into the gap between the horse and the back of the cart, shielding them both. About two seconds after he was in position, Gotto's lantern flared up.

'Not on me, you idiot,' he hissed. 'Get down off the cart and walk forward in a straight line.' For once the carter did as he was told without even arguing the toss. 'All right,' he said, 'stop there. Right, the rest of you, head for the lantern and stop where I can see you.'

(Allegory, he thought; in the dark you aren't anybody, or you're who you say you are; with all the practice I've had lately, I should be good at this.)

A face appeared in the glow of the lantern; it was young and round, topped with curly dark hair. 'I'm Captain Olens,' it said. 'We mean you no harm,' it added, rather too obviously as an afterthought for Poldarn's liking. 'Now, who in buggery are you?'

'Olens,' said another voice, 'is that you?'

(And that voice, Poldarn realised, was the stranger, the man with the broken leg. That was either good or bad, depending on context and general world view.)

'Sir?'

'Olens, you bloody clown.' (Ah. Now we're getting somewhere.) 'Will you stop prancing about and leave these people alone? They're on our side.'

'Sir,' Captain Olens replied bitterly. 'All right, fall out, over here. Sir,' he went on, 'Sergeant Gian—'

'What? Oh, yes. Excuse me, but would you mind letting him go? These people are—' A very long pause, as if the stranger was making up his mind about something. 'Well, I know them, they won't hurt us.'

Poldarn thought about that. Trouble is, people don't have their designation written on their foreheads – friend, good guy, ambusher, assassin, rescuer. Depending on what decision the stranger had come to, releasing the hostage might prove to be a bad, and final, mistake. On the other hand, he was getting cramp in his sword arm. He let go of Gian's hair, laid his left hand flat between the man's shoulder blades, and shoved. Then he followed, heading towards the light.

There was Gotto, on one side of the lantern; on the other side, four faces, almost immediately joined by a fifth. 'Excuse me,' called out the stranger with the broken leg, 'but if you could bring the light over here, Captain Olens can see it's me and maybe we can all calm down a bit.'

Even Gotto could see the sense in that. Poldarn followed, taking care to stay out of the yellow circle, determined to be nobody and nowhere for as long as he could.

'Olens,' the man with the broken leg was saying, 'where the devil did you get to? I was lying in a ditch in the fog for an hour with a broken leg. If it hadn't been for these people—'

'Sir,' Captain Olens replied. He had the knack of investing that one word with a whole language's worth of meanings. 'I think we went past you in the fog, after we got separated. Then we realised you weren't with us and went back; then I gave the order to search the ground on either side of the road inch by inch, in case you'd fallen and been knocked out, or—' Slight pause. 'Or something like that.'

'Idiot.' The man with the broken leg didn't strike Poldarn as the forgiving sort. 'Right, we can't do anything till morning. I suppose you and your men had better get some sleep. I suggest underneath the cart.'

'Sir.'

He turned his head, looking for Poldarn. 'I say,' he called out, 'you can come back in now, it's all right.'

Poldarn thought before replying. 'In a moment,' he said. 'First, suppose you tell me what the hell this is all about, and who these clowns are.'

The other man grinned. 'About time, I suppose,' he said. 'All right. My name is Tazencius – Prince Tazencius if you want to be all formal about it, which I don't. These men are supposed to be my bodyguard; which should mean,' he added, raising his voice a little, 'that they rescue me from the jaws of death, and not the other way round. But that's by the by.'

Poldarn sighed. 'All right,' he said, 'that's your name. Now, who are you?'

'Oh, for crying out loud.' Tazencius looked Poldarn in the eye and shook his head slowly, the very image of a man whose patience ran out long ago, leaving him with only a faded memory of what it was like to deal with rational, normal people. 'I'm sorry,' he said, 'I shouldn't have assumed you'd know who I am. I'm the emperor's third cousin; rather more to the point, I'm the imperial prefect of Mael Bohec – hence the splendid but utterly useless honour guard.'

Poldarn turned his head away. 'Gotto,' he said, 'have you heard of anybody called – what was that name again?'

'Tazencius.'

'Of course I have, you moron,' Gotto replied. 'But how do we know it's really you? I mean, I could put a saucepan on my head and call myself the God of Boiled Dumplings; wouldn't mean I was telling the truth.'

Tazencius smiled, rather more warmly than the joke merited. 'Quite right,' he said. 'Still, since you were willing to help me when I was just some fool who'd fallen off his horse, I hope you won't change your mind now there's at least a possibility that I'm rich and famous.'

Gotto scowled. 'I don't know,' he said. 'I reckon if you were really Tazencius, your guards would've commandeered the cart by now.'

'Oh, I think even Captain Olens knows when he's done enough damage for one night,' Tazencius replied. 'After all, this cart's not going to move any faster even if it were to become government property for a day or so; the only difference would be that I'd have annoyed two strangers who've gone out of their way to help me.'

The carter furrowed his brows. 'I still reckon—' he began.

'Gotto,' Poldarn interrupted, 'shut up. As for you,' he went on, 'what about your men? I heard the officer say something about being cavalry. So where are their horses?'

This time, Tazencius frowned. 'You know,' he said, 'that's a very good point. I hadn't thought of that. They had them last time I saw them. Captain Olens,' he called out, 'did you hear that?'

'Sir,' replied a voice, muffled by the boards of the cart. 'I left them with Corporal Vestens back where we first noticed you were missing, so we could comb the area for you. Too dark to go searching for someone on horseback.'

'That makes sense,' Poldarn admitted. 'All right, let's all get some sleep. The main thing is,' he went on, staring hard at Tazencius, 'I can't think of any reason why you or your people would want to cut our throats, so I'll trust you not to. Agreed?'

Of course, Poldarn had no intention of sleeping, even if there had been any chance that he might. As far as he could judge from the sound of their breathing, Tazencius and his escort (and Gotto, for what little that mattered) all fell asleep quite quickly and easily, but he wasn't prepared to trust his judgement on that point, or many others. It'd all be easier, he reckoned, when daylight came and gave the world back its memory. Dealing in anonymity and trust in the pitch dark was no way for grown men to do business.

He couldn't help wondering, all the same (and it was that time in the early hours of the morning when perspectives are generally different): first Chaplain Cleapho, escaping (presumably he'd escaped) an ambush by the skin of his teeth;

now the man Tazencius, whom Cleapho had mentioned (and who'd turned out to be prefect of Mael Bohec, whatever that signified), wandering about in the mist with a rather small escort, surely, for an important man (guessing that prefects were as important as they sounded); add a variety of different types of soldier, the burning of Josequin, all manner of alarms, excitements and coincidences following him round like a tripe butcher's dog—

(This man who called himself Prince Tazencius, some off-relation of the emperor himself, who reckoned that the two of them were hopelessly shackled together by some secret bond of guilt and fear . . . First the emperor's chaplain, now the emperor's cousin, claiming to be his fellow conspirators in some desperate venture. Poldarn squeezed his nails into the palm of his hand. He'd tried explaining, and asking; perhaps it was time to take the hint. The pig doesn't stop to ask the slaughterman why the abattoir gate's been left unexpectedly open.)

He yawned. All in all, he'd been happier alone in the dark, with his boot on a stranger's neck. That way, at least, he'd had some measure of control, and he'd been invisible. There was clearly a lot to be said for being nobody nowhere, at least in the short term.

Then, in spite of himself and everything, he fell asleep. If he dreamed, he didn't remember any of it when he woke up, or any splinters of memory sticking into his mind were quickly dislodged by what he saw when he opened his eyes—

—Gotto, still sitting squarely on the box but with his head leaning right back on to his shoulder blades, his throat cut to the bone, blood still glistening black in the fibres of his coat. No sign of anybody else, no horses, just himself, a dead man and – inevitably, inevitably – two crows opening their wings in exasperation as he interrupted them in their work.

Chapter Eleven

The letter was still there; so was his sword. He jumped down from the cart and tried to trace the direction the horses had been driven off in from the hoofprints in the mud, but there was just a confused mess, open to various interpretations. He looked up and down the road, right and left; two choices, back to that old game again. This time at least, he had something to motivate him: the letter, a job to do, his duty to the Falx house, their trust in him . . . He didn't give a damn about the Falx house, but it made a pleasant change to have some reason to do something. On to Mael Bohec, then. Easy.

After he'd been walking for a couple of hours, he saw three men on horses coming down the road towards him. *Not again*, he thought, but when they were close enough for him to see more than an outline he relaxed. There was a large middle-aged man in a red cloak and a broad black felt hat, and two younger men in rather less gorgeous clothes who were almost certainly his sons; the older man was leading a packhorse, unladen (so the chances were that they were on their way home). 'Excuse me,' he called out, 'but can I buy your horse?'

That got their attention. The man in the red cloak introduced himself as Cobo Istin. The other two were Cobo this and Cobo that; Poldarn didn't catch their names, and he got the feeling he wasn't missing much. Yes, Cobo Istin said, he might entertain the idea, provided the price was right. (It was a rather sad horse; it didn't take much imagination to picture the look of amazed joy on the face of Cobo Istin's wife when her husband walked through the door and announced, 'Guess what, I've sold Dobbin!') When Poldarn offered him thirty quarters he said, 'Yes,' without thinking, and his hand shot out like a lizard's tongue to receive the money.

'We haven't got any spare tack,' Cobo Istin added mournfully as soon as his fingers had clamped tight around the coins. 'Otherwise we'd—'

'That's all right,' Poldarn replied. 'I can make up some sort of bridle out of the leading rein.' The expression in his eyes warned Cobo Istin that the leading rein was included in the price; Cobo let the missed opportunity pass with only a slight twitch at the corner of his mouth.

'By the way,' Poldarn continued, 'are you going to Sansory?'

'That's right.'

'Good. I want you to do me a favour. About an hour down the road, you'll find a cart with a dead body in it. When you get to Sansory, send someone over to the Falx house and let them know about it; it's their cart and their dead body. I can't go myself. I've got things to do.'

Cobo Istin looked at him as if to say, *I knew this was too good to be true.* 'Now just a moment,' he said.

'It's all right,' Poldarn sighed. 'Don't if you don't want to. But Falx Roisin usually pays ten per cent salvage when someone helps him get his stuff back. I'd have thought you'd have known that.'

He left Cobo Istin torn between the prospect of still more free money and the threat of getting involved; he felt slightly guilty about ruining the man's day, and he hoped Falx Roisin wouldn't react too noisily if Cobo did show up at the door and start asking for money.

Gotto had mentioned something about a village with an inn and other amenities of civilised life on the road one day out from Mael. Because the horse turned out to be rather less sad than it had looked, Poldarn arrived there just before sunset. The inn wasn't hard to find (it was the first building he came to in the village and it had INN written in big letters on a hanging sign over the door) and the innkeeper was delighted to see him and take his money; as a glimpse of another, entirely different way of living, in which things generally went all right and people were still there and alive the next day, it was all painfully tantalising. For his two and a half quarters he got a stall for the horse, a genuine bed in an otherwise empty room, and a bowl of bean and bacon soup that didn't taste bad at all.

It was raining when he woke up, but nothing horrible or even unusual happened to him all that day, and he reached Mael Bohec in the late afternoon. He'd been expecting it to be another Sansory -- perhaps a little bigger, a little tidier, but basically the same sort of thing. Whether the reality of it came as a pleasant surprise or a shock, he wasn't sure for some time.

Mael Bohec started two or three miles from the walls and gates, at the point where the high, rolling moor dropped down into the flat river valley. Later, he learned that the place was known as the Crow's Nest, after the lookout platform on top of the mast of a ship; from there you could see right down the river as far as the point at which it bent round the foot of Streya, the range of tall, bare-topped hills that separated the Mael valley from Weal and the more favoured country to the west. What struck Poldarn first was the astonishing precision of the roads, walls and hedges of the rich garden country between himself and the city; they all ran for miles in perfectly straight lines, like marks scribed by a skilled craftsman on a sheet of brass. The fields and enclosures and the small woods that made up the chequerboard pattern all looked to be the same size as each other, and arranged in an orderly pattern – five fields down and you came to a hedged lane, five fields across and you came to a drain or a rine; every fifteen fields along, a road, every thirty fields down each road a building; every third field diagonal was fallow, every twelfth field a wood. In the middle of the chequerboard was the perfectly square city, with a gate in the middle of each wall flanked by two identical hexagonal towers and a great square tower on each corner. Even the river was straight, and worked carefully into the pattern so as not to offend regularity or symmetry, since it was balanced on the northern side by the road and a thick line of trees. Whoever designed this place, Poldarn couldn't help thinking, couldn't draw a curve to save his life.

As he went further down the slope, he lost sight of the pattern, and of course it wasn't visible at all once he reached the plain, at which point the flat land on either side of the road became invisible and there was nothing to see except the marching column of trees to his left and the untidy, cloud-smudged hills to the right; all he could do was carry the pattern in his mind and believe in what he'd seen, trusting his memory however improbable it might seem.

He remembered the right-angled spur that left the road and led straight to the northern gate; he took the turning when it presented itself and found himself squarely facing the wall about a mile in front of him, with the two square towers visible at the ends, the gate directly ahead of him in the middle. A blind man could have walked from the road junction to the gate without fear of straying, provided he could walk in a straight line and assuming nobody tripped him up or ran him over.

That would be a major assumption; the spur was crowded with people, on foot, on horseback or in carts and wagons. On the right-hand side of the highway, everybody was heading towards the city, on the left-hand side, they were all coming away from it, so that anybody stupid enough to try walking down the middle would've been cut neatly in two, as by a pair of shears. Virtually all the people, coming and going, were men; most of them were carrying something or leading pack mules or driving carts with broad beds and high sides, laden or unladen, all of them on business, all knowing where they were going and what they were meant to be doing. It was strange, comic, wonderful, intimidating and not a bit like Sansory.

It took him an hour to cover the last hundred yards or so to the gate. The cause of the hold-up turned out to be soldiers, who were searching carts, turning out the contents of panniers and saddlebags, and generally making nuisances of themselves. 'Is it always like this?' he asked the man next to him.

'Or worse,' the man replied. 'It's a Guild town, what do you expect?'

Not wanting to show his ignorance, he didn't ask for an explanation; instead he nodded and sighed, which seemed to do the trick. When it was his turn the soldiers waved him through, and he passed under the gatehouse, past the lodge and out into the foregate.

Inside the walls, it looked a little more like Sansory: the same crowds of people, the same slow bustle as they tried to filter through the narrow places, the same awkwardness and tension. It didn't take him long to start noticing differences, however. For one thing, there were far fewer carts, wagons and carriages, and virtually nobody was on horseback. There were no stalls or booths anywhere; instead, he saw before him what looked like a street of houses, average size by Sansory standards, but with doorways, exactly in the middle of the front elevation, two or three times as wide as Sansory's. In each doorway stood a table, with the merchandise laid out neatly in rows, small objects at the front, large ones at the back. Invariably, a small wooden sign hung over the lintel with the owner's name and trade in neat, rather pointed letters, followed by a number.

As he walked down the street he could see the workshops behind the tables, in each one a workbench, a tool-rack, the specific equipment of each trade, everything neat and tidy and in its place. It struck him that there were rather more shops than customers, but he assumed that was something to do with the time of day, week or year.

The letter inside his shirt was addressed to Cunier Mohac at the Cunier house, close under Northgate. Gotto had interpreted that as meaning due south of the foregate, not far along, on a straight line toward the centre of town. At the time he'd thought that as an address it was rather too vague to be useful, but in Mael Bohec, he soon realised, it was all the information he'd need; substantial buildings, such as commercial houses, stood at every fifth intersection and were clearly named and numbered. Ten blocks down from the gate, he saw 'Cunier Mohac 3771' inscribed in granite over a massive oak door in the exact centre of a large building with no front windows. Success.

There remained the problem of getting inside. He tried hammering on the door, but he guessed from the pain in the side of his fist that the door was three inches thick at the very least, more than enough to soak up any sound he could make. There was a wall round the other three sides, high enough to make climbing it a dangerous experience. Short of digging a sap under the walls like a besieging army, he couldn't think of any way of gaining entry, and that was ridiculous, surely.

When all else fails, ask. He explained his problem to an elderly man who'd been watching him for some time, and asked what he was supposed to do.

The man smiled. 'New in town,' he said.

'That's right.'

'It takes a while to get the hang of Mael Bohec,' the man replied, 'but once you know the ropes it's a wonderfully simple place to live. Look, I'll show you.'

He pointed to a thin slot between the door and the doorpost, just wide enough to slide his little finger into. 'You put your identification in here, see,' he explained, 'Guild ticket, trader's licence, calling tally, warrant, letter of introduction; the porter sees it, checks it against his list of expected visitors and opens the door – unless it's a government warrant or a Guild seal, in which case he doesn't need a name on the appointments list, he's got to open up, it's the law. That's all there is to it.'

Poldarn didn't say what he thought about that. 'I've got a problem, then,' he said. 'I haven't got anything like that.'

The man frowned. 'I thought you said you had business with the house,' he said.

'I have. I've got a letter to deliver.'

The man shrugged. 'There you are, then. I don't see the problem.'

Poldarn shook his head. 'My orders were to give it to Cunier Mohac in person, nobody else. I can't just go shoving it through cracks in doors.'

'Why not?' the old man said. 'This is the Cunier house, it says so over the door.'

Poldarn thought it over for a moment or so and decided what to do. He shoved the letter into the crack and waited. When he felt the pressure of someone on the other side trying to take it from him, he clung on with thumb and forefinger, put his mouth to the crack and said, 'Open up.'

'Let go of the goddamned letter,' said a muffled voice from the other side.

'I can't. Letter for Cunier Mohac's eyes only. Open the damn door.'

'No.'

Ridiculous, Poldarn thought, then the porter tried to snatch the letter with a sudden sharp tug; Poldarn tugged back and saw a vivid mental picture of the paper tearing neatly in two. Fortunately, this prophecy went unfulfilled. 'Cut that out,' he snapped. 'Go and fetch Cunier Mohac. I'll wait.'

The porter sounded horrified. 'I can't do that,' he said. 'He'll be getting ready for dinner.'

'Fine.' Poldarn exaggerated his sigh so the fine nuances wouldn't be lost in three inches of oak. 'Please yourself. I'll go back to Sansory and tell my boss I couldn't deliver the letter because some clown of a porter was afraid of disturbing Cunier Mohac while he was shaving. That'll give you three days' start before they come after you.'

The pull on the letter relaxed, and after a short but noisy interlude while the porter shot back bolts and graunched keys in stiff-sounding locks the door started to open. As soon as he reckoned the crack was wide enough, Poldarn rammed the door with his shoulder and pushed through. The porter was crouched against the lodge wall, hugging his nose.

'What did you want to do that for?' he wailed. 'Look, it's bleeding.'

'I was making a point,' Poldarn replied calmly. 'If I ever have to deliver a letter to this house again, I want to be sure you'll remember me.'

The porter scowled at him, and wiped blood off his lip with his sleeve. 'I could have you taken in charge for that,' he muttered. 'This is a Guild town, you can't just go around beating people up.'

Poldarn grinned. 'Are you sure? I like a challenge.'

'This way,' the porter said, and as soon as he'd locked up again he led the way under the lodge arch into a large quadrangle with grass and a fountain in the middle. Straight ahead were the living quarters, offices and counting-house, elegantly faced in crisply dressed, recently cleaned sandstone; the other three sides were plain brick and windowless except for narrow slits just under the eaves – warehouse space, presumably, though they might possibly be workshops. In the far left-hand corner there was another archway leading to another yard, or a cloister. Poldarn guessed that the quarters for the help were out there, and probably the stables and the coach-house and any specialised buildings needed for whatever trade the Cunier house made its living from – forge, foundry, smokehouse, curing or cutting shed, millhouse, whatever. There was, of course, a corresponding archway in the far right corner. Poldarn could see far enough through the gate to recognise that it was a formal garden.

The front door of the master's quarters opened into a smaller, enclosed version of the courtyard outside; there was a square floor, slabbed with beautifully polished and waxed slate, with doors leading off at the cardinal points and staircases in the corners that gave access to galleries on all four walls. In the exact centre of the floor there was a large round oak table, on which open-topped boxes rested, slanting inwards like the spokes of a wheel. Each box was labelled – letters out, credits, debits (paid), debits (unpaid), requisitions, memoranda, copies archive – and a third full of papers. In the middle of the table stood a life-sized statue of a crow with a ring in its mouth, exquisitely carved out of coal.

'Excuse me,' Poldarn asked the porter as politely as he could after what had passed between them, 'but that statue; is that a family thing or business or what?'

The porter laughed. 'Don't show your ignorance,' he replied. 'That's a shrine. Poldarn, patron god of hearths, forges and useful fires.' He frowned. 'You do know what we do here, don't you?'

Poldarn shrugged. 'No,' he said. 'Didn't need to know, I'm just a courier. Just interested in the statue, that's all.'

The porter headed for the front left-hand staircase. 'Coal and charcoal,' he said. 'Biggest wholesale and retail collier in Weal Bohec.' There was an almost absurd degree of pride in his voice. 'We dig coal in the Juhaim valley, north of the Mahec; we burn charcoal at a dozen camps between the two rivers; we've got seven big stores out of town and two here in Mael, besides the core stock we keep here. One of the biggest houses in Mael, we are, with six seats in Guild chapter and our own chapel in temple.'

'Good for you,' Poldarn replied, trying to sound bored. 'So where's Cunier Mohac? The sooner I can hand over this damned letter, the happier I'll be.'

The porter pulled a face. 'Like I said, he'll be in dinner, in the long hall. You want to disturb him at table, you go right ahead. I'm going back to the lodge.'

'Fair enough,' Poldarn replied. 'Which one of these doors is the long hall?'

The porter pointed to the back wall. 'Go right ahead,' he said. 'The footmen and sergeant will grab you before you've got your nose through the doorway; you can ask them to point Cunier Mohac out to you, that's assuming you don't do something to upset them and get your throat cut.'

'All right,' Poldarn said. 'Purely out of interest, what sort of thing do they find upsetting?'

'Oh, all manner of things. You'll find out soon enough.'

As it turned out, the guards didn't grab him, because he stopped as soon as he got through the door and didn't intrude on their circle. 'Letter for Cunier Mohac,' he said, 'urgent.'

A man in rather splendid blue and white livery held out his hand. 'I'll see he gets it,' he said.

Poldarn shook his head. 'Thanks for the offer,' he said, 'but I've got my orders, same as you.'

The guard didn't like that. 'He's busy,' he said. 'He's eating his dinner.'

'Fine. Let me give him this letter, then I can go and have mine. I haven't eaten for two days, and hunger makes me short-tempered.'

Another man in the same livery joined them. 'Keep the noise down, will you?' he said. 'They can hear you at table.'

'Man says he's got a letter for the chief,' the first guard explained in a tone of voice that suggested that he was reporting to a superior. 'He says it's urgent and he's got to hand it over himself.'

'I'll take it to him,' the other guard said. 'Happy with that?'

'No,' Poldarn replied.

Over the guard's shoulder Poldarn could see a long, substantial table with about two dozen people sitting round it. All the people whose faces he could see were staring in his direction.

'Oh, for God's sake,' the second guard muttered. 'All right, but you'll have to give me your sword. Or you can leave; or I can make you eat it. Your choice.'

Poldarn shrugged and took the sword from his belt. The guard laid it down on the table, then stepped in front of him. 'Follow me,' he said, and as Poldarn did as he was told the first guard fell in just behind his right shoulder. They were cautious people in the Cunier house.

The man at the head of the table had his back to them; he was talking to the woman on his left, apparently the only person in the room who hadn't been watching the proceedings at the door. The guard waited for him to turn his head.

'I'm very sorry,' the guard said to him, 'but there's a courier here, insists on delivering a letter personally. He says it's urgent.'

Cunier Mohac nodded. He was short but wide, noticeably broad across the shoulders, with a bald patch like a desert island in the middle of his thick, curly grey hair. He looked briefly at Poldarn and held out his hand for the letter. 'Wait there, would you?' he said as he took it. 'In case there's a reply.'

Poldarn watched as he broke the seal. He couldn't read the writing from where he was standing; all he could see was that the letter was short, only three lines long. Somehow that annoyed him. He thought he could make out the name Tazencius, but it could easily have been something else.

'Excellent,' Cunier Mohac said at last. 'Best news I've had all week. Pen, somebody.'

Another man in livery materialised beside him, holding a tray with an inkwell, pen, dish of sand, bar of wax and miniature oil lamp. Cunier Mohac laid the letter down on the table and wrote a few words underneath the original message, sprinkled it with sand and shook it clear, folded it and sealed it with a big fat ring he wore on his left thumb. 'No copy,' he told the man who'd brought the tray. 'Get the messenger something to eat and drink, find him somewhere to sleep. Oh, and give him fifty quarters for doing as he was told.'

The rest of the table were still staring. Nobody had spoken. If their expressions were anything to go by, they'd never witnessed such an extraordinary scene in their lives.

As he escorted Poldarn to the counting-house to get his money, the guard's attitude was rather less abrasive. 'You got any idea what was in that letter?' he asked a second time. (Poldarn had apparently not heard him the first time.)

'No. None of my business.'

The guard nodded. 'All right,' he said, 'but what line of business is your house in?'

'Shipping, transport, carrying messages.'

'Oh. So the letter may have been from somebody else, and you lot were just delivering it.'

'Highly likely.'

The guard frowned as he waited for his knock on the door to be answered. 'Ah come on,' he said. 'Are you trying to tell me you're not curious?'

'I suppose I am, yes.'

Fifty quarters, in a dear little red velvet purse, duly changed hands. 'Sign here,' the paymaster said. Poldarn took the pen without thinking, then realised that he didn't know whether he could write.

'What's the matter?' the paymaster said.

'Nothing.' Poldarn leaned over and made a conscious effort to stop trying to remember. He closed his eyes and moved his hand; it moved as if guided by the grooves of a stencil, but when he looked to see the name he'd written he saw only three loops and a squiggle.

The paymaster was looking at him curiously. 'There,' he said, 'that wasn't so bad, was it?'

'Sorry,' Poldarn replied, 'my mind just went blank for a moment, you know how it is.'

The guard led him across the yard and through the left-side arch into the far yard, which, as he'd guessed, was where the bunkhouses were. 'Guest quarters are the loft over the stables,' he said, ducking under a low doorway. 'They're all right, if you don't mind horse smells.'

Poldarn hadn't been expecting luxury so he wasn't disappointed. There was a plain plank bed, a chair and a window looking out over the yard; no lamp, but so what? 'Thanks,' he said to the guard, expecting him to go away. But he seemed inclined to linger and talk. Poldarn had no problem with that, either.

'That was quite something, the way you good as kicked the door down,' the guard was saying. 'Good fun to watch, but take my advice and don't make a habit of it, not in Meal. Not that kind of place.'

Poldarn nodded. 'All straight lines,' he said, 'nothing curved. Looks good from a distance but I don't think it'd suit me for very long. Now then,' he went on, before the guard could answer, 'maybe you can tell me something.'

'I can try,' the guard said cautiously.

'Fine. I'm new in these parts, as you've probably guessed. Who's a man called Tazencius?'

The guard looked puzzled, then laughed. 'You're serious? Guess you are new in town, at that. Tazencius was the prefect of Mael, right up to the beginning of last week. Why, what about him?'

'I heard the name somewhere, that's all,' Poldarn replied. 'Would you recognise him if you saw him?'

The guard nodded. 'Of course. Anybody who goes to

temple knows what Tazencius looks like. Smart, he always was. He had his stall built right under the skylight at the northern end of the transept so that during evensong, when it was his time to make the address, the light'd be coming through the window and catching him just right. Real impressive it was, even when you knew it was all put on.'

Poldarn smiled. 'I can believe that,' he said. 'About medium height but looks taller, middle to late forties, touch of grey in the hair but one of those faces that doesn't change much after about twenty-five; sharp nose and chin, big eyes like a horse—'

'That's him,' the guard confirmed.

'Ah, right.' Poldarn thought for a moment. 'So what happened last week?'

The guard grinned. 'Wish I knew,' he said. 'The official line – well, first it was he'd been promoted and called back to Torcea; then it was recalled to Torcea, which isn't quite the same thing as called back, and nothing about any promotion. Then there were all these rumours going around about how he'd been arrested – troop of cavalry sent specially from Boc to pick him up, only captured after desperate chase, running battle between his guards and the soldiers, you know how these things snowball. Then it was official that he was going back to Torcea to testify in front of some board of enquiry, which is just polite for "arrested". Then we started hearing all kinds of wild stuff about a big conspiracy, some stuff about the royal chaplain, Cleapho – can't see what he'd have to do with anything myself, but that's what they were saying – and then you started hearing Feron Amathy all over the place – you know, the big bandit captain – and soon they were linking him with General Cronan, who supposedly hasn't been seen or heard of in months. Last thing was that Tazencius had been rescued by the Amathy house, and either they'd got him back or he'd got away; nobody's said he's dead yet, which is odd, you usually get that when someone's arrested. Anyway, you take your pick. Something's been going on with him, but God only knows what.'

'What do you think?' Poldarn asked.

The guard pulled a face, presumably intended to convey thoughtfulness. 'My guess is he ticked off the Guild once too often,' he said. 'He was always pulling their tail, after all. But this is a Guild town and Torcea's a long way away. If the emperor's whisked him away back to Torcea, it could be for his own good. After all, they're family. Not that Tazencius was ever anybody back at the royal court,' he added, 'just some second cousin getting under people's feet. He'd never have ended up out here if he mattered worth a damn. Come to think of it, I seem to remember something about there having been bad blood between him and Cronan years ago, before the Allectus business, even; if that's true, he's lucky he's still alive.'

Poldarn nodded, as if turning it over in his mind. 'So where would the emperor's chaplain – Cleapho, did you say his name was? Where would he fit into all this?'

The guard shrugged. 'No idea,' he said. 'I think that was just somebody's imagination. Though I've heard it said that Cleapho's quite a big man behind the scenes at court; used to be thick as thieves with the emperor's brother, then switched sides after he lucked out and started running Cronan instead. Now if there really was anything going on with Tazencius and Cronan and the Amathy outfit, I suppose Cleapho might be in the middle of it somewhere.' He grinned. 'Who knows what the hell's really going on?' he said. 'Who cares, come to that, so long as they don't start another war.'

'Quite,' Poldarn said. 'Only that might be on the cards sooner than you'd think, if you believe what they're saying, about the god coming back and everything.'

'That?' The guard laughed. 'You don't believe in all that garbage, do you? Strictly for the woollybacks, that stuff.'

'Maybe.' Poldarn shrugged the subject away. 'Just out of

interest,' he said, 'is there any chance of getting something to eat?'

'At this time?' The guard stared at him for a moment. 'Sorry, I forgot, you're from out of town. No food or drink after sundown; it's the law.'

'You're joking.'

'No I'm not,' the guard replied, and Poldarn could see him consciously not taking offence. 'This is a Guild town, remember. Late-night eating and drinking leads to drunks fighting in the streets. We don't hold with that kind of thing in Mael.'

Poldarn breathed in, then out again. 'Fair enough,' he said, 'only I haven't eaten anything since this time yesterday. Nobody would know.'

'Don't you believe it,' the guard replied. 'Thirty days in the lock-up if you're caught, doesn't matter who you are. You're better off going to sleep and dreaming about breakfast.'

So Poldarn went to sleep; and perhaps because he was hungry, or because the guard had suggested it to him—

—He was sitting at the head of a table in a large tent, looking at the plate that someone had just put in front of him. A thick slab of bacon, old, cold and shiny; a narrow, deep wedge of hard, almost translucent yellow cheese; something else, either a piece of bread or a bit of broken grindstone, he couldn't be sure which; a small apple, with a skin like an old man's cheeks.

'Oh, for crying out loud,' he heard himself say. 'Hisco, this isn't fit for pigs.'

'With respect—' Hisco was the man standing behind him, who'd just put down the plate. 'With respect, that's all there is, and you're lucky to have that.'

'Hisco, you sound like my mother. What happened to all that white cream cheese we took out of that village down the valley?'

Hisco, still unseen, clicked his tongue. 'It'd gone bad,' he said, 'so I slung it out. I'd rather starve than be poisoned, thanks very much.'

'Hisco, it's *supposed* to taste like that, it's a fucking *delicacy* . . . You know how much you'd pay for a pound of that stuff in Weal Bohec?'

'The men wouldn't touch it,' Hisco replied. 'Talking of which, that's the last of the bacon. Tomorrow it'll be oatmeal and dried fish. You may want to think about that.'

He turned round in his chair, but Hisco had gone; the tent flap swished behind him. 'Bloody cook,' he said bitterly. 'Dumps a thousand quarters' worth of Mausandy cheese and threatens me with oatmeal. I ought to stick his head up on a pike.'

'It'd be good for morale,' a man three places down from him replied. 'But he was right about the cheese. We thought something had died in the wagons.'

'Barbarians. Oh well, I suppose we'd better eat this, or we'll never hear the last of it.' He pulled his napkin out of the ring – dark rosewood, carved in relief with a design of two crows holding something in their beaks; the carving was too worn for him to be able to make out the details. 'Somebody tell me there's some beer left, or I'll burst into tears.'

Someone else passed him a tall silver jug; it matched the long-stemmed goblets and the side plates. All solid silver, every inch embossed and gadrooned. He took a sip and nearly spat it out.

'That does it,' he said. 'Cold greasy bacon I can live with, but this is beyond a joke. Get me the map, someone.'

They were all dressed in the most dazzling array of silks, brocades, velvets, linens that you'd ever hope to see outside the imperial court; the effect was spoiled slightly by the characteristic red-brown half-moons left behind by rusty chainmail after a week of continuous wear. Someone reached under the table and produced a bronze tube, two feet long by six inches wide. He fished inside it and pulled out the map.

'Right,' he said, 'we're here. There's the river and there's the mountains – no, that's wrong, they're further away than that. This map's useless.'

Someone laughed. 'Imperial survey,' he said. 'In cases where the terrain doesn't agree with the map, standing orders state that the terrain must be in error.'

He clicked his tongue. 'Tell me about it,' he said. 'All right; ignoring the fact that the mountains have been sleepwalking, there's a village about half a day downstream, between this wood here – oh, for pity's sake, there isn't a wood there, we'd have seen it.'

'Old map,' the other man replied. 'Probably the wood's been felled for charcoal long since.'

'Yes, maybe. According to this map, there's a village. It's a good step out of our way, but there's nothing else this side of the river; and I don't see why we can't cut back up the other side of this combe here and get back on the road that way. Assuming the village is there, of course. If it isn't, we'll be in big trouble, since at best we'll lose a day and a half.'

'There's still the oatmeal,' someone put in. 'Sure, we'll get a bit of attitude, but we won't starve.'

He scowled. 'Besco, Besco, you don't command the loyalty and love of an army by feeding them oatmeal. No, the question is whether we can trust this stupid map. What d'you reckon?'

Silence. Then the man at the other end of the table, who hadn't spoken yet, put down his cup. 'Should be all right, Feron,' he said. 'Those maps were originally drawn for the revenue, remember. They may get the hills and rivers wrong, but they're usually pretty careful about marking the taxpayers. The only problem would be if Allectus has been there before us.'

He rubbed his chin. 'That's a good point, Mashant,' he said. 'Hadn't thought of that. Still, it's unlikely. We've got him figured as crossing the river much further up; he'll have filled his boots at Josequin, so he won't need to go stocking up in the villages.'

Mashant shrugged. 'I suppose not,' he said. 'Anyway, I don't think we've got much choice in the matter. If we're down to the oatmeal already, we'll just have to risk it.'

'It'll be all right,' he said cheerfully.

Mashant laughed. 'I'll say this for you, Feron,' he said, 'nobody could ever say you aren't decisive.'

After he'd choked down the bacon and cheese (he couldn't face the bread or the poisonous beer), he took another look at the map, with nobody peering over his shoulder. Things were starting to fall apart, mostly because he still hadn't heard from either Allectus or Cronan. It was enough to make a man paranoid; what if they'd figured out what he was up to, and were deliberately letting him kick his heels and starve while they patched up their differences before coming after him? Absurd, of course; that would be making the fatal mistake of assuming your enemies think the way you do. But it was enough to drive a man crazy, marking time like this, knowing he was down to his last few days' supplies (and the fact that nobody else seemed to have noticed that before today was hardly reassuring; the deadheads who were supposed to be running the commissary were in for a nasty surprise when the crisis was over and he had a bit of time again).

He scowled at the map, picked off a bit of frayed vellum from the edge. He really did have better things to do right now than go raiding villages for food. Quite apart from the detour, the loss of position, the risk of something going wrong, someone getting away, he didn't like the thought of doing something like this with not one but two imperial armies breathing down his neck. True, the armies were fighting each other, but they were still imperials, and both Cronan and Allectus were dutiful, honourable men, just the sort who'd leave their own war hanging in order to go chasing off after a party of raiders, if they heard there was one operating nearby . . .

It was cold, in spite of the two heaped-up braziers; he rubbed his cheeks with his palms to warm them. Part of him couldn't really believe that neither Cronan nor Allectus had yet figured out that half the attacks attributed to the raiders were the work of the Amathy house – how could they get to command armies and still be that naive? But they were imperials, Torceans, southerners; things were different down there – not better, he was sure of that, but the treachery took different forms, was played to different rules, some of which, no doubt, he'd be too naive to spot if he ever crossed the bay. No chance of that, if he had anything to do with it.

He was just rolling the map up again and thinking vague, disjointed thoughts about a variety of issues when the tent flap was folded back and a man put his head through it. 'Letter,' he said.

He looked round. 'Fine, thanks,' he said, making a point of keeping the excitement out of his voice. 'Just put it down on the chair, I'll deal with it in a minute.'

The head looked embarrassed. 'Sorry,' it said, 'but the courier says he's got to give it to you personally; orders and so forth. We tried to take it off him, but . . .'

He noticed that the head had a swollen lower lip. He managed not to smile. 'All right,' he said. 'Show him in.'

'You sure?' the guard asked. 'I mean—'

'You mean he could be an assassin pretending to be a courier.' He grinned. 'Don't worry about it, I could use the practice.'

But he wasn't an assassin, just a very thorough, dedicated courier, the kind that costs an obscene amount of money and is worth every quarter. And it was the letter he'd been waiting for.

'It's all right,' he told the guards, who were standing nervously at the back of the tent, their hands on their sword hilts. 'Thank you,' he said to the courier. 'Go and get a beer, then come back. There'll be a reply.'

The letter was, typically, short and to the point;

Cleapho, touched by the Divine, to Feron Amathy,
merchant; greetings, good health &c.

   Concerning the small point of doctrine you queried at
our last meeting; the Desert school, and Thauscus in
particular, held the view that the rising sun conveyed more
blessings on the observer than the setting sun, since it was
hotter, having come straight from the divine forge, and
more malleable, having not yet been quenched in the sea.
Both the Desert school and the Ascetics held that it was
inadvisable to wait until noon to look directly at the sun,
and the latter party attributed great virtues to observation
carried out just after sunrise, at the point when the sun's
heat dries up the morning dew. I trust that this clarifies the
matter to your satisfaction.

He grinned; Cleapho had a nice way of putting things, for a
Torcean. And it was the answer he'd wanted: side with Cronan
against Allectus and do it soon, before Allectus had a chance to
get established north of the Mahec. He scouted around for his
inkwell and pen and a piece of paper, and wrote:

Feron Amathy, merchant venturer, to Cleapho, touched by
the Divine; greetings, good health &c.

   Thauscus is, of course, an excellent authority, and your
point about the Ascetics is well made. I seem to remember
something in Pevannio's commentary about the moment
just before the sun breaks through the clouds being the most
auspicious time for reading auguries and casting lots; do
you think that might have any bearing on the matter?

He sprinkled sand and sealed it up, called for the guard—

'Wake up.' The guard was standing over him, calling him.
'It's after sun-up, for God's sake, you should be on the road by
now.'

'What?' Poldarn rolled over. 'Oh, right. Sorry, I was having a dream—'

The guard scowled at him. 'Do it on your own time,' he said. 'Cunier Mohac wants that reply on its way as soon as possible. You've missed breakfast,' he added with a definite touch of malice.

'Have I? Damn.' Poldarn yawned. 'No chance the kitchen could put me up something for the road, is there? Or would that be against the law too?'

The guard shrugged. 'I'll ask,' he said, 'no promises. Depends on whether they've thrown the scraps out for the crows yet. I told the stables to get your horse ready, there may just be time. It'll be bread and cold bacon if they can manage it, maybe a slice of cheese if you're lucky.'

'That'll do,' Poldarn said. 'I'm not fussy.'

Chapter Twelve

'Terrible,' said Falx Roisin, looking up from the column of figures he was working on. 'He'd been with the house sixteen years. I'll miss him.' He frowned, and drew a little line on the ledger to mark where he'd got up to in the sum. 'And you're sure it was just bandits?'

'That's right,' Poldarn replied. 'As soon as they attacked, I ran for it, and they didn't seem at all interested in me.'

Falx Roisin nodded. 'It was the right thing to do,' he said. 'The letter was far more important than the cargo – that's what insurance is for, after all, though in this case . . . It just strikes me as odd that they didn't actually take anything.'

Poldarn shrugged. 'Maybe they decided they didn't want twelve barrels of copper rivets,' he said.

'Maybe. But they're worth good money, there's a shortage. Of course, they may not have known that.' Falx Roisin rubbed the tip of his nose with the palm of his hand, an indication of serious thought. 'Now if they'd hit you on the way back, they'd have got a nice sum in cash and twenty bales of best Mahec valley wool. That's good,' he added, 'implies they don't have a source of information inside the house. At least, not this particular outfit. No way of knowing how many gangs there are working that stretch of road.' He glanced down at his figures, then looked up again. 'Mind you,' he said, 'it's also possible they thought Gatto was the courier, not you. Anyway, no use crying over spilt milk, as my mother used to say.'

Poldarn nodded. The dead man's name was Gotto, not Gatto; Poldarn had only known him for a couple of days, not sixteen years. Still, when it came to a good memory for names, he was hardly in a position to criticise someone else. 'Maybe it was just the horses they were after,' he said, for the sake of saying something.

'Didn't you hear?' Falx Roisin looked at him for a moment. 'We found the horses, they'd just been run off, not stolen. Hadn't gone far, either. Now there's another thing. All right, they didn't want the rivets, so they left them. But why unyoke the horses and run them off? Doesn't make sense.'

'Maybe they panicked,' Poldarn said. 'People do all sorts of weird things when they panic.'

'Maybe,' Falx Roisin replied. 'Not that I'm complaining, mind. After all that, we didn't lose the shipment, or the cart, or the horses. It's just a terrible tragedy about poor Gatto, that's all.'

Poldarn left him to his grief and went for a walk. In the back of his mind he was still a little worried about wandering about the town, just in case any of the men who'd broken up his meeting with Cleapho were still hanging around, but they weren't watching the gates now, as he'd proved when he'd passed through on his way to Mael Bohec, and since he didn't really have a clue who they were or what they wanted, it seemed pointless to spend the rest of his life hiding from them.

Nothing to do for the rest of the day, money in his pocket and all the delights of Sansory to explore. Having thought about it for a while, he decided that the only thing he really wanted was a new coat, to replace the one he'd given to the man who'd called himself Tazencius; he supposed he could go and get a replacement from the bins in Eolla's storeroom, but the idea didn't appeal to him. Just for once, it'd be nice to have something that hadn't previously belonged to someone who'd died by violence.

Buying a coat in Sansory turned out to be far more complicated than he'd imagined. At times it seemed as if the whole city was made up of clothiers' stalls, every single one of them cheaper than the last, all of them offering a better, brighter, warmer, more exactingly specified product for a fraction of the price of the one he'd just looked at and decided to buy. As if that wasn't bad enough, he found out that the act of standing in silent thought between the rows of stalls in the market was enough to attract swarms of tailors, who swooped down on him from their shops and booths like crows on a dead body and swore blind they could make him the coat of his dreams to measure for a third of what he'd pay for some piece of off-the-peg rag. Since all the coats he saw looked perfectly good and excellent value for money, he was soon utterly bewildered and bitterly regretting getting involved in such a horrendously complex issue. By noon, he'd almost resolved to give it up and make do with anything Eolla offered him that didn't have a brown-edged hole exactly halfway between the shoulder blades. Instead he bought a pancake and a mug of cider from a sad-looking man behind a barrow and sat down on the corn exchange steps to rest his aching feet.

From where he was sitting he had a clear view down a row of stalls. The stuff on them wasn't anything that interested him much – luxury fabrics, mostly, with some jewellery and almost-jewellery, a couple of men behind benches mounted with lasts who presumably made women's shoes, one or two specialising in mirrors and combs and boxes to put them in—

He looked back, and frowned. Then he swallowed the last of his pancake, got up, returned the empty mug to the man

behind the barrow (who looked sadly at him but didn't seem
to hold a grudge) and made his way down the alley until he
came to the stall he'd noticed where a woman was arranging a
display of mirrors.

'Copis?' he said.

Copis looked up at him. 'Oh,' she said, 'it's you. Hello.'

For some reason, she didn't seem particularly pleased to
see him. She leaned out over the table and looked up and down
the alley to see if anybody was watching, then scowled at him
and said, 'You can't have it back.'

That threw him. 'Have what back?' he asked.

'Don't be stupid,' she said. 'Your great big lump of solid
gold, of course, the one you hid in the back of my cart.
Bastard.'

He really couldn't see the logic. 'What's the matter?' he
said. 'What did I do?'

She looked daggers at him. 'All that bullshit about having
lost your memory. I believed you, you creep, I was actually
sorry for you. And all that time you were using me as cover to
get past whoever you stole that thing from. No wonder people
were forever trying to kill us.'

It took him a moment to catch his breath. 'It wasn't like
that—' he said.

'Well,' she went on, 'the laugh's on you now, because I
sold it and I've spent all the money – stock for this business,
for one thing, and a house, which has got my name on the
deeds and there's absolutely nothing you can do about it,
and the rest's where you'll never find it, and it wouldn't do
you any good if you did. So if you're here to make trouble,
forget it.'

He couldn't help grinning. 'Is that it?' he said.

'What?'

'That's what you're so upset about? Keep it. All yours. I was
going to share it with you anyway, but somehow I never got
round—'

'Oh sure.' She looked quite angry. 'I believe you. You were waiting for my birthday, I expect, or All Fools' Day. Damn it, I could've been killed.'

'Yes,' Poldarn said, 'but it wasn't anything to do with that lump of gold. I found it.'

She pulled a face. 'You found it,' she repeated.

'Yes. You remember that burned-out temple, in the town where they'd cut down all the trees? It was in there. I tripped over it in the dark. I didn't steal it from anybody, or at least not anybody living.'

'I don't believe you,' she said.

'Why not? Come on,' he added, 'think. Was I carrying anything when you found me?'

'It was dark,' she reminded him. 'You could've crept up and hidden anything you liked in the back of the cart, I wouldn't have noticed.'

'Could I? I was too busy killing your friend.' He shook his head and took a step back. 'It's just as I've told you,' he said. 'I found it in that temple place. And I was going to tell you about it; I nearly did, several times, but—'

'But you didn't trust me.' She was scowling again. 'That's rich. Coming from you. *You* didn't trust *me*.'

Poldarn smiled. 'Ah,' he said. 'So now you do believe me?'

'I didn't say that. All I'm saying is, if you are telling the truth, then you're still a bastard. And you aren't getting any of the money, either way. Understood?'

'Perfectly.'

She looked at him. 'That's all right, then.' She reached out and adjusted the position of a mirror that wasn't exactly in line with the others. It reminded Poldarn of Mael Bohec. 'Just so long as we're clear on that.' There was a moment of rather awkward silence; then she burst out, 'So what the hell happened to you? I was convinced you were either dead or arrested. All those soldiers running about the place, and they brought out at least four dead bodies.'

Poldarn shrugged. 'I'll be honest with you, I have no idea,' he said. 'Cleapho knew who I was, but a bunch of soldiers burst in before I could find anything out. The really strange thing was, one of them knew me too.'

'So? What did he tell you? The soldier, I mean.'

Poldarn looked away. 'There wasn't time to ask him, either.'

'Oh, for pity's sake. You mean to tell me you haven't found out anything?'

'Enough to convince me that whatever I was mixed up in, I'm better off out of it.'

'God, what an attitude!' Copis stared at him, then shook her head. 'If it was me, I'd do anything to find out who I was, I just couldn't bear not knowing. Are you really trying to tell me you simply aren't interested any more?'

Poldarn smiled, and stepped aside to allow a customer to get at the table. But the customer turned out not to be a customer, just one of those strange but ubiquitous people who picks things up off stalls, glances at the underneath and puts them back again. 'How shall I put it?' he said. 'Who's the worst person you can possibly think of?'

'What?'

'Go on, it's a simple question. Who's the nastiest, most evil man who ever lived?'

'How should I know?'

Poldarn scowled. 'In your opinion, then, who's the worst man who ever lived? Just say a name.'

'All right. General Allectus.'

'Really?' Poldarn raised an eyebrow. 'Was he that bad?'

'No,' Copis admitted, 'but you were rushing me. All right; the leader of the raiders. Emperor Vectigal. The Boc Bohec scythe murderer. Feron Amathy. My stepfather.'

'Thank you,' Poldarn said. 'Now, supposing I was one of them – Emperor Vectigal, say, whoever he was – but I'd lost my memory, and after a month or so of wandering about I settled down, got a job and started a new and reasonably happy

life. If you were me, would you want to know who you really
were?'

Copis frowned. 'I wouldn't want to be Emperor Vectigal,'
she said. 'Because he's dead. And before that he was a man. Of
course, he was also the emperor, so I could probably have got
used to it after a while.' Before Poldarn could protest, she
nodded. 'Yes,' she said, 'I can see what you're getting at. But
the odds against it are pretty damn huge, you turning out to be
some kind of evil monster. Chances are you're just some ordinary man, with a wife and kids and a nice house somewhere.
Can you really say you don't want to find out about them?'

Poldarn shook his head. 'Not worth the risk,' he said. 'Since
we – well, went our separate ways, I've got a job and a place to
live, I can start thinking about the possibility of having a
future, instead of a past I can't even remember.'

'Really,' Copis said. 'So what's this wonderful job of yours?'

'I'm a courier for the Falx house.'

Probably, Copis' attempt not to laugh was genuine, though
completely unsuccessful. 'And that's your idea of a future, is
it?'

'It's better than nothing.'

'Oh, come *on* . . . Look, I've been in this town exactly as
long as you have, and even I've learned that only real, desperate, suicidal losers end up as couriers for the Falx house. It's
what you do if you're tired of life but you're too thick to tie a
knot in a rope to hang yourself by.' She paused, and her
expression changed slightly. 'You aren't really doing that, are
you?'

'Yes,' Poldarn replied irritably. 'And it's not so bad. In fact,
it suits me fine. Nice quiet life, getting out and about, seeing
the countryside. Good money, all found—'

'You must be the one who had his driver killed the other
day,' Copis interrupted. 'It's all over town. That's your idea of
a nice quiet life, is it?'

'All right,' Poldarn admitted with a sigh, 'so it wasn't a very

auspicious start. But it can't be like that all the time. I'll bet
you nothing even remotely interesting's going to happen to me
next time out, or the time after that, or the time after that. It'll
be just fine, you'll see.'

Copis looked at him, then pulled a horrible face. 'Oh, all
right, then,' she said wearily. 'I suppose I'd feel really guilty if
you went out and got your throat cut, and I've got all your
money. I can get you four hundred quarters by this time
tomorrow—'

'No.' Poldarn realised he'd shouted, and lowered his voice.
'No,' he said, 'I don't want you to, really. At the rate I'm
going, I'll be able to save up enough money to look after
myself in no time at all. I've already got the best part of seventy quarters, and I haven't even been trying.'

'Don't be ridiculous,' Copis said, sounding like somebody's
mother. 'You can't go risking your life like that, I'm not having
it. There's plenty of money for both of us – eighteen hundred
quarters; have you got any idea how much money eighteen
hundred quarters is?'

'No,' Poldarn said quietly, 'but I can guess. Was it really
worth that much?'

Copis nodded. 'Pure gold, twelve points above imperial
standard; they haven't coined in that stuff for a hundred years.
And I was ripped off; I got paid for the weight in modern coin
metal, so you can add a fifth at least for what it was really
worth. But I was in a hurry.'

Poldarn thought for a moment then shook his head.
'Doesn't matter,' he said. 'I still don't want it, I wouldn't feel
right about it. I guess I must be superstitious or something.'

'More fool you, then,' Copis said, and he could tell that
she was offended. 'I won't offer again, and since I'll probably
be clearing out of here and heading back to Torcea—'

'That's fine,' Poldarn said, surprising himself by his own
vehemence. 'Good idea. I think you should get away from
here, go somewhere you'll be safe. I'd feel much better—'

'You want me to go.' She was positively angry now. 'Fine, I'll go. Now get lost, you're scaring my customers away.'

'All right,' Poldarn said. 'But for what it's worth, I'm very glad you're all right. You helped me out when I needed it; you deserve a bit of luck.'

'Drop dead,' Copis said.

He walked down the alley without looking round, and fairly soon he found himself in another area of the market where they sold excellent coats dirt cheap. This time he decided not to bother looking round and bought the first one he found that fitted. It was dark grey, with strings at the neck and a hood, some sort of blanket material, his for nine and a half quarters including the buttons.

On his way back to the Falx house, he heard a noise up ahead and saw that a crowd was gathering, watching something go by. It turned out to be a cart, very much like the one Copis had owned; it was being escorted by four cavalrymen in brightly polished helmets and breastplates, and in it sat a man and a woman, looking very frightened, covered with bruises, dried blood and dirt. The bystanders were yelling and jeering, and if they weren't throwing things it was only for fear of hitting the cavalrymen and being arrested.

'What's going on?' Poldarn asked the old woman he was standing next to.

'They caught 'em,' she replied with obvious satisfaction, 'and now they'll be tried and strung up, and a bloody good job. Hanging's too good for 'em, I say.'

'Really?' Poldarn caught sight of their faces again between the heads and shoulders of the crowd. 'What've they done?'

'You don't know?' (He was getting thoroughly sick of hearing those words, but he put up with it.) 'They're the two imposters who've been going all round the place in that cart, pretending to be the god and his priestess, the bastards. Asking for trouble, that is; they ought to be ashamed of themselves. And cheating honest folk out of their money and food. It's disgusting.'

Poldarn pursed his lips. 'What happened?' he said. 'How did they catch them?'

The old woman grinned. 'Got careless, didn't they?' she said. 'Tried the same trick in the same village twice. Only someone noticed there was something odd the second time, like they hadn't realised they'd been there before – well, a god'd know that sort of thing, wouldn't he? – and there happened to be a squad of the Company men riding through, so the village people turned 'em over and the Company men brought them here. There's a judge here, see, and a regular court, all legal and everything. And now they'll be strung up, and good riddance. I did hear tell there was a reward on them, but nobody said anything about who's paying it or why. Still, doesn't matter, does it? Main thing is, they're going to get what's coming to them.'

By the time she'd finished saying that the cart was out of sight and the crowd was too thick to allow him to catch up and take another look at their faces. That was probably just as well.

He got back to the Falx house about mid-afternoon to find the place in more or less complete chaos. Two carts were jammed solid in the gateway; the hub of one cart's offside front wheel was caught between the spokes of the other cart's nearside back wheel, perfectly immobilising both carts, and there was so little space left between the pillars of the arch that the house carpenters couldn't get in to cut them apart. Ignoring the protests of the carpenters, carters and sundry bystanders, Poldarn hopped up on to the boom of the outgoing cart, walked down it as far as the box, ducked under the arch and jumped off the tailgate at the other side. There was hardly enough room to jump down into; there was a line of a dozen carts wedged into the courtyard, so close that the tailgate of each one was pressing on the chests of the lead horses of the one behind. It might have been possible to clear the jam by backing the last cart in the line up into the coach-house, except that the coach-house doors opened outwards . . . On either side of the line waited men with barrows and handcarts, unable to cross from one side of the yard to the other.

Falx Roisin was standing on the box of one of the stuck carts, his hands clawing his hair. He gave the impression of having gone beyond the shouting stage and the all-right-let's-figure-this-out-calmly stage and was most of the way through the prayer stage. Eolla was standing in the doorway of the main house, yelling unheeded directions at a group of men who were trying to do something complicated with ropes and scaffolding poles. (Later, Poldarn found out that he'd been told to set up an A-frame crane to try and lift out one of the carts, thereby freeing up the others; Falx Roisin had realised how incredibly stupid and dangerous this idea was about three minutes after giving the order and had countermanded it; the clerk given the task of calling it off had told the men assigned to winch duty, but had forgotten to tell Eolla and his men. Fortuitously, they didn't even get as far as fetching the poles out of the store; otherwise, there could easily have been a nasty accident.)

Poldarn wriggled his way through the crowded yard and climbed up into the loft above the counting-house, where he had a good view of the whole thing. He lay there propped up on his elbows for half an hour, then went back down the stairs and pushed and clambered his way through to the cart Falx Roisin was standing on.

'Can I make a suggestion?' he said.

'What?' Falx Roisin looked down, staring at him as if he'd just grown an extra head. 'Yes, why not, every other bugger has, that's how we got in this mess to start with.'

'Right,' Poldarn replied. 'Here's what you've got to do.'

It took longer to explain the plan than it should have done, mostly because Falx Roisin kept interrupting and jumping forward to incorrect conclusions. When he'd finally finished his explanation, Falx Roisin scowled, closed his eyes for a moment and said, 'Oh, the hell with it, yes, give it a try. It's that or burn the whole place down and start again. You realise we've been stuck like this since just after breakfast?'

Phase one, which should have been the easiest part, turned out to be the hardest, or at least the most annoying, yet all it comprised was getting twelve men and some tools and equipment (spades, shovels, pickaxes, shauls, crowbars, buckets, planks of wood, saws, hammers, nails) out through the gate the way Poldarn had just come in. Why it was so difficult, Poldarn wasn't sure, even after he'd done it.

Phase two was digging a vertical shaft eight feet deep by four feet square. The Falx house had some fine diggers among its members, as well as four thoroughly competent carpenters, and the shaft was dug, braced and boarded in no time at all. There was a pause between the completion of phase two and the start of phase three, while Poldarn and a couple of men he didn't know but who seemed to reckon they knew something about mining operations tried to figure out a way of making sure phase five came up in the right place. The negotiations were fraught from the outset, and Poldarn eventually resolved them by unexpectedly applying the heel of his hand to the chin of one of the experts; after which, the other expert went away and left him in peace to do his calculations.

He'd expected phase three to be a real cow – digging a shaft four feet square and six feet long four feet under the gatehouse floor – but in the end it was no bother at all; the diggers dug, the dirt-haulers lifted out the spoil in buckets, while the carpenters cut and shaped the props and rammed them home. Phase four was the part of the exercise that called for precision: dig a vertical shaft upwards, to come out directly under the axles of the jammed carts, allowing the carpenters to saw through the axles, take out the two jammed wheels, and retreat. In the event the tunnel came up a foot short, which meant that phase five (sawing the axles) was trickier than it should have been, the carpenters having to work leaning diagonally with their backs braced on planks. They managed it, however, just about, and if the wheels came away rather sooner than expected and crashed down into the shaft with potentially lethal force (something Poldarn realised he should have anticipated but hadn't), it was all right, because of the shaft being offset and the carpenters accordingly just out of the way. ('Bloody clever, that was,' one of them congratulated him a few minutes later, 'the way you figured that drop just right. I was stood there while they were digging thinking, bugger me, that shaft's going to come up short, but of course I didn't realise it was on purpose. Bloody smart thinking, chum; well done.') Once the impacted wheels had been hauled back down the tunnel and out of the way, phase six, attaching ropes to the outgoing cart and hauling it clear, was easy as pie, as was phase seven, putting all the dirt back down the hole and making good so that the rest of the carts could get through without the risk of caving in the tunnels.

'Piece of cake,' Poldarn said, brushing mud off his knees. 'Don't know what all the fuss was about, really.'

Under other circumstances a remark like that could easily have cost him his life. As it turned out, however, his colleagues in the Falx house were either too busy or too exhausted to do anything more than scowl horribly at him as they scuttled or limped past.

'It worked,' Falx Roisin said.

Poldarn frowned. 'You sound surprised,' he said.

'You bet your life I'm surprised,' he replied. 'I was convinced you were going to bring the whole gatehouse down on top of your head. Still, it worked, so who the hell cares? Well done. I owe you a favour.'

Poldarn shrugged. 'Just making myself useful,' he replied. 'I think I'll get on and wash this mud off my hands.'

'What? Oh, right, yes. You know, what you did back there, it reminds me of something, but I can't think what. Bloody clever, though. If I needed a house engineer, I'd give you the job like a shot.'

'Thank you,' Poldarn replied dubiously. 'I'll be going now, if that's all right.'

It was dark before the house finally got back to normal, and dinner was delayed accordingly. Rather than spend an hour getting congratulated for his cleverness in the mess hall, Poldarn sneaked round to the back door of the kitchens and charmed one of the cooks, a massive woman as tall as he was and nearly twice his weight, into letting him have half a loaf, a big slab of the more recent cheese and a small jug of beer. He carried his trophies off to the stables, had his dinner in peace and quiet down behind the feed bins, returned the jug and went to his quarters to sleep.

Falx Roisin was waiting for him there. He'd brought a lamp, rather a magnificent object in highly polished brass in the shape of a pig.

'I remembered,' he said.

'Excuse me?'

'That trick of yours,' Falx Roisin said. 'I remembered where I'd heard about it before. It's exactly what General Cronan did at Zanipolo.'

Poldarn looked blank. 'Two carts got stuck in a gateway, did they?'

Falx Roisin frowned. 'Illanzus had been besieging Zanipolo for eighteen months, and they were running desperately short of food, half the camp was down with swamp fever and the rebels were coming up fast with a relief force twice the size of the loyalist army. Cronan was just a captain then, attached to the engineers because nearly all their regular officers had been killed or had died of the fever. Cronan had them dig under the gatehouse; calculated it so perfectly that they came up right in the middle of the lodge. A few minutes later they got the gates open and that was that. It was the making of him, of course; never looked back.'

Poldarn thought for a moment. 'That's very interesting,' he said. 'And you left your dinner and came all the way up here just to tell me about it?'

'No,' Falx Roisin replied, sounding annoyed. 'I wanted to ask you if you'd ever been in the army.'

'I see. Why?'

That annoyed him even more. 'Answer the question,' he said. 'Were you in the army or weren't you?'

Poldarn sighed. 'No,' he said.

'Really. You're sure about that.'

Poldarn grinned. 'You think I'd forget about it if I had been? Yes, I'm sure. No, I've never been in the army. Why do you want to know?'

'There was a soldier here this morning,' Falx Roisin continued, 'just before the big screw-up in the yard. Military tribune from the guards, no less. He was asking after a deserter. The description sounded a lot like you.'

'Did it? What did he say?'

'Middle-aged, medium height, long nose, pointed chin. Hair just starting to go grey.'

Poldarn smiled. 'No offence,' he said, 'but it sounds to me like he was describing you. I mean,' he went on, 'there must be hundreds of men in this city who answer to that.'

'That's what I told him,' Falx Roisin said. 'And I didn't think of you when I answered him; I mean, you've only been here five minutes, and I've got a lot of faces to remember. But then he said this deserter was one of Cronan's staff. High-ranking man, brevet-major or something like that. Not the sort to go absent without leave on a nine-day bender. So I guessed it might be something serious.'

'Sounds like it,' Poldarn said, shifting his weight to his back foot, taking himself out of the circle of light from Falx Roisin's lamp. 'But nothing to do with me.'

Falx Roisin looked at him for a moment. 'So I pressed him for some details,' he went on, 'and he replied that he couldn't tell me a lot because it's all under seal and classified. But he did happen to mention something about Prefect Tazencius; he tried to escape, apparently, and he had accomplices waiting for him on the road between here and Weal, two people in a cart. I was wondering if you knew anything about that, either.'

'Two people in a cart,' Poldarn repeated. 'You mean the two who were going round pretending to be the god?'

Whatever Falx Roisin had been about to say, he didn't say it. Instead, he narrowed his eyebrows, opened his mouth and closed it again. 'I hadn't thought of that,' he said eventually.

'Somebody else did, apparently,' Poldarn replied. 'They've caught them and brought them in. I passed them on my way back from town.' He paused, waited for a moment, then went on, 'Oh, I see. You were thinking that it was Gotto and me.'

'What? Oh, no, God forbid. The thought never crossed my mind.' Poldarn looked at Falx Roisin and was sure he could see machinery working behind his eyes. 'Damn it, if you're right, that'd make a whole lot of sense, wouldn't it? I mean, they've been going round prophesying the end of the world, spreading panic and doom and stuff, and now people are saying they had something to do with what happened to Josequin. Bloody hell,' he added, pulling a ferocious face. 'The bastards. All this time they were hand in glove with that arse-hole Tazencius – and the raiders, God damn it, just think of that. I just hope they string 'em up high, that's all, and Tazencius as well, even if he is some kind of minor royal. That's disgusting.'

'I thought so,' Poldarn said. 'Not to mention the blasphemy side of it. If that's not asking for trouble, I don't know what is.'

'Blasphemy? Oh, I see what you mean.' Falx Roisin looked at him with the atheist's gentle contempt for the believer. 'Well, quite,' he said. 'God, though, I'd never have guessed that one. Prefect Tazencius being in with the raiders. And to think I once gave him a silver dinner service.'

Shaking his head, Falx Roisin picked up his lamp and drifted away, still murmuring to himself about the iniquities of the world. Poldarn shut the door after him, kicked his boots off and lay down on the bed. Then he realised that he was still wearing his new coat, and that it was covered in dust and mud. He stood up, took it off and hung it over the back of the chair, and stretched his back, which was just starting to stiffen up.

Coincidence, he told himself. It was a fairly basic idea; if you can't get at something from straight on or above, try from underneath. Furthermore, take away the fact that both cases had involved a gateway and the similarity between them wasn't all that great. Even supposing it was, and that the idea had been in the back of his mind all along, and he'd used it for the Falx house emergency; just because he'd copied the idea, it didn't automatically follow that he'd been in General Cronan's army, or any army; Falx Roisin hadn't, to the best of his knowledge, but he'd heard about what Cronan's engineers had done; if Falx Roisin had heard of it through news or gossip, then in all likelihood so had he, and the idea had been snuggled away behind the screen along with the rest of his memories.

He pushed the whole business out of his mind and sat down on the bed. *I wonder what Copis is doing now,* he thought; and the truth was, he had no idea. What did normal people do after dark, the ones who weren't nameless strangers with no memories, the ones who didn't earn their livings in the death and intrigue business? He tried to work it out from first principles. The ones who worked hard all day would go home and sleep; if they weren't tired they'd light a lamp and mend their clothes or their tools, sing, tell stories, make love, whatever. Somehow he couldn't imagine it, any more than he could imagine what giants or elves or gods did in their spare time when they weren't being legends. Far more plausible to assume that they didn't exist in the dark, or if they didn't simply disappear when nobody could see them they sat still and quiet, inanimate, waiting for daybreak and the turn of the next page.

Pages. He wasn't tired; at least, he was very tired but he knew perfectly well he wouldn't get to sleep. But the generous and thoughtful Falx Roisin, by his duly appointed agent Quartermaster Eolla, had provided for him in just such an emergency and ordained that he should be issued with a small pottery lamp and a book. Two books, in fact. The man was all heart.

He lit the lamp, chafing a knuckle on the tinderbox in the process, sat down in his chair and examined the two books. He hadn't given them a thought since he'd received them, hadn't even opened them to find out what they were called or what they were about. That was ungrateful of him.

The first one was quite old; the ink was brown, the parchment was almost translucent in places, and it creaked alarmingly as he opened it. How do you look after books? he wondered. Are you supposed to rub the bindings once a month with neat's foot oil, the way you do with harness and boots, or would that make the ink run? Did the stitching down the middle wear out, and if so, was it easy to replace?

He chose a page at random:

. . . Two pounds of chopped leeks, three cups of light white wine, a pound of raisins, half a pound of fresh celery and six eggs. First, hang the hare for twelve days. On the thirteenth day, remove the skin and guts, fillet and coat in flour. Pour the wine into a bowl . . .

A quick flick through confirmed his suspicions; it was all like that. He frowned, closed the book and put it on the floor. One to save, he decided, until he was really desperate. That still left the other book, which was not quite as old, though somewhat shorter and thinner. He was a little apprehensive about opening it; if it turned out to be another dud, could he take them both back to Eolla and demand to be allowed two replacements, or was he stuck with them for the duration of his service? He forced himself to remember that he'd had the pick of the books in the box, and had chosen these two of his own free will, purely on the basis of size. Nobody to blame but himself, and typical, he felt, of the luck he'd had so far in making choices.

He picked up the second book and decided that it probably wasn't going to bite him. This time, he started with the very first page:

The Complete Temple Of Wisdom

(That's more like it, he thought.)

Comprising a complete digest of all the other books heretofore written that merit the attention of scholars, soldiers, government officers and those of gentle birth and breeding, including but not confined to the books of religion, natural science, medicine, philosophy, law, the skills and crafts; the best works of the finest and most acclaimed divines, homilists, commentators and grammarians, historians, poets and writers of prose fiction; also including comprehensive tables of weights, measures, rates of exchange, statutes in force, common ailments and their symptoms and cures, fasts and festivals, prosody and metre newly explained, auspicious and unauspicious days; to which is appended the complete letter-writer, comprising over two hundred model letters for all occasions; the complete understanding of the counting-board, abacus and string tally; grammars and glossaries of all the known languages; the farmer's almanac and helpmeet (newly revised); the mariner's guide, including all necessary charts and tables of tides

*and a completely new and unabridged treatise on the
practice of navigation by the stars; with over one thousand
illustrations, diagrams and maps; by A Scholar of
Sansory. Copied and bound at the sign of the Brown Dog
in the precinct of the Old and New Temples, Sansory.
Price: three quarters.*

The last bit let the rest down, he reckoned; three quarters
for all that wisdom. Admittedly the book was vilely copied in
a tiny cramped hand on low-grade mutton vellum that had
been scraped back at least three times, which probably helped
to keep the price down. On the other hand, all the answers to
all the questions in the world, not to mention ten pages of
indices and a free bookmark, all for the price of a night in an
inn – maybe that was all the concentrated wisdom of mankind
was worth. That would explain a great deal.

Having nothing better to do, he looked up 'Poldarn' in the
index. There was one listing, page 474; he flicked through,
and read:

*An obscure southern god, now neglected. Iconography: a
crow with a ring in its beak. Assigned duties: war, fire,
sundry domestic and industrial crafts, the end of the
world. Literary & cultural significance: none. Also known
as Bolodan (Sthrn), Polidan (lit.), the Dodger (colloq.).
See also: Mannerists; Life of Fthr Azonicus of Lomessa;
Enlightened thought; prophecies; end of the world, the;
Land and Sea raiders, the; carts & wagons.*

He frowned, and stuck the bookmark in to mark the place,
then looked up Josequin (two pages, mostly recommending
popular inns, taverns, brothels and carpet stalls), the Guilds,
Sansory (eight pages; lots of taverns), Mael Bohec, the empire
and a number of other things, until his eyes were too tired to
stay open and he fell asleep.

He woke up an hour later (just as he opened his eyes, he thought he saw two crows, wonderfully carved out of huge lumps of coal, come to life and flap away, croaking resentfully) with pins and needles in both feet and a sore neck, just in time to blow out the lamp before it burned up the last few drops of his monthly oil ration. Sleeping in chairs, he decided, wasn't good for him. As he stood up, he felt something under his foot (extremely painful, in the circumstances) and guessed from the size and shape that it must be the book, fallen from his hands when he dropped off. He groped around for it but it wouldn't come to hand, and he let it lie till morning.

Chapter Thirteen

'It's just as well you happened to be in the area,' the magistrate said, quickening his pace to keep up. 'We've been going through the books trying to figure out which jurisdiction these clowns fall under, and it's starting to look depressingly like they slip down between the cracks. But of course, what we know about ecclesiastical law in this town could be written on the edge of a knife.'

'Don't look at me,' Brother Monach replied over his shoulder. 'I'm not a lawyer.'

'Yes, yes, I appreciate that,' the magistrate panted. 'But you're a priest, a brother of the order, so that must make you an expert, yes?'

'On what?'

'Gods,' the magistrate said, 'and stuff like that. You see, this isn't what you'd call a passionately religious town—'

'I'd noticed.'

'Yes, well.' The magistrate was wheezing alarmingly, so Monach slowed down a little. Not too much, though. 'We all serve the Divine in different ways, don't we?'

'Do we?' Monach stopped, his progress impeded by a heavy oak door. The magistrate caught up and paused for breath before knocking on it. A panel shot back, through which Monach could see a nose and a pair of eyes, then the door opened and a guard snapped to attention. For some reason, the magistrate seemed to find that embarrassing.

'This way,' he said. 'Look, I appreciate that you may not think of yourself as an expert in this field, but you're a damn sight more of an expert than anybody else I can think of in this town. Will you help us out? Please?'

Monach, who'd come here with the express intention of getting a chance to interview the prisoners, reluctantly agreed that he would. This seemed to make the magistrate very happy.

'That's wonderful,' the magistrate said, taking a lantern from a sconce on the wall. 'Basically, we need to know if there's a case to answer on the ecclesiastical law charges – blasphemy, incitement to heresy, tempting providence, that sort of thing – because if there is, it'll be quite simple: we can hand them over to you—'

This was, of course, exactly what Monach wanted. 'Me?' he said sharply. 'What the hell am I supposed to do with them?'

'Take them somewhere and, well, try them. Put 'em on trial, lock 'em up, stretch their necks for 'em; you can even let the buggers go, if that's the right thing to do. Just so long as you get them off my slop ticket. I really couldn't care less. If you can't – meaning, if there's no case on the blasphemy counts – we're going to have to try to get them on general fraud and obtaining money by deception, and I have a really bad feeling about that on the basis of the evidence we've got. And if I put 'em on trial on secular charges and they get off, I might as well move into their cell and have the guards drop the key in the melt.'

Monach laughed. 'Which is why you're so keen to get rid of them without bringing them to trial,' he said. 'Not bad. Quite shrewd, in fact.' He altered his tone of voice a little. 'Fact is, though,' he said, 'if the evidence doesn't disclose an apparent blasphemy or other illegal act, I'm not passing false judgement just to get you out of a hole. Understood?'

The magistrate cringed a little. 'Understood,' he said. 'Still, when you hear what the witnesses have to say—'

'I'll assess it for myself, thank you very much, without any helpful pointing in the right direction from you.' Talking to the magistrate like this made him feel a bit guilty; he could see plainly enough that the fix he was in wasn't his fault, and he was pretty sure he'd be doing something very similar if he was in the poor man's position. Nevertheless, it was important to act convincingly.

The magistrate stopped outside another thick, black door. 'Here we are,' he said with fairly obvious relief. 'You want a guard in there with you, in case?'

Monach grinned and pulled back the hem of his robe just an inch or so, enough to reveal the hilt of his sword. The magistrate obviously knew what he was looking at; Monach could sense the fear. 'You shouldn't really be carrying something like that in public,' he said quietly.

'Benefit of clergy,' Monach replied. 'Besides, if they do try and attack me, all your problems will be over.'

The magistrate made a valiant effort to hide his distaste. 'Well,' he said, 'just call out when you're done. We'll be right here.'

The door opened into pitch darkness; the magistrate handed him the lantern, and he went in. He heard the door shut and the bolts go back, and lifted the lantern, extending its circle. At the extreme edge, he caught sight of two faces and took a step forward.

They were sitting on the floor (no furniture in the cell) with their backs to the wall and their legs sticking out straight in front of them. The woman just looked frightened and miserable; the man was frightened too, but some last scrap of self-respect enabled him to scowl. Their faces were mottled with bruises and scabbed-over cuts. Monach settled comfortably on his knees, in the starting position for the third sequence (draw from a kneeling posture to engage an enemy seated opposite; single-handed cut to the throat followed by two-handed overhead cut to the opposite side of the neck; he'd been doing it so often for so long that it was hard to keep his hands still).

'Well, now,' he said. 'Impersonating a god. It may be possible to get in more trouble, but I couldn't tell you offhand how to go about it.'

'It's all a misunderstanding,' the man said. 'We—'

'We didn't mean any harm,' the woman interrupted. 'We were just—'

'We were just spreading the word,' the man cut in, and Monach had to make an effort not to smile; his guess was that they were husband and wife, probably had been for some time. 'Since when is it a crime to preach the Divine?'

'Without a licence from the diocesan office,' Monach replied smoothly. 'Oh, about a hundred and fifty years, though I can't quote you the precise date or section number. Unlicensed preaching; let's see, that's an ecclesiastical felony, five years confined penance to death, depending on the facts; unless you're preaching a god not recognised by statute – basically, that means not listed in Strouthes' *Digest* – in which case it's incitement to heresy, ten years to death, with mitigation accepted from non-citizens. Failing which,' he went on with a gentle smile, 'there's at least half a dozen secular public order offences that cover the same ground, any one of which'll get you five years or more in the slate quarries. The slate quarries are marginally preferable to confined penance, because the religious orders don't have jails, only prison hulks, mines and galleys. Very few people survive long enough in the galleys to serve five years.' He shook his head. 'It could be worse,' he said. 'You could've been arrested a mile or so nearer to

Mael and ended up there. The Guild isn't nearly as humanitarian as we are. Now,' he went on after a pause, during which
neither the man nor the woman made a sound, 'since sticking
either of you two behind an oar won't achieve anything
beyond a minor reduction in the efficiency of the Fleet, here's
my suggestion. You stop trying to jerk me around and tell me
the truth; I'll see what I can do to get you out of this in one
piece. Shall we talk, or would you rather hear about the far
more serious offence of impersonating a god?'

He had their undivided attention. Good. 'Let's start with
some names, shall we?' he said pleasantly.

'I'm Tiryns,' the woman said, 'he's Louth Ressal.'

Monach nodded. 'And how long have you been married?'

'Twelve years.'

Thought so. 'Where are you from?'

'Ressal's from Josequin,' the woman told him. 'I'm from
Morsello—'

'Morsello, in Morevich? You're a long way from home.'

The woman nodded. 'It's a long story,' she said.

'No doubt.' Josequin, Monach said to himself, that's interesting. 'So, what prompted you to start impersonating gods,
and how long did you do it for?'

The man and the woman looked at each other. 'It was what
happened at Josequin, I guess,' the man said. 'We were lucky.'
He pulled a face. 'Well, we thought so at the time. We'd gone
to Weal; my mother was dying, we left as soon as we heard but
we got there too late; when we got back, the city just wasn't
there any more. Well, when we found out what had happened,
we thought, thank God we weren't there. Then we realised
that everything we'd had – the house and my workshop (I was
a glassblower) – was all gone, nothing left. We didn't have
anything, I couldn't do my work without tools, we didn't know
where to turn. Then we happened to meet up with someone
on the road who told us about the god in the cart, and we
thought – well, why not? Except of course we didn't have a

cart; but then, just as we were setting off heading for Sansory, we came across this big old farm cart tucked in under a hedge. Seemed like, you know, an omen; especially when we found a couple of riderless horses feeding nearby. We started from there and headed north – actually, we headed what we thought was north, we couldn't even get that right – and just our rotten bloody luck, the first village we tried was one where these other two had been before—'

'Cric.'

The man looked at him. 'Sorry?'

'Cric. The name of the village.'

'No, I don't think so. It was Scele or Scale, something like that. Can't remember precisely, but it wasn't Cric.'

'Oh.' Monach looked up; that had thrown him. 'And this was after Josequin? You're sure about that? Because God help me if you're telling lies.'

'Positive,' the woman put in. 'And I'm almost certain the name of the place was Scale, because it reminded me so much of my uncle Ascaltus, rest his soul. I don't think I've ever been to a place called Cric.'

Monach took a moment to consider what he'd been told. It sounded entirely plausible; the part about getting caught the first time they tried to pull the scam was particularly convincing, it was just the sort of thing that would happen to the kind of feckless losers he took these two to be. There was only one thing that snagged in the lining of his mind, and it was too insignificant to bother about.

'You're lying,' he said quietly.

For a moment it looked as if they were going to protest, declare that every word was true, maybe shout or burst into tears. He was relieved that they didn't, since he found that sort of thing rather disturbing. 'How did you know?' the man said.

'I'm not stupid,' Monach replied. 'Now, since you aren't going to tell me the truth, I'd better tell you. I don't know about you,' he went on, nodding at the woman, 'you may well be from Morevich for all I know, but you're not from Josequin.'

The man sighed and looked at his feet. 'No,' he said.

'No, My guess is you're either a deserter from the army or a veteran – early discharge for some reason or another – and you joined one of the free companies about twelve years ago – the bit about you being married a long time I do believe, not that it matters a damn. The point is, you're a southerner just like she is.'

The man nodded. 'My dad was a veteran,' he said, 'got resettled in Morsello after his discharge. And that's true.'

Monach shrugged. 'If you say so. What matters is that you come up here, north of the Bohec, deliberately intending to work this scam, and you've been doing it for at least six months. And you're good at it, too. Healing the sick – well, a woman hanging round the free companies learns a bit about setting bones and curing fevers, I guess that was your field of expertise.' The woman nodded. 'As for you,' he went on, turning to the man, 'the imperial corps of sappers and siege engineers is mostly recruited in Morevich; that's how you know about flares and bombards and other things that blow up and make a deafening noise when you set light to them. Very obscure and closely guarded branch of knowledge, that is; which makes deserter rather more likely than discharged veteran.'

'All right,' the man said. 'Yes, I ran away. Do you want the details?'

'No,' Monach replied. 'Anyway, that's what I know; everything bearing directly on your guilt and the kind of sentence you'll get. What I actually want to know is really nothing to do with that side of things, so by telling me the truth there's no way you can make things any worse for yourselves. But you could make them a lot better.'

He left the words between them in the air for a moment or so, before continuing.

'First question,' he said. 'And remember, if I think you're lying, you'll stay in the trouble you're in. All right. Why did you choose to impersonate Poldarn? Why pick a name that doesn't mean anything on this side of the bay?'

The man shrugged. 'I grew up with stories about Poldarn,' he said. 'Besides, I know he doesn't exist. I didn't want to risk pretending to be a god who might exist.'

Monach smiled. 'Nice reasoning,' he said. 'And why exactly are you so sure Poldarn doesn't exist?'

'How do you mean?'

Monach wasn't quite sure how to answer. 'I mean,' he said, 'given that you're a believer or at least an agnostic – hence the rather charming superstition – why single out Poldarn as a god who quite definitely doesn't exist? You said it like you'd seen proof somewhere.' He stopped, and frowned. 'Did I just say something funny? Must've been very funny indeed if it made you laugh, considering how much trouble you're in.'

The man looked suitably ashamed. 'I'm sorry,' he said, 'really. It just seemed so – well, odd; I mean, you're a priest, surely you know . . .'

The scowl on Monach's face set hard, like concrete. 'Enlighten me,' he said.

'It was the monks,' the woman cut in. 'At Endlupho Mountain. They made him up. They were short of money; people weren't going there any more, so they made up a god to get people to come and worship.'

Monach sighed. 'What's she talking about?'

'It's true,' the man said. 'Well, more or less. It was a long time ago, before Morevich was added to the empire. I don't know the details; it was something about the empire annexing a province, which cut right across the pilgrim trail to a famous shrine somewhere down on the coast. Endlupho was like a staging post for these pilgrims, and when they stopped going that way – started going another way so they wouldn't have to cross the bit the empire had taken over – the monastery at

Endlupho was about to die out. So they cooked up a god of their own, started a pilgrim trail. It worked really well. Then about a hundred years ago the abbot of Endlupho got in a fight with the district agent over water rights in the valley or something of the sort, and the agent got so mad he sent his soldiers up the mountain to clear the monks out, and when they got there they found all the old chapter minutes and documents like that, going back hundreds of years, and it was all in there, about the abbot and chapter deciding to invent a god, even the records from the committee they set up to choose a name. As far as I can remember, it came down to a choice between Poldarn and Bettanc, and I think the abbot flipped a coin. In fact, I have an idea they got the name Poldarn off a roof tile – you know, the name of the brickyard that made it. Anyway, the other priests had it all hushed up and I don't suppose many people outside Morevich knew about it. But that's what happened. And there really is no such god as Poldarn.'

Monach really didn't know what to say this time. 'Oh' didn't seem to cover it. It was a while before he could think of anything more impressive.

'Doesn't change a thing,' he said at last. 'Impersonating a god who doesn't exist is even worse than faking one who does; it's idolatry.' He stood up, ducking at the last moment to avoid the low ceiling. 'Still,' he went on, 'as you've probably guessed, you've told me something I didn't know. Now tell me something else. Did you go to Cric?'

The woman shook her head. 'No,' she said. 'I promise.'

'Right.' Monach sighed. 'All right, here's what I'm going to do. I'm going to tell the magistrate that you're being transferred to Deymeson for trial, which'll please him no end, at any rate. As soon as we're out of sight of the city, I'm going to turn you loose. But if I ever hear another report about gods in carts or the second coming of Poldarn – or gods who don't exist because some bloody fool made them up – I'll have a word with my brothers in the martial order, and twenty sword-monks will be sent to find you and bring back your heads, nicely packed in salt and oregano to keep them fresh. You know about the sword-monks, do you?'

The expressions on their faces suggested that they did. 'Thank you,' the man said.

Monach sighed. 'My pleasure,' he replied sourly. 'Oh, and you might as well have this.' He picked twelve gold gross-quarters out of his sleeve and dropped them on the floor. 'That way, you won't have any need to make nuisances of yourselves till you're safely across the bay. You can do what the hell you like in Torcea and it won't cause me any problems. Just remember,' he said, putting his thumb behind the guard of his sword and shifting it out half an inch so they could see it. 'Keep your faces shut, be good, or I promise you, you won't realise you're dead till your heads hit the floor. Understood?'

The magistrate was waiting for him out in the passage. 'Well?' he asked.

Monach ran his sleeve across his forehead. 'Listen to me,' he said. 'I'm taking these two with me. You don't know anything about them. They were never here. Two people might have been arrested on suspicion of blasphemy, but it all turned out to be something and nothing, a bunch of inbred rubes overreacting and wasting everybody's time. Do you understand?'

The magistrate looked very upset. 'I can't do that,' he said. 'It's common knowledge all round the city that they're here, and I'm accountable to the watch committee. If I tell them—'

'You tell them whatever you like,' Monach interrupted. 'Just so long as you do what you've been told everything will be fine and you'll never see them or me again. Mess me about, though, and you won't see me but I'll see you. If you follow me,' he added, resting his left hand on his sash, over the point where the sword hilt lay hidden.

He smiled to himself about it afterwards, of course. If there was one thing he despised as a rule, it was blustering, threatening soldiers and officials. Somehow playing at being one, and a really exaggerated, over-the-top impersonation at that, had been fun. Of course, only a gullible idiot who knew nothing at all about the Deymeson order would've taken all that play-acting at face value; the order didn't make threats, eschewed melodrama of all kinds.

Once he'd parted company from the false god and his priestess (they vanished as if by magic; one moment they were there, the next they'd gone), he turned his horse east, towards the road that led to Deymeson, rest and sanity. ('Just one thing,' the man had asked. 'What was it gave us away, when we told you the first story?' He replied that it had been the bit about glassblowing; true, there were glassworks in Josequin, but he didn't look anything like any glassblower he'd ever met, and as it happened he'd met several. Glassblowing was, however, one of the trades of which Poldarn was supposed to be the patron; hence the mental association, for a southerner. At which the man had shaken his head. 'Actually,' he said, 'that was perfectly true. Not about Josequin, I've never been there in my life. But I was apprenticed to a glassworks when I was a kid, and I passed my trade test, even stuck it there for a year or two, so yes, I'm a glassblower all right.') With any luck he'd be able to turn in his report, kid his way through his debriefing and get back to drawing and cutting practice. All in all, he decided, he wasn't suited to being an investigator: too complicated for his liking, nothing straightforward that split down the grain or cut cleanly. The Poldarn business was worse than any other investigation he'd been involved with, of course; it was a case of the more he thought about it, the more obscure it became.

The trick, as he knew perfectly well, was not to think about it. No need to, after all. He'd make his report; an investigator – somebody else, please God, let it be somebody else – would be sent to Morevich to verify the false god's story, the matter would be reported in passing in closed chapter and put aside as a dead issue. The nasty loose ends, such as who had put on the show at Cric, how he'd been able to foretell the future and raise the dead, how General Allectus had managed to survive this long without being found, who the god in the cart was if he wasn't Poldarn, these fell outside his remit and he didn't have to bother about them. Indeed, if he tried to raise any of these issues, he'd get told off by Father Tutor, and quite right, too. *It's not the place of the swordsman to fight shadows.* (Who'd said that? Somebody famous.)

For the rest of the day he kept catching sight of two black birds, rooks or crows or ravens, flying slowly alongside him a long way away. Whether they were the same ones or different each time he had no way of knowing, but most of the time he was fairly certain they were ravens, therefore not significant or a coincidence.

He reached the Piety and Poverty an hour before dark and spent the evening playing whittlejack for pleasure and profit with a party of bone merchants en route to Sansory to buy at the ossiary sale. By the time he'd finished with them, the number of cartloads of bones they'd be able to afford had gone down considerably, but they seemed good-humoured about it and even offered to buy him a drink. He refused politely, explaining that he had to be up early and clear-headed in the morning, and went to bed, wondering what on earth he was going to do with the substantial sum of money he'd just acquired. It was no conceivable use to him, and he didn't relish the prospect of explaining how he'd come by it if he turned it over to Brother Treasurer. Giving it back to the four jolly bonemen would probably be construed as an insult, and he was too tired to go back and deliberately lose it to them, even assuming he was capable of such finesse in his play. He could dump it, he supposed, or leave it in his room for the groom or the chambermaid, but the Piety was the kind of place where they might just send on a purse of money found in a guest's room, with an explanatory note ('the serving girl says you left this money on your pillow . . .', not something he'd like Father Tutor to read if he could help it). There was always the deserving poor, of course, except that brothers of the order weren't authorised to deal in largesse and charity except by special licence of their superiors, for fear of setting awkward precedents, upsetting the balance of existing aid and alms initiatives, and so on, and so on. In the end he spent a whole hour staring resentfully at the purse, wishing he'd had the moral fortitude to resist the chance of playing whittlejack with born losers . . . But he'd always been exceptionally good at the game, and he enjoyed it, and only got a chance to play once in a blue moon, and everybody knows that it's physically impossible to play it except for money.

Some god or angel must have visited him in a dream, because when he woke up he knew exactly what to do. He found the innkeeper, a man he'd known for years (though the innkeeper didn't know him from a brick in the wall, owing to the fact that each time he'd been there he'd been using a different persona) and reckoned he could trust, at least with something he couldn't give a damn about.

'See this?' he said, emptying a few of the coins on to his palm. 'Belongs to a friend of mine. He left it with me for safe-keeping and I was going to meet him here and give it back to him. But he must've got held up somewhere, and I haven't got time to hang around waiting for him. Can you keep an eye out for him, and let him have it?'

He could see the innkeeper looking wistfully at the money and resolving to be good. 'No problem,' he replied. 'So what's he called, your friend?'

Monach shook his head. 'It's not as simple as that,' he replied. 'I promise you there's nothing skew about it, only he won't be travelling under his own name.' Then he gave the

innkeeper the description of the god in the cart he'd heard
from the man in Cric who might have been General Allectus.
'He may be travelling in a cart,' he added. 'Possibly he'll have
a woman with him, or he may just send her, I can't say for certain.' He then described the priestess. 'You don't mind, do
you?' he added. 'I don't think my friend'll begrudge you two
gross-quarters for your trouble.'

The innkeeper brightened up considerably, and said no,
that wasn't necessary; Monach insisted, the innkeeper insisted
back, Monach counterinsisted and the innkeeper tightened
his hand round the purse so hard it was a miracle he didn't
bend the coins double. 'Oh, one other thing,' Monach added.
'As and when one of them shows up, if you can spare one of
your people to run out to the Joy and Sorrow at Deymeson,
leave a message for me there. My name's Monach.'

'Of course,' the innkeeper said. 'I'll send one of my boys
over. They're always glad of an excuse for a trip out.'

Monach thanked him and ordered a good breakfast. As he
ate it, he wondered whether it had been such a good idea after
all. Anybody riding east from Sansory would be sure to stay
over at the Piety, it was the only half-decent inn on a bleak and
miserable road. There was therefore a one in four chance that
the other Poldarn, the one who'd been to Cric, would end up
there sooner or later; slightly better odds that the innkeeper
would recognise him from Monach's description and send the
message. If sent, the message was almost certain to reach him,
since the Joy was owned by the Order and the people there
were used to fielding strange and unintelligible messages and
passing them on discreetly. In short, there was a remote but far
from negligible chance that he'd end up getting a lead on this
other Poldarn, the one he'd been thinking long, awkward
thoughts about, and that given such a lead he might feel a
moral obligation to do something about it. The god or angel in
his dream had reckoned that was a good idea. He wasn't so
sure.

He was still prodding at this question like a sore tooth when he reached Deymeson. As always, he had mixed feelings as he dismounted and knocked at the gate, waiting for Brother Porter to open up. It had to be admitted, he enjoyed being out in the world, free for a while from authority and the Rule, living his vicarious lives, eating good food in inns and sleeping between sheets instead of under a single blanket on a stone bench. But the soft beds never did his back any good, the food gave him indigestion after a day or so, and he'd joined the order and submitted to the Rule because this was the only place on earth where he could do what he most wanted to do, what he needed to do in order to make sense of the world. In a week's time, when he'd got back into the routine of offices, services, training, teaching and practice, the thought of going outside wouldn't please him at all; it'd be a chore to be got over with rather than an opportunity for a holiday.

'He wants to see you straight away,' Brother Porter told him, as soon as he was inside the gate. 'Been sending down, asking are you back yet, anybody know where you've got to?' Brother Porter's grin had a definite spike of malice to it. 'Said to tell you, leave your horse for the ostlers to see to, you go straight on up.'

Monach sighed. It was never personal with Brother Porter; he savoured the misfortunes of everybody with equal relish, to the point where it was hard to resent him. 'Wonderful,' he said, 'thank you so much for telling me.'

The reception he received from Father Tutor was most disturbing; no polite enquiry about his health, subtly barbed references to tardiness or ineptitude, graceful derision of his work or results, no torture of any kind. Instead Father Tutor actually seemed pleased to see him, in a preoccupied sort of a way. For his mentor and guide to come so close to acknowledging that he might actually need his services, instead of merely tolerating them, the situation must be close to catastrophic.

It was.

'I'll come straight to the point,' Father Tutor said. 'Tazencius has gone missing.'

Monach tried to stop his jaw swinging open; it was sloppy, undisciplined and sure to be commented on. Father Tutor didn't seem to have noticed.

'As far as we can make out,' Father Tutor went on, 'he was recalled, presumably in disgrace; a troop of cavalry, from one of the household regiments, was sent to bring him back, but he got past them – have you heard any of this?'

Monach shook his head.

'He got past them,' Father Tutor continued, staring past Monach's head at the corner of the ceiling, 'but they caught him up; something odd happened there, and we can't find out what it was, but the upshot was they got him back. Then they lost him again.'

'Oh.'

'Oh indeed,' Father Tutor said, and just for a moment there was a reassuring note of mockery in his voice. 'Furthermore, their bodies were found between Sansory and Mael, carved up, and no trace of Tazencius whatsoever.'

'Excuse me,' Monach interrupted, 'but when you say carved up—'

Father Tutor nodded. 'Massive cuts and slashes to the neck and upper body, consistent with the wounds typically made by backsabres. Which, as you know, could mean any one of a number of things, all of them in this context contradictory. Just the sort of vital clue we could've done without, if you ask me. Anyway,' Father Tutor said, looking away in another direction, 'I need a good eye, a fast hand and above all a sharp mind. I want you to find Tazencius and bring him back here, as quickly as possible.'

Monach realised he'd caught his breath. He let it go, and said, 'Understood. Where do you suggest I should start?'

Father Tutor thought for a moment. 'Sansory,' he replied.

'Right. Actually, I've just come from there.'

A shrug of the shoulders. 'I don't imagine for one moment that Tazencius is there,' he said, 'but I believe that you're more likely to pick up the scent there than anywhere else. I can't give you any better advice than that, I'm afraid; you'll just have to pick it up as you go along. You'll manage, though. You seem to have a flair for the work. Do you want to take anybody with you? As you can imagine, manpower is at something of a premium at the moment, but I could certainly spare you a dozen or so men at arms and half a dozen brothers—'

Just when Monach thought there couldn't be any more surprises . . . 'Thank you,' he said, 'but I'll be better off recruiting locally, if I need help; it's less awkward that way. I might need money, though,' he added.

'Whatever you think fit,' Father Tutor replied, dismissing the detail with a slight gesture of the left hand. 'And anything else you might need, help yourself. If you'll bear with me a moment, I'll write the requisition now.'

'Thank you,' Monach said in a very small voice. 'When do I leave?'

Father Tutor looked up from his lectern. 'That's up to you too,' he said. 'If you feel up to leaving straight away, that'd obviously save time, but if you want to rest and prepare yourself, I'll quite understand, you can leave in the morning.'

'I think I'll do that,' Monach said, 'if you're sure that's all right. The truth is, I haven't been able to keep up my practice while I've been away, and I'm starting to feel awkward, like my skin's shrunk.'

Father Tutor nodded gravely. 'Very sensible,' he said. 'In which case, may I recommend an hour of solitary meditation, a light meal and an afternoon in one of the private chapels working quietly and steadily through the principal sequences? I don't know about you, but I found it always worked for me.'

The principal sequences: kneeling draw, seated draw, standing draw, the eight cuts and the eight wards, the circle of life and death, the blind fencer, the sheathed sword. As he released control of his body to the memory, the instinct that guided him in the movements, he tried to clear his mind by reciting the paradoxes of defence:

> *Space is time.*
> *The circle of life is the circle of death.*
> *Sheathed, the sword is drawn back to strike.*
> *The fastest draw is not drawing.*
>
> *Only the finest master can match the skill of the novice.*
> *Only he who does not think will live for ever.*

Like the draw itself, he reflected (and his right hand found the hilt, the sword sliced the air where an enemy's neck would be and the hilt found his left hand for the finishing cut); he knew the paradoxes so well that any shred of meaning they'd once had for him had long since been ground away and they'd become nothing but noises, as instinctive to his mind as the position of the hilt was to his hand. By the time he'd worked through all the sequences it was after evensong, and as his mind came back he realised he was exhausted. He dragged himself back to his quarters, lay down on the stone ledge like a book replaced on its proper shelf, and fell asleep.

Chapter Fourteen

'Just my rotten luck,' the new man was saying, 'just my rotten bloody filthy stinking luck. Fifteen of us in the pool, and he has to pick me. Typical.'

Poldarn had been learning the art of not listening. He'd had to pick it up as he went along, but desperation is a fine teacher. He had no alternative but to learn, and learn quickly, otherwise he'd have to kill the man to save himself from going crazy, and killing him would of course prove him right.

'Don't get me wrong, I'm not blaming you,' the new man went on, in exactly the same low mumbling voice he'd been using for the last three days. 'You didn't choose me, he did. I mean, I don't suppose it's much fun for you people, having everybody you ride with ending up dead. I mean, if it was me in your shoes, I wouldn't be able to sleep nights thinking about it. I'm sorry for you, really I am. No, it's him I'm angry with, really, really angry, because he had no call to go picking me, I never did him any harm—'

It was in Poldarn's mind to point out at some stage that so far they'd been on the road together for three days and two nights, and so far the worst peril they'd encountered had been the pea soup in the Mercy and Forbearance. He hadn't done so yet, partly because of tempting providence, partly because interrupting the new man's flow wasn't going to be easy. Words poured steadily out of him like grain flowing through a hole in the bottom of a manger, and all he could do was hang on and wait till eventually there weren't any more.

Which was a pity, because if he'd been able to have a normal conversation with the man there were all sorts of questions he'd have liked to have asked about Liancor, the place they were going to. For one thing, it was south of the Bohec, and it was the first time (first time he could remember) that he'd been across the river. Things were different on this side. Instead of sprawling shapelessly, the moor was parcelled up in neat, sheep-filled squares with birch-hedged banks and dry-stone walls. Here and there he saw buildings – sheds and linhays mostly, but a few houses and yards as well, suggesting that life on this side was settled and secure enough that people dared to live outside the villages. The road was narrower, sheltered from the wind by banks and hedges, more rutted and worn, and much busier – hardly an hour went by without another cart or wagon creaking past them, going the other way. There were birds other than crows on this side of the river: big mobs of pigeons and peewits, either pitched in the trees or down on the ground, munching devastating rides through fields of young cabbage and kale; every now and then a buzzard circling high over a copse or covert; just occasionally a heron standing in the bed of one of the fast, shallow rivers that drained down to the Bohec out of the moorland hills. It was useful, productive country, on your side rather than against you, and people quite definitely lived here. As for Liancor itself, he knew absolutely nothing about it apart from the name.

'What I want to know is—' The new man stopped abruptly and sat up, staring at something on the other side of the combe; then, just as Poldarn (who couldn't see anything) was about to ask what was so interesting, he sighed. 'Oh well,' he said, 'I suppose that's it. Had to come sooner or later.'

Poldarn peered as hard as he could, but all he could see was a hillside, some walls, a couple of thorn trees bent sideways by the wind, and a small group of wild ponies. 'What are you talking about?' he said.

'Over there,' the new man said. 'Are you blind or something? Look, they're—'

Which was as far as he got. A stone whizzed out of nowhere and hit him in the middle of his forehead. His head jerked back and he fell on his back in the bed of the cart as another stone smacked into Poldarn's shoulder, wasting its force against the steel plates sewn into his gambeson. It was still enough to startle him out of his wits and move him in his seat, as if he'd been shoved. The next two rattled off the side of the cart, digging out finger-sized chunks of timber. He didn't hang around to see if the grouping improved. From the box he jumped on to the bank, scrambled over it and half slid, half fell into the ditch on the other side, which was about eighteen inches deep and full of water.

For an unnervingly long time nothing happened. Poldarn had wound up lying on his left side so that his head and right shoulder were out of the water; the rest of him was submerged. Having no reason to move, he stayed put. He was reconsidering this policy when a head bobbed up over the bank, looked both ways in a cursory fashion, and popped down again. He heard someone say, 'No sign of the bugger.' Then, after another infuriating pause, he saw a man standing up on the box of the cart. Because the bank was in the way, all he could see was the back of his head – matted, curly brown hair blowing in the wind – and the tops of his shoulders, before the man bent or knelt down and was out of his sight. While he was analysing what he'd learned, another head appeared, this time three-quarter face; same sort of hair, a thin, long face with a pointed chin scruffy with a slight growth of woolly fuzz, a very young man who probably hadn't been eating well lately.

Lying still and quiet seemed rather more attractive at this point. He'd come to the conclusion that the weapons used were most likely slings. He found that he seemed to know a lot about slings, probably including how to use one: you could make one out of anything, they were difficult to use but could be both accurate and effective, but the rate of fire was slow and up close they were useless. Just right for knocking drivers off carts, but if that was all they had, there shouldn't be any problem.

If. Time for another choice, damn it. The argument for staying where he was struck him as unusually persuasive; he was a courier, not a cart guard; he had an important letter to deliver, and getting involved in fights would only put the letter at risk; he hadn't liked the new man, not one bit. The argument for scrambling out of the ditch, vaulting over the bank and starting a fight was so insubstantial and vague that he couldn't even reduce it to words. But, he realised as his boots hit the planks of the cart bed and the two men spun round to face him, it must have had its merits, or why the hell was he doing it?

The man on the right took a step towards him. His hand may have been raised to throw a punch, or he may just have been lifting it to help him balance as he tried to jump down off the cart and escape. In any event, the step brought him inside Poldarn's circle, and he fell backwards off the cart and out of sight before Poldarn even had a chance to see what sort of wound he'd inflicted. The other man stayed very, very still.

'I'm sorry,' he said, 'really I am. I didn't recognise you.'

For a moment, Poldarn's mind was completely blank, then he decided he'd better put his sword away before he did himself an injury with it. He flicked the blood off the blade with a crisp crack of his wrist, drew the back over the web of his left thumb and slid it into the scabbard without looking down.

'What?' he said.

'I didn't know it was you,' the man said, perfectly still except for his mouth. 'All we could see was two men on a cart. I'm really sorry.'

Poldarn breathed out slowly. 'It's all right,' he said, 'I'm not going to hurt you. Just don't go away quite yet. You know who I am?'

The man shrugged. 'Yes,' he replied. 'Well, sort of. I saw you at the rendezvous when we landed.'

Poldarn stared at him a moment or so longer. 'Listen to me,' he said. 'You may know who I am, but I don't. I got a bash on the head, and when I woke up I couldn't remember anything; not my name, where I'm from, nothing like that at all. Tell me what you know, or so help me—'

'All right.' The man winced, and Poldarn caught sight of a little pool of liquid forming on the boards of the box, next to the man's left ankle. He resisted the temptation to burst out laughing, and instead said, 'It's all right, I promise I'm not going to do anything to you. Just help me out, please.'

The man took a deep breath. 'All right,' he said. 'I'm sorry, I don't know your name. I only saw you the one time. I don't even know if you're one of us or one of them; I was on watch, I saw you walking down the path from the cliffs, and before I could challenge you the skipper said it was all right, you were expected. You walked past me – close as you are now – and about an hour later you came back, went off the way you came. That's it.'

All Poldarn could do was sigh. He didn't need to ask the next question, he already knew the answer. He'd guessed it a moment ago, when he'd realised that the language he was talking and hearing wasn't the one he'd been living with for the last few weeks.

'You're raiders,' he said.

It seemed to surprise the man that this point needed confirmation. 'That's right,' he said. 'Me and Turvin and about five others, we got cut off after the battle following up too far, so when the relief came, we couldn't get back; then a squad of horsemen chased us up, and when we stopped running we hadn't a clue where we were, what direction we'd come, anything like that. Later on the sun came up, we found out we'd been going south, so we tried to head back north-west, only we walked straight into the bloody relief again. Turvin and me, we got away, the others didn't; we kept on going till we reached the river – they'd sent another squad after us, the bastards, we thought they were on our side, and we didn't give them the slip till nightfall. Well, we were so scared by then that we dumped all our kit into the river – trying to make it look like we'd drowned, though I don't suppose it fooled anybody – and swam across; we figured they wouldn't expect us to go south-east, away from the ships, so that was the only safe way to go. Anyhow, we wound up here, and here we've been ever since.'

Poldarn nodded. 'Robbing carts,' he said.

'Trying to rob carts.' The man grinned. He couldn't be more than twenty. 'Just our luck, the first time we actually connect with anything—'

'I see,' Poldarn said. 'And that's all you know about me? You're sure?'

The man dipped his head in confirmation. 'You came to the ships just after we landed. They were expecting you. At the time I guessed you were one of ours – you know, we've got scouts in deep – but I was just assuming.'

'Fine. Do I look like one of you?'

'I guess. From the south island, anyhow. But you could be one of them, too. Truth is, I haven't seen enough of them to know. This is my first time, see.'

'First time?'

'First time over here. The first expedition I've ever been on.'

'Ah.' Poldarn clicked his tongue. 'Things haven't been going well for you lately, have they?'

The young man nodded. 'It's been a thoroughly rotten year,' he said. 'First we lost twenty lambs in the cold snap, then our big shed fell in the sea during the high winds, then the sheep got into the leeks, and then we found the blight had got in the apples, ended up slinging half of 'em, and then all the bees just upped and died on us, like that, so we sold all our spare timber to get places on a ship to come here, hoping we'd be able to make enough to set it all straight, and now look. God knows what's become of Dad and Raffenkel, I'm stuck here in the middle of enemy territory, and I can't even rob a cart. It's enough to make you give up.'

Poldarn agreed that it all sounded a bit much. 'What's your name?' he asked.

'Eyvind,' the young man replied. 'And Dad's Kari. We live at a place called Ness – any of this ring any bells?'

'No,' Poldarn said. 'But that doesn't mean anything.' He thought for a moment. 'All I can suggest is that you get away from here as fast as you can, before someone comes along and finds these bodies. I'll say there was only one of you; he killed my carter, I killed him. That's all I can do for you, I'm afraid.' He paused. 'No, that's not true,' he said. He pulled his purse from his sleeve and counted out twenty quarters, leaving himself fifteen to cover his expenses for the rest of the trip. 'You could try pretending to be deaf and dumb, I suppose,' he said. 'At any rate, you'll stand a better chance than if you try and make a living as a highwayman. Do I speak with an accent?'

Eyvind nodded. 'Yes,' he said, 'but I can't place it. And there's all sorts of accents up and down the south island, depending on where people came from originally. Like I said, you could be us, you could be them. No way of knowing.'

'Fine,' Poldarn said. 'I don't think his boots'll fit you, but you could pad them out with bits of shirt. I'd leave the jacket, though.' He frowned, then said, 'You can have my coat instead, I'll take his jacket. You know, I have about as much luck with coats as you do with your life in general.'

'Thank you,' Eyvind said. 'I—'

'Goodbye,' Poldarn interrupted. He pulled the dead carter up by his arms, slid him out of his jacket and toppled him off the cart; then he wriggled out of his coat, slung it out on top of the body and walked the horses on.

Of course, he hadn't much idea of where he was, so it was fortunate that the road went straight to Liancor, with no options or choices to betray him. The first things he saw, as he laboured up a slope between two high hedges and suddenly found himself at an unexpected crest overlooking a deep, hidden valley, were two sand-yellow towers four or five miles away, their tops poking up above the folds of the ground like the heads of Eyvind and his dead colleague. Half an hour or so later the gentle hills got out of the way and he was able to look down on the whole town.

It reminded him of a lake, filling the lowest point in a valley, as if the houses and buildings had drained down the hillsides and flooded the flat water meadows on either side of the shallow, lively river that wound away at right angles to the road. Certainly, Liancor gave the impression that it had got there by some natural process of accretion, that it had grown there or been carried there like river silt over a very long period of time. The light brown stone and brown-grey thatch gave the impression of camouflage, as if the town was an animal who'd grown that way to avoid the attention of predators.

He'd made a point of finding out the correct procedure, so the first thing he did was ask the way to the prefecture, which turned out to be a doorway in the side of a long, low, scruffy-looking building with large chunks missing from the outside rendering. He gave a small boy a quarter to look after the cart and went inside. There were three clerks sitting at a bench, huddled together so as to be able to share the narrow beam of light from the one small window high in the wall to their left. One of them looked up as he walked in; the other two carried on writing slowly and carefully in big ledgers.

'Hello,' he said. 'I need to report a death.'

The clerk glowered at him as if he was a small child pestering his mother for sweets. 'Right,' he said irritably; he pushed away the ledger in front of him, stretched out an arm for another ledger behind him without looking round, laid it on the desk and let it fall open at the bookmark. 'Citizen or offcomer?'

Poldarn frowned. 'Me or him?'

'Both of you.'

'Both from Sansory,' Poldarn said.

That cheered the clerk up a little. 'Fine,' he said. 'Where?'

'Four hours by cart towards the Bohec, about a day south of the river.'

'Splendid,' the clerk said. 'Outside the jurisdiction,' he explained. 'Outside the jurisdiction, I just take names and details, check the outstanding warrants, you sign or make your mark and that's that. Inside, I have to arrest you and hold you for interrogation.'

Since the clerk was short, fat, just the right side of sixty and younger than his two colleagues, that told Poldarn a lot about the way things were done in Liancor. There was a three-legged stool against the wall next to the door. Poldarn picked it up, carried it over to the table.

'Sorry,' the clerk said, 'forgot my manners. Yes, please take a seat. Names. His first.'

As the clerk dipped his pen in the inkwell, Poldarn realised that he didn't actually know the dead driver's name; the man had been sitting on the box of the cart Falx Roisin had pointed to, Poldarn had got up beside him, the cart had moved off and the man had started moaning about how unfair it all was. Quite justifiably, as it had turned out.

'I'm sorry,' he said, 'I don't know his name. He was new; at least, it was the first time we'd worked together.'

'Oh.' The clerk looked sad. 'I need a name,' he said. 'Who do you work for?'

'Falx Roisin,' Poldarn replied. 'He runs a—'

'Unknown, Falx house, Sansory,' the clerk recited as he wrote. 'That'll do fine. You see, we pass our returns on to the prefecture in Sansory, they check them against their returns, it'll be sorted out then. Your name?'

'Poldarn.'

'Poldarn what?'

'Just Poldarn. I'm a southerner.'

The clerk looked up for a moment. 'Oh well,' he said. 'All right, just Poldarn. Now then, what happened? Accident?'

Poldarn shook his head. 'He was the driver, I was the guard. A man tried to rob the cart; killed him with a slingshot, then came for me. I killed him.'

'Right.' The clerk nodded, didn't look up. 'That's fine, then; my condolences on your loss, sign the register here—' He turned the book round and pushed it across the table, then handed Poldarn the pen. 'Oh, you can write, that's good. All right, I'll make out a certificate and forward that to the prefecture at Sansory, copy for my file, job done. Thank you, you can go now.'

'Thank you,' Poldarn replied, getting up. He put the stool back where he'd found it, then asked, 'So you believe me, then?'

The clerk looked at him. 'Does it matter?' he said.

He left the office and asked the boy who'd been minding the cart where the Fejal house was.

'What?' the boy replied.

'The Fejal house.'

The boy looked puzzled, then grinned. 'Oh, right, the *Feejle* house.' (Poldarn had pronounced it Feyjarl, as Falx Roisin had done.) 'Sorry, but you talk funny. Right, you follow this street till you come to the tannery, then twice left, right, left again by the Virtue's Own Reward, follow that road round, you'll see the old ropewalks on your right—'

'Better still,' Poldarn interrupted, 'you show me and I'll give you another quarter.'

'Sure,' the boy said and hopped up on to the box. 'So,' he said, 'what're you carrying?'

Poldarn realised he didn't know. The load was roped in at the back, covered up with waxed hides and sailcloth. He shrugged. 'You tell me,' he said. 'What do they do at the Fejal house?'

The boy grinned. 'Biggest button-maker this side of the Bohec,' he replied, 'so probably it's either horns or bones. Maybe both. I'll take a look if you want.'

'I'm not bothered,' Poldarn replied.

'Aren't you just a little bit curious?'

Poldarn shook his head. 'For reasons I won't bore you with,' he said, 'I'm not curious about anything any more.' The letter inside his shirt was for someone else, a man called Huic Penseuro, but all he had to do was hand it over to Fejal Nas, along with the stuff in the cart. 'Where's a good place to get something to eat?'

There were, it turned out, two Fejal Nasses, father and son; the father was out, but the son seemed to be expecting the letter and gave him thirty quarters for his trouble. 'Any problems along the way?' he asked.

'Nothing to do with the letter,' Poldarn said. 'Will there be a reply?'

Fejal Nas shook his head. He hadn't opened the letter. 'Just out of interest,' he said, as Poldarn was getting ready to leave, 'but have you been to the Cunier house in Mael Bohec lately?'

It occurred to Poldarn that the sensible reply would be No. 'Yes,' he said. 'Why?'

'Nothing. I just heard Falx Roisin had got a new courier, that's all.'

There was obviously a lot wrong with that answer, and equally obviously Fejal Nas didn't care. 'That's me,' Poldarn said.

'Ah. Well, I expect I'll be seeing you again, then. Safe journey home.'

Obviously more to that than met the eye, he thought, as he waited for the porters to unload the cart, but, as he'd told the boy, he didn't want to know. It was bad enough keeping himself from facing up to the implications of what Eyvind had told him. He'd been carrying that all the way from the place where the fight had happened, making him feel like an ambassador at a special reception held in his honour who can't think of anything except how desperately he needs to take a leak. Sleep, for example; he knew for certain that unless he got himself drunk enough to pass out in a chair or on the floor, he'd lie awake all night desperately not thinking about it, not endlessly turning the various explanations, likely and improbable, over and over in his mind till they'd rubbed sores on the backs of his eyes – raider, traitor, duly authorised negotiator, herald. Every conceivable possibility had flared up in his imagination long before Eyvind had finished talking, the arguments for and against each hypothesis had been analysed, correlated and compared with archived data, debated and voted on, appealed against, decided on by a whole hierarchy of levels of imagination and belief. He felt like the garrison of some small fortress surrounded on all sides by the armies of the greatest power in the world, bombarded by engines, assaulted with rams and ladders, undermined by saps and camouflets, enfiladed by archers from cavaliers and ravelins, invested and breached in every bastion, on the point of arriving at the critical moment when the losses make further defence impossible.

'That's the lot,' the head porter said, putting his hand inside his shirt to wipe the sweat from his neck and shoulder. 'Bloody lumpy stuff,' he added, 'you're not going to tell me that was just bones.'

'You're right,' Poldarn replied with a smile. 'In fact, I'm not going to tell you anything at all. Thanks for your help.'

He didn't quite catch what the head porter called after him as he drove away.

The original plan had been to hang around Liancor for the rest of the day, drinking heavily and eventually winding up in a gutter somewhere, but he had the cart to think of; Falx Roisin would probably forgive him for losing another driver, but he seemed to treat the rolling stock as if they were his own children. He didn't relish the prospect of going back the same way, probably passing the two dead bodies (he had a horrible vision of Eyvind jumping down on the cart from the branches of a low tree, missing his footing and getting crushed to death under the wheels), but he wasn't in the mood for creative navigation. In a vague attempt to keep his mind off the things it wanted to be on, he tried singing, but he only knew one song –

> *Two crows sitting in a tall thin tree,*
> *Two crows sitting in a tall thin tree,*
> *Two crows sitting in a tall thin tree,*
> *And along comes the Dodger and he says, 'That's me.'*

– and he didn't like it much anyway. Nevertheless, he sang it; and after he'd droned through it a couple of times it occurred to him that before there'd only been one crow. He decided he didn't really want to know where the other one had come from.

He spent the night beside the road, sitting with his legs spread out in front of him and his back against the front wheel, not sleeping. As soon as there was enough light to see by, he set off again, hoping to get across the river early. Fortunately as it turned out, he lost a cotter pin about an hour after sunrise and wasted a lot of time whittling a replacement out of green oak; it was just after midday when he approached the top of the heavily wooded scarp overlooking the Bohec valley, and heard the noise.

At the back of his mind he was surprised, disappointed even, that it didn't jog his memory. Given what he'd pieced together about himself, particularly the most recent evidence, he'd have thought that the sound of a battle in full swing should have been specially evocative to him, possibly enough to crack open the seal. Instead he recognised it for what it was, not because it was familiar, but because there's no other sound on earth like it.

He reined in the horses and sat still for a moment, trying to figure out what to do. Turning round and heading for Liancor as quickly as possible seemed to have a logic to it that was hard to fault. Apart from the matter of his own safety, he had a feeling that he really ought to let them know there was a war on the way. There again, however, his lack of background knowledge made him hesitate. It might well be their war, one they'd started against somebody or other, one that everybody else in the world knew about but him. There was also the possibility that the war was headed for Liancor with the intention of wiping it off the map, in which case being stuck inside the gates might not be a good idea. He could set off across country, maybe, but he had no idea what lay out of sight of the stretch of road he'd travelled along, and he was getting sick and tired of the unknown. That left the option of trying to get round the war somehow and returning to Sansory. Assuming Sansory was still there.

He pulled a face. He might not know what the best choice was, but it certainly wasn't sitting still in the middle of the road a few hundred yards away from a battle. Back in one of the identical streets of Mael Bohec he'd seen a large, ugly statue of a chunky nude female, whose inscription told him that it had been set up to celebrate One Thousand Years Of Peace. What was it like in the empire, he thought, when it was *officially* at war?

He jumped down from the cart, left the road and picked his way between the trees and brambles, heading for the crest. There was little point even trying to be quiet, with the noise of the battle so close and insistent: shouting, banging, clattering, industrial noises of various kinds. When he'd reached the top of the rise, he poked his head up to see what he could see, and realised his view of the river and the battle was blocked by a clump of young, spindly pines. He found that frustrating (he was curious; he wanted to see what a battle looked like), so, having looked round carefully for any signs of an unfriendly presence in the immediate vicinity and found none, he lowered his head, ducked under a swathe of brambles and shoved and wriggled his way to the foot of a big, bent chestnut tree. As he'd hoped, climbing trees turned out to be one of his many talents; he shinned up the trunk without thinking about how he was doing it, reached the low branches with a certain amount of effort, and found that the middle branches formed a convenient natural ladder. As he hauled himself up to the point where he could see the valley, he dislodged a very big, squat crow – practically put his hand on the bird's feet before he saw it – and nearly fell out of the tree in surprise as it shot out its wings, more than trebling its size, and flopped sullenly into the air, calling him names as it went.

Ah yes, he said to himself, grinning. *That'll be the other one.*

Then he remembered what he'd come to see: the battle. Most of all, from this height and perspective, it looked untidy, as if a naughty child had deliberately scattered its toys right across the field as a protest against being sent to bed; the black, familiar shapes lying where they'd been dropped, the toy horses, carts, wagons left lying on their sides, knocked over and trodden on and broken by a spoiled child who didn't value what it had been given. It was an affront to all his instincts of good behaviour, this wanton mess and the attitude it implied.

He didn't know, of course, how long the battle had been going on for, but it wasn't too hard to pick up the plot. The opposing sides had drawn up on either side of the river, held position long enough to plant a few flags and standards, and then, for some reason, the army nearest to him had charged down the slope and rushed the ford. They'd got a small part of their forces across by the time their enemy reached the river; but somehow or other the enemy had been able to stop them and retake the ford, cutting off the men who'd already crossed and surrounding them. That hadn't happened all that long ago, to judge by the number who were still standing and the rate at which they were going down; meanwhile, the army on his side of the river was trying rather too hard to retake the ford and rescue them, pouring men into a space where large numbers wouldn't fit, with the result that about a quarter of the men trying to push through were getting shoved out of the way and into the deep water, where the current was doing a reasonable job of flushing them away. The men defending the ford, however, didn't seem to have appreciated the strength of their position; instead of holding still and letting the enemy make trouble for themselves, they were trying to push forward and get ashore on the other side – where, surely, they'd be running the risk of repeating the enemy's mistake. In any event, the battle had lost whatever subtlety and tactical interest it might once have had, and had turned into a nasty, disorganised shoving-match, a confluence of two mistakes. Even from a distance Poldarn could see that the men involved were squashed far too close together to be able to fight. Instead they'd become soft weapons for the men behind them to barge and thrust at the enemy with, a blunt and fragile pike-hedge and shield-wall that reminded Poldarn rather too vividly of the fight between the decrepit old men he'd seen when he first arrived in Sansory. The worst part of it, perhaps, was the fact that the two sides seemed so evenly matched in numbers that he couldn't see how there could be an outcome before both had been decimated; while they were so completely engaged with each other, jammed together like the two carts in Falx Roisin's gate, even if they both agreed to stop fighting immediately it'd take hours of joint effort and a lot of imaginative thinking to get them apart again.

If he'd been hoping that watching a battle might let slip

some of his own memories, such as another battle in a river between exactly matched forces, he was disappointed, and the very act of watching like this, when he was nothing to do with either side, struck him as morbid and distasteful, as if he'd climbed up on a roof and poked a hole through the thatch to watch two extremely ugly people making love. It was also, after a while, boring; nothing very much was happening, apart from the stalemate in the ford, and he was starting to feel cramped and uncomfortable on his tree branch. The hell with it, he thought; I've had enough of this, I think I'll leave now.

He gave that some thought. Getting across the river was clearly impossible here. He could try going up- or downstream for a mile or so and looking for somewhere to cross, but downstream he stood a fair chance of running into men who'd been swept away by the river and survived, whereas upstream there was a risk of stumbling into a cavalry squadron sent to out-flank the main battle, assuming either party had the brains to think of such a move. Going back to Liancor, on the other hand, looked much more promising. If he was reading this battle correctly, by the time it was over neither side would be in any fit state to sweep down on Liancor and lay it waste, even if that was the intention. The worst that could happen, as far as he was concerned, would be for the army on his side of the river suddenly to break off and pull back, retreating up the road in panic. That didn't seem likely, though, unless some-thing extremely melodramatic and improbable happened, such as divine intervention.

He was two-thirds of the way down the tree, at a point where he was having to wrap his arms round the trunk and sidle down inch by inch towards the next convenient foothold, when he heard shouts and crashing noises disconcertingly close by. There was, of course, no way he could turn round to see what was going on. Unless whoever was making all the noise and fuss was blind, however, it was a cinch that they could see him. At the very least, it was embarrassing.

Or maybe they weren't looking, having other things on their minds. As he reached the foothold, someone screamed and then stopped screaming very abruptly. Then there was a quite distinctive sucking noise, which he couldn't remember having heard before, but guessed was the sound of a long, thin, probably fluted blade being pulled out of flesh. It was at that point that he was stable enough to turn round.

He saw a dozen or so men on foot in a circle around a single horseman; they had short-shafted halberds in their hands and were closing slowly, with the air of skilled tradesmen not about to ruin an important job by rushing it. There was a riderless horse a few yards away, standing calm and patient over a slumped body. The horseman in the middle of the ring was flailing at arm's length with a sword – one of the famous backsabres, to be precise; it was too heavy for him to use one-handed, and his swishes were uncontrolled and weak but still well worth staying clear of in the absence of any pressing reason to get close. The horseman was wearing a velvety red surcoat over some expensive-looking scale armour and a high conical helmet with a noseguard that obscured his face, but the odds were definitely against him and in favour of the halberdiers, who were also colourfully and incongruously dressed in the sort of fabric Poldarn associated with the higher class of textile stalls in the Undergate in Sansory.

Then one of the halberdiers happened to look up and see him as he reached with his toe for the next foothold. He could see the man's face, not that it was anything remarkable, and the man could see his.

'Bloody hell,' the man said, and stepped backwards out of the circle. *Not again,* Poldarn thought; the man was staring at him, as he swung the halberd single-handed overarm and back, getting ready to throw it javelin fashion. The horseman stopped thrashing about; just for a moment, nobody was paying him any attention.

'It can't be,' one of the halberdiers said, as the halberd left the first man's hand and sailed slowly, spinning, through the air. 'He's dead.' Very nearly true; Poldarn was so mesmerised, so thoroughly sick of the same thing happening, over and over again, that he left ducking to the last moment and was nearly pinned to the tree by his neck. As it was his left foot slipped off the branch and there was an awkward moment when he almost lost his balance. As he was wavering, scrabbling at the bark with the fingernails of his right hand for a grip to steady himself by, he heard someone else shout, 'You three, get after him, we'll deal with—' He didn't hear the rest; it was drowned out by the sound of splintering wood as the branch he was standing on gave way.

Hell of a time to fall out of a tree, so it was just as well he had sharp reflexes and was able to get a hand round a branch on the way down. He wasn't able to hang on long enough to pull himself back up, but at least he managed to make a controlled landing, with only about four feet to drop before his feet touched down. He stumbled immediately – he'd landed on a tree root, which did something painful to his ankle – but managed to shift his weight on to his back foot in time to swing round and face the closest halberdier in some semblance of good order.

Luckily the first man to reach him was the one who'd just thrown away his halberd; he also had a sword, but only a rather vague idea of what to do with it, and in the end he proved more of a help than a threat, since he fell straight backwards as soon as Poldarn made his draw, and the man behind him had to sidestep in order to get out of the way. Unluckily for him, this manoeuvre opened up his left side, giving Poldarn a brief but clear opportunity for a second-rib-level thrust that he didn't neglect. Number Two dropped unhelpfully to his knees, but the speed with which his two colleagues had been killed clearly stunned the third man to such an extent that he stopped dead in his tracks, thereby losing the initiative. Poldarn feinted

at him low and left, then, as the halberdier executed a slow and
clumsy block, he stepped neatly past him, kicking in the back
of his right knee as he went, and sprinted for the spare horse,
which was waiting obligingly for him with a vacant expression
on its face.

The horseman who'd been the centre of attention a few
moments ago must've had enough intelligence to know a good
thing when he saw it, because as soon as Poldarn's foot
touched the stirrup the ring of halberdiers appeared to collapse in on itself, and he caught a brief glimpse of another
horse moving off in the opposite direction just as he'd got
control of the reins. He didn't have time to see what happened to the other rider (a halberdier materialised suddenly on
his left and had to be kicked hard in the face before he'd go
away), but when he looked round again the man was nowhere
to be seen.

I know him, Poldarn thought. Tazencius?

Poldarn's own situation was far from ideal, as the only way
he could get clear of the soldiers was to ride down the road
towards the battle. But it wasn't as if he had a choice (just this
once, a choice would've been welcome), so he kicked the horse
smartly on and ducked low on to its mane to avoid an over-
hanging branch. He was congratulating himself on having
strolled unscathed out of yet another desperate encounter
when two men jumped up at him out of a clump of brambles,
waving their arms. The horse shied and reared, and the last
thing he remembered seeing was a blurred snap of a dead and
rotten tree branch growing larger in front of his eyes at an
alarmingly high rate.

Chapter Fifteen

'I thought I'd told you to go away.'

Poldarn opened his eyes, and saw half his face reflected in water. It was a familiar image, though not a reassuring one. He closed his eyes again, and immediately he realised his mistake; he wasn't the body slumped in the water at the river's edge, he was (of course) the ragged black crow circling overhead, looking warily at that same body and speculating as to whether it was safe or not (you couldn't be too careful, especially with humans; each of them a nasty little mind of its own, and all of them treacherous).

He listened to what the human was saying, though it took him a moment to figure out who it was talking to, since there was no other living human nearby. Apparently, though, it was talking to its own reflection in the water. He thought about that, and laughed. He (the greater He) had seen literally millions of humans over the years, and nothing they did surprised him any more.

'For God's sake stop following me,' the human said to its image in the water. 'I thought I made it perfectly clear, so even you could understand. I want nothing more to do with you.'

'Sure,' replied the image ironically. 'Sure you don't; at least, not till something happens; someone pulls a sword on you, or you run in with some soldiers. Then it's a different story altogether, of course. You expect me to drop everything and come running and save you, like the big, strong, brave hero I am. You know what? You want to make your mind up sometime.'

'I already did,' said the human angrily. 'And what the hell makes you think I wanted you to come barging in like that, killing people, making everything horrible?'

'Oh, right. Now you're going to say you were managing perfectly well without me.'

'I was.'

The reflection laughed. 'Like hell you were. I can't leave you alone for two minutes and you're in trouble again.'

'That's a lie,' yelled the human. 'Any trouble I get into, it's always you that causes it.'

'You want to think that, be my guest.' The reflection was calm and still, maddeningly so. 'I'd just like to see how you'd make out if I really wasn't there when you need me. Which is pretty much all the time. You want to try that? Really?'

'Yes.'

'Don't believe you. Fortunately I know you better than you do. I've accepted responsibility for you and I'm going to see you right. Whether you want me to or not.'

'Go to hell.'

'That's really sweet of you. And typical. Oh, and while I think of it, what's all this about you seeing other people while I'm not there?'

'So what if I am? Absolutely nothing to do with you. And besides, they're family. People I share in. Part of me. Which is a damn sight more than you are, now.'

'You think. We'll see. We'll see if they'll come and dig you out of the next mess you get yourself in. But,' the reflection went on, 'you needn't worry, I don't mean that. Like I said,

I'm responsible for you. I happen to take these things seriously – you know, vows, obligations. And I gave up expecting gratitude long ago.'

'Gratitude!'

'Yes, gratitude. Like, remembering me when I've gone. Staying awake. Of course, I know you still care about me.'

'Care about you . . . !'

'Of course. Else why do you keep looking for me when you think I'm not watching? And all these other people you've had in your mind, the ones you won't admit to, even to yourself. It's all just because, deep down, you're trying to make me come back.'

'The *hell* with you!' screamed the human—

—And, as Poldarn opened his eyes, he realised that he'd got it right the first time; he was the body lying in the river, and the crow up above him was just another crow. More to the point, he was looking square into the face of an extremely ugly old woman with one of those ground-down faces that could be anywhere between fifty and seventy, wearing a stiff black shawl like a crow's hood. She was strong, too; she'd hauled him over on to his back and was tugging the sword out of his sash. When she realised he was awake, she let go of the scabbard and drew the blade, pushing down on his chest with her left hand, the thumb crushing his windpipe. He managed to reach up and get the palm of his left hand under her chin; she bit his thumb with sharp, jagged teeth and he let go quickly, but he'd done enough to make her ease off the pressure on his throat. She had the sword out of the scabbard now but she was holding it awkwardly, it was too long for a straightforward underarm stab; for a moment she wasn't sure how to proceed, and the moment was long enough for Poldarn to shift hard to his left, tip her off balance and bring his right fist up hard against the side of her jaw. Something brittle gave way; she clucked with pain, dropped the sword and jumped up. Poldarn reached forward, but she kicked his hand hard and accurately, then stepped back a few paces and turned her back on him. Moaning at the pain in her jaw, she knelt down beside another body and started to search it, ignoring Poldarn as if he didn't exist.

He sat up, retrieved the sword and looked at the blood and toothmarks on his hand where he'd been bitten. There was no call for that, he thought, and if his head wasn't hurting he'd go over there and tell her what he thought about it (she was tugging a dead man's shirt off over his head as if she was skinning a rabbit). He pulled himself upright, swayed for a moment and flopped back on to his knees. Must stop getting bashed on the head, he thought; can't be good for you.

While he was catching his breath and building up his strength for another assault on standing up, he looked round again, searching this time not for similarities but differences. The first and most striking of these to engage his attention was the size and scope of the scrap pile. It was far bigger than anything he'd seen before, bigger than Eolla's collection in the stores, bigger than the whole of the salvage market in Sansory. There were certainly hundreds of bodies, possibly a thousand or more (all those shirts, trousers, boots, belts, laces, buttons, knives, purses, satchels, coats, to say nothing of the weapons and armour; looked at with the right attitude, this was better than the first week of harvest), implying that this must have been a major battle, whether it was meant to be one or not. He remembered the voices he'd heard (assuming they hadn't been a dream); something had gone wrong according to them, the battle shouldn't have happened or shouldn't have got out of hand to such an extent. He wondered where the armies were now, and why they'd had to rush off without stopping to bury their dead.

He heard a shriek of fear and looked around. He saw his friend the old woman and another just like her; his one (he could tell her from the other by the asymmetrical set of her jaw) was kneeling behind a wounded man, holding his arms

back, while the other one drew a knife from her belt. It was, of
course, none of Poldarn's business. But there was a stone of
the right size and shape right next to his hand, and he was still
annoyed about being bitten. He picked up the stone and threw
it as hard as he could. In a sense he missed, since he'd been
meaning to hit the woman with the knife somewhere on the
arm or shoulder. Instead the stone hit her just above the ear,
and she went down with a few frantic flaps of her baggy black
wings and lay still. The other woman looked up, saw him and
screamed something at him, then let go of the soldier's arms,
snatched up a bundle of shirts, boots, trousers and stockings
so fat she could hardly get her arms around it, and hobbled off
at a fair speed into the wood.

Poldarn stood up, went over and turned the other woman's
body over with his toe. She was still breathing, just about, but
there was blood pouring from her nose, mouth and ear. A
humanitarian would probably put her out of her misery, but
he wasn't in the mood.

'Thank you,' someone said. Poldarn looked behind; he'd
forgotten the soldier whose throat they'd been about to cut.
Strictly speaking, of course, Poldarn had just saved his life.

'That's all right,' he said. 'It was instinct more than anything. Maybe I grew up on a farm.'

The other man didn't know what to make of that but
laughed anyway. 'I don't know how they can do that,' he said.
'That's really terrible.' He stopped, and looked down. Poldarn
noticed for the first time that his legs didn't look right.
'Horses,' the man said. 'The last thing I remember was falling
off mine. I guess I'm lucky they only trampled my legs.'

Poldarn frowned. There was no reason why he should help;
equally, no reason why he shouldn't. Instinctively he felt for
the letter, then remembered that he'd already delivered it. In
that case, his time was his own. He went across and knelt
beside the man.

'This is going to sound strange,' he said, 'but if you want

me to help you, listen carefully and don't interrupt. I got bashed on the head a while back and lost my memory, and it hasn't come back yet. This means I don't know who you are, or what this battle was about, or whether you're the good guys or the bad guys. Understood?'

The man looked at him, and he could see him take the decision not to say anything, just nod.

'Splendid. Now,' he went on, 'it follows that I don't know who you belong to, or where I should return you to. You're going to have to tell me. It'd be really helpful if you can give me a straightforward answer.'

The man grinned. 'Easy,' he said. 'My name is Muno Silsny, I'm a junior captain in the seventh light cavalry division under Major-General Actis. If I'm right in thinking we won the battle, you'll find our camp on the other side of the river, somewhere between here and Sansory; quite close, I'd imagine, probably only a mile or so. Might as well be on the moon, of course, for a man with two broken legs, so if you don't help me I'll almost certainly die. Not that I'm trying to put pressure on you or anything.'

Poldarn nodded. 'That's lucky for you,' he said. 'I'm going to Sansory. If I take you back to your people, will they trade you for a horse?'

'Undoubtedly.'

'That's all right, then. Of course,' Poldarn went on, 'if my cart's still there I won't need one. But I have a feeling it probably isn't. Stay there, I won't be long.'

As he walked away, the man yelled out something like, 'Where are you going? Come back!' but he couldn't be bothered to reply. He retraced his steps as far as he could remember them back into the wood; there was the tree; some more dead bodies (stripped to the skin, of course); there was the road. No cart. No surprise there.

'No cart,' he told the wounded man a little later. On his way to and from the wood he'd seen at least a dozen other living men, cut up and broken in various ways, but he had to draw the line somewhere. 'Bloody nuisance. How am I supposed to get you across the river and down to your camp without a cart?'

The man looked worried. 'I don't know,' he said.

'Damn.' Poldarn sighed. 'I do,' he said. 'Just as well for you I'm at a loose end right now.'

Poldarn was impressed with how strong he turned out to be. The soldier wasn't a big man, but he wasn't a feather-weight either, yet after the initial strain and effort of getting him over his shoulder Poldarn found he could carry him without actually killing himself. The soldier did his best not to be any trouble; although the manhandling it took to lift and sling him must have been agonising for someone with two broken legs, he hardly made any noise about it.

The other side of the river turned out to be as far as he could go. 'Sorry,' he panted, 'but I've got to stop here.' Being put down probably hurt as much or more than being picked up, but that wasn't Poldarn's problem, and the soldier coped with it well enough. 'You all right?' Poldarn asked, as soon as he had some breath spare for talking. The man nodded, eyes closed, lips squeezed together. A liar, but all in a good cause.

'So your lot are presumably some sort of government army,' he went on, when the soldier had opened his eyes. 'What about the enemy?'

Captain Muno pulled a face. 'Also some sort of govern-ment army,' he replied. 'At least, about two-thirds of them were. The other third were a detachment from one of the free companies, the Amathy house. Have you heard of a man called Tazencius?'

Poldarn nodded. 'Prefect of Mael Bohec,' he replied. 'Caught out doing something illegal and arrested, so I'd heard.'

Captain Muno nodded. 'That's right,' he said. 'Unfortunately, he didn't stay arrested; some bunch of thugs rescued him and turned him loose, and he made straight for his old friend and business partner, Feron Amathy. Well, at least that's out in the open now. We've been suspecting something like that for over a year now and nobody'd listen.' Captain Muno paused and looked up. 'Sorry,' he said. 'Feron Amathy; heard of him?'

'I think so,' Poldarn replied. 'Basically an opportunist; doesn't mind changing sides. Is that the one you mean?'

'You could say that,' Captain Muno replied. 'Yes, a couple of times he helped out General Cronan; yes, on those occasions he was pretty useful – well, more than useful, he saved the day, saved the empire, however you want to put it. But he's still a treacherous bastard, and it's almost certain he's been sending his men out burning villages and massacring innocent people and pretending it was the raiders; there's evidence to suggest he had something to do with what happened to Josequin, though it's not clear whether it was his people alone or whether he was actually in league with the raiders – can you imagine that, actually helping those people? Or don't you know what I'm talking about?'

'I know who you mean,' Poldarn replied. 'So, the army you were fighting against . . .'

Captain Muno breathed in deeply, then out again. 'Tazencius showed up out of nowhere a couple of days ago just north of Liancor with about fifteen hundred Amathy house pikemen. We just happened to be at Laise Bohec, a day to the east of here, about to go off on exercises, so we were told to drop everything, get after him and bring him in. Four thousand of us; we reckoned it'd be a piece of cake. What we didn't know was that Tazencius had sorted something out with the prefect of Liancor and borrowed the garrison, three thousand men. It was a bit of a shock, coming over the crest of that hill there and seeing them all lined up and waiting for us.'

'I can imagine,' Poldarn said, inaccurately.

The captain sighed. 'Tazencius must've thought he had a chance of talking Actis into joining him, because although he had the better position and could've secured the ford before we could get to it, he just stood there and did nothing; and we stood here and did nothing back, because of course rules of engagement say we can't attack our own people first, they've got to start it before we can fight them. Meanwhile, Tazencius sends a messenger – we're standing about wondering what's going on, there's a conference or peace talks or whatever up there on the road between Actis and this messenger, and then suddenly, with no warning, some bloody fool thinks it'd be a good idea to seize the ford. To be honest with you, I don't know if it was us or them, because I wasn't watching; fact is, I was away in the bushes having a crap before the battle, it's a personal ritual of mine. Next thing, of course, everybody's scrambling down to the ford, no plan or order of battle, nothing like that, just a horrible mess and everybody piling in the river and getting trodden under or washed away. Really stupid, the whole thing. I mean, you could just about imagine the Amathy house doing something like that, but our people? We ought to've known better. I'm ashamed, I really am.'

Poldarn pulled a sympathetic face, though he had no idea whether the criticisms were reasonable or not. 'I saw the big shoving-match in the river,' he said, 'but I got distracted before the end, and when I – well, the next time I looked, it was all over. What happened in the end?'

'We did,' Captain Muno replied with a grin, and Poldarn realised he was much younger than he'd at first assumed; it was the pain and fear in Muno's eyes that had given him the impression he was dealing with a man of his own age. 'The cavalry, as always. The scouts found another ford just a mile upstream – took them bloody long enough, we'd been bashing away at each other for three hours in that damned river – so Actis called us out; we'd been fighting dismounted, would you believe, because he didn't have any light infantry and the heavies were falling over and drowning because they couldn't swim in all that ironmongery. Anyway, we were pulled out of the river, given our horses back, thank you so much, and told to get across the other ford as quick as we could, get behind the enemy and – well, do our job, that's what cavalry's supposed to be for. And we did.' A frown crossed his face, unwelcome but insistent. 'Nasty fight that was; not for us, for them, but it was pretty grim stuff up the front end. I was in the middle, of course, nothing to do once the charge had gone in; then we must've smashed through because we started moving up at the double, and that was when some bastard threw something at me and I fell off my horse, and that was that.' He sighed. 'We definitely won, though,' he said, 'because when I came round I could see where we'd been. Piles and heaps of them, maybe one or two or us – and me, of course. Just my luck, spoiling the squadron average and kill-to-loss ratio. We were at the top of the second division in the cavalry league before today, but I expect we've dropped a place now.'

Poldarn waggled his shoulders in a show of sympathy. 'Next stage,' he said. 'Sorry about all this stopping and starting, but it's the best I can do.'

It took a long time to cover a mile, but there was a steep slope to climb, and the wet ground was slippery, doubling the effort involved. By the time he reached the camp, which was more or less where Muno had said it would be, he was exhausted. Certainly, not in the mood for any aggravation from the sentries.

'Halt,' shouted a man with a spear, jumping out from behind a tree. 'Who goes there? Stand and identify yourself,' he added, levelling the spear an inch from Poldarn's throat.

'Piss off,' Poldarn replied, taking a step sideways to avoid the spear and carrying on without stopping. The guard did a double-take and came scampering after him.

'You! Didn't you hear me? I said—'

'I heard you,' Poldarn said wearily. 'Look, I've got one of your men here; two broken legs and God knows what else. You want him or not?'

The guard clearly hadn't been briefed on a situation like this. 'All right,' he said, in a tragic voice, 'but I'll have to clear it with the duty officer first. You just wait there—'

'No chance,' Poldarn snapped. 'What do you think this is, a sack of lambs' wool? Either you take him or get out of my way and tell me where you stack the wounded.'

The guard looked utterly miserable. 'Oh for God's – straight down between the rows of tents, third left, second right, look for a big green awning, that's the mess tent. Behind that on your left . . .'

'Stuff it,' Poldarn interrupted. 'You show me the way.'

'But I can't leave my post.'

'Shut up and do as you're told.'

So the sentry led the way; and whenever he tried to grab hold of someone to take over as guide, either they outranked him and told him off or dodged out of the way before he could open his mouth. All this time, of course, Poldarn's legs weren't getting any stronger and Muno carried on weighing a lot.

'There,' the sentry said, pointing at a green tent in the middle of a block. 'That one.' Then he spun round and scampered off the way they'd just come without looking back.

The surgeon was just finishing up an amputation when Poldarn came in; he was standing beside the table with a leg in one hand and a thick pad of bloodstained wool in the other. 'Who are you?' he asked as the orderlies removed the previous patient and slotted him in beside the others on the floor.

'Nobody you know,' Poldarn said. He bent down and tried to shrug Muno off on to the table without jarring or dropping him. Fortunately he'd passed out some time ago.

The surgeon glared at him. 'Can't you see there's a line?' he grumbled, indicating the row of damaged people Poldarn had just walked past.

'None of my business,' he replied. 'I said I'd get him here, and I have. In return, he said you'd give me a horse.'

The surgeon laughed. 'No offence,' he said, 'but you've been had. No chance of that, sorry. If we were back in barracks, just possibly. Right now, forget it.' He grinned, showing about four teeth. 'Now if you wanted to trade the other way round, you could take your pick.'

That annoyed Poldarn, but he was so delighted and relieved to have got rid of Muno's weight that he couldn't be bothered to argue. 'The hell with you, then,' he said, dragged himself out of the tent and flopped down on a short barrel that stood next to the flap.

For quite some time he didn't think about anything except how tired he was. Then he allowed himself to fret about getting home. Damned if he was going to walk. If they wouldn't give him a horse (his own stupid fault for being so trusting), he'd have to buy one or steal one – neither option appealed to him much – or else kid somebody into giving him a ride back to or in the direction of Sansory. That didn't seem likely to happen either.

'Excuse me.' He looked up, and saw a very young soldier in a very big, shiny helmet looking down at him. 'Excuse me,' the young man repeated, 'but did you just bring in a wounded soldier?'

Poldarn nodded. 'Maybe not the one you're thinking of,' he added. 'Mine was called Muno something.'

'Muno Silsny. My uncle.' The young man smiled. 'I was just over at the sick tent with somebody else, and they told me about you. I was really worried when I couldn't find him after the battle.'

Horse, Poldarn thought. 'That's all right,' he said. 'I found him beside the river – just in time, two horrible old women were about to kill him for his boots – and he said to fetch him here. Is he going to be all right?' he added, trying to sound as if he cared.

'We don't know yet,' the young man replied solemnly. 'Surgeon said he's got two broken ribs as well as the leg fractures, but he reckoned he'd seen worse.' He paused and added sheepishly, 'You saved his life. Thank you.'

Poldarn shrugged. 'Anybody would've done the same,' he replied, doing his best to make the remark sound like an obvious lie. 'And in case you're worried,' he went on, 'I'm not going to try and hold you to his promise.'

'Promise?' The young man looked properly concerned.

'Oh, it wasn't anything. He just said that if I brought him in he'd see to it they gave me a horse – lost mine in the fighting, of course. But really, it doesn't matter in the least.'

The young man disagreed. The young man felt that it mattered very much. And, since he was a junior adjutant on the major-general's staff, he was in a position to do something about it, so if he'd care to follow—

In the end Poldarn chose a rather magnificent chestnut mare, which he figured would fetch him at least fifty quarters in the stolen-horse market at Sansory. The young man didn't tell him who it belonged to, and he didn't ask. Instead he thanked the young man politely, took the horse by the bridle and headed for the gate.

'I really can't thank you enough,' the young man assured him for the seventh or eighth time. 'Really he's my uncle but we're more like brothers. I don't know what I'd do if anything happened to him.'

'No problem,' Poldarn muttered, wishing he'd go away before his enthusiasm and loud, high voice attracted the attention of the horse's owner. 'So which way are you people headed now?' he added, by way of changing the subject.

'I'm not sure, to be honest with you,' the young man replied, lengthening his stride to keep up. 'Either back to Laise or on to Liancor, it depends on when the reinforcements get here. I heard someone say General Cronan may be taking the field himself now that Tazencius has got involved. Apparently they've hated each other for years. I hope it's true, it'd be a real honour to serve under General Cronan.'

Wisely, Poldarn decided not to comment on that. "Well, best of luck,' he said. 'Hope it all goes well for you and your brother. I'm heading back to Sansory myself; any idea where the enemy went? I'd rather not bump into them on the road.'

The young man nodded briskly. 'I can see that,' he said. 'I don't honestly know, myself, but I could ask someone if you like.'

'That's all right,' Poldarn assured him immediately, 'I'm sure I'll manage. Thanks for your help.'

'No,' the young man replied earnestly, 'thank *you*.'

True, the young man was about as restful as a storm at sea, but thanks to him Poldarn was outside the gate with a good, valuable horse, so that was just fine. The road was straight and reasonably firm, and there was no reason why he shouldn't be able to get a move on and reach Sansory in two and a half days—

Then he saw the cart.

His cart – Falx Roisin's cart – no doubt about it, because there was the bent left-side tailgate catch, there was the impro-vised cotter pin; even the same horses, the grey and the roan. He slowed down as he passed and drew level, looking hard at the man and woman sitting side by side on the box.

'You two,' he called out.

They didn't answer, or even look round at him. The man was mostly muffled up in a dark cloak, with a broad-brimmed black hat shading his face. The woman, on the other hand—

'Copis?'

Her head cranked round so sharply he was afraid she'd hurt her neck. She reined in the cart. The man moved, was proba-bly about to say something, but she kicked his ankle and hissed at him to shut up.

'Copis,' Poldarn repeated. 'What the hell?'

'Oh,' she said flatly, 'it's you. What on earth are you doing out here?'

Somehow, he felt that that was his line. Now that he'd seen her, of course, he recognised the man's coat and hat.

'Working,' he said. 'What about you?'

'Same thing,' she said. 'You're just about to make a fuss, aren't you? Well, don't. I got a new partner once before, I can do it again, can't I?'

Not for the first time when talking to Copis, Poldarn had the feeling he'd missed out an important section. 'I suppose so,' he said. 'But what the hell are you doing playing this racket again? I thought you'd given up doing this sort of thing.'

She glared at him. 'Did you really?' she said. 'Well, you're wrong. Can we go now, please?'

That annoyed him. 'No,' he said. 'That's my cart. Where did you get it?'

'Don't be silly,' Copis replied, shifting a little in her seat. 'It's mine. I paid good money for it.'

'When?'

'Why should that matter?'

Poldarn leaned out of his saddle and snatched the right rein out of her hand with a sharp flick of the wrist. 'Because it's my cart,' he replied. 'At least, it belongs to the Falx house. I lost it when I ran into the battle back at the ford—'

'Battle? What battle?'

'—And now here it is, with you in it. Who did you buy it from, and when?'

The man on the box started to make vaguely bellicose noises, which Copis ignored. 'None of your business,' she replied awkwardly. 'Let go of the reins.'

'No.'

'Oh, this is so childish. If you must know, I bought it from a gleaning party about an hour ago, back at the camp. It was a real stroke of luck finding one there, because we had to leave

ours in a hurry when we ran into the soldiers – not those soldiers, the other ones, the ones who lost, I suppose. It had all
the props and provisions in it, too.'

'Gleaning party,' Poldarn repeated. 'Oh, you mean people
who go round robbing the dead after a battle? They actually
let them in the camp?'

'Let them in?' Copis grinned. 'They sell franchises.
Commanding officer's perk, worth good money. How do you
think all that stuff they sell in the market at Sansory gets
there?'

Poldarn could feel himself getting sidetracked. 'That's
beside the point,' he said. 'It's still my cart—'

Copis shook her head, grinning smugly. 'No it's not,' she
said. 'Articles of war; objects abandoned on battlefields. Good
title in the goods passes to a purchaser from a duly licensed
gleaner. Falx Roisin'll know what I'm talking about, even if
you don't.'

Poldarn had no answer to that, since he'd never been able to
tell when Copis was lying. Even when she was telling the
truth she gave the impression she was lying; all he'd been
able to do was make an educated guess from context. 'So what
were you doing here anyway?' he said. 'You must be out of
your mind going back to the god-in-the-cart routine. Didn't
you hear? They hanged two people for working it only the
other day.'

She scowled at him. 'So what are you going to do,' she said,
'turn me in? Why should you care?'

'I don't,' he said, wondering why she seemed so angry. 'But
you don't need to take risks like that any more, surely. I
thought—' He frowned. 'You can't have lost all that money
already, can you?'

The new god looked up sharply. 'What money?'

'You, shut up. No, of course I haven't,' Copis snapped.
'Not *lost*. It's just – invested, that's all.'

'Invested?'

'Long-term investment. It'll be a while before I can realise it again. In the meantime, I've got to earn a living, and the ivory mirror business turned out not to be any good. So.'

Poldarn could feel his temper fraying. 'So you're back to risking your life and cheating people,' he said. 'Oh, brilliant idea. Progress. Why can't you just settle down and get yourself a proper job somewhere?'

She looked at him. 'Like you did.'

'That's nothing to do with it. You can't have lost *all* the money, surely. There must've been enough left over for a barrow and a few bolts of cloth—'

'You didn't say anything about any money,' the new god persisted. 'What's he talking about?'

'Be *quiet*,' Copis hissed at him. 'And I haven't lost it, I keep telling you, it's just—'

But the new god was getting annoyed now. 'Don't you tell me to be quiet,' he said, grabbing Copis by the arm. 'What money?'

'Ow, that hurts,' Copis complained, wriggling. 'If you don't let go—'

'Tell me,' the new god insisted, 'about this money.'

It occurred to Poldarn, briefly, that maybe he ought to intervene. He dismissed the thought, since his interventions generally seemed to end in blood and carnage. Copis managed to pull her arm free, but that didn't make things any better. Instead the new god went from annoyed to angry and smacked her hard across the face, the ring on his middle finger cutting her lip. She shrieked and tried to get off the box, but the new god was quick. He grabbed her left wrist and pulled her back, and the sudden movement unsettled Poldarn's horse. He reined it back; the new god must have seen the movement out of the corner of his eye and misinterpreted it, because he shoved Copis down on to the floor of the cart, and stood up on the box, growling, 'And you stay out of it, understood?' Poldarn was still occupied with the horse and didn't answer or

look round. The new god didn't like that; he lifted the goad
out from the rest and lashed out with it, presumably meaning to
hit Poldarn's horse, but he missed and cut Poldarn across the
face instead. He flinched but managed to keep his seat on the
horse; it was only a moment later that he realised he'd grabbed
the end of the goad with his left hand after it had hit him, and
was still holding on to it.

The new god didn't like that at all. He tried to pull the
goad away; Poldarn resisted until he could see the new god
was pulling too hard to keep his balance, then let go. As anticipated, the new god fell backwards off the box and landed
hard on his left shoulder. Copis stuck her head up, yelling at
one or the other of them to stop it, then ducked quickly out of
the way as the new god scrambled back up on to the box, this
time holding the felling-axe that hung from a pair of big brass
hooks on the off side of the cart.

If the horse hadn't been skittish, it would've been perfectly
simple for Poldarn to pull away and put some distance
between them, but she wouldn't move when he tried to kick
her on, and by the time he'd tried that and failed the new god
was inside his circle and posing a definite threat. He made a
conscious decision to cut at the new god's arms rather than his
neck, but he made it too late, instinct had already aimed and
executed the shot, and while Poldarn was still thinking about
ways not to kill him the new god was toppling backwards and
the back of Poldarn's sword was pressing on the web between
his left thumb and forefinger, on its way back into the scabbard.

There was a moment's silence.

'You really must stop doing that,' Copis said, in a dull,
sullen voice.

Poldarn got off his horse and walked slowly across to where
the new god's body lay. The cut had gone right down to the
bone. 'You saw what happened,' he mumbled. 'He was going
to . . .'

'They always are,' Copis replied. 'You seem to have the knack of making people want to kill you.' She shook her head. 'He was a loud-mouthed, foul-tempered idiot you wouldn't trust as far as you could spit him and probably he'd have made a really useless god, but he was all I could get.' She sat down on the box and mopped up a splash of blood with a handful of raw wool. 'Ever since I met you, my luck's been bloody awful. None of it's really your fault, as in nasty or stupid things you've done, it just seems like you carry bad luck around with you, like the smell on a pig-breeder's boots. You always seem to come out of it just fine.'

'We'd better get out of here,' Poldarn said. 'I don't suppose another body's going to cause any problems so near a battle-field, but I'd rather not be here if a patrol from the camp comes this way. For one thing, I've got a feeling I wasn't really supposed to take this horse.'

Copis shrugged. 'Get rid of it, then,' she said. 'That's assuming you're heading back to Sansory.'

'Yes. You?'

'Might as well. No reason to go to Laise, now.'

'You wouldn't have done any good in Laise,' Poldarn said, jumping up on the box beside her. 'That's where the government army's from – that lot,' he added, waving an arm in the direction of the camp. 'They'll have left some sort of garrison there. You wouldn't have wanted to try the act in a town where there's government officers; you'd have ended up in the stockade before you knew what hit you.'

Copis sighed. 'I suppose you're right,' she said. 'Next you'll be telling me you just did me a favour.' She picked up the reins. There were a few spots of blood on them, too, and she dabbed them away with the same piece of wool. 'So what were you doing down this way? This famous respectable job of yours?'

Poldarn nodded. 'Though I'm going off it,' he said.

'Oh? Why's that?'

'What you were saying,' he replied. 'Too much of that kind of stuff. Why can't I just sit behind a stall in a market some-where all day and sell pots?'

Copis thought for a moment. 'You'd need some pots,' she said. 'And a stall. And selling stuff is a bloody precarious way of making a living.'

'More so than what I'm doing at the moment?'

'Probably,' Copis said. 'Oh sure, less chance of getting killed, but at least you get paid regularly and you've got a place to sleep provided, and probably meals too.'

'And clothes,' Poldarn put in. 'They even gave me a book.'

'A book?'

'That's right. With all the wisdom in the world in it.'

Copis raised an eyebrow. 'Must be a chunky old book, then.'

'Quite chunky,' Poldarn replied, 'though the recipe book was chunkier.' He frowned. 'Copis,' he said, 'what *did* happen to all that money?'

'You don't want to know. It was nearly a very good idea.'

'And it's all gone?'

'No, I keep telling you. It'll be back, almost certainly dou-bled. It's just going to take a while, that's all.'

'Invested.'

'Invested,' Copis confirmed. 'In a proper business. A really good business, come to that. I was lucky to have got in on the ground floor – I think that's the expression.'

'You're right,' Poldarn said, after a moment. 'I don't want to know. Besides, it's your money, nothing to do with me.'

'That's right.' Copis was quiet for some time, but she was clearly thinking about something. 'How about you?' she said at last. 'Have you got any money?'

Poldarn looked at her. 'What if I have?' he said.

'There's no need to get all defensive,' Copis said irritably. 'I was just asking, that's all.'

'People don't just ask in that tone of voice. Go on, then, tell me about it.'

'Well.' Copis breathed in deeply, then out again. 'What you were saying,' she said, 'about a stall in the market, and selling things. There's a better way of making a living than that, and you'd never have to fight anybody.'

'I know,' Poldarn said, 'it's called farming. But I haven't got a farm, or at least not yet. One day, perhaps, if I can save up some money, and some con artist doesn't cheat me out of it—'

'Better,' Copis said patiently, 'than farming. But I can see you aren't interested.'

The road passed through a gap in a hedge, where there had once been a gate, and the beech trees on either side masked the view behind them, back to where the dead god lay, and the camp, and the battle. On either side of the road there were large, rough fields, dotted with the withered stems of last year's docks and thistles. A long way down the combe on the left-hand side was a small flock of sheep, and parallel with the road ran a broken-down dry-stone wall, more bother to mend than it was worth. Someone somewhere, in some inn, had been talking about how everything was slowly running down, not just this side of the bay but all across the empire; something to do with money being cheap and commodities expensive, too many people out of work, not enough labour to get the work done. It had made some kind of sense while the man was talking.

'Tell me about it,' Poldarn said.

Chapter Sixteen

Stand with your back straight. (Monach was asleep on a hard plank bed in the only inn in Prodo, a dismal little village two hours west of Laise Bohec; but in his dream he was twelve years old, and a novice in a practice hall at Deymeson.) *Stand with your back straight—*

'. . . Your right foot slightly ahead of your left, your feet apart by the width of your shoulders.' Father Tutor walked up and down the lines, looking for a misplaced foot to smack at with his foil. Late afternoon sunlight soaked through the thin vellum windowpanes, yellow and soft, and the whole world smelt of beeswax, sweat and wet plaster. 'Now, draw your sword and hold it out in front of you, both hands on the hilt, as far as you can reach comfortably without stretching.' A hedge of wooden foils sprouted from each row—

(Across so much space and time, Monach couldn't recognise himself; they all look the same at that age, particularly in novice's robes and temple haircuts. But he knew he was there, just as he always knew where his sword hilt was, or the extent of his circle.)

—and Father Tutor went back the way he'd just come, inspecting, adjusting the height of a foil-tip up or down, until he was satisfied that he'd achieved as much uniformity as was possible with a group of human beings.

'Very good,' he said. 'Now, please listen very carefully, because I'm about to teach you the most important lesson you'll ever learn.' He waited for a heartbeat or so, just long enough to tantalise the class into paying attention. 'Moving your feet as little as you can, turn round in a circle, keeping your eyes fixed at all times on the tip of your sword.'

Of course, it was something of a shambles. For one thing, he hadn't specified clockwise or anticlockwise, and it was the first time they'd ever done the exercise . . . Inevitably, one or two novices collided in opposition, their foils meshing like the cogs of a gear-train. There was a certain amount of giggling, and the ludicrous sound of young, pattering feet on a polished wood floor.

'That'll do,' Father Tutor called out, and at once the giggling stopped and the youth in the room evaporated like water sprinkled on the bed of a forge. 'Lower your swords, stand down and listen carefully; this is very difficult, and if you get it wrong you will undoubtedly lose your first live fight and die. Now then.' He took a deep breath and stuck his thumbs into his sash, an unconscious mannerism that he hated because he knew it made him look pompous and fat, but that he had no real control over. The class was staring at him; he felt apprehension and antagonism. That was good.

'Think,' he told him, 'about the circle you've just drawn in the air.' (*Was that Father Tutor talking, or the Junior Tutor that Monach had grown into, eighteen years later, the one who copied his former teacher's words and mannerisms now that he was a teacher himself? The sword-point describes a circle—*) 'You can't see it now,' Father Tutor went on. 'You'd better learn to see it, because it's the circle of life and death – your life, your death, and the lives and deaths of others, possibly dozens or hundreds of them. So long as you're alone in the circle, you're safe, and so is your enemy. He can't reach you, and you can't reach him. As soon as either of you steps into the other's circle – and of course when you enter his circle, he enters yours – both of you are in terrible danger, both of you are a single moment away from success, from victory. The circle of life and death – there's a grand, magical-sounding name for you, but that's precisely what it is. Alone in your circle, you're safe and you can achieve nothing. Once your circle meshes with someone else's, you carry with you victory and defeat, both at the same time, success and failure, life and death.'

They were gazing at him, spellbound – all it took, he reflected cynically, was a little melodrama. He made them wait for a few more moments, then went on. 'Know your circle,' he said. 'Learn it, so that you can see it – not just when you make an effort and look for it, but all the time, whether you want to see it or not. I know it's imaginary, but you've got to make it more real than anything you can touch or see or hear or smell or taste. You've got to know how far you can reach out into the world, and how close the world can come to you, before you have to draw and cut. Does everybody understand, or shall I go through it again?'

He paused for a while, watching the ranks of novices all earnestly imagining dotted lines in the air around them, panicking because they couldn't quite see them yet. Of course, they were all convinced that they'd just learned something exceptionally profound, like the true secret name of God, when in fact he'd just given them a very useful but entirely basic and mundane lesson in swordsmanship technique. It would be years, probably decades, before they came to realise that the exceptionally profound is always, by definition, basic and mundane.

'Before the next class,' he said, snapping them back into the visible world, 'I want you all to learn your circle so well that you'll know immediately when someone breaks into it – and that includes someone behind you or off to the side, not just in front. We'll learn that until everybody's got it perfectly; then we'll do the same thing with our eyes shut. And then, when we really know our own circles, we'll learn how to see other people's.' He smiled, his most off-putting smile. 'Usually, I find it takes about ten years to get it right. And that's if you're really trying.'

The class broke up. Father Tutor drifted out of the hall, reaching the door long before any of the scampering novices, even though he had further to go, and one novice from the second-from-last row—

—Sat up in bed, bolt upright, his eyes still closed, making a noise with his mouth that had words in it but wasn't speech. Then, as his eyes opened, the dream broke up like thawing ice on a pond, and he remembered who and when and where he was, and where his circle began and ended. Not long afterwards he found out what had woken him up; there was a leak in the roof (water, not sunlight leaking through scraped lambskin windows) and a fat, wet raindrop had landed in his ear.

He stood up and opened the shutter a little, just enough to see the first stains of sunrise through the wet air. He wasn't as canny about the weather as some, but he could tell from the shape and height of the clouds that it was going to be a long, wet day, miserable for travelling in. He wasn't particularly happy to find that there was another leak in the roof directly above his right boot, which squelched loudly when he put his foot in it.

With his coat pulled round his ears and his hat dragged down over them he scuttled across the courtyard to the stables, woke up the groom by yelling in his ear, and told him to get his horse ready as soon as possible; then he scuttled back to the main building, found the landlord, paid him and demanded bread, cheese, hot milk and cider, in that order. By the time he'd dealt with them, the groom had given his horse a cursory dab with the brush and the curry-comb and slopped on the saddle and bridle (but he was always careful to check his own straps and girths, so that was all right). He left the inn just after full sunrise and followed the road west, towards Laise Bohec.

Find Tazencius, he says. Wonderful. And what if Tazencius doesn't want to be found? To which Father Tutor would have replied that Tazencius' wishes in the matter were so far down the list of priorities that he really didn't need to worry about them. Easy enough to say, in a warm, well-lit upstairs room in the keep of Deymeson.

In the seventh book of the *Dialectics*, Posuerus wrote, 'If you want to find out where someone is, ask his enemy.' Like so much of Posuerus' wisdom, it was true up to a point; it was fairly likely that Major-General Actis knew where Tazencius was, rather less likely that he'd be prepared to tell a civilian, even an accredited representative of the order with a sealed pass from Father Prior. But it was a place to start, more likely to succeed than combing the side roads looking under bushes. Major-General Actis, of course, probably wasn't in Laise right now, but that was no bad thing, since it wasn't the man himself he was planning to talk to.

Because of the rain and the churned-up roads and a bridge washed away just south of where the Lambo joined the Bohec, it took him five hours instead of two to reach Laise, and by the time he got there he wasn't in the mood for subtly picking bits of information out of junior officers like a man scraping the last bit of meat from a crab's claw. Instead he barged past the sentry in a flurry of sodden coat-tails, calling loudly for the duty officer and trying to look like a spy in a hurry. The duty officer was in the Eastgate tower, playing scuttlejack with the quartermaster and the chief engineer; they jumped up guiltily when he strode in, and tried to stand in front of the board.

Here goes nothing, Monach thought. 'You two,' he snapped at the quartermaster and the engineer, 'take a walk.' They did as they were told, giving Monach grounds to be grateful to the rain; when a man's drenched to the skin and has a suitably hostile attitude, it's very hard to tell whether he's a soldier or a civilian without asking him directly.

'Right,' Monach said, sitting down on the duty officer's stool and laying his wet, dripping hat right on top of the scuttle-jack board, 'I haven't got long – the east road's a disgrace, as I'll be pointing out in my report – so let's get straight to the point, please. Prince Tazencius. Where is he?'

The duty officer looked properly miserable. Monach could sympathise. It was the nightmare of everyone who holds a middle-level rank in a strict hierarchy to be given a direct order that contradicts another direct order by someone whose exact seniority you don't know and daren't ask for fear of sounding insubordinate; which was why he'd chosen the duty officer, of course. (*Attack your enemy at his strongest point; when attacking your allies, look for the weakest link in the chain*; Posuerus, *Dialectics*, VI, 32. Very true, up to a point, and beyond that point, lethally misleading. Typical Posuerus.)

'I'm not supposed to say,' the poor man mumbled, thereby giving away the fact that he knew the answer. He probably wasn't a very good scuttlejack player, either. 'I really need to see some authorisation—'

Monach made an ungracious noise. 'Sure,' he said, 'except that like everything else with me or on me it's soaked right through, and even if the ink hasn't run it'd take three hours to dry out enough to be legible. If I had three hours to waste I wouldn't need to be here, I'd have gone straight to Actis Fraim and asked him.'

(It was pure fluke that he happened to know General Actis' first name; not that it mattered very much, since it was a certainty that the duty officer didn't.)

'I'm sorry,' he replied, and Monach couldn't help noticing how young and generally unfinished he looked, like a clay model for a bronze statue. 'But I've got my orders, and—'

'Yes, you've got your orders. From me. Now, if you'd care to obey them, you can get back to your game and I can go and change my clothes before I catch a fever and die.' He leaned back on the stool, taking note of a rather ominous creak. 'When you're ready,' he added.

Determination drained out of the duty officer like grain from a rotten sack. 'We think he's headed north,' he said, 'looking to get across the Mahec and head north-west towards the sea.' He winced and closed his hands tight. 'We've got a very persuasive source telling us that he and Feron Amathy are planning to join forces with a large party of raiders who'll be making landfall somewhere in the north-west in about a month's time. The deal is, the raiders will take care of General Cronan, then transport Tazencius and the Amathy house across the bay for a sneak attack on Torcea; Tazencius will proclaim himself emperor, and in return for their help he'll withdraw all the imperial garrisons north of the bay and let the raiders do what they like with Mael, Weal, Sansory, Boc, all the northern cities. When they've finished and gone home, Feron Amathy will take over what's left and rule it as a kingdom.' The duty officer stopped talking and looked down, apparently studying his hands, which were shaking.

'I see,' Monach said. 'And what's Actis Fraim supposed to be doing about this?'

The duty officer looked up, puzzled, presumably, at how calmly Monach was taking the end of the world. 'There's not a lot he can do,' he replied, 'except try and cut Tazencius off before he crosses the Bohec, though there's not much chance of that. Other than that, it's a matter of staying put and waiting for General Cronan to decide what to do. Actis can't go charging off north on his own, he'd be cut to ribbons.'

Monach stood up. 'You don't have to answer this,' he said, 'but if I'm right about who this very persuasive source is, maybe the shock will make you sneeze. I think your very persuasive source is Chaplain Cleapho.'

The duty officer stared at him, remembered what he'd been

told to do, and mimed a rather unconvincing sneeze. 'How did you know that?' he asked.

Monach narrowed his eyes in what he hoped was the correct manner. 'You don't want to ask me things like that,' he said.

'Oh.' The duty officer looked away quickly. 'I'm sorry,' he said. 'I didn't . . .'

'It's all right,' Monach told him, erasing the whole conversation with a sweep of his arm. 'Just tell me this. Where, as precisely as you can tell, is Tazencius likely to be now?'

The duty officer thought for a moment, then reached behind him and picked up an old-fashioned brass map from the floor. 'Here,' he said, stabbing at the plate with a stubby finger that left a smudge on the polished metal. 'At least, that's the last place we had a sighting from. Little village called Cric, not far from Josequin.'

'Ah yes,' Monach said in a neutral voice. 'I've been there.'

'We got the report this morning,' the duty officer went on. 'He was headed in that direction, it was the only place he could be making for – well, if you've been there, you'll know that, it's all empty moorland up there. Our man reckoned he must have had barges waiting for him on the Bohec just downstream from Sansory; after we interrupted him north of Liancor, he'll have sent on a message for them to pick him up further down the river; then by barge to Beal Ford, which is due south of Josequin, and up the old cart road headed for Cric. Our man said he didn't seem to be in any great hurry, which Actis reckoned must mean he's got time in hand – for example, he's arranged to meet someone but they won't be there for a day or so. If Cle – if our source is right, that someone's got to be a messenger from the raiders.'

'Quite,' Monach said. 'Thank you.' He walked to the door, stopped and turned back. 'This is just a wild guess,' he said, 'but if I mentioned the name Poldarn, or two people travelling around in a cart—'

'Ah.' The duty officer actually grinned. 'That's them. Well, her, anyway. I don't think the man knows anything about it.'

Monach kept his face as straight as possible. 'The man,' he repeated.

'That's right. Funny, isn't it,' he went on, 'our man turning out to be a woman. No reason why not, of course, far less likely to make people suspicious; it's just the thought of a female spy, that's all.'

Monach felt lucky enough to gamble. 'That's Cleapho for you,' he said. 'Always willing to give it a try.'

'He's a very clever man,' the duty officer replied. 'I'm just glad he's on our side.'

The more I think about it, Monach told himself as his horse splashed through thick puddles of mud on the north-east road, the harder it gets. What the hell am I going to tell Father Tutor?

First, of course, he was disobeying orders; he'd been told to secure the person of Prince Tazencius, not report news – and most certainly not his interpretation of someone else's misinformation. In this case, though, he was prepared to take the risk and do the penances, if ever he got the time (five thousand draws and eight thousand cuts would be a positive pleasure if only he could stay in Deymeson and not have to ride a horse again for a year); the thought of what Father Tutor would say to him if he didn't disobey orders in this case was far more terrifying.

Cleapho; now there was a difficult man to fathom, if ever there was one. Monach wasn't sure if he was supposed to know that Cleapho was the head of his order – nearly everybody in Deymeson knew, of course, but how they ever found out was a mystery, since you never heard anybody mention it, even in the most private of conversations. It was pretty obvious what Cleapho was doing; his distrust of General Cronan was no secret either, hadn't been for many years now. Cleapho was convinced that sooner or later Cronan would turn on the emperor and make a grab for the throne; he was too much of a patriot and an idealist not to. But Cronan wasn't an idiot, and if this scheme of Cleapho's was so transparent that even a lowly sword-monk could see through it, could Cronan possibly be fooled by it?

He forded the river in blinding rain, just managing to get across (an hour later and the ford would be impassable; another damned complication), and resigned himself to a thoroughly unpleasant night ride up the ridge to Deymeson. As the ground underfoot turned from muddy slush to hard stone, he started thinking about Prince Tazencius. If Cleapho's plot really was as shallow as he was assuming, he and Tazencius had staged Tazencius' disgrace and rebellion in order to lure Cronan north of the Mahec and get rid of him – for all he knew, really with the help of the raiders, though the scary stuff about giving them Mael and Weal and Boc was clearly nonsense. Tazencius, he could safely assume, was simply doing what his cousin Galien told him to (just as he always had done, from the famous knife fight incident all those years ago right up to the present), and Galien in turn was taking his orders direct from Prince Suevio, who was doing what his brother wanted but couldn't do himself, or what Suevio thought he ought to want to do, or what Suevio had decided was good for his brother and the empire, though the emperor himself would have a fit if he ever found out . . . Monach flushed all that stuff out of his mind. Motivations really weren't important; what mattered was the deployment of forces, the collision and intersection of circles, those of Cronan and his enemies, and whether anything could be done (by, for example, one self-effacing man with a short sword) to stop it.

Far better, he decided, for him to concentrate on the smaller pieces, to keep his eye on the tip of the sword and watch for the moment when it violated the circumference. Two people, for instance, in a cart. He hadn't even considered the possibility that whoever they were – the two inadequates he'd bullied – or thought he'd bullied; perhaps they'd been playing him, rather than the other way round – in Sansory jail, or the other Poldarn, the one he'd been starting to believe really was a god in a cart – they were nothing more mystical or supernatural than a couple of spies and couriers using a confidence trick as a cover for espionage and treason. There was a good reason why he hadn't considered it; it was a bloody stupid idea, to use a dangerous and highly illegal activity as a cover for a dangerous and highly illegal activity. Then again, if the pair he'd spoken to – damn it, had given money to, out of *pity* – actually were agents for Tazencius or the Amathy house, they'd undoubtedly fooled him completely, which suggested it wasn't such a bad cover after all. And if it wasn't them but the other Poldarn, or the other Poldarn's female companion . . . He realised he was laughing out loud, though he couldn't hear the laughter over the wind and the clattering of hooves on the stony path. What if both his suspicions were true: that the man was the divine Poldarn and the woman was an Amathy house spy? What if neither of them knew?

That made him laugh so much he nearly fell off his horse, and he was still chuckling when he rode up to the main gate of Deymeson.

'You're in a good mood,' Brother Porter said accusingly as he opened the sally-port. 'What's up? Killed someone famous?'

Monach shook his head. 'Better than that,' he said. 'I've got a valid excuse for getting Father Tutor out of his pit in the early hours of the morning. Do me a favour and—'

'I'm not waking him up,' Brother Porter replied quickly. 'Last time I did that I couldn't taste vinegar for a week after.'

Monach frowned. 'I could give you a direct order,' he said.

'And I could tell you where to stick it. Goodnight.'

He took his horse to the stables, where they weren't particularly pleased to see him, and stopped off at his own quarters to dump his sodden coat and towel his hair dry. He kept his wet boots on, though; the squelching was loud enough to wake up all but the heaviest sleepers, and he'd have to walk past the quarters of several high-ranking members of the order to get to Father Tutor's rooms. He thought about the god in the cart and grinned. Then he remembered Cric, and the old man who was probably General Allectus, and the grin faded. The more I think about it, he muttered to himself, the harder it gets.

There was Father Tutor's door; dark, grubby oak, and a plain blacked latch. He balled his fist, thumped twice, lifted a lamp down from the nearest wall-sconce and pushed the door open.

The room was empty.

There were some senior members of the order who you'd expect to find absent from their beds in the middle of the night. Father Tutor wasn't one of them. Even if he had occasion to work late, he'd do it in his rooms, requiring anybody who needed to see him to come here and sit in the straight-backed uncomfortable chair while he perched at ease on the edge of the bed. Monach stood still in the doorway without a clue as to what he should do next.

'Was that you?' said a voice behind him. It turned out to belong to the Father Bursar, the particular terror of Monach's youth; he was standing in the corridor wearing nothing but a thick wool cap and holding a distinctly pornographic candle-stick.

'I'm sorry,' Monach stammered. 'I—'

'Making that bloody horrible noise,' Father Bursar explained. 'Was it you?'

'Yes.' Monach kept his eyes fixed on the wall six inches left of Father Bursar's ear. 'I need to see Father Tutor, it's—'

'You don't know? Dear God, where have you been the last two days?'

'I—' Monach forced out the words. 'Father Tutor sent me on a mission,' he said, clinging to the authorisation like a drowning man holding on to a tiny piece of driftwood. 'To Laise Bohec, and—'

Father Bursar frowned, but it wasn't anger. 'Father Coiroven died the night before last,' he said quietly. 'His heart, we think. What did you say your name was?'

Father Coiroven, Monach thought; never heard of him. He'd already told Father Bursar his name and date of orders by the time he made the connection. 'Father Tutor?' he said, his mouth suddenly dry. 'Dead?'

'That's right. I just told you.' Father Bursar fitted a sympathetic stare to his face, like someone buckling on a piece of armour. 'My condolences,' he said. 'I take it you were a pupil of his?'

'Since I was ten,' Monach replied automatically, though he knew Father Bursar didn't really want to know that. 'Was that his name, Coiroven? I never knew.'

'No reason why you should,' Father Bursar replied, in a tone of voice that suggested that this was meant to be a comfort. 'Did you say you have something important to report?'

'Yes,' Monach replied, as a terrible thought struck him. 'But who should I report to? Nobody else knew what Father Tutor was working on, not even me.'

Father Bursar smiled. 'I promise you,' he said, 'anything of importance will be known to at least one other member of senior chapter, or else recorded in his files and logs. We're a society governed by old men, we're used to taking precautions.'

Monach took a deep breath. 'I see,' he said. 'In that case, can you tell me who I should report to? It's fairly urgent.'

Father Bursar rubbed his chin. 'Not to me, at any rate,' he said. 'In the circumstances, I suggest the only person you can responsibly give this information to, whatever it is, would be Father Abbot.'

Monach's jaw fell open like a loose tailgate on a bumpy road. 'Oh,' he said. He'd seen Father Abbot nearly every day of his life but never been close enough to him to hit him with a slingshot. The thought of talking to him was terrifying. The thought of waking him up in the early hours of the morning—'I'm sure it can wait,' he gabbled. 'Really.'

Father Bursar gave him a thoughtful stare. 'I'm not sure that's your decision to make,' he said. 'You should consider the possibility that your news is far more important than you realise – unless, of course, you were fully apprised of everything Coiroven was dealing with at the time of his death, and all their implications for other areas of policy.'

It was tacitly acknowledged that sword-monks had no need to be afraid of any living thing on Earth; if it could be killed, they could kill it, so fear was irrelevant. It was generally implied that a sword-monk who'd attained orders could probably hold his own against most minor gods, given a fair fight and choice of weapons. With all his experience outside Deymeson, Monach had better grounds than most for believing in this principle, and genuine fear, as against worry or concern or apprehension, was something he'd tasted about as often as he'd drunk vintage sweet white wine at thirty quarters a bottle. But he was definitely afraid of Father Abbot.

'Right,' he said, very quietly. 'I don't suppose you could tell me where I might find him?'

Father Bursar looked at him. 'In the abbot's lodgings, of course,' he said. 'You do know where they are, don't you?'

'Sorry.' He'd been seven when the prior of novices had first pointed out to him the small grey stone box where the abbot lived; he'd been made to promise not to run or shout or do anything naughty within two hundred yards of it, on pain of vivisection. 'I forgot.'

Father Bursar didn't say anything, but he nodded slowly. He turned to go back to his rooms, then stopped and looked back. 'For what it's worth,' he said, 'I always liked Coiroven. We were novices together sixty-five years ago. If he'd lived another ten years, I might have started to get to know him, but there it is.'

Naturally, there were guards outside Father Abbot's door, two of them, lay brothers, both of whom Monach had taught, six or seven years ago. As soon as he was close enough to the door for his shadow to touch it they snapped to attention and blocked his way by crossing their pikes in front of his face. They didn't say anything, of course. That would have made it too easy.

Monach cleared his throat. 'I need to see the abbot,' he said.

The guards looked at him.

'I have a report,' he said, feeling as if he was drowning in hot sand. 'Originally it was for Father Tutor, but since he's dead—' (Did they know that? Were they authorised to know that?) '—since he's unavailable, I thought I'd better take it to Father Abbot. To be on the safe side.'

The guards continued to stare at him for three very long seconds; then one of them (Cormista, Monach remembered; good with the pike and staff, competent swordsman, hopeless at theory and protocols) reached behind him and shoved open the door. Monach, who'd been hoping that one of the guards would do the actual waking-up, felt his shoulders slump forward as he went past and into the lodgings.

From the outside, the abbot's quarters looked small and bleak. Inside they were smaller and bleaker. The room Monach found himself in was the office. Because there was only one small pottery lamp, resting on a bare board table, he couldn't make out much in the way of detail, but he could see that the walls were lined with pigeonholes, with rolls of parchment or paper shoved into them, and in the middle of the room there was a single table and a single chair. The floor was covered in neat piles of documents, arranged in arrow-straight rows. The place was as cheerful as an abandoned graveyard.

He took three steps forward, taking pains to avoid the document piles, until he was able to locate the inner door, which led to the abbot's bedroom. Then he stopped, as if he'd just bumped into an invisible wall. He could feel the abbot's circle pressing against his kneecaps, and more than anything else in his whole life he didn't want to break into it.

He'd been standing there for ten, possibly twelve seconds, when he heard a giggle.

At first he assumed it had come from outside: one of the very young novices, perhaps, who'd broken out of his dormitory and was trying to climb in through a window or the chimney. But Father Abbot's lodgings didn't have windows or chimneys, he'd spotted that by the time he was ten. Furthermore, although the giggle was as high-pitched as a child's voice, it was quite definitely female. He'd heard giggles like that many times before, while staying at inns. It was one of those sounds that you immediately recognise, like a sword being drawn behind you, or rain in a gutter.

No, he thought. Definitely not. Must've been something else.

There it was again; no shadow of doubt about it, particularly since it was followed by the sort of soft male chuckle you always hear a fraction of a second after that sort of female giggle. One of the guards, he thought; one of the guards has been stupid enough to bring his girlfriend in here – probably the abbot's a really heavy sleeper, nothing wakes him up short of the roof falling in, so it's perfectly safe, though horrendously sacrilegious and blasphemous. Somewhere in this room, unaware that he was standing there just inside the door, was a sentry and—

The giggle, again, and unmistakably coming from the other side of the inner door. There was no way past it, the conclusion was that obvious. The abbot—

The abbot was busy and not to be woken. The news would wait till morning – which couldn't be far off now in any case, and what possible difference could an hour or so make? After all, even if the news was so vital that the abbot mobilised the entire order in marching kit with three days' rations, a couple of hours would be neither here nor there. It could wait; and it was high time he got out of his sopping wet clothes and had something to eat. After all, he couldn't go in front of the abbot looking like a terrier who's just crawled out of a drain, now could he?

Very slowly and carefully, petrified in case his boots squelched or he knocked something over, Monach crept back the way he'd come in, gently eased the door open to give the guards notice he was coming out, and fled across the yard to the gate into the middle quadrangle, across it into the west cloister, and up three flights of spiral stone steps to his own door. Once it was safely behind him he let out the breath he'd taken in the abbot's office somewhere between a minute and forty years ago, and slumped on to his bed as if all his bones had suddenly melted.

When he woke up it was light, and he could tell from the angle of the shaft of light spearing through his cell's small, high window that the sun had been up for several hours. Then he realised that he'd fallen asleep in his wet, clammy travelling clothes, and that he had pins and needles in both feet.

It's difficult to hurry when you can't bear to let either foot touch the floor, but he didn't have any choice in the matter; he was washed, shaved, tonsured, respectably dressed and outside the abbot's lodgings in less time than it'd take to milk a cow. His speed and efficiency didn't alter the fact that he was sinfully, dangerously late, or that he had no idea how he was going to face the abbot after what he'd heard the previous night. At least the night watch had been relieved, and he didn't have to face the same guard who'd let him go in and experience *that*.

Somehow he found the words to explain his business to the guard, who stared at him in silence for a very long time before telling his colleague to watch Monach like a hawk until he got back from consulting the duty sergeant. The guard was gone a very long time, during which the other guard drilled fretwork patterns in Monach's face with his eyes. The duty sergeant eventually appeared looking absolutely furious (what had he been doing when the guard interrupted him? God alone knew) and forcing himself to be polite. Monach recited his speech once more, a little less coherently this time. The sergeant scowled at him and stumped off to find the duty officer. Fortunately, the duty officer turned out to be Lammis, a sparring partner from a dozen or so years ago, who vouched for him (though even he had to think about it first). At last the guard pushed the door open, and Monach went in.

Father Abbot was sitting behind his desk, sharpening a pen. Monach's first impression was that he'd somehow both aged and shrunk since the last time he'd been in chapter; he looked thinner and bonier, but there were folds of drooping, empty skin under his chin and at the corners of his mouth that suggested that he'd recently lost weight faster than his skin could take up the slack. He was genuinely bald rather than tonsured – there were a few white bristles on either side of his ears, but not enough to make a clothes-brush from – and his hands were small and plump.

'Yes?' he said.

Beyond question it was the same voice that had chuckled the night before. Monach felt his throat freeze; he could hardly breathe, let alone say anything. He knew he was staring, but couldn't do anything about it.

'Yes?' the abbot repeated.

Monach tried to remember his name, but couldn't. He could remember that he had important news to deliver, but not what it was. The abbot was frowning at him. He needed a miracle, and he needed it right away, which meant praying to the appropriate god. The only god he could think of offhand was Poldarn, so he prayed to him; and Poldarn must have heard, because quite suddenly his memory came back with a snap. He told Father Abbot his name and business without stuttering once.

And Father Abbot seemed inclined to take him seriously. 'I see,' he said. 'So, tell me what you've found out.'

Take it slowly, said a voice inside Monach's head, *you'll be all right. Don't rush the draw or you'll get your sword jammed in the scabbard mouth.* It was good advice, and he followed it. When he'd finished Father Abbot folded his hands and looked down at them, giving Monach a fine view of the liver spots on the top of his head.

'I wish you'd told me this earlier,' he said. 'I've just sent out most of the available sword-brothers; now I'll have to call them back, it'll be late afternoon before they'll be ready to go. Still,' he went on, with a remarkably human-sounding sigh, 'that can't be helped now. You'll have to go with them, of course.'

Monach shuddered, as if he'd just swallowed something unexpected and nasty. 'Me?'

Father Abbot frowned. 'Yes, you,' he said. 'I'm putting you in charge of the whole operation. Most people would be pleased.'

In charge? Me? Absolutely not. 'Thank you,' he said, with a total lack of sincerity. 'But I've never commanded a field unit before, I don't know how—'

Father Abbot smiled up at him. 'You've got four hours,' he said. 'Learn.' He rubbed his ear with the palm of his hand. 'First, though, it'd probably be just as well if I told you what you're actually going to do.'

Monach nodded. 'Thank you,' he said.

'It's quite simple,' the abbot went on. 'Find General Cronan, get him away from his men, and kill him. Try and keep a low profile if you can,' he went on, writing something as he spoke. 'A direct attack's not out of the question, of course, if there's absolutely no other way. It'd probably be the order's death warrant, we'll be disbanded, arrested and sent in chains to Datmia once the emperor finds out we've killed one of his generals, but in the circumstances, you can regard the order as expendable. Do you understand what that means?'

Yes, it means you've gone mad and we'll have to murder you discreetly and hide your body in a culvert. 'Yes,' Monach said. 'At least, I think so. This is very important.'

'That's right,' the abbot said. 'Do you know why?'

'No.'

The abbot looked annoyed. 'Coiroven was a great man and a fine strategist, but a little too fond of secrecy for his or anybody's good. Very well, listen carefully. You know, I assume, about the long-standing enmity between Cronan and Prince Tazencius. Yes?'

Monach nodded.

'Good, that's something. And you know that many years ago, Tazencius provoked – or at least tried to provoke – a duel between Cronan and himself, that Cronan humiliated Tazencius on that occasion and there's been bad blood between them ever since?'

'Yes. Yes indeed,' Monach said.

'Splendid. You probably also know that the emperor, quite reasonably, favours Cronan – he's our best general and, I believe, genuinely loyal to the emperor and the empire (not always the same thing, as you'll appreciate) – and has ignored all his brother's warnings about the danger of Cronan going to the bad and staging a coup – perfectly legitimate concerns, given the history of the last hundred and fifty years, I'm sure you'll agree.' The abbot leaned back as far as the chair's straight back would allow, and gazed for a moment over Monach's shoulder. 'The sad fact is,' he went on, 'that we have the first good emperor for at least a century, the first reliably loyal general for about as long, who also happens to be the only man in the empire who might conceivably be capable of beating the raiders, and a crown prince whose only concerns are the welfare of his brother and the well-being of the empire; and we're on the verge of probably the worst civil war in the empire's history. What's worst of all, I think, is that our only hope of averting it rests with a disgracefully conniving and devious priest who's also the head of our order, and an unscrupulous thug with a private army.'

Monach raised both eyebrows. 'Feron Amathy?'

'Feron Amathy.' The abbot sighed. 'Perhaps the anonymous god in the cart really has come again, and this is his way of bringing about the end of the world. If so, he's a rather more formidable opponent than I'd originally assumed. The point,' he went on, 'is this. I believe that Feron Amathy is planning to use Tazencius and his extremely unfortunate attempt at a coup as a means of forcing Cronan to declare war on the emperor and seize the throne.' The abbot paused. 'Why are you making faces at me?' he asked.

Monach pulled himself together. 'I'm sorry,' he said. 'But hasn't the Amathy house definitely sided with Tazencius?'

The abbot smiled. 'For the moment, yes. In fact, I'm prepared to wager that it was Feron Amathy who engineered Tazencius' coup. No doubt he filled the poor fool's mind with awful stories of how Cronan was plotting to usurp the throne and kill him for old times' sake, and goaded him into an obviously disastrous course of action he'd otherwise never have dreamed of.' He sighed. 'But Feron Amathy knows perfectly well that, with the resources available to him, Tazencius could never hope to beat Cronan. By appearing to put the forces of the Amathy house at Tazencius' disposal, Feron Amathy's persuaded the prince that he might stand a chance. He'll hustle Tazencius into an early pitched battle, during which he'll change sides and hand his supposed ally over to Cronan, who'll have no choice but to kill him. Once he's done that, the emperor won't be able to protect Cronan any longer, and he'll be forced into doing the one thing he's never wanted to do, and which Suevio and Cleapho are convinced he'll do sooner or later – attack Torcea and seize the throne. The result: the emperor will be killed, Cronan will take his place and owe his crown to Feron Amathy. Now you see why Cronan has to be assassinated, and why we're the only people in the empire who can do it.'

Monach tried to think, but it was like trying to walk through a peat bog; as soon as he tried to put his weight on some reliable known fact, it gave way and started to suck him down. 'But what about the raiders?' he asked in desperation. 'If Tazencius and Feron Amathy have really made a deal with them, they'd be strong enough to beat Cronan.'

'There's no deal,' the abbot said, smiling, as if telling a small child there wasn't really a tooth fairy. 'We know that. Unfortunately, Cronan doesn't. Oh, he's well aware how desperately unlikely a deal would be, but he doesn't know it for a fact. Which is why he has no choice but to take the bait and give battle to Tazencius, just in case the story's true; and that's why Feron Amathy started the rumour that he's implicated in the raider attacks on the cities deliberately to give the impression that he's on some kind of terms with the raiders, so that Cronan will have to take this new rumour about a deal seriously. Indeed, I wouldn't put something like that past Feron Amathy. Whatever else he maybe, he's imaginative.'

Although it was a terrible breach of protocol, Monach leaned against the abbot's desk to steady himself. 'Why can't we just tell the emperor?' he said. 'If he recalled Cronan and sent someone else to fight Tazencius—'

'Then Tazencius would win,' the abbot replied. 'And Cronan would still end up fighting him, but with the added incentive of having to do so on the south side of the bay, within a few miles of Torcea.' He signed the letter he'd been writing, sprinkled it with sand, and pushed the end of a stick of wax into the flame of the lamp on his desk. 'This is a general warrant,' he said. 'It'll authorise you to take any steps and appropriate any resources you need to carry out your mission. In theory it's restricted to ecclesiastical manpower and property only, but I think you'll find that most civilian and military authorities don't know that, so this letter and a little bluster ought to get you anything you need. You can bluster, can't you?'

'Yes,' Monach replied.

'Really? You sound like a choir novice admitting he's been stealing apples.' He poured a deep pool of wax on to the bottom of the page, then took his seal from a small wooden box on the desk and rested it gently on the meniscus. Monach had seen the print of the abbot's seal on decrees and title deeds – two ravens on either side of a drawn sword, surrounded by a circle – but not the seal itself. It was reckoned to be a thousand years old. 'Now then,' he said, 'any questions? No? That's good. I'll see to recalling the sword-monks. You go and get ready. Four hours, remember, you haven't got much time.'

'No,' Monach said, more to himself than the abbot. 'Thank you,' he added, taking the letter as if he expected it to climb up his arm and bite out his throat. He tried to think of something appropriate to say, but all he could think of was, 'I'll do my best.'

The abbot frowned. 'Your best had bloody well better be good enough,' he said. 'You do realise that you're about to take the life of the cleverest, most skilful tactician the empire's produced in two centuries. This isn't going to be an easy job, and to be brutally honest with you, if anybody else could do it, I wouldn't be sending you.' He sighed. 'I read your report about the Poldarn impersonators,' he went on. 'I'd have rather more confidence in your abilities if you hadn't got that completely the wrong way round.'

Monach's breath caught in his throat and for a moment he couldn't breathe. 'Oh,' he said. 'I mean, I'm very sorry. What did I . . . ?'

'Your research,' the abbot replied. 'Sloppy. Obviously, all you did was look up Poldarn in the Concordance; you didn't go back to the primary sources and see what the Concordance left out. Bad scholarship,' he said. 'I take the view that a man who can't be bothered to look up a reference when he's sitting comfortably on his backside in a nice warm library is hardly likely to pay proper attention to detail when he's out in the field.' He shook his head. 'For your information, if you'd taken the trouble to go back to the Morevish texts, you'd have known that one of the most important things about the second coming of Poldarn is that when he arrives, he won't actually know who he is, or that he's a god at all, until most of his work's been done. It's actually the key to the whole allegory, which is why it appealed so much to the later Mannerists.' The abbot picked up a ruler, flicked it over with his fingertips. 'You were going around looking for someone in a cart calling himself Poldarn. Anybody using the name Poldarn couldn't possibly be Poldarn, because Poldarn doesn't know that's who he is. A valiant effort on your part, but completely worthless.'

Chapter Seventeen

Vague images, changing too quickly to be meaningful, leaving only impressions, like the flashes of colour behind your eyelids when you've looked directly at the sun. Early memories, formed before he'd had the words to shape them with: lying on his back in a basket as the sky and the horizon flickered around him, feeling frightened by the jostling, wondering why his mother was running; lying in a dark place with his mother's hand clamped over his mouth, trying to pull her fingers away; a man's face directly overhead, so big that his nose and mouth and moustache seemed to fill the world, and the instinctive knowledge that something was wrong; some years later – he was standing, looking down – being shown a long rectangle of newly turned earth that looked like a freshly dug flowerbed and wondering why they'd planted his mother in the ground. Then another early one: sitting up in a cot or something of the sort, waving his hands to try and scare off the big, cruel-looking black bird that was perched on the side rail, examining him with round black empty eyes. Vague images, but for once he knew that he was there, that the eyes he was watching through had been his own: a three-legged cat crossing a paved yard, an old man with a white beard pointing at the sky, an endless journey over bumpy roads in a cart—

He woke up and opened his eyes. It was dark. He was lying on his back, just as he had been in the dream (already very nearly drained away; a few pictures clinging to his mind like limpets on a rock, but meaningless without context), and he could hear somebody breathing in the room with him.

Then he remembered. The woman lying beside him was Copis, of course, and there was nothing sinister or bad about her being there; arguably, quite the opposite, or so it had seemed at the time. Now she was lying on her left side, one arm underneath her (how can anybody sleep like that? It must be really uncomfortable), not snoring exactly, but making a gentle snuffling noise every time she breathed in – not loud at all, but once noticed, impossible to ignore. He lay still for some time, listening for the little noise, counting out the interval between. Her hair smelt like rainwater.

He closed his eyes, made a conscious effort not to listen for the noise, which was naturally self-defeating. Did this feel natural, he wondered, sharing a bed with someone? It must be something you learned how to do, the knack of keeping to your own space, like the knack of not rolling off the edge and landing on the floor. If he'd learned the knack, did he have a wife somewhere, or had he had one once? He concentrated, fishing in the dark for a face. There wasn't anything there, needless to say; the dream was long gone, and even Copis, the only woman he knew now, was hard to call deliberately to mind, so that he had to build up her face out of composite memories, eyes and nose, contours of cheeks, the radius of her forehead, the faint lines at the sides of her mouth. It occurred to him that when they'd both slept in the cart she hadn't made the snuffling noise (but they'd never slept together in a bed, so perhaps she only did it when she had a mattress and pillows, or when she was making space for someone else in a bed). He

let his thoughts stray, and after a while he found himself looking for something that wasn't there, a curved line that should
have been visible in the air, a circle.

If he had to lie awake thinking, he told himself, it'd be a
better use of the time to consider the implications of all this,
the effect it must inevitably have on the way he approached
the future. He was fairly certain that he wasn't in love with
Copis, and that she wasn't in love with him. Love wasn't an
issue here, nor was passion or pleasure or even affection. He
considered the term companionship, but rejected that, too.
Association (what language was he thinking in? He had no
idea) was closer to the mark; there was a distinctly businesslike
feel to this relationship, something to do with a contract or
agreement sealed with some formal sign of utmost good faith,
required precisely because neither of them trusted the other.
Then there was obligation, as if they were the last two of their
kind left in the world, making a mating necessary. Still no
affection, unless perhaps it was the instinctive bond between
two soldiers who meet for the first time on the battlefield, as
they stand next to each other in a hastily formed line or square
after a desperate retreat has been halted and turned into a last
attempt to hold back the enemy; arguably nothing more than
a common purpose, a shared and expedient need for help and
support in the face of a danger that can't be dealt with alone.
Comrade-in-arms, joint venturer, ally in adversity, fellow creature, joined by a shared need but still just outside the circle, or
touching it without breaking through; such delicate geometry,
and all done instinctively, in their sleep.

He was beginning to get cramp in his left leg, and needed to
shift. He couldn't think of how to move without disturbing
her, not consciously and deliberately, executing a move like a
fencer or a wrestler. That thought hung in his mind for a
moment, and somehow turned into the shadow of a memory,
of something learned so hard, so grimly that it was no longer
his to lose. *Only the finest master can match the skill of the*

novice; whatever that was supposed to mean. He gave it some thought; was it something to do with the notion that before you learn how to do something in the correct, approved manner you do it instinctively, without thinking, and that the essence of skill is to recapture that instinctiveness through endless practice and perfection of technique? Quite possibly, though what that had to do with turning over in bed he wasn't really sure.

He opened his eyes again, and this time they were used to the darkness, and he could make out the shapes of the room, the graduations of depth of shadow. This was the upstairs room in Copis' house (Copis' house, paid for with his lump of gold; who the lump of gold really belonged to was neither here nor there). They'd come here because it was raining; they'd gone to look at a cart, of all things, which Copis was interested in buying, she protesting that she didn't really know about carts and needed an expert opinion. It had turned out to be a wreck, the ghost of a cart, some scraps of plank and corroded steel strip held together by the memory of once having been a cart . . . Copis reckoned it could be fixed, and it'd be cheaper to buy an old dog and do it up as and when she had some money. It had taken him a long time over a quart jug of nasty red wine in a tavern to show her the error of her ways, and by then it was pitch dark and the rain was coming down sideways, hard enough to forge iron, and the Falx house was on the other side of town, whereas Copis' place was just round the corner. Then, properly speaking, she'd seduced him . . . but with a gravity and seriousness of manner and purpose that made him think of a craftsman undertaking an important job just inside the threshold of his competence. It would have been churlish to refuse, he told himself. And now here he was, and presumably something had changed; one set of options had been closed off, another set had opened to replace them.

It was still raining, and for some reason he found that the sound of the rain on the roof both soothed and upset him, as though it was tugging him towards a memory it knew was there but couldn't get into any more. He yawned and wiggled his toes. Absolutely no chance of going back to sleep now, but here he was in someone else's house. Probably there was some sort of etiquette or protocol governing this sort of situation, which every man of his age in the world knew, except him – under what circumstances is it permissible to leave the woman's bed before she wakes up, is it mortally insulting to get up, go downstairs, light a lamp and read a book or darn a hole in your coat sleeve – subtle points that could easily do permanent damage, at a critical point in his life where everything was suddenly in a state of flux. One moment, here and now, could change everything that followed (and for better or for worse, let's not forget that). It'd be so much simpler if he could go back to sleep, and allow his instincts and reflexes to guide him through these reefs to the safety of morning . . .

He was just trying to convince himself that she'd never know if he got up and went downstairs for a while when he opened his eyes and found them full of daylight, which was swamping the room and flushing away the shadows; he'd fallen asleep after all, and in such a way as to do serious damage to his neck and shoulders.

'Ah,' Copis said. She was up, dressed, sitting in front of a small, cheap-looking dressing-table. 'You've finally woken up, then. I was going to give it another hour and then send for the undertaker.'

He groaned and sat up. 'What time is it?' he asked.

'Four hours after sunrise,' she replied. She had her back to him, but he could see her face reflected in the mirror. 'Does Falx Roisin let you all sleep in like this? He must've got soft in his old age.'

She made it sound like she knew him; better not ask how. 'Damn,' he said. 'I was supposed to be starting out an hour after dawn. We're taking a cart out to Deymeson—'

'Left without you by now, I expect,' Copis replied. 'Was it important?'

He shrugged. 'No idea,' he said. 'Nobody tells me, and that suits me. I mean, yes, it must've been fairly important or it wouldn't need to go by special courier—'

'Special courier,' Copis mimicked, not particularly accurately. 'You do realise that's just street Weal for "someone dumb enough to take the job" – all right, all right, no need to scowl at me like that. I was just saying, that's all.'

'I wasn't scowling,' Poldarn replied, pulling a face.

She adjusted the position of her mirror so that she could see him. 'I stand corrected,' she said gravely. 'Anyway, I expect Falx Roisin's found another special courier, so you might as well take the day off. In fact—'

He braced himself. The previous night, over the wine, she'd been dropping hints heavy enough to use as anvils 'No,' he said. 'Absolutely not.'

'Oh, go on. You'd be helping me out—'

'No.' He shook his head, sharp movements to either side. 'My career as a god is definitely over.'

'You only did it once,' she pointed out. 'And you weren't exactly wonderful at it then.'

'Fine,' he said, finding himself unexpectedly put out by the criticism. 'In that case you won't want me to do it again. Which is just as well, because I won't.'

'You bloody well should.' He recognised the key change, from wounded to angry; synthetic, both of them. She was much better at angry. 'If you hadn't gone and killed my perfectly good god—'

'Perfectly good.' Poldarn laughed unkindly. 'He was a jerk. You were only too glad to be rid of him, before he cut your throat and sold your body to a tannery.'

She was about to step into his circle and fight, but she stopped and smiled. 'True,' she said. 'Which is why I need somebody who won't let me down or rob me or do anything horrible, and the only person like that I can think of is you. Please?' she added.

Somehow he found it extremely difficult to refuse.

'No,' he said. 'But,' he added quickly, before she had a chance to dodge and counterattack, 'if you're looking for a partner in an enterprise that doesn't involve gods in carts, I'd be interested in that. Like,' he went on, knowing he had her attention, 'that idea you told me about the other day.'

She didn't seem as pleased as he'd expected. 'Oh,' she said. 'That.'

Poldarn nodded. 'You wanted me to put money into it,' he said.

'That was before . . .' He got the impression she hadn't meant to say that, or at least not in that way. 'I've been thinking about that,' she went on. 'Maybe it's not such a good idea after all.'

'I think it's a great idea,' Poldarn said, making an effort to sound upbeat and enthusiastic. 'Buttons. Everybody in the world needs buttons, and the biggest button factory in these parts is right here in Sansory. We buy buttons, load them on a cart, go round the villages and sell them. On the way back, we buy bones to sell to the factory. Brilliant.'

She shook her head. 'I don't know anything about bones,' she said. 'I don't even like them.'

Poldarn laughed. 'I don't think it's absolutely necessary,' he said. 'Look, I don't know anything about bones either. Or buttons. But we can learn.'

'I don't know.' She looked away, and Poldarn found himself wondering whether he wasn't being double-bluffed, and if this wasn't a clever way of manoeuvring him into the button trade. If so, he decided, he didn't mind, because it was a good idea, even if it was one of hers. 'I just don't know,' she said. 'I don't think I'm cut out to be a trader. I haven't got the patience.'

Poldarn moved so he was facing her. 'If you can pretend to

be a priestess,' he said, 'you can sell buttons. Being a priestess was hard work, and the pay was lousy.'

'Yes, I know.' She frowned and bit her lip – the latter struck Poldarn as just a little too self-conscious, inclining him towards the manoeuvring theory. 'I can't decide,' she said. 'What if we accidentally go to one of the villages where I did the god-in-the-cart routine?'

'We'll make a special effort not to.'

By now he was convinced. 'All right,' she said, 'what do you think? After all, it's your money.'

He couldn't help smiling at that. 'I think I've had enough of the bodyguard business, and we've both had enough of the god business. And buttons are as good a thing to sell as any.'

'Quitting to go into a nice, safe, good business with a rich woman who's crazy about you,' Eolla said, examining the blanket. 'You must be off your head.'

Poldarn frowned. 'I didn't say she was crazy about me,' he replied.

'Stands to reason, doesn't it?' Eolla replied. 'Otherwise, why'd she take you in? I mean, you got no money, you don't know spit about buttons or bones—'

'Neither does she.'

'Proves my point,' Eolla said, smirking. 'If she wasn't crazy about you, she'd be looking to find someone who did know the business. Bloody good luck to you, my son.' He peered closely at the blanket. 'This tear wasn't here before,' he said. 'That'll be a quarter, dilapidations.'

If it had been anybody else, Poldarn would have had his doubts. But he could well imagine that Eolla did know every square inch of every blanket in his stores, in the same way that a god knows the names of every man and woman in his world. He paid.

'That's the lot, then.' Everything he'd been issued by the

Falx house, all the possessions considered necessary, in a neat, folded pile; except for two.

'There's the sword,' Poldarn pointed out. 'And the other book.'

To his surprise, Eolla shook his head. 'Keep 'em,' he said. 'The book's no good; there's a page missing – two hundred and forty-eight – and a big brown stain all down the outside. More trouble than it's worth to put it back into inventory.'

Poldarn had noticed the stain all right; given where everything in Sansory came from, no prizes for guessing what it was. 'Fair enough,' he said. 'Thanks. What about the sword?'

Eolla frowned. 'Don't want it,' he said. 'Just superstition, really. Bad luck.'

'Bad luck? Why?'

'Just a feeling. You get that sometimes, with things, in this job. I wouldn't want it in the rack, in case it's catching.'

Poldarn didn't like the sound of that, but he wasn't going to argue. He'd seen one just like it on a stall in the Irongate marked at two hundred quarters, and even if the buying price was only half that, it'd still be a useful sum for the business. 'Thanks,' he said. 'Right, that's everything, then.'

Eolla nodded. 'That's everything.' He turned away and started putting things back in their proper piles, chests and racks. 'Probably a good thing, really,' he said. 'For a start, you lasted longer in the job than some, and you're the only one who's left it who didn't leave in a box. And the lads—' He scratched his head. 'Nothing personal to you, of course.'

'Just superstition.'

'You know how it is. I mean, if you were them, would you want to ride with you?'

Poldarn smiled bleakly. 'I'd sooner quit,' he replied.

'There you are, then.' Eolla picked up the boots and wiped the toes with his sleeve. 'I'll tell you this and you can take it any bloody way you want. If you think you can hide in the button trade, you're kidding yourself. You're a nice bloke, always been straight with me, and I'm glad for you; you'll never come to any harm, no matter what. But God help anybody who takes up with you.'

Poldarn didn't say anything for a long time; then he opened the door. 'Thanks for the book,' he said.

'You're welcome. Mind how you go.'

The Potto house stood in the middle of a small square, almost exactly in the middle of Sansory. It was typical of the city that its middle wasn't its centre; all the markets and temples and public buildings were on the west side, in the old town, and the middle was where the second rank of merchant houses were to be found. It was the closest you'd get to a quiet, respectable neighbourhood; there weren't many fights and robberies during daylight hours and hardly anything caught fire or fell down because of the vibrations from passing carts. Potto Ilec's father had built the house forty years ago, when he'd made enough money from the button trade to get out of the north side for good. He couldn't afford to build it all at once, of course, but he had a firm idea of what he wanted in his mind, so he started on the left, with the kitchens, stables and servants' quarters, and worked his way gradually to the right as time and money allowed. When he died, twenty years later, his men were just about to fit the frame for the front door. His son Ilec had done well for himself, far better than his father, and it could only be a matter of a few years before the house would be completed with the addition of the family quarters and the master bedroom. Until then, Potto Ilec and his family slept on mattresses in the hall, while his servants, workers and clerks each had a room of their own, with a balcony. Poldarn, on hearing the story, decided that the Potto family's chief characteristic must be patience and determination. Copis' interpretation was that they were idiots.

The main door was open when they approached, and there was no porter in the lodge. They hung about for a few minutes waiting for somebody to show up, but the house and yard all appeared to be deserted, like the ghost town they'd passed through on the moors. Poldarn kept expecting to see crows. Eventually Copis' impatience got the better of her discretion, and she walked into the house. Muttering under his breath, Poldarn followed her, and they arrived in a beautifully proportioned inner courtyard-cum-cloister, with a granite fountain in the middle of a carefully trimmed lawn. The effect was spoiled rather by a large pyramid of bones heaped up in the northern corner. There was nobody about.

'Just once,' Poldarn said, 'I'd like to go somewhere and it'd all be straightforward and simple. Does that sort of thing ever happen, or am I being naive?'

Before Copis could reply, a small door opened in the cloister wall and a nondescript-looking man in a long green coat came out, holding a ledger. He looked at them for a moment and frowned. 'Can I help you?' he said.

Copis stepped forward and smiled pleasantly. 'Yes,' she said. 'We're looking for Potto Ilec.'

'That's me,' the man said. 'What can I do for you?'

'We'd like to buy some buttons, please.'

Potto Ilec sighed. 'Yes, of course,' he said. 'Any idea of what you want? Size, style, how many?'

'Various sizes and styles,' Copis replied, 'and we'll start with twelve thousand.'

'Oh.' It was as if the patient, put-upon Potto Ilec had vanished into thin air and been replaced by a totally different person who happened to be wearing the same clothes. Even his face was different; cheerful, welcoming, enthusiastic. 'No problem,' said the new Potto Ilec. 'Perhaps you'd care to follow me, my office is just through here.'

He pushed open the door he'd just come through, and led them down half a dozen steps into a large, dark room that smelt of damp, dust and cheese. There was one small window, high up in the wall, and the floor was covered in flagstones.

Potto Ilec messed around with a tinderbox for a while and managed to light a fat brass lamp and a tall, thick candle. 'Please,' he said, waving at a couple of spindly-legged stools, 'sit down, make yourselves comfortable. Can I get you something to drink?'

He didn't wait for an answer, and filled two stubby horn cups from a clay jug. There was dust in the wine, and it didn't taste very nice.

'Now them,' Potto Ilec went on, sitting on the edge of what was presumably his desk. 'Twelve thousand buttons. Yes, I'm sure we can help you out there. Would you like to see some samples?' Again, he didn't wait for a reply; he vanished behind and under the desk, and reappeared a few moments later with what at first looked like a book, but which turned out to be a slim, flat, hinged wooden box that folded open into two trays. Inside it were about twenty rows of buttons, a dozen or so buttons to each row, pinned to the box with fine brass tacks. Most of the buttons were yellow with age, suggesting that the Potto house didn't hold with gratuitous innovation in its designs.

Poldarn stared at the buttons for a while, trying to think of something appropriate to say. To him, they looked like buttons, nothing more or less. If there was anything to choose between them, he certainly couldn't see it. Copis' approach was better. He was sure she knew roughly as much as he did about buttons, but that wasn't the impression she gave; she quickly inspected each row and then let her face sag just a little, disappointed but hardly surprised, like a small child who's just been told she isn't going to be allowed to stay up late for the party after all. After holding this face for a moment she looked up, with just a glimmer of hope still smouldering in her eyes. 'Are there any more we could see?' she asked.

'I'm sorry,' Potto Ilec replied awkwardly. 'That's all the designs we carry.'

'Oh.'

'It's the best selection you'll find in Sansory,' Potto Ilec said defensively. 'And I don't suppose you'd do much better in Weal or Boc, or even,' he added with obvious insincerity, 'Torcea. Of course, if you wanted a large enough quantity, I'm sure we could turn up something to your own specifications.'

Copis shook her head. 'That's all right,' she said.' After all, it's quantity we're after, and continuity of supply. We might as well start with, say, fifty of each pattern and see how we go from there.'

Poldarn kept quiet during the negotiations that followed. Copis appeared to be doing a good enough job on her own, though of course neither of them had a clue as to what would constitute either a stupendous bargain or a merciless fleecing (and where Copis had got the number twelve thousand from, he had no idea). The outcome, good or bad, was that they ended up with twelve thousand assorted buttons for five hundred quarters.

'Have we got five hundred quarters?' Poldarn asked anxiously once they were out in the street again.

'We should be so lucky,' Copis replied. 'How much did you say you'd be likely to get for that sword?'

'Maybe a hundred,' Poldarn replied. 'And I've got a hundred. What about you?'

'In ready money,' Copis replied, avoiding his eye, 'clear and uncommitted, bearing in mind all the other expenses we've got to cover, at least thirty. But it's all right,' she added quickly, as Poldarn made a rather frantic noise, 'payment's not due for another ten days. Plenty of time.'

'Plenty of time? To raise two hundred and seventy quarters?'
'Yes.'

Poldarn frowned. She appeared to be absolutely confident about it. Then again, she'd seemed absolutely confident when she'd been haggling with Potto Ilec. 'Fine,' he said. 'How?'

She smiled. 'Come with me and find out,' she said.

Neither of them said anything until Copis suddenly

stopped outside a thoroughly magnificent house in a row of equally magnificent houses and knocked sharply on the sally-port. When the porter's head appeared through the gap, she told him that she wanted to see Velico Sudel, immediately. The porter stared at her as if she had an extra eye in the middle of her forehead and opened the door.

'Wait here,' he said, shooing them into the lodge. 'What name?'

Copis raised one eyebrow just a little. 'Oh, tell him we're from the Potto house. He'll see us.'

Velico Sudel's office was quite different. Behind the main desk was a long table, with a dozen clerks sitting round it. Beyond that there was a huge counting-board, as big as the bed of a cart, and another dozen clerks were leaning over it swishing counters backwards and forwards with long-handled rakes. All the walls were lined with pigeonholes stuffed with rolled-up papers, most of them stowed in brass or silver tubes. Velico Sudel turned out to be a thin, silver-haired man in a heavy-looking thick wool coat. He had gold rings on all eight fingers, and a massive lump of some red gemstone, carved with his seal and set in gold, on his left thumb. He looked at them carefully, as if trying to decide whether to buy them.

'Potto Ilec sent you?' he asked.

'In a manner of speaking,' Copis replied, in an incongruously cheerful, even playful voice. 'He suggested you'd be the best person to take up the loan we're raising.'

'I see,' Velico Sudel replied. 'Why?'

'I was assuming he owed you a favour,' Copis said, 'or maybe he just likes you. Now, we need to borrow three hundred quarters for two months. Can you manage that?'

'What makes you think I'd lend you three hundred quarters?'

Copis frowned. 'You're a banker,' she said.

'True. But I don't lend money to just anybody. What about security?'

'Oh, that.' Copis produced the bill of sale Potto Ilec had given them. 'Take a look, and you'll see that we've just acquired twelve thousand best-quality bone buttons from the Potto house, for five hundred quarters. Will that do you?'

Velico Sudel's manner changed slightly. 'Twelve thousand?' he said. 'What were you planning to do with twelve thousand buttons?'

'Sell them, of course,' Copis said, with somewhat exaggerated patience. 'In the towns and villages. Rock-solid proposition.'

The expression on Velico Sudel's face suggested he had his doubts about that. 'All right,' he said, 'so you own five hundred quarters' worth of buttons. Suppose you do manage to sell them. That's my security gone.'

'Ah,' Copis said, with a suffering-fools-gladly look on her face, 'but we'll use the money we get from the buttons to pay you back, and then you won't need any security. It's really quite simple when you think it through.'

Velico Sudel looked like a man trying to argue with a child who's too young to realise that the reason Daddy hasn't got an answer to his questions is because there is no answer, not because Daddy's an idiot. 'Yes, but what happens if you're robbed on the way home, or if one of you runs off with all the money? Or supposing—' He frowned, flexing his imagination like an old man stretching his legs after he's been sitting in the same chair for too long. 'Supposing you're trying to cross a flooded river, and your cart's washed away. Where's my security then?'

Copis sighed. 'My partner here was a special courier for the Falx house, so anybody who tries to rob us will end up feeding the crows. For the same reason, I wouldn't dare to run off with his money, and he won't run out on me because he's in love with me.' (That was news to Poldarn, but Velico Sudel seemed to accept it as a valid argument, so he stayed quiet.) 'And as for the third point, I promise you on my father's grave that we'll take special care crossing rivers. Also,' she added, as Velico Sudel made dissatisfied noises, 'naturally we won't be taking all twelve thousand buttons with us every time we go out; probably no more than a thousand at a time, which means that even if one of these dreadful things does happen, there'll still be more than enough buttons left to cover your rotten three hundred. Satisfied?'

Velico Sudel didn't look satisfied in the least, but he did look like someone who'd willingly pay three hundred quarters to get Copis out of his life. 'And Potto Ilec recommended you?' he said.

Copis nodded. 'He said there's a lot of thieves and lowlifes about who'd try and gouge us for five per cent on a simple loan like this, but you weren't like that, you'd be quite happy with two. Oh, he said you'd pretend to make a fuss,' she went on, as Velico Sudel pulled a horrified face and opened his mouth, 'but that's just force of habit. So,' she said, 'have you got the money here, or do you need a moment or so to fetch it?'

Velico Sudel was staring at Copis as if she were some fearsome legendary monster he'd never actually believed in but who'd suddenly appeared in his office and started building a nest. 'You haven't even told me your names,' he said, clearly aware how feeble that sounded but entirely incapable of thinking up anything better.

'I'm not sure I remember you asking,' Copis replied. 'My name's Copis Bolidan, and this is my cousin Balga.'

'Copis Balga?'

'Balga Bolidan,' Copis corrected him. 'We're from Torcea, we do names differently there.'

'And you said he's your . . . oh well, never mind.' Velico Sudel had gone a dark red colour. 'That's up to you, I suppose, nothing to do with me. And it's beside the point,' he realised, looking up sharply. 'I still can't see how I could possibly lend you three hundred quarters secured on your stock in trade alone.'

But he was fighting a losing battle, and all three of them knew it. To his credit, he kept the discussion going for another quarter of an hour before agreeing terms – three hundred quarters for two months at two per cent, secured on the buttons. When eventually he surrendered and sent a clerk for the money, Copis gave him the bill of sale so that he could endorse his loan on the back. He took a long time sharpening his pen, and his writing was tiny.

'What the hell was all that about?' Poldarn asked, as they left the building.

'It worked, didn't it?'

Poldarn shifted the bag of coins to his left hand. 'Yes,' he admitted. 'But surely you aren't allowed to do that – put something up as collateral when you haven't paid for it yet.'

Copis yawned. 'You could well be right,' she said. 'Which is why I had to rattle him. I think I succeeded.

'You certainly rattled me,' Poldarn replied. 'So now what?'

'We take this money to the Potto house – if there's one thing I can't stand, it's knowing I owe money to someone – then we buy a cart, come back, load up what they've got in stock, and work out where we visit first. No point in hanging about, is there?'

Potto Ilec was surprised but pleased to see them again, and made out a warrant to his storeman for the buttons. 'I wish I could tell you exactly what we've got in stock and what we haven't,' he said, 'but right now I can't, the stock books are at the factory.' An unmistakably wistful expression crossed his face. 'I don't suppose you'd like to see the factory,' he added.

'Delighted,' Copis said quickly, before Poldarn could refuse. 'If we're going to be selling your buttons, we really ought to see the factory.'

Potto Ilec beamed. 'Splendid,' he said. 'Right then, we'll go there straight away.' *Before you can change your mind*, he didn't need to add. The smile did that for him.

It took over half an hour of brisk walking, down narrow alleys and passages where the eaves of the houses on either side almost met in the middle, and Potto Ilec didn't stop talking until they reached the factory gate. Neither Copis nor Poldarn could make much sense of what he was saying; most of it was abstruse mechanical details of the new pattern of lathes and sawpits and mill gears he'd just had built, interspersed at very long intervals with a few oblique comments about how much he cared for his workers' welfare and how they were more like family than servants to him. Poldarn kept trying to catch Copis' eye so that he could scowl at her for getting them involved in such a monumental waste of time, but she had a knack of looking the other way at exactly the right moment.

'Here we are,' Potto Ilec announced, halting abruptly in front of a grey, split wooden door in the wall of a particularly dark and narrow alley. 'Our factory, and probably the best facility of its kind north of the bay.'

He banged on the door three times with his fist. Nothing happened. 'They probably can't hear me over the noise of the machines,' he explained. 'Can't complain, it means they're all keeping busy and concentrating on their work.' He hit the door a fourth time. A small splinter of wood fell off and landed at his feet.

Poldarn was getting bored and bad-tempered. 'Here,' he said, 'let me try,' and he gave the door a kick that would've broken a man's ribs. Something gave way and the door flew open. Potto Ilec gave him a startled look and plunged through the doorway, like a duck pitching on water.

Inside it was very dark, even darker than the office in the Potto house. 'Mind your head,' Potto Ilec said, bending almost double to avoid a very low beam. 'Oh, and watch your feet, too. An untidy shop is a busy shop, that's what I always say.'

They passed through another doorway into a large hall. It was slightly less dark; some light was managing to get through the long, thin vertical slits about two-thirds of the way up the walls that served as windows. The hall was crowded with men, women and children, most of them sitting cross-legged in rows on the ground in front of a wooden stake or stump driven into the damp clay floor. Between the rows there were duckboards, raised on bricks. The smell was repulsive: rotten meat and burned bone, sweat, urine and some kind of sweet oily smell that coated the tongue in seconds. Every surface was covered in fine white dust, like snow.

'This is it,' Potto Ilec said proudly. 'I only wish my father could've lived to see it.'

Poldarn peered at the closest squatting figure, which he was eventually able to identify as a man. In his left hand he held a button. In his right was a stick made up of plaited reeds. He was polishing the button with it.

'Horsetail rushes,' Potto Ilec explained, following Poldarn's line of sight. 'They're sharp and abrasive, just right for polishing out sawmarks, and they're free; we just send someone down to the reed beds to cut a wagonload.'

Next to the man's left knee was a large earthenware jar, full of unpolished buttons. There was another jar just like it by his right knee, half full of polished ones. Poldarn noticed that the man's fingers were cracked and bleeding.

'Over here,' Potto Ilec went on, clumping along the duckboard towards the far wall, 'we've got the saw benches, where we cut the bone into narrow sheets. Absolutely wonderful, these new saws. All it takes to run them is three men: one turns the handle, one feeds the bones into the hopper, and the third one runs them through against the fence. There, see.'

Some show of interest was obviously called for, so Poldarn took a step or so closer to the nearest saw bench. In spite of himself, he found it rather fascinating. A tall, bony child was turning a crank (he had to stand on tiptoe to bring it up to top dead centre), which powered a complicated-looking nest of gearwheels, which in turn spun the round sawblade at an astonishingly high speed. The blade was two-thirds buried in a massive wooden bench, and parallel to it was a deep keyway running the length of the benchtop, in which rode a shuttle, fitted with wooden screws and clamps artfully designed to grip various shapes and sizes of bone. A bald man in a frayed red shirt pushed the shuttle forward into the sawblade, which shot out a jet of fine white dust, like a fountain – Poldarn noticed that he was missing half the thumb of his left hand and most of the middle finger of his right – while behind him a short, fat child clamped another bone into another shuttle. The smell of friction-burned bone was sickening.

'Over here,' Potto Ilec said, 'we've got the drilling benches. Another wonderful innovation; you won't see anything like this anywhere in the world, I'm convinced of it.'

The first thing Poldarn noticed about the drilling bench was the row of what looked like miniature gallows – an upright post, about as long as his forearm, with two bars sticking out at right angles, one a hand's span above the other. There was a hole bored in the end of each of these bars, in which rode a wooden spindle with a brass collet holding a tiny flat-bladed drill mounted on the end. Five or six turns of cord were wrapped round the middle of the spindle; the ends of the cord were fastened to the nocks of a wooden bow, which a worker pushed and pulled backwards and forwards, spinning the drill in its bearings. The second man on each drill pressed down on the top of the spindle with a pad of rag or, as often as not, the bare palm of his hand, thereby pushing the drill down into the workpiece – a square of bone pared off one of the long, thin slices produced by the saw bench, held in position by two wooden clamps tightened by thumbscrews. After each hole had been drilled, the presser-down slacked off the thumbscrews and turned the bone square in its jig, ready to drill the next hole, the result being four holes in a precise square, in the very centre of the piece of bone.

'I can see your colleague shares my passion for fine machinery,' Potto Ilec told Copis happily. 'I'm just like him, I could stand for hours on end just watching.'

Poldarn, looking at the drill bench, had his back to Copis and therefore couldn't see the expression on her face, but the little grunting noise she made was enough to give him a fairly unambiguous idea of what she thought about that.

'The next process is really clever,' Potto Ilec declared, leading the way rather too quickly for comfort across the unstable duckboards. 'Our chief engineer's idea, though I must confess that some of the refinements are mine. See if you can guess which.'

Poldarn had no intention of doing anything of the sort; but the machine – for making the square blanks round – was clever enough, in its way. Mostly it was a lathe; a boy cranked a flywheel, transmitting power by means of belts and flywheels to a spindle in a sturdy oak headstock, in the centre of which was a boss with four pins sticking out of it in a square. These went through the holes in the button and located into matching holes in a revolving faceplate mounted in the tailstock. As the boy turned the handle the spindle spun round at a quite incredible rate, and the turner applied the edge of a chisel rested on a toolpost to the corners of the bone square until they'd been chipped away, leaving a perfectly circular button. This only took a few moments, after which the tailstock was drawn back, the rounded button dropped into a jar, and a new blank fitted. When the jar was full, Poldarn supposed, it was taken away and put in front of one of the polishers squatting on the damp floor. He asked Potto Ilec why he hadn't built a machine to do that job as well.

Potto Ilec looked very sad. 'God knows, I've tried,' he said. 'But the problem's holding the button. We tried modifying the pin-chucks on the lathes, but even when we found a system that worked, we could only polish the edges, and the insides still had to be done by hand, so it wasn't worth it.' He sighed. 'I mean,' he went on, 'if you can think of a way of mounting the button on the spindle I'd love to hear about it. But I don't think there is one.'

Poldarn could see one obvious solution – a shallow collet in the headstock that would grip the edges of the button, allowing the abrasive reed to be applied to the face – but somehow he wasn't inclined to mention it. 'Well,' he said, trying to sound enthusiastic, 'thanks for showing us round. Knowing how they're made makes me look at them in a whole new light.'

'Delighted,' Potto Ilec replied, then added, 'My pleasure. Now you know that when I say we can turn out literally hundreds of buttons a day and all of them identical, I'm telling the absolute truth. There's not many men in any trade, let alone the bone trade, who can say that.'

As he spoke there was a loud bang from the back of the shop, accompanied by a piercing scream and followed by some confused shouting. Poldarn spun round and saw that the long leather drivebelt of one of the lathes had snapped; the crank, suddenly freed of its load, had pulled out of the boy's hands, spun round at furious speed and cracked him under the chin, knocking him off his feet. Potto Ilec gasped with acute distress and thundered back down the duckboard, wading through the workers who'd gathered round the boy, past them to the lathe.

'It's all right,' he reported, somewhat out of breath, as he rejoined them a few moments later. 'The belt's past salvaging and the crank handle's bent, but that's all. I was afraid the changewheels might have seized and stripped their teeth.'

They'd got the boy sat up and were trying to drag his hand away from his face. There was a lot of blood, but Poldarn couldn't see the damage because of all the heads and backs in the way. 'That's all right, then,' he muttered. 'What about the kid? Is he badly hurt?'

'What? Oh, I see what you mean.' Potto Ilec sighed. 'I suppose it depends on where the crank handle hit him. Can't have been the forehead or he'd be out cold, or even dead.' A thought occurred to him that seemed to cheer him up. 'I must have a word with our chief engineer and see if he can't come up with something to dampen the crank axle, just in case something like this happens again. It'd be a pleasing challenge, I think; something with a parallel belt and two drums in suspension on either side of the axis.' He smiled beautifully. 'You know,' he said, 'with a bit of thought we might be able to come up with something we could modify to fit on to the saws as well.'

Getting out of the shop, away from the gloom and the overwhelming smell, was sheer joy. Poldarn made a fairly creditable job of hiding it. Copis didn't even try, but fortunately she was three steps behind Potto Ilec and he didn't see her. 'And now you know everything there is to know about making buttons,' Potto Ilec said. 'Now be honest, it's not a bit like how you imagined it, is it?'

'No,' Poldarn said, and left it at that.

It was dark by the time he and Copis got back to the house. 'I don't know about you, but I'm exhausted,' Copis announced as soon as the door was shut behind them. 'I think I'll go on up to bed, and tomorrow I'm going to the bathhouse. God knows if I'll ever be able to get that stench out of my hair, but I intend to try. Otherwise I'm going to have to cut it all off.'

She disappeared up the stairs, leaving Poldarn sitting in a chair beside the cold hearth. The silence suited him, after the noise of the factory and Copis' statement of what she thought about Potto Ilec and his wonderful machines, which had continued without interruption from the factory gate right up to her own door. Copis thought the button factory was an abomination. He could see her point, though he'd prefer to arrive at it by way of different reasons (she didn't hold with it because of the smell and the damp air, which made her feel dirty and scruffy); on the other hand, there was something about the machines – capable, powerful, inhuman – that appealed to a part of him he wasn't sure he was familiar with. To be able to make thousands of something so that each one of them was exactly the way you wanted it, your idea made real, and with no effort on your part, as the machines and the people who served them did all the work according to your design – thinking about it and trying to imagine what it must feel like gave him just a hint of an idea of what it must be like to be a god. A god, after all, wouldn't squat on the floor, cutting and filing and grinding each life in isolation. A god would have rows and rows of machines, shaping lives by the hundreds of thousands simultaneously (and each machine would be part of him, and no single machine would be the whole), and the essence of his divinity would be the power to build and set up the machines, work out the sequence of processes, fit together the drives and gear trains, so that the strength of a boy's hand on the crank would be amplified into enough power to shear through bone at a touch, and the holes in the work would fit the pins of the chuck exactly, every time, with no thought required, so that once set in motion (by one turn of the crank, one moment of force applied at top dead centre) the sequence of actions and processes would lead to a certain and absolutely predictable end, all while the master's back was turned and he was busy with something else. Gods, he felt, would have that same fierce, absurdly misdirected pride that Potto Ilec had displayed, a passionate love for the process and the product taken for granted, of no interest except for its value in bulk, its place in the chain of processes that moved the buttons from Sansory to the rest of the world and landed them, at the end of one sequence of functions and at the start of another, where they were meant to be, on someone's coat.

He closed his eyes. What if there are some gods who only turn the crank, operating a machine they don't understand or have forgotten about? What if someone were to build a machine and lose his memory, so that he couldn't remember how the machine worked or what it was for? But at least he'd know to turn the crank handle and set the gears and pulleys racing, and probably he'd try and figure out the workings and purpose of the machine by observing it in action, until logic and basic principles made it obvious what the process and objectives were. He worried away at this question for some time, both awake and in brief, obscure dreams, some of them involving crows and battles and men he didn't know, some of them merely mechanical, the pure machine without human hands or faces. It had been a long day and he'd had enough of it, but it didn't seem to want to let go. Bits of it were embedded in his mind, like a splinter of steel from a grindstone lodged in an eye, or the head of a tick that stays in the flesh after you've pulled off its body.

Chapter Eighteen

They dragged him, bleeding and dizzy, from the cart to the tent flap (and as his feet trailed behind him, each bump and jolt jarring the broken bone, flooding his body and mind with pain, two crows got up out of a dead spruce tree and flew away; one of them had something gripped in its beak, but he wasn't sufficiently interested to lift his head and see what it was). The sentry outside the tent blocked their way with his spear.

'What's the hurry?' he asked suspiciously. 'And what's that?'

'Top priority is what it is,' snapped the trooper on his left. 'Urgent. You know what urgent means?'

'It's all right.' The voice came from inside the tent. 'Let them through, I'm expecting them.' A hand pulled back the tent flap, and they hauled him through and lowered him to the ground like a sack of grain, gently enough to stop him splitting open, but beyond that not too bothered.

'Lift his head.' A hand gathered enough hair for a grip and pulled upwards, lifting his head enough for him to see the man in the tent. 'That's him. Fine, good work. Now, you two go and get something to eat, catch a few hours' sleep. We're moving out just before dawn.'

He couldn't see the two troopers now, so he assumed they were saluting or whatever cavalrymen did; all he could see was six square inches of threadbare carpet. But he could hear the rustling of canvas, which led him to believe they'd left the tent.

'Do you know who I am?' the voice said. A pause – he didn't reply, mostly because that would involve moving his jaw, which would be very painful. 'Hello, can you hear me? I asked you a question.'

Something hit him just above the waist, confirming his impression that at least one rib on that side was broken. He rode out the pain like a man in a small boat in a gale; so long as his connection with this body was minimal, he could stay above the breakers, not get swamped by them.

'I said, do you know who I am?' If he'd been feeling a little better, he'd have laughed. Possibly he'd have made a witty reply – something along the lines of, I don't even know who I am, or, Sorry, but my mother told me never to talk to strange men. He didn't know who he was, of course; or if he did, the knowledge had been crammed into an inaccessible corner of his mind by the pain, and he couldn't reach it. Didn't really want to, either.

'Well,' the man said, 'in case you don't know, though I'm pretty certain you do, my name is Feron Amathy. What's yours?'

Good question, and it occurred to him that if he didn't answer the man might kick him in the ribs again. He didn't want that. He couldn't remember his name, but he knew a name he'd called himself once or twice, when on a mission using a persona. He opened his mouth – his jaw hurt like hell – and managed to make a noise that sounded like 'Monach'.

'Yes,' the man replied. 'I know. Just wanted to see if you'd tell me the truth. It's what we call a control; ask questions you know the answer to, it helps you get a feel for whether the subject's likely to lie or not. So,' he went on, sitting down in the chair whose feet Monach could just make out in line with his nose, 'you're the famous Monach, are you? Bloody hell, you're a mess. What on earth did they do to you?'

He hoped that was a rhetorical question, because he couldn't remember. Generally speaking, if you want an accurate description of a fight, don't ask the man lying on the ground getting kicked and stamped on. All he can see is boots and ankles, and his concentration is apt to wander.

'Looks like you must've put up a hell of a fight,' the man went on. 'Which did neither of us any favours, of course. You got beaten into mush, I can't get a sensible word out of you. If you'd given up and come quietly, think how much better it'd have been for both of us.' He heard the chair creak, and the feet in front of his eyes moved. 'Let's get you sitting up,' he said. 'We might have better luck if you're not sprawled all over the floor like a heap of old washing.'

The man was strong, and not fussed about what hurt and what didn't. When he opened his eyes again, his mind washed clean by the waves of pain, he was sitting in a chair. Opposite him was the man who'd been talking.

'Better?' the man asked. 'All right, now, you're going to have to make an effort and answer my questions, because it's very important and there's not much time. If you don't, I'll take this stick and find out which of your bones are broken. If you understand, nod once.'

Nodding wasn't too hard. He managed it. That seemed to please the man, because he nodded back and sat down in his chair, a three-foot thumb-thick rod of ashwood across his knees. He was younger than Monach had expected, no more than forty, with plenty of curly brown hair and a slightly patchy brown beard, thick on the cheeks and jaws but a little frayed-looking on the chin itself. He had a pointed nose, a heart-shaped face and bright, friendly brown eyes.

'Splendid,' the man said. 'All right, pay attention. Do you know where General Cronan is?'

Apparently he did, because his head lifted up and then flopped back, jarring his jaw and making him shudder. The name Cronan didn't ring a bell at all.

'Yes? And?'

He felt himself trying to say something. 'At the Faith and Fortitude,' he heard himself say, 'on the road from Josequin to Selce.' That didn't make any sense. He'd never heard of any inn called the Faith and Fortitude, or a place called Selce. The man was nodding, though, as if the answer made perfect sense to him. Then he remembered the two crows, one with something in its beak. Thank God for that, he thought, it's just another dream. A real pity it's so vivid, though. A dream kick to a dream broken rib only causes dream pain, but dream pain hurts just as much as the real thing, apparently.

'I know where you mean,' the man said. 'Very good, now we're getting somewhere. Next question: have you sent some of your people to kill him?'

Just a dip of the head this time, to indicate Yes.

'Buggery. When?'

The answer, apparently, was that morning, two hours before noon.

'Which means . . . How were they going? On foot, horseback, wagon?'

He opened his mouth to reply but started coughing instead. Coughing was a very bad idea. The man didn't approve, either, because he repeated his question, loudly.

'Riding,' he managed to say. 'Not hurrying. Can't risk.'

'Were they taking the main road?'

A nod.

'That's something, I suppose. All right, stay there, don't go away.'

The man left the tent, shouting a name, and left him alone. That was wonderful, he'd have a chance to relax, to catch up with the pain, which was racing ahead of his thoughts and blocking their way. He closed his eyes – it was better with them shut, in spite of the dizziness. At the back of his mind something was protesting: no, you mustn't close your eyes, you'll fall asleep or pass out. This is your only chance; look, there's a knife on the map table, you can reach it if you tilt the legs of the chair. You can hide it under your arm, and when he comes back you can stab him or cut his throat, and that'll make up for the rest. Must do it, can't afford not to. You've done very badly, but you still have one chance. Won't get another. Must—

He stayed still, put the voice out of his mind. Maybe if he knew what was going on it'd be different; if he knew why it was so important to kill this man – Feron something, Feron Amathy, and didn't that name sound familiar from somewhere? – then maybe he might just have made the effort. As it was, no incentive. Nothing outside his body mattered, outside his body and the invisible circle of pain that surrounded it. The pain defined everything.

A while later Feron Amathy came back. He looked unhappy. 'I've sent thirty light cavalry up the old drovers' trail, so if the Lihac's fordable they ought to get there an hour or so before your assassins. Still, it's cutting it fine.'

He sounded like a senior officer briefing a delinquent subordinate, not one enemy telling another how he'd frustrated his plans and made the sacrifice of his life to the cause meaningless. It wasn't cruelty, Monach figured, just a busy man thinking aloud, as busy men so often do. Probably he found it useful having someone to talk to, even if it was only a defeated, humiliated opponent. Monach could feel his weariness, the tremendous weight of responsibility clamping down on his shoulders. 'Now then,' he said, flopping back into his chair and letting his arms hang down. 'What are we going to do with you, I wonder? My instinct says send your head back to Deymeson with an apple stuck in your mouth, to let them know I'm perfectly well aware of what they're up to. On the other hand, why give them any more information than necessary? So long as they aren't sure whether I've worked out that they're involved, they'll have to cover both contingencies, which'll slow up their planning. In which case, I can either have you strung up here, make a show of it, issue double rations, give the lads something to cheer them up; or I could keep you for later, assuming you survive. God only knows what sort of useful stuff you've got locked up in your head, but will prising it out of there be more trouble than it's worth?' He sighed. 'Truth is,' he went on, 'nobody else is fit to interrogate you; even in the state you're in you're probably too smart for them, and I can't afford to let you muck me about with disinformation. I haven't got the time or, let's face it, the energy. Besides, you've caused me a real headache, and until those cavalry troopers get back from Selce I can't be sure you haven't really screwed everything up.' He sighed. 'I think I'll knock you on the head now,' he went on. 'Anything else is just wasting valuable time.' As he said that, he stood up, drawing a short knife from the sash round his waist. One step forward, finger and thumb tightening on his face, a sharp twist sideways, the knife starting to slice the skin of his neck—

Poldarn woke up, his right hand pressed hard against his neck. Usually the dreams didn't bother him once he'd woken up; they slid away, like ducks launching themselves on to a pond, and left nothing behind. But this dream had been different, much more real and immediate, so that the pain had hurt. He'd already forgotten what had caused it, but the memory of the pain was still with him, an uncomfortable twitch every time it burst into his circle.

'You do that a lot,' Copis said.

He'd forgotten she was there. 'Do what?' he mumbled.

'Sleep with your hand under your ear like that,' she replied. 'I wish you wouldn't, it makes you snore.'

He frowned. 'I don't snore, do I?'

'When you sleep with your hand under your ear, yes.'

'Oh.' For some reason, that bothered him a lot. 'I'm sorry,' he said. 'Did I wake you up?'

She shook her head. 'I'm used to people making noises in their sleep,' she explained, with a slight narrowing of the eyebrows that made it clear that the subject wasn't to be pursued further. 'It's fairly moderate snoring, actually; cutting-damp-wood-with-a-blunt-saw snoring, not monsoon-winds-in-Morevich snoring. Are you going to lie there all day, or would you care to get up so we can go and earn a living?'

He remembered where he was: an inn called the Divine Moderation, a third of the way from Sansory to Deymeson. They were on the road, selling buttons. Yesterday had been a good day; they'd sold fifteen dozen buttons at four hundred and fifty per cent mark-up, and all the women in the village had told them how reasonable their prices were.

'This place we're going to,' Copis said, as he sat down beside her on the box, 'ought to be pretty good. Never been there myself, of course, but I've heard quite a bit about it. Apparently they've got wonderful soil, so they grow garden stuff for Sansory – fruit and vegetables, mostly, and a lot of flowers. Should mean there'll be some money about.'

The name of the place turned out to be Mestory, and it was almost large enough to be a town. The Sansory road brought them in on the south-west side, where there was a sprawl of new houses and fences that were hardly weathered at all, with the gates still hanging straight and held closed by their latches rather than lengths of fraying twine. The thatch on the roofs was still nearer yellow than grey, and all the buildings looked pretty much the same.

'Interesting,' Copis observed. 'New building. Definite sign of prosperity. We could do well here.'

More surprising still was the marketplace; that was all new, too. There was a small but handsome corn exchange in the middle of the market square, so new that the edges of the stone blocks were still sharp and clean. Opposite the corn exchange there was even a temple – a miniature temple, with a toy portico and one self-conscious-looking half-life-size statue outside, but a temple nevertheless. The scaffolding up the side of the east wall suggested it wasn't finished yet.

'All right,' Copis said, 'I'm impressed. So where is everybody?'

As soon as she said it, Poldarn realised that that was what was wrong with the place: no people. There was a fine market, but no stalls. There were temple steps, but nobody sitting on them. Half the shops in the pristine-looking traders' row had their shutters up, and there were no more than a dozen people standing outside the shops that were open. The few people he could see appeared to be acting normally – drifting, chatting, window-shopping – but there was only a sparse handful of them, and it was an hour before noon.

'There's probably a simple explanation,' Poldarn said. 'Maybe everybody's out fetching in the asparagus harvest or something.'

'Fat lot you know about asparagus,' Copis replied accurately, but she was clearly just as bewildered as he was. 'Maybe they're all indoors. Could be a seasonal thing,' she added. 'Maybe, because they grow different stuff to most places, they have their midday meal at a different time.'

Poldarn hadn't thought of that, mostly because it wasn't a very convincing explanation. The place felt empty.

'We'd better ask somebody instead of guessing,' Copis said. 'Quick, ask that woman over there.'

Poldarn pulled a face. 'You ask her,' he said.

'Oh for . . . Excuse me.' The woman stopped and looked round. 'Excuse me,' Copis went on, 'but where is everybody?'

The woman looked at her. 'Where's who?' she said.

'Everybody. The people who live here.'

The woman shook her head and walked away. 'Just my luck,' Copis said, not lowering her voice. 'I have to ask the village idiot.'

'Maybe they aren't used to strangers,' Poldarn suggested, without any real enthusiasm.

'Maybe they're just ignorant,' Copis replied sharply. 'Anyway, we're here; we might as well set up the stall, just in case. They've got a temple, perhaps they're all in there, singing hymns.'

Poldarn listened for a moment. 'Pretty quiet singing if they are,' he said.

The stall was little more than the side of the cart, which was hinged and swung down; two posts for the awning went in the canopy-rod holes, with two more rods leaning forward at forty-five degrees to support the front. All that was needed after that was a trestle table and trays for sample buttons. The rest of the stock was in jars and barrels in the back of the cart. They took their time setting up, to give the word a chance to spread. When they couldn't spin it out any longer, they sat on the bed of the cart and surveyed the empty streets.

'If we're quick,' Copis said, a short while later, 'we could be in Forial by early evening.'

'Where's Forial?'

'Next village down the road from here. I don't know anything about it except the name, but it's got to be better than this.'

Poldarn shook his head. 'I can't be bothered,' he said. 'Besides, you never know, it could pick up. I've always fancied running a stall must be a lot like decoying rooks – you know, where you find where they're feeding, hunker down out of sight and put out a few dead birds stuck up on sticks to draw the others in. Then when they pitch you pick them off with a sling.'

Copis clicked her tongue. 'So far,' she said, 'I don't get the similarity. Or are you saying we should kill and impale the next person we see? The idea does appeal to me, I'll grant you, but not on commercial grounds.'

Poldarn grinned. 'The point is,' he said, 'you can sit there in your ditch or under your tree for the best part of the day and never see anything; and then, just when you've finally decided to give it away and go home, suddenly the sky'll turn black with rooks, and next thing you know you've run out of slingstones. Patience is the key to this lark, you wait and see.'

Copis turned thoughtful for a while, as Poldarn fiddled with the trays of buttons. Eventually she looked up and said, 'Where do you get the dead ones from?'

'Sorry?'

'The dead ones you put out in sticks, for decoys,' she said. 'Where do you get them from?'

'They're the ones you killed the previous day,' Poldarn explained.

'All right,' Copis conceded. 'But in that case, how do you start off? I mean, if you need a dozen dead rooks before you can start killing rooks, how do you kill a dozen rooks in the first place?'

'No idea,' Poldarn said. 'I suppose I must know the answer, since I seem to be pretty well clued up about the subject, but I can't remember offhand.'

'Fine,' Copis said. 'In that case, let's change the subject. The thought of dead rooks really isn't one I want to hold in my mind for very long.'

Noon came and passed, during which time two old women walked past the stall, apparently without noticing that it was there. Copis made a point of standing up and staring at them as they passed, explaining that she wanted to see if they were wearing any buttons. 'They were, too,' she added. 'Which makes it odder still. Unless there's a special tree in these parts that grows buttons instead of nuts.'

Not long after that a young woman with a baby in her arms

walked by the stall, stopped and leaned over to look at one of
the trays. Poldarn and Copis snapped to attention like a couple
of farm dogs hearing a bowl scraping on the cobbles.

'Can we help at all?' Copis cooed.

'I was just looking,' the woman replied, taking a step backwards as though she'd been caught out doing something
wicked. 'Very nice,' she added.

Copis smiled at her. 'Anything in particular you liked the
look of?' she asked.

The woman hesitated and glanced down at the baby, which
was fast asleep. 'Well,' she said, hesitating. 'Those ones there,
the quite big ones with the rim on them.'

'Gorgeous, aren't they?' Copis replied, exaggerating rather.
'Made in Sansory, Potto house. You won't find better this side
of the bay.'

It was clear that the woman was tempted, and that she was
fighting the temptation. 'Those other ones,' she said tentatively, 'the little ones on the bottom row. Are they cheaper or
dearer than the big ones?'

'All the same price,' Poldarn said quickly before Copis
frightened her off. In his mind he had a picture of a black bird
putting its wings back and circling in a glide towards him.
'Two quarters a dozen.'

'I don't know,' the woman replied. 'Shouldn't the smaller
ones be cheaper?'

Poldarn shook his head. 'If anything they should be more
expensive,' he said. 'Harder to make, you see. Fiddly.'

'Oh.' The woman rubbed her cheekbones thoughtfully with
thumb and forefinger. 'If I take two dozen, would it be
cheaper?'

'No,' Copis said. 'Sorry.'

'Oh. Have you got any others, or is this everything?'

That took Poldarn rather by surprise, since he couldn't
begin to imagine what need there could possibly be for the two
hundred and forty different styles of buttons mounted on the

display board. 'Sorry,' he said, 'but that's the lot. What sort of thing were you looking for?'

The woman shrugged. 'I won't know what it is till I see it,' she replied. 'Thanks very much.'

Poldarn was too bewildered to persevere, and let it go with a smile and a dip of the head. Copis waited till the woman was about fifty yards away then stuck her tongue out in her general direction. 'Time-waster,' she explained.

'She never had any intention of buying any buttons,' Poldarn said.

'Of course not. Just passing the time. Lots of people do it, I have absolutely no idea why.' She sighed. 'This is completely pointless. Let's fold up and get out of here.'

Poldarn glanced up at the sky. 'You know,' he said, 'we've left it a bit late if we want to reach that other place by dark.'

'I'd rather sleep in the cart than stay here.'

Poldarn could see her point. But packing up would mean having to get up and exert himself, and he was feeling lazy. 'No,' he said, 'let's stick to the original plan. Stay here the rest of the day and push on to Forial tomorrow.'

'Suit yourself,' Copis said. 'But you can mind the stall on your own. I'm going to take a nap in the cart.'

Poldarn couldn't see any objections to that, so he nodded. Copis climbed up behind him, laid a blanket in the corner of the cart bed, and went to sleep. She had a knack of being able to sleep at will that he found both remarkable and enviable.

Some time later a little girl, perhaps nine years old, wandered up and stood staring at the buttons as if they were six-headed goats. Apart from the time-waster's baby, she was the first child he'd seen in town. There was something about the way she was standing and gawping that told him she was neither willing nor able to buy buttons, but Poldarn could see no reason why she should be a complete dead loss.

'Hey,' he said.

The girl looked at him and said nothing.

'Come here,' he said. 'I want to ask you a question.'

The little girl scowled at him. 'My mummy says not to talk to strange men.'

'You should always listen to your mother. But I'm not strange.'

The little girl assessed him. It didn't seem to take her very long. 'Yes you are,' she said. 'You're old and ugly and you look like a crow.'

'Thank you,' Poldarn replied. 'Now, if you don't mind, please stop looking at my buttons. You'll look all the polish off them.'

The little girl frowned. 'You can't do that, silly.'

'Of course you can.'

'No you can't. Looking at things doesn't hurt them.'

'Want to bet?' Poldarn leaned back a little. 'You know how if you leave something out in the sun for a while, like a piece of cloth or something like that, all the colour fades out of it? Same thing. The sun looks at it too long and it fades.'

The girl thought about that. 'But I don't look as fiercely as the sun.'

'Maybe. But you're much closer, so it's as broad as it's long. Go away.'

She shook her head. 'No,' she said. 'I can stay here and look at your stupid buttons if I want to.'

Poldarn rubbed his chin thoughtfully. 'All right,' he said, 'but don't come any closer.'

He made a show of fiddling with the display, shifting the boards around, rearranging the buttons, turning some of them over. When he'd been doing this for a while, the little girl said, 'What was the question you wanted to ask me?'

'Doesn't matter,' he replied, not looking up. 'You probably wouldn't know the answer anyway.'

'Bet you I would.'

He laughed. 'No point betting you, you've got nothing to bet with.'

'Yes I have,' the girl replied, annoyed. 'I've got a brass ring and a rabbit-fur hood at home.'

Poldarn shook his head. 'They wouldn't fit me,' he said. 'All right, you can push off now. I'm busy.'

'What's the question?'

He made an exasperated noise with his tongue and teeth. 'If I ask you the question, will you go away?'

She shook her head. 'You've got to bet me.'

'Oh, for crying out loud. All right, then, what do you want to bet?'

'My hood and ring against a dozen buttons,' she replied. 'Those ones,' she added, pointing. 'They're nice.'

In Poldarn's opinion the ones she'd chosen were the most hideous of the lot, although they had some pretty stiff competition. 'If you insist,' he said. 'All right, here's the question: where is everybody? Why's this village got so few people in it?'

The little girl put on a sad face, as if pulling on a glove. 'They went away,' she said. 'The grown-up men had to go and join the—' She said something that sounded like *merlicia*. It took Poldarn a second or so to work out she meant militia. 'And then the raiders came and killed them all,' she added casually. 'Mummy said they aren't dead, they just went on a long journey, but I know that's not true because I saw where they got buried, in a big pit, hundreds and hundreds.'

'Ah,' Poldarn said, feeling a little rattled. 'And what about the lady grown-ups? Did they go away too?'

'Some of them were killed,' the girl said, playing with a pulled thread on her sleeve, 'and some of them got sick and died. But a lot of them just went away. My mummy went away and I've got to live with my aunt. I don't like her very much. She *smells*.'

Poldarn nodded absently. 'That's dreadful,' he said. 'Where did they go? The ones who went away, I mean?'

'Don't know. Do I get my buttons now?'

'In a minute,' Poldarn replied. 'What do you know about religion?'

The girl looked at him. 'What's that?'

'Gods and stuff.'

'Oh,' the girl said, 'that. Well, there's lots of gods, and some of them live in the sky and some of them live under the ground or at the bottom of the sea, and the rest just sort of wander about. What do you want to know about them for?'

'Have you heard of a god called Poldarn?'

'Poll what?'

'Or a god who rides around in a cart, bringing the end of the world?'

'Oh yes, of course,' the girl said, her face relaxing as she addressed something familiar at last. 'Everybody knows about him.'

'What do they know?'

The little girl gathered her thoughts for a moment. 'Well,' she said, 'nobody knows what he's called, and he goes around from village to village, and wherever he goes gets burned down or invaded and all the people die; but it's not his fault, it's bad men like the raiders who do the actual burning and invading. He just sort of goes in front. Oh yes,' she added, 'and there's a silly bit, too, but I don't believe it.'

'Tell me anyway,' Poldarn said.

The little girl pulled a face. 'Well, they say he doesn't actually know he's a god, he just thinks he's one of us, a person. And he starts off by climbing up out of a river, and he keeps on going till he meets himself coming in the opposite direction. And then that's the end of the world. Like I said,' she added disdainfully, 'it's really silly, and I don't think anybody really believes it. *Now* do I get my buttons? You did promise.'

Poldarn found the right jar and counted out a dozen buttons. 'Thanks,' he said. 'You won your bet after all. You're clever.'

'I know,' the girl jeered, and skipped away.

By the time Copis woke up he'd got the awning down and folded up the trestles. 'You were right,' he said, 'absolutely no point staying here. We'll make a start towards Deymeson and sleep out; with luck, that'll get us to Forial good and early. Assuming,' he added, 'it's still there when we arrive.'

Forial was still there, and it was well and truly open for business. They did a very brisk trade all day, and in the rare intervals when he wasn't taking money Poldarn tried to find out about what had happened in the other village. Yes, it was true what the girl had told him; in fact the place had had a fairly dreadful time of it over the last twenty years or so. First it had been completely erased by the raiders, or by some-body – a lot of people reckoned it was the Amathy house, since they'd been in the district at the time on their way back from a war that got cancelled at the last moment, but of course there wasn't any proof; then the emperor himself had sent money and builders to restore it, by way of showing how much he cared about the northern provinces, not that anybody believed him. But it had been a good job, and quite soon they were doing a wonderful business in fruit and vegetables with Sansory and everybody was starting to get annoyingly pros-perous. Then the Amathy house had shown up – definitely them this time, they were fighting for General Allectus against General Cronan, and they needed a couple of hundred labour-ers to build a wall or dig a trench or raise a siege mound or something of the sort, so they rounded up all the men and quite a few of the women and the older children – they had the authority; some kind of general warrant issued by the pre-fect of Sansory – and marched them off to do whatever it was that needed doing, but it all went wrong; the thing they were building fell down or caved in, or the enemy attacked it sud-denly, and they were all killed. It was a terrible shame, the people of Forial told him, and a bloody good job Feron Amathy had gone there instead of here for his work detail. Feron Amathy was a menace, no two ways about it, though this new man, Cronan, he was probably just as bad, because when you came right down to it, they all were; them and the raiders and the government soldiers too. Still, at least it wasn't as bad as what happened to Vistock.

What happened to Vistock, Poldarn asked; and where was Vistock, anyway?

Ah, they told him, good question. Well, if he carried on up the road another half a day and he kept his eyes open and it was a time of year when the grass was short, he might just be able to make out some scorched patches on the ground, even now. That was Vistock. And that really was the raiders, they added. It all happened a long time ago, mind, over forty years ago, and though the land around there wasn't bad and it was all up for grabs, what with everybody being dead, nobody'd ever shown any interest at all in going out there and staking a claim. Well, apart from one old woman who still lived there, in some kind of mouldy old hut, but she was crazy, so that didn't count.

Poldarn supposed you'd have to be crazy to live all alone out in the wilds like that.

Ah yes, but she was a lot crazier than that. She figured she was the mother of the god in the cart; you know, the one who's going to turn up at the end of the world. Now that had to be a special kind of crazy, didn't it?

By nightfall they'd sold the best part of eight hundred buttons. When they'd packed up the stall, Copis asked where the inn was. There wasn't an inn. But the blacksmith might be prepared to let them sleep over in his barn for a few quarters. A few turned out to be six, rather more than they'd have spent in a reasonably good inn; the barn was cold, with a damp floor (like the Potto house) and a thoroughly objectionable goose, which brayed at them all night and managed to get out of the way of everything they threw at it.

They were ready to leave as soon as the sun rose. 'Deymeson,' Copis said. 'There's nothing to stop for between here and there, so we should be able to get there in a day if we don't hang about.'

Poldarn shook his head. 'Actually,' he said, 'I want to stop off on the way.'

Vistock wasn't hard to find. It was where a village should have been, where the road forded a small, inoffensive river. The first thing they could make out was the shell of a mill-house, with a wrecked and moss-grown wheel sunk in the water. Inside the building they found a lump of rust that had once been an anvil and the charred stump of a trip-hammer. There was only one other structure still standing: half a barn (the other half had fallen in a long time ago, there were still signs of fire on the rounded ends of the rafters) surrounded on two sides by an overgrown wall.

'Over there, I suppose,' Poldarn said.

'What the hell could there possibly be in there worth stopping for?' Copis asked.

'No idea,' Poldarn replied. 'Come on.'

Someone had made a half-hearted attempt at boarding in the remaining half of the barn. There was even a door, hanging out of the fence of rotten timbers on two straps of mouldy rope. There really didn't seem to be much point in knocking, since you could get through the gap between the door and the fence if you went sideways and held your breath, but Poldarn knocked anyway.

'Go away,' said a voice from inside.

'Good God,' Copis whispered. 'There's someone in there.'

'I know,' Poldarn replied. 'That's why we're here.'

He opened the door into darkness. An egg hit him in the face.

Luckily it caught him on the chin, so he didn't have to worry about razor-sharp splinters of shell in his eyes. He wiped it away with the back of his left hand and called out, 'Hello?'

'Piss off. I got a knife.'

Poldarn peered round, but it was very dark indeed inside and he couldn't see anything. 'Can I come in?' he asked.

'No. Get lost, before I stick this knife in you.'

'There's no call to be like that,' Poldarn said.

'Yes there is. Get out, or I'll kill you.'

Poldarn was using the voice to find whoever it was. It was low for a woman's voice, rather breathy in a way that suggested some kind of chronic lung trouble. 'We don't mean you any harm,' he said. 'I'd just like to ask you a few questions.'

'Get out. Go away, before I set the dogs on you.'

It was fairly obvious that there weren't any dogs. 'Really,' he said, listening hard, 'we aren't going to hurt you or steal your stuff. We've come a long way.'

'I don't give a damn if you've come all the way from bloody Morevich, you're not—' That was enough for Poldarn to get a fix; he reached out quickly into the dark and grabbed, and connected with a thin, tight arm. He could feel small muscles, as hard as rope, under old skin.

'Sorry,' he said, dragging on the arm, 'but I do need to ask you some things. Won't take long.'

She may have been lying about the dogs, but not the knife, but Poldarn knew the moment her hand violated his circle, and he caught her wrist easily. A quick twist, enough to hurt without damaging, was enough to make her drop the knife. He pulled firmly, overcoming rather more resistance than he'd expected, and led her out into the light.

Not a pretty sight. It was fairly evident that she didn't feel the cold, since she wasn't wearing any clothes; as a result, it was hard to miss the shiny white scar that ran from her left hip almost to her navel. She had a fuzz of tangled grey hair, with things in it, and a jaw that had set badly after being broken a long time ago. She stopped struggling when Poldarn let go of her, and sat down on a log that looked as if it had done long service as a chopping-block.

'Who the bloody hell are you, then?' she asked, and sneezed.

Poldarn grinned. 'You know,' he said, 'that's a very good question. But if you don't mind, I'd like to ask you a question of my own first. Is it true you've got a son?'

She scowled at him, and wiped her nose on the back of her wrist. 'Come to make fun, have you?' she said. 'I know your sort. You'll be old too one day, and then you'll be sorry.'

Poldarn shook his head. 'I'd really like to know,' he said.

'All right.' She reached down behind the log and produced a small axe – Poldarn could have sworn it hadn't been there a moment ago. 'But you lay off me, or so help me I'll smack your head in. You got that?'

'Sure,' Poldarn replied. 'So, is it true?'

She nodded. 'I did have a son once, yes. Had him for all of ten days, before they came over from Vistock; said they reckoned it was about time for the kid to be born, and it wasn't right, trying to bring up a kid out here. They told me I had to go with them, I said I wasn't going. One of them grabbed him, my baby, so I cut his throat.' She paused to pinch something out of her eye; she was very delicate and precise about it, nipping whatever it was off her eyeball with the ends of her jagged nails and flicking it away. 'Well, that was him dealt with, and they went away. But they took the boy, and I've never seen or heard of him since. That was a long time ago.'

Poldarn, who was kneeling down beside her, nodded. 'What about this story I heard in Forial,' he asked, 'about the god in the cart? How did that start?'

She turned her head and looked at him. 'Oh, that's who he was, all right,' she said. 'He told me so himself.'

'I see,' Poldarn said, without emphasis. 'When he was ten days old.'

'No, of course not,' she replied, frowning. 'Don't talk so stupid. No, it was in a dream. I saw him.'

'You saw him,' Poldarn repeated. 'As a baby, or was he grown up?'

'Oh, he was all grown up,' she replied. 'But I knew it was

him. And he knew who I was, too. He stopped the cart and got out – he was standing about where that stone is.' She pointed with her left hand, but Poldarn didn't turn to look; the axe was still in her right hand, and he didn't want to take his eye off it just yet. 'Anyway, he smiled at me – always did have a nice smile, of course – and then he got back in and rode away. The smile's from my mother's side, though he had his father's nose.'

'His father.'

'Yes, him.' She frowned. 'One of Feron Amathy's men, he was,' she went on, looking down at her feet. 'It was them burned the village, you know, and killed everybody. Never knew why; I suppose we were in the way or something.'

'Oh,' Poldarn said. 'I'd heard it was the raiders.'

'That's right. Feron Amathy's men. From across the sea.' She found a stub of twig and started whittling at it with the hatchet blade. 'When he was finished with me he was going to kill me, but I was too quick for him. Always was quick with my hands,' she added with a smile. 'That's how I got my knife. Been a good knife over the years, I'd be lost without it. It was lying there on the ground, he was reaching for it, but I got it first and stuck it in his ear. Just there,' she added, 'where you're kneeling, that's where he fell. Landed on his face, and I pulled the knife out and ran. One of his mates was just by the door, he took a swing at me with one of those big inside-out swords of theirs – that's how I got this, in case you were wondering.' She drew a fingertip down the line of the long scar, tracing it by feel, almost affectionately. 'And this was later,' she added, touching her jaw, 'when the government soldiers came through. Was that what you wanted to ask about?'

Poldarn nodded slowly. 'So your son, the god in the cart – his father was a raider, and you killed him.'

'That's right.'

'But he's the god in the cart.'

'I just told you that. You think I'm mental, don't you?'

Poldarn shook his head. 'I can't see any reason not to believe you,' he said. 'Do you think you'd know him again if you saw him, after all these years?'

She scowled. 'My own kid? Of course I would. He's got my mother's chin and his father's nose. I'd know him anywhere.'

Poldarn stood up. 'And you've been here ever since,' he said. It wasn't meant as a question. 'How do you manage? What do you live on?'

She smiled. Once upon a time, it would probably have been a very nice smile. 'I trade,' she said.

'I see,' Poldarn said. 'What do you trade?'

'None of your business.'

'I agree,' Poldarn replied. 'There's no reason why you should tell me if you don't want to, I'm just interested.'

With a turn of her wrist that was too fast for Poldarn's eye to follow, she flicked the hatchet into the log, right between her knees. 'I trade with Master Potto Ilec of Sansory,' she said proudly. 'He sends a wagon up here four times a year, with jars of flour and some cheese and bacon. He needs me,' she added, 'he can't get the good stuff anywhere else, for fear of people knowing. He sends his own son and his two brothers and his uncle, because he won't trust anybody else not to tell.'

Poldarn was holding his breath without knowing it. 'Would you like to tell me what you give him in return for the food?'

She reached down, pulled up the sole of her foot, like a farrier shoeing a horse, and examined it. 'Master Potto Ilec makes buttons,' she said. 'For the really special buttons he likes to use a special kind of bone, with a fine, straight grain and a good feather. It's got to be properly dried and seasoned, and it's got to be the right colour, dark brown. It's the colour that makes it so hard to find.'

'I think I see,' Poldarn said.

'You can't stain it,' she went on, 'it only goes that colour when it's charred in a fire – that dries it up, see, gets all the grease out – and then left to weather, out in the wind and the

rain. Takes a long time to cure, according to Master Potto
Ilec, you can't rush it. Very hard to find these days.'

'Thank you,' Poldarn said, 'you've been very helpful. Can
I ask you one last question?'

She looked up at the sky. 'Don't see why not,' she said.

He took a step closer. 'Your son,' he said, 'did you give him
a name, by any chance?'

She shook her head. 'Didn't get round to it. I had other
things on my mind, really.'

'Right. Does the name Poldarn mean anything to you?'

'Poldarn.' She thought for a moment. 'No,' she said, 'does-
n't ring any bells.'

Poldarn felt in the pocket of his coat. 'Those special buttons,' he said. 'Are they anything like these?'

She glanced at the buttons he'd taken from his pocket and
shook her head. 'Too pale,' she said. 'And they're not quite as
big as that. They showed me one once, so I could be sure to
match the colour.'

Poldarn stepped back towards the cart, still facing her every
step of the way. 'Thank you,' he said. 'Is there anything you'd
like us to bring you? We'll be passing here again on our way
back in a few days.'

She shook her head. 'I got everything I need right here,' she
said, 'thanks to Master Potto Ilec, and Feron Amathy.'

Poldarn looked at her. 'You didn't need the kid, then.'

'No.'

'Ah. Well, thank you for talking to us.'

'You're welcome. And now you can piss off and leave me in
peace.'

Copis didn't say anything for a long time, not until the
ruins of Vistock were out of sight behind the horizon. It was
as if she was afraid the mad woman would hear her. 'You
didn't ask her name,' she said.

'You're right,' Poldarn replied, 'I didn't.'

'Oh. Why not?'

He shrugged. 'I forgot. I suppose I figured it wasn't important. Talking of which, is Copis your real name?'

She laughed. 'No,' she replied.

He didn't make any comment about that, which annoyed her. 'Aren't you going to ask me what my real name is?', she said.

'No,' Poldarn replied. 'You can tell me if you want to.'

She scowled. 'If you must know, it's Xipho Dorunoxy. And I'm not really from Torcea, though I did live there for years, when I was a kid. I'm from Exo.'

'I see,' Poldarn said. 'Where's that?'

'Oh, a long way away, inland to the east. It isn't even a province of the empire any more. I think it broke away about sixty years ago, though our people still come and go quite freely across the border. You aren't interested, are you?'

He shook his head. 'One thing I've learned lately,' he said, 'is how little it matters what people call themselves or where they come from. They seem to have an idea that without things like that they'll lose their shape and collapse, like a bowl of water if you suddenly take the bowl away. Well, I'm here to prove it isn't true.'

She looked at him in silence for a while. 'You're really trying hard to believe that, aren't you?' she said.

'Yes.'

'Any luck?'

'Not really, no.'

She laughed again. 'Did I ever tell you what the iron-master told me?'

'What iron-master.'

'Ah.' She took off her shoe and shook something out of it, then put it back on. 'Well, I've told you that some of the customers where I used to work liked to talk sometimes, tell me things. I haven't a clue why; I suppose I had a knack of looking like I was interested, and men who're important in business like to talk about what they're doing, stuff they're pleased or proud about, but of course it's usually technical, so nobody outside the shop can understand what they're talking about. Anyway, they used to explain things to me – how things work, how they're made, that sort of stuff.'

'And you listened.'

'It was better than work, that's for sure.' She pushed her hair back behind her ears. 'One of them was an iron-master, like I said. He had a big foundry for brass and copper, and an enormous furnace and great big trip-hammers for the iron and steel – apparently you can't melt iron, the fire's not hot enough, you can only make it soft and squeeze it out of the ore into big lumps, what they call blooms. Then if you want to make plates or bars or whatever, you've got to get it hot till it's soft and beat it into shape.'

'I see,' Poldarn said. 'How fascinating.'

'Shut up, I'm getting there. With scrap, you see, it's different. You sort it all out into piles – soft iron in one pile, hard steel in another, and the soft iron that gets turned into steel, like old horseshoes and wheel tyres and stuff, in a third; and then what you do is you get them all hot and you hammer them and hammer them until they're all welded together into the shapes your customers want – bars and plates and rods. Ever such a lot of work, he told me.'

Poldarn yawned. 'I can imagine,' he said.

'The point is,' Copis went on, 'when you make steel hard, you make it able to hold a shape. That's what hard is, really, being able to stay the same shape even if you get bashed on, unless you're too hard and brittle, in which case you shatter. Anyway, this being able to hold a shape; according to him, the word they used for it was memory. Like a cart spring or a crossbow prod, or a sword; if you bend it, it can remember the shape it used to be and go back into it, exactly the same shape it used to be before you twisted it back on itself. Or, if the memory's really strong, you can hammer and file at it all day and all you'll do is wreck your tools, because it won't budge.'

She was looking straight ahead, not at him. 'But if you heat it up, past sunrise red and blood red and cherry red to orange, it'll lose its memory just like you lost yours, and then it stops being hard or springy and turns soft, so you can bash it and shape it and do whatever you like with it. Then, if you just let it cool down slowly in the air, it'll stay soft; but if you take it all red and bloody out of the fire and dip it straight into a pool of water, it'll immediately freeze hard, like the Bohec in winter, and then it'll have a memory all over again. Do you see what I'm getting at?'

'It'd be difficult not to,' Poldarn replied. 'You believe in the sledgehammer school of allegory, I can tell.'

She looked offended for a moment, then shrugged. 'I was just trying to be nice,' she said.

He nodded. 'It's the thought that counts.' He rubbed his face with the palm of his hand. 'So why did you start calling yourself Copis?'

'Because nobody could be bothered to say Dorunoxy,' she replied. 'So they called me Xipho, which of course is my last name, not my first, and where my family come from it's really rude to call someone just by their last name unless you know them really well, and even though I knew they didn't mean anything by it, it used to upset me a lot. So I changed it.'

'Fair enough. What about Copis?'

She laughed. 'Oh, it's a common enough name in Torcea, particularly,' she added, with a grin, 'in that line of work. It's the sort of name the customers expected me to have, so it was easy.'

He nodded. 'And now,' he said, 'what do you think of yourself as, Dorun-whatsit or Copis?'

'Copis.' She pulled a face. 'Which is really bad, because – well, a Copis, you can be pretty sure what kind of person a Copis is.'

'And you're not.'

Her expression changed. 'No. Well, what do you think?'

'Does it matter what I think?'

'Why are you deliberately trying to annoy me?'

He shrugged. 'I don't think you're a Copis, no. I'm just disproving the point you were trying to make at such interminable length a moment ago, that's all. You've changed your name and the shape you appear in, but you've still got the old memory; you're not a Copis, you're a – whatever it was. However hard you try to be a button, you're still a bone.'

She shook her head. 'Whatever,' she said. 'This is all getting a bit too involved and personal for me. I suggest we talk about something else, before we fall out.'

'All right.'

'That woman,' Copis said. 'Who was she?'

'I don't know. I forgot to ask her name, remember?'

'Be like that.' She turned her head away and pretended to look at the scenery for a while. There wasn't any, just a flat plain, and some mist where the Deymeson hills should have been. 'So why did we go out of our way to see her?'

'I was curious.' Poldarn shivered a little. 'Back in the other place, where we sold the buttons, they said she reckoned her son was the god in the cart. The subject interests me. Should be fairly obvious why.'

She raised an eyebrow. 'I thought you said you didn't ever want to do the god act again.'

'I don't. I'm just interested in finding out who I've been, that's all.'

Chapter Nineteen

Monach drew and cut, and as he watched the soldier drop to his knees and slump forward he thought, *I can't believe I've made such a mess of it. Everything's going wrong, and it's all my fault.*

The other three soldiers were closing in; one dead ahead, one on either side. He took a step back, sheathing his sword – this was a standard exercise he'd learned in third grade, but the sequence started from rest, sword sheathed, and he wasn't in the mood for improvisation. As soon as they impinged on his circle, the sequence began; it was as if it couldn't wait and had started without him. The knuckles of the right hand touched the sword handle; as the hand flipped over and the fingers found their place around the handle, the left foot came back half a step, then turned inwards, placing heel against heel at ninety degrees, so that as the sword left the scabbard, the body pivoted towards the left-hand target and the cut slid out into the space the oncoming target's neck was about to occupy. No time to waste looking to see if the cut had connected; the back foot went forward in a hundred-and-eighty-degree arc, swinging the body round to face the right-hand target, while the arms lifted the sword up and back till the point touched the base of the spine, at which moment (like a mechanism engaging an escapement) the left-side diagonal overhead cut launched the sword into a perfectly located slice (number four in the manual, 'dividing the earth from the heavens'); the momentum pivoted the right heel as the arms followed through and used the spare energy of the last stroke to reset the correct position as he turned to face the enemy in front; another perfect cut, to be taken on trust since there still wasn't any time to waste on gawping; pivot once again to face the first target and deliver a conclusive, if redundant, finishing cut down the line of the collarbone. A simple but impressive sequence; a good sixth-year should be able to complete it and return to rest, sword flicked free of blood and back in the scabbard, in the time it takes for an apple to drop from a tree.

Monach felt the sword click back into the tight jaws of its sheath, and looked to see what had happened just as the first target hit the ground. The other two followed a fraction of a second later. There was still a fine mist of blood hanging in the air.

That appeared to be that. A threat had presented itself and been dealt with quickly and efficiently; he could be forgiven for thinking that he'd actually got something right, for a change. But he hadn't. The plan had been to sneak up on the patrol, grab one of them and force General Cronan's current location out of him. As it was, all four of them were dead, and in no position to tell him anything. Screwed it up *again*.

It wouldn't be so bad if he had a clue where he was, but he didn't. Somewhere in the woods below the hilltop village of Shance, where Major-General Ambosc's cavalry detachment was spending the night before pressing on, probably just after first light, to meet up with the main army, and the general, at Cric. Put like that, it sounded precise and entirely sufficient; but the whole truth was rather different. In practice he had no idea which direction to go in, or where he was in the wood. He was lost.

. . . Which was infuriating, because there wasn't time for any such nonsense, not if he was to stand any chance of intercepting Cronan on his way to Cric (when he'd be at his most vulnerable, with only an honour guard of half a dozen cavalrymen, out in the open with nowhere to hide). He didn't even know for sure whether that plan was still feasible, since he wasn't very clear about how long he'd been in this damned wood, let alone how long it was going to take him to get out again. Of course the soldiers he'd stumbled across on the edge of this small, deceitful clearing could have told him, if only he'd had the wit to pretend to be a wandering trader or a government courier or something. Instead he'd killed them all. If it wasn't such a nuisance it'd be a joke.

He sat down on a moss-covered log and applied his mind to the problem. Now, unless the soldiers were lost too, it stood to reason that they were passing through the wood on their way somewhere, presumably following the track that he could just make out between the trees. Whether they'd been going up the track or down it was a secret they'd taken with them to the shadows; likewise, which direction led to Shance, and which ran straight back to Mahec Ford, where he'd just come from. Choices, options, decisions; Monach shook his head, he couldn't be doing with them. There's nothing on earth as helpless as a man lost in a wood, he reflected bitterly. It's as bad as losing your memory; you're left with nothing but what you're wearing and carrying, cut off from everything that might help you, with no very clear idea of what to do next or for the best.

Nothing else for it, he was going to have to guess. He pulled a face; ordained sword-brothers of the order didn't guess; either they knew or they found out. He wasn't even sure he knew how to go about it any more. Should he just close his eyes and start walking, or would it be more appropriate to use some formal method – tossing a coin, blowing a dandelion clock, observing the flight of roosting birds? Undoubtedly it was a point addressed somewhere in Doctrine, though he didn't know where was the best place to start researching the point. Genistus' *Observances*? The Secondary Digest? *Lathano on General Procedure*?

Roosting birds would seem to be the best bet; it was starting to get dark, and the sky was full of rooks and crows, wheeling and shrieking all around him. He chose a tree at random. If ten birds flew past it on the right before an equal number went by on the left, he'd go up the track, and vice versa. The idea had a certain charm; he could pretend it was an omen from the divine Poldarn, master of crows, rather than a wild, feckless guess.

Nine to the right, all in a clump, and only three to the left. One more needed on the right; but instead, a mob of seven flew left while the right side stayed clear. He followed the seven; six of them carried on but one peeled off, circled behind him and came back in on the right. Monach sighed. Did that one count, or would it constitute cheating? He shrugged. The way things were going with him, if he'd decided to flip a coin instead the wretched thing would probably have ended up landing on its edge.

Just to be awkward he went down the track, realising after a few yards that it was probably a mistake. After all, Shance was on the top of a hill, so didn't it stand to reason that he'd have to go uphill to get there? Unfortunately it wasn't quite as simple as that. He'd been going uphill whenever possible for a long time now, several hours at least, and where was he? Lost.

But he carried on nonetheless, and was rewarded by a sudden violent change in gradient. No question about it, he was going uphill now, for sure. This was promising, even if he did have to stop and lean against a tree for a few moments to catch his breath. The comforting width and straightness of the trail was reassuring too, a trail that gave every sign of knowing where it was going. Or coming from.

But it wasn't in any hurry. Once again he lost track of how long he'd been walking, and he couldn't help thinking that Shance Hill hadn't looked anything like this high or steep when he'd seen it in the distance from the road that morning. He was wondering whether it wouldn't be better after all to give up and retrace his steps when he came round a corner and saw a house.

Not just a shack or a shed, a real house, with a chimney and a porch, large enough to be a farmhouse or something of the sort. Better still, there was a cart outside, conspicuous in the small bald patch immediately surrounding the building. Monach got closer, and was rewarded with the sight of four horses tethered to a rail. It looked very much as though somebody was at home.

He knocked at the door — oak, grey with age but hanging straight and recently scraped clean of moss and lichen — but nothing happened. He couldn't quite understand that; the horses hadn't got there by themselves and tied their halters to a post, so it stood to reason that whoever had brought them here was still in the immediate vicinity. He pushed the door gently with the edge of his left hand, waited for a moment in case there was an ambush or booby trap, and walked quietly inside.

Ah, he said to himself, *that would explain it.*

There were two people sitting in chairs on opposite sides of a table, a man and a woman. The man had been killed by a single thrust to the heart, and was lolling backwards, his arms hanging down parallel with the legs of the chair. The woman's skull had been split by a square-on overhead cut, delivered with a sharp weapon and a lot of force. He recognised them as the god in the cart and his priestess, the two frauds he'd interrogated in the prison at Sansory.

Well, they weren't going to tell him the way out of the wood. He sighed, and made a closer examination. From the tone and texture of the dead flesh, not to mention the smell,

he reckoned they'd been dead for two or three days, just conceivably longer since the house was more than a little chilly—

In which case that cart might well be their cart, but those
horses weren't their horses, or if they were, someone else had
fed and exercised them recently. Monach frowned. There was
a reasonable chance that this mystery was nothing to do with
him, and he certainly didn't have time to indulge his curiosity.
On the other hand, if these two characters were spies or agents
who'd been masquerading as frauds (a thoroughly unsuitable
cover, but possible, and the manner of their deaths suggested
something other than robbery or mere dislike), they might
turn out to be very relevant indeed. Or not. He found he
wanted very badly to know who'd been looking after the
horses.

It was also curious, to say the least, that they were sitting
facing each other, since the wounds that had killed them were
the sort almost invariably inflicted from in front, and the table
didn't look ferocious enough to have killed both of them
before either of them had a chance to run away. Deliberately
propping up dead bodies in chairs so as to give someone else a
shock, or a warning? Monach shook his head. There was a lot
of evidence to be read here, but he wasn't in the mood.

A horse, on the other hand, would come in handy. He shut
the door quietly behind him and headed across the clearing
into the trees, then made his way round in a circle through the
briars and saplings and other tiresome undergrowth to a point
where he could watch the horses for a while; the concept of
bait was floating about in his mind, and he wasn't in such a
tearing hurry as all that.

True, he'd had an exhausting time of it lately and not
nearly enough sleep, but his first reaction, on waking up with
a crick in his neck and one leg completely numb, was self-
disgust and shame. That was quickly followed by fear; he'd
been woken up by the sound of something coming towards him
through the wood, and with his right leg asleep he couldn't

move. Everything wrong, he told himself resentfully, all my
fault. Of all the stupid things to happen—

He'd managed to crawl-hobble a few yards towards the
edge of the wood when it occurred to him that he was going in
the wrong direction. Out in the open, he'd be even more vulnerable, unless he had time to get to one of the horses – but
even if he did make it that far, how was he proposing to get on
the creature's back with one leg out of commission? He
stopped, leaning against a tree as the pins and needles surged
up his leg as far as his groin. He couldn't face going back,
directly towards whatever was making the noise (more than
one of it, whatever it was). Going forward didn't appeal.
Staying put was very probably a bad idea too, but he didn't
feel up to anything else. He closed his eyes and begged for it
all to have been a dream.

They came out of the undergrowth around him as if by
magic, like fish jumping up through the mirror surface of a
still lake; eight men, armed. 'Where the hell have you been?'
one of them asked.

Monach slumped a little against the tree he was standing by.
'I could ask you the same question,' he said. 'I got fed up
waiting for you, so I set off on my own. Bloody fine back-up
squad you turned out to be.'

They were, of course, sword-monks, eight of the ten men
he'd chosen specially for the job of tracking down and killing
the commander-in-chief of an imperial field army. He'd
posted their orders on the chapter door two hours before he
was due to leave, and they hadn't shown up. Now, apparently,
they were here, having followed his trail and tracked him
down in the depths of this impenetrable wood, where even he
hadn't a clue where he was. He couldn't help feeling
impressed. 'All right,' he said, 'we'll go into all that later.
Which way is Shance?'

One of them grinned. 'You mean to say you're lost?'

'Yes,' Monach admitted, tentatively pressing the sole of his foot on the ground and wincing. 'And we're very short on time.' He paused. 'Do any of you know anything about the two dead bodies in that house?'

One of the monks shook his head. 'We've only just got here,' he said.

'Oh.' He thought for a moment. 'You three, you're coming with me. Get that cart spanned in, and you'd better know the quickest way to Shance. The rest of you, follow on as quick as you can. And keep your eyes open; somebody killed a man and a woman, possibly spies, in there; those are probably their horses.'

'Our spies or theirs?' one of the monks asked.

'Haven't a clue,' Monach replied (define ours; define theirs). 'Don't get sidetracked, mind; if you see them, keep out of their way, that's all. Understood?'

He didn't explain why he had to hobble slowly to the cart, and they didn't ask. Neither did he ask, or they volunteer, how they'd found him. He let one of the brothers drive; he wasn't very good at it, never having had much experience.

The brother found it humiliatingly simple to get out of the wood; he just followed the road, which came out on the top of a ridge. Less than half a mile away was a walled town, coiled round a spur like a length of rope. Shance, presumably.

'So,' the brother said (nobody had said anything since they left the house in the wood), 'what happens here?'

Monach, who'd been half dozing again, sat up sharply. His leg was fine now, but his neck was still painful. 'We need to find a prefect or a duty officer, someone who can tell us where Cronan's going to be coming from.'

'Coming from.' The brother thought for a moment. 'So we know where he's going, then.'

Monach nodded. 'Cric,' he replied. 'Of course, there's every chance he's there already, but it's worth a try. Certainly better than trying to get at him in the middle of a military camp.'

'Agreed,' said another brother in the back of the cart. 'So how do we go about it?'

Of course, Monach hadn't given it any thought. He wasn't inclined to try barging in and beating it out of them, whoever they were. Far better to be subtle, using some persona or other – superior officer, government courier, spy, something from his usual repertoire. He half turned.

'Scout around in the back there,' he said, 'see what you can find in the way of clothes and stuff. We've got to pretend we're staff officers or messengers or imperial agents, something like that, and right now we're unmistakably scruffy monks.'

A little later, the brother reported back. 'There's clothes in here all right,' he said, 'but I don't think they'll really be all that suitable for what you've got in mind. This stuff is *weird*.'

He held a sample up for Monach to see: a black velvet robe embroidered with glass thread, further decorated with paste gemstones and sequins forming mystic-looking symbols. 'Bloody hell,' Monach sighed, remembering who the cart had formerly belonged to. 'That's no use, then, unless one of you jokers feels up to impersonating a god.'

The monk frowned. 'Do gods wear this sort of thing, then?' he asked. 'I'd have credited them with better taste, personally.'

Monach laughed. 'Don't you believe it,' he said. 'Not any gods I've ever come across, anyway. Well, if we can't be gods, we'll just have to be spies. All comes down to the same thing in the long run.'

The sword-monks looked at each other but didn't say anything, and the cart rolled up to the town gate. A bored-looking halberdier waved them through – just as well, Monach realised; his imagination wasn't up to the task of concocting a plausible explanation for a cartload of illegal divine vestments.

At least finding the prefecture wasn't a problem. It was where it ought to be, in the old, thick-walled tower overlooking the road, at the weakest point in the town's natural defences. A clerk told them the prefect wasn't there; he was out with the garrison on exercises, and hadn't said when he was likely to be back. No, he couldn't see the duty officer, the duty officer was a busy man . . . Monach handed him the pass, signed by Father Abbot and wearing the Great Seal of the order. Suddenly, the duty officer's schedule turned out to be far less hectic than the clerk had first believed.

'I'm sorry,' the duty officer said, plainly terrified at the thought of four sword-monks in the same town as himself, let alone the same small half-circular room at the top of the tower. 'I really wish I could help, but I can't, I've got specific orders not to release the general's itinerary to anybody with-out—'

'You idiot,' Monach growled. 'How many times have I got to explain this before it seeps through the cracks in your brain? *They're going to kill the general.* They're going to ambush him somewhere on the road, cut his head off and take it to Feron Amathy in a jar of spiced honey, unless *you* stop fooling around and tell me which road he's going by, so we can get to him, warn him and fight off this ambush. Do you under-stand? If you don't give me that itinerary, the general is going to *die*, and it'll all be *your* fault.'

The duty officer looked as if the whole town had just been buried by a landslide and he was the sole survivor, the man who'd set it all off by throwing a pebble at the side of the cliff face. 'Well, I suppose it'll be all right,' he said at last, 'since you're religious, after all; I mean, if you can't trust a priest, it'd be a pretty poor show.' He pulled a brass tube out of the jumble on his desk and fished out a roll of thin, crisp paper. 'All right,' he said. 'I don't know much, no reason anybody should tell me, after all, but before he left the prefect got this.' He unrolled the paper, which proved to be a map. 'He had orders from Cronan to meet him with the garrison at this vil-lage here, Cric. The orders said that Cronan would be coming up the north-west road from Lesar's Bridge – that's down here, see, that squiggle; you can just make it out if you look closely. And here's the road – well, it isn't actually marked on this map, but it follows the line of this little river here; if you find the river, you'll find the road.' An unpleasant thought struck him, and his face changed. 'What if you're too late and they've already ambushed him? God, that'd be terrible.'

Monach requisitioned the map, together with another one that had rather more places and things marked on it, and left the tower as quickly as he could without drawing attention to himself. 'Right,' he said, as they clambered back into the cart, 'here's what we'll do. You four, find whatever passes for a horsefair in this town, get yourselves four horses and cut up across the top here.' He prodded the map. 'If you get a move on and don't stop to admire the scenery, you might just catch up with him. I'll head for Cric and see what's happening there. If he's already arrived, of course – well, we'll skin that goat when we get to it.'

The monks nodded agreement. 'Just one thing,' one of them asked. 'Can you give us a few more details? I mean, all we really know about what's involved is what you told the man back there; someone's going to try and kill General Cronan, we've got to stop them—'

'What?' Monach looked up. 'No, you've got that completely wrong. Didn't anybody tell you?'

The monk looked puzzled. 'We assumed—'

'Don't. Our orders are to kill General Cronan. Got that?'

There was a moment of complete silence. 'Understood,' the monk said. 'Any other considerations?'

'You aren't monks, you don't belong to the order, you've probably never even heard of the order. Try not to get captured or killed if you can avoid it. That's it.'

'Understood,' the monk repeated, and it was as if his former impression, his misunderstanding of the object of the mission, had never existed. 'We'll need some money for the horses.'

Monach searched in his sleeve and took out a small cloth bag. 'Twenty gross-quarters,' he said. 'While you're at it – this is a long shot, so don't waste too much time on it – see if you can lay your hands on at least one raider backsabre. You see them in markets sometimes. If you can get one, use it for the kill. A little confusion never hurt anybody.' He looked at each of the monks in turn. 'Does anybody have a problem with any of that?' he asked.

'Not really,' replied one of the monks, a newly ordained brother tutor. 'It's just that I can't help wondering what all this has got to do with religion.'

Of course, Monach knew the answer to that, and recited it to himself several times as he drove the cart north towards Cric. In its simplest form:

1. The order is the world's most important centre for the preservation, study, teaching and development of doctrine; therefore –

2. The survival of the order is essential to religion; therefore –

3. Any steps taken to preserve, protect or strengthen the order are by definition beneficial to the order and acts of grace.

Simple. Even second-year novices could grasp the logic. As for 'steps taken to preserve, protect or strengthen', the only definition of the phrase that a brother tutor needed to know was 'whatever a superior officer tells you to do', the argument being that if the superior cleric was in error and the mission turns out not to qualify as an act of grace, the brother carrying out his instructions nevertheless enjoys as much grace and absolution as if the mission had been legitimate. Without a provision like that, the work of the order simply couldn't get done; you'd have brothers and brother tutors and canons and possibly even novices questioning every instruction they were given, from *kill the general* down to *it's your turn to bale out the latrines* on the grounds of imperfect doctrine and heresy. Religion in the empire would collapse inside a year.

In which case, why did his mind keep returning to the question, like a child picking at a scab?

It was the fault of these confoundedly slow carthorses, giving him too much leisure to worry away at things he shouldn't even be thinking about. Religion, after all, was something quite specific and concrete as far as he was concerned. Religion was the ultimate grace expressed in the form of the perfect draw, in which there is no delay whatever between the infringement of the circle and the cut; the draw that is no draw, because it's too fast to be perceived with the senses and therefore by any reasonable criteria doesn't exist.

(So too with the gods; the gods are beings so perfect that they can't be perceived with the senses and can therefore only exist inside the grace of impossible perfection; the eye can't see everything at once, the ear can't hear every voice simultaneously, the body can't be everywhere at the same time; accordingly, the all-seeing, all-hearing, omnipresent must be divine, as invisibly real as the city just out of sight over the horizon, or land that can't be seen from the crow's nest; the faster the draw, the nearer to God, and to be impossibly close to God is to be God. Nothing could be more straightforward than that.)

Monach frowned. He'd made that speech to five years' intakes of novices, and it had made sense even to them, implying that it had to be true. Now, though, it made him think about the god in the cart, what he'd heard from Allectus, and the two dead bodies in the wood. What is perfection, he asked himself, but the elimination of everything that isn't the true essence, the fluxing off and purging away of all impurities from the meniscus of the molten metal (metal that's lost its memory in the fire; the divine Poldarn, who doesn't know he's a god)? To become perfect, to become God, you must eliminate thought, fear, memory, anything and everything that lies between the sheathed and the unsheathed sword—

And instead, here he was out in the world, sitting in a cart behind four of the slowest horses in the empire, on his way to murder a general. Good question: what did all this have to do with religion? Except that instinctive, unthinking obedience is grace, just as much as the instinctive, unthinking draw. The hand doesn't need to know why the enemy has violated the circle, or where the merits of the quarrel lie, and neither does the sword-monk. God draws us, and we cut.

One good thing about these speculations was that they kept his mind occupied all the way to Cric.

At first glance he didn't recognise the place. For one thing it was full of soldiers. There were tents everywhere, and spear stacks and carts and shovels and pickaxes and mattocks leaning against the sides of half-finished trenches. There were portable forges for the farriers and cutlers and armourers; a stack of cordwood taller than any of the houses; rafts of posts, piles and rails from which the carpenters were building a corral for the horses; a big round tent that didn't need a sign or board outside – the smell alone announced that it was the field kitchen. Above all there were men, each of them busy with some task or other. They made the place look like a city. A soldier came up and asked who he was and what he was doing there, but that was all right, because he'd prepared an identity. He told the soldier some name or other, ignored the rest of the question and asked if the general had arrived yet.

'Why do you want to know that?' the soldier asked. He had an accent that Monach couldn't quite place.

'None of your business,' Monach said. 'Is he here or isn't he?'

The soldier shook his head. 'He's expected,' he added. 'Any time now, in fact. What's it to you?'

Monach pulled a face. 'All right,' he said, 'which direction is he coming from? I'd better go out to meet him, this can't wait.'

'Messenger, are you?' Monach didn't answer that. 'All right, please yourself,' the soldier went on. 'He ought to be coming in up the east road.'

Monach knew that already, of course. Still, it did no harm
to verify. 'East road,' he muttered, 'that figures. Right, thank
you, I'd better get moving.'

An hour up the road, he was overtaken by a horseman
riding dangerously fast on the sloppy, stony road. It turned out
to be one of the sword-monks he'd sent after Cronan.

He pulled up and waited for the monk to come back and
talk to him. 'What the hell are you doing here?' he asked him.

The monk was grey with exhaustion. 'Came back to find
you,' he said. 'Bad information. Cronan wasn't coming this
way after all. Wild-goose chase.'

Monach scowled. 'Bloody hell,' he groaned. 'Where did
you get that from?'

'Courier,' the monk replied. 'Carrying a letter under
Chaplain Cleapho's personal seal, telling Cronan to sit tight at
the Faith and Fortitude till he's told otherwise. Here,' he
added, pulling a rolled-up page from his pocket; he tried to
hand it down and dropped it instead. Monach retrieved it and
read it quickly.

'Buggery,' he said. 'That screws up everything. Where did
you find this courier, then?'

The monk closed his eyes, struggling to find the words.
'Back along,' he said, 'maybe an hour up the road from here.
Courier said he was coming down from Toizen.'

'What? Toizen's on the north coast. What in hell's name is
Cleapho doing all the way up there?'

The monk had just enough strength to shrug his shoulders. Monach shook his head. 'I'm not sure about this,' he
said. 'Yes, that looks like Cleapho's seal, and I've seen it once
or twice before, but it could be a good fake. Then again, why
would anybody *want* to fake a message like that? If Cronan's
not at the Faith and Fortitude, he'll know that a letter telling
him to stay there must be phoney. I don't get this at all.'

The monk sighed impatiently. 'Well, he's not where you
said he'd be. We've been up and down this road, no sign of

him. Nobody's seen anything like a troop of cavalry, either. So, that letter may or may not be bad information; what you got from the captain in Shance definitely was. Go figure.'

Monach thought for a moment. 'All right,' he said. 'Where's this courier now?'

'Ah.' The monk grinned. 'That's more a matter of theology than geography.'

'You mean you killed him?'

'Wouldn't hold still,' the monk explained. 'It was that or let him get away.'

Monach shook his head. 'Just for once,' he said, 'wouldn't it be nice if something turned out the way it's supposed to? All right, not your fault. Where are the others?'

'Heading for the Faith and Fortitude,' the monk replied, 'Wherever the hell that might be. Brother Aslem reckoned he knows where it is.'

'Halfway between Josequin and Selce,' Monach said. 'Please, tell me that's where they're headed.'

'I think so. Doesn't mean a lot to me, because I haven't a clue where Selce is, either, but I'm fairly sure that's what Aslem said.'

Monach sighed. 'That's something, I suppose,' he said. 'All right, here's what I want you to do.' He clicked his tongue. 'First,' he said, 'find a tree or a bush or something and rest; I'd say come with me back to the camp at Cric, but I don't think you'll make it that far in the state you're in. When you're feeling better, I want you to head back to Shance, find that little snot of a duty officer and put the fear of the gods into him – tell him he's a traitor, deliberately misleading us, put it on thick as you can, because I need to know where this CO got his false orders from; someone's playing games with someone else, and if we can find out who, we might stand a chance of figuring all this out. When you've done that, get back here to Cric; if I'm not there, you can bet I'll be at the Faith and Fortitude. If I'm not, get yourself back to Deymeson and tell them there's something very screwy going on, and to make ready for an attack, just in case. I don't think either Cronan or Tazencius has tumbled to what we're up to,' he added, as a look of fear crossed the monk's face. 'I certainly can't think of any way they could've found out, and we haven't actually done anything yet, so it couldn't be educated guesswork; still, better safe than sorry, and if all this is deliberately to mislead us, somebody must know what we're up to and they may just possibly consider a direct attack on the order. Not worth the risk. You got that?'

'I think so,' the monk replied, yawning hugely. 'Sorry,' he added. 'And you're right. I've got to stop for a rest, before I fall off and break my silly neck.'

Monach left him to it, turned the cart round and headed back to Cric. It was just his rotten luck, he reflected, to find himself in the middle of a situation that was far too complicated for him to manage, with responsibility for the survival of the order, possibly the empire as well, and nobody to tell him what to do or how to do it. All his life he'd been taught *not* to think for himself – better still, not to think, just draw and cut, guided by faith and instinct. All his life he'd been warned that the overall view, the big picture was not for the likes of him, at least not until he'd achieved enlightenment and been promoted to Father. All his life, he'd been trained to believe in the value of instinct and ignorance, two qualities which weren't likely to get him very far in his present situation. No wonder that he felt such a strong affinity with the divine Poldarn, harbinger of confusion, the god who didn't know he was a god.

A bizarre thought occurred to him, and he laughed out loud. Maybe *he* was Poldarn.

The more he thought about it, the more obvious it became. Here he was, driving through the northern villages in a cart, liable at any moment to make a mistake that would plunge the empire into war, bring about the destruction of the order (which would mean the end of religion, since it was an article of faith in the order that nobody else knew the most fundamental bases of doctrine) and quite possibly open the gates to the enemy incarnate, the raiders – how they fitted into the picture he wasn't sure; but then again, if he was Poldarn, that was to be expected; that they were involved in some way he was absolutely certain.

It started to rain, but he hardly noticed. Of course; that solved everything. Had Father Tutor known who he really was? Of course; Father Tutor knew everything, and that was why he'd chosen him for the mission, sent him to find out the truth about rumours of his own (false) appearances. Unfortunately, he'd been too stupid to make the obvious connections at the time, and Father Tutor had died before he'd had a chance to explain – or perhaps it was essential that Poldarn should remain ignorant of his true identity until the end of the world had been successfully encompassed – in which case something had gone wrong, he'd failed; had Father Tutor sent him on the mission on purpose to expose him to the truth and therefore make the end of the world impossible? Just the sort of thing you'd expect a father tutor of the order to do – frustrate destiny, save the world from its appointed doom. Had he always been Poldarn, he wondered, or was divinity something that happened to you later in life, like puberty or baldness; was it something you were chosen for, on merit, like the priesthood? If so, what had he done to deserve it? Had he been chosen out of all the world because he was the only man alive *stupid* enough to become a god and not realise it? Above all, what ought he to do next? As Poldarn, it was his duty to bring about the end of the world, but Father Abbot had ordered him to kill Cronan because that was the only thing that could save the world from ending. Which took precedence, his duty as a god or the direct orders of his superior officer? Or had Father Abbot sent him to kill Cronan because killing Cronan was the event that would bring about the end of the world – which would mean that Father Abbot had deliberately misled him; until recently, that would have been inconceivable, but now he knew that Father Abbot fornicated with loose women in the dead of night, he had to admit it was possible.

What should he do next? Trust his instincts, of course. Have faith. Above all, resist the disastrous temptation to *think*, because thought allows a moment to slide in between the breached circle and the draw, thought negates faith. To become God, you must become perfect, eliminate the moment, eliminate thought . . . Was that why he'd been chosen? Because he was the best of his year at swordfighting?

. . . And if my sister had six tits she'd be a cow, as they said in Sansory. He sighed, and shook his head. For a moment, he'd almost believed it, proving how easy it can be to pick up a bloody stupid notion, like a nail in the sole of your boot. Whoever he was (and at times it was hard to keep track, what with his true name and his name in religion and all those aliases), he was pretty certain he wasn't a god; and if he was a god he wouldn't be Poldarn, not if you paid him. The plain fact was, the gods didn't exist, as he'd known in his heart since he was a second-year novice. Religion wasn't about gods, it was all in your own mind, it was the self-denying moment between the instinct and the draw, nothing more or less than that. He grinned. A god who didn't know who he was, maybe. A god who's an atheist, no.

'Besides,' he said aloud, 'if I'm Poldarn, where's the crow?'

Whereupon not one but three crows erupted out of a tall, skinny ash tree beside the road and paddled noisily away through the wet air. For a moment, Monach sat quite still with his mouth open, then he burst out laughing.

He was still chuckling when he rolled into the camp at Cric. It was beginning to get dark, and the campfires stood out in the gloom, their light reflected in glowing clouds of smoke. The rain was falling steadily now, hard enough to make it difficult for Monach to think much further than shelter, warmth, food and sleep. He was wondering how these objectives might best be achieved when a soldier stepped out beside the cart and grabbed the lead horse's bridle.

'You're back, then,' he said. It was probably the man he'd spoken to earlier, he wasn't quite sure. 'You'd better get down and come with me. The general wants to see you.'

Monach woke up out of his train of thought with a snap. 'What?' he said. 'General Cronan?'

There were several soldiers now; lots of soldiers, a dozen at least and more coming. Two more were holding the horses, one was climbing up on to the box of the cart beside him, at least three behind him in the bed, and as many again closing in round him in a rapidly shrinking circle. While he sat still and tried to figure out what was going on, the soldier sitting next to him reached across and pulled the sword out of his scabbard, before he could do anything about it.

The first soldier's face broke into a grin. 'No,' he said, 'not General Cronan. General Feron Amathy. You coming quietly, or what?'

Chapter Twenty

'I've never seen anything like it,' Poldarn repeated.

'You can't remember seeing anything like it,' Copis pointed out. 'In your case, that doesn't mean much. For all you know, you used to live there.'

Poldarn frowned; he wasn't in the mood. 'It's amazing,' he said. 'And you honestly believe we're going to be able to sell them buttons?'

From the top of the rise they could see Deymeson, dramatically backlit by the sunset: the town, slopped round the foot of the hill as if it had seeped out under the walls of the castle; the fortress, with its double wall and star-pattern bastions; the abbey and the citadel, topped with a massive low, square tower. Nobody in their right mind would ever call it beautiful. It made Poldarn think of the machines in Potto Ilec's factory: entirely functional, designed to execute some process or operation he couldn't begin to understand. If Copis had told him that the gods lived there, he'd probably have believed her.

'For what it's worth,' Copis was saying, 'I've never seen it before either; but I've heard about it, of course, and I'd have recognised it at once because there's a picture of it on the back of the silver hard-quarter. Doesn't do it justice, of course; makes it look pretty.'

Poldarn shook his head. 'I don't believe that anybody who could build something like that uses buttons. Or clothes, even. They're probably covered from head to foot with scales, or feathers.'

Copis sighed. 'We aren't here to sell to the monks, silly,' she said. 'You may not have noticed, but there's a fair-sized town as well as that granite monstrosity. That's where they keep the people who do all the work – you know, scrub the floors, slop out the latrines, cook the food. And do you know what makes them special, as far as we're concerned? They get paid, in money. Therefore,' she concluded with a smile, 'we can sell them buttons.'

They stopped for the night at an inn down in the valley, where for some reason they seemed to cause something of a stir; the grooms and the servers looked at them oddly and wouldn't say why. That made Poldarn nervous, but Copis swore blind she'd never been there before, let alone tried out the act. 'I'd remember,' she said, 'trust me.'

In the morning they drove up the hill to the Foregate. The Foregate was a gate, but there was no town wall, just an arch, at least fifteen feet high and twelve feet wide, made up of mirror-smooth granite blocks with no decoration or embellishment of any kind, free-standing in the patchy grass. No walls, but two sentries.

'That's silly,' Poldarn pointed out. 'You could just drive round the whole thing.'

Copis shook her head. 'Wouldn't advise it,' she said. 'If you did that, they'd call out the guard and you'd find yourself in a cell in the watch-house, if you were lucky.'

Sure enough, the four carts that had been ahead of them on the road were drawn up in line, waiting to go through the gate, while the sentries questioned the drivers. 'Symbolism, you see,' Copis explained. 'Deymeson doesn't need a wall, because its defence is the awesome reputation of the sword-monks.'

'Fine,' Poldarn said. 'Then what's all that masonry further up the hill?'

'Walls, of course,' Copis replied. 'Symbolism is all very well, but some people are too stupid to understand it. The walls and towers and stuff are for their benefit.'

Apparently the sentry hadn't heard of buttons, or else didn't believe in them, because he insisted on opening all the barrels and rummaging about inside, like a man loading grain with his empty hands. He gave up eventually, but there was a resentful glow in his eyes that suggested that he didn't take kindly to being baffled, and would be keeping a very sharp eye on them in future.

Beyond the gate and the scrappy five-acre parcel of scuffed grass and bare mud it stood in were the first houses of the town, warehouses or granaries if their windowless facades were anything to go by. The main street led straight up the steep hill, and the buildings on either side of it gave no indication of what they were used for; two narrow windows per frontage, like scratches or blisters in the blank grey stone, and even those were all on the second or third floor. Some of them had no visible doors or windows at all. There were no people to be seen anywhere.

'I knew this was going to be a waste of time,' Poldarn muttered, 'as soon as you told me this was some kind of religious place. They're probably all at prayers or doing meditation or something.'

'Not the ones who live down here,' Copis said firmly. 'For a start, the order doesn't pray in the sense you're thinking of, they prance about hitting each other with wooden swords. And they live up in the castle, not down here. I don't suppose they see a monk in this part of town from one year's end to the next.'

Just then Copis noticed a turning on her left. It was an archway, just wide enough for the cart to get through if they weren't too fussy about scraping the wheel hubs. 'Let's try this,' she said.

'We can't. For all you know, that could be somebody's private courtyard.'

'Then they ought to put up a gate and lock it,' Copis replied, pulling the cart out in the middle of the street to give herself the right angle to get through the archway. 'Besides, I've got a theory.'

Poldarn signed. 'More symbolism?'

'We'll soon see.'

The archway led into a narrow passage, paved with slate and roofed over, very high up, with dark red tiles. After a very sharp bend, it led into a square.

'Now that's more like it,' Copis said.

It was as if the street had been turned inside out, the way a cushion is turned to hide the seams. In the middle of the square was a fountain, flanked by two statues of young women playing harps. All four sides of the square were lined with open doors; some were shops, with trestles covered with merchandise standing under oilskin awnings; the rest were ordinary houses. Why their owners bothered having them wasn't clear, since it was fairly obvious that everyone spent most of their time out in the open air, standing on one side of the traders' trestles or the other. There was one boy with a tray of evil-looking sausages; another sitting on top of a huge barrel, his legs swinging, his hands cradling a big tin cup; on the side of the barrel was chalked a tariff – a quarter a cup, or six for a turner. As for the stalls, pretty much anything you could ever want to buy was there, in every possible permutation of size, colour and quality, from coarse white sailcloth to seven-colour brocade ('First time I've seen that north of the bay,' Copis whispered in awe), from cheap pine-handled beanhooks to pattern-welded walking-swords, from clogs to court slippers with absurdly long toes and savagely tight gussets, from green-turned wooden bowls to four-handled pewter goblets, from blanket-cloth ship-jackets to the sort of complicated audience gown that needed two strong maids and a three-foot-long buttonhook to install – everything, in fact, except for buttons.

('Now are you glad we came?' Copis muttered.

'All right, yes.')

The nearest thing to a button in the square was a card of sand-cast brass toggles, rough and unfinished and priced at five quarters. Copis grinned like a dog smelling blood. 'No competition whatsoever,' she sighed happily. 'The one thing I was afraid of was that there'd be a deep-rooted button cartel who'd run us out of town for trying to shove in on their pitch.'

'Doesn't look that way,' Poldarn replied. He'd tied up the horses to a conveniently placed rail and was unstepping the awning poles. 'This is extraordinary. Nothing at all like this in Sansory.'

Copis nodded. 'And this is the first place we came to. For all we know, the whole damn town could be like this. You know, we should've brought all the stock.'

They set up the stall, expecting a soldier or bailiff to arrive at any moment and demand to see their trading permits, but nobody paid any attention, apart from a few good-natured enquiries about what they were selling. To their relief, when they replied, 'Buttons,' they weren't stared at or asked what a button was; in fact, quite a crowd had gathered by the time they opened the stall for business. By noon, the table was looking decidedly threadbare.

'Definitely coming back here again,' Copis said, during an uncharacteristic lull. 'And we can easily jack the prices up a quarter or so; to judge from what they've been saying, they reckon we're practically giving the stuff away.'

'We'll see,' Poldarn replied. As far as he was concerned, their mark-up was steep enough as it was without increasing it further. In fact, there was something about trade in general that struck him as rather dishonest, only a step or two removed in legitimacy from the god-in-the-cart scam. 'I figure luck's a bit like a cart. Pushing it when you're struggling uphill is usually all right, but when you're coasting gently downhill it's probably not a good idea.'

Copis shook her head. 'Don't believe it,' she replied. 'I know this kind of people, they're like we used to get in Torcea. The more expensive something is, the more likely they are to buy it. I mean, look at some of the stuff on these stalls. This lot aren't short of a quarter.'

Poldarn shrugged, not being inclined to take the subject further. He beckoned to the boy sitting on the barrel and held a coin up in the air. The boy duly brought him a tin cup, which turned out to be full of quite palatable wine, not stale beer as he'd expected.

'And a quarter a cup, too,' Copis remarked, after she'd had a mouthful. 'That's very reasonable. You know, we could do worse than buy a barrel or two while we're here and sell it on in Sansory. No point taking the cart home empty.'

'We could,' Poldarn replied without much enthusiasm. Something was definitely making him uneasy, though whether it was Deymeson, the morality of commerce or something else he couldn't quite put his finger on, he wasn't sure. 'Next time, maybe,' he added, 'once we've had a chance to find out if there's actually a market for the stuff there. And we'd better look into things like excises and tariffs if we're going into the wine trade.'

Copis sighed. 'That's the problem with you,' she said, 'no spontaneity. I think you were probably a counting-house clerk in your previous life. And I'll bet your books always balanced at the end of the day.'

'And that'd be a bad thing?'

'You know perfectly well what I mean,' Copis replied. 'Still, I suppose it's a good combination, one brave and impetuous and the other sensible and boring.'

Poldarn looked up. 'That's how you see us, is it?'

Copis nodded. 'I was exaggerating a bit,' she said, 'but not that much. The thing about you is, I think that deep down you've got this urge to live a really dull, ordinary, commonplace life, which suggests that to you it's all new and fascinating, being ordinary, and that before this you used to be something dashing and dangerous.'

'You just said I was probably a clerk.'

'Changed my mind.'

Poldarn clicked his tongue, a habit he'd picked up from Copis. 'If I'm going out of my way to avoid excitement and adventure, I'm not making much of a fist of it,' he said. 'Except for the last week or so, I suppose, that's been refreshingly quiet. In fact, it's been days since I last killed anybody.'

'My heart bleeds,' Copis replied gravely. 'You'll just have to make do with fleecing people instead. Not as effective as killing them, but it means you can carve off another slice or two the next time you're passing through. I guess you could say it's the difference between hunting and rearing livestock.'

The market dissolved abruptly an hour before sunset, like a giant turned to stone by the first light of dawn. The stallholders lifted their tables off the trestles and carried them, still laden with goods, back into their houses, while their wives and children scurried backwards and forwards with table legs, stools, barrels and bales. It all happened so quickly that if Poldarn had happened to be kneeling down lacing his boot at the time, he'd have missed it and stood up again to find the square suddenly and inexplicably different (ah, the difference one moment can make . . .).

'You'd better get a move on,' someone said as he stood gawping at the empty square. 'If the bailiffs come round and catch you still trading, you'll be for it.'

'Oh,' Poldarn said. 'Thanks. Why?'

'Curfew,' the stranger replied, and hurried away.

'Wonderful,' Copis muttered, grabbing dishes and trays of buttons and pouring them into jars at random. 'Well, don't just stand there, tear down the stall. And if you can stop someone and ask, find out if it's a general curfew or just trade.'

She seemed to be taking it very seriously, so he dismantled the canopy and unshipped the poles as quickly as he could. Nobody came close enough to the cart to be stopped and questioned; in any event, they were moving too fast and too purposefully towards their houses, which suggested that the curfew was general and that they really didn't want to get caught. That, of course, presented them with a fresh problem.

'There'll be an inn or something,' Copis reassured him. 'Nothing to worry about.'

As soon as they had the stall down and packed away in the cart, they headed across the square to the inn (the Dogma and Doctrine), arriving a couple of heartbeats after the door bolts went home and the shutters were snatched in with a bang. Knocking on the door proved to be a complete waste of time.

'Marvellous,' Copis said edgily. 'Now what?'

Poldarn wasn't listening; he was watching three robed men with staffs walking across the square towards them. Since there was nobody else in sight, it wasn't difficult to guess what they wanted.

'I suppose they must be sword-monks,' Copis whispered. 'You hear all sorts of things about them, of course, but I've never seen one before.'

'Well, they don't seem to be carrying swords,' Poldarn said. 'I'll have to take your word about the monk part.'

'Quiet,' Copis replied. 'I should be able to handle this.'

Sword-monks or not, the three men didn't seem to be in any hurry; they were strolling rather than marching. 'Hello,' one of them called out from about fifteen yards. 'You're strangers in town, aren't you?'

'That's right,' Copis said. 'We're terribly sorry, we didn't know about the curfew.'

The monk who'd spoken to them shrugged his shoulders. 'That's all right,' he said. 'We aren't going to lock you up for ignorance. I take it you haven't got anywhere to stay.'

Copis nodded. 'We tried the inn over there, but they've locked the doors.'

'Don't worry, we'll see to that,' the monk said, and nodded to one of his colleagues, who set off quickly across the square towards the inn. 'Right,' the monk went on. 'The rules are pretty straightforward. Nobody on the streets after curfew – that's three-quarters of an hour before sunset, there's sundials in every square, so knowing the time's easy enough. All inns and shops closed and locked on time; all foreigners registered with the prior's office and able to show proof of accommodation for the night. You aren't either of those, are you?'

Copis shook her head.

'Not to worry,' the monk said, and nodded towards the inn. 'It's perfectly straightforward; I issue a vagrancy notice and billet you in the nearest registered accommodation. If they're full you might have to put up with a night in the stables, but it's bound to be better than the watch-house lock-up. I'll trust you to report to the prefecture by an hour after sunrise tomorrow morning; just tell them who you are and why you're here and that you didn't know the rules before you arrived, and they'll issue you with the necessary passes and stuff. Quite painless,' he added, 'so long as you follow procedure.'

The innkeeper and his wife weren't overjoyed at having a sword-monk hammering on the door, and would probably have harboured a grudge against them if it wasn't for the fact that earlier in the day they'd bought six sets of buttons for the price of five (Copis had been feeling generous) and were quite delighted with the bargain. Accordingly, although the inn was full, the innkeeper's younger son was turned out of his room and sent to sleep under the table in the kitchens, while Copis and Poldarn got a bed for the night, albeit a small one, and a view out of the tiny fifth-floor window over the bleak main street down towards the gate-with-no-walls and the moors beyond. By the standards of Sansory or any of the main-road inns they'd stayed in it was damp, cramped and miserable. On the other hand, it could easily have been far worse.

'Actually,' Copis was explaining, while Poldarn leaned his elbows on the window ledge and watched the last glow of sunset fading in the west, 'curfews aren't all that uncommon, but mostly you get them in Guild towns, so it didn't occur to me that there'd be one here. Of course, it's like a Guild town in ever so many ways, so maybe I should've suspected. Never mind,' she went on, 'there's no real harm done and we can find somewhere better in the morning.'

'Doesn't bother me,' Poldarn replied truthfully, as he watched a distant glimmer of light. 'But I guess the innkeeper's son would like us to go away so he can have his bed back. Are we allowed to move on, though? I got the impression that once we're registered somewhere, we've got to stay put till we leave.'

Copis frowned. 'Not sure,' she replied. 'The impression I got was that we aren't committed to staying anywhere till we register in the morning; so if we get up good and early we can scout around and find somewhere before we sign in at the what's-its-name, prefecture.' She yawned. 'This is an odd town,' she said. 'Not the oddest I've ever been to, not by a very long way, but still odd. Good for business, though.'

'That's true,' Poldarn said absently. He was still watching the light. 'One of these days, you'll have to explain to me about Guild towns. I've heard people talking about them, but all I've gathered so far is that they're different and not all that pleasant to visit.'

'You've been to Mael,' Copis said sleepily. 'That's a Guild town.'

'True. Now that was an odd place.'

'Tell you about it in the morning,' Copis sighed, and turned over on to her side. She was occupying the whole bed, and

Poldarn didn't feel like bickering, so he grabbed the cushion off the chair for a pillow and lay down on the floor. Just before he fell asleep, he thought he heard something moving about in the thatch directly over his head, but he wasn't sure; it could just as easily have been the crows in his dream, spreading their wings and launching themselves wearily into the darkness of his mind.

'It's him, isn't it?' one of them said.

'It's him.' The speaker, an old man with a thick bush of unruly white hair, rested both palms on the table-top. 'No doubt about it whatsoever.' He paused for a moment, catching his breath, then went on: 'I was more or less sure when I heard the report from Sansory, about the man who met with Chaplain Cleapho but escaped before they could catch him. Then there was the message from the inn – full marks to your sword-brother, by the way, it was an inspired idea to set the innkeeper to watch out for him – and I was almost certain. Now I've seen him with my own eyes. It's him.'

There was a long silence. 'That's settled, then,' the abbot said at last. 'Now that we know it's him, what shall we do?'

There were no suggestions. Father Abbot leaned forward a little in his chair, elbows on the table. 'The obvious solution would be to kill him, or to load him with chains and send him to Torcea. I'm not sure what we could charge him with, but there's bound to be something. In any event, I don't suppose the emperor will be very particular about details.'

He paused, waiting for someone to contradict him. Nobody seemed inclined to say anything. Father Abbot frowned. For once, unanimous agreement with his decision wasn't what he wanted.

'With respect.' At last, the abbot thought. More than anything else, he wanted a way of not having to do what obviously needed to be done. 'With respect,' the man who'd spoken repeated, 'I don't believe either of those courses of action is either necessary or advisable.'

Father Abbot gestured to him to continue.

'The point is,' the speaker continued (he was a short, fat monk with very curly grey hair and a rather babyish face; he was also the deacon in charge of security and defence), 'we have excellent grounds for believing that – well, we may know who he is, but he doesn't.'

That wasn't what the abbot had been expecting to hear. He was interested.

'My agents have been looking for him for some time now,' the deacon went on. 'The plain truth is, they couldn't find him, except for one; and for practical reasons that agent was in no position to file regular reports. I've now had an opportunity to piece together what we've learned so far. I think you'll agree, it puts a different complexion on the matter.'

'Go on,' Father Abbot said. Nobody else spoke.

'To cut a long story short,' the deacon said, 'we believe that on his way from here to Boc he was ambushed by an enemy unit sent specially to find him – how they knew where to look I'll deal with later – and there was a short but very fierce fight. We believe that he was the only survivor of that battle; what's more, we're almost certain that during the fighting he took a heavy blow to the head that knocked him out. When he woke up, he found that he'd lost his memory. He didn't know who he was, where he was, or even what language he was speaking in. We believe that he still hasn't got his memory back; in fact, I've taken advice from my colleagues in the infirmary and one or two lay experts in the field, and they assure me that the most likely outcome will be that unless he's suddenly presented with the truth about his past, he'll quite likely never remember, neither who he is nor what he's done. To all intents and purposes, he's a different man altogether. And as such,' the deacon said, 'not only would it be wrong for us to kill him or betray him to the authorities; it would also be a wickedly negligent waste of a remarkably useful opportunity to make use of him.'

'Well,' said the abbot, 'we can't have that, can we? Perhaps you'd better explain your idea to the rest of us.'

The deacon made a short, crisp bow. 'By all means,' he said, and proceeded to tell the chapter what he had in mind. At the end of his presentation, Father Abbot was wearing a very slight smile.

'A very elegant solution to the problem,' he said, 'provided, of course, that your information is accurate and you can get him to do what you have in mind. It's also the nastiest, most vindictive punishment I've ever heard anybody suggest, and therefore entirely suitable. As long as you're sure on those two points, I'm quite happy for you to proceed. Opinions, gentlemen?'

Nobody spoke for a long time. Then one of the monks shook his head.

'I'm not sure,' he said. 'I know who he is and what he's done – more to the point, what he would've done if it wasn't for this freak accident we've heard about. Even so, I wouldn't do that to my worst enemy.'

Father Abbot breathed out through his nose. 'Your humanity does you credit,' he said. 'All in favour.'

The vote was, of course, unanimous; every vote of the chapter in council since the foundation of the order had been unanimous, or at least that was what it said in the minutes. Nevertheless, Father Abbot wasn't blind or stupid. He could see that at least one of the councillors was unhappy with the decision, not counting himself. (But then, if he'd opposed every sensible measure that he found morally repugnant, the affairs of the order would've ground to a halt ten years ago.)

Poldarn woke up, and found that he was sitting upright, both hands clenched. He assumed that it was because he'd been having a bad dream.

This time there was definitely somebody moving about, and not just outside, actually in the room with them. He glanced over at Copis; she was fast asleep, lying diagonally across the bed, one foot and one arm sticking out from under the covers. Just to be sure, he kept still and waited to hear her breathe. It seemed to be a long time before she did.

Whoever it was moved again. Poldarn stretched out with his fingertips until he identified the hilt of his sword, and carefully teased it towards him until he could get his left hand around it and pull it smoothly across the floor. He wasn't wearing a belt or a sash, so when he got to his feet he held it pressed to his waist with his left hand in exactly the right place.

He closed his eyes – it was too dark to see anything, and somehow he knew he'd be able to make more sense of what was going on if he shut off his vision and relied entirely on hearing and touch. He had an idea he'd practised fighting blindfold or in a darkened room at some point in his life.

Curiously, as soon as he closed his eyes he could see his circle. It was like being back in his dream, the one he'd just come from (it wasn't the dream, because there weren't any crows; at least, he didn't think there were any crows. Of course, he wouldn't be able to see them even if there were any, in the dark with his eyes shut). The circle was as clear as anything; he knew where it was in the same way that he knew where his feet were, without needing to look or listen. He applied his mind to the presence of his enemy, feeling for his circle—

—And found it, a fraction of a second before it burst in on his own. The draw happened; but instead of the firm, soft resistance of flesh, he felt the sword in his hand spring back, like a hammer dropped in its own weight on to the face of an anvil. Whoever it was had parried the cut.

While he was still figuring out what was going on, his legs and arms were busy; he discovered that he'd jumped back the full radius of his circle and was standing in a position that came instinctively – feet a shoulder's width apart and at right angles, heel to heel; body chest on, with the arms extended equally, outstretched but the elbows slightly bent, the pommel of the sword level with his navel; it came as naturally as breathing, and suddenly he felt secure, in control, powerful, like a captain on the bridge of his ship. It had taken no longer than a single heartbeat. His circle blazed and flowed around him like a burning moat, like the invisible walls of Deymeson, and quite suddenly he knew he was *home* . . .

The attack came in on his left side, at sixty degrees to his sword blade. He could feel the violence of it before his circle was even breached. His left foot went back and behind his right heel, and at the moment when his enemy had to be raising his arms for the cut he launched his own sword at the place where the other man's hands must inevitably be (*the best defence is no defence; the best attack is no attack* . . . maxims that had always been there in his mind, asleep or silent) and felt the curve of the tip, the optimum cutting point, biting into the soft iron of a hilt. The right idea, then, but he'd missed by perhaps as much as an inch; by the time he realised that, he'd already wheeled his circle through ninety degrees to the right, reading everything there was to know about his invisible enemy from that one instant of contact. He knew that he was fighting someone so close to him in skill and experience that he might as well be fighting against himself; each could read the other's mind as clearly as his own thoughts, and nothing he or the other man could do would surprise or deceive the other. It was as if the darkness in the room was a mirror, and he was facing up to his reflection.

('. . . *When will I know that I've learned the draw?*'
'*When you can outdraw your reflection in a mirror.*'
'*But that's impossible.*'
'*If you really believe that, it's not the end of the world. You're still young enough to get indentures with a clerk, or learn how to mend saucepans.*')

A cut was on its way, slanting in from the right, aimed at

the point where the collarbone faded into the shoulder. He stepped forward, knowing exactly where the point of the curve would pass, and as its slipstream cooled his cheek he swung low for the knees, bracing himself for the shock that would travel up the blade as the other man parried with the flat. He used it to spring his sword up, racing the other man to see who could get there first as he turned his wrist for an upwards flick at the underside of the jaw. The other man stepped out of the way, of course, and he gave ground himself to avoid the riposte, a side-cut that would have sheared through his hip into his spine if he'd been there to receive it. He was like a man reciting a poem he'd learned by heart so long ago that the words no longer mean anything, and as his body made each inevitable movement his mind began to wander, drifting into a state between sleep and waking, the place where the crows roosted.

'Stop,' said a voice in the dark. He stopped, knowing he could trust the voice implicitly. 'Is there a lamp or a candle in here?'

Before he could reply Copis grunted and woke up. 'Who's that?' she mumbled, in a voice still saturated with sleep.

'It's all right,' Poldarn replied. The other man's voice had only confirmed his position; Poldarn already knew exactly where he was. Nevertheless, by speaking the other man had pinpointed his location, an act of truce as clear and eloquent as dropping his sword on the floor. The least Poldarn could do was reciprocate by answering. Besides, if Copis was awake, it changed the whole nature of the fight. If she chose to stand up and wander about, she stood a better than average chance of getting in the way and being cut in half. 'Who are you?' he asked.

For some reason the other man laughed. 'I could ask you the same question,' he said. 'Is there a lamp or a candle? We'll probably understand each other better if we can throw some light on the subject.'

'No,' Poldarn replied. 'At least, I don't remember seeing anything like that.'

'Pity.' Poldarn heard the click of a sword being returned to its scabbard. 'Still, it's not essential. You'll just have to use your imagination.'

'Look,' Copis interrupted, 'who the hell are you, and what are you doing in our room?'

'Listen to me.' The voice had changed a little. 'You don't know who you are, do you?'

'No,' Poldarn admitted. 'I lost my memory a while ago—'

'When you woke up beside the river, after a battle. Yes, I know all that. I'm a little vague about what you've been up to since, but I – we know pretty well everything about you up to that point. Would you like me to tell you?'

Poldarn hesitated two, perhaps three heartbeats before answering. 'Yes,' he said.

'Then I'll tell you. But first—'

'No. *Now.*'

'First,' the voice said emphatically, 'I've got to warn you. Tomorrow morning, some senior officers of the order will send for you and have you taken up to the chapterhouse. There they'll tell you all about yourself, in great and very plausible detail. They'll tell you that your name is Brother Stellico, that you're a renegade monk of this order and therefore – technically – an outlaw already sentenced to death; that before you left the order, you were a father tutor – that's a very high rank indeed – and the senior deacon of applied religion, which is our term for swordfighting. According to what they'll tell you, I was your immediate subordinate and your pupil, and you taught me everything I know about the subject.' He paused. 'None of this is true,' he said.

'Oh,' Poldarn said.

The voice laughed softly. 'It's all entirely possible, of course,' he went on. 'And it fits everything you'll have learned about yourself. They'll go on to offer you amnesty and an impressive-sounding title and privileges, provided you stay here for the time being and send away your friend here – Copis, isn't it? And before that, you were called Xipho Dorunoxy, when you worked in the brothel in Josequin. That's not your real name, of course.'

He'd pronounced Xipho Dorunoxy perfectly, or as well as Copis had, at the very least. 'How clever of you,' Copis said. 'I won't ask how you know.'

'Thank you,' the voice replied. 'We prefer not to explain how we come by our information. It's not a dreadful dark secret, quite the opposite, in fact, all perfectly straightforward and unimpressive. Which is why we don't explain; it ruins the mystique.'

Poldarn breathed in slowly. 'Why would they want to tell me all these lies?' he said.

'Let me tell you who you really are,' the voice said reasonably, 'and you should be able to work it out for yourself. You'll also see why, even though I have every reason to hate you and see you come to harm, I couldn't stand by and watch them do this to you. I may not respect you, but I respect our order; if we stoop to acts of pure malice, such as what they have planned for you, we stand to lose everything we are.'

'All right,' Poldarn said. 'Now, tell me who I really am.'

Chapter Twenty-One

They dragged him, bleeding and dizzy, from the cart to the tent flap (and as his feet trailed behind him, each bump and jolt jarring the broken bone, flooding his body and mind with pain, two crows got up out of a dead spruce tree and flew away). The sentry outside the tent blocked their way with his spear.

'What's the hurry?' he asked suspiciously. 'And what's that?'

'Top priority is what it is,' snapped the trooper on his left. 'Urgent. You know what urgent means?'

'It's all right.' The voice came from inside the tent. 'Let them through, I'm expecting them.' A hand pulled back the tent flap, and they hauled him through and lowered him to the ground like a sack of grain, gently enough to stop him splitting open, but beyond that, not too bothered.

'Lift his head.' A hand gathered enough hair for a grip and pulled upwards, lifting his head enough for him to see the man in the tent. 'That's him. Fine, good work. Now, you two go and get something to eat, catch a few hours' sleep. We're moving out just before dawn.'

Monach opened his eyes, and shivered. He couldn't see the

two troopers now, so he assumed they were saluting or whatever cavalrymen did; all he could see was six square inches of
threadbare carpet. But he could hear the rustling of canvas,
which led him to believe they'd left the tent.

'Do you know who I am?' the voice said. A pause – he
didn't reply, mostly because that would involve moving his
jaw, which would be very painful. 'Hello, can you hear me? I
asked you a question.'

Something hit him just above the waist, confirming his
impression that at least one rib on that side was broken. He
rode out the pain like a man in a small boat in a gale; so long
as his connection with this body was minimal, he could stay
above the breakers, not get swamped by them. In seventh
grade they'd studied the classical techniques for enduring and
ignoring pain. He'd done all right in the seventh grade, enough
to scrape a pass, and the high marks he was getting in swordsmanship and religious theory made up for it.

'Well,' the man said, 'in case you don't know who I am,
though I'm pretty certain you do, my name is Feron Amathy.
What's yours?'

Good question; and it occurred to him that if he didn't
answer, the man might kick him in the ribs again. He didn't
want that. He couldn't remember his name; but he knew a
name he'd called himself once or twice, when on a mission
using a persona. He opened his mouth – his jaw hurt like hell –
and managed to make a noise that sounded like 'Monach'.

'Yes,' the man replied. 'I know. Just wanted to see if you'd
tell me the truth. It's what we call a control; ask questions
you know the answer to, it helps you get a feel for whether the
subject's likely to lie or not. So,' he went on, sitting down in
the chair whose feet Monach could just make out in line with
his nose, 'you're the famous Monach, are you? Bloody hell,
you're a mess. What on earth did they do to you?'

He hoped that was a rhetorical question, because he could-
n't remember. Generally speaking, if you want an accurate

description of a fight, don't ask the man lying on the ground getting kicked and stamped on. All he can see is boots and ankles, and his concentration is apt to wander.

'Actually,' the man went on, 'your name isn't Monach at all. It's confusing, because all you damn monks have so many names – the one you were born with, the name-in-religion you get given when you're a kid novice, the other name-in-religion you take when you're ordained, not to mention the names you use when you go out into the world making trouble for regular people.' He sighed. 'In your case,' he said, 'I know them all. First you were Huon Josce. Then you were Valcennius – named after the author of six obscure commentaries on the Digest, though you didn't know it at the time. Then you were Brother Credizen; and when you're out murdering people, you're Soishen Monach.' He smiled. 'Took my people weeks to find all that stuff out. You should be flattered.'

Monach felt sick, as if all the skin had been flayed off his face and the man had just drawn his fingertip across it. It was absurd, of course, to feel shocked and horrified about the violation of his names, bearing in mind what was about to happen to him. But he couldn't help it; it was instinct, like everything that mattered in religion.

'Looks like you must've put up a hell of a fight,' the man went on. 'Which did neither of us any favours, of course. You got beaten into mush, I can't get a sensible word out of you. If you'd given up and come quietly, think how much better it'd have been for both of us.' He heard the chair creak, and the feet in front of his eyes moved. 'Let's get you sitting up,' he said. 'We might have better luck if you're not sprawled all over the floor like a heap of old washing.'

The man was strong, and not fussed about what hurt and what didn't. When he opened his eyes again, his mind washed clean by the waves of pain, Monach was sitting in a chair. Opposite him was the man who'd been talking.

'Better?' the man asked. 'All right, now, you're going to

have to make an effort and answer my questions, because it's very important and there's not much time. If you don't, I'll take this stick and find out which of your bones are broken. If you understand, nod once.'

Nodding wasn't too hard. He managed it. That seemed to please the man, because he nodded back and sat down in his chair, a three-foot thumb-thick rod of ashwood across his knees. He was older than Monach had expected, at least forty, with plenty of curly brown hair and a slightly patchy brown beard, thick on the cheeks and jaws but a little frayed-looking on the chin itself. He had a pointed nose, a heart-shaped face and bright, friendly brown eyes.

'Splendid,' the man said. 'All right, pay attention. Do you know where General Cronan is?'

Apparently he did, because his head lifted up and then flopped back, jarring his jaw and making him shudder. Once he'd nodded, he remembered who Cronan was, and the vital importance to the order and the empire of not answering the question he'd just answered.

'Yes? And?'

He felt himself trying to say something. 'At the Faith and Fortitude,' he heard himself say, 'on the road from Josequin to Selce.' The words came out fluently, like a child wetting his bed in spite of his best efforts to control his bladder. He couldn't help thinking that if only he still had his names, that wouldn't have happened.

'I know where you mean,' the man said. 'Very good, now we're getting somewhere. Next question: have you sent some of your people to kill him?'

Just a dip of the head this time, to indicate Yes.

'Buggery. When?'

'This morning,' he answered. No hesitation now. 'About two hours before noon.'

'Which means – how were they going? On foot, horseback, wagon?'

He opened his mouth to reply but started coughing instead. Coughing was a very bad idea. The man didn't approve, either, because he repeated his question, loudly.

'Riding,' Monach managed to say. 'Not hurrying. Can't risk.'

'Were they taking the main road?'

A nod.

'That's something, I suppose. All right, stay there, don't go away.'

The man left the tent, shouting a name, and left him alone. That was wonderful; he'd have a chance to relax, to catch up with the pain, which was racing ahead of his thoughts and blocking their way. He closed his eyes – it was better with them shut, in spite of the dizziness. At the back of his mind something was protesting: no, you mustn't close your eyes, you'll fall asleep or pass out. This is your only chance; look, there's a knife on the map table, you can reach it if you tilt the legs of the chair. You can hide it under your am, and when he comes back you can stab him or cut his throat, and that'll make up for the rest. Must do it, can't afford not to. You've done very badly, but you still have one chance. Won't get another. Must—

He stayed still, put the voice out of his mind. Objectively he weighed up the conflicting demands on him. On the one hand there was the future of the order and the empire; on the other, the thought of the effort and pain, and the even worse pain if he tried and failed. It wasn't a difficult choice. Nothing outside his body mattered, outside his body and the invisible circle of pain that surrounded it. The pain defined everything.

A while later Feron Amathy came back. He looked unhappy. 'I've sent thirty light cavalry up the old drovers' trail, so if the Lihac's fordable they ought to get there an hour or so before your assassins. Still, it's cutting it fine.'

He sounded like a senior officer briefing a delinquent subordinate, not one enemy telling another how he'd frustrated

his plans and made the sacrifice of his life to the cause meaningless. It wasn't cruelty, Monach figured, just a busy man
thinking aloud, as busy men so often do. Probably he found it
useful having someone to talk to, even if it was only a
defeated, humiliated opponent. Monach could feel the other
man's weariness, the tremendous weight of responsibility
clamping down on his shoulders. 'Now then,' Feron Amathy
said, flopping back into his chair and letting his arms hang
down. 'What are we going to do with you, I wonder? My
instinct says send your head back to Deymeson with an apple
stuck in your mouth, to let them know I'm perfectly well
aware of what they're up to. On the other hand, why give
them any more information than necessary? So long as they
aren't sure whether I've worked out that they're involved,
they'll have to cover both contingencies, which'll slow up
their planning. In which case, I can either have you strung up
here, make a show of it, issue double rations, give the lads
something to cheer them up; or I could keep you for later,
assuming you survive. God only knows what sort of useful
stuff you've got locked up in your head, but will prising it out
of there be more trouble than it's worth?' He sighed. 'Truth
is,' he went on, 'nobody else is fit to interrogate you. Even in
the state you're in you're probably too smart for them, and I
can't afford to let you muck me about with disinformation. I
haven't got the time or, let's face it, the energy. Besides, you've
caused me a real headache and until those cavalry troopers get
back from Selce I can't be sure you haven't really screwed
everything up.' He sighed. 'I think I'll knock you on the head
now,' he went on. 'Anything else is just wasting valuable
time.' As he said that, he stood up, drawing a short knife
from the sash round his waist, and stepped into Monach's
circle.

Monach closed his eyes. Dying in a manner befitting a
member of the order had been covered in some detail in eighth
grade, and he'd come third out of twenty. The key to the

approved technique was dignity, acceptance, faith in a higher purpose.

Keeping his eyes closed, he visualised the course the knife and the hand holding it would have to take (assuming Feron Amathy was proposing to sever his jugular vein). He saw the left hand spreading to press down on his ear, to keep his head steady while the right hand cut; it was the obvious vulnerable moment, because it's always a mistake to place your body into the enemy's circle unless it's led by your weapon. At the perfect moment he reached up with his right hand, caught hold of the other man's left index finger, pressed it back sharply and broke it.

Feron Amathy squealed, his instinct making him try to pull away. That was good. Monach increased his grip on the broken finger so that Feron Amathy, trying to yank his hand back, put most of his body weight into the area of maximum pain. Excellent: in tight corners, use pain to confuse the enemy, force him to overlook his advantage and his opportunity for a single finishing cut. In the meanwhile Monach had time to shift his position on the ground (not that he wanted to, but he supposed it had to be done), enough so that he could get his left hand round the other man's right wrist and shake the knife out of it. At some point during this manoeuvre a spike of pain made him open his eyes and he found that he was looking directly at Feron Amathy's face. He saw the fear and smiled, just as the knife hit the ground.

He let go of the other man's wrist and gathered up the knife. As anticipated, Feron Amathy pulled away with all his strength, freeing his broken finger and screaming as the pain lit up his whole body. Monach took advantage of having his right hand free again by slamming the heel of it up under the other man's chin. Quite correctly, Feron Amathy slumped backwards, landing on his broken finger and howling.

In Monach's mind, the calm, contemptuous voice of Father Tutor told him to assess the situation objectively. For the moment he had a total ascendency, but it was a moot point whether it would last long enough for him to get in close and kill the enemy, especially given his own wretched condition. Any attempt at a finishing cut would only provoke a furious instinctive resistance, like the one he'd just put up, which could easily lead to disaster in spite of his superiority in technique and firm grasp of theory. If, on the other hand, he chose to get up and leave the tent, it was highly unlikely that Feron Amathy would try to pursue him personally. Instead he'd yell at the top of his voice for the guard, and by the time they arrived anybody who'd attained a pass in grade five, let alone a second-class distinction, ought to be among the shadows and halfway to making a perfect escape, regardless of any previous injuries.

As always, Father Tutor was right, and the idea that here was a moment of destiny, when he had the crucial Feron Amathy at his mercy and could kill him easily, was just an illusion. Someone with less discipline, less training, less skill in the interpretation of theory might be fooled into thinking that this was a point at which the world would change for ever, but Monach knew better. Only a god could do something like that.

An intriguing thought occurred to him. Not all that long ago he'd almost managed to convince himself that he was the god Poldarn. He'd talked himself out of it, reasonably enough, but somewhere in his mind there lingered just a smear of a suspicion. Now, if he really was a god, surely all he'd have to do was say the word, or just think it, and his injuries would miraculously heal. Gods, after all, can't be injured; they can project an illusion of injury, possibly well enough to deceive themselves, but no actual harm could come to them. It was worth a try.

He thought the command, and waited. For one very brief moment, he wasn't sure; then the pain reasserted itself, and he knew. Another theory knocked on the head. Never mind.

He made it to the tent flap before Feron Amathy started yelling for the guard. Any kind of movement was fairly close to being unbearable; walking should have been technically impossible, let alone running. Looked at from another angle, he had the time it would take for the guards to enter the tent and get their orders in which to get through the camp and into the village. He ran.

At exactly what point the idea took shape in his mind he couldn't say. It might even have been before he broke Feron Amathy's finger; certainly it had very nearly evolved into its final form when he stuck his head out of the tent and looked for an escape route. Partly it was desperation – who else did he know in Cric, after all? Of course, there was no reason whatsoever to suppose that the old man who might just be General Allectus would be inclined to help him. But if his guess was right, the old man would have nothing to lose by harbouring a fugitive, since if he was caught and recognised by a soldier from the Amathy house he'd be killed immediately in any case. A lot would depend on whether General Allectus saw it that way, of course. Always assuming he really was General Allectus.

It was a stupid idea; but it gave him something to focus on, a purpose. They'd taught him that long ago, at an age when other boys were still playing with wooden swords and fighting make-believe enemies: if you have to run, run towards something, not just away. The slightest trace of purpose will often keep back the smothering blanket of fear, which is nearly always a worse enemy than the source of danger itself, just as more people are killed by the smoke in a burning house than the actual fire.

His sense of direction was hazy, but he had an idea that when he'd been brought in he'd made a note in his mind that the general's tent was at right angles to the road through the camp, on the left-hand side. Find the road, turn left and keep going, parallel to it, picking a way through the rows of tents . . . He staggered as his knees and his breath collapsed simultaneously, but he managed to keep his balance by swaying wildly, like a drunken old man.

That was a thought. He tried to picture them in his mind, vague figures he'd seen in every town and city he'd been to; the mind filtered them out after a while, since they were of no possible importance and an eyesore into the bargain. He analysed their way of moving – unselfconscious, confident in a twisted sort of a way, since men with neither past nor future are rarely afraid of anything. He remembered one or two who were familiar sights from the lower town in Deymeson. Cripples, both of them; one, now he came to think of it, must have broken both legs at some point and had them heal without being set; the other had wrecked his back, or been born like it, so that he always walked along with his nose right down by his feet, the knuckles of his fingers dragging along the ground. As he adjusted his stance and posture to copy them, it occurred to him that they must spend their entire lives in something like the pain he felt now, and for a moment he was filled with admiration for their courage and endurance (because he would either die or escape, be rescued and healed; they would be here for ever, in the confined area of pain, the circle).

Whatever else he wasn't, Monach was a fine actor. The guards passed him three times: once, at the run, going towards the town; once, at the double, coming back; the last time, walking dejectedly, going out again. The third time he called out to them, a vague loud noise that was composed half out of words and the rest of mere roaring. They swung out a few yards further into the road to avoid him.

Cric village was deserted. Of course, it always would be at this time of night, since hard-working farmers rise and go to bed with the sun. Nobody here wasted good tallow by burning a lamp or a candle. There was just enough starlight to mark the difference between emptiness and the shadows of buildings. As he trudged and swayed and staggered, Monach found that although he felt the pain with each step, it wasn't actually troubling him – because it wasn't his, it belonged to the persona of the old drunk, a character he'd dragged into the world to carry his sufferings for him like a porter. Instead he used each ache and wrench and spike of pain as a foundation for his performance – *the more it hurts, the less you feel it*; that still made no more sense than it had twenty years ago, but the order had been of the opinion that learning it by heart would make him a better monk, more able to make the draw and understand the nature of the gods.

He hadn't been counting doors and there weren't any visual landmarks to guide him, but he knew which house belonged to the man he was looking for, because his instinct and intuition told him which one it was, and he believed in them as a true monk should. He felt for the latch and lifted it. It wasn't locked or bolted; Cric wasn't that sort of place.

'Hello?' He stepped inside, resisting the temptation to stand up straight in spite of the pain in his back and shoulders. Stay in persona until the very last moment, just in case. 'Hello,' he repeated, 'is anybody there?'

'All right, I can hear you,' replied a voice in the darkness. 'There's no need to shout.'

It was a voice he thought he recognised, at any rate. He tried to remember the name the old man had been using the last time he was here. Jolect; Jolect something or something Jolect, and he'd claimed to be a plain, ordinary retired soldier.

'Sergeant Jolect?' he said. 'Am I in the right house?'

The voice chuckled. 'What if I told you that you weren't?'

'That would depend,' Monach croaked as a surge of pain too broad and grand for him to ignore swept up from his knees to his chin.

'Depend on what?'

'On whether you're telling the truth.'

The voice chuckled again, this time with a little more colour. 'Yes, I'm called Jolect,' it said. 'But I was never a sergeant.'

'Would it be all right,' Monach asked, very quietly, 'if I sat down on your floor? Just for a moment or so.' Before the old man could answer, Monach pressed his back against the wall and slid down to the floor. It took him a great deal of effort not to yell and scream.

'By all means,' the old man said. 'I won't press you for your name,' he went on, 'but as and when you feel like mentioning it—'

'Vesser,' Monach said. 'Vesser Oldun. I—' He coughed, and took advantage of the pause to think. 'I was on the road, on my way home – I'm a trader, you see, I deal in small household stuff, buckles and pins and brooches and buttons, that sort of thing – and I was just a mile or so north-west of here, shortly before sunset, when some men on horses overtook me and – well, you can probably guess the rest. I lay there for a while until I felt strong enough to move, and made my way into town. Is there an inn here?'

'I'm afraid not.'

'Oh. Oh, that's a nuisance. I'm sorry,' Monach added, trying to ignore the pain in his jaw that came from so much talking, 'you must be wondering why I came bursting in here like that. The truth is, I was looking for an inn, as I said just now, and then all of a sudden I started feeling so weak and faint I simply couldn't stand up any more. So I pushed on the first door I came to, and it turned out to be yours. I'm terribly sorry if I'm causing you a lot of trouble or anything.'

'Not a bit of it,' the voice replied. 'Well, well, that is a surprise. I don't think anybody's been robbed in these parts for forty years, or at least that's what my neighbours have told me. Of course, I was away for a great many years and only came back here – what, a dozen years ago? Less than that, probably, I can't remember. Anyway, I can't vouch for it personally, for the reasons I just gave, but I'm fairly sure what they told me about the lack of robberies is more or less true.

So, if someone's just set up in that line of work nearby, we'll have to do something about it.'

'Yes,' Monach said, struggling a little. 'Yes, you really should.' He could feel himself sliding into sleep, there was a dream already open and waiting for him to fall into it. 'Well, if there's no inn . . .'

The voice laughed. 'Don't worry about that,' he said. 'You're welcome to stay here for the night, or as long as you want to. In the morning, though, when the boy comes with my breakfast, I'll send him for one of my neighbours. She's very good with broken bones and medicines.'

Monach managed to thank him before his mind tripped and went sprawling into the dream—

Monach opened his eyes, and saw bright daylight. Instinctively he looked up, and saw a blue sky with a few smudges of high white cloud. The position of the sun told him it was mid-morning. It was very quiet, but he could sense that he wasn't alone. Something was about to happen.

He looked over his shoulder, and saw an army. They were drawn up in line of battle, and their formations stretched away on either side as far as he could see, thousands of men, standing at parade ease, all staring straight ahead. He turned back and tried to make out what it was that they all found so fascinating.

He couldn't see it. He and the army were just below the crest of a hogsback ridge, looking down a fairly gentle, even slope of what looked to him like average-to-good sheep grazing towards a quite substantial wood at the foot of a steep hill. There were no houses, barns, linhays or other buildings in sight, no walls or hedges or livestock. As views went it was pleasant enough, but rather dull.

I wonder who I am, he thought, but didn't allow himself to dwell on the point. He was sure he'd find out soon enough, and besides, it was only a dream.

'There, look,' somebody said, a few yards away on his right. He looked at the man who'd just spoken; his arm was out-stretched and he was pointing. 'Just coming round the edge of the wood, look,' the man went on. Monach followed the line of his finger, but couldn't see anything. 'Can you see it, General?' the man went on, and Monach perceived that the words had been addressed to him. 'Outriders, probably,' the man went on, 'or mounted pioneers. Do you want me to send out a cavalry squad, see if we can cut them off?'

Damn, he's asking me a question, Monach thought, slightly flustered. *If this dream is something that really happened, what if I give the wrong order, and we lose the battle? Or win the battle, for that matter, when we should've lost it? Would that mean I'd be trapped in this dream and unable to get back out again?*

'It's funny you should say that.' Monach looked round; standing right next to him on his left was the old man from Cric, the one who might once have been General Allectus, the one on whose floor Monach's body was sleeping.

'I'm sorry?' Monach said.

'It's quite all right,' the old man said. 'And I shouldn't have startled you like that. No, it's all right. No matter what orders you give them, I'll still lose the battle, history will take its course. Those men there—' he gestured to his left with the back of his hand, 'the Amathy house,' he went on, 'they'll change sides as soon as things start to go wrong for me, and that'll be that. But we're drifting away from the point, I apol-ogise. I just wanted to set your mind at rest, so you can enjoy the dream without fretting about getting home again after-wards.'

'Thank you,' Monach felt obliged to say.

'My pleasure. Now, what was I about to tell you? Oh yes.' The old man wiped a strand of fine white hair out of his eyes; the wind was getting up, and here on the slope they were in a position to catch the worst of it. 'This idea of yours about get-ting trapped in a dream.'

'What? Oh, right, I see.'

'It's not a new thought,' the old man went on. 'In fact, in some versions of the Poldarn myth, that's what happens to him; he falls asleep under a lime tree on Deymeson Hill and in his dream he suddenly finds himself sitting on the box of a cart, dragging across the moors to a place called Cric. But he doesn't remember who he is or where he came from, or anything like that, let alone the fact that he's a god, not a mortal.' The old man laughed; he seemed to be in rare high spirits. Of course, he was younger than Monach remembered him. 'Anyway,' he went on, 'what my men – sorry, your men – are looking out for is the first sign of General Cronan's army, which is due to come out from behind that wood any moment now. When it does, you'll give the order to stay put and receive them here. It's a very sensible order, and even now I can't help wondering what'd have happened if they'd obeyed it.' He sighed, and suddenly he was an old man again, though only for a moment. 'They don't, of course,' he went on. 'They let Cronan's men get halfway up this slope, and suddenly take it into their minds to charge. That works very well to begin with, until Cronan springs his trap and two thousand heavy cavalry come out of the wood, race up the hill on the flanks and cut us in half. The lower half keeps on pushing forward, bursts through the line and carries on down the slope and into that wood. They don't come out again, ever. The top half – well, Feron Amathy changes sides, and the rest of them pull back in good order to the top of the ridge and withdraw from the field. I – you – *we* stay here, trying to rally enough men for a stand; the enemy cavalry catch sight of us and at the last minute we break and run away – you and me with them, of course, which is why I'm alive and trapped here. If for some reason you decide to stay, please try not to win the battle. As I told you a moment ago, winning'd be the easy option. And it wouldn't matter, even if you did win. You'd still lose, but it'd all take longer and the casualties would be higher.

Ah,' the old man said sharply, 'they're here, and about time too.'

As the enemy army became visible inside the wood, they put up a colony of rooks and crows that flew ahead of them for a while, like the slow, shallow wave that comes before the breakers. 'In a sense,' the old man was saying, 'all battles are just unpleasant, conscience-stricken memories, just as this one is; they've all happened before, and the only difference lies in who's dreaming them this time. Then again, you can pass off all kinds of old rubbish by tacking *in a sense* in front of it.'

Monach squinted; the wind was making his eyes water. 'I can see them now,' he said.

'Can you? Splendid.' The old man was looking at them too. 'Interesting, I suppose, that you chose to come here, before the battle started. My guess is that your instincts led you to the moment before the draw, the point where they violate our circle. Since you believe in religion, the next part, the battle itself, doesn't really exist; there's just the moment before and the moment after. Or am I oversimplifying?'

'Yes,' Monach replied, 'you are. The battle wouldn't exist only if this was a perfect world, which it isn't, or if you and I were gods, which we aren't.'

The old man grinned. 'I'm not, for sure. As for you – well, I can't see that it matters all that much, one way or the other. If I told you, Yes, you're definitely a god, take my word for it, you wouldn't believe me, after all. You'd say this is just a dream, and your dream at that.'

Monach wasn't sure whether that was a divine revelation or simple teasing. He thought it best to ignore it, on either count. 'So,' he said, as his instincts urged him to counterattack, 'you really are General Allectus, then? May I ask, what're you doing hiding out in a wretched little dump like this?'

'I was born here,' Allectus replied. 'Not in the village, you understand; my grandfather owned the whole valley and half the moor – it was more trouble and expense than it was worth, which is why when he died my father just forgot about it, stopped trying to collect the rents, let the house fall down; at the best of times the income from the estate wasn't enough to pay the gardeners at our main house, in Torcea.' He wiped something out of the corner of his eye, a speck of dust or grit, or a small gnat. 'But yes, we had a house here. If there's time, you might make a detour and take a look at the ruins, if there's anything still there to see; the villagers have been tearing it up for building stone for forty years, so there's probably not much left. And yes, I was born here, while the family was spending the summer out here one year. We moved around a lot then, tracking from estate to estate, like a bunch of itinerants roaming the countryside with all our possessions packed in a cart. Of course it had to be a very big cart to get all our stuff inside. But a cart's a cart.' He shook his head. 'Anyway,' he continued. 'When I lost the battle and my army and found myself in these parts, alone and with a price on my head, I suppose a sort of homing instinct drew me back.' He smiled. 'And it helped that I could remember a few bits and pieces from our visits here when I was a boy. I remembered the name of a servant we hired from this village who was just about my age, by the name of Jolect. He left with us, caught a fever and died. I hardly knew him. But when I came here, I decided to be him, coming home after a lifetime of service in the army. Fortuitously, the Jolect family had died out in the meanwhile, so nobody was left to say I wasn't who I claimed to be; besides, nobody cared. I had twelve gross-quarters in gold coin when I arrived here – it was my pocket change, the day I ran away from this battle, but enough to represent a time-expired veteran's life savings, enough to make me a rich man in Cric. I gave it to my neighbours so they could buy all the things they couldn't grow or make – iron and steel for ploughs and tools, mostly, and some other materials, enough to last all of Cric for a generation – and in return I have this fine house, and they'll feed and clothe me till I die. What more could a god ask?'

Monach didn't say anything.

'Besides,' Allectus went on, 'there's a beautiful symmetry about it. I was born the son and heir to this huge demesne – worthless, maybe, but vast by any standards – and now in my old age here I am again, the squire, the old master, loved, respected, tolerated and put up with by my faithful tenants.' He pulled an exaggeratedly sad face, as the sun flashed alarmingly on the spears of Cronan's army, far away in the distance. 'We have a habit of turning out to be what we're supposed to be, regardless of whether we like it or not, or know it or not. If you understood religion instead of just knowing all about it, you'd see that that's what the Poldarn story's all about, an allegory for that simple fact. Of course the Poldarn story also happens to be true, every word of it, but that doesn't stop it being an allegory as well. You can stay here as long as you like, you know.'

Monach didn't quite follow. 'What, here, you mean? This battle?'

'No, of course not. In Cric. At my house. After the pounding you took from the Amathy house, it'll be a week at least before you're fit to move, and besides, it won't be healthy for you in these parts until Feron Amathy moves on. Escaping was bad enough; breaking his finger into the bargain – that's a bad loss of face, he'll be taking it very seriously. But you'll be safe here.'

'Thank you,' Monach said, as General Cronan's army began to climb the slope. It was large, but not as big as his, Allectus', own. In the middle was a hedge of pikes, with a wispy line of skirmishers strewn untidily in front of it and blocks of armoured foot soldiers and cavalry on either wing. Behind the pikes he could see the baggage train, a sloppy column of carts and mules, packed too closely together. 'That's very kind of you.'

'On the contrary,' Allectus replied. 'After all, you're the man who's undertaken to kill my deadly enemy, General Cronan – not that you'll succeed, of course, but it's the thought that counts. If anything happens to me, by the way, don't panic. Just keep out of sight when they bring in the food, and leave the dirty plates and the washing. Sometimes I stay in the back room sulking for weeks on end, so they won't think anything of it; and as for the smell – well, who's going to notice, in here?'

'Thank you,' Monach repeated. He was aware of the army above and around him starting to get restless, muttering and shuffling. 'Am I really going to fail in the mission?'

'Yes,' Allectus told him, 'but not for the reason you think. You see, nobody knows where Cronan is; that's why he wasn't here, wasn't on the road where he should have been, wasn't where he told his people he was going to be. The plain fact is, he vanished a couple of months ago, on his way to Josequin, and nobody's seen or heard of him since.'

'What?' Monach shouted, but he couldn't make himself heard; his army had decided to ignore his orders and charge down the slope, and a moment later he was on the ground, his arms over his head to protect it from the boots and knees of the soldiers all around him. Allectus had vanished, in any case. Monach wound himself up into a ball, squeezing his legs and elbows in as tight as he could to get them out of harm's way, but a man running flat out tripped over him, and the men behind piled up on top of him, until Monach was buried under a mound of jerking, squirming bodies (*a living grave*, he thought, *now that's original*). He tried to breathe, but it rapidly went from difficult to impossible, at which point he suffocated and died—

—And sat up, to find both hands clamped tight over his nose and mouth, which would explain the asphyxiation. Thin spikes of sunlight were intruding under the door and between the gaps in the old, warped timbers of the shutters. He felt cold, probably because he was soaked in sweat. He tried to remember the dream he'd just tumbled out of, but it had passed by.

Next he tried to move, and that was a very bad idea. In eighth grade they'd done wounds, including how to recognise your own; they'd been taught a cumulative assessment system – ten points for a broken collarbone, thirty for an arm, fifty for a leg; you chose your course of action on the basis of your running total, and if it came to more than two hundred there was no recommended course of action. On that basis, he scored somewhere between one hundred and eighty and two hundred and fifteen, depending on whether there was major internal bleeding around the smashed ribs.

'Hello,' he called out. He could remember his host saying something about some local wise woman or witch doctor; country medicine wouldn't have been his first choice, but it was better than dying or (worse still, in a way) healing up with unset bones and being a cripple for the rest of his life. Not that he wanted to impose on his host in any way, but that was one offer of help he could reconcile himself to accepting.

'Hello,' he repeated, and then he realised that the shape in the corner, which he'd been assuming was a sack or a pile of old clothes, was a body.

He sighed. Too much to hope for, obviously, that the old fool could somehow manage to stay alive long enough to arrange for the doctor to call. That would've been too easy, not a sufficient challenge for a brother tutor of the order. The statistical probabilities intrigued him; of the two of them, he'd have bet money on who was more likely to survive the night, and he'd have lost.

If anything happens to me, by the way, don't panic. Just keep out of sight when they bring in the food, and leave the dirty plates and the washing. Someone had said that to him recently, but he couldn't remember who. He frowned – even frowning hurt, the tightening of the skin across his forehead tugging apart the lips of a gash that was only just beginning to knit together. Maybe the old man had said it last night, when he was drowsy and half asleep.

In the ninth grade they'd taught them basic field medicine and surgery, with a short and mostly hilarious session on how to set your own bones and bind your own wounds. It had been too close to the end of the term; they'd all been worn out with study, saturated with too much information, and nobody had really made any kind of an effort to learn the stuff properly. For the rest of the day, therefore, he was forced to rely on trial and error and instinct as much as authorised procedures. That was a great pity, since experimenting on one's own broken bones is a painful and demoralising experience. For bandages he had to use strips of the late General Allectus' threadbare and filthy carpet – a genuine Morevish tent rug, no less – which he slowly sawed and hacked to shape with Feron Amathy's impractically shaped knife. All day he was pitifully thirsty, and there was a water jug no more than ten feet away, but somehow he never got around to crawling across the room and fetching it.

Eventually the splinters of light began to fade, suggesting the onset of evening. He wasn't conscious when the food arrived – he passed out at least a dozen times that day because of the pain and his general condition – and he woke up out of an involuntary doze to hear the door closing. Once he'd got the panic under control, he listened for the sound of someone moving about or breathing; while he was holding still and doing that, he had time to work out the various possible explanations for what he'd heard and the odds on each of them. The likeliest explanation was that the villagers were used to Allectus being asleep or crazy out of his mind, and left the food and the house without saying a word or making a loud noise. That would suit him just fine, of course. The food and the water and the clean clothes would be left beside the door; all he had to do was get from the inner room to the main room without tearing the loose confederation of injuries he called his body.

And if he *didn't* do that, of course, he'd be in desperate trouble, because if they came in and found that the food and drink hadn't been touched they'd be concerned (good, caring neighbours that they were), and would put their heads round the partition to make sure he was all right, and they'd find Allectus dead and a strange man propped up next to him.

So, taking advantage of their good nature was suddenly compulsory. Monach laughed; the whole thing was ludicrous, especially for a good monk and a student of ethical theory. He couldn't wait to get back to Deymeson and pitch it to his ethics class for discussion: *Under what circumstances are deception and theft justifiable in the name of expediency? What difference does it make that the intended recipient of the charity is dead? That the deceiver's life is at stake? That the intended recipient gave his permission for the fraud?*

Had he? Monach seemed to remember that he had, but not the exact context. Either Allectus had told him so, in unambiguous terms, or he'd dreamed it (*Discuss, with reference to the moral ambiguity of unsubstantiated perceptions . . .*). Remembering was difficult, and getting more so. It was just as well he'd had such a firm foundation in mental discipline.

He closed his eyes. Outside it was raining, but he couldn't hear that. He couldn't hear the sound of boots squelching in mud, or cartwheels in the street, as the Amathy house left Cric and went to war.

What difference would it make if the deceiver acts in furtherance of the general good? Of a manifest destiny? What difference would it make if the deceiver incorrectly but sincerely believes that he acts in furtherance of a just cause or a manifest destiny? What difference would it make if the deceiver commits the deception knowing that the legitimate just cause or manifest destiny so authorising his deception has failed? Assuming that the deceiver is so justified, would that justification extend to fraudulent use or consumption of articles conducive to mere physical comfort, as opposed to the bare essentials required for survival? In such context, what would such bare essentials consist of?

What difference would it make if the deceiver were a god?

Chapter Twenty-Two

They came for him the next morning, just as the voice in the night had said they would, and they took him to the abbot's lodgings, where the abbot told him all the lies the voice had warned him to expect. He pretended to believe them, just as the voice had advised him to do: *Of course,* he said, his voice low with wonder, *it's all coming back to me now. I remember this place – over there's the drill hall, where I did my twelve grades, and the novices' dormitory's in the next yard over, and opposite that's the dining-hall.* The voice had drilled it into him the night before, made him repeat it all a dozen times, to make sure the geography of the place was firmly fixed in his mind.

Listening to the deceptions, knowing the truth, Poldarn couldn't help feeling a sense of elation, of release – partly because he was the one who was deceiving them, not the other way round, mostly because now, for the first time in a long time, he knew who he was. To begin with it had come as a complete shock; then he'd started to remember – not actual memories, but fragments of dreams in which he'd been the man he now knew he was, in which he'd heard and seen and known things that couldn't possibly have been picked up by eavesdropping on stray conversations or extrapolating from what Copis had told him. Also, it made perfect sense, explained so many of the strange, meaningless things that had happened to him – the attack on the cart by the three horsemen, shortly before they reached Cric; the meeting with Chaplain Cleapho in Sansory, and the soldier who'd recognised him in the kitchens of the inn, the one he'd had to kill before he could make the man tell him his own name. Most exhilarating of all was the realisation that his life had meant something, that he'd attempted and achieved things worthy of his talents and abilities, that he was on the right side.

(And now he was about to achieve something else, far more important and beneficial than anything he'd ever done before; furthermore, he'd have the opportunity to punish the order with appropriate savagery for trying to trick and use him. No wonder he was the sworn enemy of these people, or that they'd been so keen to get him out of the way.)

He listened carefully to what they had to say, while speculating as to which of the grave, solemn men sitting round the table was the voice he'd heard the night before. Only one of them spoke, making it possible for Poldarn to eliminate him at once (the prior of observances; and he was too tall, anyhow), which left him nine to choose from. Five of them were the right height and build. He'd have time and opportunity to figure it out over the next few days, and then he'd be able to make direct contact with his ally and put into operation a plan of his own that ought, if everything went as it should, to set everything right.

(*Your name*, the voice had told him, *is Cronan Suvilois. You were born on the sixth day of the Ninth, in the fourth year of Emperor Massin Dasa, in Torcea. Your family are southerners. Your father's name was Lalicot, and your mother, before her marriage, was called Actin Doricalceo. Your family was comfortable rather than wealthy, minor provincial nobility, of no great account in the capital; your father felt, correctly, that in order to make your way in the world you would need to follow a career, either the army or religion. Accordingly, when you were six years old, he sent you to the Paupers' Institute at Collibortaca—)*

'Of course,' the abbot was saying, 'we appreciate the fact that you probably won't remember the details of what you used to know for some while yet; as it happens, we have doctors here who've made a study of your sort of condition and probably know more about it than anybody else in the empire. When there's time, we'll send them to take a look at you, see if there's anything they can do. I believe they've managed to cure some pretty stubborn cases in the past.'

'That'd be wonderful,' Poldarn said, making a mental note to add this to the list of crimes for which these people had to be punished, this wanton planting of false hopes. 'You don't know how much it means to me, even the hope of someone finding a cure. It'd be something to live for.'

The abbot nodded. 'Plenty of time for that later,' he said. His face was stern but sympathetic, wisdom, justice and mercy combined in it like three elderly sisters sharing a house, ideal for the role of father, or god. 'First things first; we've got to get you back to where you're needed. Probably best if we supply you with an escort – trying to keep track of where you'd be likely to run into one of Cronan's scouting or foraging parties is a sure way to go mad, the way this war's going. With fifty horsemen along for the ride, it won't actually matter who you run into, short of a full cavalry squadron or a field army.'

Awkward, Poldarn thought, but he had the presence of mind to appear pleased and grateful. He did it very well, and that seemed to disconcert the monks. No bad thing, needless to say.

'Talking of which,' he asked as a diversion, or the equivalent of a rest in music, 'how is the war going? Has anything much been happening?'

The abbot smiled. 'That's a very good question,' he said. 'If you mean battles and sieges and the like, then no, not much. It's what's not been happening that's so confusing.'

It wasn't just the abbot who talked like that, of course. These monks all seemed to have the annoying habit of being gratuitously cryptic. He wondered what it was like in the dining-hall, when the grand prior wanted to ask the dean of the archives to pass the horseradish.

(*You graduated with honours from the Academy of Arts and War at nineteen*, the voice had said, *the youngest officer ever to join the service. Your first command was a platoon of pioneers attached to a frontier station on the Morevich border – no accident that you were given such a miserable assignment, you'd made enemies as well as friends at the Academy. That was the year the raiders sacked Malevolinza; with the main provincial garrison wiped out to a man, your station was the only Imperial resource left between the mountains and the sea. The Morevich rebels and the mountain tribesmen saw their chance; a dawn attack came within a hair's breadth of forcing the gates. They were beaten back, but all the station's command staff were killed in the first hour, leaving you in charge of a desperate, impossible defence—*)

'When do you think I should leave?' he asked. 'From what you've just told me, it'd better be sooner than later, surely.'

The abbot dipped his head in agreement. 'Quite right,' he said. 'There are a few things we'll need to sort out in due course, and when you get back we'll have to give you a quick refresher course on being a sword-monk, and a good bit of additional background material on Brother Stellico, to make up for what you can't remember yet. But there really isn't time for any of that now.'

What if they were telling the truth, and the voice in the night had been lying?

He let the thought sit quiet for a moment, afraid of waking it up. 'What about my—' Involuntary hesitation; couldn't

think of the right word. 'Wife' wasn't true; 'friend' was fatu-
ously coy. 'What about my business partner?' he asked. 'I
haven't seen her since this morning.'

The abbot frowned. 'Oh, she'll be all right,' he said. 'Of
course,' he went on, 'it'll be awkward for her, losing her associate so suddenly, but we'll see to it she's not out of pocket.'

That was the first time that it occurred to Poldarn that
there wouldn't be a place for Copis in this new old life of his.
Was he still married? He didn't know; oh, he knew all manner
of things about himself just from having overheard them in
inns and bakers' shops, besides what the voice had told him,
but the things he wanted to know weren't the sort of thing that
anybody else could possibly know.

'That's all right, then,' he said. 'So what'll you do? Let her
go back to Sansory?'

The abbot nodded. 'If you like, we can provide her with an
escort,' he said. 'Probably just as well, if she's carrying a large
sum of money and with the roads as they are.'

'I'd appreciate that,' Poldarn said, wondering if he'd just
made a serious mistake. They couldn't help but have heard the
note of concern in his voice, the one that proclaimed, *I care
about this person, who would therefore make an ideal hostage,*
loud enough that they'd probably heard it in Boc. If he'd kept
quiet and not mentioned her, perhaps they'd have forgotten
about her and left her alone – no, precious little chance of
that. He had an idea that the order made a virtue of scrupu-
lous attention to detail. Still, going on about her now would
only make things worse, and it wasn't as if he was in any position to do anything constructive for her.

*(Your first marriage, to Bolceanar Hutto, was purely a polit-
ical affair, and ended in divorce once you achieved your first
prefecture, to the great satisfaction of all parties. When you
were twenty-six, however, and just about to leave Torcea to
assume command of the expedition against the Fodrati, you
made the drastic mistake of marrying for love. Sornith Eollo was*

*the daughter of a prosperous building contractor rather heavily
involved in bidding for military contracts – not to put too fine a
point on it, for a master tactician you were either blind or deliberately obtuse. It didn't help that your feud with the young
princes was just starting to become a major annoyance – it was
the year of your infamous duel with Tazencius, which led to his
disgrace and earned you the undying hatred of the entire
Revisionist faction—)*

'Well,' the abbot said, 'I think that's more or less everything. Welcome back to the order, Brother Stellicho, and the
best of luck for your mission.'

That signified the end of the interview; he could feel them
turning over his page and moving on to the next item of business. He allowed himself to be politely shooed out of the room
by the four sword-monks who hadn't left his side since early
that morning, and went with them across the yard, through a
couple of arches, past the stables and the coach-house—

He didn't stop, because he didn't need to. When a man's
been jolting and rattling along muddy, rutted roads in a cart
for any length of time, he gets to the point where he can recognise that cart by the thickness of its tyres or the degree of
warp in the side panels. Definitely his cart, their cart, but it
was backed in and surrounded by a dozen others in the coach-
house, suggesting it had been subsumed into the transport
pool, to be booked out and assigned to the duty carter next
time a load of charcoal needed to be fetched or two dozen
crates of chickens brought up from the market.

Attention to detail, just as he'd guessed. Easy enough to
reconstruct what had happened. A monk would have come
back from the lower town that morning and sent for a carter,
explaining that there was a cart down at the inn, and that its
owners wouldn't be needing it any more; if it stayed there, the
innkeeper might get to wondering what had become of the
man and woman who'd brought it in – he wouldn't say anything out loud, of course, but loose ends like that are bad for

morale. So the monk would have given the carter some kind of warrant or letter of authority, and the carter would have given it to the innkeeper, and the innkeeper would have told his groom to get the cart ready, and the carter would have turned it over to the transport officer or the duty officer, who would have told him to put it away with the others (waste not, want not; men and women die every day, but a functional cart is valuable property), and the cart itself would henceforth serve the order, purged of its identity and memory, because a piece of equipment is there to serve and be used by whoever has a right to it.

'Just a moment,' he said, slowing down without stopping. 'I left some things in my cart last night. Would it be all right if we stopped off at the inn and picked them up?'

'Don't worry about it,' one of the monks replied. 'We'll arrange for all your stuff to be collected and kept for you till you get back. If there's anything you need, we can stop by the quartermaster's.'

They were in perfect position, two in front and two behind, just outside his circle. If they'd been closer or there had only been three of them, he'd have given it a try. But the order wouldn't make a mistake like that. Poldarn shrugged. 'No, the hell with it,' he said. 'It wasn't anything important.'

'There'll be a horse waiting for you at the gate,' the monk continued. 'You'll have three days' rations, money for expenses in the saddlebag, change of clothes, blanket, water bottle, all the usual kit. Is there anything else you might need, do you think?'

Poldarn didn't smile, though he felt moved to do so. 'Well,' he said, 'there's my book. Normally I wouldn't go anywhere without it, but just this once won't hurt.'

The monk was curious. 'Book?'

Poldarn nodded. 'Marvellous thing,' he said, 'contains all the wisdom in the world. Still, I won't be needing it for this job, I don't suppose.'

'All the wisdom in the world,' the monk repeated. 'Must be a big book, then.'

'Quite big,' Poldarn replied. 'Not as big as the recipe book, but it makes a good pillow.'

The cavalry escort was waiting for him: fifty sword-monks, in dark brown and grey coats drawn from the quartermaster's bin marked 'Riding Coat, Civilian, Nondescript'. Would they be wearing armour under them, he wondered, or didn't sword-monks feel the need of steel rings and scales when they had their invisible circle of sharp steel around them at all times? If getting away from four monks on foot was beyond him, escaping from fifty of them on fast horses wasn't going to be any easier. Falx Roisin would have been delighted to give any one of them a job riding dangerous cargo.

On an impulse he turned to the monk he'd already talked to and asked him, 'What do you know about a god called Poldarn?'

The monk hesitated for a moment, then grinned. 'Bit late to be asking that now, isn't it?' he said. 'Besides, it should be me asking you, shouldn't it?'

Poldarn shrugged. 'Well, you know,' he said. 'I always like to know who I've been.'

'You were pretty good at it, by all accounts,' the monk replied. 'But really, she should've known better, or else she didn't know. Talk about tempting providence.'

'I don't quite follow,' Poldarn said quietly.

'Oh, no, of course,' the monk said. 'I forgot, sorry. The thing about Poldarn is, you see, that anybody who gets up in the cart with him always dies.' He made a vague gesture with his right hand. 'You could just about come up with a worse omen, but it'd take some fairly serious research. Still, there you are.'

'Quite,' Poldarn replied. The monk had moved very slightly out of position, no more than a single step, but enough. He could see the sequence perfectly clearly in his mind's eye, as if he was remembering something that had already happened. From the draw, he cut the side of this monk's neck and carried on, so that the curved tip sliced into the soft skin under the second monk's chin as he stepped away and left. By this time the two monks behind him had drawn and were one step of the right foot forward, which was why his turn pivoted around his left heel, bringing the overhead diagonal slash perfectly in line with the left-side monk's right wrist; then the clever move, dodging left to keep the wounded man between himself and the fourth opponent, just long enough for a feinted lunge to make him shy backwards into a right-side rising cut to the chin; the wounded man, dealt with at his leisure, completed the pile of bodies, all four dead before the first hit the ground. And Father Tutor, looking on with grudging approval—

'Is something the matter?' the monk asked him.

Poldarn looked up sharply. Last time he'd looked, the monk had been toppling over backwards with the white of his spine showing through the red lips of the cut. Then he remembered: that hadn't actually happened, or not yet. On the other side of the yard, three birds pitched on the ridge of a roof. He looked again, and saw that they were pigeons.

'This may sound like a silly question,' Poldarn asked slowly, 'but do we know each other?'

The monk actually smiled. 'You're remembering, aren't you?' he said. 'Go on, see if you can . . .'

'No,' Poldarn snapped. 'You tell me.'

'All right.' The monk was still smiling. Three of them were now out of position, as good as dead; in another part of his mind he could see a fine mist of a few drops of their blood, hanging for a tiny moment in the air. 'My name's Torcuat. Ring any bells?'

Poldarn shook his head. 'Names don't mean anything to me. Tell me how long we've known each other.'

'Since sixth grade, actually,' Torcuat replied. 'At least, we were in the same class, but so were a hundred other kids. You were always the high flyer, of course; four months in sixth grade and then straight on to seventh. I was stuck in sixth for another two years, and by then you were a junior proctor. Then you were my—'

'Tutor in swordsmanship for six months,' Poldarn said. 'You were clumsy. In fact you were worse than clumsy, you were a menace to yourself and others. You even dropped your sword once, I wanted to have you thrown out of the school—'

The monk grinned, and pulled up the left leg of his trousers to show his ankle. 'There,' he said, 'see it?'

Poldarn saw it very clearly indeed: a crescent-shaped pink scar, just above the bone. He could remember the same mark when it was gushing blood; how he'd almost panicked, for just a moment convinced himself that one of his students was going to bleed to death right there in the schools, and that'd be the end of his teaching career. He looked up at Torcuat's face.

'I remember you,' he said. 'You used to keep—'

He couldn't say the words.

'A crow in a cage,' Torcuat said. 'Horrible, mangy old thing, and it wouldn't eat table scraps – just my luck, a gourmet crow; I had to go scrabbling about in the cellars hunting mice for the useless bloody creature, and even then it wouldn't touch them till they were three days old.'

Poldarn took a step back and to the side, putting all four monks back into position, like a king granting a reprieve to condemned men already standing on the gallows drop. 'It had a gold ring round its neck,' he said.

Torcuat laughed. 'Brass, actually,' he said. 'It was a curtain ring, from the big hall at home. About the only thing I ever had to remember home by, actually; I left when I was six. It was you held that damned crow still while I shoved that ring down over its head—'

'Poldarn. It was supposed to be Poldarn's crow.'

Torcuat was beaming now. 'You do remember,' he said.

'Yes, that's right. We had that southern kid in the dormitory with us, we wanted to scare him out of his wits because he believed in Poldarn, and seeing the crow . . . You know, I'd forgotten that myself till you reminded me.'

Poldarn took a step forward and left. 'The woman I came with,' he said. 'What's happened to her?'

The abrupt change of subject seemed to take Torcuat a little by surprise. 'I don't know,' he said, fluently enough. 'I guess she'll be going back to Sansory, unless she feels like staying here for a while. Weren't you two doing a good trade down in the town? Maybe she'll be hanging on for a day or so, carrying on the good work.'

That would, perhaps, explain the cart. 'I think I'd like to go back for my book now,' Poldarn said.

Torcuat shook his head. 'Sorry,' he replied, 'but we've kept the escort hanging about long enough as it is, standing around chatting like this. Under the circumstances, of course—' His eyes lit up. 'I know,' he said. 'What if I were to change places with the escort sergeant? Then we could carry on talking about old times, and you—'

He didn't draw. Instead, he swung his fist, smacking Torcuat so hard on the point of the chin that the monk dropped immediately, like a sheaf thrown out of a hayloft. For a moment the other three hesitated, unable to cope with an assailant who hadn't drawn and therefore couldn't be restrained with deadly force. The moment was long enough for Poldarn to take four quick, short steps backwards, clearing their circles.

'What the hell do you . . . ?' one of them shouted, and the captain of the escort lifted his head and stared. By then, though, Poldarn was standing beside the horse so thoughtfully provided for him (but there would always be a horse standing by when he needed one, and a sword ready to his hand when he felt the inclination to spill blood). He mounted awkwardly, his foot slipping out of the stirrup at his first attempt, but he still had time in hand when he grabbed the reins and pulled the horse's head round, facing it away from the gate and towards the inner yards. Tactically it was a mistake – not running to any place in particular, just running away – but just for once, when he wanted choices there weren't any.

As he passed under the gate arch, a monk with a staff stepped out of the shadows about twelve yards in front of him. He pitied the poor fool as he reached for his sword, but the monk took a step forward, turned sideways and threw the staff at him like a javelin. The squared-off point hit him in the middle of his chest; he felt his feet drop out of the stirrups, then all he saw was dancing sky, until something very broad and fast-moving slammed into his back.

The monk put a boot across his throat before he could move. Neither of them said anything.

'Well done.' He couldn't look round, of course, but he recognised Torcuat's voice. 'Is he damaged?'

The monk shook his head. 'Shouldn't be,' he said.

'That's all right then. Bastard nearly broke my jaw,' Torcuat went on, his voice suggesting that he found it hard to understand how anyone could bring himself to resort to violence. Someone stooped down and relieved Poldarn of his sword. *So this is what losing feels like,* he said to himself. *Actually, it's even worse than I'd imagined.*

They lifted him up, and two monks held his hands behind his back while a third tied his wrists together with thin, sharp cord. 'What was all that about, anyway?' Torcuat asked. 'One moment we were talking about the Poldarn legend, the next you were trying to ram my teeth down my throat. Was it something I said?'

They turned him through ninety degrees so that he was facing the main gate. Of course, the fifty horsemen, his cavalry escort, had been watching the whole time. Most of them hadn't moved. He wondered what they were making of all this.

'I told you,' he replied. 'I want to go back for my book.'

'What? Oh, there really is a book, then. I thought you were joking.' Torcuat rubbed his chin thoughtfully. 'Why didn't you just say so?'

'I did. You didn't seem to be listening.'

'Oh, for pity's sake.' Torcuat shrugged, then turned to one of his colleagues. 'Be a good man, run up to the provost's office, get him to open up our friend's locker and find this book of his.' He looked back at Poldarn. 'You haven't got more than one book, have you? I wouldn't want him fetching the wrong one.'

Poldarn shook his head. With his hands tied and the monks bracing his feet with their own, it was about the only part of himself he could move. *Curious*, he thought. *When I didn't know who I was, I could do any damn thing I liked. Now I'm me again, and I can't even wipe my own nose.*

'That's all right, then,' Torcuat said. 'Otherwise, we could be here all day. Right, if you'd be kind enough to follow me.'

They marched him across the yard and lifted him like a dead weight into the saddle. Two monks passed a rope around his waist and tied it to the pommel (attention to detail . . .). By the time they'd finished, the monk was back with Poldarn's book and had tucked it into his saddlebag.

'Cheer up,' Torcuat called out after him as the escort moved off. 'You'll probably find you like it when you get there.'

Six horsemen held perfect position around him: two in front, two behind and one on either side, making rescue as impossible as escape. They'd put his sword back in its scabbard, but since he couldn't even reach it with his teeth, thanks to the rope around his waist, he couldn't imagine it being much use to him. The main street of the lower town was just as empty as when he'd last seen it, but there was quite a long line at the gate (they rode round it) and most of the people waiting in it seemed to be staring at him as he went past. He assumed that they were looking at the monk's habit and issue boots he'd been given to wear, and were wondering what a brother of the order could possibly have done to warrant forcible restraint and expulsion under heavy guard. Their faces suggested that they were watching a god being thrown out of heaven. That reminded him; he looked up at the branches of the trees beside the gate. No crows anywhere.

(*Figures,* he thought. *No cart, no priestess, no superhuman strength and skill with weapons. Why would a crow waste his time looking at me now?*)

He wondered what they would do to Copis; whether they'd done it yet; whether he'd ever find out. What a terrible thing it must be, he thought, to be a soldier dying in the middle of a battle, never knowing whether his side won or lost. Victory in war must go to the party the gods favour most, the one with right on its side (or where was the point in it?); to die without knowing if you'd been right or wrong was a special kind of torture that the gods must reserve for only the most hopelessly evil and depraved.

An hour after Deymeson dropped down out of sight behind the horizon, the column stopped suddenly. It was open country, apart from a large wood a few hundred yards away on the left and a small, steep hill crowned with five spruce trees beyond that. There was no obvious reason for stopping here.

A horseman detached himself from the front of the column and rode back to the middle, where Poldarn was. He stopped his horse a yard or so away.

'Recognise me?' he said.

Poldarn nodded. 'You were at the council meeting in the abbot's lodgings,' he said.

'That's right. And?'

Poldarn thought for a moment. 'Say something else,' he said.

The monk was short and fat, with very curly grey hair and a rather babyish face. 'All right,' he said. 'What'd you like me to say?'

'I don't know. Anything that comes into your head.'

The monk shrugged. 'All right,' he said. 'Two crows sitting in a tall thin tree. Two crows sitting in a tall thin tree. Two crows sitting in a tall thin tree. And along comes Lucky—'

'It's you,' Poldarn interrupted. 'You broke into my room at the inn last night.'

The monk's expression didn't change. He was definitely the right height and build. 'Did I?' he said. 'I don't think so. You probably had a dream.'

'I'm sure it was you. Why have we stopped?'

The monk grinned. 'Do you really want to go and join up with Prince Tazencius? I have an idea that the welcome he'd give you would be enthusiastic but probably not enjoyable.'

Poldarn shook his head. 'You know,' he said, making an effort to move his arms and failing. 'You know, I don't think I'd really have much of a choice in the matter, even without all these damned annoying ropes. You could call it predestination, I guess.'

'You haven't got any choice,' the monk said. 'Luckily for you, though, I do. Several choices. For instance, I could have you killed, right here and now, or I could let you go free on your solemn undertaking not to be a pest in future. Or a nice sensible compromise, later on when we've finished and we don't need you any more. Wouldn't that be best?'

'No,' Poldarn replied. 'Letting me go's still the best one you've mentioned so far.'

The monk laughed. 'No, you're too valuable,' he said. 'But as it happens, that's exactly what I'm going to do: cut the ropes and let you go free. I'll even ride with you to Cric, make sure you get there.'

The name Cric was, of course, very familiar. 'What would I want to go there for?' he asked.

'Don't worry,' the monk replied. 'It's where Cronan's camp was, last time I heard. I don't suppose anybody's going to take issue with you because of what you did and who you were the last time you were there, and even if they did, it wouldn't do them any good. It's Cronan's personal guards you want to worry about.'

Poldarn frowned. 'Why?' he said. 'Won't they recognise me?'

This time, it was the monk's turn to look confused. 'Surely that's the point,' he said. 'What we've got to do is try to get you past them before they recognise you. I'm sorry if this sounds unduly negative, but being handed over to Tazencius would be a positive pleasure compared with what Cronan'd do to you. And when all's said and done, you can't really blame him after the way you've treated him.'

Ah, Poldarn thought. Not the same voice, then, after all. He looked round for a crow with something in its beak, but there wasn't one anywhere to be seen. Then another explanation occurred to him. 'Just remind me,' he said. 'My memory's been weak for so long I don't seem to be able to remember anything for very long. What was my name again?'

A long moment of silence. 'Stellicho,' the monk said. 'How could you have forgotten that?'

Poldarn nodded. 'That's right,' he said. 'And why am I going to General Cronan's camp?'

The monk sighed impatiently. 'To kill him, of course. We sent our best man, but he's obviously failed. Then suddenly you turn up again out of the blue – either by coincidence or Poldarn heard our prayers and sent you. Can't you remember *anything*?'

'It's coming back to me,' Poldarn said, 'I just need to be reminded. So why did the abbot say I was being sent to Tazencius?'

The monk scowled. 'Because of what you did,' he said, 'the reason you ran away in the first place. Don't say you've forgotten that too.'

'I'm not sure. I mean, I may not be remembering it straight. You tell me.'

'You killed – sorry, let's not mess about. You *murdered* a brother; your father tutor, not to put too fine a point on it.

Which is why the abbot sentenced you to death. Sending you to Tazencius because you'd lost your memory and didn't know what you'd done to him – well, Father Abbot has a weakness for poetic justice. For my part, I think it's a waste of resources. As far as I'm concerned, the deal is that if you manage to kill Cronan you'll be the saviour of the order and the empire and the abbot's bound to give you a free pardon. If not – well, you're dead already, and the term "no great loss" springs readily to mind. Does that seem fair to you?'

Poldarn nodded. 'So the abbot doesn't know you're doing this. You're disobeying orders.'

The monk smiled. 'I'm a member of chapter and a councillor,' he replied. 'I do what's best for the Order. Now, you have a choice. Don't take too long about it, I'm getting cold hanging around in this wind.'

Poldarn glanced at the escort. They were sitting still, quiet, upright in the saddle as good troopers should. If the monk's story was for their benefit, they didn't appear to be paying much attention. On the other hand they were sword-monks, probably trained from childhood in secret unobtrusive eavesdropping techniques. 'That's not my idea of a choice,' he said. 'If I manage to kill General Cronan, will you let me go? Really let me go, I mean.'

'Of course,' the monk replied, 'if that's what you want. You can go back to Sansory and your lady friend and spend the rest of your life selling buttons, if that's what you want.'

Copis, Poldarn thought, but of course he couldn't trust anything the monk had told him. 'I think so,' he said. 'If this was my old life, I reckon I'd be well out of it. Horrible way to live, if you ask me.'

'I'm sorry to hear you talk like that,' the monk replied, and he sounded quite sincere. 'You were my student, you know, for two years. I'd never met anybody that age with such an intuitive grasp of abstract theology.'

'Thank you,' Poldarn said. 'What's abstract theology?'

The monk kept his promise and had one of the horsemen untie the ropes. Poldarn hadn't realised how cramped and painful his arms had become until he had the use of them again. 'Of course,' the monk warned him, signalling the column to move on, 'if you even look like you're thinking about trying to escape, I'll kill you myself. Please don't make the mistake of thinking I *like* you,' he added, with a little smile. 'I don't. In fact, it's only the extreme unlikeliness of your getting out of Cronan's camp alive that's reconciling me to doing this. If I thought there was a serious risk of you surviving, I'd cut your throat now and deal with Cronan myself. I just thought I'd tell you that,' he went on. 'Just in case nobody's thought to mention it to you.'

After that nobody said anything for a long time. They were making good progress without hurrying unduly, which suggested to Poldarn that they had a long way to go. He still didn't have a very clear picture in his mind of where Deymeson and Cric were in relation to each other; his mental geography was calibrated in other units besides measurements of physical distance. He let his mind wander – very easy to do when you're riding a horse and not having to navigate for yourself – and found himself humming a tune. It was, of course, the only tune he knew:

> *Old crow sitting in a tall thin tree,*
> *Old crow sitting in a tall thin tree,*
> *Old crow sitting in a tall thin tree,*
> *And along comes the Dodger and he says, 'That's me.'*

The monk had made him think of it, of course, by reciting the words just now. He hummed it a little louder, and suddenly realised that all the horsemen near enough to be able to hear were staring at him.

'Sorry,' he said. 'It wasn't that bad, was it?'

None of them said anything, but the look on their faces was

pure hatred. But, since Poldarn had decided by now that he didn't like them either, he carried on humming even louder. Needless to say, they were too well trained and disciplined to rise to the bait, which was fine, too, since he didn't want to fight anybody, just be annoying. He started to sing:

Old crow sitting in a tall thin tree,
Old crow sitting in a tall thin tree—

He wasn't, he realised, a particularly good singer. He resolved not to let that deter him.

Old crow sitting in a tall thin tree—

'Do you mind?' said the horseman to his left. 'If you must sing, perhaps you'd care to sing something else.'

'I don't know anything else.'

'Oh, come on.' He could tell that the man was furiously angry about something, for all that he sounded like a man discussing the best way to grow carrots. 'Of course you do. The Vespers hymn. The "Come, Shining Light". How about "There Is No Rose"?'

Poldarn shook his head. 'Sorry,' he said. 'Don't know any of them.'

'You must do, you're a brother of the order.'

'What, are they religious songs or something?'

That, apparently, made the man too angry to speak at all. Poldarn shrugged and went back to singing the song about the crows, softly, under his breath, but just loud enough that the horseman would know what he was doing. At one point he noticed the monk looking round at him and frowning, but he pretended he hadn't noticed.

Old crow sitting in a tall thin tree,
Old crow sitting in a tall thin tree—

It was the kind of tune that works its way into your head and stays there, itching and annoying, like a burr in your shoe or a little strand of meat lodged between two teeth. It was getting on his nerves now. He made a special effort to stop singing it and put it out of his mind. A few minutes later he realised he'd started singing it again.

Old crow sitting in a tall thin tree—

There was an old dry-stone wall on the north side of the road, and behind it a stand of spruce trees; seventy years or so ago, someone had planted them out for timber, but he'd died or gone away before thinning the stand out, and the trees were far too crowded and close together; they'd grown up spindly and crooked, no good for anything. Poldarn could see where a few of the tallest and weakest had blown down, falling halfway before their branches fouled in those of their neighbours and stopped them, allowing briars and other green rubbish to spring up and tangle their shoots in the thin, dead twigs. Holly and birch and hazel had sprung up to fill in the gaps, turning the copse into a fortified position. Poldarn smiled; talk about your tall thin trees—

Two crows got up and hung circling in the air, almost directly above his head, screaming abuse at him—

He was still singing, instinctively, without thinking. And so was somebody else:

> *Old crow sitting in a tall thin tree,*
> *And along comes the Dodger and he says, 'That's me.'*

Somebody else was singing the song, from behind the wall. At once the monk yanked back on his reins, making his horse rear, and started shouting orders. The monks were drawing swords – why? There wasn't anybody to fight—

—Yes, there was. From over the wall, and from a ditch on

the other side of the road that Poldarn hadn't even noticed, there came a great crowd of men, a hundred, perhaps two hundred, all standing up at the same time, like soldiers performing a drill. But they weren't armed—

The horseman on his right yelled something and started his draw. Difficult to gauge circles on horseback; Poldarn threw his weight to his left and slid off his horse, the quickest way of getting clear, and as his shoulder connected painfully with a large stone in the road, the horseman's sword sliced through the parcel of air where his head would have been. As he tried to get up and found that for some reason (some reason that hurt a lot) he couldn't, he saw another horseman slashing down at one of the men who'd come from behind the wall; some cut, clean through the spine on the diagonal, missing the collarbone, uncharacteristically wasted effort. Poldarn couldn't see any reason why the horseman should attack like that—

> *Old crow sitting in a tall thin tree,*
> *Old crow sitting in a tall thin tree—*

—The same tune, he realised. The other voice had been singing the same tune and words that meant the same thing, but in a different language.

Something hit the ground a few inches behind his head. He jerked his head back and bent his spine, and found he was nose to nose with a dead man, the monk who'd been riding on his right. A pair of boots stepped over him; it was one of the men from the ditch, and he wasn't unarmed by any means. He was swinging a short, fat sword with an unmistakable curved, concave blade, what Poldarn had come to know as a backsabre. The leg of his horse was in the way and he wasn't able to see the blow land, but he heard it, a sucking, hissing sound, like a man pulling his boot out of deep mud.

I think I probably know who these people are.

He'd been planning on lying still and pretending to be dead, but the horse backed up and scuffed him in the face with the back of its hoof, not hard, but enough to make him wince. He noticed one of the strangers watching him, and figured he must have seen the movement.

He knew the man's face: long, with a pointed chin and straggly, wispy hair. He was holding a backsabre, letting it hang by the rear horn of the hilt from two fingers. A sword-monk, on foot, stepped quickly up behind him – Poldarn couldn't see the sword in his hand, but he knew where it was from the position of the monk's arms.

Eyvind; that was the stranger's name. Pointless, remembering it a heartbeat before the poor fool had his head cut off—

Later, Poldarn figured that Eyvind must have seen a change in the look in his eyes and somehow realised what it meant; something must have warned him of the danger, because he spun round astonishingly quickly, using the speed and momentum to swing the backsabre in a down-slanted side cut that opened the monk up a finger's breadth below his ribcage. The monk noticed what had happened, but he'd already embarked upon his own cut, which should have split Eyvind's head in two, like an apple. When it arrived, however, somehow Eyvind wasn't there. Poldarn didn't see him move, he just seemed to relocate, materialising instantly a yard to the monk's right. He tugged the backsabre out of the wound like a tired woodcutter freeing his axe, and let the monk flop to the ground; the next moment he was busy again, but Poldarn couldn't see, there was a boot in the way.

By the time it moved, it all seemed to be over.

Chapter Twenty-Three

He was standing on a cliff, with thin, wiry grass under his feet and a brisk, cold wind on his face, staring out at a blue-grey sea the colour of steel in the forge fire, just before it turns red. In the middle of the sea, he could see the white sail of a ship. Fifty yards or so to his left, two crows were pecking at something he couldn't quite see.

When he looked up again, the sail had disappeared; but he was minded to walk down the steep, rather terrifying path that ran diagonally across the cliff face, like the cut of a sword-monk's blade on a man's neck. At the bottom of the path there was a little triangle of shingle, folded in the arms of two spits of rock: a private one-berth harbour set in a fortress wall of gleaming yellow sandstone. You'd never find it if you didn't know exactly where to look.

Either the ship couldn't make it in, or it was in a hurry; instead they'd lowered a little frail boat, leather hides stretched over birch ribs and sewn up in thick, well-greased seams. Two men were rowing, two others sat with their backs to him. The boat was lower in the water than it should have been.

While he waited for the boat to crawl through the lively waves, he took a moment to admire the ship, not that he knew anything much about ships, but it was the aesthetics rather than the technicalities that appealed to him. Long and sweet it appeared to him; the castles at either end melodramatically high, the wide, fat middle absurdly low. It was built to roll with the waves without capsizing, even he could see that; as it bobbed and wallowed in the water, its lines seemed to flow unceasingly, sinuous and meretricious as a dancer.

You'd never get me out in one of those things, he told himself. Not if you paid me.

Then he felt impatient, without yet knowing why, so much so that he splashed several yards into the water, wincing as the cold unpleasantness seeped in round his toes and ankles. The boat was still a long way out when he took a deep breath and shouted, 'Have you got it?'

One of the men with his back to him turned half around; the movement was ill advised and nearly swamped the boat. The oarsmen yelled at him to sit still at the same time as he shouted something inaudible, presumably a reply to the question.

He found this extremely frustrating. 'I said, have you got it?' he yelled, even louder. This time he could just make out the man's reply. 'Yes.'

That was evidently the answer he'd wanted to hear; he could feel joy flooding his heart, as palpably as the sea had flooded his worn-out boots. Of course, he hadn't got a clue what *it* was.

Perhaps it was because this was a dream, and in a dream things happen at extreme speed, so that you can dream a week in a few minutes of real time, but the minute or so it took for the boat to reach the shore seemed to last an entire lifetime. Just before the brittle prow bit into the shingle, a single crow dropped down on the rock beside him and turned its head away.

'Well?' he shouted.

The man who'd answered his question hopped over the side into the water, then reached back into the boat and picked up a familiar-looking bundle. 'He's asleep,' the man said, 'for a change, the little bastard. You're bloody lucky we didn't pitch him over the side.'

'It's a boy, then.'

The man scowled. 'Well, of course it's a boy. Do you think we'd have bothered otherwise? Here, you take the dirty little snot. If I never see him again, that'll suit me just fine.'

Stepping a yard or so further into the water he took the bundle from the man's outstretched hands and at once felt an all-consuming sense of relief that nearly stopped him from breathing.

'My grandson,' he murmured.

'Yes,' the man from the boat confirmed. 'Almost as big a pain in the bum as his grandpa, if you ask me. Next time you want a kid fetched from a long way over the sea, do it yourself. Now, if you don't mind getting out of the way, we've got *valuable* cargo to land.'

Some other men had come down the path; they were helping the men from the boat with barrels and jars and boxes. The baby in his arms looked like some exotic wild animal.

'Thank you,' he said, and the man from the boat nodded.

'That's all right,' he replied. 'Tursten was a good lad, I'm sorry.'

He turned away and started on the long, painful climb back to the top. He didn't notice the gradient, or the treacherous footing, or the wind that tried to comb him off the side of the cliff. He was utterly fascinated by the way the strange creature was opening and closing its tiny five-fingered hands, almost but not quite the way a human being would do it. It occurred to him that if some inhuman thing, a monster or a god, were to take a human body to live in for reasons of expedience or policy, probably it would familiarise itself with the way the thing worked by flexing the muscles and testing the nerves and tendons, just as this strange object seemed to be doing. The thought made him stop for a moment and frown. The idea had been that his dead son would somehow have found his way into this small body (because Tursten couldn't really be dead, that would be unthinkable; there had to be a way round it), but now that he was actually holding it, he wasn't sure. Maybe something else was in there, as well as or instead of Tursten.

Well, he thought, it'll be interesting finding out. Even if it is my son, he can't be expected to remember anything of his previous life, it'll be as if Tursten had come home but with all his memories wiped away – in which case, of course, he wouldn't be Tursten at all any more. Take away someone's memories and all you've got left is an empty bottle, a piece of scrap only fit for putting in the fire and bashing into something else.

At the top of the cliff he paused and looked back. There was the sail, more or less exactly where it had been when he first looked down from there (but since then, everything had changed; the old world had come to an end and a new one had slipped in and taken over the physical remains). He noticed something yellow and shiny in the child's left hand, just visible through the gaps between the soft, damp fingers. A gold ring, or something of the sort; he wondered where that had come from, and what it meant.

The child opened its mouth, miming a cry though no sound came out. He cast about in his mind for a nice soothing lullaby, but all he could think of was:

> *Old crow sitting in a tall thin tree,*
> *Old crow sitting in a tall thin tree—*

Hardly a wonderfully apt choice; but the kid seemed to like it, so he carried on:

Dodger sitting on the red-hot coal,
Dodger sitting on the red-hot coal,
Dodger sitting on the red-hot coal,
Then he jumped in the slacky-tub to save his soul.

The child started to howl, which suggested a certain degree of taste, if nothing else. He laughed, and started to sing 'Sweet Meadowgrass' instead, but found he could only remember the first two lines.

He took his time walking home, as if part of him didn't really want to get there. At the top of Enner's Steep he stopped and leaned against the orchard gate, looking down over the sprawl of thatched and tiled roofs of the farm. For some reason he felt a need to preserve an image of it in his mind, as if something he was just about to do would change it for ever. He made a careful mental note of the position of each building, taking the main house as an obvious datum and locating the barns and outhouses in relation to it, then he looked up at the sun to check the time, though that was hardly necessary. At Enner's, you didn't need the sun to tell you the time, you looked up at the thin, spindly fir trees and then down at the yard. If the crows were roosting, it was early morning, midday or evening. If they were in the yard, mobbing the stalls, it was morning or afternoon feed. If they were pitched out on the grass in the long meadow, it was mid-morning or mid-afternoon; and if they were crowding together on the branches of the apple orchard, it was morning or evening milking and the boys had driven them off the yard as they walked the stock through. As often as not, you could tell the time with your eyes shut just by listening to them. All the years he'd lived here, he'd been aware of them nearly all the time, their single cold mind reaching into his, groping in the dark for his thoughts – where was he going, what was he doing, was it safe to be out or was it time to fall back to safe positions and wait for him to go away? Once a year, ever since he was old enough to toddle and throw a stone, they'd assaulted the castles and cities in the fir copse with every weapon at their disposal, from pebbles and slingshots to blunt arrows and twenty-foot poles, trying to break up the nests while the season's children were too young to fly; every year, no matter how hard they tried to wipe them out, they killed or drove off a third of them, thereby preserving an exact balance with their normal rate of population growth. It was the only time they could even pretend to win a victory against the rookery; the rest of the time, the raiders raided, stole, wrecked and withdrew, undefeated and unassailable.

(Tursten hated the crows, always had; he could remember him as a small boy, standing in the yard screaming at them. As he got older he stopped screaming and went quiet, his cold, savage mind devising some better way, and as always he'd found one. He collected twelve birds whose wings he'd managed to break with stones, and pegged them out a dozen yards out from the meadow hedge, their legs tethered to short sticks. At midday, the birds in the trees flew down and pitched next to them, assuming they were the scouts sent out to find safe pasture; Tursten was waiting for them in a hide of freshly cut hazel, perfectly still, with his forty-pound bow and plenty of lead-nosed blunts. Every bird he stunned, he pegged out, until he had dozens of decoys; and the more decoys he put out, the more birds came to join them. At dusk he went out and killed them all, apart from half a dozen he kept for the next day. After three days the survivors got wise and circled above his head all morning, screaming at him the way he'd screamed at them; he appreciated that. It was the greatest victory ever achieved in the war, but he never managed to repeat it; and two years later, the numbers were back to where they'd always been.)

'Your dad was a clever man,' he told the child, who was asleep now. That was no lie, he reflected. Tursten could be a vicious little bastard when he wanted to, but he was clever.

Probably would've made a good soldier, if he'd hated the enemy like he hated the crows.

As he walked down the meadow slope he caught sight of a face framed in the upstairs window, but at that distance he couldn't be sure who it was, Elgerd or Bergtura. Probably not Elgerd. It occurred to him that he hadn't really considered how she'd take it, being expected to bring up her dead husband's child by some foreign woman whom he'd raped and who'd then killed him. Come to think of it, he couldn't remember any occasion when anybody had stopped to consider Elgerd's feelings about anything, so it was probably safe to assume that she didn't have any. Not that it mattered, Bergtura had enough for both of them (Gods help us all!). It was a safe bet that the face in the window was hers.

Well, he thought, for some reason, it's too late now. He pushed open the back door with his left hand, and heard his wife's clogs clumping down the stairs. He wondered what on earth he was going to say to her; something utterly banal, probably, such as, 'Here he is,' or, 'I'm home.'

'Here,' someone called out, 'you missed one.'

Poldarn opened his eyes, the dream exploding like a glass bowl dropped on a stone floor. He started to get up, but someone behind him put a heavy boot between his shoulder blades, forcing him back down into the mud and perceptibly stretching his bones. Out of options once again, and this time he was on the ground and couldn't move. He made himself relax, theorising that the pain would be less if his muscles were tense and stressed when the blade cut into them. He felt surprisingly, agreeably calm.

'Hold on.' The voice could have been Eyvind, but he didn't know him well enough to be sure. 'Leave him alone, will you? I know him.'

'You sure?' A different voice, puzzled. 'He was with the column.'

'Yes, well, he would be. Byrni, stop treading on the poor bugger.'

The pressure relaxed. 'What's all this about, then?' Another voice, this time directly above him.

'You'll see. Hey, whatever your name is. Say something, that'll prove you know Western.'

That made sense; nobody in the empire knew the raiders' language, which was what he assumed they were all talking. 'Is that you?' he managed to say. 'Eyvind? The man I met on the road?'

'That's him,' said the voice. 'Yes, it's me. Don't just stand there, you bloody fools, help him up.'

They hauled him to his feet as if he was a dead weight, an inanimate object of some kind. He saw the man who'd called himself Eyvind, the same one he'd seen before, on the road and later in the battle. *Please,* he prayed silently to the divine Poldarn, *don't let anything happen to this man, not until I'm safe and out of here.* All around, the raiders were stripping the dead, bending to their work like field hands pulling carrots. He noticed one of them dead on the ground; all the other bodies were sword-monks, carved with deep cuts sloping diagonally inwards from the junction of shoulder and neck.

'Yes,' Eyvind said, 'I definitely know this man. Saved my life.' That was an exaggeration, as Poldarn remembered it; all he'd done was refrain from killing him when he killed his companion. But his memory was tricky, at the best of times. 'He's one of us, I promise you.'

'Really?' The man who'd been treading on his spine sounded good-natured, curious. 'Then what was he doing with all these freaks?'

Poldarn remembered something. It came as a flash of bright light in his mind, blotting out everything around him, even the fear of dying that was still clouding up his mind; but it wasn't anything special, just a memory of himself standing next to an older man in a ditch beside a bank – the man with

him was draping a little net across the mouth of a rabbit hole
with his right hand; his left was down by his side, holding the
back legs of a furiously kicking rabbit. He wasn't taking any
notice of the animal; a methodical man, one thing at a time.
Get the net back in place first, in case the dog flushed another
one out, then kill the one you've got in hand. While he was
resetting the net, the man was talking about something else,
some routine job they'd have to start tomorrow if the weather
held off. That same calm, detached, methodical economy of
movement that the raiders displayed as they searched the dead
bodies for articles of value (things trivial enough: a penknife,
a sharpening-steel, a belt buckle, a dozen horn buttons; obviously valuable enough to these people to be worth killing for,
as the rabbit's meat and fur were to the old man), and carefully
and thoroughly despatched any monks who were still alive.

Eyvind was saying something to the other man, Byrni.
Everybody else had lost interest and gone back to work. 'My
guess is,' Eyvind was saying, 'Uncle Cari'll know who he is.
He was much more involved in all the preparations than I
was; at least, I was there but I wasn't listening half the time.'

Byrni laughed. 'Sitting still's never been your strong point,'
he said. 'All right, can't see any harm in it. If he does anything
I don't like, mind, I'll cut him in half.' He turned his head and
looked Poldarn in the eye. 'Did you hear that, mister?' he
said.

Poldarn nodded, to indicate that he had. 'Don't worry
about Byrni,' Eyvind interrupted, 'he just likes scaring
people.'

'He's very good at it,' Poldarn replied.

For some reason, Byrni thought that was enormously funny.
'He's a smartass and no mistake,' he said, clouting Poldarn on
the shoulder with his left hand. In his right hand he held a
backsabre, its cutting edge dirty with blood, dust and grime.
He looked as if he'd just been trimming back a hedge, and had
paused for a whet and a sly mouthful of beer.

'You two.' Someone else, further up the road. 'Whatever you're doing, do it later. We've got a war to fight, or had you forgotten?'

The raiders weren't hurrying, just doing their work more quickly. Poldarn noticed how little effort they wasted, like old men doing a familiar job. Mostly they were young, between nineteen and twenty-four, but they looked older; they had the broad chests and thick necks of hard workers, square heads and solid jaws, small noses and broad foreheads, and their skin had been burnished by long exposure to cold, hard winds. They didn't look like him at all, but the way they moved and stood and walked seemed *right*, in a way that none of the other people he'd come across did. The monks, for example, moved with almost excessive grace, as if everything they did had been practised for hours in front of a mirror – the grace wasn't inherent but painfully acquired. In Sansory, people moved too quickly; in the villages, they lumbered, as if they were forever carrying heavy sacks on their shoulders and wearing lead-soled boots. In Mael, they'd walked about like factory hands or field workers coming home after a double shift. Copis – she'd been different, her movements were like someone dancing the steps of one dance to the tune of another, and making it work thanks to an amazing natural ability to improvise. These men, he realised, moved entirely naturally, the way humans were meant to move. He couldn't imagine one of them slipping in mud or catching his foot in a tree root or accidentally barging into a heavily laden trestle in a market.

Eyvind grabbed his arm and pulled him to one side. 'I think it'll be all right,' he said. 'I don't suppose you've been able to remember anything since the last time I saw you?'

Poldarn shook his head.

'Oh well. So what were you doing with this bunch of old women?' He prodded a dead man with his toe by way of illustration.

Poldarn cracked his face with a grin. 'Actually,' he said, 'I was on my way to be killed. They were to make sure I didn't get away.'

'Ah.' Eyvind nodded. 'Aren't you the lucky one, then? What did you do to get them so annoyed at you?'

'I wish I knew,' Poldarn replied. 'They knew who I am, that's for sure, but I don't believe what they told me.'

'Really? What was that?'

Poldarn smiled. 'Oh, they said I was one of them, and I murdered a brother. And then they said I was the empire's most famous general. And then they said I had to go and murder the empire's most famous general, or they'd cut my throat.'

Eyvind gave him a startled look. 'Fine,' he said. 'They enjoy playing games, obviously. You know, I have a feeling you'll be better off with us.'

'Me too. But what makes you think I'm entitled?'

'You don't know, do you?' Eyvind grinned. He had straight, white teeth, unlike most people in Sansory. Of course, Poldarn had good teeth too. 'You talk our language; not only that, you talk with a strong South Island accent. Even if you were one of them who'd learned Western (and we've never heard of any of 'em who's lived long enough to do that), you couldn't do the woollyback voice, not unless you were born and bred within fifteen miles of Eddinsbrook.' He thumped Poldarn between the shoulder blades with the flat of his hand; deceptively strong. 'I don't know who you are now, friend, but I can tell you who you were once. And this lot know it as well as I do, or you'd be dead on your face right now.'

Poldarn let what he'd been told sink in for a moment. 'But they don't look anything like me,' he said.

'So what? We're all North Islanders. On South Island, they're all as ugly as you are; and on Unnskerry too, but they don't talk like that. More nasal, if you know what I mean, like they've always got a half a carrot shoved up their noses.'

Poldarn considered that. 'All right,' he said. 'But if I'm one of you, what the hell was I doing wandering around on a battle-field surrounded by dead people?'

'I've been thinking about that,' Eyvind replied. 'And there's at least one perfectly simple explanation. For years, you see, we've been planting a few of our people here, to spy out the land, let us know what to expect and where the good prospects are, keep us in touch with the traitors on their side who think they're on our side, if you can follow all that. My guess is that you're one of them. It all fits quite neatly,' he went on, pulling an earring out of a dead monk's ear like a man picking blackberries. 'If you think about it, one of us who's spent a year or so pretending to be one of them – well, he couldn't help getting just a bit confused, having to be two completely different people at the same time. Then, suppose he gets a bash on the head and can't remember for sure whether he's who he really is or who he's been pretending to be – well, you get the idea, I'm sure. And that's who I think you are.'

Abruptly they left the road and plunged into the wood. Poldarn found it very hard to keep up – where Eyvind and his people always seemed to find deer tracks and gaps in the brambles, he kept blundering into thorny tangles, tripping and staggering and ripping his hands and face against trailing fingers of briar. He had a feeling that he wasn't at home in woods.

'Of course,' Eyvind told him, when he said as much. 'No woods worth talking about on South Island.' He shook his head. 'I keep forgetting, you don't remember it at all.'

Poldarn decided to change the subject. 'So how did you find these people?' he asked. 'Last time I saw you, you were on your own on the other side of the Bohec.'

Eyvind nodded. 'That's right,' he said. 'But thankfully I got it in my head that I should keep going north; crossed the river and started walking in as straight a line as I could manage.

Then one day I came over the top of a hill and there they were. It was enough to make a man religious, I'm telling you.' He shook his head again; it was a common enough gesture among these people. Poldarn had caught himself doing something similar once or twice. 'This lot's just one scouting party,' he went on. 'Apparently the army that's over here at the moment's the biggest expedition ever to leave the islands. Ever hear of a man called Feron Amathy?'

Poldarn nodded. 'All the time,' he said.

'And nothing good, I'll bet. Well, he's the brains behind all this, apparently. He's got some scheme or other for taking over the empire; we don't give a damn about that, goes without saying, but his plans fit in perfectly with ours, and he's given us all kinds of useful information, things our own spies would never have found out – sally-ports, blind spots, soft spots where you can dig under walls, you name it. He says he learned it all back when he was hired by most of these cities as a mercenary soldier, at one time or another. You can believe that or not, whichever way suits you best. Personally, I figure anybody who'd sell out his own people like that doesn't deserve to live.'

Poldarn didn't express an opinion. 'And where are you off to now?' he asked. 'Joining up with the rest of the army and going home?'

'Don't you believe it. We've hardly started yet. Talking of which, as far as I'm concerned you can hang on with us and we'll give you a ride home – back to the islands, I mean. Best offer you'll ever get.'

Poldarn thought for a moment before replying. 'I'd like that,' he said.

For men who didn't appear to be in a hurry, the raiders moved deceptively quickly. Poldarn soon came to understand how they achieved their effects of suddenly vanishing from one battlefield and miraculously appearing at the next. Magic had nothing to do with it; instead they used the terrain, following river valleys, crests and ridges to stay out of sight, and marching at top speed whenever they had no alternative but to cross open ground. They never seemed to get tired, either.

'After all that,' said one of them, coming back from a cautious glimpse over the top of a ridge, 'we're early.'

'Typical,' said another. 'They must've stopped for a rest, or picked a fight somewhere. That's the trouble with the Green River boys, they won't take these things seriously.'

Poldarn didn't need to look over the ridge to know where he was. On the other side of the hill was Deymeson, and the raiders were here to attack it. He hadn't needed to be told that, either.

'You're not going to be much use with nothing but sweat in the palm of your hand,' one of them said to him. 'Here, try this for size.' He reached over his shoulder and wriggled out of a strap, from which hung a cloth bundle about as long as Poldarn's arm. Under the cloth was a backsabre.

'Belonged to my cousin Bearci,' the man went on, 'but he didn't make it this far. I'll have it back when you've finished with it.'

It would have been rude to refuse outright, and he couldn't explain – *I'd rather not, thanks; you see, as soon as I can get away from you people, I'm going to run to Deymeson as fast as I can go and warn them you're coming.* 'Thank you very much,' he said. 'I'll try and take good care of it.'

'Oh, it's nothing special, not old or anything. Fits you nicely, though.' He was looking at Poldarn's hands. 'Lucky to find one your weight.'

Poldarn realised that, without thinking, he'd been doing back flips, letting the sword flop backwards through his fingers and then bringing it back up again with a sharp snap of the wrist. He frowned and tried the other way, the widdershins flip (harder to control and flashier). He was very good at it, a fact that wasn't lost on the man who'd just lent him the sword.

'That's hours of practice, that is,' the man said. 'I couldn't do that, even when I was a kid.'

'Thank you,' Poldarn replied. 'Obviously there was a stage in my life when I had way too much time on my hands.'

The man wasn't quite sure what to make of that. 'My name's Sitrych,' he said. 'From Anniswood, in Blackdale. Do you know those parts at all?'

'Anything's possible,' Poldarn replied, 'apparently.'

Sitrych gave him a strange look, part concern and part amusement, as if he'd encountered a two-headed mouse. 'Well,' he said, 'best of luck with it. Watch out, it's sharp.'

'Poldarn wasn't sure whether that was some ancient customary joke or well-meaning advice to a presumed idiot. 'Thanks,' he said, 'I'll be careful with it. Don't want to do anybody an injury.'

Sitrych frowned, shook his head and walked away. The raiders were doing something, though it wasn't immediately apparent what it was; they were falling into groups – not hurrying so you'd notice, but in a few minutes they'd all found their places and formed ranks and files – and they were all looking up at the ridge, preparing their minds. They stopped talking without anybody telling them to; in fact, Poldarn realised, he hadn't heard anybody give any orders, and he had no idea who their leader was, assuming they had one.

Then they started to move. It wasn't walking or running; they seemed to flow, like an incoming wave on the beach that's lapping round your ankles before you realise, and by the time Poldarn had figured out what was going on, they were over the ridge and vanishing out of sight. 'Come on,' someone said cheerfully behind him – not someone he'd spoken to – and he felt a broad hand in the small of his back pushing him forward. Whoever it was didn't seem to be running, but Poldarn had to run to keep up with him.

Over the ridge; and he saw Deymeson in the valley below, the gate in the invisible wall and the town rearing up out of the plain like a shying horse. The rest of the raiders were definitely running now, with the gradient to help them; they were covering the ground ridiculously fast, moving easily and gracefully, like deer. Not running away, Poldarn thought, running toward; here were people who knew exactly what they were doing and why. He wondered what that must feel like.

The man who'd encouraged him over the ridge was right behind his shoulder, keeping perfect pace with him, unobtrusively deliberate on the extreme edge of his circle. There was no possibility whatsoever of getting away, he was committed to these people and their course of action; they'd swallowed him up and absorbed him as easily as the incoming tide absorbs a rockpool. That was disconcerting; right up to the moment when they'd cleared the ridge he'd been reassuring himself that as soon as an opportunity presented itself he'd sneak away and warn the monks – his people – and help them fight, as he was morally obliged to do (after all, these were the raiders he'd heard so much about, the common enemy, the forces of evil). But something had happened, so subtle that he hadn't noticed it happening, and now that was out of the question. He was committed, he'd already taken sides (without knowing it, apparently) and here he was, part of the unstoppable onset of darkness—

(Except that, if he allowed his concentration to slip for a moment, he could already see himself thinking of these people as his friends, his people, his own; it was as if he'd slotted into place, suddenly and in the dark, or as if he'd been wandering in circles in a blinding fog on the moors and finally stumbled on a house, and only discovered when he pushed the door open that it was his own.)

Academic, in any case, since even if he managed to outrun the man behind him and the rest of the raiders, all of whom were faster than he was, and got to the abbey gates and raised the alarm, it'd only be a matter of moments before the raiders caught up with him, and what could the sword-monks do to save themselves in that time? Besides, if he had enough time to achieve anything he wouldn't spend it warning the abbot, he'd waste it looking for Copis (waste it, because he was sure she was dead, or too heavily guarded to be rescued).

There was nothing he could do for the monks. Unless they could outfight the raiders, they were already dead. In fact, he could see them now, their bodies draped and dumped and piled and dropped in the streets and over and behind walls, under tables and beds where they'd tried to hide, heaped up in stairwells or at the foot of towers they'd fallen or been pushed from. He could see the dust and dirt forming a skin over pools of their blood, the caked and clotted blood masking the tremendous backsabre cuts, from the side of the neck to the middle of the chest; quite vividly, like a man recalling some traumatic memory, he saw them, most dead, a few still dying, painfully dragging breath into punctured lungs, dribbling blood from their mouths like old men or children trying to drink soup. He saw Torcuat, the monk who'd arrested him when he tried to run, lying on his back on the dorter steps, his head lolling at an impossible angle to his shoulders, his eyes wide open. He saw the abbot himself, only just visible under a pile of arms and legs and trunks and heads, all haphazard and confused, like the scrap in Sansory market; a cut had split his face on a diagonal running from the right eye socket to the left corner of his mouth, though the stroke that killed him had been a stab just under the ribcage, with the palm-wide point of a backsabre. He saw Copis, still alive, one leg severed at the knee, her back broken over the side of a cart—

That'd be right, he thought; I can't remember the past, only the future.

The raiders were at the invisible wall already. The guard at the gatehouse took one look at them and ran, but the foremost raider caught up with him before he reached the bottom of the hill, grabbed him by the left shoulder, spun him round and ripped him open with a short, quick flick of the wrist. As

usual, the street leading up the hill was empty; the raider
who'd just killed the guard didn't stop or even break stride,
but started to run up the hill, hardly slowing down in spite of
the gradient. Meanwhile, five other columns of raiders had
appeared out of nowhere and were streaming across the open
ground; Poldarn was sure there were others that he couldn't
see, approaching the hill from the north, west and east. He
could almost see them, or at least he remembered seeing them
pouring into the abbey courtyard, like floodwater overwhelming a house. At some point he'd quickened his pace so that he
was almost keeping up. It hadn't been a conscious decision,
but he found he didn't feel tired or short of breath, it was as if
he was drawing on a shared strength that came from the others
all around him. He saw Sitrych, the man who'd lent him the
sword, dodging round the side of the gatehouse and lengthening his stride as he approached the hill, and another man
he'd spoken to on the way there – Engfar, his name was –
only a pace or two behind him, and gaining. If he'd had the
breath, he'd have been tempted to cheer them on, as if he had
money on the outcome.

By the time he reached the bottom of the hill he could just
hear the sound of something going on at the top over the
pounding of his own heart. He kept running, without knowing how; he was a boat on the back of a big wave, arching its
back like a cat before jumping on its prey. At one point he had
to jump over the dead body of a monk to keep himself from
tripping and sprawling. Someone was screaming somewhere,
but he had no way of knowing what it was about.

The next monk he met was definitely still on his feet, a lay
brother who stepped out of a house a yard or so in front of
him holding a short pike. Yesterday he'd have stopped and
taken guard, knowing how difficult it is for a swordsman to get
the better of a spearman in a one-to-one fight. Today he
swerved round him, slashing wildly as he went past to ward
off any thrust the man might make – no intention of killing

anybody, just defence. He didn't feel any shock of contact run up his arm from the sword blade, and he didn't have time to look round. The lay brother was dead anyway, he'd already seen it, so there didn't seem to be much point.

His magic strength evaporated, suddenly and completely, about fifty yards from the top of the hill. Without warning his knees folded under him, and once he'd stopped he felt a pain in his chest so severe that nothing else could possibly matter. When he could at last see again he watched the raiders engulfing a couple of lone sword-monks who'd stood and waited for them instead of running away. When the raiders had passed them by, they were still there, but broken and cut up, ground into the dirt until their shapes ceased to be human.

(So this is how the raiders win all their battles, he decided; the deadly secret of their success. What would General Cronan have thought of it, he wondered; would he have realised that there was nothing at all to be done about it, this ability to run past and through their enemies as if they weren't really there? He dismissed the thought abruptly.)

'Dawdling again.' His self-appointed shadow, directly behind him. 'What's the matter, stone in your shoe?'

'Worn out,' Poldarn replied. 'All this running about is too bloody energetic for me.'

The voice laughed. 'You need to get yourself in shape,' it said. 'You'll miss out on the good bit if you aren't careful.'

'There's a good bit?'

'Oh yes,' the voice replied, 'there's a good bit.'

Poldarn found the good bit soon afterwards, after he'd dragged himself up the rest of the slope and into the abbey proper. The porters hadn't had time to close the gates; the raiders had streamed past them, cutting them down as they went almost as an afterthought. The monks were spilling out into the yard singly or in groups of two or three, apparently not realising what was going on – many of them weren't wearing their swords – and the raiders were surging up round them, six or seven to one. That was beyond the limits of religion; even the most advanced forms, practised by the upper ten per cent of the order, only envisaged facing four opponents at once. Faced with such blatant violation of the rules, such an abomination, the monks weren't even trying to draw, and those that did found their cuts parried with moves that weren't on the syllabus, while illegally placed enemies stepped up behind them and severed their necks. True, a group of about twenty monks were crowded together in the doorway of a janitor's hut and were standing shoulder to shoulder, their drawn swords forming an impenetrable fence; but the raiders were standing off fifteen yards or so and pelting them with bricks from a pile left over from some minor building works. Poldarn watched, fascinated; for the first dozen seconds or so, the monks managed to bat the bricks out of the air with their swords (those lovingly nursed cutting edges, sharpened with a steel instead of a stone and lightly anointed with camellia oil every night and every morning), but then there was one brick too many, and it cracked a monk just about the right eyebrow and he grunted and folded up; one gap compromised the wall, and five seconds later the raiders rushed in to chop up the fallen. They're overwhelming the monks, Poldarn thought, just as they overwhelmed me. They don't fight, they simply prevail. Like gods.

A monk came running straight at him. He recognised him: Torcuat, who'd presided over his defeat and humiliation, back when he'd tried to escape. Torcuat's face was distorted into a mask of sheer hatred; it was the masterpiece of a great artist who'd spend his entire life trying to paint the pure essence of an emotion. His sword was drawn and he was holding it in both hands over his head as he ran. Poldarn turned to face him and flipped the backsabre over the back of his hand – showing off, and he didn't know why, it had just happened – and just as the monk edged against the outer limit of his circle, like a runner breasting the finishing rope, he stuck out his hand with the sabre in it, a very short, mundane little movement, the sort of thing a novice would do from pure instinct on his first day in the schools. Torcuat's momentum drove the broad point deep into his stomach until it jarred against bone, whereupon the shock of contact shot up Poldarn's arm to his elbow, making him let go. Torcuat fell forward on to the sabre hilt, and as he landed, the sword-point burst through his back like a crocus.

I didn't do anything, really, Poldarn thought, as he rolled the dead monk on to his side with his boot. He had to stand on Torcuat's chest to get enough purchase to haul the sword out again (but he couldn't just abandon it, it didn't belong to him). *I suppose that counts as revenge, but I wasn't really all that fussed. I didn't blame him, personally.*

'Nicely,' said the voice behind his shoulder. 'These freaks, they think they know it all, but when it comes to a real fight, they haven't got a clue.'

Poldarn straightened his back. 'No,' he said, 'they haven't.'

'Goes to show,' the voice went on. 'If you'd been one of them, I expect you'd have tried to have a fencing match. But you sorted him out just like I'd have done, so I guess you're one of us after all. So that's all right.'

'Good,' Poldarn said. Part of him seemed to mean it.

'Right,' the voice went on, 'now that I've seen you kill one of 'em, not much point in me hanging round you any more. You carry on, and have a good time. Any idea where they keep the small, valuable stuff?'

Poldarn thought for a moment. 'You could try the abbot's lodgings,' he said. 'I saw some nice inkwells and candlesticks and small silver lamps.'

'Sounds good to me,' the voice said, and someone brushed past Poldarn's left shoulder. He got a glimpse of the man's back as he strode away.

This, then, was the good bit. Judging by the number of bodies scattered round the main yard, most of the monks must already be dead; certainly, their numbers had to have fallen below the critical point where they could no longer mount any kind of meaningful resistance. Poldarn guessed that there would now be a short interval for looting, after which they'd burn the place down and be on their way – down the hill into the town, maybe, or perhaps their schedule wouldn't allow it. Over at the coach-house, they were backing out carts ready to be loaded up with good things (harvest festival, bringing home the fruits of hard work and divine favour). And for his own part, he was on his own, with nobody watching. Copis, he thought.

Of course, he had no way of knowing whether she was still alive, or still in the abbey, let alone where to find her, but instinct had served him well this far, and he had nothing else to do. If she was still alive, chances were she'd be in whatever the monks used as a prison or dungeon. From what he'd seen of the order, he figured it was a safe bet they had something of the sort.

A live monk would be able to tell him where to find the dungeons, but there didn't seem to be any of them left. Poldarn looked round, wishing he knew what a dungeon looked like, and suddenly felt an urge to try a small door at the back of what he'd assumed was some kind of store, because it only had two small, barred windows high up in the wall. *Divine intuition,* he muttered to himself, and walked quickly across the yard, stepping over the dead where necessary.

The door was open. There was a monk in the small outer room; he was sitting on the floor with his back to the wall, both hands pressed to his stomach. When he tried to stand up, his knees buckled and he flopped down on his face. Poldarn put a foot on the back of his neck and stabbed him once through the ear, after which he stopped moving. Then he frowned and flipped the backsabre over a couple of times, wondering if there was something familiar about the monk's face. Probably just his imagination.

Whoever I used to be, I know who I am now, and that's all that matters.

He liked the sound of that; it was simple, and positive. He saw another door in front of him, and kicked it open.

It wasn't a dungeon, it was a store. The wall opposite the door was covered from floor to ceiling with shelves, lined with thousands of neatly folded blankets. Against the wall to the right there stood five enormous wooden bins, heaped almost to overflow point with charcoal. To his left was a large pile of kindling, tied up in small bundles, enough to light one regulation fire. Standing in front of the kindling was Copis, and she was holding a sword in both hands.

'Stay away from me,' she said. 'Or I'll kill you.'

Poldarn hadn't been expecting that. 'Copis, it's me,' he said. 'I've come to rescue you,' he added, feeling extremely foolish.

'Go away,' she said, then her face relaxed just a little. 'You bloody fool, haven't you worked it out yet?'

Poldarn shook his head.

'Then you're even more stupid than you look,' she snapped. She looked embarrassed, as if he'd caught her stealing from the cashbox. 'You don't still think we came here by accident, do you?'

'Accident,' he repeated. 'What are you talking about?'

She sighed, as if he was a small child being deliberately obtuse. 'I brought you here,' she said. 'You still don't get it? I'm your *keeper*.'

She wasn't making any sense. No, he didn't want what she'd just said to make sense. 'You knew?' he asked.

'All right.' She lowered the sword, but he recognised the position of the blade as a hidden guard. 'I'll spell it out for you, shall I? I serve the order. Do you want me to go on?'

'Yes,' he said.

Copis scowled. 'If you insist,' she said. 'I was assigned to you. Mostly just to keep an eye on what you were doing and report back, but if necessary I'd be there to protect you from being assassinated, or kill you myself if that's what they wanted me to do. When your escort was attacked beside the river – by these people, damn it, the raiders – I admit I panicked and stayed out of it; actually it wasn't me so much as that waste of space they'd paired me with, the man you killed—'

'Hold on,' Poldarn said. 'You're talking about the first time we met, just after I woke up—'

'Of course I am,' Copis replied. 'What else did you think I meant?'

'So you knew all along.' Suddenly he couldn't breathe, but there were more important things than breathing. 'You *know* who I am. You can tell me—'

Copis shook her head. 'I'm sorry,' she said. 'But I have no orders to give you that information.' Her words were stilted, out of character; she was quoting from some general order. 'I'm sorry,' she said again.

'Copis, for God's sake.' He started to move towards her; the sword swung up and pointed at his heart. 'Don't you understand?' he said desperately. 'The Order's gone, they've been wiped out. Look out the door if you don't believe me. We've killed them all, so it doesn't *matter* any more.'

She gave him a look that was as cold as ice, or a dead man's face. 'Not all,' she said. 'For a start, there's me. Or are you going to kill me too, you *barbarian?*'

She spat the word at him, and behind it he could feel the weight of months of hatred, repressed and hidden away in a part of her mind that even she hadn't been able to get into until now. It wasn't just hate, it was contempt and disgust, the unappeasable loathing of complete opposites. He took a step back, as if afraid of getting burned.

'Besides,' she said, 'I wouldn't tell you even if I was allowed.' She was looking at the backsabre, and the red smear. 'I should have killed you when I had the chance.'

Poldarn stared at her, his mouth open. 'Why?' he asked.

She laughed. 'You'd like to know, I bet. That way, you'd have a clue, you'd finally be able to figure out who you are. Sorry, no chance, but I'll tell you this much. This is an imperfect world, and most people are partly bad. Sometimes, depending on the way things happen, they find themselves in circumstances where the bad part of them comes to the top and they do terrible things, because they have to, or because it's safer or easier. You can't really blame them, because you can imagine circumstances where you'd do the same yourself, they're a mirror you can see yourself in, and all you can do is hope that you'll never end up in their shoes, do the things they found themselves doing. But you aren't like that. You're a core of evil with a few layers of flesh and skin, just for show. Everything you did you did because you wanted to, and that's where I can't even begin to understand you, because you didn't stop at greed or ambition or advantage, you just kept on going, like you wanted to be the end of the world.' She caught her breath, and laughed shrilly. 'That's why I decided you had to be the god in the cart, Poldarn the Destroyer. It seemed so appropriate at the time, and even when you'd lost your memory and suddenly you'd stopped being yourself, everywhere you went there was killing and burning and things falling down. And now,' she added, letting the sword drop to her side, 'here you are. Why am I not surprised?'

Poldarn took a deep breath, like someone waiting for a wave to break all round him and drag him under. 'Whoever I used to be, I know who I am now, and that's all that matters,' he said. 'And if you stay here, they'll kill you.'

'We'll kill you, you mean.'

'They'll kill you,' Poldarn repeated. 'I came here to rescue you, because—'

She laughed. 'Yes,' she said, 'quite. So, if you really love me, hold still while I cut your head off. Will you do this one small thing for me?'

He opened his mouth to speak, but nothing came out.

'Well?' she said. 'Is that too much to ask?'

'No,' he replied.

She took a step forward, into his circle. He stayed perfectly still, either because he didn't care if she killed him or not, or because it was too early to assess where her attack was going to come from, so that choosing a guard now would prejudice his defence. 'It's one of those dreams we all have,' she was saying. 'You die, but you rid the world of an unspeakable monster, so it's all right really. Something like that would give your whole life some degree of meaning. Seven-eighths of humanity would love to be where I am now.'

'Go on, then,' he said. 'If it's what you really want.'

She swung the sword over her head, taking a step forward. Poldarn read the move just in time, stepped back and to the right with his right foot and angled his sword down to deflect the cut. She recovered well and threw a backhand side cut at his neck. He'd read that too, and went back out of the way, reverting to a plain forward guard. She glared at him, her expression almost comical, then swung a looping cut that started out aimed at his face but curved in at his hands. He dropped his guard just in time and the tip of the cutting edge glided past his knuckles, missing them by the width of a coin. She took two steps back and resumed her guard.

'Your money,' she said, 'the gold you found in those ruins. I tried to tell myself it wasn't dirty, you'd just found it, I could give it to the Order where it could do some good. But I couldn't, so I threw it down a well. At least you'll never have it now.'

He didn't answer; instead he started walking backwards towards the door. 'No you don't,' she yelled, and came at him again, this time feinting high and pulling the cut back in to bring it down at his knees. He parried instinctively, and whatever it was he did, it worked. 'Please,' he said. 'Stop it. I can get you out of here alive.'

'I wouldn't take my life from you,' she replied. 'It wouldn't be worth having. And for God's sake fight back.'

He realised. 'You can't read me,' he said. 'You don't know how to fight someone who only defends and won't attack. Those moves aren't in any of the forms you learned.'

She scowled. 'Congratulations,' she said. 'You've just attained the fifteenth grade, summed up in the maxim, *The best fight is not to fight.* I never got further than the twelfth grade myself, but I'm just a woman, I was lucky to get that far. The depressing thing is, you worked it out for yourself. You never went any higher than the tenth grade.'

She swung at him, a cut that started waist high but changed into an uppercut to the chin as she turned her wrists. He parried it without thinking and took a step closer to the door. 'I don't want to leave you,' he said, 'but I will. I don't want to die today.'

'Tough.' She attacked again, a rather clumsy lunge that told him she was losing her temper and her patience. 'So many others didn't have the choice, because of you. And now—'

He saw the moment and took it. As she drew back from the lunge he hopped sideways and slashed hard, turning the sabre at the last moment so that the back of the blade cracked her across the knuckles. She dropped the sword; he jumped forward and kicked it away. She spat at him, but he dodged easily.

'Last chance,' he said.

'Go to hell,' she replied, and before she could move he slammed the lower horn of the hilt across her jaw. In retrospect he realised he'd hit much too hard; he felt the jawbone break, the moment of yielding transmitted through the steel into his hand. Apart from that, it worked fine; she was out cold, and he caught her before she hit the ground.

Outside, he ran into Sitrych.

'Bloody hell,' Sitrych said, looking at the unconscious woman in his arms. 'Where'd you find one of them in a place like this?'

He smiled. 'Just a matter of knowing where to look, I guess,' he replied.

Sitrych pulled a face. 'Jammy bastard,' he said. 'All I've found is a few pairs of old boots and a set of fire irons. Though,' he added, peering past Poldarn's elbow at her bruised, swollen face, 'maybe I haven't done so badly after all.'

'I'm not swapping, if that's what you mean,' Poldarn said.

Sitrych shrugged. 'Worth a try,' he said. 'Anyway, you'd better stash her somewhere safe, we've got to burn this place down now. God knows how, it's all stone and slate and tiles.'

Poldarn looked up at the sky. He remembered a dream he'd had, involving a captured woman and a village that wouldn't burn. 'At least it isn't raining,' he said.

Chapter Twenty-Four

'We found this in the muster yard,' reported the duty officer, signalling to the guards with a nod of his head. 'Fell off his horse at us while we were on our way to the mess tent.'

The guards brought forward a mess of clothing, mud and blood and let it slide gently to the ground. The general looked up from his map and sighed. 'Can't you deal with it?' he said. 'I'm rather busy.'

The duty officer shook his head. 'I think you'd rather talk to this one yourself,' he said.

From experience, the general trusted the duty officer's judgement. 'If you say so,' he said. 'Well, come on, find him a chair or something. I can't very well interrogate a heap on the floor.'

They fetched a folding chair and loaded the prisoner into it. They were surprisingly gentle, for soldiers.

'All right,' the general said, putting down his ruler and compasses. 'Who are you?'

The prisoner lifted his head. Most of his face was an open wound, with soil and dust ground into it. 'My God,' the general said, 'what happened to you?'

It was more in the nature of a rhetorical question, since he couldn't believe that someone so badly smashed up would still be able to talk. In fact, the man's voice was calm and steady, if a little weak. 'Like the man said,' he replied, 'I fell off my horse. Almost fell off,' he added, moving the corner of his mouth into what would have been a smile, 'except for one foot, which I carelessly left in the stirrup. Wouldn't have been so bad, only these idiots were chasing the poor brute all round the square.'

The general, who had seen more slaughter than most men, couldn't help shuddering a little. 'Get the doctor,' he said. 'This man needs attention.'

'Later.' The prisoner could still raise his voice. 'I've got to ask you something. Who are you?'

There was a brief silence.

'Banged his head, probably,' muttered the duty officer. 'You, get the surgeon.'

A guard hurried away, while the general looked at the prisoner. 'My name is Cronan Sulivois,' he said. 'Are you telling me you didn't know that?'

The prisoner tried to laugh, but couldn't. 'Well, there you go,' he said. 'I've been looking all over for you. My name's—' He hesitated. 'My name's Monach,' he said. 'I represent the order of Deymeson. Would you like to know why I'm here?'

General Cronan frowned. 'Where's that doctor got to?' he said. 'This man's off his head.'

'No,' the prisoner replied. 'And you didn't answer my question. Would you like to know—?'

'Yes,' General Cronan interrupted. 'Since you seem determined to tell me, yes, I would.'

The prisoner let his head slump forward. 'I was sent to kill you,' he said.

General Cronan looked up. 'Were you really?' he said. 'Well, I don't think you'll be up to killing anybody for a while. I hope that's not a problem.'

'It's all right,' Monach said, 'there's been a change of plan. You need to go to Sansory, immediately.'

'Do I?' Cronan sighed. 'And why would I want to do that?'

Monach grabbed the sides of the chair with his tattered hands and pulled himself up straight. He managed to hold himself there for a second or two before his strength gave way and he slid back. For some reason Cronan found the gesture impressive. 'Because,' Monach said, 'Feron Amathy and the raiders are going to burn it down if you don't. Do you understand me?'

Cronan leaned forward. 'What makes you say that?' he said.

'Because he told me so himself. I was holding a knife under his chin at the time. I'm inclined to believe him.'

Outside a sergeant was shouting at his platoon about something or other. 'You got close enough to Feron Amathy to hold a knife on him?'

Monach shrugged. 'Yes,' he said, then he winced and raised a hand to his right eye, slid it back past his ear to the nape of his neck. Just as the duty officer realised what he was doing, he thrust his arm straight up in the air and snapped it down through ninety degrees; the knife missed Cronan's head by the width of a thumb and split the headrest of his chair.

'No,' Cronan shouted, as the duty officer started to draw his sword, 'leave him alone. He just got my undivided attention.'

Monach smiled, and the duty officer took a step back, his hand still resting on the pommel of his sword. Cronan turned round in his chair and tried to pull out the knife, but it was too deep. Also, his hands were shaking.

'The same knife you held up Feron Amathy with?' he asked, in a rather awkward voice.

Monach was kneading the tendons of his forearm. 'Yes,' he replied. 'And before you ask, it's the only one I had on me. I'm a priest, not a cutlery stall. Keep it,' he went on, 'I've decided you can carry on living. But you've got to move now if you're going to stand a chance of reaching Sansory in time.'

Cronan stood up, and motioned to a guard to get the knife out of his chair. 'Admit it,' he said, 'you just missed. That's fair enough; you're obviously not at your best right now.'

Monach smiled. 'Sansory,' he said.

'How do I know you aren't leading me into an ambush?'

This time Monach managed to laugh, though the sound was more like the shrieking of crows. 'I suggest you follow your instincts,' he said. 'Or you could pray for divine guidance. Tell me, do you ever dream about crows?'

Cronan frowned. 'No,' he said. 'At least, I don't think so.' He nodded to the duty officer. 'General muster,' he said, 'quick as you like. Then I'd better see the captains of division, and you can get me the bigger map of the Bohec valley, the old one with the cart tracks on it. And get a messenger off to Sansory, tell them to shut the gates.' He turned back to face Monach, who'd slumped back in the chair. He looked like a sack of old junk dumped carelessly in the corner of a room. 'You're really a sword-monk?' he asked.

Monach laughed. 'What's left of one,' he replied. 'It'd be nearer the mark to say that you could make up a whole sword-monk out of me and a dozen yards of bandage.'

'Fascinating,' Cronan said. 'I've never met a sword-monk before, at least not to talk to; I've seen a few of your lot strutting about in the background at big receptions and temple services, but that's all. Were you really sent here to kill me?'

'Yes.'

'Oh. Why?'

Monach shrugged. 'There was a reason. Probably. Will you settle for God moving in a mysterious way?'

'No,' Cronan replied, 'but if you don't know, you don't know, and there's no point badgering you about it.'

Monach nodded. 'You believe me, then. That's good.'

'I haven't got the time or the energy not to believe you,' Cronan replied. 'If I wasn't so busy, maybe I'd have the guards beat the truth out of you with big sticks, but the secret of being a good general is keeping your priorities straight. What made you change your mind about killing me?'

'Who said I changed my mind? But first I've got to save Sansory.'

'You've got to save Sansory?' Cronan smiled gently.

'That's right. And I've got to use you to do it, since I can't think of any other way of going about it. I'm allowed a certain degree of discretion, as a senior field officer and honorary deacon.'

'Interesting,' Cronan said. 'You remind me of me. Do you think I'd have made a good sword-monk?'

'No,' Monach replied. 'You're a bit too tall, and you'd have difficulty with the theoretical side. The secret of being a good sword-monk is the ability to concentrate on meaningless tiny details at the expense of the main issue.'

Then the doctor arrived, with four orderlies and a stretcher; they lifted Monach out of the chair and laid him on his back. 'Thank you,' he said, just as they were about to carry him away.

'My pleasure,' General Cronan replied.

The cavalry went on ahead. Not that they'd be any use against the raiders, or much good against the specialist horsemen of the Amathy house (who paid better and weren't so fussy about rules of engagement and plunder), but they could find out what was going on and report back, which was rather more important.

General Cronan's coach had shed a wheel the previous day, and the wheelwrights hadn't got round to fixing it, so he rode at the head of the baggage train, in the same cart as the wounded monk. For some reason the monk found this highly amusing, though he also seemed to feel that no good would come of it. Two large crows followed them all the way.

A scouting party from the main cavalry unit reported in, saying that they'd ridden past Sansory (which was still there, and yes, they'd sent a detachment to check the gates were shut, and they were) and carried on east towards Deymeson; about four miles short of the town, they'd seen columns of smoke in the sky directly above where the abbey should have been. No, they hadn't had sight of the raiders, but on the other hand their orders had been not to engage the enemy unless absolutely necessary, and they didn't want to risk disobeying those orders by going any further . . . The main body of the cavalry had fallen back to guard the east–west road, with skirmishers out deep on either side, given the raiders' apparent tendency to come across country whenever they could.

Cronan spread out the map on his knees – the wind tried to tug it away, but a couple of guards jumped up and held the corners down – then sent word down the line that they'd be missing out Sansory and heading for – he glanced down to read the name – Vistock, a village roughly halfway between Sansory and Deymeson. 'We won't bother looking for them,' he explained, 'they'll come looking for us. Or they'll just vanish into thin air and turn up somewhere else next month. At any rate, they won't attack the city with us at their backs.'

It hadn't taken long for word to spread through the army that they were on their way to fight the raiders, and the sergeants were having to shout and call time to keep up the usual pace. That was understandable enough, but annoying, and the general's temper started to fray. This was unusual enough to provoke further doleful commentary up and down the column, until the sergeants had to order silence in the ranks, which didn't do much for morale. At this point some captain or other thought it might be a good idea to get the men singing, to cheer them up and quicken the pace. He didn't take the trouble to check with the general first, assuming he wouldn't want to be bothered with such trivia. The men were in no mood to sing, but they couldn't disobey a direct order; so they sang:

Old crow sitting in a tall thin tree,
Old crow sitting in a tall thin tree,
Old crow sitting in a tall thin tree,
He'll make his dinner of you and me.

'For God's sake,' Cronan shouted, standing up on the box, 'tell them to stop making that bloody awful noise.'

The monk, who'd been asleep for some time, opened his eyes. 'Now there's a tune I haven't heard in a long time,' he said.

Cronan looked down at him. 'You know it then, do you?'

The monk nodded. 'Used to hear it a lot when I was a boy. It's a very old song, I believe.'

'Really,' Cronan said. 'How would you know that?'

The monk coughed painfully. 'I'm a scholar, don't forget,' he said. 'First recorded as a marching song in the reign of Tercennius, which I hardly need tell you is over four hundred years ago, and the text implies it was an old song then. A commentator from the reign of Cadentius – a mere two centuries back, which makes it slightly suspect, but he could well have been drawing on earlier sources – says that it refers to the defeat of Sclerus Acasto by the south-eastern nomads, which would put it back nearly six hundred years; far-fetched, perhaps, but by no means impossible, since another popular marching-song, "Lady With the White Felt Hat", can reliably be dated to the accession of Loriscus, nearly seven hundred and fifty years ago. Which goes to show, soldiers like the old tunes best.' He closed his eyes again. 'Amazing, isn't it, the garbage that makes it down the centuries intact. Did the doctor happen to say how he rated my chances?'

Cronan looked away. 'Not good, I'm afraid,' he said. 'But not hopeless either. There's some internal bleeding—'

The monk shook his head. 'Doesn't matter,' he said. 'I knew I'd be too late to save the order. Even if I hadn't been, you'd never have risked your army for us. I expect you're glad we're out of the way.'

'Well, they did send you to kill me. A man can take offence at that sort of thing.'

'There was a very good reason for it,' Monach replied, 'though of course they didn't explain it to me. We act in the best interests of the empire. Always.'

'Really.'

Monach nodded. 'Properly speaking, the best interests of religion, but the one includes the other. The idea was, since we're free agents and dedicated to the greater good, we can do the difficult, unpopular things that emperors and governors and generals daren't do. It's a privilege and a responsibility. We're well aware of the implications.' He started coughing again. 'At least, we were,' he said. 'But then the god in the cart showed up, and here we are, the end of the world. Arguably, that's why I had to kill you, to make sure the world came to an end. I mean,' he went on, turning his head a little, 'it'd be ridiculous if the armies of darkness were defeated, just because the dying empire happened to throw up an unusually talented general. It'd make a mockery of religion; what my old tutor used to call an abomination. How being destroyed would be good for the empire I couldn't rightly say, but I don't suppose I have all the facts at my disposal.'

Cronan grunted and went back to his work. The soldiers had stopped singing and were trudging along even more slowly than before. The monk went back to sleep, and muttered from time to time about something or other.

A squadron of cavalry brought in a further report. No sign of the raiders, they said, but when they'd ridden up to Vistock Beacon, the highest point for miles around, they'd seen what looked like a big mob of armoured horsemen riding in from the north-west. They were seven, perhaps eight hours away, assuming the Visk was still fordable at North Hey.

'The Amathy house,' Cronan said, frowning, searching the map. It didn't show a River Visk, let alone a ford or a village called North Hey. It was a new map from the cartographer royal's office in Torcea.

'Could be,' said one of his staff. 'Or it could be Tazencius, coming from that direction.'

'More likely to be Feron Amathy, if they're cavalry,' Cronan pointed out. 'In any event it's bad news.'

'What do you think he's planning to do?' someone else asked.

'Either join with the raiders and make us fight on two fronts – tactically his best option, but he may have another agenda besides mere victory. Otherwise, he could hold off while we fight the raiders, and then attack whoever's left standing.'

One of the senior officers frowned. 'I can see why he'd attack us,' he said, 'but why pick a fight with them? I thought they were in this together.'

Cronan shook his head. 'Only as far as it suits him,' he replied. 'No, if he can step in after we've been wiped out and drive the raiders back into the sea . . .'

'I follow you,' the other man said. 'The long-term view. You think this may be what he had in mind all along?'

'Possibly.' Cronan shrugged. 'I think he's more of an opportunist than that. For one thing, I don't know how he's planning to handle that idiot Tazencius. He'll be glad of a few more infantry regiments, and it could be that he's planning to set up Tazencius as a puppet emperor, at least in the short term – you know, to make his coup look more legitimate. Or maybe he isn't bothered about that, in which case he'll probably send Tazencius and his people in first to get chewed up, and finish off the rest of them along with the rest of us. Or the raiders, depending on who wins the main battle.' Cronan yawned, and stretched his arms. 'The likeliest bet is that he's keeping all these options open, and he'll make his final choice as late as possible. The one thing I do know about Feron Amathy, he loves having as many choices as possible.'

'So what are you going to do?' someone asked.

Cronan smiled. 'I haven't got any choices at all,' he said rue-fully. 'I've got to press on to Vistock and take on the raiders, stop them getting to Sansory. Of course, while I'm doing that, Feron Amathy may stave off boredom while he's waiting by sacking the city and burning it to the ground, something else to blame on the raiders. It depends on what's most important to him: giving his people a good time, to keep them happy for the next stage of the plan, or being the saviour of Sansory and the last, best hope of the empire. At the moment I'd be inclined to favour the latter, except that Sansory's small but rich, which makes it eminently suitable for feeding to his dogs. There's plenty of other cities he can save, after all, whereas sacking, say, Mael or one of the other Guild towns would be a bigger job with a lower return per man hour expended. So I really don't know. Anyway,' he went on, 'there's nothing much we can do about that, so it's best not to think about it. After all, our chances of still being on our feet after we've picked a fight with the raiders are small enough, God knows.'

That wasn't the sort of thing they wanted to hear; mostly because Cronan had a reputation for telling the truth, even when it wasn't the wisest thing to do. 'What about Tazencius?' someone said, after a long silence. 'I know it's a long shot, but he can't be completely stupid, he must realise that playing along with Feron Amathy's a wonderful way of getting killed before your time. Could we talk to him, do you think?'

Cronan shook his head. 'Highly unlikely,' he said. 'He does-n't like me very much, you see. And he's just cocky enough to think he can finesse his way past Feron Amathy when the time comes. Of course, his plans may be seriously adrift by now; supposing he was banking on our sleeping friend here having done his job – get rid of me, and there's no reason why he shouldn't desert the Amathy house and change sides, thereby making himself the champion of legitimate govern-ment and his imperial cousins' new best friend – it's reasonable to expect a sword-monk to be able to pull off a simple assassination after all. If my guess is right, he talked the order into believing that killing me was the only way to save the empire. His bad luck, I suppose; you can't really say he was stupid for gambling on what should've been a certainty.' Cronan smiled, and held up his thumb and forefinger, three-quarters of an inch apart. 'He came this close,' he added, 'assuming the monk really did miss.'

Only one or two of the staff knew what he was talking about; the others didn't ask. 'So we can't expect any help from Tazencius,' someone said. 'Even if we beat the raiders, we'll have the Amathy house and Tazencius' infantry at our backs. No disrespect, but it's not sensible to stake the future of the empire on your tactical ability. You may be able to pull off a miracle, but then again you may not.'

'Very tactful,' Cronan sighed. 'I put our chances at something less than a hundred to one.'

'Fine,' said an officer. 'You're as good as saying you're resigned to this army getting wiped out, Sansory falling, and Feron Amathy with nothing between him and Torcea but a handful of third-string garrisons.' He hesitated, then went on, 'There is an alternative, you know.'

Cronan nodded, looking away. 'Sure,' he said. 'We simply withdraw, refuse to play. Sansory falls – but it'd have fallen anyway, in all probability; Feron Amathy doesn't get an opportunity to stab the raiders in the back, he doesn't get rid of Tazencius; the raiders get as much loot as they can carry and go home. Feron Amathy's campaign loses momentum, giving us time to pick off Tazencius, maybe patch up a pardon so he can go home, and then deal with the Amathy house once and for all. Apart from Sansory getting burned to the ground, it's a good result. And, as you say, our chances of saving the city even if we do press on and fight are next to nothing, so to all intents and purposes they're already dead, we can't save them.' He picked at a thread on the knee of his trousers. 'Also, true courage and service don't lie in making the heroic gesture; fighting and dying here would be the easy way out. The truly brave and loyal thing to do would be to walk away. Did I leave anything out?'

'I think that covers it,' someone murmured, 'more or less.'

'Splendid,' Cronan replied. 'Well, we'd better be getting along. If this pathetic excuse for a map's anything to go by, it's still nearly two hours to Vistock.'

Just over two hours later they came to a ford over a small, inoffensive river.

'North Hey?' Cronan asked the captain of pioneers, who claimed to know the area.

The captain shook his head. 'Vistock,' he replied.

The first thing they could make out was the shell of a mill-house, with a wrecked and moss-grown wheel sunk in the water. There was only one other structure still standing: half a barn (the other half had fallen in a long time ago, there were still signs of fire on the rounded ends of the rafters), sur-rounded on two sides by an overgrown wall. Outside the ramshackle doorway someone had driven a stake into the ground and stuck on it the head of an old woman with long, matted grey hair. The blood running down the stake was still wet. The body was nowhere to be seen.

'Raiders,' someone said.

'Or Feron Amathy,' someone else suggested, 'pretending to be the raiders. Not that it matters, I suppose.'

Cronan stopped the cart and climbed out to take a look. He didn't seem shocked or revolted, just curious. 'Actually,' he said, 'it doesn't look like either of them to me. I guess we may just have tripped over a good old-fashioned private murder, nothing to do with the destiny of nations and none of our business.' He knelt down and stared up at the base of the neck. 'It's a clean cut,' he said. 'Just one cut; which could mean a backsabre, I suppose. Or a sword-monk; they're sup-posed to be able to chop off heads with one mighty blow, in fact I think it's on the syllabus. Or it could just be some lunatic loose with a felling axe.' He stood up and looked round. 'This is Vistock? The map says it's a medium-sized town.'

'Raiders,' the pioneer captain told him. 'Forty-odd years ago.' Something caught his eye and he stooped to pick it up: a single bone button. 'Let me see that map of yours a minute.'

Cronan reached up into the cart for it and handed it over. 'And some of you bury that,' he said, pointing to the head, 'before the crows get at it. I don't know about you people, but I find this place depressing.'

He walked over to the barn and told a couple of his guards to help him on to the roof, where the rafters were bare and he could hold on and look around. From there he could see a fair way up and down the road. The obvious point was the ford, but he wasn't convinced, so he called down to some scouts and told them to look for crossing places a couple of miles in each direction. If not the ford, then what? He'd been assuming there would be a town: houses, walls, gates, a wide variety of obstacles to break up a charge, cover behind which he could hide reserves. Instead he'd committed himself to fighting on a level plain, with nothing to play with except a river that he suspected wasn't deep enough to slow down a determined advance, let alone block it. His suspicion proved to be correct.

'Wonderful,' he said. 'All right, if there's nothing here, we'll have to make something of our own. Somebody help me down, there's a lot to get done.'

They weren't finished by nightfall, so Cronan called for big fires and all the available lamps and torches. The men weren't in the mood, not after a long march, and it was fairly obvious they didn't have any faith in what Cronan was doing. He couldn't really blame them; he was being thorough and workmanlike but unimaginative; there was nothing in his plans that another general couldn't have thought of and carried out just as well. If he was going to be the first man in the history of the empire to beat the raiders in a pitched battle, he was going to have to come up with something better than that. Unfortunately he couldn't think of anything; and besides, they were running out of time.

'You look awful,' someone told him. 'You want to get your head down and sleep for a few hours, or you'll be no good to anybody when they do show up.'

'Yes, Mother,' Cronan grunted, but he couldn't think of anything else to do, and he was very tired. They offered to pitch his tent for him but he told them he couldn't be bothered; he'd just lie down in the cart for a while and go over the maps one last time, in case he'd missed something. When they came back with the lantern he'd asked for, he was fast asleep.

Monach woke up with a start, and wondered if he was dead. He was feeling much better, almost no pain – entirely consistent with death, from what he'd read about it, rather less likely if he was still alive, considering the gravity of his injuries.

But he was alive. He was also alone, in a cart, about four hundred yards away from a great deal of noise and movement. They'd started the battle while he was still asleep, and nobody had thought to wake him up. Bastards!

It hurt a lot when he raised himself on one elbow, to where he had a view of what was going on, but it was worth it. He could only see about a third of the action, because the units in the centre of the battle were blocking his view of both wings to some extent; however, not only was the imperial centre still there, it was moving forward at a calm, brisk walk, and the bodies being stepped over weren't all imperial soldiers, by any means.

Intriguing development. He resolved to make the effort, and dragged himself up on to the box of the cart. That really did hurt, and for a moment or so he thought it'd be the death of him, since breathing became almost more trouble than it was worth. But that passed, and he found that he was looking

at a fairly straightforward three-sides-of-a-square envelop-
ment procedure, with the raiders penned in the middle, a
massive central block of infantry herding them back, and two
hedges of cavalry on either side doing the killing and the
wounding—

Cavalry. Far more cavalry than General Cronan had had at
his disposal on the way here. Another, more careful look at the
backs of the infantry in front of him confirmed it; at least a
quarter of the centre weren't wearing Cronan's arms or livery.
He squinted (the sun was inconveniently placed) until he
recognised the flamboyant outfits of the Amathy house, and
old-fashioned imperial patterns, which could only be the foot
soldiers from Tazencius' garrisons.

Very strange indeed, he thought; Feron Amathy and Prince
Tazencius were fighting with General Cronan against the
raiders. How on earth had that happened?

There hadn't been one single factor that turned the tide,
simply the cumulative effect of small, common-sense precautions and preparations, combined with a certain amount of
flair in the leading and handling of troops.

It was, of course, pure Cronan, all of it. His basic idea was
to fool the raiders into thinking that he was planning to defend
the ford. They'd know perfectly well that the river could be
crossed in at least two other places, and they'd split into two
units and make a rush for them, with the aim of getting across
the river and round behind Cronan's infantry before he could
withdraw or react. They'd meet brief, futile resistance from
the cavalry on the wings; they'd charge through them, scattering them, and rush down on the infantry – only to find
that the cavalry had deliberately given up too easily and were
coming back to take the raiders in flank and rear, while the
heavy centre unfolded to receive them with prejudice. That
was good tactical thinking; the part that might almost qualify
as genius was the caltrops.

('Caltrops?' the colonel of engineers had said, when he got his orders. 'Oh, you mean those little three-legged wire things about the size of your fist, with spikes sticking out, the ones you hide in long grass or something, and when the enemy treads on them – yes, I suppose we could, if we had enough wire.' Cronan had, of course, seen to it that there was plenty of wire suitable for improvising caltrops out of in the field, using only basic tools.)

Genius, because Cronan had guessed that what gave the raiders the edge was their unstoppable charge, the impetus that carried them on, through and over any obstacle, no matter how dense or determined. Unstoppable, he'd said to himself, but supposing they wanted to stop. Could they?

In the event, it turned out that they couldn't. As the dozen or so men in the lead suddenly collapsed to the ground, screaming with pain, the main body of the raiders guessed something wasn't right. But they were committed to the charge and couldn't stop; they ploughed on into the caltrop field, driving the finger-long tines of the caltrops clean through bootsole and foot, and fell to the ground like ripe corn under the thin slice of a sharp scythe. When they fell, they landed on more caltrops, which stabbed them in the stomach and the chest and the face, and the boots of the men behind them landing on their backs and necks drove the tines in further still. As the charge continued to falter and pile up, still a dozen yards or so short of the enemy line, the cavalry crashed into the rear of the mob, stampeding them, and now the great wave of the raiders was smashing into the sea wall and disintegrating into fine spray, vaporised by its own impetus. Cronan saw that and muttered a quick prayer under his breath, to Poldarn the Destroyer; at the heart of all inspirational tactics lurks a small kernel of poetic justice, of the strong undone by their own strength. Then he looked up and saw the Amathy house, heading straight at him.

Oh well, he thought, *it was a moral victory, I suppose.* But

the Amathy house cavalry swung further than he'd anticipated they would when he saw them line out; instead of
charging his squadrons, they wheeled and crunched into the
raiders' flanks, stoving them in like rocks crushing the side of
a ship. Not far behind came Tazencius' infantry, with the
Amathy foot soldiers bringing up the rear; they moved in to
reinforce his own troops as if they'd been practising the move
as a drill for a year. They'd figured out about the caltrops for
themselves and stayed clear of the few patches where the
spikes hadn't been clogged and rendered safe with a mat of
dead raiders.

It was at this point that Cronan finally realised how few of
the enemy there actually were. Spaced out in open order in the
full flight of the charge (like a flock of birds flying) was one
thing; crowded together in a narrow space (like the same flock
roosting in a few tall trees) was quite another. And, of course,
the best part was still to come—

Poldarn didn't get to fight in the battle. One moment he was
running forward, the backsabre held over his head in both
hands; the next he was lying on his side, his whole body ringing with some terrible shock that hadn't yet started to melt
into pain, but that paralysed him nonetheless. He only just
had time to locate the source of the trauma – the spike of a
caltrop poking up through the top of his right foot like a
crocus, the feel of something pricking his ribs through his
upper arm – before heavy bodies thumped down on top of
him, squashing his face down among the heather stems and
blotting out the light. The last thing he saw was a huge flock
of crows congealing in the sky directly overhead—

—And they were talking to him, one voice coming together
out of the multitude, announcing itself as the god whose name
he'd borrowed or stolen. He wished he could see, but that was
apparently out of the question.

To be certain, he asked: Who are you?

The voice answered: Oh, you know us, you've known us ever since you were a boy. We've been enemies for years.

He didn't like the sound of that. Have I actually done you any harm? he asked.

The voice answered: It depends on how you define harm. You've killed hundreds of us, possibly thousands, but that's all right, you can't hurt *me*; not on your own, there's simply too many of us for you to make a perceptible difference. Don't worry about it; I forgave you years ago.

A window opened in his mind, and through it he could see a level field, muddy, with small pools of rain standing on the surface here and there. From a distance it was brown with a faint sheen; as he grew closer he saw that it was covered with ranks and files of tiny green spearheads, driven up through the mud like caltrop spikes. He saw a gate, and beyond that the stump of an old dead tree in the hedge, where someone had built a very fine hide out of green branches and briars. Fifteen yards out from the hide, four or five crows were hopping round in small, furious circles; looking closer he could see that each of them was tethered by one leg to a stick driven into the mud. From time to time each captive bird would open its wings and manage to rise a single wingbeat off the ground before flopping back down again and continuing its small, circular dance. Further out, scattered at random within a twenty-yard radius, he could see a couple of dozen more crows, but when he looked closer he saw they were dead and pegged out, a slender thorn twig stuck through their lower jaws and into the dirt to keep their heads up and make them look as if they were contentedly feeding.

He asked: Am I doing this?

The voice replied: This is who you are, it's the answer to your question. The boy in the hide is you. Now look up and to your left.

He did as he was told and saw a stand of seven tall, thin ash trees, leafless. In the branches sat a dozen fat black crows, and as he watched one of them got up and flew straight towards him, gradually getting lower in the sky as it battled against the stiff wind. It gained a little height as it flew over the decoys, turned a tight circle and came in against the wind, wings back. As it pitched, an arrow with a thick blunt tip shot out of the hide and knocked the bird over in a tangle of outstretched wings, then the bird scrambled up and hopped towards the trees, one wing trailing. Meanwhile the rest of the crows in the trees got up and sailed over; two of them pitched straight away, and an arrow flew out and knocked it down, while the others veered sharply and rode the wind back to their trees.

The voice said: That's how clever you are; you noticed how, when you put one of us down, the others didn't see the arrow, they only saw one of their own dropping in and staying down. I saw that and thought that must mean it was safe, which is why the others came over too. Because you're patient as well as clever, you were able to kill scores of me in a single day, until eventually I realised what you were doing and learned to avoid you.

He said: I'm sorry.

The voice said: I told you, don't worry about it. I admire intelligence. Consider this: you're the only human ever to defeat the great army of the crows, just as Cronan is the only general who's ever beaten the raiders. Consider this: if you hadn't won your famous victory against me, I'd have stripped this field bare – that's your grandfather's spring barley, which he can't afford to lose if he's to feed you and the rest of the farm. Compare General Cronan again: if he hadn't won his famous victory against the raiders, they'd have burned Sansory and killed everybody inside. Does the morality bother you, now that you've decided to become a crow?

He replied: I suppose not. There's a sort of poetic justice to it.

The voice replied: A great man once said that there's a kernel of poetic justice inside every famous victory. Consider this: you and Cronan are the only men in history to have defeated the divine Poldarn. Who do you think you are, the boy or the crows?

He said: Didn't you just say I'm the boy in the hide?

The voice replied: Consider this—

—And he was sitting in the hide watching the crows flying slow, cautious circuits around the trees. After a while, one crow peeled off from the mob and flew straight towards him, heavy and straight, like his own blunt-headed arrows (as if the crows were shooting at him, not the other way round). He watched the crow come within seventy-five yards, then suddenly shear off screaming and fly back the way it had just come.

The voice said: Consider – before I assemble to feed, I send out a scout (the scout is also me, of course) to see if it's safe, to lead the way. Ask yourself this – when the divine Poldarn manifests himself as the god in the cart, leading the way, scouting ahead for the end of the world, are you the crow or the boy in the hide?

He thought before replying: Perhaps you could tell me, he said; does the crow that leads the way know it's a part of you, or when it leaves the trees and the rest of the mob does it think of itself as an individual?

The voice laughed, and said: Think about this—

—And he was standing on the top of a cliff watching a sail ship slip away into the interstice between sea and sky; when it had gone, he turned and walked across the downs towards the lights of a town in the distance; and he was repeating to himself his new name, his new history, the details of his new persona—

The voice said: There's your answer; you're the crow flying away from the trees, the spy sent out to find a good place to feed. When you leave the trees and the rest of the mob, do you think of yourself as an individual? And if so, which one?

He said: I don't know. The person I'm about to become is a stranger to me.

The voice said: When the divine Poldarn manifests himself as the god in the cart, leaving the mob and flying away from the trees, does he know he's me or does he think he's just an individual whose mind happens to be empty of memories because of some accident?

He thought hard before answering: Do you just send out one spy at a time, he asked, or are there many of us?

The voice became hard and cold, as if it was angry at having been tricked into giving away too much. Consider this, it said—

—And he saw his mother as a young girl, standing up with the knife in her hand, her skirt wet and filthy falling back down to her knees, as his father tried to breathe but couldn't, his throat having been cut; and he saw her as an old woman, coming out of the barn because she'd heard voices and assumed it was the bone cart from Sansory (she wasn't afraid of a man in a cart rolling up to her door) and hardly seeing the backsabre before it severed the veins and tendons of her neck and bit into and through the bone, and the last thing she heard was an old man talking about his dead son.

The voice said: Consider this, since you're so clever: Copis is carrying your child, he'll be born in just over seven months. When he's born, you'll be a long way away, or dead. As he leaves the mob and flies away from the trees, will he think of himself as an individual or merely a part of the pattern?

He replied: What'll happen to her? Will she be all right?

The voice laughed, and said: Consider the five dozen crows you killed when you won your famous victory, when you pegged out all of me that was in that place, so that the roosting trees were empty and the nests were deserted. Consider the one crow that didn't fly into the decoys, and so survived, when all the rest of me was dead. Do you think she considered herself still to be part of the mob, or an individual?

He replied: But she's not the last survivor of the order. There are others, scattered about.

The voice replied: On the day you won your famous victory over the divine Poldarn you killed all but one of me that were in that place, but there were others of me, hundreds of millions, scattered about. Do you think she considered herself still to be part of them, or an individual?

He said: I don't know. But I never meant her any harm. I'd never do anything to hurt her.

The voice said: Consider this—

—And he saw himself standing on the cart on the road to Laise Bohec, facing Eyvind, the last survivor of his party. And he saw himself standing up out of the mud and staring at the two dozen dead men, not knowing who they were or who he was.

He said: I think that the scout believes it's an individual, but it's wrong. It's still part of the mob.

Thank you, the voice replied, that's better. Is there anything else you'd like me to tell you, or shall I send you back to the battle?

He shouted, Yes; but the sky exploded into light, and he saw the heel of a boot come down and skin his cheek, shearing away the skin. The sky was bright and empty. Another boot crashed into the back of his head, and everything went away.

Chapter Twenty-Five

'For the very last time,' said the body lying in the water, 'go away. I won't tell you again.'

'Oh sure,' sneered the reflection. 'Wasn't it going to be the very last time the last time you tried to get rid of me? And the time before that?'

He was in the air, feeling the crisp breeze in his wings and against the feathers of his belly. He was happy now that he'd rejoined his people, been allowed back into their mind, and would soon be flying home. Meanwhile, he spared a moment to look down at the body lying in the water (but it was still alive, so no joy) and its reflection, which was apparently talking to it.

'I'm not going to listen to you any more,' said the body to its reflection. 'I can't hear a word you're saying.'

'Oh, please,' said the reflection, scornfully. 'Try and act like a grown-up.'

'Anyway,' the body went on, 'fairly soon I'll be rid of you once and for all. I'm going home.'

'Home?' The reflection laughed. 'No such place.'

'Yes there is. I've found my family and I'm going home over the sea, where you can't follow me.'

'Want to bet?'

'You can't follow me,' the body repeated, 'and even if you could, you'll never find me there, not just one among so many. It'd be like trying to find a leaf in a forest.'

'I'll find you,' said the reflection, 'bet on it.'

'You can try,' replied the body. 'I expect you will, it's just the sort of nasty, obsessive behaviour I've come to expect from you. But you'll fail.'

Silence, just for a moment.

'You don't need to do that,' said the reflection. 'Talk about cutting off your nose to spite your face. And anyway, it's not what you really want.'

'How the hell would you know?'

'I know everything about you. I know everything from the moment you were born. Before that, even. Every single thing there is to know about you, I've got it in here. Safe, where you can't lose it or get rid of it. It's my duty,' it added, 'as your better half.'

'You've never known me,' said the body, furiously angry, 'you don't know the first thing about me. All you know about or care about is you. All these years you think you know me, but all you can see is your own smug grin in a mirror. You think I'm just a polished surface you can shine in. Well, that's all over. I'm leaving. And without me—' Great pleasure in the voice, suddenly. 'Without me, you'll be dead. You'll just stop existing and fade away.'

'You really believe that? God, you're stupid.'

'All right, we'll see who's left once I've gone, and taken the baby with me. Back home—'

'Don't be ridiculous.'

'Back home, to his family, where he belongs.'

When Poldarn woke up, he panicked: God help me, he thought, where am I, who am I, God damn it, I can't even remember my own name . . .

He lifted his head and looked round. He'd been lying in

blood-soaked mud beside a river, and all around him lay the bodies of dead men; some dressed one way, some another. A crow glanced up from its meal and smirked at him, one professional acknowledging another.

It's all right, he told himself, as the mist cleared in his mind, you're home. Very much home, you were born here (in that barn over there, in fact), and in a few minutes Copis will be along with the cart and you'll be off about your missionary work; unless, of course, the world ended while you were asleep, and this is the brave new world—

—Same as the old one, only more painful. The last time he'd been here, at this point of departure, he hadn't had a pair of three-inch spikes stuck through his foot and his arm. This time the blood in the mud was his own, which at least afforded him a sense of belonging, almost equivalent to citizenship.

Must've missed the major veins, he rationalised, or I'd be dead. Unless I am dead, and this is heaven; or unless I'm a god, in which case they could drain all the blood out of me to make sausages, and it wouldn't make a whole lot of difference.

It would have been nice, he thought, if there'd been someone he could have asked; he was tired of having to rebuild the world from scratch practically every time he opened his eyes, it was a scandalous waste of mental energy that could have been used for more positive, constructive purposes.

He shifted a little, wondering how he was going to get the caltrops out without making everything worse. It was a highly intriguing combination – left foot and right arm – likely to present a worthwhile challenge to even the most ingenious (as if he'd gone up a grade since last time, and had been set a fittingly ingenious puzzle as a reward).

Come on, Copis, you're late. No, she wouldn't be along this time. He remembered about her now; he'd dragged her out of the store room at Deymeson, splashed water from the stable trough on her face until she'd woken up; before that he'd found a horse nobody seemed to want and he shunted her up on to it; she was still dizzy and confused, unable to talk because of her smashed jaw; he'd put the reins in her hand and led the horse by the bridle out of the abbey gate, given it a hard slap to make it walk on. She hadn't looked back at him as the horse carried her away down the hill. He'd made sure there was some food in the saddlebags, and six gross-quarters he'd found in a dead monk's sleeve. Then he'd gone back inside, before he was missed, and helped out with the looting and burning.

And now here he was, and she wouldn't be coming to rescue him from the field of battle; there was no guarantee that she was even still alive, and if she was, the only reason she'd come looking for him would be to kill him (and he could do without that kind of rescue, even now). He tried to think practically, one stage at a time. First grade: get the caltrops out. Second grade: crawl off the battlefield and find some cover. Third grade: find some food and something to drink. Fourth grade: don't bother your head with fourth grade until you've passed first, second and third.

He tried five or six times, but he couldn't reach the caltrop in his foot, and that was the one that mattered, because he couldn't crawl away from there until he'd got rid of it. The one in his arm was far less important; once he was off the field and inside the barn over there, he could attend to it at his leisure, if only he could find some way of getting this other one out of his foot . . . He considered trying to kick one of the other spikes into the ground, anchoring the caltrop firmly enough so that he'd be able to draw his foot clear (like a man drawing a sword from a scabbard, given that he would be the scabbard). The pain caused by one gentle, tentative attempt was enough to convince him to forget about that idea. He let go, sinking back into the mud.

What had happened, he wondered, in the battle? Who'd won? When he left it, the raiders (his side?) appeared to be losing or about to lose, but they were the raiders, the invincible, nearly supernatural enemy he'd heard so much about; it was almost impossible to believe that they'd choose this one occasion to go against the grain and fail for the very first time. Besides, he'd only seen one small part of the battle, and his impressions could therefore have been entirely misleading. In any event, the battle was over, or it had moved a long way away. Perhaps each side had wiped out the other, down to the very last man, leaving him as the sole survivor.

If that was the case, he didn't want to know.

Didn't matter in any event. The battle, the war didn't mean anything to him, and he belonged to neither side, or both. True, he had a strong intuitive feeling that the raiders were his people, but it wasn't very long at all since he'd had exactly the same feeling about the sword-monks. They couldn't both be his people, since the raiders had hated the order so much they'd frittered away time and energy wiping them out; how could there be any common ground between two such deadly enemies?

Since he couldn't see anything but mud, he closed his eyes for a while and tried not to think about the pain (which only made it worse; he could feel every nerve in his body each time his heart beat). It was some time before he realised there was someone else moving about.

He kept perfectly still. Helpless as he was, there was nothing he could do to save himself if whoever it was turned out to be the enemy, or even just some scavenger from a nearby farm, picking through the dead for scrap. On the other hand, if it was a friend and he kept still and quiet, he could escape notice and miss out on his only hope of being rescued. He thought about that; if nobody rescued him, he was probably going to die here, and it would take a long time and be unpleasant. Since the worst that could happen was going to happen anyway, why the hell bother with caution?

He tried to sit up, but it hurt so badly that he cried out at the pain. That, however, was all that was needed; a moment later he found himself staring at the toes of a boot.

'Is that you?' someone asked.

—Which was a very good question, given his circumstances. But the voice was, once again, familiar.

'Eyvind?' he asked.

'Yes, I thought it was.' The voice was much closer; whoever it was, he was kneeling down. 'God almighty, look what happened to you. Here, hold still. I don't know if this is the right thing to do, but I expect we'll soon find out.'

It was annoying and illogical that he'd hardly felt the caltrop spike go in, but the pain as it left his foot was almost enough to stop his heart. 'Damn,' said the voice he believed was Eyvind, 'it's started bleeding. I don't know; do I leave the other one where it is, or do I pull it out? Well?'

He realised that the voice had asked him for a decision, a choice between options. That hardly seemed fair, to his way of thinking. 'Haven't a clue,' he said. 'I have a feeling that if you make the wrong decision I'll probably die, but that's about as helpful as I can be. Sorry.'

There was definitely an edge to the voice as it replied, 'All I wanted was a straight answer to a civil question. Damn it, I suppose I'd better leave it in there for now. Seems to me that if you've lived this long with it in, a few more minutes won't kill you. We'll see.'

He thought about the implications of that. 'Who won the battle?' he asked.

'Quiet a moment, I'm going to try and get you up on your feet.'

He saw two hands passing in front of his face, then he felt them each gathering a fistful of his shirt and he was lifted up off the ground like a sack. Eyvind was apparently stronger than he'd looked.

The pain as he tried to put weight on his pierced foot was enough to make him squeal, but a hand grabbed his left arm and draped it round a pair of broad, thin shoulders, and he was able to lift his foot off the ground and still stay upright. He opened his eyes, which he'd instinctively closed when the pain started.

'Right,' Eyvind said, 'that was probably the difficult part, we'll see. Gently now, there's no need to rush.'

Behind the barn was a cart. Needless to say, a crow was perching on the box; he was sure that given time he'd be able to remember its name. It flew away as they approached, ploughing a weary line across the broad sky.

'They did,' Eyvind said, dumping him down on the box and scrambling up beside him. 'It was a massacre.'

'Oh,' he said.

Eyvind picked up the reins. 'We don't even know how many of us made it,' he went on, urging the horses into a brisk walk. 'We haven't had time for a head count. Best guess at the moment is that half of us got killed. It was a nightmare.'

He nodded. 'What happened?'

'They decoyed us into the trap, basically,' Eyvind said with a sigh that was more disgust and disappointment than anything else. 'We were suckered in; those bloody spike things were what did it. After they'd got us bottled up, they pushed us back to the river, at the deepest point, needless to say, where we couldn't get across. That was a mistake on their part,' he went on, 'because we managed to pull ourselves together, counter-attack. We were so badly outnumbered by that stage that it should've gone the other way, but they lost their nerve when we started cutting them about; we punched a hole right through their centre and started to pull out, which was when the horse-men started carving us up; we lost it and started running, and of course that was the worst thing we could've done. End result was, by the time they realised they'd gone too far and called off the pursuit, we were scattered all over the place in fives and tens or just one man out on his own, no chance of regrouping or anything like that. They gave it up and went back towards

the big town; we've been blundering about trying to find each
other ever since. The idea is to get back in some sort of order
and follow a straight line back to the ships, assuming they're
still there.' He scowled ferociously; his expression was almost
comic. 'Since our so-called best friend knows where the ships
are, that's by no means guaranteed. All we can hope for is that
he wants us to get away, since he won't want it coming out that
it was him who set all this up in the first place.'

Poldarn nodded again. 'You mean the Amathy house,' he
said. 'They changed sides, didn't they?'

'Is that what they're called? I can't seem to remember these
foreign names. Yes, that's exactly what they did. Of course, it's
our own damn silly fault for being so trusting. I've said it
before, these people aren't like us, you can't believe a single
word they say.'

Poldarn thought about the monks of Deymeson, and Copis.
'Are we any better?' he asked.

'Of course,' Eyvind replied. 'We don't even lie to our enemies. Not that we ever need to, of course; if you don't talk to
them, you can't lie to them. Saves a lot of trouble in the long
run.'

'I suppose it would,' Poldarn said. 'Where are we headed?'

'Over there.' Eyvind indicated the direction with a vague
dip of his head. 'There's a little combe, well hidden, you
wouldn't know it was there unless you were looking for it.
Mercifully we happened to find it on our way up here, and
after they'd stopped chasing us we all had the wit to head for
it. The general idea is to hang about there till it gets dark
and then sneak back up the way we came, past that religious
place we took out, and find the north-west road in the morning. If we keep going after that, we ought to have a clear run to
the coast, provided they don't figure out what we're up to and
cut us off. But I doubt they will, they aren't organised enough.
Probably be back to fighting among themselves in a day or so,'
he added contemptuously. 'They always seem to be doing

that, and what it is they're actually fighting over, God only knows. I don't suppose they do.'

Poldarn shook his head. 'It's complicated, certainly,' he said. 'While I think of it, I never did get to ask you what happened to you after that first time we met—'

Eyvind laughed. 'Amazing stroke of luck,' he said. 'The day after we ran into each other I walked straight into a scouting party – they'd have killed me, only I recognised one of them from back home and yelled out his name. It's like some providence is looking out for me,' he went on. 'And the same with you, I reckon; if I hadn't happened to see you there when we attacked that column of horsemen you were with – well, you'd be feeding the crows right now, no question about that. And again just now; pure luck I found that cart, just standing there empty on the road with the horses still between the shafts. And I didn't set out to look for survivors, I just happened to look in your direction and there you were, so I went to see if you were still breathing. No idea why I did it, it just seemed like the right thing to do. I reckon you've got someone up there looking out for you, in which case I'm going to stick close to you, hope some of it rubs off on me. That's what they say, isn't it? Stay close to a lucky man.'

'That makes sense, I suppose,' Poldarn replied. He hadn't thought of himself as unusually lucky before, but he could see Eyvind's point. And there are several different kinds of luck, some more desirable than others. He thought for a moment, then asked, 'When you get back to the ships, can I come with you?'

Eyvind gave him a curious look, then laughed. 'What a strange question,' he said. 'Yes, of course you're coming with us, you're one of us. All right, so you may have lost your memory; doesn't alter the fact that you're clearly one of our own. We wouldn't dream of abandoning you here.'

Poldarn nodded. 'Thank you,' he said. 'So what'll I do when I get to your country? Our country,' he amended.

Eyvind shrugged. 'My guess is, either you'll remember who you are and where you live, or somebody'll recognise you soon enough. Failing that, you'll come and stay at our place for as long as you like. Trust me, as soon as you're home in the islands, it'll all come flooding back. I mean, think about it. The only reason why you'd lose your memory for so long is because you're in the middle of this totally foreign, alien country, among all these people who're nothing at all like us, so naturally nothing's familiar, there's nothing to jog your memory, break the ice. I can see that clearly enough after being lost and alone in this country myself; I tell you, there were times when I reckoned I was having trouble remembering who I was and where I came from; when I closed my eyes and tried to think of home there was just this vague blurry picture, like seeing it all through autumn fog. Bloody disconcerting that was, I can tell you, scared the life out of me. What it's been like for you, after several months of it – makes my blood run cold thinking about it.'

It wasn't far to the combe Eyvind had been talking about, and he'd been right; it was so well hidden that they were rolling down the sheep track into it almost before he realised it was there. It was much larger than he'd imagined, and nearly full of people, most of them lying or sitting on the ground, talking to their neighbours or dozing or playing dice or knucklebones, as if they were at some kind of festival or outing. He wondered what it would take to make these people act miserable—

(Kill half of them? No, that didn't work. Kill the other half, maybe? No, then they'd just be cheerfully dead. Are I really seriously contemplating going to live in a place where everybody's cheerful all the bloody time? If I'm not mad now, I soon will be . . .)

Someone looked up and called out, 'Eyvind, over here.' Eyvind stopped the cart – a couple of men stood up and started seeing to the horses; nobody had told or even asked them to – and jumped out. 'This way,' he said. 'I want you to meet my uncle Sigfus.'

There was something bizarre, almost dreamlike, about the overwhelming wholesomeness of it all; Eyvind didn't say, 'Uncle, this is my new best friend,' but the genial smile and the firm handshake were straight out of some daydream of the bright, impossible Better Place where everybody's learned to get along just by being nice to each other . . . On the edge of a battlefield, with a caltrop stuck through his arm, he wasn't sure whether he could cope with it.

Eyvind was asking his uncle what he reckoned; and Uncle Sigfus was saying that pulling it out now might easily set off a lot of heavy bleeding, but on the other hand it had to come out eventually and the longer it stayed in there the worse it would probably get. He made it sound like a bad tooth. 'Uncle Sigfus knows all there is to know about wounds and serious injuries,' Eyvind told him. 'He'll have you fixed up in no time flat.'

Uncle Sigfus reached his decision quickly and very abruptly, suddenly plucking the caltrop out of Poldarn's arm like a man picking an apple. 'Bloody things,' he said, frowning as he held the caltrop up and examined it, 'that's no way to fight a war.' Poldarn was still reeling from the pain. 'Quick,' Sigfus went on, 'run and find something we can use for a bandage. It may hurt for a while,' he told Poldarn, 'but you'll just have to put up with that, I'm afraid.' (*If he calls me a brave little soldier,* Poldarn decided, *I'll have no option but to cut his throat. You can't just let something like that go by.*)

Then he felt painfully weak, and Eyvind and Sigfus took his arms and carefully lowered him to the ground, as if he was a slightly cracked jar. 'You stay put and get some rest, now,' Sigfus told him. 'There's still a couple of hours before sunset, and closing your eyes for a bit will do you the world of good.'

But Poldarn didn't want to close his eyes or sleep; in fact, it was out of the question—

'Well,' said the crow, 'here we are again.'

Poldarn looked up, and round. His instincts shrieked at

him to run or hide, but he discovered that he couldn't move. 'Dream?' he asked.

'Are there many talking crows where you come from?' the crow asked patiently. 'Well, then. At least you can be fairly sure you're awake. Whether this is strictly speaking a dream or a vision, I can't tell you, I never did go to college. A sword-monk would know, if you should chance to see one anywhere.'

That was presumably a pointed reference to his part in the attack on Deymeson, so he decided to ignore it. 'What's going on here, anyway?' he asked.

The crow hopped through forty-five degrees. 'Over there,' he said, 'is the destruction of Sansory. You'll observe that they broke through at the Southgate—'

'Who did?' Poldarn asked.

'—Which,' the crow went on, 'is a fine example of the old military adage about attacking your enemy's strengths, not his weaknesses. Over here—' It hopped round another twenty degrees. 'Over here, we have the riots in Mael, just before the rebels open the gates to the enemy—'

'Who are the enemy?'

'—A bad mistake on their part, since once the enemy get inside they kill everybody they can find regardless of which side they're on and set fire to the place, thereby making the civil war supremely irrelevant. Next to that—' Another fifteen degrees. 'Next to that, there's the razing of the walls of Boc Bohec; just beyond that, if you look closely, you can see the smoke from the fires of Torcea, right off on the other side of the bay, which goes to show what a big fire it is. All those thatched roofs, you see, and all those old wooden buildings in the shanty towns round the base of the walls; any fool could've told you it was a disaster waiting to happen, but of course nobody ever wants to hear uncomfortable stuff like that. Finally,' the crow added, hopping round to within a few degrees of where it started from, 'smaller but just as significant as far as you're concerned, the burning at Turcramstead – there, you can just make out the people trying to get out through the hole in the roof, and the enemy with their long poles pushing them back in again. Which brings us back to Sansory, of course.'

Poldarn turned round slowly, studying the patterns of destruction by fire, the constants and the variables. 'It looks like the end of the world,' he said.

'Very good,' replied the crow. 'And all your fault, of course; all directly your fault. I want you to be sure and remember this moment, later, when all this happens.'

Poldarn looked round again, taking careful note of various details – a building collapsing in a shower of sparks, a mob of soldiers dragging a woman out of her house, dragging the baby from her arms and tossing it like a log of firewood into the flames, noteworthy items that would jog his memory when he came to witness them. 'What do you mean, my fault?' he asked. 'Is this to do with who I was, or what I'm going to become?'

The crow looked past him. 'Same difference,' it said. 'You'll be who you always were; wiping our your memory hasn't changed who you are, all it's done is rearrange the schedule a little, added a few refinements, tinkered a little with a few of the causality chains. I mean,' it went on, 'you haven't really changed a bit, in spite of this wonderful fresh start you were given, this chance to stop being you. You've acted differently, mostly because you haven't been in much of a position to do harm deliberately, but you still have the same mind, the same temperament.'

'I see,' Poldarn said. 'Well, if you can show me the future, can you show me my past as well? I'd like to be able to see that.'

The crow didn't move, but everything else changed around it; now they were standing in a prison cell, lit by one window very high up in the wall. Through it Poldarn could just make out the legs and feet of passers-by. He found that he was sitting in the middle of the floor, secured with chains to the point where he could hardly move, let alone accomplish anything. 'That's the essential you,' said the crow, 'trapped in a prison in your own mind; and you know why? Prisons can be ambiguous things, you know; maybe this one isn't what you assume. The man in the middle there is you. Some prisons aren't built to keep the inmates from getting out, you see, they're to keep everybody else from getting in, with a rope and a chair, to deal with you as you deserve.'

'Who are you?' Poldarn asked.

'That,' the crow answered, 'is a very good question. You ought to ask him that,' it added, opening its wings and pitching on the chained man's shoulder. 'He could tell you that, if only you could reach him. But you can't, because deep down – as far below the surface as this prison is – you don't want to find out, because you already know. Oh sure, not a name or any memories, but you can feel the sort of man you are, and really, you don't want to go back. Understandable, God only knows, but it isn't going to do you any good.'

The crow suddenly vanished, in less time than it'd take a sword-monk to draw, and where the chained man had been Poldarn saw a sword-monk. He was in a bad way, with blood on his face and seeping through the cloth of his shirt. 'Who are you?' Poldarn asked.

'You know, I can't seem to remember,' the monk replied. 'But lately, I've been using the name Monach. It's just the word for monk where I came from originally.'

'Monach, then,' Poldarn said. 'All right, do you know who I am?'

The monk laughed. 'Of course I do,' he said. 'You're the evil bastard who did this to me. At least,' he added, 'I think you are. Your face is different, but I can see you very clearly hiding behind its eyes.'

'I don't understand,' Poldarn said.

The monk shrugged. 'Doesn't matter,' he said, 'it's what you've done that matters. Would you like to see that? Some of it, anyway, there isn't time to show you more than a few examples.'

Before Poldarn could reply, the monk vanished. Poldarn looked round to see where he'd gone to, and realised that he was flying, a long way up above the ground. All around him were columns of smoke, and when he looked down he saw that they were billowing up out of cities.

'Not bad,' said a voice that seemed to be coming from between his shoulder blades. It sounded like the monk he'd just been talking to. 'Considering that when you first arrived in this country you had nothing but the clothes you stood up in and a backsabre bashed out of an old beanhook, it represents a fairly impressive achievement. There's Culhan Bohec, look – of course, you've never heard of Culhan Bohec. Not many people have, these days. And there's Sirouesse, that used to be on the north-west coast, where the Mahec meets the sea; your first major work, and there's many as reckon it's still your best. Oh, and there's Josequin. I guess you could call that your posthumous masterpiece, since strictly speaking it happened after your death-of-memory. But even though you weren't there in person, it was definitely all yours, conceived, planned, realised and produced by you, got your signature all over it. And another thing you've got to bear in mind is how quickly you achieved all this. Twelve years; dammit, if you'd stayed a monk, like me, what would you have accomplished in those twelve years? Maybe, if you'd practised really hard and brown-nosed your way round the faculty, you might just have gone from ninth to twelfth grade, to the point where you'd be allowed to learn how to fight three imaginary enemies at the same time.' The voice sighed wistfully. 'Amazing, isn't it, the different ways our lives turned out. You went on and made something of yourself, out here in the world: burned cities, killed thousands – make that tens of thousands, hundreds of thousands even – made and overthrew emperors, played knucklebones and bouncing-bunny with the destinies of millions. I stayed in the abbey, cutting neat slices of empty air, to the point where I was allowed to go outside and kill – what, two dozen? Three? Can't actually remember offhand, but it can't have been more than five dozen, and that's including guards, witnesses and other dross. As for making a difference and diverting the course of history's river, forget it; all right, I may have wasted a few big-noses here and there, but I never had the faintest idea who they were or why they were important, so I really can't claim any of the credit.' The voice made a tut-tutting noise. 'Got to face facts,' it said. 'If there's a life after death and we all meet up in some sulphur-pit for a class reunion, no prizes for guessing who'll get the lifetime achievement award. I mean, who else in our year went on to become a god? No, I wouldn't do that if I were you,' the voice added, as Poldarn felt himself losing height, swooping down on wide, scraggy black wings towards the burning roofs of Josequin. 'No offence, but you don't want to go there. Might prove bad for your health, if you see what I mean.'

'I can't help it,' Poldarn replied. 'I can't seem to climb.'

'Oh,' said the monk. 'Oh, that is a pity. My weight, probably, forcing you down. Never mind, it'll probably be quick, if that's any consolation. Of course, if you could see your way to waking up at this point, you'd save us both a lot of bother.'

'I can't,' Poldarn said.

'Damn. The closer we get, you see, the sharper the focus gets; they stop being tiny little scurrying dots and start turning into people. Hey, look at that, will you? That's really recent. Today, in fact. Look!'

A gust of wind caught hold of him and dragged him down; beating his wings didn't help, and he couldn't turn into the wind to slow down. On the rapidly approaching ground below him he could see the derelict barn at Vistock, the crazy old woman who sold bones, and four men dragging her out into the light. He saw a fifth man: bald, with a brown, liver-spotted head, clearly not a day less than eighty years old but still tall, upright, imposing; he was absent-mindedly doing backflips with a mirror-burnished backsabre as he waited for the old woman to be brought to him and crushed down to her knees by skilful pressure on the joints of her outstretched arms; she was cursing and screaming in a language he didn't understand; she was in the middle of a sentence when the old man swung the backsabre smartly back to gather blade-speed and cut off her head in one fluid, graceful movement.

'Got to admire that style,' said the monk approvingly. 'Never had a day's formal tuition in his life, I don't suppose, but did you see that inswing? Damned if I could do that, even with a proper sword, not one of those overgrown hedge-trimmers. I guess that's what they mean when they talk about the true skill being no skill, only instinct.' One of the men had stooped down, picked up the head by its hair. 'Well,' the voice went on, 'you wanted to find out more about your family.'

They'd fetched a stick, a clothes prop. One of them was sharpening the end with a little knife.

'Do you remember,' the voice continued (and the ground kept on getting bigger and closer), 'how you used to stake out the dead crows, with a sharpened stick shoved up through the underside of the jaw, to keep the head up and make the decoy look lifelike? Maybe that's where he got the idea from.'

'Who are those people?' Poldarn asked; any moment now they were going to crash into the ground, but although he could feel the speed and momentum gathering they didn't seem to be moving—

'One of the paradoxes of religion,' the monk explained. 'Best exemplified in the moment of the draw, but it's a fundamental rule of how we view the universe. The fastest movement is no movement at all – like, for example, the movement of the hand to the sword hilt, so fast it doesn't actually happen, that moment never exists. What would it be like, we speculate, if somehow one found oneself trapped in that not-moment for ever? Maybe, we speculate further, that's what it means to be a god. Of course,' he added, as they hung still and the rest of the world raced past them, 'it's only a theory. Absolutely no means of proving it, one way or the other.'

They'd stuck the old woman's head on the pole; one of them had knelt down, holding the head neck uppermost on the ground, while the other had stabbed the clothes prop into the stub of the windpipe. Now they were hoisting it up and planting it in the ground.

'You see?' the monk said, as Poldarn finally managed to bank into the wind, and felt the shock of the air in his wings, cutting his speed enough that he could put his wings back and glide in to pitch. 'This decoying method of yours, it works every time.'

He woke up with a start, sitting forward and raising his hand to guard his face. Someone leaned over him and pushed him gently back.

'It's all right,' the voice said, 'you were having a bad dream, that's all.'

The sky was overhead again, back where it should be; but he could feel the memory of the dream rushing past him, as if he was falling out of it. A man was looking down at him, a worried look on his face. He was old, at least eighty, with a bald, wind-tanned head and huge shoulders.

'Is he going to be all right?' the man said.

'I should think so.' That sounded like Eyvind's uncle Sigfus. 'Just tired out, I think. God only knows when he last had anything to eat, either.'

The man stared at him for a few moments, then said, 'Do you recognise me?'

'No,' Poldarn said, then, 'Yes, you were in a dream I was having. You cut off an old woman's head.'

The man nodded. 'That's right,' he said. 'How did you know that?'

'Who are you?' Poldarn asked.

The old man's voice was very deep, and his eyes were sunk right back into his skull. 'My name is Halder,' he said quietly. 'I'm your grandfather.'

Poldarn thought for a moment. 'Are you sure?' he said.

This time the old man smiled, just a little twitch at the side of the mouth, but his eyes glowed warmly. 'Yes,' he said. 'Do you know who you are?'

'No,' Poldarn said.

The old man nodded. 'You're called Ciartan,' he said, 'after my father; so your full name is Tursten's Ciartan, of Haldersholt. Tursten was my son,' the old man went on. 'He died before you were born; oddly enough, not twenty yards from this very spot.'

Poldarn breathed in slowly, then out again. 'The old woman—' he said.

'Yes,' the old man said. 'She killed my son. Not that I blame her, but things have to be done. I'm just sorry it took so long.'

Poldarn thought about that, and he remembered what the old woman had said, about selling the old bones that lay in the ashes to the Potto house, to make buttons from. 'It doesn't matter to me,' he said, 'at least, at the moment it doesn't, I can't remember anything.'

The old man straightened up a little and rubbed the small of his back. 'So I gather,' he said. 'Strange business, that, but I've heard of cases like it over the years. Well,' he went on, 'here's something, I must say. Never thought I'd see you again after nigh on twenty-five years.'

I must know this man, Poldarn thought, because although there's no expression in his voice or his face, I know him well enough to recognise joy when I see it. Something in his eyes, and the set of his lips. He's telling the truth.

(And then a door opened in his mind, only a crack between door and frame, through which he could see a small part of the landscape behind: a high, square-cut hedge running down a steeply sloping hill, an old man trimming back the hedge with a brush-hook while the boy raked up the spoil; winter, nothing else to do around the farm, so time to tidy up, impose a few straight lines and square edges on the curved and rounded forms of nature; the old man was all straight lines and square edges, he remembered. Of course, he hadn't really been old then, Poldarn realised, he couldn't have been much more than twelve years older than I am now, but to me he was as strong and stern and remote and timeless as a god, undisputed master of two enormous valleys, and everybody else around the place called him the boss, or the owner. He's hardly changed at all in thirty-odd years, but the boy – that's me, I recognise that old green shirt – something must've happened to him between then and now, some great sorrow or trial, or an unwanted apotheosis.)

'I think I remember you,' Poldarn said. 'You had a grey felt hat with a very wide brim. I borrowed it once and left it out in the rain, and it was ruined.'

The old man laughed, a brittle, unhappy sound. 'You were a terror for taking things without asking,' he said, 'and then you'd bust them and pretend it wasn't you. God, how we used to argue about that; you'd never listen, it was like I was talking to myself.'

(That's right, we were never close, never really comfortable with each other. Nothing that mattered to me was ever important to you, and you never even tried to understand me. I was always the next best thing, the grudged and meagre compensation for your fine, dead son. I remember we rode together once in the cart from our farm to somewhere two days' ride away, and we never said a word to each other the whole way.)

'That sounds familiar,' Poldarn said. 'But the name – Ciartan, you said; that doesn't really mean anything to me.'

The old man shrugged. 'Figures,' he said. 'Don't suppose anybody ever called you that above once or twice a year. Mostly you were boy, or you there; son, maybe, when I forgot or I was trying to be nice. Don't remember you ever calling me anything, now I come to think of it. You never did talk much, anyhow.' He sighed. 'But you were a good worker, I'll say that for you, and a quick study, when you could be bothered. God help us, what've you been doing all these years?'

'Well,' Eyvind interrupted (Poldarn had forgotten he was there), 'obviously you two'll have a lot to talk about, so we'll leave you to it. Remember, we're pulling out as soon as it gets dark.' He turned and walked away, grabbing his uncle Sigfus firmly by the elbow as he did so. Uncle Sigfus didn't look like he wanted to go, but he didn't have much choice.

'I don't know,' Poldarn said. 'Sorry, I thought Eyvind had explained. You see, I got bashed on the head and lost my memory—'

'Yes, I heard about that,' the old man interrupted, 'I mentioned it a few minutes ago, or weren't you listening? But you must be able to remember *something*.'

'No. Well,' Poldarn qualified, 'almost nothing. Just now I remembered a few things about when I was a kid. But they were just scraps, bits and pieces, pictures. I can't remember names of people or places, or anything useful like that.'

'Not much help, then, is it?' The old man shook his head. 'It'll be different once we're home. Soon as you set eyes on Haldersdale and the farm, it'll all come right back, you'll see. You always were mighty fond of the valleys.'

It was starting to get cold, and Poldarn had nothing except what he was wearing. He considered asking the old man if there was a spare coat or blanket, but he decided against it. Showing weakness at this stage of their relationship would probably lead to repercussions later – the old man didn't look like the sort of person who'd forget something like that in a hurry. 'Tell me something about myself, then,' he went on, 'see if that works.'

The old man considered this for a moment, said, 'Very well,' and squatted down on the ground, balanced on the balls of his feet as if he was expecting to have to jump up and fight at any moment. That made him wonder what kind of place this Haldersdale was.

'Well,' the old man said, 'when you came to me you were just a baby; no use to anybody. Had you doing chores round the yard when you were five and old enough to hold a rake; the sort of thing that needs doing, but it's a waste to set a grown man on the job. You were doing things like scraping the yard, turning the apples, fetching the stock in and out of the pens. And that was it, really, till earlier this year. Winds were bad, see, we had to launch the ships early if we were going to get out at all. Same as the year you were born, come to think of it; we left early that year, too, and that was another time everything went wrong. A judgement on us, I guess, for being in such a damn hurry all the time.'

'What about my father?' Poldarn asked quietly.

'Tursten, his name was,' the old man said, looking down at the ground between his knees. 'He was a good boy, Tursten, and just shaping up to be a good farmer. Only his second year out,' he went on, 'and that bitch murdered him. There was no call for her to go doing that.'

My mother, Poldarn thought. *Who died today, the day I found my people and family again. Best not to dwell on any of that.* He looked up, wondering how the old man would look now that he'd faced that particular issue. To his surprise there was no perceptible difference. *Not so strange, at that,* he rationalised, *since I only met her the once and I couldn't get away from there, here, fast enough. Or maybe I'm just naturally callous. That's possible, too.*

'Are there any more of us?' he asked. 'Family, I mean.'

The old man nodded. 'Cousins,' he said. 'My brother Turcram's boy, almost exactly the same age as your father, and he's got four sons – Cari, Stearcad, Healti and Oser. Then there's Eolph's son Turliff, he's got two girls, Renvyck and Seun; and there's the other cousins, over at Colsness. It's not a big family or particularly close, but it's better than being alone.'

'That's good,' Poldarn said, wondering what it must be like to know someone all your life. Very strange, he decided, like being part of a herd of animals or a flock of birds. 'I'll look forward to meeting them,' he added. For once, he seemed to have said the right thing.

'They'll be surprised as all hell to see you again,' the old man said, and this time there was just a little warmth in his grin. 'Which is just as well,' he added, 'it'll take their minds off all this. There won't be a family on the island except ours that won't have lost someone. And we'll be one stronger, instead of two or three less,' he went on, looking over Poldarn's head at the gradually setting sun. 'Well, they say even in the worst times there's always one good thing to every half-dozen bad. Reckon someone must be looking after us, the way things've spun out.'

It was getting noticeably darker, and some of the men were getting to their feet, picking up their things, tightening their bootstraps and hanging the straps of their luggage round their necks. *I wonder,* Poldarn thought, *what it'll feel like, flying back towards the trees and rejoining the mob. Will I still be an individual, or just part of the family? Of course, nobody else in the world but me would ever ask a question like that.*

'Is it far to the ships?' he asked.

The old man shook his head. 'Couple of days, day and a half; if we can cover some ground tonight, so much the better. It's their damn horsemen we've got to worry about. One of these days they'll build ships so we can bring our horses with us when we come over, and then we'll show them something,

I'm telling you. But you can never find horses in this damn country; probably the government takes all the useful ones for their army.'

They were starting to move out. Nobody gave a signal or blew a horn, nobody specified a direction. 'You dropped this,' the old man said, producing the borrowed backsabre. 'You may need it before we're done.'

Poldarn stood up. 'Tell me about the farm,' he said.

That pleased the old man. 'Haldersholt,' he said. 'It's not a big spread, but it's plenty for us. There's a small river runs down the middle of Haldersdale; that's about a thousand—' The old man said some unit of measurement; it meant nothing to Poldarn, of course. '—And at the end of the valley there's a deep old combe, more or less at right angles; all wooded on the north side, with a little stream in the bottom, good pasture up the other side, but steep. The farmhouses are where the combe stream meets the river. We've usually got a couple of hundred sheep, a hundred beef stock, thirty-odd milch cows, a few dozen horses; west side of the dale's in plough, we switch ends around every year, plough and fallow. Wheat never comes to much, barley's all right, and there's gardens for greens and stuff out back of the houses; orchards too, and a hop garden. Got our own quarry on the patch, which is a blessing, and a little mill on the combe stream. There's always a few goats and pigs and chickens about the place, but the women see to all that. We had grapevines on the south side of the combe when I was a boy; my father grubbed them up one year in a bad season, but they'd probably take again. There's a few deer in the wood, birds in the season; used to be a salmon weir at the south end of the dale, but we haven't bothered with it in years, not since the Barnsriver people built theirs and fished the river out. Still, we haven't had to trade for anything outside the farm for sixty years, to my certain knowledge – got everything we need, and what we don't need we do without. And that's not much, either.'

'I like the sound of that,' Poldarn said. 'You must have a fair few men working for you.'

The old man gave him a strange look, then shrugged. 'Really have lost your memory, haven't you?' he said. 'That's not how it is back home; I'll explain it to you later, when there's time. But there's, what, fifty or sixty of us at the farm, maybe another half-dozen up at the hill station or the coal pits; like I said, it's not big but it's big enough. You want to meet some of the hands? Left most of 'em behind this time, thank God – so far, we only lost one, back there in the battle. Here,' he went on, lengthening his stride; Poldarn had to trot to keep up, like a little boy. Suddenly the old man stopped, put two fingers in his mouth and whistled. Two men ahead of them in the group turned their heads and looked round; the old man waved at them to come over.

'This is Raffen,' the old man said. 'You may just remember him; no? Shame. You used to play together when you were kids.'

The man called Raffen was very tall and broad-shouldered, bigger even than the old man. He was bald as well, with a springy ruff of greying black hair ringing his head from ear to ear, and a short, neatly trimmed beard. He didn't say anything, but he nodded, and his eyes said that he recognised Poldarn after all this time, was even glad to see him again. 'Raffen's the head shepherd,' the old man went on, as the two hands started to walk alongside them. 'Only the second time he's been off the farm in his life; figuring it'll be the last, aren't you?'

Raffen nodded again, and pulled a wry face. Poldarn wondered if he was capable of talking.

'The other one's name is Scaptey,' the old man went on, and the tone of his voice changed a little; disapproving and indulgent at the same time, implying that Scaptey was some kind of tolerated rogue, put up with for the sake of some special skill or quality. He was very short for a raider, with bushy fair hair, bright blue eyes and creased brown skin, and he almost seemed to bounce along as he walked. 'Scaptey's a pain in the backside most of the time,' the old man went on, 'but only because he knows he can get away with it. Isn't that right, Scap?'

The little man shrugged. 'Whatever you say,' he replied. 'You know me, never one to argue.'

'When he's not being a pain in the backside,' the old man continued, 'he's a half-decent carpenter, general mender and fixer. Which is to say, he built a new barn last winter and it hasn't fallen down yet. Oh yes, and he's your cousin, two or three times back; he's the grandson of my aunt Ranvay, who married out on the north coast, at Locksriver. I figure we only took him in because it's not right that one of ours should be living with foreigners.'

Poldarn decided that must be some kind of old, familiar joke or taunt between them, because Scaptey pulled a face and even Raffen smiled. For some reason Poldarn felt vaguely annoyed at being left out.

They were setting a brisk pace; he could feel his knees and the calves of his legs aching already (too much riding around in carts, not enough walking . . . The voice in his mind that said that sort of thing to him was already starting to sound like the old man, like his grandfather. Very briefly, he thought he heard the voice of the god of crows, welcoming him). It was already too dark to see clearly, but he could make out the head of the man in front of him, who seemed to know where he was going, so he followed that. Soon, there was nothing left to see at all, but somehow he knew where the man in front was; the technique worked, he didn't trip over or put his foot down a rabbit hole, and after a while he stopped feeling the pain in his legs as the rhythm of the pace took over.

When they stopped, he stopped, not knowing why or even how he knew to hold still and stay quiet. Something was going on, somewhere up ahead. He closed his eyes and tried to catch some sounds, but he couldn't even hear breathing.

*They've run up against something, we've run up against some-
thing, so we're sending out our scouts. When they get back, we'll
know what it is and decide what to do.* He concentrated on
standing perfectly still; naturally, the harder he concentrated,
the greater was the urge to shift his feet and fidget, so he tried
to think of something else instead. He thought about the farm.
There was already a picture of it in his mind, but it was flat
and artificial, like the paintings on the wall of the inn at
Sansory. There was the river, there was the stream, medium
blue for water; overhead the sky was bright light blue, and the
grass was a uniform fresh green, inlaid at appropriate intervals
with fluffy white sheep. He tried thinking about the two men,
Raffen and Scaptey; God help me, he thought, I'm about to
get on a ship and sail away to the Land of the Archetypes,
where everybody's either a strong, silent, faithful retainer or a
lovable rogue. He thought about the old man, but somehow
his mind skidded off the surface of that thought, like a file on
a hardened steel edge. He tried to remember something about
home, but he didn't like to get too close to the pictures that
came into his mind, for fear that the paint was still wet and
might smudge.

Suddenly there was some movement, and up ahead, shouting and thumping. Something fell over with a bump he could
feel through the soles of his feet; somebody yelled in pain, at
which point he started to walk forward, his hand tight on the
sabre hilt, feeling a hard edge where the wood had shrunk a
little away from the tang. Someone had lit a torch, several
torches, forming a circle of light around a dozen men, and a
cart.

'Talk about a slice of luck,' someone was saying, in our language. 'Anybody know who these clowns could be? They look
important enough.'

Eyvind's voice: 'Here, somebody find Tursten's Ciartan.'
Who? Poldarn realised with a jolt that that name meant him.
'He knows their language, he can translate.'

It was as if someone had put a hand between his shoulder blades and pushed him forward. Men got out of his way without looking round (so how did they know he was coming through?). When he reached the edge of the circle (reached it but hadn't violated it, he was still just about in the dark) he called out, 'I'm here.'

'Splendid,' Eyvind's voice said—

(Was Eyvind in command? He didn't think so. At least, he hadn't been in command before, but now here he was, deciding what was to be done. Poldarn made a slight effort and adjusted his mind. Eyvind was in command *now*, for this particular job. When it was over, he'd be subsumed back into the group, the mob, the melt. Apparently, that was the way we do things.)

'Splendid,' Eyvind's voice said. 'All right, I'll say the question, you translate it into their language, then tell me what they say. Ready? Right, here goes. Who are you?'

Poldarn had to think this time, he couldn't just put his hand to his side and draw the words instinctively. 'Who are you?' he said.

No reply. His first instinct was that he hadn't translated it properly, then he realised they'd understood just fine, but they were refusing to say anything back. That struck him as downright rude. He improvised. 'Unless you tell us,' he said, 'we'll take that tall man on the extreme left and cut his hands off. Now, who are you?'

He already knew part of the answer; they were soldiers, probably imperial rather than Amathy house: eight cavalry troopers, four men who looked like officers. One of us was standing up in the cart; he called out, 'Hey, there's another one in here, but he looks like he's sick.'

Poldarn thought for a moment. 'You in the cart,' he called out, 'who are you?'

'That,' replied a weak, ragged voice, 'is actually a rather complicated question. But my name's Monach.'

One of the troopers tried to get up into the cart, presumably to shut the voice up. One of us grabbed him by the shoulder and compressed him to his knees, apparently with no effort at all.

'Monach,' Poldarn said. 'Are you a soldier too? I can't see you.'

'Me? No, I'm a civilian.' There was something about the voice; it was telling the truth, but it was telling it for a reason of its own, probably not fear of death or torture. It was up to something.

'All right,' Poldarn said. 'So who are these people you're with, and what are you doing with them?'

'Why the hell should I tell you that?'

Poldarn had to search his minds for the right words. 'Because if you don't, we'll kill you. Is that a good enough reason?'

The voice laughed, and the laugh broke up into a cough. 'Not really,' it replied. 'Why don't you come over here where I can see you?'

Why indeed? For some reason, Poldarn felt apprehensive about stepping into the light. 'I can talk to you perfectly well from here,' he replied.

'Please yourself. Your voice sounds a little bit familiar, that's all.'

'Yours, too, come to that.' Poldarn frowned. This wasn't helping, and he could feel Eyvind frowning at him. 'Answer the damn question,' he said. 'Who are these people?'

There was a brief silence, then the voice said, 'The medium tall one in the middle is General Cronan.' Two of the troopers twitched, as if they'd been meaning to have a go at rushing the cart, and their nerve had failed at the last moment. 'I don't know the names of the other three, but they're senior staff officers. Congratulations, whoever you are, you've thrown a double nine. I think that means you get a free go.'

Poldarn assumed he knew what that meant. 'What about you?' he said.

'If you must know,' the voice said, 'I'm a monk of the abbey of Deymeson. Possibly even the last one, I don't know; not that it matters, I'll be dead fairly soon.'

'All right,' Poldarn said. 'So why should I believe you're telling the truth?'

'You can if you like; I suppose it's like religion, a matter of faith. But if you want to know why I'm betraying the general, truth is I'm following orders. The abbot sent me to kill him, you see. Well, I haven't had the chance up till now.'

The man who was supposed to be General Cronan turned his head and swore at the man in the cart; one of us stepped forward and punched the back of his head, dropping him sprawled on the ground.

'Wouldn't have been right before the battle, anyhow,' the voice called Monach went on. 'We needed him, you see, to deal with you. But he's done that now.' The voice sounded very tired, but it was still clear and audible. 'Don't suppose any of this'll mean anything to you, but I'd like to tell someone how clever I've been. You want me to explain?'

'If you like,' Poldarn replied.

'How gracious of you. Right, then. I needed Cronan to beat you, because nobody else could and you had to be stopped. But now he's done that, he's definitely got to be killed; the only man to fight and defeat the raiders, that makes him the most terrible threat to the safety of the empire. He'd only have to say the word, and the whole imperial army would go over to him without a moment's hesitation. So we take him out of the picture, who does that leave? Tazencius is a nonentity, nobody's going to trust Feron Amathy; the government troops have fallen back on Sansory, which means the Amathy house can't sack it like they were planning to do. It's all turned out pretty well, if you ask me.'

Poldarn wasn't sure if any of that made sense, but it was none of his business anyhow. He turned his head in the direction that Eyvind's voice had come from. 'This is a slice of luck,' he said in our language. 'Seems like we've tripped over the enemy general, the one responsible for what happened. The other three are his advisers, and the man in the cart's a traitor. I think he's telling the truth.'

'Dear God,' Eyvind said. 'Well, things are looking up. What do you want to do with the traitor?'

Poldarn considered the matter. 'He reckons he's going to die anyway,' he said. 'Leave him be, I would.'

'Why not?' Eyvind replied, and while he was still speaking a backsabre chewed through General Cronan's neck. The sound carried a long way in the dark. One of the other staff officers tried to say something, but he wasn't fast enough. All the rest of them died in silence.

'Thank you,' said the voice from the cart. 'It's just like they said, everybody who rides with me gets killed, sooner or later. The unsettling thing is, what if I've averted the end of the world? I don't think I was supposed to do that.'

For some reason Poldarn knew it was safe to enter the circle now. He walked up to the cart and peered in. There was just enough light to see the man's face.

'Excuse me,' Poldarn said, 'but does the name Poldarn mean anything to you?'

The man looked back at him. 'Are you trying to be funny?' he said; then his face crumpled up with pain, and he passed out.

Chapter Twenty-Six

It was a long walk to the ships. Shortly after the first dawn they reached the Mahec, which made navigation extremely simple but increased the risk of detection by enemy cavalry. A few days before, of course, they'd have regarded a chance encounter with the enemy as an opportunity rather than a threat, but attitudes had changed. The main thing now was to get home quickly and safely, without further loss.

'I don't suppose I understand these people any more than you do,' Poldarn said, as they followed the riverbank on the second afternoon. The man he was talking to (he hadn't caught his name) shook his head and smiled, but he persisted. 'No, really,' he said, 'you've got to bear in mind, when I woke up I couldn't remember anything. I've been learning about these people from scratch, just like you.'

The man clicked his tongue. 'There's a difference, for a start,' he said. 'We don't want to learn about them, at least not more than we need to know so we can beat shit out of them. I mean, why bother? It'd be like learning to speak sheep.'

Poldarn let that go by. 'My guess is, though,' he went on,

'they aren't going to bother us any more; I mean, why the hell should they? They'd have to be crazy. They've beaten us once and we're going home. If they fight us again, there's a good chance they'll lose, now they haven't got their military genius any more, and that's the advantage they've gained gone for ever.'

The man wasn't convinced. 'You're assuming they're smart,' he said. 'You can get in a lot of trouble making assumptions like that. No, it's just as likely that they're too dumb to figure out what you just said, and they'll come after us to try and score another victory. Whoever their new commander is, won't he want to prove he's every bit as good as the dead guy?'

Poldarn had to admit that was quite likely from what he'd gathered about the way the empire's mind worked. 'Still,' he went on, 'if they do attack, we'll be ready for them. Last time they only won because they'd had time to plant those damn caltrops.'

His foot didn't hurt nearly as much as it had the previous day, which in turn had been an improvement on the first night. He'd had help, of course; men he didn't know but who seemed to know who he was had taken it in turns to lend him a shoulder; that, combined with the unrelenting pace of the march, had turned the whole business into some kind of deadly serious three-legged race. His arm was a different matter, unfortunately. Someone who seemed to know about such things had announced that the wound had gone bad. He'd known the cure, of course – seven different kinds of poultice, all involving garlic and bread mould, neither of which was available in the middle of nowhere, with the enemy possibly hot on their trail. 'You'll probably be all right, even so,' the man had told him, 'it'll just take longer, that's all.' He'd got the impression the man was trying to be positive rather than tiresomely accurate.

On the third evening they reached a village. For once news

of their approach had preceded them, and the place was deserted. All traces of food had been cleared out of the houses, but they found apples on the trees in a big orchard, and several plots of leeks and onions more or less ready to be pulled. That was just as well; they'd had precious little to eat since the battle, though nobody had actually gone hungry. A dog followed them down the street as they left, wagging its tail but keeping a good twenty-five yards clear at all times. Poldarn noticed it, and for some reason realised that he hadn't seen a crow for days, and not many birds of any kind.

On the fourth day he was able to walk on his own, though Halder and Raffen took it in turns to walk on his lame side, keeping perfect step, in case he stumbled. Raffen didn't say anything, but Halder told him more about the farm; how he'd found the site himself when he was twelve, moved there when he was sixteen and built his first house, floating the timbers down the combe stream one at a time. His father had a fine place a day's walk to the east, he explained, but he'd never been comfortable at home; he had three elder brothers and he wanted somewhere of his own, so one day he followed the river until he came to the place where the house now stood. It was a hot day and he felt thirsty, so he lay down to drink. Somehow, when he stood up again, he knew that here was the place he was meant to be. He wasted the rest of the day walking the valley and the combe, and spent the night lying on his back beside the watersmeet, trying to count the stars. He woke up soaked with dew, and by the time he reached home he was running a bad fever that nearly killed him, but as soon as he was fit to be out again he took his father and brothers to see the place and formally laid a claim by raising a stone and cutting his name on it. When his father died, his brothers and their people helped him raise the house, gave him his share of the flock, the herd and the seedcorn, and left him to it. That suited him fine. The next time he left the farm, except to borrow tools or scrounge for iron, was three years later, when he walked down the river for two days to Gynnersford, where he'd been told they had a spare daughter. Her name was Rannway, and some useful stock and a serviceable cart came with her. Their son, Tursten, was born a year later. The day after he was born Halder started planting a pine copse on the rise opposite the farm, the idea being that by the time Tursten was old enough to want a house of his own the trees would be the right age for felling and logging; the copse was called Tursten's Wood, and it was still there, since Tursten never showed the slightest inclination to get married or leave the main house. Nobody had ever got round to thinning the trees out, so they'd grown tall and spindly; there was a rookery on the southern edge, and the birds had an aggravating habit of pitching in when the men fed the calves and robbing the feed from under their noses.

(And when I was a kid, I declared war on those crows, and won a single glorious victory, Yes, I know all about that.)

'How old was my father when he died?' he asked.

Hallder counted backwards for a moment. 'Nineteen,' he replied, 'just about to turn twenty.'

Poldarn nodded. 'And how long ago was that?'

Halder looked at him, then realised the point of the question. 'Forty-one years ago,' he replied, 'give or take a month. The woman was ten years older than him, they reckon. When I heard what'd happened, I looked up the men who'd been with him at the time – they were from Colscegsbridge, on the other side of the island – and made them promise to take me there the next year when they went, in case there was anything left to see. We found her there, among the ruins, with the baby. We tried to creep up nice and quiet but she must've heard us. She was in the barn, and there was a hole in the back wall we hadn't spotted. By the time we figured what had happened, she was out back and running, with you tucked under her arm like a parcel. We saw her just in time, and chased after her; I fell behind, but Asley and Turcram, two of the men, were good runners, they were closing in; suddenly she stopped – I saw this myself – and she put you carefully down on the ground, then she ran off, fast as she could.'

'Oh,' Poldarn said.

'Well,' Halder went on, 'Asley carried on after her, Turcram stopped to pick you up. To cut a long stick short, Asley tripped on a molehill and twisted his ankle, she got away, and we were left with you. Of course, soon as I saw you I knew you were Tursten's boy; so I brought you home, and handed you over to Rannway – that's your grandmother—'

'Yes, you told me that,' Poldarn said.

'So I did. Anyway, she died two years later, but there were women at the farm to look after you, you never wanted for anything, and that's all there is to tell. At least, that's all till you were just turned nineteen, old enough to go abroad for the first time.' The old man shook his head. 'Should've known better, of course,' he said, 'but you were wild keen to go, and I couldn't see the harm. Worst thing was, I was laid up that season, I'd fallen out of a pear tree, of all the damn fool things to do, and broken my leg. So I didn't go, and you didn't come back. That's something to think about,' he added. 'There's only been two years since I turned twenty-three that I didn't go abroad; the first time I lost Tursten, the second time I lost you. I guess that's why I'm here now, for fear of what'll happen if I miss another year, because the only one I'd got left to lose by then was me.'

That night they slept in the ruins of a town, long since overgrown. Halder said he had an idea that he'd been with the expedition that burned it, forty-seven or forty-eight years ago, but he couldn't be sure. The wind was coming up from the east, but there were some bits and pieces of wall still standing, enough for most of them to get behind. Poldarn fell asleep as soon as he lay down, and had a dream in which his mother appeared to him and forgave him for something he couldn't remember having done, but she didn't look anything like the old woman from the barn at Vistock, and he couldn't help wondering if the dream had really been meant for somebody else.

The next day, just after mid-afternoon, they reached the coast (which was good), at least half a day south of where they thought they'd come out (which wasn't); the confusion turned out to be the result of following the southern fork of the Mahec at the point at which it split into two. Everybody in the party seemed very upset and disappointed, though nobody blamed anybody else; they seemed to regard it as an omen or a punishment from heaven, and none of them seemed to be in any mood to talk about anything for the rest of the day. They pressed on, apparently hoping they'd be able to force the pace enough to make the ships by nightfall, but they'd underestimated the terrain and ran into complications they didn't appear to have been expecting: boggy ground, woods, places where the path ran along the cliff face and occasionally crumbled away into the sea. Five men left the main party of their own accord and went ahead to scout out a safe route; they hadn't come back by the time the main body decided to stop where they were and wait for morning.

Poldarn lay down and went to sleep lying on a flat rock. When he woke up he realised that the rock sloped downwards at a sharp angle, and was perched on the end of a spur hanging out over the sea.

The next morning they set out early, the consensus of opinion being that they couldn't be more than an hour from the ships, if that. Four or five hours later they still hadn't found any ships, or even any landmarks they recognised, nor had the scouts come back. This didn't make sense, so another five men set off to find the way and see if they could figure out what had happened to the other advance party. They came back soon afterwards and announced that they'd seen the ships, and they weren't far away, but there was a problem. Between the raiders and the ships was the mouth of the main spur of the Mahec River; it was too wide to cross, and there didn't seem to be a ford or a bridge. Rather than muck about and waste time following the river upstream looking for one, they'd come back to report and warn the others, who would doubtless be able to think of some way round the difficulty.

At that point everybody started talking at once, and it wasn't long before Poldarn came to realise that this was a sure sign that nobody had the faintest idea what to do. Of course, he didn't either. If the nearest crossing place was a day's march upstream – well, that was two days wasted, during which time the enemy might show up at any moment. (Did they have ships of their own? Nobody knew. If so, were they patrolling the coast in the hope of finding the beached ships? If so, why hadn't they already done so?) To make matters worse, they'd be kidding themselves if they reckoned they had enough food left for a square meal, so there was a very real prospect of a long detour on an empty stomach. A few enthusiasts started talking about swimming out to the ships and bringing them into the mouth of the river. Others, more sensible, explained why this would be a bad idea. It was the first time Poldarn had seen them disagreeing among themselves, and it struck him that they weren't very good at it, presumably through lack of practice. Nobody particularly wanted to listen to anybody else's views or suggestions, they were too busy shouting out their own, with a degree of vehemence that suggested that fairly soon they'd reach the conclusion that words weren't going to be enough, and start reaching for their backsabres.

Someone asked why they hadn't considered this problem when they beached the ships there in the first place. The explanation seemed to be that they hadn't anticipated coming back that way. It had been assumed, reasonably enough in the light of past experience, that they'd be following the north bank of the main spur of the Mahec, having come down on it from the north about a day out from the sea. The river hadn't been an issue since the trail they'd been planning to follow both going out and coming back sheared off north-east from the river road, and nobody had actually carried on that way far enough to notice any fords, bridges or ferries.

By this point the argument was going round in circles, but there wasn't anybody either willing or able to stop it and bring the discussion to order. Poldarn, who didn't feel he was qualified to join in, wandered away and sat under a thorn tree, one of the few windbreaks on the open moor. He rested his head against the trunk and closed his eyes—

Don't I know you? he thought.

The woman from his previous dream was standing in front of him, while the obligatory crow flew in overhead and pitched in the spindly branches of the tree. Poldarn stayed where he was.

I don't know, the woman replied, do you?

That didn't seem very helpful. The woman was about forty years old, with a thin face, very pale, and a small, sharp nose. This time, apparently, she wasn't his mother.

I'm sorry, he said, but I don't know who you are. Not that that means anything, I don't even know who I am, let alone anybody else.

Well, you should know me by now, the woman replied, I'm your wife.

Oh, Poldarn thought; and he said, I'm sorry, I hadn't realised I'm married.

The woman gave him an unpleasant look and said, Well, you aren't, not any more. Poldarn said, I'm sorry, I don't quite follow. The woman shook her head and said, That's a joke, when you think that it was you who had me killed. Murdered, she amended; you had me murdered, because I'd become a nuisance and you wanted to marry someone else, Prince Tazencius' daughter, who's less than half your age. So you had two of your men push me down a well, and I remember floating there, after I got too weak to swim any more and drowned, and I was listening to you telling everybody that there'd been a dreadful accident, you were bawling and sobbing – I'll bet you managed real tears, somehow or other – and they all believed you, or they put up a bloody good show; and all this time I'd been thinking, at least he remembers, at least his conscience must be ripping into him sometimes, probably in the early hours of the morning, when you wake up and can't get back to sleep again. Now it turns out you've forgotten, and that makes me feel so angry—

I'm sorry, Poldarn repeated, but I honestly don't remember. I don't know your name, even.

She grinned at him unpleasantly. I like that, she said. My name's Faleris, and we were married for seven years. We have a son, who's five, and a daughter who's just turned three. At least, that's how old they were when I died. You have no way of knowing when that was, and I'm damned if I'm going to tell you. I'll leave you to think about that in the early hours of the morning, that time when you've woken up and you can't seem to be able to get back to sleep. That'll give you something to think about other than wars and fighting and plundering, assuming you're capable of doing that.

He reached out a hand towards her, to see if she was real; but she seemed to melt and soak away into the ground, leaving behind nothing but a noise in his head that was somewhat like her voice. He looked directly overhead, trying to see the crow in the branches that would reassure him it was all just a dream—

'I said wake up,' Halder repeated. 'Or we'll go without you.'

He sat up. 'I'm sorry,' he said. 'I think I fell asleep.'

'You were always doing that,' Halder told him, reaching out a hand and pulling him to his feet. 'Leave you alone for ten minutes, come back and there you'd be, dead to the world. God only knows how anyone could sleep at a time like this, but if anybody could, it'd be you.'

It turned out that they'd decided there was nothing for it but to walk alongside the river and look for somewhere to cross. Nobody was happy about it; the pace of the march dwindled away into a slow trudge, that of weary men with half a day's work still to be done. No one spoke. Poldarn's foot and arm were both hurting, but he felt he couldn't say anything.

Late in the afternoon they came over a blind ridge. For some reason they hadn't sent out scouts (nobody had wanted to go), so the first they knew about the army in the valley was when they cleared the ridge and looked down at them.

'Who the hell are they?' somebody asked.

The soldiers down below were looking up at them, plainly stunned; this wasn't an ambush, Poldarn realised, just a chance meeting that nobody had planned. Of course, there was no reason why they should fight each other.

'Well, just standing here isn't going to do any good,' someone said, and a moment later they were charging down the hill, sabres drawn and swung above the head, ready for the downstroke. Damn, Poldarn thought, and he started running as well so as not to be left behind. He carried on running until he crashed into something; the something turned out to be a man, one of the enemy, who'd dodged sideways to get out of the way of someone else. Both of them hit the ground and rolled; Poldarn was the first on his feet, and his bad arm screamed with pain as he swung the sabre, a fraction of a second quicker than the man he'd just collided with could snatch his sword up from the damp grass and thrust at him. Poldarn was quicker, but he botched the cut. Instead of connecting with the junction of shoulder and neck, he cut through just above the elbow joint. The man opened his mouth to scream, but nothing came out. It was at that moment that Poldarn recognised him, even recalling his name – Captain Muno, the man he'd rescued from the old women who were robbing the bodies, after the battle by the river; the man he'd carried back to camp, and been given a horse in exchange for.

Captain Muno sank to his knees, his mouth still open, like a fish drowning in air. Poldarn swung again, this time getting the cut in exactly the right place; he felt the jar as the blade hacked into bone, running up his arms and filling him with pain. Muno fell forward, making the backsabre twist; Poldarn yelped and let go, but not before he felt something tearing in his bad arm. Trying to ignore it, he reached down with his other hand and picked up the sword, which wasn't his and therefore couldn't just be abandoned.

He'd been left behind, of course. He tried to run, but could only hobble along behind the great, splendid surge of the raiders' charge, like a very old, grey-nosed dog pottering along behind a cart. More than once he tripped over a dead body or a stone.

Whoever these people were, they were fighting to the last man (ridiculous, Poldarn thought; this is an *accident*), as if something vital was at stake. A bunch of them had drawn back to guard a line of carts. They'd formed a circle around them, but at least a third of them were facing inwards, as if they were expecting to be attacked from both sides. *Prisoners,* Poldarn guessed, *they've got prisoners in those carts and they daren't let them get away.* But he didn't have the mental resources to spare for mere curiosity. The main thing was to get out of the way of this pointless fighting before it ruined everything. He had an unpleasant vision of his newly acquired grandfather coming in a trifle too late with his guard, or failing to notice the man immediately behind him. The way his luck had been running, for himself and everybody he'd been in contact with, he reckoned he had cause to be apprehensive.

But he couldn't see the old man, or Raffen or Scaptey-the-lovable-rogue. They weren't hampered by infuriatingly inconvenient injuries, and had rushed off down the hill and merged in with the rest of the battle scene, flying back towards the trees and dissolving into the mob. For a brief moment they'd been individuals, with names and histories, but now they were part of the wave, and he couldn't make out their faces at this distance, not even to watch them die.

He stumbled on as best he could, but the pain in both his foot and his arm was reaching the point where he couldn't just shove it out of his mind; it was insistent enough to control him, the way a baby's crying controls its mother. Long before he reached the bottom of the slope and the battle, he gave in to it and sat down, letting it sweep through him simply because he couldn't resist it any longer. *This isn't right*, he thought, *being separate, not being in there with them*. He felt ashamed, but there was more to it than that. He felt lonely, sitting by himself on the wet ground surrounded by dead bodies; and he thought, *Well, that suggests I've come a certain distance from the place where I woke up first. It's probably better to belong somewhere, on balance.*

'There you are,' said a voice behind him.

He looked round. How the hell did they manage that trick of sneaking up behind him? 'Eyvind?' he said.

'Are you all right?' Eyvind said.

Poldarn shook his head. 'Did you come back just to look for me?' he asked.

'Sort of,' Eyvind replied. 'Actually, Halder sent me. He couldn't see you, wondered where you'd got to.' He smiled. 'I guess he's scared to let you out of his sight now he's found you again.'

'That's nice of him,' Poldarn said. 'You'll have to help me up, I'm afraid my foot's gone useless again.'

'That's all right,' Eyvind said, pulling him up by his good arm and taking his weight across his shoulders. 'It's pretty well all over anyway. What we can't figure out is why they're making such a big deal about those carts. Must be something worth having in there, which means,' he added with a grin, 'that once we've shooed off those few, we might end up with something nice to take home with us after all. Nearly broke our hearts, having to dump the proceeds of all that hard work.'

Poldarn shook his head. 'Don't get your hopes up,' he said. 'I have an idea it's people in the carts, not things. Here, look; can you see the inner ring of soldiers?'

Eyvind looked, then sighed. 'I see what you mean,' he said. 'But that can't be their own people they're guarding.'

'Prisoners,' Poldarn replied. 'Probably they've got it into their heads that we're here to rescue them.'

Eyvind looked thoughtful. 'Think about it,' he said. 'Who would we go out of our way to rescue? Our own, of course. Maybe they've got some of our people down there. Survivors from the battle, maybe.'

Poldarn frowned. 'Unlikely,' he said. 'Why bring them all the way up here, north-west? I'd have thought that if they'd caught any of us, they'd either kill them out of hand or ship them off to Torcea as quickly as possible.'

Eyvind considered that. 'Exactly,' he said. 'Ship them off, by sea. Maybe they've got ships of their own waiting up the coast a way, and that's where they were taking them.'

'Maybe,' Poldarn conceded, though he wasn't convinced. 'Anyway,' he added, 'it won't matter, will it? Like you said, it'll be all over pretty soon. Almost certainly by the time I could get there.'

'Damn.' Eyvind looked troubled. 'That's awkward. I think I should get down there, just in case I was right about them having some of our people, but I promised Halder I'd look after you.' He shrugged. 'Can't be helped,' he said. 'Besides, you and I won't be the only ones who've drawn that particular conclusion. Still, we'll get down there as quickly as we can, I think. Who knows, they may manage to spin the fighting out for long enough.'

It was a painful walk, and Eyvind's impatience didn't make it any easier or noticeably faster. But they got there in the end, just in time to see the circle of soldiers breached and crushed, like the man who draws a little too slowly. After that it was like watching the sea rush in through a hole in the wall: quick, efficient, rather depressing.

'There's Halder, look,' Eyvind called out. That was a relief, though Poldarn hadn't been thinking much about him at that particular moment. He followed the line Eyvind was showing him, and saw the top of the old man's head; beside him he saw Raffen, so that was all right. He couldn't see Scaptey, but he wasn't really bothered about him.

The fighting petered out quite quickly after that; here and there Poldarn could see rapid scuffling movement, an arm upraised for a moment as some leftover enemy was disposed of, but mostly the raiders were standing about or sitting on the ground, resting sociably for a moment or so before moving on to the next job of work that needed to be done. Two men were pulling down the tailgate of the nearest cart. The prisoners, Poldarn thought, assuming there are any, of course.

One of the men took a step backwards and raised his sabre. 'Hold it,' Poldarn called out; the man hesitated and looked round to see who'd spoken. Poldarn hobbled over as quickly as he could.

'There's some more of them in there,' the man explained. 'I saw something move under that pile of old blankets.'

'I thought there might be,' Poldarn replied, and he explained his prisoners theory.

'It's possible,' the man admitted. 'All right, let's shift the blankets and have a look. Though if it was one of us, surely he'd have called out as soon as he heard our voices.'

Nobody else was paying them any attention; mostly they were wandering round the battlefield picking up weapons and pieces of armour, anything made of metal. Poldarn eased in front of the man he'd just been talking to, picked up a spear and used its point to flick away the blankets, revealing a man's head. The face was familiar.

'I know you,' he said. 'You're Tazencius.'

The man under the blankets sneezed, then stood up. Poldarn had been right; it was the same man he'd picked up off the road, on his first trip out for Falx Roisin. He looked very sad; there was dried mud in his hair, and he had a black eye. His left leg was tightly wrapped in cloth, with two splints to keep it straight. 'That's right,' Tazencius replied. 'What happened?'

Poldarn frowned. 'You tell me,' he said.

Tazencius sat down on the edge of the cart, his bad leg stuck out straight in front of him. 'After the battle at Vistock, you mean?' he said. 'I thought you'd have figured that out for yourself. The Amathy house sold me to the imperials; no idea what the price was, I was in no position to ask.' He frowned. 'But you should know that,' he said. 'After all, if you didn't know I'd been captured, how'd you know to rescue me?'

Poldarn grinned. 'What makes you think you've been rescued?' he replied.

'Hey,' asked the man who'd discovered him, 'what are you talking about?'

'It's all right,' Poldarn replied without turning round. 'It so happens that this is a very important man. The emperor's cousin, I think.'

'Quite right,' Tazencius said.

'Doesn't matter,' the raider broke in. 'You know the rules: no survivors, no witnesses. Now, are you going to deal with him, or shall I do it?'

'Just hold your horses, will you?' Poldarn said. 'Or doesn't the concept of ransom mean anything to you?'

'The what?' the man asked, and Poldarn realised that he'd used the imperial word for ransom, since there wasn't an obvious equivalent in his own language. Anyway, that answered the question fairly well.

'I know him,' Poldarn said, not really sure how this was supposed to justify breaking what was presumably a cardinal rule by sparing a witness. 'It's all right,' he added.

'Please yourself.' The man slid his sabre back on to his belt. 'All yours,' he added, then turned away, having apparently lost all interest in the matter. His colleague had already wandered away, and was trying on a dead soldier's boots.

'Thank you,' Tazencius said. 'I couldn't understand what you were saying to that man, but I could guess pretty well.'

'He wanted to kill you,' Poldarn replied.

Tazencius sighed. 'I have an idea that puts him in with the majority of the human race. Are you in charge of these people?'

Poldarn frowned. 'Good God, no. They're taking me along for the ride. Apparently, some of them are my relatives.'

Tazencius was looking at him oddly, as though what he was saying didn't make any sense. 'Whatever you say,' he replied. 'Anyway, I owe you another favour. That makes it twice in a matter of weeks you've saved my skin. It's good to know there's someone on my side.'

'Am I?' Poldarn asked. 'Not that it matters particularly, since I'm getting out of here. Which is what I'd do if I were you,' he added.

Tazencius grinned and patted his broken leg. 'I agree with you,' he said. 'If you could just explain how I'm supposed to go about it—'

'Your problem,' Poldarn replied.

For some reason Tazencius looked as if he'd expected rather more. 'If that's the way you want to play it, fine,' he said. 'Like I said, I owe you my life, and I don't want to make things difficult for you with your friends here. The fact remains, if I'm left hobbling about the place, there's a better than even chance I'll get picked up by the imperials pretty quickly – or the Amathy house, which amounts to the same thing, apparently – and then everything we've both been working for these past few years'll have been a waste of time and energy. I really don't want to be a burden to you, but it's in your interests just as much as mine. And there's Lysalis to

consider, just in case you'd forgotten. We've had our differences, sure, but I don't suppose she'd be pleased if she found
out you'd left her dear old dad out on the battlefield to die.'

Poldarn thought for a moment; then he hauled himself up
on to the cart and sat down opposite Tazencius. 'I haven't got
a lot of time,' he said. 'They'll be wanting to move out soon and
I don't want to be left behind. Do you know who I am?'

Tazencius scowled at him. 'What's the matter with you?' he
said. 'It's all right, there's nobody watching. And even if there
was, they can't understand what we're saying. Can they?'

Poldarn leaned forward quickly and grabbed Tazencius by
the throat before he could get out of the way. 'That name you
just said.'

'What? Oh, you mean Lysalis. My daughter. Your wife.'

'My wife,' Poldarn repeated. 'Prove to me that she's my
wife. Prove she even exists.'

'But I don't need to. You know . . .' Tazencius tried to
shake himself free, but Poldarn was too strong for him.
'Look,' he said, 'what the hell's come over you? Everything
was going so well. First you led these people of yours into an
ambush, just as we'd planned, so I'd have my victory. Then
you managed to catch Cronan and kill him – and I'm really
grateful to you for that, you don't know how much it means
to me. And now you've saved me again, just like you did that
other time; it's like having my own personal guardian angel,
it's wonderful. Best thing I ever did, letting you marry
Lysalis. And now you're acting like you've gone mad. What's
got into you?'

'Don't you understand?' Poldarn said. 'I've forgotten everything. I can't even remember who I am. I only know who you
are because I heard someone mention your name—'

He stopped. Tazencius was grinning. 'Is that right?' he said.
'You know, I believe you. What, you can't remember anything? Anything at all?'

'No. For God's sake, you've got to tell me.'

Tazencius was laughing. 'I don't think so,' he replied. 'My God, talk about a stroke of luck,' and as he spoke he leaned back a little, picked up a long knife that was lying on the bed of the cart, and poked Poldarn quite hard in the ribs with it. It was very quickly and neatly done. 'Now let go,' he said. 'Gently, that's right. Thank you. Now I suggest that you find a way to get me out of here. Otherwise, we'll die together.'

Quickly, Poldarn assessed the position. One very slight movement, and he'd be dead; it doesn't take much to push a sharp, thin knife up under the ribcage and into the heart. 'Why won't you tell me who I am?' he asked.

Tazencius smiled maliciously. 'Mostly,' he said, 'because I don't like you very much. To be perfectly honest – and there's no reason why I shouldn't be, not any more – I never could stand the sight of you; the thought of you with my daughter, it's enough to make me sick. Actually, I'm doing you a favour, because if I was you, I really wouldn't want to know who I was, if you see what I mean. Ignorance is bliss, as the poet says. So what happened? Bash on the head, was it?'

'What harm have I ever done you?'

'What harm? Do me a favour.' Tazencius shook his head. 'Just associating with you, it's like wallowing in blood and shit. Did you just say you're going away?'

'Yes.'

'Wonderful. With the savages?'

'Yes.'

'Absolutely splendid. Give it a week or so, you'll have them all at each other's throats, with any luck they'll wipe themselves out and leave us all in peace. You know, this is quite extraordinary. In a way, it's even better than killing you.'

'You want to kill me?'

Tazencius shrugged. 'Who doesn't? In fact,' he went on, 'about the only person I can think of who wouldn't want to kill you on sight is my poor besotted child – and that, my dear son-in-law, is the one thing I'll never be able to forgive you for.

Oh sure, I was the one who sold my poor innocent lamb to the most evil man in the world, just so as to get his help in stealing the empire; the very thought of what I did disgusts me so much I can't bear to think about it. But that she should go and fall in love with you – you, for God's sake – that was my punishment, of course, that was divine retribution, as cruel and vicious as they could make it. It means I can't kill you – here we are, you and me and a nice sharp knife, and the pointed end actually facing in the right direction, and I can't rid the world of you. Isn't that something?' He sighed. 'No, instead you'll help me escape, I'll let you live – I'll owe my life to *you*. Again. That's my punishment too. You know what? You're like spilt honey; the more I try and clean up the mess, the stickier I get. You're all over me. Because of you, in everything I do, evil sticks to me and I can't wipe it off. Well.' He smiled. 'Now, just possibly, things are about to get better. You're going away. You don't know who you are. You don't know what we've done together, so you can't hold it over me. And when I'm emperor – and I will be, you can count on it, God help me – when I'm emperor you won't be there to torment me any more, because you won't know who you are. It's priceless, really it is. You know, for the first time in years I'm actually feeling optimistic.'

Poldarn tried to move, but he couldn't; the knife point was precisely in position, leaving him room to breathe and nothing more. Out of the corner of his eye he could see his people harvesting steel from the dead, working steadily, cheerfully; they wouldn't be able to help him, they couldn't see that anything was wrong. 'Please,' he said, 'I promise you, I'm going away, you'll never see me again. At least tell me my name.'

Tazencius smirked at him. 'All right,' he said. 'Your name's Ciartan. But that's only the name you came with, not the one everybody here knows you by. And if you think everybody's an exaggeration, you're wrong. There can't be anyone – well, certainly this side of the bay – who hasn't heard of you. And if

I said your name and asked, "Who's he?" you know what they'd all say? "The most evil man in the world," that's what. And they don't know half of what you've actually done . . .'

Poldarn breathed in and out, slowly. 'What do you want me to do?' he asked.

'Easy. Get me out of here.'

'How can I? I can't move.'

'Think of something. Didn't I mention, you're the most brilliantly innovative strategist the world has ever seen? Something like that, anyway. Just don't try and get away from me, not till I tell you. The only way I'll trust you is if I know I can kill you with a flick of the wrist; and if I'm going to die, one thing I'll make sure of is taking you with me.'

'What if I told you I didn't care?' Poldarn said.

Tazencius shook his head. 'I wouldn't believe you,' he said. 'I know you too well. You'll do anything to stay alive.'

Poldarn thought about that and realised it was true. He didn't want to die. 'If you kill me,' he said, 'they'll tear you to pieces. You realise that, don't you?'

Tazencius shrugged. 'It won't come to that,' he said. 'You're going to save me. Like I said just now, you're my guardian angel.' He put a tiny amount of additional pressure on the knife handle, just enough to hurt. 'You're afraid,' he said. 'That much pain's enough to make you afraid of dying. Am I right?'

'Yes,' Poldarn replied.

'Another thing I can't forgive, by the way, is that you really do love my daughter. You have the capacity for love, you see; I think that's obscene. It devalues everything. Have you thought of something yet?'

Poldarn nodded. 'I'm going to ask one of my – of these people to hitch up the horses to this cart,' he said. 'I'll explain that I can't do it myself because of my bad arm. I'll say that you're my friend, you were kind to me when I got stranded here, and I said I'd make sure you got out all right, I'll vouch for you. If I say it just right, casually enough, it ought to work; you don't know these people but they're like that, they trust each other.'

Tazencius raised an eyebrow. 'You like them, don't you?'

'Yes,' Poldarn replied, 'I do.'

'That figures. They're monsters, and so are you. I'm not sure I like this idea. I won't be able to understand a word you're saying; you could tell them something quite different, like the fact that I'm sticking a knife in your ribs, please help—'

'I won't,' Poldarn replied. 'It'd be too much of a risk.'

'I think so too,' Tazencius said, 'I just wanted to be sure you did. All right; once the cart's moving, I suppose I'll let you get down. What's to stop you sending your friends after me? The moment I stop prodding you with this knife—'

Poldarn shook his head. 'I don't wish you any harm,' he said. 'I mean that. All I want is for you to tell me my name.'

Tazencius nodded. 'And I won't be able to do that if I'm dead, of course. All right, I don't see how I've got any choice; but remember, if you mess me about, I will kill you.'

Much to Poldarn's surprise and relief, it all worked out as he'd hoped. A man he'd never seen before (but who seemed to know him, as they all did) hitched up the team with a cheerful smile, and stopped to wave as the cart started to roll. Nobody else seemed interested.

'Can I get down now, please?' Poldarn said.

Tazencius frowned. He was managing the reins with one hand, holding the knife with the other. 'Not yet,' he replied. 'I want a bit more space between them and me before I give up my only advantage. Of course, if I was in your shoes, I'd be thinking about the fact that once this cart's out of sight of your friends there's nothing to stop me killing you and shoving your body off the cart and down into the ditch. In fact, bearing in mind my position here, it'd make much more sense for me to kill you than let you go. Have you considered that?'

'Yes,' Poldarn replied. 'But it's not as though I've got a lot of choice in the matter.'

'You haven't. Just think,' he went on, 'after a lifetime of making choices for other people – Γ I like living in this city? Why should I live at all? Would I ᴠe better off dead? – now here you are, with no choices whatsoever, no responsibilities, no indecision, nothing. How do you feel?'

'Frightened,' Poldarn replied. 'And alone. I don't like either of them much.'

'You'd better get used to it,' Tazencius said, 'if you're really going to go and live among the savages. Imagine what it'll be like, the only human being, surrounded by two-legged wolves. Though I can't think of a better place for you, at that.'

The cart rolled on. One wheel was squeaking. Poldarn thought of Copis, but he was having difficulty remembering what she looked like. Besides, apparently he had a wife. Children, too? It would probably not be a good idea to ask.

It was a long time before the cart was out of sight of the battlefield; when the moment came, Tazencius looked at him and frowned. 'Here we are, then,' he said. 'Well, I suppose you could say you've done your good deed for the day.' Something about that remark seemed to amuse Tazencius; he grinned suddenly. 'I don't know if it counts, since you weren't acting of your own free will. But then, that'd go for most of us, most of the time. Still, I don't mind thanking you for saving my life, again. If I don't, nobody else will, that's for sure.'

'Don't worry about it,' Poldarn replied.

'Oh, I'm not worried,' Tazencius replied. 'You should be, of course. You do realise that by letting me live, helping me get away, you'll be directly responsible for thousands of deaths, tens of thousands, probably. A whole civil war. You see? Even when you do something good, it turns into evil. Your fault. Like everything.'

'Everything,' Poldarn repeated. 'Well, I wouldn't know about that.'

'Your good luck,' Tazencius said, 'at least for now. You know that? The day will come when you do find out, and I'd like to be there, to see your face. I'll be the one sitting on a big cedar-wood chair, my feet level with your head, while a beefy sergeant sharpens a sword on a stone. Till then, you can sweat it out.'

He squirmed sideways, raised his left foot and kicked hard against Poldarn's thigh, shooting him off the box. Poldarn landed on his bad arm and yelled, and then the cartwheel rolled over the ankle of his good leg. He heard the crack a fraction of a second before he felt the pain rush up through his body, flooding it, like a river in spate. From a long way off, he heard Tazencius whooping with delight – 'Yes! Neat trick, huh?' – and then his eyes closed.

When he woke up, the first thing he noticed was movement. It felt familiar.

He opened his eyes, and saw Halder's face, looking down at him. 'Grandad?' he said.

'I'm here,' Halder said.

'Are we on the ship?' Poldarn asked; then he added, 'The *Long Dragon.* Are we on the *Long Dragon*?'

Halder smiled, genuinely warm, like a good fire in the hearth. 'No, son,' he said, 'the *Dragon* was sawed up for floorboards fifteen years ago; this is the *Raven.* But you remembered the name.'

Poldarn nodded. 'I helped you build the *Dragon*,' he said. 'We sawed the timbers together; me up top, you down in the pit. I was fourteen. The big saw broke, and you had Ginlaugh weld it at the forge.'

Halder nodded. 'Ginlaugh passed on the summer before last, rest his soul,' he said. 'Now then, can you tell me who'd have the forge now?'

Poldarn thought for a moment, looking past his grandfather's face at the soft white clouds against a rich blue sky. Although the sun was bright, he was comfortable in the shade cast by the broad grey sail. He could hear voices, and although he couldn't quite make out what they were saying, he recognised the tone and pitch; familiar voices, his own people talking to pass the time. The smell of the sea made him want to sing. 'Asburn,' he said, the name slotting into place like a tenon into a well-shaped mortice. 'Asburn, his sister's boy. My age, or a few years younger. Is that right?'

The old man nodded. 'Welcome back,' he said. 'God, I wish I had a mirror handy, I'd like for you to see your face. You've got that look you always had when you were a kid. First time I've seen it since we found you again.'

Poldarn laughed. 'It's all right,' he said. 'I can remember. I can remember all sorts of things, right up to—' He frowned. 'Leaving home,' he said. 'On the *Dragon*, and you stayed home, after you fell out of the pear tree. And that's all.'

Halder shifted a little; he was sitting on a pile of empty sacks, with his back to the mast. 'That's all you need to remember,' he said, 'for where we're going. Anything that happened back there—' he made a vague gesture, presumably in the direction of land, 'all that, it doesn't matter any more, whatever it was. Where we're going, it's all different.'

There was something about the way he'd said that. 'Grandad,' Poldarn said (and for the first time he knew that his name really was Ciartan, and that he was going home), 'do I talk in my sleep?'

Halder looked away. 'Always did,' he replied. 'Bloody nuisance it was, too. Still, nobody's perfect.'

'Have I been talking just now?' He knew the answer from the way the old man didn't look at him. 'Have I been saying things about—?'

Halder shook his head. 'Nothing that made any sense,' he said. He was lying. 'Just a load of nonsense, not even in our language. Doesn't matter.'

Poldarn thought for a moment. 'If you do know,' he said, 'or if you ever find out, will you promise not to tell me? I have a feeling I'd be better off not knowing. Probably we'd all be better off.'

'I promise,' Halder said. High overhead, Poldarn could see

two seagulls riding the warm air currents. 'We won't talk about it any more.'

'Thank you,' Poldarn said. 'Where's Raffen, by the way? And Scaptey?'

Halder looked past him again. 'Scaptey's dead,' he said. 'He didn't make it through that last battle. Raffen's here, it's his shift on the tiller.'

'I'm sorry,' Poldarn said. 'About Scaptey, I mean.'

Halder shrugged. 'It's been a bad business all round,' he said. 'Just on half of us aren't coming back. Never been anything like it in my time, or my father's, that I can remember. In fact, I'd say finding you again's about the only good part of it. And you know what? Far as I'm concerned, it's worth it. I thought I'd die alone, you see. Never could bear the idea of that.'

Poldarn looked at him, and saw fear in his eyes: fear of that loneliness, which no longer threatened him; fear of what he'd done – in those eyes, Poldarn could see a reflection, the crazy old woman from Vistock at the moment when the backsabre started to come down. All that was to be expected, it belonged there and was all quite right and proper. Beyond that he could see another fear, dividing the two of them like a wall of ice. Halder was afraid of him.

'You won't,' he said, 'I promise you.' He started to reach out, to put a hand on the old man's shoulder. Halder evaded his touch, with a small, subtle movement. Somewhere behind them, someone was singing. Poldarn couldn't catch the words, but he knew them already:

> *Old crow sitting in the tall mast-tree,*
> *Old crow sitting in the tall mast-tree,*
> *Old crow sitting in the tall mast-tree,*
> *Of the ship that carried Dodger home across the sea.*

'It's all right,' Poldarn said, nevertheless. 'Everything's going to be fine now, you'll see.'